Martina Reilly, formerly writing as Tina Reilly, is the author of six successful novels: *Flipside*, *The Onion Girl* and *Is This Love?* published by Poolbeg in Ireland and *Something Borrowed* and *Wish Upon A Star* published by Time Warner Paperbacks. Her most recent novel, *All I Want is You*, is published by Sphere. She has also worked as a columnist for the *Irish Evening Herald*. At the moment she freelances for the newspaper while concentrating on her novels. She is a mother of two and in her 'spare' time she teaches drama at the Maynooth School of Drama, writes plays and helps out with her son's under-11s soccer team!

For more information see www.martinareilly.info.

Praise for Martina Reilly

'Clever, frank and funny' – *Bella*

'Hard to put down, laugh-out-loud funny . . .
perfect holiday reading' – *Woman's Way*

'Reilly is a star of the future' – *Belfast Telegraph*

'A rollicking good yarn' – *Irish Evening Herald*

'Reilly has a wonderful comic touch, both in the way she draws her characters and in her dialogue . . .
A brilliant read' – *U Magazine*

Also by Martina Reilly

Flipside
The Onion Girl
Is This Love?
Wish Upon A Star
All I Want is You

MARTINA REILLY OMNIBUS

Something Borrowed

Wedded Blitz

sphere

SPHERE

This omnibus edition first published in Great Britain by
Sphere in 2007

Previously published separately:
Something Borrowed first published in Great Britain in 2004
by Time Warner Paperbacks
Published by Time Warner Books in 2006

Wedded Blitz first published in Great Britain in 2005
by Time Warner Paperbacks
Published by Time Warner Books in 2006
Reprinted by Sphere in 2007

A CIP catalogue record for this book is available from the British Library.

ISBN 978-0-7515-4020-8

Papers used by Sphere are natural, recyclable products made from
wood grown in sustainable forests and certified in accordance with
the rules of the Forest Stewardship Council.

Printed and bound in Great Britain by Mackays of Chatham Ltd
Paper supplied by Hellefoss AS, Norway

Sphere
An imprint of
Little, Brown Book Group
Brettenham House
Lancaster Place
London WC2E 7EN

A Member of the Hachette Livre Group of Companies

www.littlebrown.co.uk

Something Borrowed

This is dedicated with thanks to all those who have bought and read my books in the past – hope yez enjoy this one!

Acknowledgements

Thanks, as always, to my family for their support, for buying my books and for trying not to look too bored every time I talk about my writing. Thanks to Claire for reading and helping me proof the final drafts of *Something Borrowed.*

Thanks to all my mates, especially Margaret for her sales patter to the good folk of Tesco, Kathleen for her lovely peaceful house, Imelda who I miss, Irene who I met because of Imelda, and Mary, my lovely neighbour with the fab garden that keeps my daughter entertained. Also to Gaye for her belief in me and all my neighbours who buy my books and ask 'how's the writing going?'. Thanks too to the parents of all the kids at Maynooth Drama – you've been brilliant over the years, especially the 'long-termers'.

Thanks to all my writer friends – you're a great bunch and deserve huge success: Catherine Barry, Colette Caddle, Dawn Cairns, Denise Deegan, Claire Dowling, Catherine Dunne, Anne-Marie Forrest, Marisa Mackle, Marita McConlon McKenna, Jacinta McDevitt and Annie Sparrow. Special thanks to two other wonderful writers: Sarah Webb, who gave me her agent's number (forever grateful!) and Martina Devlin (who knows that if she gives up the writing she can be my PR woman anytime!).

To the gang at the *Evening Herald* for all the help with the last book – thanks a million, guys.

Thanks to the bookshops, especially Eason's, and most especially to Adrienne in Liffey Valley – you've no idea how much pleasure it gives me to see the books as I pass by. I'm mostly too shy to sign them!

Thanks to the Adoption Board for their help with my research and to Helen Scott at the Adopted Parents Association for her frank and honest observations of the adoption process. Thanks to everyone who gave me an insight into adoption. While I know tracing is a lengthy process, for the purposes of the novel I had to speed things up a lot – any mistakes are my own.

Loads of grateful thanks to Ali Gunn, my agent, who worked tirelessly on my behalf to make my dreams come true. Thanks also to my new publishers for having faith in me, especially to Tara Lawrence for her brilliant suggestions and to Joanne Coen for her patience with the editing.

For my lovely family – Colm, Conor and Caoimhe.

And finally – thanks to you for choosing this book. Without readers, I wouldn't be here – enjoy!

Something Borrowed

Prologue

THERE IS A silence. A really bad sort of silence. The kind of silence that makes me want to hide.

Tommy gawks at John.

John stands with his arms folded, surveying me. Then he sort of swaggers a bit. 'Betcha didn't know that now.'

All my cousins are looking at me and I don't know why.

'Ready made,' John says again, sniggering.

Auntie Julia looks at Uncle Dessie.

Dessie is snoring on the couch, an opened bottle of Guinness clutched in his hand and beginning to spill all over the floor.

Auntie Julia wallops him awake then grabs John's arm and wallops him across the head. Then she drags John howling out into the hall. I can hear her slapping him all the way up the stairs.

Dessie blinks and looks slowly around. 'That young fella in trouble again.' His voice is all slurry.

'Let's go home now,' my mammy says in a high, bright voice. 'Time to go now, Vicky.'

Silence as I'm bundled into my coat. It's the nicest coat of all my cousins and they're all dead jealous.

'What did John mean?' I ask.

Mammy looks at Daddy. Daddy turns away.

'We'll explain when you get home,' Mammy says firmly. 'Let's go now.'

That night was the worst of my life.

Chapter One

Sixteen years later

EIGHT O'CLOCK, CHRISTMAS Eve. Sal, my flatmate, skidded to a halt beside Toys Galore – the toy shop I manage. She threw open the door of her VW Beetle and yelled at me to 'effing hurry up'.

When Sal tells you to 'effing hurry up', you do. Throwing my case onto her back seat, I leapt into the passenger seat and fastened my belt.

'I've circled the block twice,' Sal moaned, shoving her blonde hair behind her ear and glaring out at the rain that had just started to fall. 'Where the hell were you?'

'It's Christmas Eve, Sal,' I said mildly, unwrapping some chocolates I'd been saving for the journey. 'I work in a toy shop.'

'So?'

'Toy shops sell toys?' I arched my eyebrows. 'Christmas is all about toys.'

'Yeah?' Sal made a face. 'I thought it was about boozing and listening to your rellies singing stupid songs.'

'Mmmm.' Sal has this awful sceptical view of life. 'D'you want some chocolate?' I held out some Cadbury's Roses to her.

Sal shook her head. 'The tissue they're wrapped in kind of spoils my appetite.'

'I only wrapped them in tissue to stop them getting lost in my bag,' I said, exasperated. 'They're perfectly safe.'

She didn't bother to reply. I popped a caramel one into my mouth and followed it up with a coffee flavour.

'Why do you always eat the minute you get into a car?' Sal asked, sounding annoyed for some reason. 'I mean, can you not wait until later? We've a four-hour journey ahead, you know.'

'I have crisps for later.' I pulled out a six-pack of Tayto. Then, in case she thought I was a right pig, I explained, 'Bridie and I had a little party for the kids that came into the shop today – you know, a few lollies and crisps and stuff. So this is what's left.'

'So why didn't Bridie take them home?' Sal asked, braking hard and throwing us both forward. 'Bloody traffic. Jesus!'

'Bridie would never eat six packets of crisps,' I quoted Bridie.

'But she'd use them over Christmas?'

'Dunno.' I didn't know. Bridie never talked about her family or friends or anything.

'Yeah, well, you should have left them there,' Sal remarked. 'You're eating too much. I think you've put on weight.'

'Thanks.' She was in a bad mood for some reason.

'You always put on weight before you go home,' Sal continued. 'Are you afraid they won't think you're eating properly up in Dublin if you don't?'

'Don't be stupid.' Now *I* was getting in a bad mood. Maybe because she was edging too close to the bone. I did tend to eat a lot just before I went home. I ate a lot before my leaving cert too. And before I ditched college.

I ate when something made me uneasy.

We made it to Cork in under four hours. Sal drives like a maniac. She drives the way she lives her life, I guess – fast and furious. Knowing where she is going and just wanting to get there. Anyway, she had just pulled away from me in a huge cloud of dust when my mother began legging it down the driveway, her arms out in a huge embrace.

'She's home, she's home,' she yelled out. I guessed she was telling my dad. He soon appeared at the front door, paper in hand, pipe in mouth, and stood beaming at the two of us as we made our way towards him. Another hug from him. 'Welcome home!' He patted my back. 'And how's the toy shop manager today?'

They were inordinately proud of me. I used to be 'The Student' before I flunked out of college, then I became 'The Traveller' for the five years I backpacked about the world, then 'The Flower Girl' for my flower shop job, then 'The Travel Agent' – and now I was 'The Manager'.

'Well?' Dad asked, smiling away at me.

'Fine,' I muttered.

'Will you let the girl breathe.' My mother pushed him out of our way as we entered the hallway. She was breathless from her run to meet me. 'Let her get a cuppa and some food into her before you start quizzing her.'

It was always the same. The dinner, the chat. I was escorted by both of them into the big, stone farmhouse kitchen. Mam pulled out a chair for me at the wooden table and before I had a chance to adjust my seat, a huge slush pile of stew was ladled onto a large plate and slapped down in front of me.

'I'll have some of that.' Dad winked at me as if asking for some food was a risky business.

Mam, only too happy to oblige, gave him even more than she'd given me and made a production of laying it in front of him.

'Ta.' Dad slapped his stomach and began to eat.

Mam pulled down a warm plate from over the range for herself and soon the three of us were eating in silence.

I never talked much in the house. To be honest, ever since I was a kid, I've been sort of scared by it. And it's not because it's old and creaky, though that may have something to do with it, it's more because everything about the house is so HUGE. And I mean *everything*. From the granite stonework on the outside walls to the flags on the kitchen floor. Even the table I'd sat at for years looked as if it was hewn from an enormous oak.

Mam and Dad suited the house. They looked as if they'd been born out of the masonry, both of them tall and brawny and sort of ageless, while I, small and skinny, am like some kind of freak compared to everything around me. I stand out, you know. But in the wrong sort of way.

I've always stood out in the wrong sort of way from the rest of the McCarthy clan. So it was a relief when at twelve I found out that I was adopted. Don't get me wrong; it was an awful shock, but a relief as well. At least I had a reason for feeling that I was always the odd person out – and it wasn't just in the family, it was everywhere. In school, with friends, even in crowds at gigs I've always felt apart somewhat, like I'm not quite anchored.

Stew finished, Mam cleared the table and an enormous strawberry cheesecake was brought from the fridge and dumped in front of me. 'Your favourite.' She smiled delightedly at me. 'I made it specially.'

'Ta.' Oh God, I didn't much like cheesecake. I hadn't ever liked it really. But when I'd returned from my travels, Mam had attempted to make something a bit different. Something to show me that fancy cuisine could be made anywhere, not just in 'foreign hot places where the women don't even cover themselves up properly'. And I'd raved over the cheesecake – well, I would, wouldn't I, when I'd lived on pennies for a whole month and eaten bits of stale bread to keep me going? A bit like I did now, actually.

Anyway, ever since then, Mam has made me a cheesecake and she and Dad eat a small portion each, protesting that fancy food brings on their indigestion while I gamely shove a quarter or so into me to keep them happy.

'Daddy?' Mam asked, knife poised. 'Would you like a piece?'

Dad rubbed his stomach and eyed the cake suspiciously. 'Oooh, I dunno. Brings on a lot of wind, I find.'

'I find that too,' Mam said, setting down the knife. 'It repeats on a body.'

'Belching and farting, that's what happens when you eat strange food. No,' Dad waved his hand about, 'none for me, thanks.'

'I won't either,' Mam said.

Both of them looked at me.

So now, I was expected to eat something that made them belch and fart? 'A small piece,' I murmured.

'A small piece,' Mam scoffed. 'When was ever anything small in this house? You'll have a piece to fill you up, so you will.' With that she hacked off at least half of the bloody cake and offered it to me.

They watched while I cut into it. They watched as the first piece went into my mouth. They watched as I swallowed. I swear, if they could have seen me digest it, they would have. 'Gorgeous,' I pronounced.

Mam laughed and clapped her hands. Dad lay back in his chair and lit his pipe. 'I think we'll have a cup of tea, Evelyn, and some mince pies.'

Mam jumped up like a jackrabbit to meet his request.

Tea was laid before him. Tea was put before me.

A huge plate of mince pies and a big bowl of cream were laid on the table and while they ate that, I did a Bruce Bogtrotter on the cake.

Tea over, we all retired to the dining room.

This was the part where I had to entertain them with all I'd done since the last time I'd been down. No matter what it was, they thought it was wonderful. It was embarrassing how much they loved me. It poured out of them with every look, every gesture, every smile.

I hadn't much to tell them, which was a bit embarrassing seeing as I hadn't been down in about four months. But Dad was still reeling over the fact that I was a manager. It didn't matter that there was only Bridie and me in the shop, it was still an honour. A *huge* honour.

'O'Neill hadn't anyone else he could pick.' I hated all this false praise. 'There weren't many in for the job.'

'Mister O'Neill,' Mam corrected hastily.

'Mister O'Neill,' I muttered.

'He chose you,' Dad said vigorously, 'because you are so good.'

'I don't think—'

'You're exactly like your mother, too modest by half.' Dad smiled fondly at Mam who flapped him away.

'Tell her.' Dad nodded at Mam.

Mam turned red. 'Well, I—'

'You'll get a surprise when you hear this.' Dad jabbed his pipe in my direction.

'I entered the—'

'This is good now,' Dad nodded. A big beam. 'Just you wait till you hear this.'

'I was in the—'

'It's a good one, mind.'

'I won—'

'She only went and won the parish flower show,' Dad said loudly. He beamed at Mam who beamed back at him.

'I did a winter bloom display,' Mam said to me. 'D'you remember?'

Vaguely. 'Oh yeah.'

'Well, first prize I got.'

'And that's not all, is it?' Dad gave Mam a nudge. 'Go on, tell her the rest.'

'Well, Amanda Sweeney—'

'This is the icing on the cake,' Dad interrupted.

'Amanda Sweeney—'

'Amanda Sweeney was so impressed by the winter blooms that she asked your mother to do her daughter's wedding in the summer.'

'No!' Now that was news. Amanda Sweeney was the parish snob, not to mention rich chick. 'You're doing her daughter's wedding?' I gawked at Mam. 'You?'

'There's no need for that tone,' Dad chastised me. 'Your

mother is well able for it, aren't you, Evelyn? Go for it, I told her. Show those bloody Sweeneys.'

Mam laughed, flapped her arm at him. She always did that. Sometimes he caught it and they went all lovey-dovey on each other, which was a bit embarrassing.

'Two wonderful women!' Dad looked proudly at us. 'What did I do to deserve such luck?'

In my case, I guess, he'd just forgotten to take his rose-tinted glasses off.

I couldn't sleep at all that night. Coming home is never the return to childhood that other people write about. There's no soothing reassurance in sleeping in my old bed, looking at my patterned wallpaper and hearing the familiar tick of the grandfather clock on the landing. Even though it's always the same, it still never lies easy on me. I normally get up some time in the night and grab a glass of milk from the fridge. I spend the rest of the night watching the dawn creep over the fields beyond the house. It reminds me that there's a big wide world out there and I can disappear into it whenever I want.

Chapter Two

CHRISTMAS DAY DAWNED bright and clear. I was up before Mam and Dad, which wasn't surprising as I'd never actually slept. I got their presents out from my case and laid them under the tree in the dining room. They were all wrapped up in traditional red with big white bows. My mother likes tradition a lot, and despite the fact that she'd told me exactly what dressing gown to buy her, I still had to wrap up her present and pretend that I had a major surprise for her.

Once the presents were under the tree, I poured myself a glass of whiskey and hacked off a lump of Mam's pudding. Feet up, I flicked on the telly and waited for the two to get up.

Dad was up first, which was unusual. Normally Mam beats him to it. He walked in on me just as I was cutting myself another slice of pudding. 'Aw, now, Vic,' he scolded. 'You won't eat your breakfast at that rate.'

He didn't know me very well. I grinned at him and offered him a piece.

'Not at all.' He shook his head. 'I'm saving myself for the fry-up.' He took rashers and sausages and pudding from the fridge and flicked on the grill. I filled up the kettle and began to set the table. I felt a bit guilty that I hadn't thought of it before now.

'That's the girl.' Dad looked at me in approval. 'Now, only a glass for your mother, she's cutting down on the auld tea and coffee.'

'What?'

'Aye,' Dad nodded, deftly turning a sausage, 'she says the stuff is bad for her.'

'Since when?' My mother was the world's biggest tea drinker. If she gave it up, half the world's exporters would go bust.

'Since a few months ago,' Dad said. 'She just decided all of a sudden. She only drinks it at night now.'

'Right.' I removed Mam's cup from the table and put a glass there instead. 'So what does she drink instead?'

'Orange juice,' Dad said as if it was some kind of an exotic beverage. 'Imagine replacing tea with orange juice.'

'Is he laughing at me again?' Mam's voice came from the stairway.

'He is,' I called back.

Mam appeared in her oldest dressing gown. That was to make my present seem extra good. 'Happy Christmas, love,' Mam said as she embraced me.

'Happy Christmas, Mam.'

She turned to Dad who took her hand in his and they looked at one another for a few seconds before kissing each other tenderly on the lips. Happy Christmases were exchanged.

I turned away. I always felt weird looking at them – as if I was in the way or something.

'Aw, who's been eating the pudding?' Her annoyed tone made me flinch. 'Sean,' she demanded, glaring at Dad, 'have you?'

He pointed at me.

Her face sagged with disappointment. 'Aw, Vic, could you not wait? I wanted it to be whole for the dinner.'

'Sorry, Mam.'

She 'tisked' a bit.

'Didn't I tell you?' Dad said righteously to me, acting like the big class swot.

'And you could have stopped her.' Mam belted him with her hand.

'Hadn't she half it eaten by the time I came down?' Dad held out his hands in an appealing gesture. 'How could I stop her?'

'I needed something to wash the whiskey down,' I grinned, knowing they'd be shocked.

'Vicky!' they both exclaimed.

'You'll be drunk in mass,' Mam pronounced. 'That's not a fit way to turn up in the house of God.'

'Well, if God laid on a bit more entertainment I mightn't need the drink to get me through it,' I shot back. I knew they'd laugh. They always do. Sort of shocked and horrified yet loving the fact that I'm a free spirit.

That's what they think I am, you see.

After breakfast, we opened our presents and after that we went to mass. It lasted for ages. There was a choir singing and everything. Mam thought that it was beautiful. Dad, like me, had spent most of the time looking around to see who was there. Amanda Sweeney had turned up, her horrible family in tow. The daughter, the one who was getting married, had been in my class in school. We used to be mates until I'd stolen her Barbie doll one year and then her mother wouldn't let her play with me again. Unfortunately I had to shake her hand at one stage during the mass and it was like holding a dead fish. A huge diamond ring glittered like a Christmas light on her left hand.

'A lovely-looking girl,' Dad whispered loud enough for the whole parish to hear, 'that's the one that's getting married.'

'Yeah, Dad. Thanks.'

Mam and Dad loved weddings. Any time someone got married, Mam procured their wedding album and kept it until I arrived home and then I was duly shown photographs of people I didn't know with bright sunny happy smiles on their faces, surrounded by family and friends.

Sometimes I liked looking, sometimes they made me sad. I guess Lisa Sweeney's wedding album would make me very sad, especially for the poor sucker she was getting hitched to.

After mass, I waited in the car while Mam and Dad did the usual hugging and kissing with the neighbours. They also caught up on all the week's gossip. Honestly, that part of Cork was unbelievable for scandal – I don't think anyone slept with his or her actual spouse.

'Well, well, well,' Dad whistled as he started the car. 'Could you credit that?'

'What?' I asked, agog.

'Never you mind,' Mam tutted. 'It's Christmas. It's not spreading scandal about the neighbours we should be.'

'June Crowley slept with Dr Jones.' Dad couldn't wait to get it out. Honestly, he was like a clucking hen. 'Can you credit that now?'

'June Crowley that's married to the solicitor?' I asked.

'The very one.'

'And she's leaving him for the doctor,' Mam added, in case Dad forgot.

'Leaving her husband and two little kiddies,' Dad nodded. 'Isn't that a scandal now?'

'Terrible,' my mother agreed.

And it was, I thought.

'The country is going to the dogs,' Dad said, as he drove at a safe twenty miles an hour home. 'Imagine June Crowley, a married woman, sleeping with Dr Jones.' He shook his head. 'Imagine doing the likes of that.'

'Yeah,' I muttered, 'Dr Jones is a horror.'

'That's not what your father means,' Mam said, totally missing my joke. 'He just can't believe that June would do such a thing. I mean, all she went in for was a check-up.'

'And instead she got something else up,' I grinned.

Shocked expressions before Dad began again. 'You young folk,' he said, carefully avoiding a pothole, 'you take nothing seriously. Marriage breakdown is rife in this society and it's the children that suffer.'

'They don't take marriage seriously any more,' Mam said, nodding vigorously in agreement. 'They don't take relationships seriously any more.'

'Yes they do.' I felt I had to stick up for my generation. Mam and Dad were always at this, completely out of touch. Sometimes I felt suffocated by their attitudes. 'Everyone marries for love – no one can see into the future. Things happen.'

'Aye. Things happen.' Mam looked at me. 'They happen because they're let happen. Dr Jones and June knew exactly what they were at, I've no doubt about that.'

'They made a mistake.'

'A mistake that hurt her husband and two children, that's the mistake they made.'

I glared at her. Jesus, they always had the answer for everything. There was never any bend in them. 'Well,' I fired one last shot, 'if my' – I didn't know what to call her – 'my birth mother hadn't made a mistake, I wouldn't be here with you now, would I?'

Mam blinked. Once. Twice.

'That's not what we were discussing,' Dad said quietly.

Naw, they never discussed that, did they?

'And we're glad you're here,' Mam said, in an even quieter voice. 'And you're not a mistake.'

I just stared out the window.

Mam chose that Christmas Day to show me how to cook. I was quite happy to peel a few spuds and chop a few carrots, but Mam had something more exotic in mind.

'You can make the sauces,' she instructed, handing me the flour and butter and milk for the white sauce. 'Now, the first thing is to make a roux.'

No such thing as packet sauce in our house, unfortunately.

Anyway, I made it all lumpy and it burned a bit.

Then I had to cream the spuds.

Too much milk went onto them.

Dad and Mam laughed.

'Hot ice cream,' Dad pronounced as he lifted up a dripping spoonful of spuds. 'Ha, ha, ha.'

Mam giggled and flapped at him. 'Oh, you'll never make a cook,' she muttered fondly to me.

'You don't take after your mother, that's for sure,' Dad said, as he deftly began to slice the turkey. 'Smell that.'

I made a big production of sniffing the turkey and spice-scented air but inside I wasn't even smiling.

I knew I didn't take after my mother.

How could I?

Chapter Three

THE FOLLOWING DAY, Saint Stephen's, was normally spent in Aunt Julia's and this year was no exception. The invites had been sent out months ago, and Dad liked to joke that the RSVP on the invitations meant Respond So Very Positively. You just did not dare to miss Aunt Julia's Christmas party. A family member had a better chance of being forgiven for murder than a 'no-show' at the event of the year.

The party always started at three, when the family, the whole massive extended family, sat around and ate finger food, and normally finished up twelve hours later after the stories and gossip and the jokes had been swapped.

Despite Dad's joke about the invite, it's the highlight of his and Mam's year and it's the curse of mine. All five foot nothing of me sitting around with the towering hugeness of the McCarthy clan. That, plus the fact that I don't get on very well with my cousins. Ever since we were kids, Aunt Julia's two boys, Tommy and John – he's the same age as me, twenty-eight – have teased me. And because they're so funny and witty and everything, all the others tend to side with them. And though I know I should be past all that at this stage in my life, I'm actually not.

Maybe it's just delayed maturity or something.

Anyway, Dad and Mam were dressed in their best. Mam wore her brand-new Christmas dress and the new shoes that Dad had bought her. They didn't match, exactly, but she hadn't the heart to tell him, though how he couldn't see it for himself, I don't know. A green dress with red shoes does look weird, I think.

Dad had his brown suit on, the one he wears to every important occasion. He looked quite handsome in it, actually. But then again, all the McCarthys are handsome, even the women.

I wore a pair of black trousers that I'd worn to Bridie's and my Christmas party. We'd gone to see Joe Dolan because Bridie loves him. And, as I was the manager, I did have to consider what my one member of staff wanted. And Bridie wanted Joe. In fact all the wrinklies there wanted him – it was quite an eye-opener actually to see women that could barely throw a shape on a dance floor throwing their knickers up at a man in a tight white suit.

I swear, I couldn't even eat the dinner I'd been served up.

'You look lovely,' Mam said approvingly as she eyed my very conservative top. 'Green really suits you. It sets off the red in your hair.'

If there was one thing I did not want to draw attention to, it was my red hair. Against the dark looks of the McCarthys it stands out something rotten. Still, there was nothing I could do about it now. 'Ta,' I smiled at her. 'So, are we off now?'

'But where's your coat?' Mam looked horrified. 'You can't go out in just trousers and a light top.'

I held up my black jacket.

'That's too light. You can't wear that. Look,' she held open the front door, 'look at that for rain!'

'Well, it's all I have.'

'You'll catch a nasty cold if you don't put on something a bit heavier.'

'You can't catch a cold from the wet, Mam.'

'Indeeden you can.' Mam looked sternly at me. 'Didn't my own sister, your Auntie Olive, die from getting wet one summer? If she had only dried herself when she came back from the blackberry-picking she would have survived but she thought she knew better.'

'Mam, don't be ridiculous, no one would—'

'Coat,' Mam said imperiously.

You just did not argue with her when she spoke like that.

We arrived ten minutes late because no coat I had was warm enough for braving the Corkonian weather. In the end, I'd been forced to wear a see-through raincoat of my mother's. Can you imagine the embarrassment of arriving into a party in a see-through raincoat in front of all your sniggering cousins?

'Nice one, Vic,' Tommy, the most obnoxious of Aunt J's brood, called out when he saw me. 'Is that the fashion now?'

A laugh. At my expense. As usual.

Well, I'd had it with him.

'This?' I pointed to the coat. Nodded. 'Oh yeah.'

He looked a bit thrown. I think it was because I normally ignore him.

I made a big deal of taking the coat off as if every squeaky, sweaty inch of it was precious. 'Is there somewhere safe I can hang it?'

Now they were all gawking at me. Mam and Dad had gone to wish Aunt J a Happy Christmas. 'Well?'

'I'll take it,' Lydia, the youngest cousin, said breathlessly. 'I'll hang it in my room.'

'Be sure and keep it away from fibres,' I told her sternly. 'It tends to pick them up very easily and it'll ruin the line.'

'Sure.' Lydia, who was only ten, walked with great importance out of the room.

'My arse that's the fashion,' Tommy said, grinning.

'Big arses are becoming fashionable all right,' I told him pleasantly.

He laughed.

'And how's Vicky?' Aunt Julia's voice rose as she spotted me. 'Come over and talk to me, child, I haven't seen you in so long.'

I joined my folks at her side, relieved to be getting away from the cousins.

'You've got bonnier,' Aunt Julia said.

I presumed she meant I'd put on weight. Aunt Julia had a knack for cloaking her insults in the thick velvet of compliments.

'Hasn't she,' my mother cooed.

Thanks a lot, I wanted to say.

'You've got older,' I said to Julia. And she had. She didn't look as straight-backed as the last time I'd seen her.

Give her credit, she laughed. 'I have, just like yourself,' she smiled. 'Sure aren't we all getting on?'

'Mmm.'

'And how's the job? Your dad tells me you're still in the toy shop.'

'Yep.'

'*Managing* the toy shop, Julia,' Dad said.

'Isn't that nice.' Julia clapped her hands. 'A manager in the family. Your Uncle Ted was a manager.'

'Was he?'

'He was. Very responsible job. Tommy is a manager too.' She shot a smile over at her vile son. 'He manages some kind of big corporation, I don't know all the details.'

'Well, Vicky has her foot on the corporate ladder now,' Dad said, beaming. ''Twon't be long before she's climbing to the top.'

'Aw,' Tommy joined us, 'so that's why she needs the big raincoat!'

Mam and Dad stared, puzzled, at him.

Aunt Julia tittered. She laughs at him no matter what he says. 'Nothing wrong with a good warm coat,' she said then.

'Nothing at all!' Tommy grinned at me.

I didn't smile back. 'I'll just go get a drink.'

'You do that,' Julia said. 'And after the food, sure maybe you'll give us a song?'

It wasn't a request, it was an order.

I hoped that I could get good and drunk before that happened.

The caterers cleared away the food, pulled Aunt J's table over to the edge of the room and we all sat down to await whatever was going to happen next. There were about thirty of us all cramped together around the table. Everyone was getting relaxed and stories of family outings and family disasters were being swapped. Drink was being swilled down and Tommy and a few of the cousins had started up a game of Twister in another part of the house. Their laughter could be heard all over the place.

'You should go and join them,' Mam whispered to me. 'They sound as if they're having a good time.'

I didn't answer. Up in Dublin, I'd have had no problem making an eejit out of myself in front of a group of people, but here, well, I just couldn't. I know they all thought I was a dry shite and to be honest, I probably was. I just felt so self-conscious in front of them all.

'Vicky's not going anywhere,' Julia said, a bit drunkenly. 'She's going to sing for me. She promised.'

I was hoping she'd have forgotten. 'Well,' I muttered, 'I didn't *exactly* promise.'

'But you will,' Uncle Dan, Dad's brother, grinned at me. 'You know how Julia loves a good song.'

A chorus of 'oh yes' followed and a few bits of clapping and then a cheer arose. I had no option but to get unsteadily to my feet.

'Smile,' Mam hissed at me. 'You look so much nicer when you smile.'

I dunno if the grimace that made its way across my face could have been construed as a smile but I did my best.

A song had to be decided upon.

'Raglan Road' was picked. It's basically a Patrick Kavanagh poem set to music. Luke Kelly of the Dubliners did a great job of it. It was a sad song, full of loss and longing, and I loved it but I hated singing it.

'Up there now, good girl.'

'Give it a belt, there's the girl.'

'Aw, she's a great singer is our Vicky.'

The last from my dad who was well gone.

A big 'shushing' campaign began in earnest as I began to sing.

I was a bit shaky on the first verse but by the middle of the second, I'd forgotten about the whole lot of them. There is something about that song that wraps me up and carries me away. I sang about the queen of hearts making her tarts while I wasn't even making hay, I sang about the snare set by the dark-headed woman and the fact that it didn't matter. Nothing mattered except love.

When the final note died there was a silence. The cousins had even stopped playing their game of Twister to listen. They were all looking at me, looking at me as if I was some weirdo in their midst.

Tommy broke the spell. Turning away from me, he asked loudly, 'Who's on red? Come on, who's the bastard on red?'

That shocked everyone. 'Language, Tomas,' Julia hissed sternly.

Tommy winked at her and she 'tisked' him. Then one of Uncle Dan's lads admitted to being the bastard on red and the Twister game started up again.

Aunt Julia turned from him and smiled at me. Pressed her hand into mine. 'Lovely,' she whispered. 'That was lovely.'

'Ta.'

'Where did you get that voice?' Uncle Dan chortled. 'And the rest of the family like rusty gates every time they open their mouths.'

A laugh.

A bloody laugh.

I don't know if it was the drink or the sheer hell of always being different that finally got to me but I said, really loudly, 'I dunno where I got my voice, Dan. I don't bloody know.'

Then I left the room.

Apparently the party died soon after that. I don't know because I left the house, minus my see-through rain jacket, and just walked and walked and walked. I don't know where I went, I don't even know if I got wet, all I know was that I'd had it with pretending. I'd had it with trying to be a daughter when nothing about me matched with anything about them.

I did love my parents. I couldn't but love them. But I owed it to myself to find my place in the world. To find out where I belonged. To find out where I got my voice from.

I owed it to myself to find my mother.

Chapter Four

'THAT WASN'T A very nice way to treat your Auntie Julia last night,' Mam chastised me the minute I got up. She laid a plate in front of me and asked, 'Toast?'

'Pardon?' My head was banging. My eyes had sandpaper under the lids and all I wanted to do was to get back to the flat I shared with Sal and forget about here for another while.

'I asked if you wanted toast.' Mam quirked her eyebrows. '*And* I also said that leaving Julia's party was very rude of you. *And* as for the way you snapped at Dan, I don't know!' She shook her head and shoved some bread into the toaster. 'You've been very edgy since you arrived. I should have known you were in bad form when you started drinking the whiskey the other morning.'

'Oh for God's sake, Mam, I had a whiskey because it was Christmas!'

'Really.' She sounded as if she didn't believe me. 'And why did you leave Julia's party, so?'

Silence.

'Because,' I bit my lip, 'I just felt like it.'

'You felt like it!' She put her hands on her hips and glared at me. I can honestly say it was the first glare she'd ever given me in the whole of my life. 'Well, you ruined it for us all, do you know that?'

'No.' I stared sullenly at my plate.

'Your dad was worried sick about you. He and Tommy went out in the car looking for you.'

'I'm a big girl, Mam, I don't need people looking for me. Especially not that big eejit!'

'Don't you dare call your father that!'

'I meant Tommy!'

'Oh.'

She didn't say much more after that, just went around making too much toast and too much tea. I ate about ten slices while she began tidying up the kitchen. From outside, the sound of cattle being brought back out into the fields could be heard. The rain was falling, hitting off the kitchen window and making the world appear all grey and sullen. A bit like me, actually. Thank God I was leaving that evening. I figured that I'd tell them just as I was going out the door; that way there'd be no scene, no begging me to reconsider, no well-meant advice.

I was just finishing up the last slice of toast when Dad came in, banging his boots on the step and clapping his hands together to get them warm. 'Aw,' he winked over at me, 'there she is, The Wanderer!'

I smiled briefly and ignored Mam as she crashed a cup into the dishwasher.

'So where did you go?' Dad asked. 'Tommy and I drove up and down the road looking for you.'

'She just felt like leaving,' Mam said then, sounding more exasperated than annoyed. 'Can you believe that?'

'I can,' Dad nodded. 'Sure I've often felt like it myself, only I'd never have the nerve. You're like me like that, Vic,' he grinned. 'Not the one for the big family thingamajigs!'

That did it. In my head, somewhere, I knew he was just trying to cajole Mam into better form. But every other part of me refused to co-operate. It was like, I dunno, a red mist across my real self, and stuff that I'd buried for years erupted from somewhere inside me. 'I am not like you!' I remember that I stood up. I remember the look of shock on his face. But even that didn't stop me. 'I *can't* be, don't you see?' I glared at the two of them. 'You didn't *have* me. You didn't carry me inside you. All that I am, I owe to someone I don't even know!'

Silence.

Mam moved towards Dad. He was still staring, shocked at me.

'Can you imagine how that makes me feel?' I took a step nearer them, trying, I suppose, to make them understand. 'I don't know where I come from. I don't know if I get my curly hair from him or her or my grandfather or maybe an aunt or someone. I don't know if she can sing like me. I don't know if she's small like me or stupid like me or—'

'You are not stupid,' Mam spoke up, loudly. 'Don't say that.'

'And all that you are you owe to us.' Dad spoke in a hard voice. 'We're the ones who' – he gulped and put his arm about my mam – 'we're the ones who kissed you and cuddled you and let you sleep in our bed when you had nightmares as a kid. We're the ones—'

'I know. I know.' I paused. This wasn't coming out right at all. In fact, I hadn't planned on saying it like that. I took a slow breath in and said levelly, 'I know what you mean, Dad, and I am grateful for it. I am. But—' I paused, gulped, tried to think of a way to explain and only ended up with, 'but I have this need to know where I come from – don't you see? I've been thinking about it for ages.'

And I had, I realised. I'd just never admitted it to myself.

'You want to find your birth mother?' Mam spoke softly. 'Is that it?'

I took a look at her soft face and wanted to hug her for saying it for me. 'I *need* to find her.'

They took a moment to digest this.

'It's just to see where I fit in,' I explained, trying not to show how desperate I felt because I didn't want to hurt them. They had never understood my square peg attitude. 'I can never fit in anywhere until I know where I come from.'

Dad thought it was bullshit. I saw it in the way he raised his eyes. But Mam surprised me by catching my hand in hers and squeezing it. 'You're right, Vic. Everyone needs that.' Her voice wobbled a bit. 'You do what you have to do. We'll help if we can. If it makes you happy, then do it.'

'Thanks.' I squeezed her back. Turning to Dad I gave a hesitant smile. 'Dad?'

'You're loved here,' he said, folding his arms and glaring at the two of us. 'That's all I know.'

'I know that,' I said.

'And this is your home.'

I didn't reply to that. Trouble was, it had never felt that way. 'It won't make a difference to how I feel about you both,' I said. Jesus, this was getting a bit sloppy. 'I mean, you'll still get on my nerves and all.'

At least they laughed.

Even if they didn't feel like laughing.

The rest of the day dragged. Conversation was stilted. They didn't know what to say to me and I didn't know how to bridge this distance that had suddenly sprung up between us. It was like all of a sudden they realised that I'd grown up. That I was making my own decisions.

Dad was the worst; he didn't even come to the door to wave me off when Sal collected me, saying that he had to check on the cattle.

Mam walked me to the door, her arm on my elbow. 'You'll ring when you get home?' she asked.

'Uh-huh.'

'You know how I worry with Sally driving.'

'Uh-huh.'

'And about that other thing, I meant what I said. We'll help you in any way we can. Just tell us what information you need and I'll dig it out.' A smile. 'We only want you to be happy, Victoria.'

She always called me Victoria when she was really upset.

'Thanks, Mam.'

A hug.

Then she was gone.

Sal was blasting the horn for all it was worth and making gestures at me to hurry up. And like I said before, when Sal says to hurry, you hurry.

Chapter Five

SAL AND I go back a long way. We met in primary school; she was the sulky kid with the plaits and the 'I-hate-teacher' attitude. I was the awkward, thick-at-maths kid with the 'I-hate-school' attitude. We hit it off straight away and spent our time dreaming up weird and wonderful ways to earn our living once school was over for ever. Secondary school was spent smoking fags and eyeing up the lads. Sal always scored every Friday night at the discos while I wilted like the wallflower I was beside her. I soon learned to spend the slow sets in the loo doing my hair.

To everyone's surprise, including my own, I managed to get enough points in my leaving to do Arts at UCD while Sal, to my surprise, got Journalism in Rathmines. Mam and Dad spent a blissful year boasting about their student daughter while I slowly went mad in a grotty bedsit listening to all the other students rave on and on about how much they loved the student life. In the end, I told Mam and Dad that I couldn't seem to hack it and that maybe some travel would broaden my mind. I got a loan from the bank, then worked my way around most of the world. It was the best and the worst time in my life. Great because I was finally free, horrible because I didn't find anywhere I really wanted to be. So, after five years, I came home to try and find work and pay off my loan.

I've had a selection of jobs culminating in the managership of Toys Galore. And for the first time ever, I really loved being somewhere. It's great seeing kids coming in with their parents, looking for something to buy and going out with smiles plastered to their faces. Or seeing kids choosing presents for their mates, or brothers buying for sisters.

It's dead nice.

And I love toys. Not just dolls and teddies, but everything. The Meccano sets, the wrestlers, the swings and slides.

It's such a happy place to be.

I didn't tell Sal about my decision to look for my mother. It's not that she doesn't know I'm adopted, I think the whole of Cork knows, it's just that Sal doesn't know what to keep to herself and what to blab to everyone else. I guess it comes from working in tabloid land for a living – any bit of news is money in her pocket. Anyway, I decided, there was no point in telling her anything unless I'd actually got something to tell her.

A search wasn't exactly major news.

For the time being, I vowed, I'd find out how to start my search.

It'd be my New Year's resolution.

Chapter Six

'SO,' SAL ASKED, the day after New Year's, 'any New Year resolutions?'

Her question startled me, though I have to admit it wasn't entirely unexpected. I'm a great one for the NY's resolutions. I gave a sort of a giggle. 'Resolutions?' I said it as if the thoughts of making some had never even occurred to me. 'Nope. None. I'm not bothering with that this year. In fact, my resolution is not to make any resolutions.' I made a big deal of zipping up my anorak and wrapping my scarf around my neck. I was due into work in an hour.

'Really?' Sal sounded surprised. 'Wow.'

'Yep.' I couldn't look at her. 'Resolutions are a load of crap.'

'They are for you, aren't they?' Sal said matter-of-factly. 'I mean, what was it you were going to do last year? Learn to drive or something, wasn't it?'

'Dunno.'

'And didn't you crash your dad's car and didn't the driving school tell you not to do your test?'

They'd practically *begged* me. 'I'd better go.' I shoved my scarf into my jacket. 'Bye.'

'And you've none this year?'

'I dunno why you're so interested in—'

'Tell you what mine is,' Sal interrupted, lighting up a fag. 'I'm going to be full-time on *Tell!* before the year is out.'

'That's good.' *Tell!* was a magazine that Sal sometimes free-lanced for. A downmarket version of *Hello!*, their whole budget was spent on writing titbits on the jet set. No one was safe – that was their slogan. Along with 'If you tell it, we'll sell it!' Sal did the odd piece for them and got paid handsomely for it.

Her real job, and one she loathed, was working for a local paper. She was their head reporter and, as such, got the plum interviewing jobs – she'd done pieces on the local parade being cancelled due to the mayor having food poisoning, or the local boy making good in England, or about the joy of having a twenty-first in the local pub. I thought it was an OK job myself – all she had to do was sit at a desk and make phone calls or travel to an interview and claim expenses. But according to Sal, there was no buzz in it, no thrill of the kill.

She was mental.

'And what's more,' she went on, holding her fag aloft, 'I'm gonna marry someone rich and famous and they'll buy the magazine for me.'

'And are pigs gonna fly as well?'

'Bitch!' She picked up her cigarette packet and fired it at me but I managed to leg it out the door before it hit the wall.

It pissed rain all the way from the bus stop to the shop – about twenty minutes' walk. My scarf, being the vibrant spirit that it was, unwrapped itself from my neck and danced away down the street. I just could not be arsed chasing after it, especially as the rain had managed somehow to invade my waterproof trainers and I was literally squishing along. My hair, which I'd blow-dried that morning, frizzed out all over the place. My hair does that in the rain, believe it or not. In fact, I can actually tell when rain is on the way because my hair begins to get fuzzy in advance. On top of all this, my anorak, which was an expensive one, but unfortunately a suede one, got completely and utterly ruined.

I arrived into work in very bad form.

As you can imagine.

Bridie was there. She always gets in before me. When I first started work, I actually had suspicions that she was sleeping in the place because no matter how early I'd be, Bridie would be there, sitting in her favourite chair and nursing a cup of tea. It was kind of spooky actually. Every morning it was the same, she'd look up at me as I came in, her brown eyes smiling, and say, 'Hello, Vicky, the kettle's boiled,' and scurry around fetching me biscuits and making sure I was looked after.

Groundhog Day for ten minutes every morning.

That day, though, she excelled herself. She made me take off my shoes and socks and put them by the heater. Then she made me tea and told me to drink it up nice and slowly and to relax and get dry.

'You'll catch a cold by getting wet,' she clucked.

I smiled to myself. She was so like my mother that that was scary too.

We sat in silence for a few minutes, her sipping and me sniffing.

'So,' she smiled, 'did you have a good New Year?'

'All right,' I admitted. 'Nothing major.'

'So you didn't go home?'

'Naw, I usually just go home for Christmas.' I didn't want to elaborate. 'You?'

'Oh. You know me,' she looked at her hands, 'I like the quiet life.'

Bridie was the only woman I knew who'd suit being dead. She did absolutely nothing. As far as I could gather, she never went anywhere or had any friends. I sort of felt sorry for her so I always asked her to go for a drink on Friday nights after work. Not that she ever took me up on the offer. 'So what did you do?' I asked. 'Throw yourself a party?'

She laughed at that, a sort of gentle laugh to herself. Bridie laughs at a lot of the stuff I say, which is nice. 'I suppose I did,' she smiled. 'I sat in and watched RTE counting down and then when it was midnight I went to bed.'

'Right.'

I'd gone to a club with Sal and a few of her pals, drunk too much, sang 'Auld Anis Ine' in the middle of O'Connell Street to lots of applause and then got a taxi home.

'Now' – Bridie stood up and I winced as her legs creaked and popped – 'I'll open up. We shouldn't have too many in today, God willing. You stay there and get dry. God knows, we can't afford for either of us to be sick.'

'Ta, Bridie.'

I watched her shuffle out of the room and heard her go out into the main shop and begin unlocking the doors. It was a bit of a nuisance all right, just the two of us. I'd been on to Albert O'Neill, the owner, to get me a third member of staff but he'd snorted and said something about me getting a boyfriend if I wanted to dominate any more people.

I have to say, I was offended at that.

Bridie told me not to worry. 'He's a bit of a moody man,' she said. And I guess she should know, having worked for him for almost thirty years. So I took it on the chin and didn't ask for any more staff after that. I just made myself unavailable whenever he rang looking for me, telling Bridie to say that I was dealing with deliveries or on my lunch.

He could wait, I decided, until I was ready to talk to him. My unavailability would show how busy I was.

And it worked, only not exactly in the way I'd expected.

Chapter Seven

'BRIDIE, WILL YOU go down and keep an eye on the shop, I've, eh,' I indicated the phone, 'to make a call about a delivery.' My face got all hot. I've never been the greatest fibber in the world.

'A delivery?' Bridie frowned. 'Which one would that be now? All our deliveries are coming in Friday.'

I searched my mind for an order. Blank.

'Just one of the Friday ones.' I gave a false smile. 'Have to confirm it.'

'The Barbie one?'

'That one, yeah.'

'I already did it.' Bridie beamed at me. 'I *told* you that.' She gave a bit of a laugh, took another bite out of her egg sandwich and shook her head fondly. 'Honestly, I don't know what's happened you – you haven't been yourself since Christmas.'

'I need to confirm it again.' I kept my voice firm. Jesus, Bridie was way too efficient. 'Please go and keep an eye on the shop, will you?'

She looked a bit put out at that. She replaced her sandwiches in her brown paper bag and, standing up, dusted down her tweed skirt. 'I'm on my lunch,' she muttered. 'It's a terrible thing when you can't even enjoy your lunch.'

'You can come back up once I've made the call.'

'Can't you make it from the shop?'

'No. It's busy. I'll be disturbed.'

Still muttering, Bridie slipped her feet into her spongy shoes and shuffled out the door, clutching her sandwiches in her hand. She'd have no time to eat them; the place was beginning to buzz down there.

Once I was sure she was out of earshot, I closed the door and took a slip of paper from my pocket and dialled the number scrawled across it. Well, tried to dial – my fingers were shaking so much that I mis-dialled twice. When eventually the phone did begin to ring at the other end, my heart started to jack-hammer. I closed my eyes and told myself that what I was doing was no big deal. Thousands of people had done it before. It didn't help. I thought I was going to be sick. What, I wondered, would I be like when I'd actually contacted my mother, if this was the state I was in before I'd actually done anything. I sat weakly down on the chair and waited for my call to be answered.

'Hello. Adoption Board. How can we help you?'

I froze. Completely.

'Hello?'

I wanted to hang up. I was on the verge of putting the receiver back into its cradle when it hit me. If I hung up now, I'd have to make the call at another time. Next week, next month, next year – it didn't matter, I'd have to do it eventually.

'Adoption Board?' the woman spoke again. 'Hello?'

'Hello?' I could barely get the word out, my voice had gone all shaky.

'What can we do for you?'

She sounded so efficient.

'Well . . .' I licked my lips, clenched the phone tighter to my ear. Jesus, I hadn't thought this out at all. 'I'm, er, adopted.'

'Yes?'

Polite interest.

'And, well, I, eh, want to trace my parents.'

Saying it was weird. It made me realise that this was what I'd wanted since I was twelve. All my life, I'd felt as if something was missing and this was it. 'I'd like to trace my birth parents,' I said again.

'I'll put you through to someone,' the lady said, and there was a sudden silence on the line.

More heart hammering.

More clenching the phone really tight.

'Hello?'

And so I began again, slightly more confidently.

'OK,' the man at the other end said, 'well, the first thing you need to do is to formally request, in writing, details of your birth mother.'

'OK. Do I write to yous?'

'No. Write to your placement agency.'

'Sorry? My what?'

'The placement agency – the agency you were adopted from.'

'Oh.' Who the hell were they?

'Your adoptive parents should know it,' the man said, as if reading my mind, 'and if not, we can find out for you.'

'Oh. OK.' Jesus, it'd mean a call to my mother. I wasn't sure if I wanted to do that. I hadn't really talked to them since Christmas.

'When you know where to write,' the man continued, 'you can request two types of information. Non-specific information is the first type. That can be given out very quickly. That includes the name of your birth mother, the place—'

A *name*. I could find out her name. Even that would mean something.

'—up to two years—'

'Sorry, I didn't catch that last bit.' There was a huge chunk in the middle I didn't catch either but I hadn't the nerve to admit it.

'I said that it can take up to two years to trace a birth parent.'

'Two years?' No way.

'People move on,' he said gently, as if sensing my shock. 'Some people might not want to be found.'

'Really?' My voice was small. 'Would that be normal, like?'

The guy's answer was drowned out by the sound of the door

crashing open and a booming northern voice yelling, 'I hope you're giving the delivery boys hell, Vicky!' A slap on my back that almost shattered my entire spine. A large, vulgar, expensively dressed man plonked himself onto the seat on the other side of my desk and, spreading fleshy lips, gave me the benefit of his white and gold smile.

How the hell had Albert O'Neill managed to come into the shop without my hearing him? There was no way I could continue my phone conversation now. I cut the nice man off mid-flow at the other end of the line. 'Well, thank you for your time,' I said, in as crisp a voice as I could, 'I'll have something into you soon.'

'As the bishop said to the altar boy!' Albert gave me a lewd wink, then he laughed. It sounded as if a car bomb had gone off in the street.

I gave a bit of a laugh too as I replaced the phone and folded up the paper I'd been doodling on. The words 'placement agency' were scrawled across it. Shoving the paper into my pocket, I stood up from the desk and held out my hand. 'Hi, Mr O'Neill – Happy New Year.'

'And to you too, Victoria,' he grinned, pumping my arm up and down. It was like shaking hands with a wet dishcloth. 'And to you too.' He let my hand drop and I had to stop myself from wiping it down my jeans.

Albert O'Neill is my boss. Mine and about five thousand other people's. He's one of the most successful businessmen in the country. Probably one of the most successful businessmen in Europe, seeing as how he has toy shops in France, Spain and Italy. He's loud and crude and from all accounts keeps himself fit by chasing women. As far as I could see, he'd be very fit because if they'd any sense, they'd be running very fast in the opposite direction. The man was a horror. Fat. Wobbly in all the wrong places, with a dyed black head of hair on him that was thinning quicker than the ozone layer.

'So' – I gave what I hoped was a businesslike smile. It was

best to play it cool with him – 'to what do Bridie and I owe the pleasure?'

'The pleasure is all mine,' he chortled.

I made a superhuman effort not to look alarmed. 'Oh, now!'

'I have news that should make you both very happy,' O'Neill said, crossing towards me.

'Really?'

'Oh yes. You know how I like to put a smile on my employees' faces.'

I did know and that was why I decided to try and make an exit. 'I'll just get Bridie and tell her that—'

'Stay here!' The order was sharp. The jovial smile was gone. 'I'm telling you, you're the manager. You can pass the news on to Bridie later.'

'Oh, oh, right.' I shrugged, moved back into the office. 'I just thought Bridie—'

'You'll have a new member of staff from next Monday.'

'Sorry?' I thought I'd misheard.

'I said, you'll have a new staff member from next week.' O'Neill shoved his hands into his trouser pockets and gave himself a good scratch. 'Isn't that what you wanted?'

'Well, yes—' I tore my eyes away from his trousers. 'Yes,' I said in a stronger voice, 'that's, that's great. Thanks very much.'

Scratch. Scratch. Scratch. 'Oh, now don't ever say I don't listen to my staff.'

'I'd never say that.'

'Now,' O'Neill went on, 'he won't have much experience.'

'Oh, well, we can train him in.'

'Good.' O'Neill smiled and, his itching over, he began patting down his black hair. 'Work him hard. Make use of him.'

'Definitely.' I allowed him a genuine smile. 'Another staff member is just what we were looking for.'

'I'll be checking up on him from time to time, making sure he's pulling his weight.'

'Aw, well, I'm sure—'

'No son of mine is going to get away with shoddy work.'

'Who? Sorry?'

'My son,' O'Neill nodded grimly. 'Your new employee.'

With that he shook my hand again, his sweaty palm making me cringe, and left the office, booming out his goodbyes to Bridie, who was too awestruck to reply.

I had to sit down.

I could not believe it.

I could not believe that I was going to be stuck with his son as an employee.

For one thing, if he was as bad as his da, I'd spend more time avoiding his advances than actually working and, even worse, what happened if he was totally crap? I could hardly fire him now, could I?

Jesus.

Sal was agog. 'His son?'

'Yep.' I broke open a can of Bud – that was how pissed off I felt. I had made it a rule, some time ago, only to drink at weekends, but I hadn't envisioned this scenario. I deserved a drink. 'His son is coming to work in our toy shop.'

'Wow!' Sal rolled her eyes. 'He's probably loaded – Jesus, if you played your cards right, Vic, you could get in there.'

'Sal, I don't want to get in anywhere. All I want to do is run the shop and I won't be able to do it with the bloody boss's son breathing down my neck.'

'And I thought you said you didn't want to get in anywhere!' Sal rolled her eyes and grinned broadly. 'Jesus, old biddy Bridie will be getting pretty steamed up with that kind of carry-on.'

I had to laugh. 'Stop it!'

Sal turned back to her laptop. 'That's what you'll be saying all right,' she said, still grinning. 'Well, if you're lucky that is!'

Lucky my arse. 'You have not seen the holocaust that is his dad,' I fired back. 'If he's anything like him I—'

'Hey!' Sal interrupted me. 'D'you know something, I think

I've a picture of your boss and his family in a back issue of *Tell!* In fact, I'm sure I have!' She almost knocked over her laptop as she legged it into her bedroom. 'Back in a sec.'

Sal has a great memory for all things celeb. She knows who's married to who, who's living with who, who's having affairs with who. She knows all the members of the royal family and for some reason she has a mad fixation on Dustin Hoffman. The *South Dublin Journal* really didn't use her talents at all. It was no wonder she wanted to be a *Tell!* girl.

I had just opened another can of Bud when she arrived back, waving the magazine about. 'It's this one, I'm sure of it.' She started flipping rapidly through the pages. 'I remember we did a big toy special just before Christmas on the most expensive toys to buy and your boss, I'm positive it was him, agreed to pose for a photo with his family.'

'And he didn't shatter the camera?'

'You are bloody cruel, so you are.' Sal was busy flicking. Then, a sort of recoil before she muttered, 'Ugh, I see what you mean.'

She'd found the page and there, sure enough, was Albert posing with his wife and son. It was under an article entitled *Toys Galore* and it showed Albert and his family in the middle of lots of expensive gear. Albert was dressed casually in a blue shirt and jeans. A stupid Santa hat was perched on his head and it looked as awkward on him as a pair of underpants would on a naturist. Beside him sat his wife, her hand in his. She was a dark, not unattractive, anxious-looking woman. She wore a ridiculously expensive dress.

'John Rocha,' Sal said, drooling. 'It's wasted on her, isn't it?'

In front of the two of them, cross-legged on the ground, was Albert Junior. He was dark like his mother, but he was big like his dad. Big and surly, as if nothing in life made him laugh. There was nothing redeemable in his features at all. In fact, he looked downright scary.

'Mmm,' Sal muttered, screwing up her perfect face, 'maybe it's a bad photo.'

'No maybe about it,' I said.

Sal gawked more closely at the picture as if somehow that would make it morph into something nicer.

'Can you imagine that guy working in a toy shop?' I asked. 'I mean, he'll scare the kids away.'

'I'm more interested in trying to imagine him in bed,' Sal said. 'I mean, looks don't matter in the dark, do they?'

'I'm not interested.'

'Yeah, but I am.' Sal smiled cockily at me. 'You never know, I could call into you one day looking for an intro.' She studied the photo again and groaned. 'Aw damn – he's RFP.'

Ring finger positive.

'Now,' she said, 'isn't that just a bummer?'

Chapter Eight

BRIDIE WAS DRIVING me mad. She thought it was wonderful that O'Neill's son was coming to work with us. 'I'll just go and dust the shelves at the back of the shop,' she twittered, scrimmaging under the counter and locating the feather duster that hadn't been used in my whole eight months as manager. 'It wouldn't do to show ourselves up.'

'He's not a health inspector, Bridie,' I said, grinning. 'He's not going to be interested in the state of our shelves.'

Bridie looked as me as if I'd just crawled out of the swamp. 'He'll be the owner of those shelves one day,' she nodded, 'so he'll want to see that we have respect for them.'

'Respect for a shelf?' I rolled my eyes. 'Suit him better if he's got respect for us.'

'He will if we keep the shop nice.'

And with that gem of pointless logic, off she went, as fast as her legs would let her.

I began flicking through a toy catalogue while all the time she shouted bulletins on her progress.

'Spiders as big as rats!'

'What? As big as O'Neill?'

A shocked silence for a few seconds, then a small titter. 'Oh, Vicky, you are awful. You'll have to stop saying those things when the son comes!'

I allowed myself a grin. Bridie was old school. She simply did not give out about 'the boss' or 'the job' or about anything really. As far as she was concerned, you did your job and got your pay and anything else was a bonus. The manager she'd had before me must have been a slave driver. Bridie had almost fallen off her chair the first morning I arrived and suggested that maybe it'd be nice to have a tea break in the middle of the morning. Then when I'd suggested one after lunch too, she'd shaken her head. 'You take one if you want,' she'd said uneasily, 'but I'll keep working.' So I had to keep working too. Bridie was too conscientious by half. I sometimes wondered who was managing who.

'I'm going to give those shelves a bit of a wash,' Bridie called out. 'A bit of washing-up liquid will do wonders for them.'

'You don't need to do that.' Honestly, I was beginning to feel guilty at her activity. Half afraid too that she'd want me to help her. I hated cleaning at the best of times.

Bridie emerged, flushed, from the back of the shop. 'I do so. You haven't *seen* those shelves. Honestly, they're begging for a good scrubbing.'

'I don't think anyone will notice, Bridie.'

'You young people' – Bridie flapped her hand, reminding me of my mother – 'you *don't* clean so that people will notice. It's about having pride in things.'

'Mmmm.'

'My house, now, I do my windows, inside and out, at least once a week. I hoover every evening when I go home. My brass, now, I do that—'

'Sorry, your what?'

'My brass.'

'You have a special day for washing your bras?'

'*Polishing*, Vicky. You *polish* brass, you don't wash it. It'll tarnish that way.'

'Oh.' I grinned, suddenly realising my mistake.

Bridie continued. 'Brass needs special attention, I find. I always do it on a Monday, after the weekend.'

'Right. So your brass needs special attention after the weekend?'

'Yes.'

Lucky Bridie, I wanted to say, but didn't. A little respect, after all. 'Well, look, Bridie, you wash away – I just want to make a quick call, so if someone comes in, you'll look after them, will you?'

'I'll do my best.' She shook her head. 'Those shelves are very dirty.'

I ignored the hint and exited.

In my office, I dialled home. I'd been putting off the phone call all morning but the sooner the better. I told myself that I'd feel relieved when I'd done it.

Dad answered. His 'hello' sounded a bit flustered.

'Dad,' I said, 'it's me.'

Pause. 'Vicky, is it?'

'Yeah. Is anything wrong?'

A bit of a laugh. 'Wrong? No. Why?'

'You just sounded a bit, I dunno, flustered.'

'Well, I'm not,' he said adamantly. 'So, how's my girl? I heard from Sally's parents that you had a great night on New Year.'

'Yeah. Sal and I went to a club.'

'Lovely.'

He didn't mean that. He was always giving out about those *Ibiza Uncovered* programmes, convinced that they reflected life in the clubs of Dublin. If only it were true.

'So what is it you wanted? If it's a chat with your mother, she's not here.'

'Oh, right.' I paused. Bit the bullet. 'Well, maybe you can help me. I'm looking for the name of my placement agency.'

Silence.

'You know, the one where I was—'

'I do know what a placement agency is, Vicky.' His voice had gone all hard and I flinched.

'Oh, well, good. So . . . will you find out for me? It's just that I need—'

'Aaah, do you need to be doing all this, Vicky?' He attempted a laugh. 'I mean, what do you want to go dragging up the past for?'

I gulped. Blinked hard. 'I thought I explained this,' I mumbled. 'I just need—'

'You just need to cop on, that's what you need. There's no point in trying to find—'

'Well, Dad, I think there is.'

If I could have seen him, I reckon his face would have flushed and his hands begun clenching and unclenching. He always did that when he was threatened. Either that or tried to cajole someone to his point of view.

'You think there is,' he repeated slowly.

'Yes, Dad, I do.' My voice caught. I hadn't expected him to be like this. 'I don't want to hurt you, you know that, it's just—'

'I'll see what I can do,' he said abruptly. 'Now, is there anything else?'

Even if there was, I wouldn't have had the nerve. 'No. Just say hi to Mam for me.'

'Right.'

He didn't put down the phone.

Neither did I.

Both of us said 'well' together.

He began again. 'Well, bye-bye, Vicky.'

'Yeah. Bye.' Pause. 'And thanks, Dad.'

He mumbled something and hung up.

Chapter Nine

MY DAD DIDN'T contact me all weekend. And it wasn't that he couldn't have. He had my mobile number, my work number *and* the number of the communal phone in the hall of the apartments. He even had Sal's mobile number for some obscure reason. In fact, given the chance, he'd have had the contact numbers of everyone I knew. So for him not to ring was deliberate. I began to wonder if he'd even told Mam that I'd been in contact, but I decided to give him the benefit of the doubt at least until Tuesday. If I didn't hear from him by then, I'd get back on to him.

If I had the nerve.

'Ready?' Sal poked her head in my bedroom door. Long blonde hair, coloured that very day, fell across her face. She brushed it back impatiently and looked at me in exasperation. 'Jesus, Vic, what is the hold-up in here?'

I'd been sitting cross-legged on my bed, headphones shoved in my ears, listening to a CD I'd bought on the way home from work. Between the first track and the fourth, I'd painted my nails and attempted to blow-dry my hair. It hadn't been the most successful of efforts. My hair stuck out everywhere, but then again, it always did.

'You haven't even got dressed yet!' Sal glared at me. 'Mel is on her way over.'

'Sorry.' I jumped up from the bed, my Walkman clattering to the floor. Bits of fluff from the bedspread duly embedded themselves on my wet nails. 'Oh, shit!'

'We're not going to wait.' Sal gave me another of her expert glares and slammed the door.

I stuck my tongue out at the closed door and grumpily began to look through my wardrobe for some inspiration. There wasn't really much point. Sal always outshone me in the fashion stakes. Not that I was in competition with her or anything, it was just that even when I'd made a humongous effort, she still looked heaps better than me.

'Where are we going anyway?' I hoped it was a pub. I had jeans for that.

'Club Zero.'

Great. I morosely discarded the jeans. Club Zero was only the newest, trendiest place in town. It had been opened a month ago by some famous film star or other. Trust Sal to want to spend a Saturday night posing and flirting. I'd be far happier sitting in a pub, drinking a Bud and having a bit of craic. But unfortunately, if I didn't go out with Sal, all I'd be doing was watching TV and wondering if my folks were ever going to ring.

I began a search for trendy clothes. The first thing I found was a tiny black skirt hiding away at the back of the wardrobe. But the fake-tan issue reared its ugly head and I decided against it. A few minutes later, I located a pair of red jeans that I'd forgotten I had. They'd looked good on me the last time I'd worn them. Laying them on my bed, I began a search for a matching top. The only one I had was orange with a big red sun.

Red and orange.

Mmmm.

'Vic? I'm waiting!'

I dressed hastily. Well, as hastily as I could seeing as how I had to lie on the bed to pull my zip up. A cut finger later and I surveyed myself in the mirror. The colours didn't look too bad together actually. At speed, I braided my hair into two plaits to keep it in check and let the side bits fall down around my face. A pair of boots and I was set.

'Are you not wearing make-up?' Sal asked accusingly when I walked out.

'I wasn't sure I had the time,' I muttered. Mel hadn't yet arrived.

'You've always time to put on make-up.' Sal rolled her eyes. 'Honestly, Vic, we're not heading to a grotty little pub here.'

'Yeah. I know.'

'So, put on a bit of make-up, would you. Jesus, your skin is so pale they'll quarantine you when you arrive.'

Red-haired, pale-skinned, that was me. Sal on the other hand had a constant tan from spending all her free time on a sunbed. Her hair was bleached to a bright yellow and she looked every inch a 90210 babe. And, as usual, she'd outdone me in the clothes stakes. A pale blue miniskirt, white, tiny, tight top and powder blue slip-on shoes. Her hair tumbled down around her diminutive shoulders and just looking at her made me feel like a hick.

Who was I kidding? I *was* a hick.

I shoved on some foundation that instantly caked on my face. Yep, I'd forgotten the moisturising trick Sal had taught me. Still, at least I looked healthy. Some eye shadow and lipstick were also applied along with plenty of red blusher.

Mel buzzed up just as I finished.

Sal opened the door to her and there was lots of squealing and giggling and air-kissing. I dunno, maybe I'm just not girlie enough but to me that sort of stuff makes me laugh.

'Hiyaaaa, Vicky,' Mel cooed, waving all her fingers over at me. 'Ready for some fun?'

'She's only putting on her make-up.' Sal rolled her eyes. 'I had to tell her to do it.'

I smiled cheerily over at them.

Mel looked shocked. 'No. No way. You *forgot* to do your make-up?'

'I didn't forget,' I said. 'Sal wanted me to hurry up and it was a toss-up between getting dressed or doing my make-up. I reckon I stood a better chance of getting into Club Zero with clothes on.'

Mel screeched with laughter. Sal tossed her blonde mane and managed to look disgusted. 'Come on, let's go. There'll be a queue a mile long if we don't hurry.'

There was a queue two miles long. Sal hopped from one foot to the other, trying to pretend she wasn't freezing. Mel pulled her fake fur around her and started to tell Sal all about her week in work. Mel worked on *Tell!*; Sal was carefully cultivating her friendship in the hope that it would lead somewhere.

'So,' Mel finished up a story about having champagne with Nicole Kidman at the premiere of some film, 'what did you work on this week? Any interesting pieces?'

She'd done a dead funny one about the rats in the local canal.

'Mmm. Some.' Sal managed a mysterious, casual shrug and changed the subject. 'How long will it take us to get in, do you think?'

'Ages,' I said.

She shot me a withering look.

'This is a great place' – Mel lowered her voice – 'all the celebs come here. Great for gossip too. It's worth waiting ages to get into.'

'Absolutely,' Sal nodded.

There was a silence. Sal took out a cigarette and lit it.

The queue moved forward another inch.

'They all call her Nic, you know,' Mel said then.

'Who?' Sal asked.

'Nicole Kidman,' Mel said. 'All her family.'

'Mine call me Vic,' I offered.

Mel guffawed.

Sal puffed a long stream of smoke into the air.

The queue moved forward a good bit.

'Nearly there,' Mel said.

We were about two feet from the top of the queue when one of the bouncers spotted Mel.

'Mel?' he said. 'Is it you?'

'Oooh!' Mel frightened the life out of both Sal and me by her squeal. She sounded like a pig in its final moments. 'Gregory! Hey, how *are* you.' Air-kiss. Air-kiss.

'You should have come straight to the top,' Gregory said. 'Come on in.'

'And my lovely friends too?' Mel asked.

'This way, ladies.' The bouncer gave Sal an appreciative look as she wiggled on past him.

He barely glanced at me.

Well, I thought, he wasn't worth looking at either.

Club Zero was gorgeous. Called Zero, I guess, because there was very little in it. Minimalist décor – all brushed steel and light wood. Most of the tables were taken when we got in but we managed to find one, right at the back of the room. A glass-topped table with steel legs. We sat on hard steel chairs and Mel offered to buy us all a first round.

Well, I presume she did; it was hard to hear over the music pumping out of the speakers.

'So, a Bud, a tequila and a Red Bull and vodka,' she shouted, taking her tiny, glittery purse out of her tiny, glittery bag. 'Back in a sec.'

Sal and I watched her totter off.

'Isn't this fab?' Sal was busy looking around. 'Honestly, Mel can get into some great places. That'll be me someday.'

I smiled. I had no doubt about it. Sal was a great writer. Her pieces for *Tell!* were hilarious.

'Oh, isn't that your man?' Sal sat up straight in her seat. 'The guy from that new boy band?'

'Where?'

'Just over your shoulder,' Sal said. 'Now don't look too – Jesus!'

I had done a complete swivel about and located the boy band member. He raised his glass to me and I grinned back.

'Did you have to make it so obvious?' Sal snarled when I

turned back. 'Honestly, Vic, you always do that. I tell you not to look and wham, you go and look.'

'Sure he doesn't care' – I shook my head – 'he thinks it's great being recognised.'

'Yeah, well, it's not exactly cool, is it, to go gawping at famous people?'

'Who cares about being cool?' I rolled my eyes. 'Sure we're only having a laugh.'

To prove my point, I turned back to boy band member and gave a little flirty wave.

'Jesus!' Sal glared at me.

It was just as well Mel arrived back with our drinks 'cause I think Sal would have stalked off in a huff. She was dead conscious about her image. I guess it was because she *had* an image. Maybe I did too, only I'm not too sure what mine was. I didn't care about keeping it either. All I wanted was a good time.

'Bottoms up,' Mel said, raising her glass. 'To the girls.'

Now, wasn't that a ridiculous toast?

To the *girls*?

Sal repeated it after her as if she'd just toasted world peace.

I clinked my bottle off their glasses and took a huge slug of Bud. They sipped decorously and draped themselves elegantly over their seats while I leaned elbows on the table to see if I could spot any more famous people.

There were piles of them. A few made their way to our table to talk to Mel. She 'darlinged' them to extinction. Then Sal shook their hands and gave her perfect smile. And giggled a lot. Then I did. Shook their hands, I mean. Then when they left, we all went back to drinking again while Mel explained what they were really like.

'He's mad,' Mel confided to us about one of the stars of a British soap. 'D'you know, on set he won't let anyone sit on his seat. And if anyone does,' she looked at us and whispered, 'he fires them.'

'Asshole,' I muttered.

Sal and Mel looked at me aghast.

'It's because he's *creative*,' Mel explained. 'Creative people are like that.'

'Well,' I raised my eyebrows, 'I've never met a *creative* asshole before. Sounds dead promising. Better than any of the fellas I've been with recently.'

Mel guffawed. Sal didn't.

I drank some more.

'Men are assholes, though, aren't they?' Mel said casually. 'At least all the ones I know are.'

'Except Lorcan,' I grinned.

Lorcan was Mel's really strange boyfriend.

'Yes,' Mel agreed, 'except Lorcs.'

I swilled my drink around. Listened to Sal and Mel tear their previous guys to shreds. I dunno what Sal was on about really. Most of the guys she went out with were mad about her. She always did the dumping.

I tended to do the dumping too. But that was because the guys I picked up were complete eejits. The ones that weren't eejits dumped me.

Wasn't that always the way?

'Who was your last fella?'

I became aware that their attention was focused on me. Obviously they'd spilled their emotional baggage.

'His name was Ron, wasn't it?' Sal said. 'Ron the Ride, that's what we called him.'

'Because he worked in Funderland,' I clarified to Mel, who was looking impressed. 'He operated the Bone Cruncher.'

'Lovely,' Mel winced.

'He offered to paint Vic's name on all the carriages, didn't he?' Sal giggled.

'Yep.' I rolled my eyes. 'I mean, can you imagine it – people puking up all over my name?'

Sal and Mel laughed.

I didn't. That suggestion had been the beginning of the end for us and thinking about it still hurt a bit.

'And he even—' Sal was preparing to divulge all the nitty-gritty details of my love life when she noticed that Mel wasn't paying attention any more. I was glad because I knew what she was going to say. And it wasn't Mel's business.

'Hey, Mel, what's up?'

Mel was smiling quietly to herself. She turned towards Sal and said 'Bingo' very quietly.

'Here?' Sal looked confused.

Then Mel looked confused.

Then both of them said, 'What?' together.

Then Sal said, 'What do you mean, "Bingo"?'

Mel 'tisked' as Sal looked contrite.

'See that gentleman over there,' Mel gave a discreet point.

I swivelled once again in my chair. 'The one in the—?'

'For goodness' sake.' Mel's hissed whisper caught me by surprise. This was ferocious. 'Will you just stay where you are!'

Sal glared at me.

'The man in the blue denim jacket and red shirt,' Mel said again to Sal.

'I see him.' Sal looked at her curiously. 'Why?'

Mel winked. 'Tell you Monday,' she said.

'Aw, Mel—'

'No,' Mel said, quite sharply, I thought. Then she flung a look at me.

Then Sal looked at me.

So I knew that whatever it was had to be top secret and that I was in the way.

'I can get out of your way if you want,' I offered.

'Monday,' Mel said, to Sal, ignoring me. 'Gimme a call.'

Sal's face lit up like Sellafield. 'Oh, great, yeah, sure.'

Then they both smiled at me.

'Here's to a great night,' Mel called another toast.

We clinked our drinks.

Chapter Ten

THE NIGHT GOT a bit weird from there. Weird for me, I mean. The way my nights out always tend to be.

It started off with my being abandoned by both Sal and Mel. Mel left to go chat with some weirdos wearing tablecloths and lampshades. There was a lot of drawling and 'Oh yaahing' from them. Along with the obligatory kisses.

Sal then decided to get closer to the red-shirted, denim-jacket man, so off she went to the bar and began to flirt with about half the place. She could bat for Australia. Bat her eyelashes, that is. Before long, she was chatting away to some hunk of testosterone at the bar. I could tell by the way she was touching him ever so casually that she was lining him up to pay for her drinks.

'Hey, you're looking kind of lonely, girl, do you need someone new to talk to?'

It was boy band member. He'd slid in beside me with just about the crappiest chat-up I'd ever heard. I sang back, deadpan, 'Oooh, oooh, I don't want to share the night together.'

Boy band winced. 'Ha!' He tried to make a joke of it. 'Wouldn't have had you down for a Doctor Hook fan.'

'I'm not.' I stared into my drink. Handsome eighteen-year-olds are not my idea of a good time. I was no cradle snatcher.

And besides, I wanted to go home. Now that Sal had decided to flirt, there wouldn't be a guy left in the place for me.

'Oh.' Boy band paused. Flicked his floppy red, gold and brown highlighted hair from his face. 'So you won't like our new single then. That's what we're doing. A cover of "Sharing The Night Together".'

'Great.' I managed to look as if I was pleased for him. 'Good luck with it.' Why on earth was he talking to me? There were plenty of nubile miniskirts his own age about.

He beamed at me. 'Ta.' Then, 'Are you famous or what?'

'Sorry?'

His baby blues studied me intently. 'Are you famous?' He gawked around him. 'I mean, most of the people in here are.' An impressed sigh. 'It's, like, mega, isn't it?'

'Mmm.'

'So?' he looked at me expectantly.

'Well, I can't be that famous – I mean, you don't know who I am, do you?'

Frown. 'We-ell, you look like yer one, you know, the one that does be in the films.' He nodded sagely. 'That's who I thought you were straight away.'

'What one in the films?' Despite myself, I was flattered.

'Yer one, the dark-haired one, what's her name?'

'Sandra Bullock?' I despised the hope in my voice.

He exploded with laughter. 'Naw.' He displayed his American-ised mouthful of teeth. 'She is *gorgeous*. I mean the other one.'

'The ugly one?' I couldn't help it. He'd walked himself into it now.

He missed my irony. 'Not *exactly* ugly.' His face crinkled up with the effort of thinking. 'She's sort of fat sometimes.'

'Oh. Right.' I was beginning not to want to know.

'Not Minnie Driver,' he said. 'You're not Minnie Driver, are you?'

'Nope. I'd be an Audi driver though, given half the chance.'

He laughed in such a way that I knew he didn't really find it funny. It was the sort of laugh that didn't know when to end, so it was all loud and hearty one minute and the next – nothing.

'OK.' He tried to make out that he was holding the chuckles in check. 'Yer wan I'm thinking of has a baby. Have you a baby?'

'Nope.'

'Oh.' His handsome face fell. 'So you're not her.'

''Fraid not.'

'So, who are you then?' He looked wonderingly at me.

'Victoria McCarthy.' I said my name as if it should mean something.

Blank. Then, 'Related to the Paul McCarthy?'

Yep. I had an obnoxious cousin called Paul. 'Uh-huh.'

'The singer?' Before I could answer, he said consideringly, 'Yeah, you do look like him, come to think of it.'

He couldn't be serious. I searched his face for some sign that there was a joke going on.

Nothing.

I leaned towards him, waved my glass. 'What's this you were saying about a new single?'

He took the hint. Asked me if I wanted a drink and promised that we'd talk as soon as he came back.

I almost felt guilty but then again, he'd thought I was a fat film star.

It didn't take long to realise that I had just met the thickest guy on the whole planet. If he'd been a magician, he'd have made a fortune because he could swallow everything. I guess I did know a bit about music but hey, I'd never sat in on a Lennon-McCartney recording session. In fact, I was a bit insulted that he thought I was that old. *And* I hadn't ever backed Leonard Cohen up in concert because one of his backing singers was sick. 'They're always pulling that one,' I said airily to him.

'Right,' he nodded, as if picking up life tips from the master. I don't actually think he knew who Leonard Cohen was.

And I honestly expected him to guess I was spoofing him when I told him that I'd once been in a Michael Jackson video.

I was the stand-in dancer.

For Michael.

'Hey,' he said instead, 'that must be where I recognise you from. I just, like, love that guy's videos.'

I'd done it now. Dug myself in so deep that there was no way I could get out without making an idiot of the kid.

And he was so innocent and accepting that I couldn't do that.

So I just kept digging.

His name was Cliff, after Cliff Richard. His hero was Ronan Keating and his favourite song was 'Uptown Girl' – the Westlife version. He was eighteen, had just reached number thirteen in the charts with his cover of 'Sharing The Night Together' and the other guys in his band were all former models. 'But they can sing,' he assured me.

'Great.'

Maybe I could escape to the loo and climb out a window? The guilt was killing me. I mean, I couldn't even look him straight in the face any more.

'So, maybe you'll tell Paul to look out for us?' he asked. His voice had gone a little breathless; the way voices do when they believe that Nirvana is just within reach.

'I don't talk to Paul that much,' I said. The look of devastation on his face prompted me to add, 'About once a month or so, so I'll mention it next time. All right?'

'Ace. Classy.' He nodded and grinned. 'Classy,' he said again. He offered to buy me another drink. 'A Bud, is it?'

'Aw, no.' I shook my head and stood up. There was no way in good conscience I could let him buy me another drink. It was best to get away from the kid now. I'd hide in the toilet until the place closed down or something. 'I'd better go.'

'Suppose you've got a big limo waiting for you,' he said wistfully.

'Nope. Just a plain old taxi,' I grinned.

'Oh, well hey' – he waved wildly at a guy across the room – 'let my manager give you a lift home. He drives us everywhere. Hey, hey, Marti!'

His manager!

'Marti, over here!'

'Aw, no, Cliff, I honestly—'

I saw Marti excusing himself from a group of people and coming towards us.

'Cliff, I'd better—'

Cliff smiled at me. 'Marti, Victoria McCarthy' – 'he stressed the McCarthy – 'wants a lift home. Will you give her one?'

It was on the tip of Marti's tongue to make a rude comment to that. Don't ask me how I knew, I just did. I blushed and he blushed and then we both began to grin.

'She knows Paul McCarthy,' Cliff said then. 'She's related to him.'

'Paul McCarthy?' Marti raised his eyebrows. 'Who the hell is that?'

Cliff looked embarrassed for his manager. 'The Beatles,' he hissed, poking him with his finger.

'That's McCartney,' Marti snorted. 'Jesus.'

Cliff's face dropped.

I smiled as best I could. 'Sorry.'

'And the Michael Jackson thing?' Cliff sounded wounded.

'Sorry,' I said again.

'And, yer man, Leonard Comb?'

'Cohen,' Marti snapped. 'Jesus.'

All I could manage was a 'ha'.

As Cliff slunk off, I was left with Marti.

The manager.

He stared at me. I stared, uncomfortably, back.

'Suppose the lift is out of the question,' I joked feebly. Not that I would have gone with him anyway. With my bad luck, he mightn't even have tried to kiss me.

He grinned. 'Forget the lift, let me buy you a drink to make up for my totally thick lead singer?'

It was an offer too good to refuse.

Chapter Eleven

Marti was thirty-four and five foot six. He'd worked with loads of bands and he named them off like a kid would the alphabet. Not that he was boasting or anything, he just told me because I asked him if being a manager was his full-time job. Yep, a stupid question but hey, you try making conversation with a dark, though much smaller version of Brad Pitt. I mean, these type of guys just don't talk to me when Sal is in the room. But the chances were that he hadn't spotted her yet.

'Let's see' – Marti lay back in the hard metal chair and sprawled his legs under the table – 'I started out in the business about five years ago when a band I was in went belly-up. You might have heard of us – we were called Low Life.'

'Naw,' I said. Then to ease the blow, I joked, 'But I've met loads of guys matching that description.'

Marti guffawed. Took a slug of his pint. 'Anyways,' he said, 'I got fed up of the music scene and I decided that I'd take a more background role. So, I found a little band that were going nowhere and I nudged them in the right direction.'

'Really? What band was that?'

He waved his hand about. 'Aw, now, you wouldn't have heard of them. They made it big in Dubai. Never did the business over here. I've a lot of contacts in Dubai.'

'Oh. Right.'

'Hey, don't knock it, Dubai is a good market.'

I wasn't going to knock anything. 'And then?' I asked.

I watched as Marti lifted his pint to his lips. He had nice lips.

Sort of pouty but not in a girlie way. His hair was dark and floppy, cut in this really cool style, all choppy and edgy. His skin was spot-free and had just the right hint of stubble. His eyes though were a mystery 'cause the flashing lights made them look purple. And he was loads taller than me. I liked the way he sprawled about in his chair. It had an easy-going air about it. Marti licked the foam from around his mouth and sighed deeply as if it was the best pint he'd ever tasted.

'And then,' he said, 'I found other bands, did the same thing. I've had a guy, Emilio Byrne, make it big in Nigeria. Now, how many managers have you heard do that?'

'None,' I said truthfully.

Marti nodded in satisfaction. 'There now,' he said, as if he'd just proved his worth as a human being. 'There you are.'

'That's great,' I said.

'Then I got married,' Marti went on.

It took a second for me to digest that bit of information and, before I fully had, he added, 'And then I had a son.'

'A son?' I virtually squealed out the word. 'Great.' My first thought was Jesus Christ Almighty get me out of here. My second one was – no wonder he's chatting me up.

'Then she left me.' Marti added.

I suppose it was some consolation. 'Did she?'

'Holding the baby.'

'Aw, God.'

''Course he wasn't really a baby, he was five. He'll be five and a half now tomorrow.' Marti drained his pint and looked at me. 'What do you think of that?'

I thought it was awful. That's what I thought. I didn't know how he could be so matter-of-fact about it. 'And does your wife ring your little boy or anything?'

'It only upsets him.' Marti banged his pint in front of me. 'So I disconnected the house phone. Only use this now.' He tapped his breast pocket. 'The mobile.'

'Poor little kid,' I said.

'She'll come crawling back now that I've made it with Boy Five,' Marti said, wiping his mouth with his sleeve and leaning towards me. 'But she's wasting her time. I don't need her any more.' He thumbed in the direction Cliff had gone. 'Thick as a plate of cold custard but a great voice on him. They'll go far. Tell you what, we'll give Louis Walsh and the boys a run for their money.' He grinned, showing even, white teeth. 'Connections, that's what you need in this business. I brought the boys here to make a few connections. Cliff though wouldn't recognise a connection if it came attached to a plug socket.'

I didn't know if I should laugh.

'Good singer though.'

'He said the song is number thirteen.'

'And rising,' Marti said.

'Congratulations.'

'Ta.'

'Want another beer to celebrate?'

'I wouldn't say no.'

On the way to the bar I wondered if I was stupid. The guy was married, for God's sake. Married but separated, another part of me said. And we were just chatting. OK, he was chatting, I was listening. But I liked it like that. I've never been one for talking about myself.

'So tell us about yourself?' Marti asked.

'Nothing to tell,' I grinned, slugging back my fifth Bud. Or was it my sixth? 'Your average Irish Catholic twenty-something.'

'I like the Irish twenty-something part,' Marti said. 'So two out of three ain't bad.'

I grinned.

'You're not from Dublin?'

'No. I'm not.' More drink. 'Cork.'

'I managed a band from there once. You might have heard of them – the Rosslare Rockers?'

'Nope.' I frowned. 'But isn't Rosslare in Wexford?'
'That was the joke of it,' Marti said.
'Oh.'
'They were pretty big at one stage.'
'Well, I never heard of them.'
'You're probably just not into music,' Marti said knowledgeably. 'A lot of women aren't.'
'Well, maybe—'
'My wife, now, she wasn't into music. Wasn't into a lot of things, come to think of it.' Pause. 'Which I'd rather not.'
Both of us looked into our drinks.
The silence grew a bit uncomfortable with both of us trying not to think of his wife.
'What do you do?' Marti asked then. In a slightly bitter voice, he added, 'Betcha you're not married.'
'Good bet.'
'Are you here on your own?'
'Well, I came with a flatmate and her friend but they've deserted me.'
'Ouch.'
Shit. I'd made myself sound like a loser. 'Yeah,' I managed a passable scoff, 'they can't stand the competition. With me about they've no chance with fellas.'
Marti smiled. 'I can believe that,' he said, looking at me in a funny way.
Yeah. Right. I drank some more and laughed a little.
'So, what else do you do?' Marti's eyes were still giving me *that* look. 'Besides hook vulnerable guys?' Before I could answer, he held up his hand. 'Nope, don't tell. Let me guess.' He studied my red jeans and orange top. 'You look like the sort of girl that works in a trendy juice bar or something.'
It was said in all seriousness.
'Or a vegetarian place,' he added.
'I work in a toy shop,' I told him.
He laughed. 'Nah.'

'I do,' I said. 'Honestly. Toys Galore in Yellow Halls.'

'Adult toys?' His eyes sparked with interest.

'Well, if you're into Barbie, maybe. Otherwise it's kids only.'

'Aw, that's—'

'Hey, hey, Marti!' A kid, barely out of nappies, was calling Marti over. 'Come here, willya?'

Marti rolled his eyes. 'Can't even chat up a nice-looking girl in peace,' he said, standing up as prepubescent scurried over. 'What's the problem?' he asked.

'I've made a connection, Marti. The editor from *Tell!* is here. She wants to talk to you.'

Marti dusted himself down.

'I know her,' I said.

Marti chortled. 'I'm not as stupid as Cliff, you know.'

'I do know her.'

''Course you do,' he winked one of his purple eyes. 'Look, back in a sec. Just let me talk to this woman, will you?' Without waiting for my answer, he turned to the young lad. 'Good work, Robin,' he said.

Robin looked thrilled.

The two walked off together.

To my surprise, he actually did arrive back. Rolling his eyes, he sat in beside me.

'Not the best pitch I ever made,' he muttered, placing his pint back on the table. 'I'll have to do better next time.'

'Hard luck.'

'And speaking of next time,' he grinned at me, 'I'm making a pitch now. D'you fancy coming out with me at some stage?'

I was caught on the hop. I hadn't expected him to ask me out. Granted, we'd chatted most of the night, but he was married, for God's sake. 'Aw, I dunno.' If my folks found out they'd die.

'Please?' His purple eyes looked so appealing. 'OK, maybe I shouldn't have told you about having the wife and the kid, but at least you know what you're getting into.'

That's what worried me. I mean, what if I had to meet his kid? What if his wife was the jealous type?

'Just one night?'

He looked so appealing that I found it hard to refuse him.

'Tickets to see Boy Five live?' He rummaged about in his pocket and pulled out a wad of tickets. 'As you can see, they're going fast.'

I laughed.

'And to be honest, any connection with Paul McCarthy is valuable to me.'

'All right then,' I found myself saying, attracted by his humour. 'Let's see how it goes.'

We swapped phone numbers and he said he'd pick me up the following Saturday at seven.

Chapter Twelve

MONDAY MORNING.

The office was shining.

Bridie, for some bizarre reason, had decided to clean it.

She'd obviously come in appallingly early and now the room reeked with the smell of vinegar and polish. My desk, which up to this had been a dull brown, was now a less dull brown and all my baskets and order forms had been neatly piled one on top of the other. There was even a desk tidy that hadn't been there before and the black filing cabinets glinted with the winter sun pouring in the newly polished window.

Bridie virtually stood to attention as I entered.

'Hey,' I said, 'the cleaning fairies must have been in during the night.' I dumped my bag onto the desk and grinned at her.

'Oh, I just decided to do a bit of housekeeping in the office,' Bride tittered as she removed my bag from the desk with as much tact as possible. 'It'll smear the wood,' she said as she apologetically placed it on the floor.

'Is O'Neill paying you extra to do this?' I asked.

'Oh *no,* and I wouldn't *ask* for it.' Bridie was shocked. 'I just thought with,' lowered voice, 'the son starting that we could put on a decent show.'

'Well I can sing – what do you do?'

'I meant—'

'Let me guess' – I did a big psychic thing on it – 'you are an acrobat. The triple somersault a speciality?'

She gave a weak laugh.

'A lion tamer?'

'Oh now, you're too smart for me, so you are. Too smart.'

We smiled at each other. Bridie began to pack her dusters away in a brown bag. The sight of her frail bent body rummaging about in a tattered bag touched me.

'Look,' I said gently, 'don't be worrying yourself about this fella, *he's* the beginner. He won't know anything.'

She coloured. 'Who's worried? I'm not worried.'

'We'll beat him into shape.'

She ignored me. 'I mean, if I can't polish up without you thinking I'm worried, when can I polish? I'm not the sort that worries. All I want to do is to—'

'Create a good impression. I know.'

'Good.' She folded her arms tightly about herself and stood looking at me. 'What time's he coming anyway?'

'O'Neill said midday.'

'*Mister* O'Neill,' Bridie corrected. 'You can't go about calling him O'Neill when the son is here.'

'Midday,' I said, ignoring her. 'What sort of a time is that to start a job? I dunno. Well, it'll be his last midday, that's all I can say.'

'You wouldn't want to be going getting his back up, now,' Bridie said. 'Creating tension.'

Bridie was creating enough tension for the two of us. I decided to change the subject. I plugged in our white kettle – it had always been a beigey colour before – and asked, 'So, how'd the weekend go? Any mad parties?'

She laughed, as I knew she would. Bridie has a very simple sense of humour. Anything mildly risqué and she titters uncontrollably. 'Oh now, I'm well past the mad party stage. No' – she found a cup and handed it to me – 'I did a lot of cleaning on Saturday night – hoovering and dusting and such like. Then on Sunday, I went to eight mass, bought the papers and sat down for the afternoon. I had a nice bit of chicken for my dinner.

The butcher I go to does a lovely bit of chicken. I could get you some if you like. Very reasonable.'

'Does it come in tin foil with curry sauce and rice?'

'Oh now.' A titter before she straightened the desk tidy. 'And you – how was your weekend? Did you go home?'

'Went to a club with Sal.'

'Is that your reporter friend?'

'Uh-huh.'

'Well, you can tell her from me that her piece on sponge cakes was first-rate.'

Sal? Sponge cakes? She'd obviously cogged it from someone else. 'I will.'

Bridie looked at her watch. 'Well, better get some work done. You finish your tea, don't drink it too fast, it'll burn your mouth. Sit there now and I'll open up.'

She always said that.

I watched her leave.

There were plenty of customers in that morning, which was good. Bridie was showing one boisterous kid the joys of wrestling rings. I wish I'd nabbed him first – the wrestling rings were cool.

Dominic, a small three-year-old, was over playing with the opened box of Lego. His mother hovered around, pretending to look at the shelves but really in the shop for the warmth. The two came in every second day for a couple of hours, having being thrown out of their B&B. The mother, with her tight jeans and crop tops, was a tough-looking woman who never talked much. Dominic was cute, though. Sometimes I'd buy him a lollipop and, if his mother was in good form, she'd let him take it from me. If she wasn't, she'd tell me that she didn't take charity.

I was a bit scared of her, to be honest.

At eleven fifty-five, despite my best intentions, I was getting as edgy as Bridie. At least I'd dressed a bit more upmarket that day. There was no way this guy was going to think Bridie and

I were a couple to be messed with. I'd power dressed and power blow-dried my hair. It now just frizzed out a little.

I'd blind him with knowledge. I'd be brisk, efficient and managerial.

Jesus, I hoped he'd be on time.

I didn't know if I'd have the nerve to give out to him if he wasn't.

The second hand on my watch was ticking off another minute when the phone rang. Thinking it would create a good impression to see me too busy to talk to him when he did arrive, I answered it.

'Hello?'

'Oh, hello, love, it's me.'

It was my mother. 'Mam. Hiya.'

I was vaguely aware of someone coming in the door. I did a quick check and it wasn't the dreaded O'Neill. The someone stood beside the counter and I indicated the phone. He shrugged and, shoving his hands into his pockets, slouched against the counter.

'I'm sorry for ringing you at work, love,' Mam said breathlessly, 'but I think your mobile might be dead or whatever it is they say.'

Damn! I was always forgetting to charge the bloody thing. 'Could be,' I said. My heart began a slow pounding. 'Sooo?' I didn't want to ask why she'd rung. I was afraid it might hurt her feelings. She never rang me in work. Ever. 'How's things?'

'I found that information you were looking for.' Mam ignored my question as she rushed on. 'I just wanted to ring and tell you.'

'Oh.' I didn't know what to say to that. 'Great.' I began to fumble among the junk on the desk for a pen. Papers flew everywhere. Eventually my sweaty fingers found a Biro lodged against the till. 'That's great. Have you the details there?'

I wished the fecker would move away from the counter. If I didn't know better, I'd swear he was earwigging on my conversation.

Bridie was signalling me in agitation.

'Well, no.' Mam sounded flustered. 'I sent all the documents up with Tommy. He was down the—'

'Tommy?' I paused. Took a breath. 'You've *told* Tommy?'

'Well, no, love.' She was struggling now. My tetchy tone had upset her. But, hell, how could she have done that? It was my business. *Mine.*

'It's my business, Mam.'

'I know it is, love, but you see, I didn't exactly know what to look for so I just sent it all up to you. Tommy's just delivering it. He won't look at it.'

Tommy of all people. Tommy, my childhood tormentor. My adulthood tormentor, come to think of it. 'He'd better not.' They'd known I didn't like him. How could they have—?

'I just thought it might be safer than posting it,' Mam said then, after a pause. 'I mean, if you came home every weekend I could have held on to—'

'I come home when I can.' I turned away from the guy and muttered furiously into the phone. 'I'm very busy up here.'

Bridie was going red in the face, pointing and gesturing.

'I know you are, love.' Mam's voice was contrite. 'And I'm sorry if I've done the wrong thing.'

'It's fine,' I muttered, though it wasn't. Tommy? For Christ's sake! 'So when will he give it to me?'

'Today, most likely. He said he'd drop it into you in work. He works near you, you see. Just around the corner, he said.'

'Right.'

Bridie was now scuttling towards me. She had a piece of paper in her hand and, covering it, like a kid in school, she shoved it in front of my face. *The son*, it said. A big arrow pointed at the guy at the counter.

I shook my head. Rolled my eyes and pushed her paper away. Honestly, she was getting on my nerves now. 'Bridie, see to this man, will you,' I said.

'I hope it's all there,' my mother was saying. 'If it's not you can ring me on Thursday. I'll be away for a few days.'

'Hiya,' the young guy was saying to Bridie. 'Ed O'Neill.' He offered her his hand.

I dropped the phone.

'Vicky?' my mam was saying anxiously as I picked it up from the floor. 'Are you there?'

'Yeah.' I was staring askance at the fella, willing Bridie to say something instead of staring awestruck at him. 'Listen, Mam, thanks a lot. I've to go now.'

Before she even said her goodbyes, I'd hung up.

'Don't hang up on my account,' Ed O'Neill said, looking at me with these amazing blue eyes. They flicked from one to the other of us. 'I won't tell Dad, you know.'

Bridie gave a false whoop of a laugh that embarrassed everyone.

'I'm Vicky.' I held out my hand to Ed. Determined to ignore his last comment, I said coolly, 'The manager.'

He took my hand in a firm grip and gave a small grin. 'I'm Ed,' he said, nodding slightly. Pointing to Bridie's discarded bit of paper, he added, 'The son.'

Bridie shuddered.

Either this guy took a terrible photo or it was another son. 'I didn't know O'Neill—'

Bridie gasped.

'Mr O'Neill,' I corrected, flushing, 'had two sons.'

Ed shrugged. 'Well he does.' His voice had the slow cadences of the north. 'Only' – he shrugged again – 'I'm the son he doesn't talk about.'

'Oh now,' Bridie gave another slightly hysterical laugh, 'I'm sure he does. Sure he can't deny you anyway – you're the spit of him, so you are.'

Well, that was an insult if ever there was one.

That fat, balding, slobbering Albert O'Neill had ever looked like his son was hard to believe. It was like saying that a big slug of a caterpillar looked like a butterfly. To put it bluntly, Ed

O'Neill was a fine thing. Completely different from what I'd been expecting. He looked nothing like his dour brother. The only thing they had in common was their dark hair. However, where his brother had been clean-shaven and manicured, Ed was not. His whole appearance was unruly, from his close-shaven head to the casual way he was dressed. An orange jacket thrown over a black T-shirt with the band Picture House on the front. He wore grey combats and a pair of expensive trainers. His face was handsome though not in a traditional, strong-jawed model way. Cute, I guess would describe him best. Where he resembled his father most was in his eyes. An unusual shade of pale blue. Shiny eyes. But even there, the expression in them was different from his father's.

Ed turned his attention from me to Bridie. He bestowed on her a devastating smile. His voice all warm and creamy, he said, 'You must be Bridie. I've heard about you.'

Bridie melted. I swear, it was like watching a snowman dissolve into a puddle. Her brown eyes were like two saucers in her face as she beamed at him. 'Well,' she gushed, 'I am *so* pleased to meet you. Vicky and I were *so* looking forward to it.'

'Because we're overworked here,' I said swiftly. 'We hope you'll take some of the burden off us.'

Bridie laughed again.

Ed said nothing.

'I've a file here.' I reached in under the counter and took out a yellow file marked *Training*. I'd spent all last week running it up on the computer. I'd made it as long and as easy to follow as possible. I hoped its length would frighten the shite out of him, make him realise how much we did, and that its simplicity would guarantee us an able worker. 'I'd like you to read it.'

His expression told me that its size had the desired effect. 'All of it?'

'Yes.' I was proud of my casual tone. 'Is that a problem?'

'Is there going to be a sequel?'

Bridie clapped her hands. 'Ha, ha, ha, ha, ha.' Shaking her head, she muttered, 'A caution. A caution.'

'You can read it up in the office,' I said frostily. 'I'll be up in a bit.'

Ed took the file from me and tipped his forehead in a half salute.

'There's biscuits in the red box,' Bridie called after him. 'You can open the new packet.'

Ignoring the incredulous glare I gave her, she turned her back on me and waltzed back down the shop.

Chapter Thirteen

WHEN EVENTUALLY I got a chance to slip upstairs to the office, I was pleased to see Ed busily reading the training file. To my horror, though, he'd also managed to munch halfway through the luxury biscuits that Bridie had bought in honour of his arrival. He was reaching for another when I came alongside him. It was then I noticed that he was drinking coffee from *my* mug.

'That's my mug,' I couldn't resist pointing out.

He looked at the mug and then looked at me. 'Oh. Sorry. I didn't—'

I waved him away, half ashamed of my childishness, but it had suddenly seemed vitally important to let him know that I was in charge. In charge and in control. For some reason his presence in the shop was freaking me out. I dunno if it was the way Bridie had totally capitulated to him or if it was the fact that now he was here, I didn't quite know where I stood. He was the boss's son, for God's sake. One day he'd own this shop.

How much power did I have over him?

I had to start as I meant to go on.

I sat down opposite him and tried to look managerial. It was hard because I'd never done it before. Clasping my hands together in front of me, the way I'd seen O'Neill do, I began laying down the ground rules. 'You'll have to get your own mug for tomorrow and we have a fund for the biscuits, so you'll have to contribute to that.'

'No problem.' He nodded and indicated the training file. 'I

would've given money only I haven't reached that part yet.'

'And you won't either – it's not in it.'

He laughed slightly. 'Aw well, even if it had been, I probably wouldn't have got to it until next year. I mean, who put this together?' He flipped through the pages of the file, a bemused grin on his face. 'It's like *War and Peace*, for God's sake.'

'I put it together. Actually.'

The grin died on his face. 'Oh.'

'And no one has had any problems with it before.' Which was true, as it happens.

He had the grace to look shame-faced. 'Massive apologies then.' A charming smile. 'Boss.'

I was about to smile back and then decided not to. He might be able to charm old ladies like Bridie but I wasn't such an eejit. 'Now, work starts at nine sharp with an hour for lunch and a tea break in the morning.'

'Do we get an afternoon break?'

'Eh—' I was tempted to say yes, but then had the horrifying thought that maybe he was testing me. 'No,' I managed to gulp out. It was the hardest decision I'd ever made. 'No,' I said more firmly, trying to convince myself, 'one break is enough.'

He didn't look impressed.

'You get one day off a week seeing as there's three of us now. I take Monday' – I allowed myself a little smile – 'because I'm the *boss*. Bridie says she'll have Tuesday so you can take one other day.'

'Thursday,' he said without even bothering to think about it. 'I'll have that day.'

'Well, you can think about it. You don't have to decide—'

'Naw, Thursday's great. Shops are open late in Dublin.'

Well for him, I thought. Spending his daddy's money.

'Good for busking,' he added.

'Busking?'

'Uh-huh,' he nodded. 'Dublin's great for busking and I've done it most everywhere.'

Despite my desire to create a professional image I was seriously impressed. I'd always admired buskers. '*Really?*'

'Uh-huh. Worst place I found was Vienna. I got robbed and beaten. Didn't put me off, though.'

'Wow. So you didn't always work for your dad then?'

He flinched, as if I'd hit him. 'I've never worked for my dad until now,' he said. He held my gaze for a second before glancing back down at the training manual.

'Oh.' I wasn't sure if I'd offended him. He certainly *seemed* offended. 'So what did you do? Just busk?'

'I wish.' He grinned ruefully. 'Nah, I worked in London for a while then I came back here.'

'Oh right.' I waited for him to elaborate and when he didn't, I found myself asking, 'Doing what in London?'

'Work,' he said casually.

Well, that was *me* told. I felt myself flushing madly. So, if he wanted it strictly business, strictly business it would be. I'd blind him with knowledge.

A while later, I offered him a tour.

'Right,' he said, looking a bit dazed at all the information I'd managed to impart. 'I'll, eh, just wash your cup first.' He spent ages washing it and then replacing it in the exact same place he'd found it. 'Lead on.' Slight hesitation. Big grin. 'Boss.'

'My name is Vicky,' I said.

He nodded. Didn't reply.

We'd just got out of the office when Bridie accosted us. She almost bowed in front of Ed and blinded us both with the smile she gave him. 'Oooh,' she said, her voice all quivery, 'did you find the biscuits?'

'Aye. Thanks.'

'I bought chocolate ones especially,' Bridie said to me. 'Men like their bit of chocolate.'

God, she was going to get on my nerves bigtime if she kept looking at Ed like that.

'Do they,' I said. 'That's nice.'

Bridie smiled again.

We both waited to hear what she had to say.

'Bridie,' I prompted, 'what do you want?'

'Oh, oh yeah,' she tittered. 'I only came up to tell you that there's a young gentleman to see you.'

I didn't know any gentlemen. 'Are you sure it's for me?'

'Well' – Bridie blinked rapidly – 'he asked for you. He seems like a nice man.'

Definitely not for me.

'Thanks, Bridie.' I indicated Ed. 'Will you do me a favour? I was about to show Ed around – will you do it?'

'Everywhere?'

'Uh-huh. The shop floor, the stores, the lot.'

'Ed,' she beamed, 'if you'll come with me.'

As I watched the two of them descend the stairs, him making her laugh with some comment or other, I wished that he hadn't come.

'Aw, there she is, my favourite cousin.'

Tommy bellowed it out all over the shop so that heads swivelled to look in my direction. Well, two heads actually – Dominic's and his mother's.

'So this is the place you manage, is it?' Tommy bellowed again.

'Uh-huh.'

'I didn't realise you worked so close to me.' Tommy leaned his elbows on the shop counter as I neared him. 'I'm only over the road.'

'Really?'

'Yeah.' Tommy grinned. 'We'll have to do lunch sometime – hey?'

'Sure,' I smiled, knowing that I'd do a runner quicker than I'd do lunch.

'Anyway' – Tommy dug into the folds of his fancy coat and

took out a brown envelope – 'Auntie Evelyn told me to give you that. Said it was important.'

I snatched the envelope from him and shoved it under the counter. 'Yep. Thanks.'

'She said if it wasn't what you wanted to ring her.'

'Great. Thanks.' I looked over his head to a customer coming in the door. Buy something, I willed. Buy something. Anything to get Tommy out of the shop.

'And John only works in Kildare Street,' Tommy was saying, oblivious of my surliness. 'I'll give him a buzz and see if he's interested in meeting up.'

John was almost as bad as Tommy on the appalling cousin scale. In fact it had been John who'd told me that I was adopted. Well, he'd told me I was a 'ready made', which had hurt even more. And OK, so he'd been grounded for a week and he'd been only twelve, but it had hurt and to be honest, it still did.

'So what's the best time for you?' Tommy asked.

'My lunchtimes vary,' I said as apologetically as I could, 'I probably wouldn't be free.'

'You're the manager, aren't you?' Tommy said. 'Suit yourself. That's what I do.'

I had no doubt about it.

'Here.' Tommy drew out a business card. 'Gimme a ring whenever you want to meet up – eh?' He didn't wait for an answer, assuming that I'd be delighted. 'And ring your mother if that stuff isn't what you want,' he said. 'Talk again.'

Not if I could help it, we wouldn't.

I watched him leave and then turned my attention to the brown envelope. I couldn't wait to get back to the flat and tear it open.

Chapter Fourteen

Dear Sir/Madam,

I was adopted through your agency and I would be interested in having more up-to-date information on my background please. Below, please find my personal details. I listed my name, my date of birth and the address of my parents. I put down my mobile number on the letter in case they wanted to contact me. On the calendar near my bedroom door, I wrote, in massive black marker, CHARGE MOBILE. Turning back to the letter, I read it through. Then, hand shaking, I wrote: *I'd also be interested in making contact with my mother with a view to a meeting.*

I liked the way it looked on the page.

I had a mother.

Somewhere out there I had a mother.

I signed the letter.

Sealed the letter.

And kissed it for luck.

I posted it the next day.

Chapter Fifteen

SATURDAY NIGHT.

Marti was strolling up and down the pathway outside the flat, his hands sunk into black trousers. Black trousers with bright green stripes. A green shirt, open to the chest hair, mercifully covered with a green and black leather jacket. My first and very disloyal impression was that he looked like a clown. I tried to think what he'd worn the night I'd met him in Club Zero and couldn't. 'Hey,' he smiled at me as I emerged. 'You look great!'

'Hey,' was all I could manage back.

The garishness of Marti's clothes sort of swamped him. He looked like he was drowning in a sea of green. I shook the thought away. Clothes were so superficial anyway. Still, I didn't want Sal to see him looking like that, she'd die laughing. She'd nearly died when I'd introduced her to him last Saturday night. 'But he's so *small*,' she'd whispered.

'You – look – stunning,' Marti said, admiring me with what I noticed, in horror, were purple eyes.

'Well,' I joked, trying to salvage some humour from the situation, 'I decided I'd go all out and match your eyes.' I indicated my new purple jeans and red top. And OK, maybe my stuff was a bit off, but I liked it.

He laughed loudly. A little too loudly. He was probably as nervous as I was.

'You're in for a treat this evening,' Marti said as he led me to a black car. 'We've VIP tickets, right at the top of the hall.'

'Eh, great.' I wasn't much into boy bands but it had seemed

a good idea last Saturday. It must have been all the Bud I'd drunk.

'That's why I've got this stuff on,' Marti indicated his clothes. 'People will remember me. The same for the eyes.'

'What?'

'Why I wear the purple contacts. No self-respecting record producer will remember the name Marti Hearty, but they'll remember me because I've purple eyes, see.'

Marti Hearty would be a hard name to forget, I reckoned. Still, I could follow his logic. I just wished he hadn't been so logical on our first date.

'So,' Marti asked, snapping his seatbelt on, 'is this OK by you?' He looked anxiously at me, and I saw that he was nervous. 'I mean,' he went on, 'we could give the concert a miss but the lads need my support and I thought you'd like to hear a good band.'

I tried not to smile. My idea of a good band was drummers and guitarists and singers all sort of working together. 'This is fine by me,' I said and he looked relieved. Sure if nothing else, I thought, I could sit and admire Marti's lovely-looking face, which mercifully hadn't changed from my drunken memories.

It was a sort of showcase for new bands. Boy Five were headlining. 'We can go after they perform,' Marti said, shoving the programme into his jacket pocket and striding ahead of me to the backstage entrance. 'I'll just go and wish them luck.'

In the dressing room four of the lads were sitting around in ridiculous silver cowboy costumes.

'Cost a bomb, those outfits,' Marti informed me before asking the lads, 'where's Cliff?'

'In the jax. Puking,' said one of the guys who I later learned was Keith.

As if on cue, there came the sound of vomiting from the toilet.

'Calm down, man. Calm down,' Keith called.

'But we've never sung live before,' Cliff moaned. 'All we ever did was mime.'

'Jaysus!' Marti rolled his eyes at me and strode over to the toilet door. 'Come out, you twat!' he ordered, hammering on it.

'Aw, Marti, I can't.' Retching sounds.

'Are you such a big blouse that you're afraid of a load of ten-year-olds?'

'Me ma and all is out there. And me girlfriend.'

'Right, eleven-year-olds then.'

The other four lads exploded in laughter.

'Feck off,' Cliff moaned.

'Get out of there or you're out of the band.'

'It's not a band – it's just singers.'

'Mimers,' Keith called helpfully.

Marti scowled furiously at him. Then he began to wheedle. 'Look, Cliff, you're on the crest of a wave here. Number thirteen again in Ireland this week. Who knows what's next? England maybe? Come on, you'll be minted. But fall now and Jaysus, it'll be like Eamonn Coughlan and the Olympics.'

'Eamonn who?'

'Fucking thick,' Marti mouthed to me. Back to the toilet, 'Sonia O'Sullivan then.'

'What was she – a one-hit wonder or something?'

Pause. 'Look,' Marti began again, 'first you were afraid, you were petrified. But now, right, you will survive? D'you get me?'

A man poked his head in the door. 'Ten minutes, folks.'

'Oooh,' Cliff moaned.

The other four lads looked at Marti. Big trusting eyes. I even looked at Marti. I felt sorry for him. This, according to him, was his big chance. But the evil part of me hoped that Cliff would stay in there and Marti and I could go somewhere else.

'If you don't get out of there,' Marti yelled, 'I'll give you such a root up the hole, you won't be able to shag that sweet little girlfriend of yours for a month.'

'She won't let me shag her anyway.'

Laughter.

'Jesus!' Marti began to stomp about the place.

'Cliff, will you bleedin' get out of there!' Now it was Keith's turn to hammer on the door. 'How the hell do you think the rest of us feel? I promise, right, that if you do it, I'll give you the twenty euro I owe you.'

'It's thirty.'

'Right, thirty then. Only come out, for God's sake.'

Silence.

'If I forget the words, you'll jump in and sing them, will you?' Cliff called out.

'Yeah. Yeah, I will.'

'Well, then we're really fucked,' one of the other guys muttered dryly.

From behind the toilet door, Cliff laughed. 'Just let me wipe my face,' he said. 'I'll be out in a bit.'

'Come on,' Marti took my arm. 'We'll sit in the wings so I can push the bastard on if he won't go.'

I laughed, but I don't think it was a joke.

Five minutes later, the drum rolls started. From behind the stage, I could hear the crowd out front going wild. Kids screaming, others hooting. The music getting more and more frantic. The drum roll again and Boy Five standing beside me and Marti and sweating buckets. Cliff was being supported by Keith and one of the other lads.

'Yez look fantastic.' Marti clapped each one of them on the back. 'Super.'

They looked like those cheap white Christmas trees my mother had years ago.

'Don't they look super, Vicky?' Marti asked.

'What can I say?' I spluttered. The whole thing was a gas and, to be honest, I was enjoying the excitement of it all.

'Nothing.' Cliff had recognised me and was scowling. 'It's bound to be a lie, anyway.'

'Now, now,' Marti admonished, 'Vicky is my girlfriend.'

The lads gawked at him.

'And when we meet up again, I'll introduce her properly to you all.'

They didn't seem too thrilled at the prospect. Maybe they were just nervous. The compere was building them up.

'Deep breathing,' Marti said urgently. 'In. Out. In. Out. That's the lads.'

'. . . BOY FIVE!'

A huge cheer tore the place apart.

'Run, acknowledge, take your places,' Marti urged.

The five lads jogged onto the stage, waving and smiling.

Screams. Whistles. Some advanced ten-year-old kept yelling out the word 'Rides' over and over again.

They took their places as the backing track began.

And they sang and danced their way through 'Sharing The Night Together'. Keith tripped up on the fringe of his silver trousers during one very complicated lassoing routine but other than that they went down a storm.

And Cliff was a singer.

Completely wasted in a boy band.

They came off the stage to massive cheering.

'They've made it,' Marti whooped, clapping and cheering along with the rest. 'They're going to be stars!'

And even though I'm a music snob at heart, I liked the way Marti danced about the place. I liked it even better when he hugged me to him. Hard.

And at that moment, I fell a little in love with him.

The lads were elated. They opened the bottle of champagne Marti had had delivered to the dressing room and they generously shared a glass with me. Even Cliff managed a smile. Then a press photographer came into the room and took a few snaps. I had to stand at one end of the group while Marti stood at the other. It was all very exciting.

'So.' Marti put down his glass as the photographer left. 'I'll love yez and leave yez, lads. I'm heading out with Vicky now. See yez Tuesday for a review. Right?'

'Ah, but Marti,' the smallest member of the band spoke up. He had baby blond fluffy hair and a baby squeaky voice. 'Me mudder wants to talk to you about something.'

'Tell her to ring me Tuesday.'

'I told her she'd get you tonight. Aw, Marti, don't go. She'll murder me. You know me mudder.'

'Aw, yeah, you know his mother,' Keith said. 'She'd rip the balls off a prize bull.'

Sniggering.

'Lads, lads.' Marti held up his hand. 'We've a lady in the room.'

'Who? Me?' I said.

The lads laughed again.

Marti sighed. Looked at me. 'D'you mind, Vicky? D'you mind if the lads come with us? You'll understand when you meet Adam's mother.'

The last thing I wanted to do was to sit in a pub with a load of kids and their families. My spirits, which up until then had been rising steadily, sank drastically. How could a guy expect me to spend a first date in a pub with a crowd of teenagers? Sal would break her heart laughing when she found out. 'Maybe I'll go home,' I said. 'Let you get on with the business of managing.' I picked up my bag from a chair. 'You can gimme a call during the week.'

'Aw, now, Vicky, don't be like that.' Marti looked upset. 'You'll have a laugh.'

'I don't think I will.' I looked at the lads. 'No offence, lads.'

'None taken,' Adam squeaked.

Marti grasped my arm. He pulled me about the room. 'You will have fun, you will,' he said, sounding so insistent that I had to smile. It was like when I was a kid and I'd fight with one of my cousins. They'd always say, 'You're not my friend,' and I'd hit them a belt and yell out, 'I am your friend.'

'Look,' Marti went on, 'I'll introduce the lads to you now and we'll all get to know one another. It's important you get on with them, Vicky, I'd like you to.'

I wondered what he meant by that.

'This fella here is Cliff, but you already know him, this is Keith, this is Adam, this is Robin and this is Logan.'

'After Johnny Logan,' the guy said proudly.

I tried not to grin.

'It'll just be this once.' Marti looked at me appealingly. 'Don't get annoyed.'

'I just don't think chatting to mothers and fathers and stuff is quite my thing,' I explained. 'I don't know anything about the music business. I just wanted a quiet drink.'

'My da's a great laugh,' prepubescent Adam called out. 'You won't be bored with him. He works in the zoo.'

Marti nodded. 'Funny stories about animals,' he said jovially. He looked beseechingly at me. 'And anyway, you won't have to talk to them. Promise.'

I guessed it might be OK. The lads seemed nice enough and after all they were number thirteen in the charts – almost pop stars. And to be honest, I found it quite glamorous, being with them and having my photo taken. And Marti was fun and how many times had a fun guy begged me to go anywhere? And Marti made me feel that it would be a laugh – he was all manic energy and enthusiasm. I put my bag down.

'OK.' They all grinned back at me – well, all except Cliff.

'Brilliant!' Marti gave me another hug, which I rather liked, and handed me another glass. 'Drink up now.'

So I did.

The pub we went to was very upmarket. You know the kind of place, no furniture and freezing cold with madly over-priced drinks. 'Important for the lads to be seen in the right places,' Marti said as the bouncer let us in. 'Does wonders for the image.'

We found seats and Marti ordered a round of drinks. The

lads talked among themselves so it *was* kinda like Marti and I were on our own. He told me a bit about each of the lads and about his plans for the future.

'We need another hit single,' he said, 'then the album. After that, we'll do the tours and the rest of it. For now, though, it's important to make it in this country.'

'It must be hard,' I said, 'what with having to look after your little boy and everything.'

He said nothing for a few seconds. Then shrugged. 'That's where family comes in,' he muttered.

'Sorry?'

'My mother lives with us so she minds him.'

'That's good. At least he's not fobbed off on some babysitter.'

His eyes lit up as if I'd just said the most wonderful thing. 'That's exactly how I figure it,' he said. 'Of course it's not the same as having his mother around.'

I guess that was true.

'Still,' Marti shrugged, 'if his mother left him is she any good anyway?'

He had a point. What sort of a mother leaves her kid?

Poor little lad, I thought.

'And how's my boy!' A huge woman with an even bigger husband barged towards us. 'Where's my Cliff?' Cliff was enfolded in a huge hug in breasts that swallowed him whole. 'You were wonderful! Wonderful! I was crying when I saw you.'

'Yeah. Real neat costume, Cliffy.' A young girl punched him on the arm. 'I was bleeding crying too. Laughed my arse off, I did!'

'I'm going to have to do something about that relationship,' Marti whispered to me. 'That girlfriend of his keeps denting his ego all the time. It's no wonder he was sick tonight!'

I was doing my best not to laugh.

More people joined us. Among them Adam's ball-breaker mother. And yep, she was scary. And yep, if I were Marti, I'd never have broken an appointment.

Soon a whole section of the bar was full of proud parents and blushing kids.

He drove me home. Talked more about his band. I was glad of that because I was exhausted. I guess it was from trying to smile and trying to remember who everyone was and trying just to appear *nice*. Being nice was bloody hard work. Especially as I hated crowds and being stuck in the middle of them. And I had a pain in my face from smiling.

'Logan can't get the high notes, I'm gonna have to work on that. And Cliff—'

'Cliff is great,' I said, meaning it. 'Really great.'

'Yeah, but he needs to work on the relaxation. Gets too tense.'

We were outside my apartment by now. Marti cut the engine and turned to me. His hand rested across the back of my seat and I could feel his breath on my face. 'So, how'd you enjoy yourself?' His hair flopped forward over his eye and his mouth quirked upwards in a grin. 'Good, wasn't it?'

'I liked the concert, it was a laugh,' I said.

He looked puzzled.

'And the pub was mostly good,' I went on hastily. 'Except for the extra company.'

He grinned. 'You don't bullshit around, I like that. The next time, there won't be any extra company.'

'Good.' My heart was beginning a slow, heavy beat. He was dead sexy-looking, despite the vertical green stripes.

'So you'll come out with me again?'

'If I'm not too busy.'

He gave a rumble of laughter at that. 'I'll ring you.'

'Do.'

We smiled at each other. I didn't know if I should ask him up. I didn't know what he'd take it to mean. I liked him a lot. He was zany and fun, but I don't sleep with guys that quickly. And besides, if Sal saw him in his green stripes she'd have a field day.

The choice was taken from me. Marti smiled ruefully and said, 'Well, I'd better get back to the sprog.'

I liked that he'd said that. 'OK, so.'

Pause.

We looked at each other.

He leaned towards me. I leaned towards him. Our lips met. Softly. Gently. He cupped my face in his palm. Ran his hands through my hair. I moaned slightly because I love my hair being stroked.

'I'll call,' he said.

'Yeah. Great.'

And I meant it too. I reckoned it would be great.

Maybe this was the real thing?

Chapter Sixteen

It was Monday of the following week before Sal remembered to ask about Ed. Normally if there was half a chance of Sal meeting a guy with money, she'd have been sniffing around within nanoseconds but her piece for Mel, which I assumed was about the guy in Club Zero, seemed to be taking up all her time.

When we were in school, Sal used to always say that she'd marry for love but that any prospective hubby would have to have money, a good job and a nice car. I used to think that was hilarious. I mean, I used to ask her, what if you fell for a guy that hadn't any of those things? What, like, if he was just nice and kind and considerate? Sal used to look at me as if I was the one that was mad. 'Mr Nice, Kind and Considerate might dry the dishes but the guy I'm looking for will have a state-of-the-art dishwasher.'

I used to think it was all crap until Jorge had come to visit. Jorge was a German guy I'd met when I'd been in Egypt. He'd been a great mate to me over there because Egypt hadn't been lucky for me at all. I'd had my credit card stolen, lost my sleeping bag and, a week later, my tent had gone for a hike. No pun intended. Jorge, for some reason, had found this dead funny and, after dubbing me the 'Egypt Eejit' he'd subbed me, shared his tent and bag with me (it was a double – in case he got lucky) and even cooked meals for me during the two great months we'd travelled together. Eventually we'd split and gone our separate ways – he to Australia and me to South America. We'd kept in touch by e-mail and eventually, when I was settled, I'd invited him to Ireland.

Despite the fact that he was tall, blond and quite passably handsome, Sal hadn't paid any attention to him. As far as she was concerned he was just another weirdo hitchhiker. Only mental people slept in tents, Sal stated. Jorge had been about as interesting to her as a piece of cold cabbage.

Until he mentioned to me that his dad was some big financier in the German stock market. And I, knowing that Sal would be impressed, mentioned it to her. And suddenly Jorge morphed from a piece of cold cabbage into a gourmet meal.

And Sal ate him for breakfast.

My German friend was no longer mine. He and Sal spent the rest of the holiday together and I was suddenly the leftover on the plate.

It was the biggest row Sal and I had ever had.

'Well, you weren't interested in him,' Sal had said in a big bored voice when I'd attacked her for seeing him off at the airport. 'So what's the problem?'

I didn't understand how she had to ask. 'He was *my* guest.'

'So he's not allowed to get off with anyone – is he not?'

'He was my guest.' It was all I could say. I'm useless at fights. I could feel the tears welling up and I blinked really hard to get rid of them. 'I was the one meant to be showing him around. I should have been the one seeing him off.'

'Well,' Sal shrugged, 'he wanted me to – what was I to say? No?'

'Yeah. Yeah actually.'

'That's what I did say.' Sal gave a bit of a laugh and quirked her eyebrows. 'And anyway, we did ask you to come with us and you wouldn't.'

'I don't do gooseberry.'

'Well, you're green enough with jealousy now.'

I, madly mature individual that I am, stormed out of the room. I didn't talk to her for ages. I think her and Jorge e-mailed one another for a while but it petered out. And even though he'd copped off with my friend, he still had the cheek to e-mail me. I never bothered replying and he gave up writing about six months ago.

I think if he'd really wanted to keep in touch, he would have.

Anyway, there I was, flicking through an issue of *Hello!*, my feet curled up on the sofa, when Sal asked, out of the blue, 'Hey, how is rich boy working out?'

She was filing her nails and doing 'the Mel piece' on her laptop. I wasn't allowed to go near it. The whole project was top secret. Anyway, she must have read what she'd written, liked it and decided to file her nails. While filing her nails, she wanted to be entertained. 'Well?' she asked.

How was Ed working out? 'All right,' I muttered grudgingly. 'I mean, he can sell toys better than anyone else I've seen. Bridie likes him.' I paused. Shrugged.

'And you?' Sal prompted.

I shrugged again. 'Dunno.' Pause. 'He's the boss's son, isn't he?' Sal kept staring at me. 'I'm scared he's after my job,' I finally admitted. 'I mean, when you think of it, why else would O'Neill put him in the shop?'

'Because you need an extra worker?'

I half-laughed. 'Aw, come on, Sal, we could pick up an extra worker no problem. This is the guy's *son* we're talking about.'

Sal was silent for a bit. I watched her study her nails and knew she was thinking about what I'd said. Sal was dead wide about business and stuff like that. She was the kind of person who thought things out before speaking. The sort of person that scared me stupid because I tend to jump right in and say what's on my mind. Then regret it. Sal regretted nothing. 'Mmm,' she eventually pronounced. 'Maybe he's just in your place to be trained in from the bottom up. Maybe his dad just wants to give him some experience in a shop before he does anything else.'

'He's come back from *London*,' I said. 'He wouldn't just come back for a crummy old job in a shop. *And* this is his first time to work for his dad.'

Sal looked puzzled. 'London? What was he doing over there? I thought he was working in accountancy or something. At least that's what it said in *Tell!*'

'The guy in our shop is another son,' I explained. 'A younger son. He was in London – he told me. I'm telling you, there's something going on.'

'A younger son?' Sal gawked at me. 'What's he like?'

'I already told you – he's a good salesman but—'

'Naw – is he married?'

'Sal, I'm worried here and all you want to know is if he's married!'

Sal laughed a bit. 'Look,' she said, 'if you're so worried – just ask him or his dad straight out. You're entitled to know.'

'Oh, I couldn't—'

'Well, that's your problem then, isn't it? Now.' She put down her nail file and sat in beside me. 'Go on – is he married?'

'You think I should ask Ed if he's planning on taking over my job?'

'Well, why not? Don't let them think you're a fool. Now, is he married?'

She was right, I suppose. That's what I should do, but the very idea of it made my stomach churn. What if I made a fool of myself? But there was something up, I knew it.

'Vicky!' Sal poked me. 'I've told you what to do – now 'fess up – what's this fella like – is he married?'

'Single,' I answered. 'But not your type.' *What the hell would I say – 'Are you taking over my job?' sounded a bit bald. I'd have to think about it.*

'What do you mean "not my type"? If he's the son and heir of Albert O'Neill, he's right up my street.'

'Yep, but he's living at the wrong end of it – he's the guy with the stubble and the combat jacket.'

Sal made a face. She liked her men well groomed. 'Is he

good-looking? On a scale of Troy to Brad Pitt, where would you place him?'

Troy was our neighbour.

'The Brad Pitt end.'

'Wow!' Sal gawped at me. Thumped me. 'What the hell are you waiting for – get in there!'

'All I want is my job,' I answered. 'And I have a nice man, thanks.'

'That small little fella you went out with on Saturday? Aw, Vicky, come on.'

I ignored the jibe about Marti. 'You go for Ed,' I joked. 'Maybe he might find it harder to do the dirty on me if he's seeing my best friend.'

Sal laughed. 'Who knows – I might just do that. A rich, handsome, single man – if I can't get him, no one can.'

I know she was only joking but she really did believe it. I'd have loved to have her confidence.

'And I'll bet,' Sal went on, in a sort of dreamy voice, 'with that Omagh accent, he sounds dead sexy!'

'Yeah, it's nice,' I admitted. 'There's a bit of London in there now, though.'

Sal tapped her nail file up and down on the palm of her hand. 'Lucky you. How come I never get to work with guys like that? He sounds very fanciable.'

'Huh, if he takes my job, he wouldn't be fanciable if he was dipped head to toe in chocolate.'

'Ugh,' Sal giggled. 'For such a puritan, you've an awful kinky mind.'

I wasn't a puritan, I thought as I left the flat to buy some stuff in the local shop. Sal had promised to help me phrase my 'Are you taking my job?' request if I bought her some fags.

It was beginning to drizzle and immediately, as if I'd been struck with about a million volts of electricity, my hair frizzed out. I hate the drizzle. Give me a good old-fashioned storm any day. At least that way my hair ends up flattened and I don't look like Marge Simpson.

I shoved my hands into my coat pockets and, head down, I began the walk to the top of the road. Even though Sal had been joking, the puritan remark stung. I'd had very few relationships and those that I had had always ended badly. I found it hard to keep interested in a guy once I began to know him. Boredom set in, boredom with a capital ZZZ in front of it. Within every funny, spontaneous guy I picked there seemed to be a slipper-and-pipe man just bursting to get out.

And it wasn't that I didn't want to fall in love and do the whole settling down thing – I did. But the idea of it being so *long-term* revolted me.

'Hey, *coooooool.*' The voice came from behind. 'I didn't know you were a Trekkie!'

It was Troy – the nice but visually challenging guy from our landing. He was a gasman, slightly batty. He was trotting along beside me. 'You rock.' A pair of Bugs Bunny teeth were revealed to me in what I suppose was an admiring smile. 'We can travel together.'

'Sorry?'

'On the bus. To the Trekkie convention.'

'You've lost me, Troy.'

'Trekkie convention?' His eyes flicked up to my hair. Stayed there.

It took a couple of seconds.

Both of us were embarrassed at the same time.

'I've just ruined any chance I ever had with you,' Troy said glumly. 'Beam me up, Scotty,' he chortled, snorting with embarrassment. 'Huh, if only I could – hey?'

Beat him up was more along the lines I'd been thinking.

'Anyway, gorgeous,' Troy nodded, attempting to recover, 'I've got to go. The convention starts in forty.' And off he strode in what I noticed now was a tight gold babygro.

'I hope you get eaten by the Borg,' I yelled after him.

He turned to face me. 'The Borg don't eat,' he said, 'they amalgamate.'

'Well, it'll be the only mating you'll ever get!' I yelled after him.

He laughed loudly and blew me a kiss.

Chapter Seventeen

MY HEART WAS booming as I walked up the stairs to the office the next day. 'The sooner you ask him the better,' Sal had briefed me. 'Otherwise there'll just be bad feeling.' So I'd chosen the very next day – Tuesday – which happened to be the day that Ed and I were on our own in the shop.

'Now be calm and in control,' Sal advised. 'Think before you speak and for God's sake, Vic, don't say anything in the heat of the moment.'

That was fine advice for me. I am a very emotional person. It had got me into trouble my whole life.

'Count to ten,' Sal continued, 'and remember, even if he is going to take your job, it's not personal. Be detached.'

If Ed was going to take my job, I told her, he'd be the one that'd be de-tatched. 'I'll pull the hair out of his head.'

'Classy,' Sal had mumbled.

So, now, here I was, on Tuesday, dressed in my best manager's clothes, looking very efficient with my heart about to explode in my chest. I made myself a cuppa and couldn't drink it. I sat, sweaty-palmed, waiting for Ed to appear.

He arrived about ten minutes later. Dressed in what seemed to be his only jacket – the orange one. 'Hiya,' he smiled at me as he took it off, revealing a navy T-shirt with a denim shirt half unbuttoned. He wore a pair of distressed denim jeans that accentuated the length of his legs and the narrowness of his hips. I love nice hips on a guy. 'Good weekend?' He grabbed his mug from the shelf and poured some boiling water into it.

'Great, yeah.' *Ask. Ask. Ask.*

'How so?' Ed dunked a teabag and squished it out with a spoon.

'I went to a gig.'

'Yeah?' He looked interested. 'Who?'

I wasn't admitting to going to see Boy Five. 'Dunno – can't remember.' My heart was hammering, pounding. I told myself that when he'd poured in his milk and sat down, that I would ask.

'That good – eh?' He grinned and poured his milk and sat down.

I remained frozen.

'Where did you go?'

'Sorry? What?'

'The gig,' Ed prompted. 'Where was it?'

'Oh, eh, the Northside somewhere. Ed, can I ask you something?'

He looked mildly curious. 'Fire away.'

'Eh, well, eh.' *This was it. This was it. Take it easy.* 'Action Men,' I gulped out, sweat glistening on my forehead. 'Where'd you put the Action Men?'

I cursed myself.

'They're on the lower shelf,' he said. 'No need to panic. I just thought that the young kids wouldn't be able to see them where they were so I moved them.'

'Right. Right. Good idea.' Too good an idea, I thought suddenly. He *had* to be after something. 'What are you doing here?' It came out sounding completely hostile.

The hand holding his cup jerked and tea slopped onto his jeans. He didn't seem to notice. He was staring transfixed at me. I dunno if it was the question or the way I'd asked it. 'Sorry?' He laid the cup carefully on the desk and, looking at it rather than at me, he said, 'What was that?'

'You heard me – what are you doing here?' More hostility.

'Drinking tea,' he answered with the grin he'd been using on the customers all week. 'Why?' The nervous look in his eyes belied the grin, though.

'I mean in this shop.' I was going to start hyperventilating. I wanted to know his answer yet I dreaded it. 'Why'd your dad put you here?'

He blinked. Once. Twice. 'To work,' he answered.

I tried to remember what Sal had told me to say in the event of an evasive answer. 'I'm no fool,' I went on, my voice stern. 'If it's my job you want, I want to know.'

He stared incredulously at me. So much so that I felt myself redden. I think I'd just proved myself to be a fool.

'After your job,' he said slowly. 'What gave you that idea?'

'You. Being here.'

A slow smile broke out on his face. 'So that's why you're being so snotty to me, is it?'

'I'm not snotty to anyone,' I said snottily.

He laughed a little, then at my lack of response, he leaned forward in his chair and, sounding really sincere, but still with that grin on his face, he said, 'I'm not here to take anyone's job. I just want to work.'

'But you were working in London.'

He nodded. 'Aye.' His smile disappeared. 'I, eh, left my job over there and it was hard to find another. I was busking but not making a whole lot of money. Dad offered me this.'

'Working under me? And Bridie? And you don't mind?'

He flinched. 'It's work.'

He seemed genuine. But, I wondered, would he actually *admit* if he was taking over? Probably not. Again I felt sick. I'd have to keep an eye on things. 'You being here,' I went on, determined to set some ground rules, 'I suppose you realise that it's awkward on me and Bridie. I mean, you're the boss's son.'

'Yeah.' He nodded, shrugged. 'There's not a lot I can do about it. And Bridie doesn't seem to mind all that much.'

Was he saying that it was *me* that minded? When in doubt, say nothing, Sal had advised. It was hard but I did it.

'I am not a spy,' he went on quietly, his eyes holding mine. 'I just want to work – OK?'

I wished he'd work somewhere else. 'OK,' I muttered, not too sure if I completely believed him though he seemed genuine. 'Just so we know. You work here and no matter what happens it doesn't go back to O'Neill.'

'I won't tell O'Neill a single thing,' he grinned. 'Cross my heart.'

'And you are not after my job?'

He grinned that grin again. 'Looking at you, it's definitely not your job I'd be after.'

I reddened. Half flattered. Half annoyed that he should flirt in what had to be the most stressful conversation I'd ever conducted. Still, I thought, like father, like son. I tossed him the keys. 'Well then, you can open up.'

He caught them mid-air. 'Ta, Vicky,' he said just as he was leaving. 'I'm glad we cleared that up.'

I wasn't too sure anything was cleared up. He was too bright not to want more. Way too bright.

Then it hit me. Ohmigod – I'd called his dad O'Neill.

'Mad,' Ed said, surrounded by bits of a transformer that had just come in. 'How do they expect kids to do it when I can't? Honest, the instructions are crap, Vicky.'

'Maybe it's just you,' I said dryly. He'd suggested that we do a transformer window and, while admitting to myself that it was a good idea, I didn't want to encourage his ideas.

He laughed. 'Maybe,' he agreed good-naturedly.

'Might have to scrap the window,' I said, trying to sound sad about it.

Before he had a chance to reply, Dominic hurtled through the door, determined to make it to the Lego before any other kid got there.

'Slow down, Domo,' his mother called as she followed him. 'It's not a bleeding race, ya know.'

Dominic, still running, turned back to her and ran slap bang into a shelf. He walloped his head and fell face first onto the floor.

'OHHH GOD!' his mother screamed.

'MAMMMYYY!' Dominic screamed.

Ed and I rushed towards them. Dominic was howling as his mother picked him up off the floor and held him to her.

'Is he OK?' I asked.

'No, he's not bloody OK,' she snapped at me, her eyes watering. 'Can't you *hear* he's not OK?'

I flinched.

Ed knelt down beside them. 'Let me have a look,' he said gently. 'Just let me see his face.'

'Noooo,' Dominic cried. 'No, Mammy, don't want to!'

'Leave him alone!' the mother barked, rubbing his back with the palm of her hand. 'Bleeding shelves. What was that shelf doing there anyway?'

I looked hopelessly at Ed.

'Holding up toys,' Ed answered mildly. 'Now, are you going to let me look at him or not? My guess is that he's fine. He'll probably just have a massive bruise, that's all.'

'Dat's all?' Dominic's mother said sarcastically. 'Wonder-bleeding-ful.'

'Better than him having concussion,' Ed said. 'And if you let me look at him, I'll tell you for certain.'

'What? Does this toy shop have its own bleeding doctor now? Are yez going to charge me?'

Ed managed a laugh. 'Dominic,' he said; 'let's see you. Let's see if that bruise looks as if you've been hit by The Rock.'

The Rock was Dominic's favourite wrestler.

Slowly Dominic pulled himself out of his mother's embrace. His bruise was looking pretty big all right.

'Cool!' Ed said in an admiring voice.

'For Jaysus' sake—' the mother snarled.

'Is it big?' Dominic asked half fearfully, half hopefully. He scrubbed his eyes with his tiny fist. '*Really* big?'

'Massive,' Ed answered.

Dominic gave a little laugh and turned to his mother. 'Is it, Ma?'

She nodded, glancing suspiciously at Ed.

'Vic, d'we have an ice pack for this tough guy?' Ed asked, without taking his eyes from Dominic.

'Sure.' Jesus, some manager I was. An ice pack should have been the first thing I'd fetched. I legged it upstairs to the office. In the first aid kit was a chemical ice pack. The one with the liquid and the stony bits that freeze up when you press it.

When I came back down, Ed was still hunkered on the ground beside Dominic and his mother. He was telling her that as Dominic's pupils had not gone small, it was unlikely that he had concussion. 'Just let him hang around with me for an hour or two,' he said. 'I'll keep an eye on him, just to be certain.' Then he added, 'You've not got anything urgent on, have you?'

I smiled. It was nice of him to ask her that.

The mother pretended to consider. 'Naw. Anyway, seeing as that shelf was there, Domo falling was yer fault, so I reckon yez owe us one. You can have him for the couple of hours.'

I handed the ice pack to Ed who winked at me. He told Dominic to hold the pack to his forehead. Dominic, his eyes wide, did as he was told.

'And d'you know what, Dominic, I reckon Vicky there has something dead nice for you under the counter. She's got lollipops for kids that hurt themselves, you know.'

'She gives me lollies anyway,' Dominic answered proudly.

'No way!' Ed sounded impressed. 'She must like you, so.'

'Yeah. Yeah.' Dominic smiled. Then asked shyly, 'D'you like me?'

'Absolutely,' Ed grinned and tousled his hair. 'I'll like you even more if you help me stock some shelves.'

'I'll just get my lolly first,' Dominic said.

He followed me back to the counter and I handed him a big green one that I'd bought the previous week but had chickened out of giving to him. His mother helped him unwrap it.

'Would you like a cuppa?' I asked her then, feeling sorry for her. 'You must have got a shock.'

She bit her lip. 'Need more than a cuppa to get me over the shock,' she muttered.

'Oh, well—'

'Black, plenty of sugar,' she said.

'I think I could do with one too, boss,' Ed called after me. 'Let's have an afternoon cuppa just this once.'

'Yeah,' I agreed, trying to sound as if I was torn with indecision, 'I think that's a good idea. We've all had a bit of a fright.'

Ed chortled.

'You've a fan for life there,' I remarked as Dominic left at closing time, his hand clasped tightly in his mother's, a big purple bruise like a beacon covering most of his little forehead.

'Nice kid.' Ed pulled on his jacket. 'Crap life.'

'Is he really all right? I mean, how do you know?'

'Ach, he's fine.' Ed turned in the door. 'Most bumps to the front of the head are harmless. He's grand.'

I nodded, not wanting to thank him but knowing that I had to. 'You did well with him.' I couldn't look at Ed. 'Did you do first aid or something?'

'Aye.' He smiled a little wistfully. 'Anyway, see you tomorrow.'

After he left, I sat down and surveyed the shop. He could sell toys, he could deal with difficult customers, he could calm down hysterical kids – was there nothing he couldn't do?

And then, I did something so completely childish that I surprised even myself. I located the transformer that he'd been working on earlier that day and began to try and figure it out.

I left the shop some time later, the aeroplane/robot proudly sitting beside the till.

Jesus, I was knackered.

Chapter Eighteen

THERE WAS A letter waiting for me when I got in. I'm one of those pathetic people that love getting letters. Most of the time, they turn out to be bills or organisations looking for my money but I don't care. It's the fact that I've been written to that counts.

'Letter,' Sal indicated the table. 'For you.'

She didn't take her eyes off her laptop as she spoke. Her fingers flew over the keys and I knew better than to disturb her. For some reason she gets really narky if I make a noise in the middle of her writing a sentence. I mean, it's OK for her to tell me I've got a letter but not for me to say 'Where is it?' or anything like that.

I tiptoed across to the table and picked up a white handwritten envelope. My head was so full of gloating thoughts about what Ed would say when he came in and saw my transformer all made up that I ripped the letter open without realising exactly what it was.

It was the non-identifying information on my natural mother.

At least that's what it said. Somewhere in the middle of the first page. The words sort of leaped out at me. Hit me. And jammed themselves back into the sentence. I stood there, paper trembling in my hand, not able to think.

Sal kept typing.

Noises receded and whooshed back again.

The words of the letter danced in front of my eyes before I squeezed them tight shut and told myself to calm down.

I calmed down by folding the pages up and jerkily, it seems to me, walking into my room and shutting the door.

I don't think Sal even noticed.

My hands were trembling as I unfolded the letter again. There were two pages. The first was a note from the Adoption Board, saying that they'd received my request, warning that it could take up to two years to trace a person and that once traced, they advised counselling for all concerned. *Meanwhile*, the letter went on, *please find enclosed some non-identifying information on your birth mother*. The letter finished with a '*Yours sincerely, Valerie Coogan*.'

I placed this on the bed and focused on the second page.

Her name was Barbara.

My birth mother, I mean.

Barbara. I rolled the sound of it on my tongue. Found I couldn't say it without gulping.

She'd been nineteen.

Only young. But old enough to work. Maybe.

Today she'd be forty-seven.

Her hair was red.

My hand stole up to touch my frizzy locks.

I wondered if I looked like her at all.

I couldn't sleep that night. When I was a kid, I used to lie in bed and conjure up images of my mother. She'd be warm and welcoming and smiling. She'd have Barbie's figure and wear cool clothes. We'd go on holidays and I'd meet my dad. The three of us would realise that we belonged together. I'd look around my attic room and know that it wasn't really my attic room. It could have been anyone's.

Now, the image had changed. Now I knew she had red hair and would be forty-seven. She might even have a tooth missing the way I did. For some reason, one of my back teeth had never come up. The dentist at the time said quirky teeth ran in families. I remember my mother saying swiftly that she had all her back teeth and then I remember her looking at me and smiling, sort of sad. As if she'd forgotten that I wasn't really her daughter.

I lay in bed that night and hugged the letter to me. No matter how fragile, it was the first link in a chain that would lead me to her.

That would lead me to who *I* was.

Chapter Nineteen

THE BUS INTO town the next morning was packed. Hot. And comfortable. Basically, after a night spent tossing and turning, I fell asleep. I woke up when the driver decided to play his music at top volume. Thin Lizzy's 'The Boys Are Back In Town'.

'Jesus!' I jerked awake.

A round, bald guy was peering down at me. 'Sorry, luv, but it was the only way I could wake you. Women dese days are awful sensitive to strange men touching them.'

'I haven't been touched by a strange man in a long time,' I said back as I gathered up my coat and bag from where they'd fallen on the floor. 'Would have made a nice change.'

He chortled good-naturedly. 'Take care,' he said as I left. 'It's raining hard out there.'

Raining hard was an understatement. And the fact that I'd slept past my stop and had to walk almost a mile in the hard rain made it worse.

And then, to arrive in, drenched to my knickers, only to see Bridie fussing over Ed as he tapped away furiously on the computer.

I was virtually ignored as she laid a cup of coffee in front of him and asked him if he'd like a 'special nutty biscuit'.

'Ta.' He didn't even bother to look at her and off she went, filling cups and getting biscuits. All the while she did that she hummed away to herself.

What did he think she was anyway? Some kind of a maid?

'Paralysed, are you?' I asked in a friendly voice, so he wouldn't think I was getting at him. 'Forgotten how to make coffee?'

Both of them looked at me.

'Ed made me a nice cup yesterday, Bridie.'

'Aw' – Ed had a smile in his voice – 'but you said yourself, it wasn't as nice as Bridie's.'

'Ooohh.' Bridie almost wet herself. 'Did she really say that? Did you really say that?' She beamed at the two of us.

I didn't bother to answer.

'I'll make you a cup too, shall I?' Bridie asked me. Then, 'Oh, you're soaking. Oh, take off those wet shoes.'

'I'm fine.' I squelched past both of them and got my own cup down from the shelf. 'Don't worry about me. I'm fine.'

It seemed that they weren't anyway.

'I'll make my own coffee.'

'And how are you coming on there?' Bridie deposited Ed's biscuits in front of him. Without waiting for an answer, she turned to me. 'Ed's working on the computer, doing something fancy, aren't you, Ed?'

'Just showing how best you could use your window display space, Vicky.'

I froze. 'Pardon?'

'Well, see here.' He pointed to our computer screen, which, instead of having a Toys Galore logo dancing across it, was now covered with little diagrams and measurements. 'If you—'

'What have you done to our computer?' I gasped. 'Where have our account files gone?'

'They're still there.' Ed looked slightly amused. 'I only loaded this program onto it this morning.'

'You can't go doing that!' I gawped at him. 'It's a Toys Galore computer system. What happens if—' I sought my computer-illiterate mind for something horrendous, 'if a virus gets into our files? You're putting our files at risk with all your fancy messing about.'

'Oooh yes.' Bridie looked alarmed now and I was glad. 'I never thought of that.'

'The program is safe.' Ed bit into a biscuit and looked at the two of us. 'A mate of mine designed it – he lent me the disk. Yez should be glad of it. It's dead handy.'

'Yeah, well.' I tossed my head. 'We don't need a computer to tell us how best to use our window space. All we have to do is look.'

Ed shrugged. 'So you just haven't bothered to look at it in the last eight months, have you not?'

The nerve! The cheek! 'We've been *busy*,' I said back, flushing. 'Waiting on our new member of staff to arrive.'

'Oooh, yes,' Bridie nodded. 'We've been very busy.'

'Well now you can take a break.' Ed smiled sweetly at me. 'After all, that's why I'm here.' He pointed to the computer. 'And if you'll just look, Vicky, you'll see what I'm talking about.'

I desperately didn't want to look.

'Because,' Ed went on, 'I was thinking last night, that if only I could get that transformer made we could do a mega window on them. And what do I find when I come in today – the transformer all made up.'

'Yeah,' I said airily, 'it was no problem.' To do it in two hours, I should have added.

'So *look*,' Ed indicated the computer, 'you make up the transformers and this is what we can do.'

Jesus, the idea of making up loads of transformers brought me out in a sweat. But if I didn't look, it'd seem petty. 'I'll still have to think about it,' I muttered, crossing towards him.

'Absolutely,' he nodded with enough deference to keep me happy. 'Now, see here—'

To my horror, he began to talk about measurements and depth and horrible mathematicky things. I kept nodding and acting like I understood, but I hadn't a clue. Bridie looked at the two of us proudly before saying that she'd go down and open up.

'We'll have a great shop by the time you're finished with us, eh, Ed,' she giggled before leaving.

She didn't notice the glare I gave her. Neither did Ed, he just smiled absently at her before re-launching himself into the figures again.

Eventually, I had to stop him. 'Who'll do all this work?' I asked.

'Me,' he said. 'It just means pulling out the partition and sticking in a shelf. That way, see, we can get two levels in, whereas before we only had one.'

That made sense. 'OK,' I said, hating that he was right. 'Leave it with me.'

'I'll just do out another proposal,' Ed said, pressing the print button. 'That way you can decide which one you want. OK?'

Jesus, I thought, I hadn't even managed to think up *one* proposal.

The only good thing about Ed working on the computer was that he was upstairs all morning while Bridie and I had the shop to ourselves. If I concentrated very hard, I could just about fool myself that Ed wasn't actually among us at all.

'So,' I asked Bridie as I counted out the bags of small change, 'did you enjoy your day off yesterday?'

'I did.' Bridie was dusting the counters. I'd swear the counter was higher when I'd come here first. Bridie was eroding it with all her cleaning. 'I got up at eight, went to mass and then got all my washing out. Isn't it great when you can get all your washing out?'

'I prefer to have all my nights out, actually.'

I liked to hear her laugh at my jokes. She hadn't bothered all last week since *he'd* arrived. I think she thought he was funnier than me. 'Oh, you're a one,' she said, flicking her duster at me. 'Did you go out last night then?'

'Nah.' I shoved the bags of change into the till. 'But I went out last Saturday.'

'With your journalist friend?'

She always called Sal that. I think she thought being a journalist was a big deal.

'Nope. With a man.'

'Boyfriend?'

'I guess he is now.'

'Oooh,' Bridie giggled. She looked at me with glittering eyes. 'Did you meet him in here?'

'Nah, I met him at a nightclub two weeks ago.'

Bridie shook her head, her mouth slightly open. 'Isn't that lovely,' she sighed. 'Just shows how wrong they are – they say nightclubs are the worst places to meet people.'

'Well, mainly they're the places to meet the worst people,' I smiled. 'But he was nice.'

'Well, I'm delighted for you. You haven't been out with anyone since you came here. A lovely girl like you deserves a lovely man.'

I didn't tell her about him being separated or about his little boy. It'd spoil the romance for her. 'Aw, thanks, Bridie.'

We smiled at each other.

'But you'd want to be careful all the same,' she said then. 'I mean, you don't know this chap very well, do you?'

'Careful?'

'You know, make sure you tell someone where you're going when you're out with him. Keep the mobile phone handy. I mean, I'm not one for technology, but the mobile phone is a wonderful thing.'

'And your computer is too.' Ed startled us by arriving down. He looked tired. He was rubbing his eyes and blinking hard. 'Eyestrain,' he muttered as he saw me looking. Then he pushed a few bits of meaningless paper at me. 'For you.'

I felt I'd better thank him. 'Ta.'

Almost as if he knew it choked me to say it, he ignored it. 'I've put in a screening program for e-mail,' he said to no one in particular. 'It's a download.'

Bridie and I looked at each other.

What the hell was a download?

'Seeing as you were so worried about computer viruses,' he went on.

Rather than show our ignorance, Bridie said, 'Wow, you certainly know your way around a computer, eh? A download – sounds almost rude.'

Ed laughed.

'So' – Bridie turned her attention back to me again – 'where did you go with this man?'

'A gig,' I answered, flushing. It was one thing telling Bridie about my private life but I wasn't about to announce it to Ed.

'A gig?' Bridie's brow puckered. 'That was unusual, wasn't it? Was it not a bit cold to be out on a horse and cart?'

Both Ed and I cracked up laughing.

Bridie looked confused.

'A music gig,' I giggled. 'As in a concert.'

'So call it a concert.' Bridie puckered her lips, embarrassed. 'A gig, how are you?' She dismissed me and turned to Ed. 'So, how about yourself? Did you go out with anyone the weekend?'

'Just some mates.' Ed was still grinning.

'No girl then?' Bridie asked.

'Girls don't interest me, Bridie,' Ed leaned on the counter and winked at Bridie. 'It's women I go for.'

'And why not!' Bridie giggled like a schoolgirl. 'So, have you a *woman* at all?'

'Unfortunately' – Ed looked dolefully at her, his blue eyes all shiny and round – 'the last time I fell for a woman I hurt myself really bad.'

'No!'

'Aye.' He was grinning. 'Skinned my heart and my knees and everything.'

Oh *please*, I thought.

Bridie was dripping sympathy. 'That's dreadful. Poor you.'

'Aye. So I've no one now at the minute.'

'Can you believe it, Vicky?' Bridie said. 'Can you believe that Ed has no one?'

Yes, yes I could actually. 'No.'

I made it sound unconvincing. Both of them looked at me. 'No,' I said again, brighter.

'Aw, sure, once I can cook some beans and iron a shirt, I'll get by – huh?'

'You won't attract too many women eating beans,' I said.

Ed laughed. He had a nice laugh. Really sunny or something. Worst thing was, though, I hadn't actually meant to be funny.

'And it's great you can laugh at it, too.' Bridie was gushing compassion. 'That's the spirit.'

He laughed again. I had to smile too.

'And have you anyone special yourself, Bridie?' Ed asked, teasing her.

Bridie tittered. 'I'm too old for all that.'

'Ah, you're never too old. I'll bet you're a right raver when you get going.'

'Indeeden I'm not.' She looked thrilled that he thought so, though.

'I bet all the old lads whistle when you walk by!'

'Stop!' Bridie was tittering with laughter. 'Will you stop it.'

'It'd be your legs. You've fine legs, Bridie.'

'Will you stop it!' Giggling, she flapped him with the duster.

'Aye.' He was all bewildered seriousness. 'I don't know what you're laughing at. You wouldn't see better crafted legs on a table, so you wouldn't.'

That cracked her up. I left the two of them and noisily began restacking the Lego sets. Legs like a table. Jesus, it was no wonder he hadn't got a girlfriend.

Chapter Twenty

'OOOH.' MEL BURST into the flat at seven on Saturday, arms outstretched in a big hug. 'Where is she? Where's my girl?'

I presumed she meant Sal.

'In the kitchen.'

I watched her totter into the kitchen on heels high enough to make it as a tall man in a circus. A lot of squealing and screeching followed. I wondered what the big occasion was. I was just shutting the door, about to join them, when Lorcan slithered in. Lorcan was Mel's partner. The first time I'd met Lorcan, I'd been convinced that Mel was having me on. 'Sure he's your boyfriend,' I'd sniggered when Lorcan had gone to the bar to get in a round of drinks. 'Sure he is.'

Mel had turned white. 'Yes,' she'd said, 'of course I'm sure. Why – what have you heard?'

'Oh nothing.' Hastily I tried to backtrack. 'I just—'

'That fling with the actress was just a rumour. You're reading the wrong papers, Victoria.'

And she hadn't talked to me for the rest of that night.

Lorcan was not what you'd expect Mel to go for. He wasn't a human dynamo, he wasn't even borderline good-looking. He was basically a prissy, twitchy, anally retentive snob. And that was when he let himself go. Short, skinny, with thinning brown hair, he favoured polo necks and polyester. OK, so they were BT's polo necks and polyester, but they still did nothing for him. And maybe there might have been a chance I could have liked him, but how do you form a relationship with someone when you hardly understand what they're talking about?

Mel doted on him.

So Sal and I put up with him.

'Hello, Victoria,' Lorcan nodded to me as he came in. His voice was deep and chewy.

'We're on a flying visit – Mel just wanted to offer her congratulations to Sal on her extremely erudite and engaging piece for the magazine.'

'Oh. Right.'

'She loves it apparently.'

More squeals from the kitchen.

'Right. I'd never have guessed.'

Lorcan thought this was funny. He chuckled a bit. Then nodded. Then nodded some more. Then asked, 'Are you going somewhere?' His nondescript eyes looked me up and down. 'You look very fetching.'

'Ta.' I have to say I was flattered. I'd never got a compliment from Lorcan before. So I joked, 'Once I'm not the one *fetching* the pints from the bar.'

He looked blank. 'Oh.' Pause. 'I meant fetching as in—'

'I know.' I felt stupid now. 'It was a joke?'

'Oh.' Weak smile. 'Ha, ha. Very good. Clever wordplay.'

'I'm just heading out for a drink with a guy I met a few weeks ago.' His eyes had already glazed over. Not for Lorcan the mundane everyday lives of others. So I pointed to the kitchen. 'Mel is in there.'

'Marvellous or' – wink, wink – 'should I say *Mel*vellous?' He laughed slightly at his wit, rubbed his hands together and left me staring after him.

Even his walk was odd. He half-hopped, half-loped along, almost as if he was conscious of me looking at him.

I heard him gravely congratulating Sal on her wonderful work and Sal telling them that it was nothing. It was a pleasure. It was what she was getting paid to do.

'And,' Mel said loudly, before taking a deep breath and

pausing dramatically. The air in the flat seemed to vibrate with what she was about to say. I shoved my head in the kitchen door. 'We are running it as our headline piece!'

'Oooh!' Sal almost dropped the bottle of wine she had in her hand. 'No!'

'Yes! Yes! Yes!' Mel did a little jig and blew kisses everywhere. Then she spotted me. 'Vicky, did you hear that? Did you?'

'Congrats,' I grinned in at Sal. I was really pleased for her. She'd worked so hard on the bloody thing. 'Can't wait to read it.'

'Oh' – Mel tapped the side of her nose – 'you'll be reading it all right. Everyone will be reading it.'

'So can we ask what it's about now?'

'No.' Mel shook her head. 'You never know who's listening or who you might tell that will tell someone else and before we know it, the whole world is writing the same thing. Next week. All will be revealed.'

Mel and Sal grinned at each other.

Lorcan sighed dramatically. 'There's no secret so close as that between a rider and his horse.'

We all looked at him.

'Are you calling Sal a horse?' I asked.

'Metaphorically speaking, yes.' Lorcan smiled.

Sal pursed her lips but said nothing.

'Well, I hope you're not suggesting that Mel and Sal are riding one another?' I couldn't resist it.

Lorcan flinched as if someone had just farted; Sal looked at Mel for her reaction before both began to laugh.

'That was a quote from R. S. Surtees – an English sporting journalist and novelist,' Lorcan said, offended. 'I thought you of all people would know that, darling.' He shot an accusing look at Mel.

'Well, I didn't, but I do now.' Mel tweaked his ear.

He blushed and pushed her off.

'Anyway,' I said, 'I must be off.'

'Yeah, Vic's got a hot date tonight,' Sal said to Mel.

'Really?' Mel raised her eyebrows. 'So that's why you've' – she made motions with her hands – 'washed your hair, is it?'

I might have taken offence from that, only I knew what she meant. I'd got my hair straightened that morning. It lay all sleek and shiny over my shoulders. Unfortunately it was still red, but my budget didn't extend to colouring it. 'Yep.'

'Anyone special?' she asked.

'Only the manager of some band,' Sal said.

'Boy Five, actually,' I put in.

'Oh, let me guess.' Mel closed her eyes. 'They're five boys who sing.'

I ignored the sniggering from the other two. 'You've met him,' I said. 'He talked to you at the nightclub we went to a few weeks back.'

She looked blank. 'I talk to a lot of people, dearie.' She blew me a kiss. 'It's the nature of my job.'

'Purple eyes?' I said.

'What?' That was Sal and Lorcan.

'He wears purple contacts,' I explained.

I saw Lorcan shiver.

'Oh, yes, I remember him now.' Mel made a face. 'Wanted me to do a spread on his band. I told him we were a celeb magazine not some *Hot Press* outfit.'

'They were number thirteen,' I said. 'Surely they're famous now?'

Mel rolled her eyes. 'Oh, innocence,' she sighed.

I was not staying around to be patronised by Mel. 'Well, I'll bid the horse' – nod at Sal – 'the rider and trainer farewell.' I gave them a little wave. 'I've to get ready to go out.'

'Enjoy!' Mel called after me. 'Make good use of the boys five!'

Huh, they could laugh!

It was so good to be in a relationship again – I'd almost forgotten what it was like. Normally, I'd have had to go out with

Sal and Mel and feel like a hick beside them as they talked about deadlines and journalists and editors. Their jobs sounded so important beside mine. I mean, who wanted to hear about how many transformers fitted in a shop window when they could hear about the latest exploits of tabloid hacks with celebs?

The answer, by the way, is fifty. Ed managed to shove fifty transformers into our toy shop window when I finally gave the go-ahead on Friday. Fifty transformers, made up by me on Thursday night – it had taken me hours – fifty transformers transforming into aeroplanes, boats and guns. Ed had worked all day on the window, with Dominic helping him. Dominic had taken quite a shine to Ed and followed him about the shop telling him stories about his B&B. Ed used him to find out what his favourite toys were and made a point of displaying them in the 'Under fives' section. He'd even bought Dominic a little toy for himself. 'It's just a thank-you present,' he explained to Dominic's prickly mother. Bridie kept cooing about how lovely it was of Ed to do that. Huh, I'd been buying the kid lollipops for ages and she'd never remarked on that.

Anyway, Marti called for me at eight. To my relief, he was dressed normally. Well, in tight black leather that squeaked when he walked, but it was better than green vertical stripes. 'How's things?' he grinned when he saw me. 'Thought you might like to grab a beer in town somewhere.'

'Great.' Sounded like my kind of night. I grabbed my coat and flicked on the alarm.

'Lead on.'

'Had a good week this week.' Marti strode ahead of me, towards the lift. 'The lads got a booking doing support to The Chillies so we'll be touring for next week. They're dead excited about it.'

'The Red Hot Chilli Peppers?' I was impressed.

'Naw, The *Chillies*,' Marti replied. 'The man band.'

'Oh.' I didn't want to say that I'd never heard of The Chillies. 'That was short notice, huh? I thought you'd have to book a support act weeks in advance.'

'Aw yeah, well, no one wants to tour with these guys,' Marti said off-handedly, pressing the button to bring us to the ground floor. 'The lead singer is a bit of a wanker apparently. Smashes things up and incites riots at his concerts. Just done to get publicity, you know.'

'Right.'

'So I told my lads, I told them not to get involved in stuff like that. They need a clean image.'

'Good.'

The lift pinged and we both got out. 'And I got my car adapted as befits my status as manager.'

Visions of sleek and sexy flashed before my eyes.

Reality beckoned as I spotted Marti's car underneath an enormous double-sided billboard of Boy Five. The lads' young, fresh faces beamed out from one side of the board while the words *Boy Five – The Best Band Alive* were splashed in lurid red all across the other side.

'Great, innit?' Marti said proudly. Then, without waiting for my answer, he went on, 'I got loudspeakers attached to the roof so that I can play the song as I drive along and everyone gets to hear it. So, what do you think?'

'Well . . .' I bit my lip. 'It'd be great if the lads were going up for election.'

Marti laughed. Then he stopped. His face fell. 'You hate it, don't you?'

'Look, it's your car . . .'

'It's too loud – yeah? It's overboard – yeah?'

'It's—'

'Linda was always telling me I didn't know when to stop,' he muttered. 'Jesus, maybe she was right.' He looked up in anguish at his car. Then he turned his eyes on me. 'D'you still want to be seen in it? I can't take it all down now, it'd cost me a fortune.' He paused. 'We can get a taxi if you like – what d'you say?'

I'd have liked a taxi but he looked so crushed and it was all my fault. 'I don't mind,' I lied, 'just, eh, well, maybe don't play any music – OK?'

A smile lit up his face. 'Aw, no, I wasn't going to anyway.' He caught my hand. Reddening, he muttered, 'I like you, Vicky. You're the first woman I've been out with since Linda left. I don't want to scare you off.'

It was, I learned later, not often that Marti spoke like that, but when he did, he meant it.

'You won't.' I went around to the passenger door of the car. 'Not unless you've a Boyzone tape hidden somewhere in here.'

He laughed loudly. 'No chance.'

It was a perilous journey. Marti's poster seemed to attract a lot of unwanted attention, especially from rough-looking teenagers. Chunks of earth smashed off the sides of the billboards as we made our way into town. Marti's car seemed to be shuddering as each ball of clay made its impact.

'Little useless wankers,' Marti fumed, unable to get the car to go above forty. 'Jealous, that's all they are.'

He manoeuvred his car into a multi-storey car park with inches to spare at the roof and we got out. 'Daly's is a nice pub,' Marti said, locking the car and patting it as one would a pony. 'How about we go there?'

Daly's was nice. It was always good for a bit of a laugh. 'Brill.'

That evening Daly's was packed. There was a sort of karaoke thing on and people were being asked to get up and sing for a pint. A gang of lads beside the door were shoving a guy up as we arrived in. 'Go! Go! Go! Go!' they were chanting.

Marti and I took our seats across from them and Marti went up to the bar to order the drinks.

'And now,' the DJ said, 'we've Ed O'Neill up. Give him a hand.'

The guys beside the door erupted in cheers.

I hardly heard them. It was typical, going into a pub and meeting a guy I could barely stand to work beside. I only hoped he didn't spot me. He didn't seem to. Mouthing the word 'fuckers' at his friends, he went up to take the microphone from the DJ.

'I'm told Ed busks around Grafton Street on Thursday evenings,' the DJ went on. 'He's very popular, by all accounts.'

More cheers.

Marti arrived down with the drinks.

'A guy I work with,' I told him.

'Oh, right, great.' Marti took a gulp of his pint. 'Good singer, is he?'

'I have no idea.'

'He'd look good in a mature sort of boy band,' Marti said idly.

I grinned, trying to imagine Ed in a white Lycra cowboy suit.

Ed had decided to sing 'Big Yellow Taxi'.

Another cheer from the lads he was with. Ed grinned down at them and the music began. It was a brilliant performance, helped, it has to be said, by his mates all yelling out the '*Don't it always seem to go, you don't know what you've got till it's gone*' chorus. Soon most people in the pub were clapping and singing along. And Ed just dripped sex all over that stage. Well, to me there is nothing so much of a turn-on as a man with a guitar in his hand. Not that Ed even had a guitar, but if he had, he would have been irresistible.

There was lots of clapping and laughter when he'd finished.

'I think that deserves a pint,' the DJ called.

A Guinness was handed to him to roars of approval from the crowd.

It was on the way down that Ed spotted me. He smiled and crossed towards us. 'Better say hello to the boss,' he grinned.

To my horror, I blushed. 'Yeah, hi,' I stammered out.

'Hey, great song.' Marti thrust out his hand. 'Marti Hearty, manager, Boy Five.'

Ed grinned. 'Ta. They' – he thumbed to his mates who were all staring curiously at us – 'me flatmates, always make me do it when we go out. It's just a laugh, really.'

'You were good,' I said.

'Ta.' Ed grinned at me, indicated his mates again. 'Anyway, I'd better get back.'

'Nice voice,' Marti said to me when he left. 'Pity I'm so tied up with Boy Five 'cause I'd sign him.'

Ed's arrival back at his table was met with a 'whoooo' followed by loads of laughter.

Marti drove me home. This time I did ask him back to the flat and he accepted. As I was spooning the coffee into the cups, he came behind me and wrapped his arms about me. 'Give us a kiss,' he whispered.

I turned around and wrapped my arms about his neck. Slowly he brought his mouth to mine. Soft, gentle kisses. I was just beginning to wish he'd do a bit more when Sal burst in.

'Ooops, sorry, folks.' She grinned hugely. 'Didn't mean to interrupt. I'll get out of your way.'

'Naw, naw, no need.' Marti pulled away from me. 'I'd better go. The sprog will be missing me.'

Sal looked puzzled.

'I'll see you out.' I virtually shoved him out the door.

Then, when he'd gone, after a few more limp biscuit kisses, I legged it into my room before Sal could ask me anything.

Chapter Twenty-one

IT SEEMED THAT everyone in the world got up before I did. As I stumbled out of bed the next day, I heard Sal humming away to herself in the kitchen. I use the word 'humming' very loosely. Sal hasn't a note. And whenever I slag her over it, she always replies that they're not the sort of notes she's interested in having anyway. So there I was, having been in bed by one, feeling completely knackered, and there she was, hardly having been in bed at all, eating breakfast and looking radiant.

How does everyone do it?

Iron tablets?

The 'tonic' my mother was always referring to? 'Vicky, you'd want to get yourself a good tonic.'

'I don't drink gin,' I'd told her.

It had made my dad laugh.

She hadn't looked impressed.

'So,' Sal asked as I shambled in past her, 'how'd the date with Purple Eyes go?'

I stiffened. So far I'd avoided telling her of Marti's marital status. 'Marti,' I corrected. Without looking at her, I popped some bread into the toaster. 'And yep, it went well.'

'Not that well.' Sal sniggered into her bowl of healthy something-or-other. Then made a big deal of looking all around her. 'He's not here this morning, is he?'

She was a great one for measuring the success of a date in terms of how long it took to reach shagging stage. If it didn't happen until the third date it was a mega slow starter.

'If he was here this morning,' I said back, 'he certainly wouldn't be here next weekend or the weekend after.'

'Puritan!' Sal scoffed. 'You've been brainwashed by your mother. If he likes you, he'll be back, simple as that.'

I was not getting into the puritan debate again. It had nothing to do with my mother's dire warning of men not respecting me; it was all a lot more practical than that. Sal could take a guy home and shag his brains out and he wouldn't believe his luck. He'd come trotting back the next week to see if it had really happened, whereas if I took a guy home first date he'd think I was desperate. And where would he be the next week? Running for his life, that's where. Or, if he didn't go heading for the hills, he'd start reading more into the relationship than I wanted him to and then *I'd* have to do a runner.

Relationships, for me anyhow, were a minefield. And it wasn't just the love ones.

'He left pretty quick after I came in last night.' Sal was licking her spoon and looking speculatively at me.

'He had to go home.'

'Home?' she scoffed. 'No man goes haring home unless his mammy warns him not to be out late. Now, he's hardly still living with Mammy, is he?'

I didn't answer.

'He *isn't*!'

I didn't like the 'are-you-completely-mental' look on her face. 'She lives with him,' I clarified. 'And she was babysitting his little boy.'

Her spoon clattered to the floor. For a fleeting second I enjoyed her look of shock before she said incredulously, 'Come again?'

'You heard him last night,' I said. 'He had to go home to his little boy.'

'Jesus!'

I felt like I was back in school being grilled for having no homework done. I tossed my hair back in what I hoped was a defiant gesture, before saying nonchalantly, 'Nope, just an ordinary little boy.'

Sal did smile before declaring, 'That is so not something to make a joke about. Oh God!' She pulled an anguished face. 'A kid. How awful.'

She made it sound like AIDS. Seeing as I'd come this far, I decided to go the whole hog. 'He has a wife too.'

'Jesus!' Now she really looked gobsmacked. 'He's *married.*'

'Separated.'

For the first time ever, Sal was speechless. It didn't last long though. 'I take it back. You're not a puritan. You're a gobshite.'

Her words stung. 'He's *separated.*'

'So? He was married, wasn't he? He has a kid, hasn't he? That woman will be in his life for ever.'

'She left them.' I furiously buttered my toast. I didn't want to hear this.

'There'll always be that tie there.'

I shrugged. 'It's not that serious, anyway.'

'It's bloody dynamite!' Sal stood up from the table and brushed by me as she dumped her bowl in the sink. 'There's no future in that. For one thing, he'll always have two houses to support – hers and his.'

'She *left* him.'

'Doesn't make a difference. He'll have no money to make a decent life.'

It always came down to money with her. 'I'm not like you. I don't think of money all the time.' I hoped it would hurt her the way she'd hurt me. I *wasn't* a gobshite. I liked Marti, he liked me. It wasn't as if it was an affair or anything as seedy as that.

'Well' – she fingered my tatty dressing gown and arched a perfect eyebrow – 'maybe you should.' She swished past me, her own silk designer gown fluttering out behind her.

I couldn't eat my toast.

* * *

We didn't say much to each other for the rest of the day. She lolled about in her pyjamas, flicking through the Sunday papers and drinking glasses of water. I, after trying to read my latest self-help book and failing, decided to get dressed and go for a walk. The atmosphere in the flat was so bloody cold, I'd have been deep frozen by nightfall.

It wasn't a bad day for February. It was dry and bright and the birds were singing. For the first time that year it looked as if spring was a definite possibility. I decided to head towards the park. Walking alone in the park would look slightly less suspect than tramping the streets of Yellow Halls on my own.

There were a few people milling around in the park. Couples entwined, OAPs with their arthritic dogs, families with kids throwing bread to lethargic ducks. The ducks were the fattest ones I'd ever seen. One little fella was aiming great hunks of bread directly at them and scoring every time.

'Oh, yeah,' he said as he hit one particularly obese duck on the back.

His mother smiled fondly at him.

Little brat, I thought. He reminded me of my Cousin Tommy. It's exactly the sort of thing he would have done. But it was nice the way his mother thought he was great. It gave me a sort of pang to see it. Right in the middle of my chest.

'Vicky!'

The voice startled me.

'I didn't know you were a Sunday stroller!'

What an old-fashioned name. How like a complete dork I sounded. But then again Bridie was an old-fashioned sort of woman. 'Bridie, hi.' I was quite glad to see her. Now, with a person walking beside me, I wouldn't look like such a saddo. She was dressed in her brown tweed coat and old lady button-up boots. Where do old people get stuff like that? Is there some secret shop you only learn about as you get older or something? Anyway, she folded her arms and smiled up at me. 'I'm just taking a stroll while my chicken cooks. It should be ready around half-four, so that gives me just enough time to walk to the swings and back.'

She was the exact same as in work. Everything timed to perfection.

'I like looking at the kiddies in the playground. So I spend about ten minutes there and then I turn back. I live just across that way.' She pointed in a vague sort of way at the trees across the green. 'I always go for a stroll on a Sunday. Do you?'

'Nah.' I began to walk alongside her. 'It's my first time in the park actually. It's nice.'

'It's more than nice. It's a lovely place to blow the cobwebs away. I come here most days. On my day off, I walk the whole park. It takes about ninety minutes. That's what you should do – you'd enjoy it.'

Maybe I would. When I'd been away, I'd walked and walked and thought and thought and there'd come a stage when I'd walked so far that my mind would switch off and that was the best time. Just walking and enjoying the moment. I guess at heart I'm a bit of a loner. I don't mean in an antisocial way or anything, I like a night out as much as anyone, it's just that I always find myself alone at some stage in the night and I enjoy it. I enjoy being a saddo. What I don't like is others *thinking* I'm a saddo.

'Sunday is my favourite day,' Bridie went on, 'going to mass, getting the papers, having a walk, enjoying my dinner, watching the television. Just, you know, relaxing.'

My Sundays were usually spent drinking copious amounts of water to rid myself of the banging headache from the night before.

'So what brings you out here?' Bridie asked.

'Oh' – I made a face – 'my flatmate isn't talking to me.'

'The journalist girl?'

'The one and only.'

'Oh dear.' Bridie made clucking sounds. 'And on a Sunday and everything.'

I don't know what Sunday had to do with it.

'So I came out to get away from her,' I said, trying to sound happy about it. 'If anyone can create a bad atmosphere it's her.'

'Mmm,' Bridie nodded. 'Journalists are very temperamental people.'

I was glad she was on my side.

We walked along side by side until we came to the swings. Well, it was more than swings, it was one of those dinky wooden playgrounds with climbing nets and huge slides and wooden climbing frames. Bridie sat down on a seat and I joined her.

'The kiddies have great fun here,' she said, half wistfully.

'The adults could have too,' I muttered. 'Look at the size of that slide. Betcha it'd be great to go down backwards on it.'

She laughed. 'I'd break every bone in my body.'

I watched the kids running up and down and envied them. 'One day, when it rains and there's no one else here, I'm going to come back and go on that slide,' I said.

Bridie smiled.

'I am. Honest.'

'You'd get stuck halfway down,' she giggled childishly.

I have to say I was insulted. 'I'm not *that* big.'

'No,' she was still giggling. 'I meant with the rain.'

'Oh. Right.'

We didn't say much after that. Just looked at the kids.

'Playgrounds are happy places,' Bridie remarked suddenly. 'That's why I come here.'

'Just like the toy shop,' I said.

She looked at me, surprised. 'Yes, I suppose.'

'That's how I got the job, I reckon,' I told her. 'In my interview they asked me why I'd like to manage a toy shop and that's what I told them. I said that toy shops are always happy. I like happy places.'

'Who doesn't?' Bridie stood up. 'Who doesn't?'

She sounded sad.

I walked her back to the park entrance. She was quiet and didn't say much. I was wondering if she wanted to get rid of me.

Maybe she hadn't wanted me to follow her in the first place? After all, would I want my boss with me on a Sunday? I was about to say that I had to be going when she asked, 'D'you want to come for dinner – I'll have enough for two?'

I hadn't had dinner since Christmas. Not a proper spuds and two veg dinner anyway. But maybe Bridie was only being polite. She was an awful polite person. 'You don't have to,' I protested, 'I know you like being on your own and stuff.'

'Being on my own?' She looked surprised. Then shrugged. 'Well, yes, yes, I suppose I do but, well, with your friend not talking to you, I just thought—'

'Don't worry about me.' *She was having roast chicken. Mmmm.* 'She'll probably talk eventually.'

'There's plenty,' Bridie went on. 'I usually get a chicken big enough to last a few days. That way I can have chicken sandwiches for lunch in work. And I've put on extra potatoes because I was going to make a bit of potato salad, but you can eat them. And I can always put on a few extra peas and carrots. I use the tinned ones, you see.' She sounded as if she really wanted me. And I didn't have anywhere else to go. And I hadn't realised how much I wanted a dinner . . .

'If you're sure,' I said.

'Of course I'm sure.' She smiled at me. 'A bit of company would be nice.'

Bridie's house was a tiny two-up two-down affair. Her garden consisted of grass and rose bushes. Her front door was brown with the brass knob shining like some kind of a homing beacon in a street of tarnished knockers. Inside, her hall was cream and brown and her kitchen was cream and brown. The whole place was clean, but it didn't sparkle. I guess it was because everything looked so brown.

The smell of chicken was lovely, though. And she had potatoes gently boiling.

Sticking a fork into them, she pronounced them almost done.

'Now you sit down and make yourself comfortable while I lay the table and get some vegetables on.'

I sat on one of her brown kitchen chairs. It felt a bit weird to be in Bridie's house but it felt nice as well.

'Can I do anything?' I asked, knowing that if my mother heard me she'd keel over and die.

'No. No.' Bridie waved me off. 'Just relax. I want you going home ready to make up with that friend of yours.'

I felt really awkward as she fussed about, handing me a napkin and a fancy glass.

Then came the dinner. A massive plate for me. Honestly, I'd say she gave me all her lunches for that week.

'Eat up now.' Bridie smiled at me from across the table. 'I don't often get company but when I do I like them to go home full.'

After dinner, she led me into her 'good' room. She didn't say it was good but I knew by the smell of polish and the lonely look of the furniture that it hadn't been used for ages. There were pictures up on the mantelpiece. As Bridie went to get me a coffee, I studied them.

There was one of Bridie taken years ago that still looked like her. She was standing on a beach somewhere with the wind blowing her hair and she had a hand up to keep it down. She was laughing into the lens. Beside her stood a man, laughing too, his hands casually jammed into his trouser pockets. He had dark hair and was quite handsome in a nineteen-fifties type of way.

'Who's that?' I asked as Bridie came in. 'Your husband?'

She put down my coffee and took the photo from me. 'No.' She smiled at the frame. 'He would have been if he'd lived.' I saw her stroke his face.

'Oh. I'm sorry.'

'Not at all. It was a long time ago now.' She put the photo back in its place. 'I just like that photograph. Mainly because I look nice in it – don't you think?'

I grinned at her vanity. 'You're a real babe, Bridie.'
'Legs like a well-made table,' Bridie smiled back.
'Sorry?'
'Ed. He said that.' Bridie giggled. 'He's the funniest lad. I have to admit I was a bit worried at the start but he's working out well, don't you think?'
I was glad she thought so. 'I think he's a bit' – I didn't want her to think I was a bitch or paranoid – 'a bit overpowering.' The word didn't do him justice. 'Back-stabbing bastard' would have done the job.
Bridie looked puzzled. 'Oh no.' She shook her head. 'He's a nice quiet lad and the kids love him.'
'Do they?' That was news to me.
'Oh yes,' Bridie nodded. 'He knows all the PlayStation games and all the wrestlers and everything. I think he does nothing bar watch TV and play computer games in his spare time.'
'And you wonder why he hasn't a girlfriend.'
That was bitchy, I know.
'A boy like that won't be single for long,' Bridie said with a confidence that annoyed me. Then with a bit of a whoop she said, 'And I almost forgot – how did your night out go last night?'
'Great.' I was delighted that she remembered.
'And him?' Bridie asked. 'Do you still like him?'
'Very,' I nodded. 'He's a bit eccentric – you'd think he was odd but he's not. He's' – I looked at her cream ceiling and tried to think of how to describe him – 'colourful. He's got a big loud personality.'
'Oh.' She didn't look too impressed.
'He's not like anyone else I've ever been with. I like that.'
'Well, I'm glad.' She picked up my coffee and handed it to me. 'It's important to be happy, to make good choices.'
She sounded a bit sad as she said it.

I stayed in Bridie's until after seven. She was all set to make me tea but I couldn't hang around any longer. Part of me is ashamed to admit that I didn't want to have to tell anyone that I'd just spent a Sunday with a sixty-year-old woman who wasn't even my mother. I think she was disappointed that I couldn't stay but I pretended to her that I was going out with some friends.

If only.

Instead I pulled up my hood – it had begun to rain – and I walked home prepared to brave the atmosphere.

Sal was surprisingly polite when I came back.

'You had a phone call,' she said tersely, watching me shake all the drops from my mac onto the kitchen floor. 'From the purple-eyed, separated father.'

'I did?' I forgot about my mac and tried to look nonchalant. I figured that if I looked desperate, Sal'd string me along for ages. 'What'd he say?'

'He said that he'd ring you on your mobile.'

My mobile. My very *immobile* mobile. I legged it into my bedroom and, locating my haversack, tore it open. My phone was sitting serenely in its groovy holder, as dead as a Dodo.

The calendar on the wall seemed to mock me with its big CHARGE MOBILE sign. When I emerged from the room, Sal was holding out my charger. 'Figured you'd need this.'

I tried not to grin as I took it from her. Even if she was a cow, she knew me well.

'You'll never have a relationship without a mobile phone,' she warned as she stood behind me.

I said nothing, just plugged in my phone and prepared to wait at least an hour until I could access it.

'Sorry about earlier,' Sal said. 'It was none of my business.'

Apologies from Sal were about as rare as French cooked steak. ''Sfine,' I muttered, trying not to sound too gobsmacked. Uneasily, I wondered what she was up to.

'I mean, if you want a relationship with a married man with a kid, you go right ahead.'

'I will. Thanks for your permission.'

'And if I want a relationship with a young, hunky, rich guy, you won't stand in my way either, sure you won't?'

'Nope.'

It was only after she'd waltzed out of the room that I realised what she'd meant. She was going in after Ed.

I wondered what had brought that on.

There were two messages on the phone.

Two voicemail messages.

The missed call part told me that I'd missed a call from Marti and another one from a number that I didn't recognise.

Dialling the number, I attempted to access the messages.

And guess who hadn't topped up her credit?

Chapter Twenty-two

THE FOLLOWING DAY, I broke all records and got up at ten. On my day off!

Normally, I'd lie in bed telling myself over and over that I was going to get up, but the fact that I was unable to access two messages on my mobile was driving me mad. I got up, pulled on my jeans and a yellow sweatshirt, pulled a comb through my hair and, donning socks and trainers, legged it out the door and up the road to the corner shop.

'Call card.' I shoved my money to the guy behind the counter. 'Fifteen euro.'

He seemed to be a slow starter like me. He took my money, looked at it for ages, put it in the till, spent ages looking with narrowed eyes at what he was supposed to do next while I hopped impatiently from foot to foot.

'Hi there.' A face poked itself into mine. Buck teeth gleamed in the dusty light. 'Day off, eh?'

'You got it.' I smiled briefly at Troy, hoping like mad he wasn't going to talk to me.

'Cool sweatshirt.' Troy nodded at my sweatshirt.

'Ta.'

'You always wear big, bold colours, don't you?' Troy leaned his elbow on the counter and poked his face even further into mine. 'I've noticed that about you.'

'That's me, big and bold,' I said. I deliberately didn't look at him. Troy was like a stray dog; if I showed him any interest at all, he'd follow me home and hover about all day.

He was snorting with laughter over my comment and saying that he hoped I wasn't too bold when the guy behind the counter said in a bored voice, 'Was that fifteen euro?'

'Yes.'

A piece of paper with a number was passed over to me. 'There.'

'Ta.' I took it up and shoved it in my pocket. I'd dial once I got out onto the street. My heart had begun to hammer and I felt a bit sick. I told myself it was because I hadn't had any breakfast. 'Bye, Troy.'

'Aw, no, awww, look,' Troy called after me, 'I've to just get a packet of Star Trek cards and I'll walk home with you.'

I pretended not to hear. I took off down the road and crossed into the park, knowing Troy would think I'd gone back to the flat. I sat down on a mouldy-looking seat and inputted my credit number. Once that was done, I dialled up for my messages.

'You have two new voicemail messages. First message. Left Thursday seventh of February.' To my crushing disappointment, I heard my mother say, 'I don't think this auld thing is working at all.' My father's voice rumbled from somewhere in the background. 'I'll leave a message, so,' my mother said a bit narkily. Then, sort of breathlessly, she said, 'Hello, love. It's me. Mam.' A bit of a laugh. 'I've got this new mobile phone from Tommy. He gave it to us, he didn't need it. Anyway, I'm trying it out. Just to tell you that I'm up in Dublin next week. Tuesday. And I'll call into work to see you for lunch. Bye-bye now.' A load more fumbling before it went dead.

The second message came on. I hardly heard Marti as he thanked me for a great night and promised to call me again.

It had been my mother.

The unknown number had been my mother.

All last night, I'd envisioned that it might be the adoption board. That they'd got news for me.

And all along it had been her.

I don't know how long I sat on the bench with the stupid phone to my ear but it was ages.

I was so devastatingly, terribly disappointed.

Chapter Twenty-three

MY MOTHER SAT across from me, tucking into her enormous salad roll. She looked well. She was wearing her green suit, the one she'd bought for Christmas, and a white blouse. Green suited my mother. Most colours did really. On the table in front of her sat the newly acquired mobile phone. 'In case your father rings,' she'd said, placing it reverently beside her plate.

'And why would he?' I asked, amused.

'Oh, no reason.' She gave a short laugh and indicated the phone. 'They're great things, aren't they?'

I hadn't really thought about it. 'Suppose.'

'I mean, if you'd had one when you were on your travels, it would have made things so much easier.'

I ignored that. There was no point in explaining to her about the difficulties of charging a mobile whilst crossing the desert in a tent.

Mam gave her phone another fond look.

I don't know what was so special about it. It was last year's Nokia. 'I would have bought one for you if you'd wanted it,' I said. Then added, 'A new one.'

She rolled her eyes and laughed a bit. 'Don't,' was all she said, but I knew what she meant.

I have a thing about accepting second-hand stuff. 'False pride,' my mam calls it. 'Having too much money,' my dad says. It's neither. I just don't like feeling that I owe someone.

'Don't,' Mam said again. Then, in a wonderful, subtle change of subject, she asked, 'Are the chips nice?'

'Lovely, yeah.'

Silence.

'So, what brings you up here?' I shoved a chip into my mouth to show her that I did like them. 'It's hardly just to see me.'

'I like seeing you,' she said defensively. 'I'd like to see a bit more of you.'

I flinched. 'I'm just busy,' I mumbled.

'I know that,' she said in such an understanding voice that it made me feel like the worst daughter in the world, 'but surely not too busy to come and see us once in a while?'

I said nothing.

Her hand crossed the table and clasped mine. 'What is it?' she said softly. 'Why won't you visit?'

I was caught off-guard. Her hand felt funny on top of mine. It gave me the sort of claustrophobic feeling that the family gatherings did. 'I do visit,' I muttered. What did they want? 'I come home as often as I *can*.'

I don't know what it was I saw in her eyes. They sort of flinched and wavered and then it was gone. She took her hand away. I was glad. 'Well, I hope you'll come down next month. It's your dad's sixtieth and I'm throwing him a surprise party.'

'Of course I'll be there.'

'Good.'

She held my gaze for a bit before turning her attention back to her lunch.

'So that's why you're up here, is it?' I asked, striving for normal once again. 'You're buying Dad a present.'

'Among other things,' she answered.

'Yeah?'

I saw her gulp. 'Well,' she floundered, 'I, eh, I was in the markets looking at flowers for Lisa Sweeney's wedding. They've fabulous colours here. I just want to get an idea of what's available.'

'She's getting married in late *summer*. Those flowers won't be around then.'

'They'll be around for the right money,' Mam answered. 'And the Sweeneys said to spend what I like.'

'Well, you'd better not do the flowers too nice or they'll outshine the bride.'

'Stop!' Mam flapped her hand at me and laughed. 'You really are awful!'

'It was just a joke.' For some reason I felt ashamed of myself. 'I didn't mean it.' But I had.

Mam smiled.

There was silence as we began to eat our lunch in earnest. It was nearly two and I had to go back and relieve Ed. No point in giving the guy *excuses* to shaft me.

'So' – Mam poured the last drop of tea from the pot into her cup – 'have you' – she paused and flushed – 'found out anything about your, your' – she bit her lip – 'birth mother?' She busied herself stirring milk into her tea.

God, she was really getting personal today. 'A bit.' It was funny that she'd asked. Like I said before, my folks don't like to bring the issue of my birth into the spotlight. I glanced quickly at my mam and she was giving me this encouraging look, as if she wanted to know, so I gulped out, 'Her name is Barbara.'

'That's a nice name,' Mam whispered.

'Yeah.' I paused. 'And she has red hair.'

Mam laid down her spoon. 'Like yours,' she said softly.

'Uh-huh.' Without thinking, I curled some of my hair about my finger.

Mam smiled a little. Sort of sadly, I think. After a few seconds, she asked, 'Anything else?'

'No.' I studied my fingernails. 'Finding someone can take up to two years, you know.'

'Really?' She made some sort of a surprised gasp. 'I didn't know that.'

I wished she hadn't brought the subject up. All I wanted was for this lunch to end. All the guilty feelings were grabbing me and making me feel awful.

'If you do find out something, will you tell me?' Mam asked then. Her voice was soft and low. 'I'd like to know.'

'Would you?' My eyes unexpectedly filled with tears. I didn't know if I felt awful or relieved or what. 'Really?'

'Yes. Really.' I think she was about to touch me but one of the waitresses came over.

'Are yez finished?' She stood beside us with a cloth in her hand. 'There's a bit of a queue waiting for a table.'

We ignored her. 'OK?' Mam said.

I just nodded.

I couldn't say much.

Sal, of course, chose that day to breeze into the shop in search of love, romance and a big fat chequebook.

'Hiiii,' she said chirpily as she came in. 'How's things?' She sashayed towards the counter in a pair of red jeans and a white Calvin Klein T-shirt that dipped in a plunging V neckline. A tiny red denim jacket clung to her upper body and her light blonde hair tumbled around her shoulders. She looked windswept and vibrant and part of me envied her her easy confidence. She was here to get a man and get a man she would.

'What are you doing here?' I hissed at her. It was bad enough seeing Ed in work and hearing about what a wonderful guy he was from Bridie, without having to listen to it at home too.

She tossed her head. 'I'm looking for a toy,' she said, all mock-innocence. 'What else?'

'A boy?' I virtually shrieked. 'Stop it. Now!'

'Toy,' she repeated, reddening slightly. Then, lowering her voice, she hissed, 'You said you wouldn't care.'

'Of course I care,' I hissed back. 'Jesus, will you get out!'

'Oooh.' Sal suddenly smiled and it was as if the sun came out in the shop. 'Hi, you must be Ed.'

Ed, who had just appeared from the back, dirty and dishevelled, looked confused. 'Sorry, do I know you?'

'I'm Vicky's flatmate.' Sal flicked her razor-straight hair back from her face. 'She's told me all about you.'

'I haven't,' I put in quickly.

Both of them looked at me.

'She says you're an expert on boy's toys,' Sal went on, tittering. 'Can you help me choose something for my nephew?'

'What nephew would that be?' I asked, trying not to grin. Honestly, she was such a cow but she had such nerve.

'My brother's kid, the eight-year-old,' Sal lied charmingly.

'You sure you don't want Vic to show you?' Ed asked, completely oblivious of Sal's intentions.

'She said you're the expert,' Sal twinkled.

Ed shot me a sceptical look, which I returned with a shrug. Then he turned his full attention to Sal. He gave her *the* smile. I had got to call it that because of all the times he used it on the customers. It was a smile that said, 'You are, hand on heart, my number-one priority.' And Sal, not to be outdone, gave him her smile. The one that says, 'Hey, I'm only a helpless woman and I need a man like you to *make* me your number-one priority'.

'This way, Vicky's friend.' Ed was now giving her his wink. 'You'll probably find something suitable back here.'

'It's Sal,' Sal said pertly, using her eyes to dazzle him, 'and yes, I'm sure you're right. I'll bet there's something very suitable back there.'

He grinned and strode on ahead of her, leading the way.

'Cor,' Sal mouthed to me but I pretended not to notice.

She came back about ten minutes later with two PlayStation games and a whole heap of wrestlers and transformers. Ed, depressingly enough, was the best salesperson of the lot of us. The *crap* he persuaded parents to buy for their kids was unbelievable. And it wasn't as if he did a hard sell or anything. He had a sort of easy charm that made you believe he was kosher. All he had to do was recommend something to a customer and t was sold. I think part of it was that Ed loved toys and so he nade our customers love them too.

He helped Sal carry her purchases to the counter. 'Honestly,' she was saying to him as she dumped them in front of me, 'you are the most helpful assistant Vicky has ever had in here.'

Like she would know, I thought in amusement.

'And you must be the most generous aunt on the planet,' Ed grinned.

For a second Sal looked puzzled.

'The toys,' I supplied helpfully, 'for your nephew?'

'Oh those,' Sal laughed. 'They're nothing, he deserves all of them. I just love kids.'

I bit my lip to try and stop giggling. 'They'll cost about eighty euro worth,' I said, beginning to cash them up. 'Are you sure you want them all?'

'Sure. Sure I do.' She smiled bravely as I ran them through the till. 'Ed recommended them all.' She smiled at Ed who, completely missing the fact that he was being flirted with, shrugged modestly. 'Here.' Sal handed me her credit card. 'Put them on that.'

Another customer came in. Sal looked meaningfully at me.

'Ed,' I said, 'will you finish this sale while I see to this lady?'

'Ach, no.' Ed shook his head. 'Sure you talk to your friend there, I'll go and see to this one.' He nodded amicably at Sal and sauntered off.

I tried not to giggle.

'Is he thick or what?' Sal hissed, rolling her eyes. She pulled some wrestlers out of the way. 'You can take those wrestlers out. There is no way I'm buying them. They're completely overpriced.'

'And the PlayStation games?'

'Just pretend like I want them. I'll give them back to you—'

'She doesn't want any help.' Ed arrived back. 'Hey' – he looked at the discarded wrestlers – 'what's wrong with them?'

'Oh, nothing.' Sal gave her tinkly laugh. 'I just thought I'd

bought two the same.' She hastily began to shove them toward
me again.

'Two the same?' Ed shook his head and grinned. I could se
Sal melting. 'Not at all. Sure this fella here is Triple H.' He hel
up my favourite wrestler. 'This other one here is The Rock, he'
the one most of the kids love, and the one you just put back
he's . . .'

I walked off and left him discussing the merits of one wrestle
versus the other with Sal.

To be honest, if she could survive the conversation, sh
deserved him.

'I think we should do a wrestling window,' Ed said when Sa
finally left. 'The wrestling rings are cool – have you seen them?

'I ordered them,' I said, a bit snottily. 'I know how good the
are.'

'Then you'll definitely have thought that we should do
window at some stage – yeah?'

He looked at me like a kid hoping for sweets.

'I might have,' I shrugged. 'Could never get around to i
though.'

'I'll do it if you like,' Ed offered. 'That's what I'm here fo
isn't it?' The pale blue of his eyes lit up his face. 'It'll be *grea*
I'll put the backstage mayhem and the studio wreckage on eac
side of the ring. Honestly, they'll sell a bomb once the kids se
it. The transformer sales have really picked up – yeah?'

'Yeah,' I muttered with bad grace.

Ed grinned delightedly. 'Told you. And see, the problem wit
the way we're displaying the wrestlers at the moment is that they'r
all in the boxes, except for that one over there, and the kids don
see that unless they come in. This way, they'll all come in.'

Of course he was right. And I'd lied, the idea of doing
window had never occurred to me. I gritted my teeth – ye
another little defeat in what was turning out to be a bit of
list. 'Fine,' I muttered.

'Don't be so sceptical,' he grinned, 'it'll boost the sales no end.'

I'm glad he took my resentment for scepticism. 'Just make sure Triple H is the one that's winning,' I said gruffly.

He looked at me in surprise. I dunno whether it was because he couldn't believe that I actually knew the name of a wrestler or because I wanted Triple H, The Rock's arch enemy, to be the victor.

'I was going to have—'

'The Rock, yeah, I know, but he's an arrogant shit.' I smiled at him, hoping he'd make the connection between himself and The Rock. 'It's Triple H, the much maligned underdog, or no window.'

A slow grin spread itself across his face. 'Yeah,' he nodded, 'I can see why you'd like wrestling.' Before I had a chance to reply, he said hastily, 'Triple H it is.'

I was horrible enough to hope that the sales of wrestlers would go down.

Chapter Twenty-four

'I JUST DON'T get it.' Sal slugged back her martini and regarded me as if it was all my fault. 'I go in at least once a week and he smiles and laughs and tells me how lovely I look and that's it.'

'The guy is gay,' Mel said with such authority that I almost believed her. 'He has to be. There you are, offering yourself on a plate—'

'I don't "do" offering myself on a plate,' Sal said a little sharply.

''Course not.' Mel blew a long stream of smoke upwards and flicked the ash all over the table. 'Bad, bad choice of words. Anyway, he's gay, that's all there is to it!'

'Why didn't you tell me that he was gay?' Sal demanded of me.

'He's not,' I shrugged. 'Maybe he's just not interested.'

'In *that*?' Mel jabbed her fag towards Sal. 'Of course he is.'

I groaned. This night out was shaping up to be a 'wish I had stayed in and clipped my toenails' type of night. It was meant to have been a celebration of the publication of Sal's piece in the February issue of *Tell!* but instead it was turning out to be an in-depth analysis of Sal's failure to land The Big One. She and Mel had been obsessing over it since we'd left the flat. I dunno why Mel was so bothered; she'd never cared about Sal's love life before. Even the fact that Sal's story was splashed across the front of *Tell!* was no consolation to either of them.

And I mean *really* splashed across the front of the magazine.

Sex Scandal for Soccer Star was the headline. And the piece she had written was about how Denis McCoy, a football sensation in England, had been caught snogging a twenty-year-old beauty while his wife 'played happy housewife in England'. Sal had done her work well. Her descriptions of Denis's mad nights out sounded fantastic. (I wouldn't have minded going on a bender with him.) The pictures that accompanied her story left nothing to the imagination and, unsurprisingly, Denis McCoy had refused to comment on the story. And while Sal and Mel celebrated, I just had an uneasy feeling that though well written, the whole story was just tacky tabloid-ism. Of course, I couldn't say that – I mean, it was Sal's big break and I didn't want to hurt her – but surely she could do better than to wreck someone's life?

'What you want to do,' Mel said, blowing smoke straight into my face as she talked to Sal, 'is to find out what he's interested in and be interested in it yourself.'

I gave a bit of a snort.

They both looked at me.

'Eh, music, wrestling and soccer,' I provided.

'And haven't you just done the exposé on the soccer star!' Mel shrieked, causing people to look over. 'You can talk about that.'

Sal would ruin any chance she ever had with Ed if she told him she was responsible for that piece, I thought in alarm. Ed hadn't been a bit impressed with it. Denis McCoy, a Liverpool player, was one of Ed's heroes. 'Would you look at that?' he'd said to Bridie when the story had been taken up by other newspapers. 'Wouldn't you think a guy's life is his own private business?'

Bridie agreed.

'I mean, a guy makes a mistake, he doesn't need it splashed all over the papers.'

'But he was unfaithful to his wife,' I'd argued, just for the sake of arguing and I guess to be a bit loyal to Sal. 'If he's in the public eye, he can't do stuff like that and not expect to be caught. I mean, people are interested in these things.'

Ed looked at me, his blue eyes narrowed. 'That's not being interested,' he said coldly, 'that's being vindictive. I mean, what is the point in a story like that – hey?'

'I guess the point is that it sells papers,' I said mildly, getting a tiny kick out of annoying him.

'Oh aye, once we sell papers, who cares if we ruin the guy's career?'

'Oh, he'll still play, never fear,' Bridie said lightly. She laughed a bit. 'That's all you're worried about. That it'll stop him scoring for Liverpool.'

Ed threw the paper onto the table. 'Yeah. Yeah, right, Bridie.' He dumped his tea down the sink. 'I'll go down and open up.'

'Oops.' Bridie made a face at me as he left. 'A bit touchy, wasn't he?'

'Mmm.' I grinned slightly. 'I wonder where he tethered it?'

'What?' Bridie asked. 'Tethered what?'

'His high horse.'

She couldn't stop laughing all day.

I grinned as I remembered.

'What are you smirking about?' Sal asked. 'Are you laughing at me?'

'Naw, but I wouldn't tell him you did that story on McCoy – he happens to love the guy.'

'I told you he was gay!' Mel clapped her hands together. 'What did I say?'

'Apparently McCoy is Liverpool's top scorer,' I explained over Mel's triumphant cackles, 'and the whole thing has affected his goal-scoring ability or something.'

'Oh.' Sal looked crestfallen. 'Well, can't he go and cheer on another team?'

'That's not the way it works, apparently.' I slugged down the last of my Bud and sought a way to explain. 'It's like, it's like you being married for twenty years and suddenly deciding to have sex with someone else.'

'Listen.' Mel flicked her ash all over the table. 'A guy I'm married to suddenly loses his scoring ability, I'm outta there, you know what I mean!'

We laughed.

'Look,' I said, when they'd stopped making crude comments, 'why don't you just ask him *out*?' I stood up. 'Anyone want a drink?'

'Just ask him out!' Sal was aghast. 'I've never done that in my life!'

'Tacky,' Mel agreed.

'Well, it's either that or become a soccer fan,' I grinned, 'and I just can't see you as that, Sal.'

'You'd be surprised.' Sal tapped her glass. 'Make mine a double.'

'You'll need it.' I ignored both their exasperated looks and went to the bar.

I got manky drunk. As far as I can remember Mel and Sal had remained sober enough but that's only because they had so much to talk about. They knew the same people and hated the same people. They roared with laughter over stories that I couldn't even understand. And so, for lack of anything better to do, I drank too much.

Sometimes when I drink, things become really clear to me. It's like I can see into the future and into who I really am, inside, underneath all the wisecracks. And as I was sitting there, downing another Bud, it suddenly occurred to me to wonder just what on earth I was doing with Sal and Mel. There they were, two glamorous, career-minded women on the opposite side of the table, laughing and sniggering at everyone. And here I was, a woman who felt about twelve years old, with not a clue of what she was about at all. In my drunken fug I managed to smile every now and again whenever they broke into laughter, but really, I didn't find anything they said a bit funny. Not. At. All.

Before I had a chance to think about it, I rose up. ''Scuse me,' I said, all self-righteous. 'I'm going home. You two just talk crap.'

They laughed.

'Drunk!' Sal said fondly. 'As usual.'

I resented that. 'I re-sent that.'

'Oooh,' Sal and Mel went.

I stumbled off. Got a taxi and came home. 'Vicky,' I thought to myself as I lay down, just before the room began to spin at about a hundred miles an hour, 'you have gotta get out of here.'

Of course, the next morning I woke up with a hammering head and the vague notion that I owed Sal an apology.

And, many months later, I thought that if only I'd listened to the voice of drunkenness, things might have turned out a lot better.

Chapter Twenty-five

I'LL ALWAYS REMEMBER Wednesday 25th February of that year. It's like one of those pop-up cards – everything about the days leading to it and from it are sort of background decoration while this day stands out in 3D, Technicolor. To be more precise, it's about five minutes of that day that stand out.

It was after lunch and I was talking to Dominic, who'd come out of his self-imposed shyness to ask me why Triple H was beating up The Rock in our front window. (Yep, it was going a bomb, the wrestlers were selling out and so I'd reluctantly left Ed's display in place for another month.)

'The Rock is better than Triple H,' Dominic was saying earnestly as my phone began to ring. 'I don't think that it's fair to have him getting all beat up.'

I would swear Ed had put him up to it. He stood at the other side of the shop, leaning against the shelves, grinning broadly over at me.

Dominic's mother was smiling shyly too.

'It's only a window display,' I said in my nice patient voice. 'And Triple H has to win sometime.' I reached under the cash desk to get my mobile out of my bag.

'No, he doesn't,' Dominic said back. 'Triple H could never beat The Rock. Not in a million years. Not ever. Not in this lifetime.' His voice rose. 'Can you smell what The Rock is cooking?' he yelled out all over the place, causing a little baby in a pram to start shrieking.

Ed laughed and Dominic turned and gave him the thumbs up.

'Ed,' I said, 'will you please go into that window and make Dominic happy.'

'Aw, you're so good.' Ed winked at me. He caught Dominic by the hand. 'Come on, Dom, let's show Triple H what The Rock is cooking – huh?'

Dominic squealed.

'That fella is crackers,' Dominic's mother said fondly, looking after Ed. 'I dunno who's de bigger kid.'

'I do,' I smiled.

She laughed. She looked suddenly much younger and nicer.

'Triple H is crap, isn't he, Ed?' Dominic could be heard saying as he looked at Ed moving about the window display.

'He's tragic!' Ed agreed.

'Not quite so tragic as your orange jacket,' I said back, flicking on my mobile.

Ed laughed loudly and I found myself grinning. He never seemed to take offence at anything I said.

'You shouldn't criticise a man's clothes,' Bridie whispered. 'Maybe his dad bought it for him – did you think about that now, miss? You'd want to control your tongue, you'll—'

'Hi,' I said into my phone. I did not want to hear what I should and shouldn't say. She was always telling me off these days.

'Vicky McCarthy?' It was a woman's voice.

'That's me.'

'You shouldn't be on your mobile.' Bridie poked me in the ribs. 'What if Mr O'Neill comes in?'

'Sorry, sorry, I didn't hear you,' I said to the woman as I moved away from Bridie towards the office. 'What did you say?'

'My name is Helen Devine, I work for the Adoption Board. I have some news for you about your mother.'

Time stopped.

It was as if everything receded and still I was walking towards the office.

'Vicky?' the woman said. 'Are you there?'

'Yes, yes.' My voice was feathery. My heart was hammering as if it was going to break up into a thousand pieces. I felt numb. 'My mother.' I closed the office door on Bridie and sat down in the computer chair. 'You have news?'

Beyond the door, Bridie had begun muttering loudly about certain people only wanting to walk into trouble despite her best efforts.

'You've made enquiries about tracing your birth mother – is that right?'

'Yes.'

'Well, it's policy here to ring with any news we have – it's a little more personal, we'll be sending you a letter in a couple of days, OK?'

'Right.' I felt sick, for some reason.

'We have information for you about your birth mother.'

'Yes?' It came out as a whisper.

'We have on file the name of a third party—'

'Sorry?'

The woman's voice was gentle. 'I can tell that this has been a shock for you, hasn't it?'

'I just wasn't expecting—' I gulped. 'So soon.' My voice went a bit wobbly.

'Of course.' Helen stopped and then asked tentatively, 'Have you had counselling?'

'Nope.' Pause. 'What about my, my' – it was weird, saying it – 'my birth mother?'

She ignored me and went on, a bit sternly, I thought, 'From here on in, you should definitely consider getting some counselling. It's not like seeing a therapist or anything, your counsellor will be a social worker who's dealt with these situations before. I'll send you the phone numbers of these counsellors in my letter. It's a big thing this, Vicky. Getting counselling lets you explore your feelings. Helps you think about the what ifs.'

'Yes,' I said, hardly hearing her, 'but my mother?'

Helen didn't say anything immediately and when she did begin to speak, it was in a slow, measured way that had me wishing she'd hurry up.

'We have on file the name of a third party,' she began, 'and we have contacted this person and they, it seems, have agreed, in the event of you wanting to make contact with your mother, to act as an intermediary between the two of you.'

I didn't get it. 'What?'

'Your mother nominated this person a long time ago to act as a sort of go-between – carrying messages from you to her.'

I felt as if my heart was being squeezed too hard. 'She doesn't want to know me?'

'No, that's not it at all.' Helen's voice was reassuring. 'It's not uncommon. Your mother might be nervous about meeting you or she might just want to see how she feels about things. It's very rare on first contact to have a full-blown reunion, you know. These things take time.'

I hadn't known that. I felt sick and stupid and naïve and—

'I mean,' she went on, 'you must be nervous at the prospect of meeting her yourself.'

I hadn't actually thought about it. 'I dunno, I never—'

'These are the things counselling *makes* you think about,' Helen said. 'It's important you go.'

'Yes.' I bit my lip, just to feel the pain of it, so I'd know I was really there. 'I guess.'

Silence.

'So what happens now?'

'Well,' Helen said, 'this third party, his name is Jim, has told your mother that you've been in contact. I think she's sending a letter to us to forward on to you.'

So it was to be letters. Letters after this long time.

'In time, you could call her or send photographs.'

'How long does it all take?' I couldn't bear this. I'd waited twenty-eight years already.

'It depends on the people,' Helen said.

'But she might never want to meet me!' The words tore out of some part inside me. I couldn't take rejection, not again. 'That's not fair!'

Helen remained calm. 'It's a step-by-step process, Vicky. Just take it that way. Talk to your counsellor. Talk to your parents. And don't forget, you can write back to your mother – OK?'

The tears were starting in the back of my eyes. 'Sure.'

Helen said a few other things but I hardly heard her. In the end, she said, 'It's good news, don't forget that.'

I flicked off the phone. I stared at the computer screen. I didn't know how I felt.

I left work early. I ignored Bridie as she scurried after me enquiring anxiously if I was OK and then Ed as he wondered if maybe I could do with a taxi to get home. I just walked out of that shop, red-eyed, snotty-nosed, and walked and walked and walked. It was drizzling as I found myself in the park. Without thinking I made my way towards the playground. There were very few kids about and so I sat down on a swing and began to go to and fro, to and fro. Soon, I was so high I could see the whole playground spread out in front of me and then I was back down again, among the pebbles and the sand. And then up again. And then down again. That's the way I felt, I realised.

High and low.

And maybe a little bit scared of letting go and falling flat on my face.

Chapter Twenty-six

Vicky,

I've been composing this letter in my head for the past twenty-eight years and yet when I try to write, the things I want to say are coming out all wrong – they either look too formal, too absurd or too pathetic when written down. I don't even know whether to say 'Dear Vicky' or even if I have the right to.

I don't know what it is you want from me and that too makes it hard to write. Whatever it is, I'll do my best. If you want some background on why I gave you up (and I hate that word – I didn't give you up, I never stopped thinking of you all these years) I'll provide it.

I don't want to go on and on in this first letter, I just want you to know that when I heard you'd made contact, I cried for days. You were alive. You were well. My biggest fear was always that by letting you go, something terrible might have happened to you and it would be my fault.

Thank you for doing this – it means more than I can say.

With love,
Barbara

I read that letter over and over, especially the bit about her never stopping thinking of me. I touched the ink, rounded my finger along the words, held it to my face. It was the closest I'd been to my mother in twenty-eight years.

Then I sat down and dialled a counsellor. I was crying and hopeless and beside me on the bed were sheets of foolscap notepaper with letters begun and crossed out and begun again. Like Barbara, I simply hadn't a clue what I wanted to say.

Chapter Twenty-seven

FRIDAY EVENING. THE shop was quiet. Bridie was dusting some shelves while Ed was assembling a swing I had ordered a few weeks before. It was the coolest swing ever – instead of consisting of two ordinary swings and a see-saw, this one had a swing, a see-saw and a roundabout! The roundabout was brilliant. It was circular and could fit up to three kids. Using a handle, the kids could make the roundabout spin up into the air while at the same time spinning around like mad.

Kids were going to go for it bigtime.

'Kids will go for this bigtime,' I'd told Ed and Bridie. 'Wait and see.'

Bridie had agreed but Ed had hummed and hawed and got on my nerves. Then he'd said that the kids wouldn't go for it unless they could *see* it. And I made some smart remark about them being able to see it on the box. And he'd said that that wasn't what he'd meant and I'd said that we hadn't the space for showing off swings. So he'd presented me with some fancy drawings he'd done on the computer (yep – using his mate's wonderful program) demonstrating how the space in the shop could be used much more efficiently if things were moved about a bit.

And I had to give in.

Again.

I'd given him permission to rearrange the whole shop and watched while he sweated buckets lifting stock and rearranging shelves. I wanted him to regret ever suggesting the idea.

'Hand me that nut and bolt, will you, Vicky?' Ed broke into

my thoughts as he pointed to some bolts that were on the floor. 'Once I have that in, I'm all finished.'

Oh, if only that were true.

I handed him the things he wanted and he nodded his thanks. Bending over, he began to screw them in.

The only consolation of being upstaged by the assembly of the swing was that Ed had a great-looking backside. It looked so firm and grippable in his black Levi's. I couldn't help myself, I just had to keep peeking at it. It was a pity that such a great ass should be owned by such a great ass, I thought. It was a complete waste. Sort of like a good-looking guy being gay or someone being offered the perfect, salted bag of chips in the middle of the desert or being a big fat juicy pig in the middle of Israel—

'Vicky!'

Marti's voice made both Ed and me jump as it echoed around the shop.

'She's down the back.' Bridie sounded quite disapproving. She's always telling me that she doesn't understand the need for shouting. 'And there's no need for shouting, you know.'

'Right,' Marti boomed as he began striding down towards me. 'Oy, Vicky!' he bellowed, once I was in sight. 'Get the finger out, would ya. I'm double-parked.' Marti had agreed to give me a lift to the bus station. It was my dad's sixtieth that weekend.

I gave him a bit of a wave before legging it up to the office to grab my weekend bag. When I got back down, Marti was admiring the swing. Ed was standing beside him, spanner in hand. 'I'm not sure,' he was saying to Marti. 'You'd have to ask the boss.'

'Ask me what?'

'How much that swing is?' Marti turned to me.

'Five hundred euro,' I said, quoting the staff discount price.

'Mmmm.' Marti made a face. 'Expensive. Still, Leo would love it.'

'And who's Leo?' Bridie asked, coming up behind us.

'Aren't you double-parked?' I cut in before Marti could enlighten her. 'We'd better go.'

'Uh-huh.' Marti strode before me up the shop. 'Bye, folks.'

Behind me I heard Ed and Bridie muttering their 'goodbyes' and 'have a nice weekends'.

It was a relief to get out into the street. I still hadn't told Bridie anything about Marti's circumstances. Well, it wasn't really her business; I mean, it wasn't as if she was my mother or anything. But, then again, I hadn't told my mother either. I hadn't even invited Marti down to the party. Time enough, I kept telling myself. No point in shocking the folks too much.

'I've Leo looking after the car in case I get clamped,' Marti said as he powered along, me running to keep up with him.

'Leo,' I said breathlessly. 'Your Leo?'

'Yep.'

I stopped walking. I soon found myself staring incredulously at his back as he kept up the pace. 'Marti!'

The tone of my voice halted him. He spun around. 'What?' he sounded impatient. 'Come on. I'll be clamped.'

'You can't just drag me into your car and expect me to talk to your son,' I said, not able to believe that he hadn't given it a thought.

Marti looked baffled. 'Why not?'

'I've never met him, for starters. You should have *warned* me. I mean, who does he think I am? You can't just go shoving us both together like this. Will he know that—?'

'He knows you're my friend,' Marti said. 'I told him I've to pick up a friend. He's cool about it.'

'A girlfriend?' This was not happening. I'd planned on giving Leo a little toy or something when we'd meet. Something to buy his affection.

'Girl, boy, doesn't matter. He's only five, for Christ's sake.' He glanced at his watch before grinning hugely at me. 'Now, come on.'

I had no choice but to follow him. I'd never make the bus

station otherwise. Dragging my bag, I clumped alongside him, hoping he wasn't parked too far away. As I spotted his car ahead – it was easy to spot, it had the enormous Boy Five election poster thingy up on the roof – my heart began to hammer. Even my palms broke out in a sweat.

Marti seemed oblivious. He crossed to the driver's door, opened it, reached over and popped the lock on my door. 'Park yourself down,' he grinned.

I gingerly climbed into the car, my bag at my feet. I was afraid to look behind at the little boy, scrunched up in a corner.

'Any trouble, bud?' Marti asked Leo as he fired the engine.

'Well,' Leo began and I could sense him looking at me and I still didn't know what to do, 'a man came by and he was putting something on your window so I pretended to be sick, like you said. And I said that you were gone to the chemist to get something for me.'

'Good lad!' Marti chortled. 'Isn't he great, Vicky?'

'Yeah.' I took this as my opportunity to turn around and smile. Even as I did so, I felt my smile wobble all over the place as it was met with a sullen glare from an attractive kid hugging a brown teddy bear.

'Leo and me are going to McDonald's, aren't we?' Marti said then as he overtook a truck to vicious blaring of horns from every motorist in the vicinity.

'Yeah, Daddy.'

'I *love* McDonald's,' I said, my voice hysterically cheerful.

'Well, you can't come,' Leo said, narrowing his eyes. 'It's just me and my daddy.'

There was a silence.

I decided to change the subject. 'I like your teddy.'

Leo held it closer to him and glared at me as if somehow I was plotting to take it away.

'What's his name?'

Silence. Then, 'It's a *her*.'

Dressed in dungarees and a straw hat, the teddy didn't look

much like a her. 'Sorry.' I gave an apologetic smile. 'What's *her* name?'

'Linda.'

It was said with such calculated aplomb that despite feeling as if I'd been punched in the chest, I had to admire the kid. 'Nice,' I muttered, turning away from him. Linda was Marti's wife's name.

'Don't mind him,' Marti whispered, patting my leg. 'That teddy used to be called Marv.'

'Did not!' Leo said.

'Did so,' Marti said back, a bit narkily, I thought.

'That was another teddy!'

Marti slammed on the brakes and threw us all forward. 'Don't you lie to me,' he snapped. 'Don't you dare!'

Leo bit his lip and tears welled up in his eyes.

'Well, I think the name Linda suits her,' I put in, hoping to diffuse the situation. I smiled at Marti. 'Don't you?'

He turned from me and shrugged.

Leo gulped and stared out the window away from me.

I decided to shut up.

Thirty minutes later we arrived at Busarus. Marti pulled into the bus lane and jumped out of the car. 'I'll see you to the door,' he said.

'Can I come, Daddy?'

'It'll only be for a few minutes,' Marti answered. 'You stay here and mind the car. Then we'll head to McDonald's – OK?' He reached in and ruffled the top of Leo's head.

The boy smiled, showing the perfect teeth of his dad. 'OK.'

'Say bye to Vicky.'

'Bye, Leo. It was lovely to meet you.'

His voice was barely audible as he muttered his 'bye-bye'.

'Say it properly,' Marti ordered.

'It's OK—' I began, knowing that the kid would hate me for sure now.

'It's not OK.' Marti glared at Leo. 'He has to have manners. Now say goodbye to Vicky.'

'No.'

'Right. No McDonald's for you.' Marti slammed the car door on his protests. 'Come on, Vicky.'

I could still hear him howling as Marti walked me to the door.

'Sorry about that,' Marti said, looking completely fed up. 'He's been very difficult recently. I don't know what to do with him – he wouldn't go to school for me this morning or anything. Normally he's a great kid.'

'He's probably just missing his mother,' I said. 'You can't expect him to—'

'His mother is gone months now,' Marti said abruptly. 'He should be over it.'

Some people never get over it, I wanted to say, but didn't. 'He's only five.'

'Yeah . . . well . . .' He let his voice trail off and his eyes slid from my face to his feet. He looked defeated. All his cockiness seemed to have deserted him. His eyes met mine. 'Look, have a great weekend, all right?' He leaned over to kiss me. His lips brushed mine and I put my arms about him.

'Bring him to McDonald's, all right?'

His voice was muffled in my shoulder. 'You think?'

'I think.'

He gave me a small smile. Another soft kiss. 'Ta.'

I watched him walk away. There was something sad about him that I hadn't noticed before.

As I walked into the bus station, I heard the jangly sounds of Boy Five being played from Marti's loudspeaker. It made me smile as people groaned all around me.

Chapter Twenty-eight

THE PARTY WAS in full swing. Dad, who'd been completely taken by surprise, was dancing with Mam, holding her close and smiling like a lunatic. All he kept telling everyone was that it was 'mighty'. 'This is mighty,' he said, over and over again. All the cousins from both sides of the family were mingling and chatting to one another. Drink was flowing faster than the Nile in heavy rain and the food, which had been prepared by my mother and her army of sisters, was almost gone. The table I sat at sported six empty plates and two miserable cocktail sausages. I sort of felt sorry for the sausages, being rejected and left to grow cold, so I speared the two and shoved them into my mouth.

I washed them down with a mouthful of Bud and watched as my father kissed the tip of my mother's nose. Some part of me remembered Sal saying that it was bad luck to be kissed on the nose and I shivered slightly.

'Hey, has someone glued your arse to that chair?' Tommy, grinning, slid in beside me.

'Yes,' I answered shortly. I did not want to be dragged up onto the dance floor by him.

'Really?' Tommy feigned surprise. 'Have they invented industrial-size Superglue then?'

'Nope.' I regarded him over the rim of my glass. ''Cause if they had, someone would surely have used it on your mouth.'

He laughed. 'You're dead funny, Vicky,' he grinned. He held out his hand. 'Dancing?'

'Drinking.' I held up my glass.

'Aw, come on,' he pleaded, 'one dance.'

The DJ was playing 'La Bamba' and everyone was doing weird things with their bodies. In the centre, my mother and father danced a waltz.

'Maybe later,' I muttered, hoping he'd forget. 'I prefer to look.'

'OK.' Tommy didn't move. Instead he followed my gaze and looked too. He spotted my folks. 'Are they really that happy?' he asked, sounding wistful. 'Or, like, is it for show?'

I was insulted for them. That was typical of Tommy, trying to belittle everything.

'They don't put on a show,' I snapped back, realising it was true. What you saw was what you got.

'No, I guess they don't.' He paused. 'It must be nice for you,' he said then, 'to have happy parents.'

'I never much thought about it.'

'Well, maybe you're used to it.'

There was a silence. I wondered if he was thinking about his dad, who had died years back. Aunt Julia had thrown him out of the house for drinking and a few months later he'd been found dead from alcohol poisoning. He'd been a gentle guy but had spent every penny on booze. Tommy and John had grown up wearing hand-me-downs. Still, I thought, looking at him, he hadn't done too badly for himself. He was dressed that night in really nice gear – the kind of stuff women like men to wear – cream combats and a black Tommy Hilfiger shirt. There was nothing to think that he'd had a hard upbringing.

'And now,' the DJ roared into his microphone, 'everyone up on the floor.'

Tommy jumped up and looked questioningly at me. I wasn't going to follow him until I saw the staff wheeling out an enormous cake in the shape of the number sixty. It was obviously a 'Happy Birthday' moment.

My dad looked gobsmacked at the size of the cake. My mother began pushing him towards it, laughing as she did so.

Dad didn't need a push. He took his place at the top of the room, beside his cake, his face red with pleasure. 'Well,' he said, 'this is mighty.'

People were clapping and I thought his face would split in two from smiling.

'And now,' the DJ continued, in his deep, American voice, 'I've been asked to request his daughter, Vicky, to lead us in "Happy Birthday".'

More cheering.

I wanted the ground to swallow me up. Tommy, roaring, shoved me forward. I plastered a smile on my face and took the microphone from the DJ.

Dad reached out and clasped my hand. I don't think he'd ever looked happier. 'That would be wonderful,' he whispered, so that only I could hear.

I wanted to make it wonderful for him. He'd been cool with me ever since Christmas and I saw this as a way to repair things. I began to sing and it wasn't so bad because everyone joined in. The whole room resounded to the sound of 'Happy Birthday' and 'Hip Hip Hooray'.

More clapping and cheering.

My mother hugged me and hugged my dad and then they both hugged me. It was mortifying. But nice.

'And now,' the DJ said, 'another request has come in for Vicky to sing her dad's favourite song – "Nancy Spain".'

Emotional blackmail, that's what it was.

Dad was beaming at me. 'Go on there now,' he coaxed, 'there's a great girl.'

I rolled my eyes at him and once again took the microphone. I didn't really need it because my voice was quite strong but I took it anyway; I'd feel naked standing up in front of them all with nothing to hold on to.

I didn't understand why everyone always asked me to sing the sad songs. My dad says it's because I look so forlorn singing that it makes people want to listen, my mother says it's because

I 'do' sad so well. But I 'do' happy good too. I can belt out a pop tune with the best of them.

Everyone began 'shushing' each other but I started to sing before the whole room was completely quiet. I knew in my heart that they'd become silent once I sang. I wasn't being big-headed, I just knew it from experience. I could make anyone listen to me. My voice has a rough edge, a sort of hoarseness that bleeds into noise and makes it silent. And I sang the song about Nancy Spain and about how impossible it was to forget about her no matter where life led me. I let my voice soar before curbing it. The words of that song have their own music, I couldn't trample all over them.

When I finished, there was a silence.

I hated that silence. In that silence, people look at you differently, as if they've never quite seen you before.

Then the applause, which embarrassed me.

Eventually, I was mercifully able to sit back down at an empty table and resume my drinking.

'You should sing professionally,' the manager of the hotel said as I was leaving.

I smiled politely.

'My brother runs a hotel in Dublin,' he said, thrusting a card into my hands, 'and he's looking for a singer for the weekends to entertain the guests. You'd go down a bomb.'

'Naw.' I attempted to give the card back to him. 'I don't think so.'

'Oooh, Vicky!' My mother poked me in the back. 'You hold on to that card. You could become famous.'

I laughed at that idea. Becoming famous was not something I would particularly want.

'Look,' I explained to both my folks, who were looking chuffed at the very mention of me singing in a hotel, 'doing a stint at a party is completely different to singing professionally.'

'And you'd know, would you?' Dad chortled. 'You who knows all about professional singers.'

Mam tittered.

The hotel manager looked taken aback at my lack of enthusiasm. 'Well, think about it,' he urged. 'The Glen Hotel.'

'Ta.' I shoved the card into my bag, watched by three beady pairs of eyes.

'You'd be fantastic,' the manager called as we left.

'You would too.' Dad slung his arm about my shoulder and one about Mam's shoulder. He smiled at both of us. 'Well, that was a great night. Fantastic. Thanks very much.'

'Yes,' Mam agreed, 'I think everyone enjoyed themselves.'

'And to think I thought you were just bringing me out for a meal!'

We laughed.

'Not that I would have minded that either,' Dad went on. 'My two favourite women in the whole world on either side of me – now what can be nicer than that!' He pulled us closer to him.

The sound of our footsteps was the only thing to disturb the perfect silence of the night. In the sky, pinprick stars peeped down on us.

It was a perfect moment.

The kind of moment when nothing else matters except the silence and being there, exactly where you are.

Then as soon as you begin to think, 'I like this moment', it disappears.

But what matters is that it was there in the first place.

Chapter Twenty-nine

After the usual restless night, I eventually conked out around three and slept until midday. When I awoke, a weak spring sun was doing its best to creep through the room. I lay in bed for a while, warm and snugly under the covers, and thought that of all the things in the world to do, this was my favourite. Just to lie in bed and not to think too much. It was glorious, just savouring the warmth of the sun in the room and the soft silence of an empty house.

Of course, like all lovely things, it never lasted. Five minutes later the front door opened and Mam and Dad entered the hall talking in loud voices about who they'd seen at mass. And who was wearing what and who was not talking to whom. Then Dad went into the kitchen and I heard him pulling on his boots to go check on the cattle. A slam of the kitchen door as he left. Then Mam began rattling pots and pans in preparation for the dinner.

The same thing every week.

I must have dozed back off because the next thing Mam was tapping gently on my door, bearing tea and toast. 'Thought you might like your breakfast in bed,' she said, balancing a big flowered tray on the bedside table. She wiped her hands down her apron before pouring me a cuppa and milking it. 'You're such a big lazy lump in the morning.'

It was said fondly as if being a lazy lump was something rather endearing.

I rubbed my eyes and grinned at her. Pulling myself up in the bed, I took the tea from her. 'Ta.'

She sat down on the bed beside me and watched as I sipped.

'You make the best cuppa in Ireland,' I said. She loved when I told her that.

'So' – she folded her hands in her lap and looked so fondly at me that I had to look away – 'how are you? We didn't get much of a chance to talk on Friday, what with organising the party and everything. How's the shop going?'

'All right.' I didn't want to tell her how I was being upstaged time and again by Ed, because if I was upset, she'd only worry. And she'd tell Dad and then he'd worry. And I'd never hear the end of it. 'We're selling more toys than we did this time last year.'

'Isn't that great?'

'Yep.'

Then I told her about Bridie and her constant cleaning and she laughed and said that maybe I could learn a thing or two from her. I told her about Sal trying to get off with Ed and she clicked her tongue and said that Sal was way too forward and always had been. And I told her about Marti – a sanitised version. She was dead impressed to hear he was a boy band manager. 'Well, at least you've that in common,' she said, 'you're both managers.'

'Yeah.' I managed not to smile too much.

'And—' I put my cup carefully down on the tray and reached under the bed to my haversack. Taking a blue crumpled envelope from it, I nervously held it towards her. 'I got this in the post – from my birth mother.'

My outstretched hand holding the envelope remained between us for what seemed like ages. I could hear Dad coming in downstairs and the tramp of his feet as he walked to the bathroom to wash himself down. The clock on the landing loudly ticked off the seconds and still Mam made no attempt to take the letter from me.

'Don't you want to see it?' I asked. I desperately needed to share it with someone.

'Sure.' Mam smiled a little uncertainly. 'It's just, well, it's a bit sudden, isn't it, I thought—'

I explained about the third party and what the woman in the Adoption Board had said. Not very well, I think, because my words were spinning about all over the place and all I kept worrying about was what if Mam refused to read the letter.

But by the time I'd got to the end of my rambling explanations, Mam had taken the envelope. I watched as she slowly drew out the note. 'Nice writing,' she said, as if it were a compliment to me. She smoothed out the page and began to read. It took her ages; she kept having to go over the words.

'Isn't it a very nice letter?' I asked eventually, dying for some sort of a verdict. 'Doesn't she sound . . . nice?'

Mam looked up at me. Her eyes were bright. She reached out and clasped my hand. Holding it tightly, she said earnestly, 'She's your mother – how could she be any other way?'

I blinked. Once. Twice. Gulped. She just couldn't have said anything nicer. I put my other hand on top of our joined ones. Like the time in the coffee shop, I couldn't speak.

We sat there, like that, for a long time.

Dad made the dinner. While Mam and me were upstairs he'd roasted the chicken, over-boiled the carrots and mashed the spuds. He'd poured us both a glass of wine and announced that dinner was ready by shouting up the stairs for us to hurry on down before it all got colder.

'Sounds ominous,' Mam giggled like a schoolgirl and scuttled from the room.

I got dressed quickly and shoved my feet into a pair of Poochie slippers. I was downstairs just as Dad was taking the carrots from the oven.

'They did too quickly,' he said to Mam and me as he began to poke at them with a knife, 'so I shoved them in the oven to keep them warm but—' Pause. Poke. 'They don't seem too good now.'

'A bit on the dry side,' my mother said.

'Like that Sweeney wan,' Dad chortled, tipping the carrots into the bin.

Mam began to examine the chicken, which did look nice, and then she turned her attention to the peas. 'They're cold.'

'Aye.' Dad made a face. 'They did awful quick.'

'He does this every time,' Mam chuckled. 'Every single time.'

Dad looked sheepishly at her. 'Amn't I doing my best?'

'You are, pet, you are.' She tapped his cheek lightly. 'So – what – we have chicken and some spuds and I'll reheat the peas?'

'I'll reheat the peas.' Dad pushed her out of the way. 'You sit and relax, like you were told to do.'

My dad was never what you'd call a new man. All my life he'd tended the farm and done the 'man' things while my mother had cooked and cleaned and washed and polished. As far as I knew they'd been happy in their stereotypical roles but now, for some reason, Dad was branching out and Mam was letting him. It made me admire them in a funny way. I wondered if I'd see her in the tractor the next time I came down and the thought caused me to grin.

'Are you laughing at me?' Dad demanded, pointing to a chair for me to sit down. 'She of the "take-away" mentality.'

'Swear I'm not,' I grinned again.

'Then sit and eat.' Smile. 'Eventually.'

Eventually was ten minutes. There wasn't a sound as we scraped our plates clean. And just when I thought that it wasn't going to make an appearance, an enormous strawberry cheesecake was pulled out from the fridge like a rabbit from a hat.

'And you thought we'd forgotten,' Mam beamed.

'Yeah.' The thing was bigger than ever before.

'I had to buy it,' Mam said, laying it in front of me. 'I didn't have time to be making one, you know, with the party and everything, so I bought this instead. I hope it's all right.'

'You shouldn't have bothered.' She had no idea how much I meant those words.

'Oh no, now, never let it be said . . .' She pulled a knife out from the block on the counter. 'And you'll have a big slice now, won't you, because your father and me, now, we'd never eat that.'

'Cheese in a cake.' Dad made a face. 'It's like putting jelly in spuds.'

I had the uneasy feeling that jelly in spuds would be nicer for me to eat than the bloody cheesecake.

After the dinner, it was show and tell.

So, after a bit of chit-chat, I showed him my letter.

'From her mother,' my mother said. She smiled a sort of brittle smile over at me as he opened the envelope. 'It's a really nice letter.'

Dad opened the page but before he read it, he said, 'Sure aren't you her mother?'

Mam flinched.

'My birth mother,' I said softly.

'Oh aye.' Dad raised his eyes. 'That one.' He sort of spat the words out. 'Well, let's see what she has to say for herself.'

There was no mistaking the tension that had entered the room. It was as if someone had taken all the air out and we were afraid to breathe. As if someone had laid heavy weights on my arms and legs and chest.

Dad was mumbling the words of the letter to himself. Then, he calmly folded up the paper, placed it back in the envelope and handed it back to me. 'Great,' he said. 'Great.'

I took the letter back and glanced at Mam. The indifference hurt.

'She hasn't written back yet,' my mother said with false brightness. 'She's going to see a counsellor.'

'There'd be no need for counsellors if people would be happy with what they've got.'

'Ah, now, Sean—'

'I'm going out.' Dad didn't even look at me as he left, banging the door harder than necessary.

'He didn't mean it,' Mam said quickly. 'You know your father – he takes a while to adjust to things.'

'He doesn't want me to look, does he?' It was a stupid question. Of course he didn't.

'He's not *you.*' Mam knelt beside my chair and looked up into my face. 'He doesn't understand.'

'And you do?'

She shrugged. 'I understand that I want you to be completely happy, Vic. That's what I understand. And if this makes you happy, well then . . .' Her voice trailed off.

'Thanks.'

Like that morning, she caught my hands in hers. 'He'll come around. He always does.'

'I hope.' My lip quivered and I bit down on it.

'He will.' She smiled slightly. 'D'you remember the time, when you pestered him and pestered him to let you drive the car because you'd had lessons?'

'That was—'

'And you wrote off his car?'

'—different.'

'And he swore that he'd never let you near his car again but he did.'

'It was different.'

'He did it because he knew it'd make you happy. That's why the man does everything. He'll come around.' She stood up and ruffled my hair. The subject was closed. 'Now come on, I'll wrap up the cheesecake. You pack your bags and I'll drive you to the bus station.' She smiled. 'Or you can drive me.'

Travelling back to Dublin, the cheesecake at my feet in a freezer bag, I felt guilty.

Guilty that Mam was being so reasonable. Guilty that Dad wasn't.

Guilty that I was going to go my own way anyhow.
Guilty that maybe I'd hurt them.
Guilty because I'd decided that I couldn't handle the guilt.
I'd stay in Dublin as long as I could before going home again.

Chapter Thirty

I WAS LOOKING forward to getting back to the flat. To just dumping my things, grabbing a can and plonking myself down in front of the telly. That way I could forget about the weekend and forget about the fact that tomorrow would be my first meeting with the counsellor. I was kind of regretting calling her now – I mean, I wasn't too sure what to expect. What if she wanted to hear my darkest secrets or something? I could hardly tell her about the time I stole Lisa Sweeney's best Barbie doll, could I? Or the time I ran away from home when I first found out I was adopted? Or—

'Stop,' I told myself as I inserted the key into the lock of the apartment. 'Just take it as it comes.'

'My thoughts exactly,' Troy chortled from behind, so close that he was virtually breathing down my neck. 'I always knew you were my type of girl, Vicky.'

'But you're not my type of boy,' I said back, trying to sound mournful. 'You're too forward for me. I prefer my men quiet and docile so I can boss them around.'

'I quite like the sound of that,' he said as he followed me up the stairs. 'You could be the Captain Picard of the relationship.'

I grinned.

'You could command my machine anytime.' A revolting thrust of denim-clad pelvis.

'And what machine would that be?' I had my hand on the apartment door, ready to leg it. 'Your washing machine?'

I slammed the door to the sound of him laughing.

'That Troy is getting more suggestive every time I meet him,' I yelled out to Sal. She was always in on Sunday nights, finishing off stories for the paper which was 'put to bed' the following day. That's newspaper jargon for finishing something, apparently. I dumped my case on the floor and carried the freezer bag in so that I could put the cheesecake into the fridge.

Sal was in all right, standing at the table, a cuppa in her hand.

But that's not what stopped me dead.

Ed was sitting down at *our* table, nursing a cuppa himself.

'Hiya,' Sal said, smiling broadly. 'How was the weekend?'

I didn't answer. I couldn't take my eyes from Ed.

'I'd introduce you to Ed only you already know each other,' Sal giggled.

'From somewhere,' Ed grinned. He raised his cup to me. 'Cheers, Vicky.'

I still couldn't speak. How had it all happened? There was nothing doing on Friday when I left.

'Ed and I are heading out to the pictures,' Sal said, sitting in beside him.

'Right.' I was shell-shocked. I didn't know if I was pleased or what. 'So . . . what happened . . . how did you . . . ?'

'She asked me out,' Ed said, thumbing to Sally as if I wouldn't know who "she" was. 'Just came into the shop yesterday and asked me to go out with her.'

Sal gave a throwaway laugh.

'Wow!' I smirked over at Sal. 'That is impressive. She *never* asks anyone out, you know.'

'Ha, ha.' Sal stood up abruptly, almost upending her tea. She looked sensational in a long navy denim skirt, split at the sides, which gave flashes of her neat ankles and her tiny tiny feet. A royal blue gypsy top completed the look and she'd tied her long hair back with a blue and navy scarf.

Ed looked good too. Black denims and an orange T-shirt. I reckon he had a bit of a fetish for orange. He wore a gorgeous black leather jacket.

'Let's go.' Sal picked up her cup and dumped the remainder of her coffee down the sink. Ed followed her lead.

'Bye, Vicky,' Sal said, almost dancing out the door. 'Don't wait up.'

'See ya, boss.' Ed tipped me a grinning salute.

'You better not be late in in the morning,' I grouched. As soon as I said it, I wanted to kill myself. What was I like?

He laughed. Closed the door.

Bloody wonderful.

Marti rang me later that night. He was in great form. He didn't mention Leo and I didn't ask. 'Listen Vic,' he said, 'the lads are doing another tour this week, I'll be back on Sunday and I'll have a surprise for you – right?'

'A whole week?'

'Yep. Great, isn't it?'

I hadn't meant it that way. 'Suppose.'

'See you Sunday! Listen, have to go!'

He blew me a kiss down the line and was gone.

Chapter Thirty-one

MY COUNSELLING APPOINTMENT was at ten-thirty in the local health centre. It was a bit early, seeing as Monday was my day off, but apparently mornings were all this woman social worker did.

It meant that I had to get up at nine, have a shower, and blow-dry my frizzy red hair, which took *ages* because in order to de-frizz it, I had to blow-dry the roots first and then the outside and then rub some gel into it to keep it that way. I was seriously considering getting it all chopped off and doing a Sinead O'Connor on it. On top of all this, I had to choose my clothes. Now, maybe this sounds mental, but I did not want this woman thinking there was something wrong with me. Not that there was, you understand. But I figured that if I wore my normal attire of red or purple jeans and a bright sweatshirt, she might get the wrong idea about me. I had to pick something that screamed 'sober citizen'. I eventually settled for a pair of navy jeans and a red and navy T-shirt. It looked normal enough. Shoving my feet into a pair of red trainers, I had just enough time to grab a cup of coffee before I left.

'You're up early,' Sal remarked. She was tapping away furiously on her laptop, a big frown on her face. 'Jesus, I'm way behind.'

I said nothing. When Sal was working – and especially when Sal was 'way' behind' – you did not talk. I watched her furiously banging away on her keyboard and I wondered how the night with Ed had gone. He wasn't in the flat that morning anyway, which wasn't a great sign. And gazing at Sal as she pounded the letters with her French-manicured fingernails, I had to admit that she did not look like a woman who'd enjoyed coital bliss with the rich man of her dreams.

Mind you, even if she'd had sensational sex, she'd still be narky. Her mood had been pretty crap recently, mainly because *Tell!* hadn't yet offered her a position.

'What are you looking at?' she snapped.

Definitely no sex.

'Nothing.' I smiled brightly and poured some coffee into a cup. 'Want one?'

She held up her mug. 'Nope.'

More keyboard sounds.

I sat down at the table and began to flick through a magazine. It was one of Sal's. An old issue of *Hello!* with a big feature on Dustin Hoffman in the centre pages. I didn't know what she saw in him. Maybe it was the big nose.

'You ruined my night last night,' Sal said suddenly, startling me. I'd been so determined to read all about Dustin's on-set exploits in order to get this damn counselling appointment off my mind that I hadn't noticed that she'd stopped typing.

'What?'

'I said that you ruined my night last night. Ed wouldn't stay. And I know why.' She leaned forward in her chair and glared at me. 'It's because he didn't want to run into you this morning.'

'Really?' I hadn't known I was that intimidating. It made me feel like a heel. 'Well – I guess that I am his boss and—'

'Yeah, and I was his date.'

My grumpy parting shot to Ed rang in my ears as I stared at Sal's glum face. I felt sorry for her. First Mel messing her about and now this. 'Sorry,' I said meekly. 'You know I—'

'I mean, he came up here and then after a bit he just legged it. It had to be because of you. What other reason would there be?'

'Well, maybe he doesn't want to rush things.'

She laughed at that. 'What man, given the opportunity, wouldn't want to rush things?'

'You hardly know each other—'

'Puritan.'

That was it. I turned back to my magazine, determined to ignore her.

'You better hide the next time he comes. I'll pretend you're not in or something.'

Thoughts of cowering away in my bedroom while she and Ed went at it in front of the telly or in Sal's room made me wince. How would I look at them again? 'Why not go to his place?'

'What?' Arched eyebrows, a scornful tone. 'With a pile of guys there? I don't think so.'

'Sorry.' I felt stupid. Sal ignored my apology and crossed to the kettle with her empty mug. I tried to get back to reading about Dustin, but I couldn't concentrate. For one thing, Sal was still glaring at me, and for another, the hand on my watch was slowly creeping towards the ten mark.

'If he'd liked me enough,' Sal said, just as I'd given up my reading and was preparing to leave, 'I reckon he would have stayed, even if you were here. Don't you think so, Vic?'

I shrugged. What did I know? Marti hadn't stayed over yet and according to himself he was mad into me. But, as Sal said, maybe he was just mad, full stop.

'He hardly even kissed me goodbye,' Sal went on. 'Isn't that a bit weird?'

'I *told* you he was weird.'

'No, you told me he was trying to steal your job.'

Same difference as far as I was concerned.

'Then I began to wonder was it something I'd said, the way he rushed out of here last night.'

So it mightn't have been because of me after all. I was a bit annoyed at her trying to make me feel guilty. 'So you don't know that it was my fault?' I asked sweetly.

'And I went over everything I'd told him and drew a blank,' Sal continued. 'So it had to be you.'

'Did you tell him that you were the one that wrote the football fella piece?' I asked suddenly. If anything, that wouldn't have gone down well.

'The *Tell!* piece?'

'Uh-huh.'

'The scoop of the year?' Sal said. I think she was a bit offended by me referring to it as the football fella piece. 'That brilliant story that Mel still hasn't hired me for?'

'That's the one,' I said.

'No, I never mentioned it. You told me not to.'

'Good – so it can't be that then.'

'Though I don't know what the big deal is,' Sal continued. 'It was a perfectly honest story about an unfaithful shit . . .' Her voice trailed off. 'Hey, he probably didn't like it because his auld fella got caught a few years ago.' Her face lit up. 'Didn't he have it off with his manageress and didn't she kiss and tell?'

She had too. That must have been awful for the family.

'That was some story,' Sal said, remembering. 'I mean, nothing was left to the imagination, d'you remember?'

'I wouldn't go saying that to Ed.'

'I'm not stupid!' Sal scrunched up her dainty little nose. 'Well, so, I won't tell him I did that piece on McCoy.' She tossed her fab, unfrizzy hair back over her shoulder. 'But he'll have to accept my job sooner or later. I mean, I am who I am.'

'Yeah, well, just make sure he's fallen for you first.'

'Huh, the only thing he seems to have fallen for so far is that cheesecake of yours. He ate practically the lot of it last night.'

'My cheesecake?' I suddenly noticed the box sitting in the bin. And Sal looked as if she wished she'd kept her mouth shut. 'He had no right to eat that.'

Sal gave a false laugh. 'I mean, have you *ever* tried to get romantic when your other half is shovelling strawberry cheesecake into his mouth?' She was deliberately ignoring me.

'He shouldn't have been, though. It was *my* cake.'

'Which you don't eat,' Sal said, sounding pissed off.

'That's not the point.'

'Oh, Vic, don't start. Just don't.' She slammed her mug onto the table and closed her eyes.

'I don't like people taking my things without asking. That's all.'

'So what? He should have woken you at two this morning, should he?'

'Yes. Yes, he should.'

'Oh, come on . . .'

I buttoned my coat up all wrong in my haste to get out. There'd be a row if I stayed. Sal knew I couldn't bear my stuff being touched when I wasn't around. She *knew* it. She'd known it for years and yet she had to go and offer my cheesecake to someone. Yeah, I know, it's all a bit paranoid, but I can't help it. I cling on to practically everything I have. I've stuff dating back years in my room – clothes from when I was a teenager even. I hate throwing stuff out. Even cheesecakes. I would have eaten it.

'I'm going out.'

'It was only a bloody cake!'

'It wasn't a bloody cake. It was a *cheese*cake.'

'Vic . . .'

'You had no right.'

'For God's sake – it was something you didn't like.'

'How would you like if I gave . . .' I searched my mind – 'your laptop away to someone?'

'Completely different,' she said in a big bored voice.

I sort of knew it was. I knew I was being a big kid but I couldn't help it. 'Yeah, well, you'd better watch out.'

And with this stunning comment, I picked up my bag and stalked from the room.

Behind me I heard her going, 'Cop on!'

Once outside, I was suddenly consumed with what I can only describe as terror. The disappearing cheesecake dilemma receded as my heart began to slam about in my chest. Every step I took towards Yellow Halls' health centre made my stomach lurch something awful. I was convinced that great big patches of sweat were forming under my armpits. Even my fringe, which was unfrizzy, was beginning to curl up because of the beads of sweat on my forehead.

I arrived at the clinic five minutes early and found my way to the counsellor's office. Taking a seat, I began to pray feverishly that no one would see me. I did not want anyone to think that I was in need of counselling, even strangers. *Especially* strangers.

At ten-thirty, a small woman, even smaller than me, approached the office. She was dressed in a slate grey tailored jacket and trousers. Underneath her jacket, she wore a white silk blouse. Her dark hair was caught up in a ponytail, which made her appear younger than I'm sure she was. And her smile was gap-toothed. A reassuring sort of a smile that I'm sure she'd practised in front of a mirror.

'Victoria McCarthy?' she asked as she began to unlock the office.

'Vicky,' I said. I hated the name Victoria. It reminded me of some old dried-up prune of a person.

'Vicky, then,' she said. Inside the office, she flicked on the lights. 'Sorry about this, I'm normally in around ten but this morning everything went wrong. I'm Lucy, by the way.' She held out a tiny, manicured hand and I clasped it. It was warm. Her grip was tight. She gestured towards a comfortable green chair. 'Take a seat.'

Well, at least I didn't have to lie on a couch.

I sat gingerly down, right on the edge of the seat, clutching my haversack between my hands the way you'd grab onto a raft in an ocean. I watched as Lucy pulled up the blinds, flicked on her computer and adjusted her chair. Eventually, she clasped her hands together and smiled at me.

I managed a smile back.

'You look nervous.'

I flinched.

'There is nothing to be afraid of, Vicky,' she said gently. 'All we're going to do is have a chat about how you feel about things. It's not therapy or anything like that. It's just so that you know how to deal with all that's happening to you.'

I knew all this. I hoped she wasn't going to go on and on.

'I believe you've made contact with your mother.'

Her directness caught me unawares. 'Yeah. Yeah, I have.'

'And that she's written you a letter?'

'Yes.' I'd brought the letter with me, just in case. 'D'you want to see it?'

'If you want me to. If it's not too private.'

I did want her to see it. I was hoping she'd tell me what to say back. 'It's a nice letter,' I babbled as I opened my bag. 'Friendly.'

She took it from me and had a read. 'It is nice,' she agreed. 'How does it make you feel?'

'What?'

'The letter? How does it make you feel?'

I blinked. Once. Twice. Thought for a bit. She didn't hurry me or expect an instant answer. I'd spent the last while wondering how I felt. I mean, I thought I'd be overjoyed, but it went deeper than that. 'I dunno,' I finally said.

'You don't know?' She paused. 'How about what she says in the letter? How does that make you feel?'

I thought about what my birth mother had said. I knew every word off; I'd read it that many times. In the end I settled for a very inadequate, 'Good, I guess.'

'Good? In what way?'

'Well, you know, it's—' I did some more blinking. 'It's nice to think that she hasn't forgotten me.'

'That's true.'

'And, well, it's good to know that she wants to write to me at all.'

'Why wouldn't she write?'

Because she'd given me away, I wanted to say, but didn't. I just shrugged and looked at Lucy's tiny clasped hands. She had an engagement ring – a solitaire. They're my favourite rings.

'In my experience,' Lucy said, after a bit of silence, 'most mothers never stop thinking about the child they've given up. How could they not? It's a huge thing to have done.'

I didn't answer. I wished I had nice neat hands like Lucy's. Instead I had square hands with huge veins that made kids gawk when they saw them.

'So, what now?' Lucy asked. 'Are you planning on writing back?'

I was forced to look at her. I shrugged and muttered, 'I guess so.'

'You don't sound too sure.'

Her voice was quiet, probing. I bit my lip. My words rushed over themselves. 'I dunno what to say. I mean, I thought I would but, then, well, I couldn't just get it down. That's why I came, you see,' I explained. 'To see if you knew.'

'I can't tell you how to write a letter, Vicky.'

'Oh.' I was back to staring at her hands. What was the use of being here then?

'How long do you think your mother spent writing that?' She pointed at my letter. 'My guess is that she slaved over it too and she still probably wasn't satisfied with the result.'

I hadn't thought of that. Even though it had been one of the things she'd written, I hadn't actually *believed* it.

'My advice is to write what you feel, Vicky. Tell her her letter makes you feel good. Tell her you're glad she hasn't forgotten you. Things you've just told me.'

That made sense. Even to my muddled brain, that did make sense. 'I'll try that.'

'Do.' Then she chatted a bit more about how the letter made me feel. Drew stuff out of me that I hadn't planned on saying.

'Think about things,' she advised at the end. 'Think about where you want all this to go. Think about why you initiated contact in the first place.' She wrote something down on a piece of paper. Then she stood up. 'And that's it,' she smiled. 'It wasn't so bad, was it?'

I shook my head. It hadn't been too bad, but it hadn't been too helpful either. I still had to write the letter when I got back.

'It was lovely to meet you, Vicky, and we'll talk in two weeks, when you've had a chance to think – OK?'

'Sure.'

She held out her hand and we shook again. 'You have my number if you need me during the next couple of weeks, OK?'

'Yeah. Thanks.'

'Bye now.'

'Bye.'

I left her waiting for her next client.

But it had been good to talk.

I hadn't talked about things like that in twenty-eight years.

Chapter Thirty-two

Dear Barbara,

Thank you for writing back and it means a lot that you want to be in contact with me. Your letter and the things you said made me feel good. I know that reads badly but I honestly am finding it hard to express myself properly.

You asked me in your last letter what I wanted from you and the truth is I don't really know yet. I would love some background information on who I am. It's hard going through life not knowing stuff like that – at least I think so.

In time, I guess I'd like to meet you.

I hope this will be possible.

Vicky

Chapter Thirty-three

'HERE.' A BOX was placed under my nose.

'Oooh,' Bridie squealed. 'What's this? A present for Vicky, is it?'

I'd just arrived in, last as usual, and Ed had waited until I sat down before presenting me with an enormous box. He grinned down at me, his eyes made even bluer by the tie-dyed cerulean T-shirt he wore. 'Go on,' he urged, his hands jammed into the pockets of his combats, 'open it.'

'Yes, Vicky, open it!' Bridie nudged me with her elbow, her voice breathless, her eyes out on stalks. 'What could it *be*, I wonder?'

It didn't take a genius to work it out. A white box, tied up with a gold string and bearing the words *Carey Cakes*. I gulped, ready for humiliation.

'Go on.' Ed nudged me lightly with his elbow.

'So you were in touch with Sal,' I said, stalling for time.

'Rang her Monday night,' Ed nodded, a broad grin on his face. 'Seems she's all booked up until Saturday so I'll be seeing her then.'

'You and Vicky's journalist friend?' Bridie looked from him to me. In a teasing manner, she asked, 'Is there something going on?'

'She asked him out,' I said, my finger twiddling with the twine on the box and wondering how I could get out of this. I had a picture of Sal and Ed laughing away over the wobbler I'd thrown over the cheesecake. I could literally feel my guts cringing with shame.

'Well, isn't that great!' Bridie laughed, oblivious of anything but the romance of the situation. 'First you get asked out and then Ed.' A clap of her hands. 'Maybe I'll be next!'

'No maybe about it,' Ed grinned.

Bridie giggled, blushing. She really did love Ed.

'So, are you going to open the box or not?' Ed asked. He sounded amused.

'Oh yes, open it.' Bridie nudged me. 'It looks like a cake we can all share!'

Ed gave a splutter of a laugh but tried to turn it into a cough.

'I know what it is,' I said sullenly to them both. 'It's a cheesecake, right?'

'Wrong!' Ed smiled delightedly and pulled at the string himself. 'Da-na-nananh.' He lifted the lid and I saw the most enormous chocolate cake, smothered in cream and nuts and bits of flake.

He was grinning like a big kid at me. I gulped.

Bridie literally dribbled all over the place. 'Gorgeous,' she cooed. 'Isn't that lovely, Vicky? Oh Ed, that's so *kind* of you.'

Chocolate cake was my favourite. Sal must have told him that too. I didn't know if he was getting a dig at me or if the gesture was genuine.

'It's not kind at all,' Ed said. I sensed that he was looking at me, but I kept staring at the table. 'I ate all Vicky's cheesecake last Sunday and now I'm making it up to her.'

'You didn't have to.' I stood up. It sounded petty when he put it like that.

'Well, it's gorgeous,' Bridie declared. 'Will I put it in the fridge for you, Vicky?' Without waiting for an answer, she picked the box up and toddled towards the fridge.

'I'll open up,' I said, wanting to be out of there before Ed said anything else. To my horror, he followed me out of the room.

'Am I forgiven?' He gave a rueful smile. 'I didn't know the cake was yours, Vicky. Honestly.'

'Joke over.' I walked rapidly in front of him.

'I'm not joking.' There was something oddly arresting in his voice and I turned about to find him staring down on me with an intense look on his face. 'I know it's horrible when someone takes your stuff without asking. It's crap.' He gave a shrug. 'And I apologise.'

Something in me told me he really meant it. Some other part of me said he was only keeping me sweet because he was seeing Sal. 'Apology accepted,' I said. 'Forget about it.'

His smile, warm, lopsided and completely sincere, took me by surprise. I had to turn away.

'Forgotten, boss,' he shouted after me, spoiling everything as usual.

'Here, Dominic,' I said, pushing a plate of cake towards him. He was busy building something completely weird out of the Lego. 'That is for you.'

'Me?'

'Uh-huh,' I smiled at him. 'All yours.'

'Aw, no.' Dominic's mother legged it over towards us. It was as if I'd just offered her kid a plate of arsenic. 'Naw,' she shook her head vigorously. 'Domo doesn't need dah.'

'I know he doesn't need it,' I said, watching poor Dominic's face fall as his mother grabbed the cake from under him. 'But it's just that I got a cake this morning and it's too much for me, Bridie and Ed to eat and it'll be gone off by tomorrow so I thought you and Dominic might like to share it?'

'I *would* like that,' Dominic nodded vigorously. 'I like that cake, Mammy.'

'How'd you know you'd like it?' she spat at him. 'You've never eaten it before.'

Dominic's face crumpled.

'Well, maybe he could *try* it,' I suggested tactfully. I wasn't as scared of her as I used to be, mainly because Ed seemed to be able to get around her and if he could, well, I figured that I could too. 'It'll only go to waste otherwise,' I added.

The woman looked at the plate. Looked at Dominic. And finally, looked at me. 'No more after dis,' she finally said, shoving the cake towards Dominic. 'Dat's enough for him.'

Dominic began to eat it with his fingers, cramming it into his mouth. 'It's nice, Mammy.'

'Is it, luv?'

'Will you have some?' I asked. 'Honestly, Ed bought this enormous cake—'

'He bought a cake for you?'

'Well, yeah.'

She smiled suddenly, showing crooked teeth. 'He likes you, you fucking lucky bitch.'

The poor woman was definitely losing it. 'Well,' I shrugged, 'will you take a piece of cake from this fucking lucky bitch?'

Dominic giggled.

His mother managed a reluctant smile. 'Just a small piece. I'm full after me breakfast.'

Chapter Thirty-four

LATER THAT AFTERNOON, Albert O'Neill paid us one of his unannounced visits. 'Hello! Hello! Hello!' he shouted as he barged through the front door. 'And how's everyone?'

Bridie, the ever conscientious, was first on hand. I heard her answer in a high-pitched, nervous voice that she was 'very well and thank you for asking, Mr O'Neill'.

'And those legs?'

'Very well, thank you for asking, Mr O'Neill.'

'And the boss?'

'Oh, she's very—'

'Right here,' I interrupted, knowing that O'Neill would keep asking Bridie questions until she grew uncomfortable. 'Hi, Mr O'Neill.'

'Albert!' he roared. 'You can call me Albert. How many times do I have to keep telling you?' He boomed out a laugh. Then barked out, 'And where's himself?'

'He's setting up a display in the Football section,' I said.

'Good. Good. Keep him working hard.' O'Neill rubbed his hands together. 'By the way, brilliant window, Vicky.' He jabbed a finger towards the wrestling ring.

'Ed's,' I said shortly. Huh, typical. I'd slaved over the Barbie display and he bloody well hadn't noticed. In fact I don't think anyone had noticed, what with all the wrestling stuff Ed had managed to jam into one tiny slot.

'Oooh.' O'Neill looked surprised. 'Well, I'm sure you had something to do with it?'

I was tempted to say that it had been my idea, but Bridie was there and she'd know I was lying. 'Nope. All your son's.' I gave a forced laugh. 'He's quite the salesman.'

O'Neill's face glowered. 'He's quite a lot of things,' he muttered, rather nastily, I thought.

Bridie and I looked at each other.

'Can I have a word, Vicky – upstairs?' So saying, he dismissed Bridie with a glance.

As usual, the office was a tip. O'Neill almost tripped over the radio as he entered. Papers and files were strewn all over the desk and the computer was displaying a picture of Boy Five which I'd managed to scan in last week.

'Tea?' I asked, knowing O'Neill would forgive the state of the office if he could be persuaded to try a piece of the chocolate cake.

'Were you robbed?' O'Neill said instead, surveying the debris.

I forced out a laugh. 'Chocolate cake?'

'OK.' He sat himself down on the computer chair having removed a pile of files from it. I felt incredibly self-conscious as I made him a cuppa and cut him a generous slice of cake. The man was a lecher; with every glance, I felt as if I was being mentally undressed. I put the tea and cake in front of him and remained standing. I did not want to sit on one of the soft chairs and look in any way vulnerable. I wondered what he wanted. Maybe he was going to warn me that I was to lose my job. Well, I vowed, before he left that evening, I'd ask him straight out.

If I had the nerve, of course.

'Something wrong?'

I jumped, realising that I'd been glowering at him. I readjusted my face into something resembling a smile. 'No.' Pause. 'Nice cake, isn't it?'

'Lovely. Yes.'

I watched as his fleshy lips sucked another bite into his mouth. He chewed like a cow munching on grass. Eventually, finishing up, he sucked all his fingers, one by one, making funny kissing sounds as he did so. Then, fat fingers splayed on brown trouser legs, he said ponderously, 'I wanted to have a word with you about himself.'

My stomach heaved. 'Who? Ed?'

'Yes – how's he getting on?' His blue eyes studied me and I squirmed. His resemblance to Ed was quite striking when you looked closely. O'Neill had probably been a fine-looking man in his youth, before flab and hair loss and bad dress sense got to him. This was it, I found myself thinking in despair. The beginning of the end. 'I want to ask you about him myself,' I heard myself saying, hardly daring to believe it.

His brows came together ominously. 'What's he done?' The words were spat out.

'Nothing,' I said, startled. 'It's, eh, what he's going to do that worries me.'

'Join the club,' O'Neill said bitterly.

'Is he being groomed for my job?'

There was a moment's silence.

'I mean, I asked Ed when he started first and he denied it and I just wondered—'

O'Neill looked at me as if I was a complete moron. 'Groomed for your job?' he asked slowly.

'Yeah, I wondered if he was going to take over—'

'I would not let that son of mine take over on a motorway let alone take over one of my shops.'

'Nice to hear you still think the same of me, Dad,' Ed spoke from the doorway.

Neither of us had heard him and we both jumped.

O'Neill's face darkened.

'And I already told *you*,' Ed went on, looking at me and sounding strangely hurt, 'I told you all I wanted to do was work.'

'Yeah, I know,' I said, feeling terrible and going red. 'It's just that—'

'Oh, don't apologise to him, Victoria,' O'Neill boomed, pushing past Ed. 'It's his speciality, making everyone suffer. Don't mind him.'

'You never did, that's for sure,' Ed said, stopping him in his tracks.

O'Neill whirled on Ed. He was about two inches shorter than his son. 'Don't even go there,' he warned. 'I only financed every bloody thing you wanted to do.' He poked Ed in the chest. 'Computer courses, construction job. Every bloody thing you dropped out of.' He looked at me. 'Medicine – that was the last thing he fucked up.'

'I paid to do that myself,' Ed muttered mutinously.

'Damn right you did. I wasn't throwing any more money away on you. Christ!'

O'Neill, after giving Ed a final prod, stomped off.

'Bastard,' Ed muttered. I think he'd forgotten that I was there. He stood staring after his dad for ages.

I didn't know what to do. So I stayed very quiet, hoping that Ed would go on down.

He didn't. Instead, he turned back to me. 'So now you know,' he muttered. 'I am the O'Neill family fuck-up.'

'Oh no—'

'Oh yeah. Betcha glad you asked about me now.' He took his orange jacket down off its hook.

'Where are you going?'

'Just staying with the habits of a lifetime.'

'You're leaving?'

'Yep.'

I stared, horrified, as he shoved his arms into his jacket. Since he'd been with us, the sales of the wrestlers had tripled. He was a damn good toy seller and all the profit he'd make would ultimately reflect well on me. But over all that was the fact that he'd bought me the chocolate cake. Crap, I know. But I was pathetically grateful to him for admitting he was wrong to take my stuff, for admitting that he didn't like it when people did it to him. For not making me feel weird to be so obsessive. I'd spent most of my life feeling weird. 'You can't go. Don't go.'

He zipped up his jacket. Looked hard at me. Said quietly, 'Tell me one good reason why I should stay.'

'You're a good salesman.'

He laughed slightly. 'That's not much use when you don't trust me.'

'Yeah, well, I know different now. I guess I should have believed you.'

'Yeah, you should have.' Ed pinned me with his stare. 'And that's the problem, see, no matter what I do or say from now on, you'll double-check with me dad.'

'I won't.' He was making me feel guilty. 'I promise I won't.'

'You will.'

'I'm not a liar.'

'Neither am I.'

'I never said you were.'

'You just didn't believe me.'

'How could I?' I snapped. 'I figured if you were eyeing up my job, you wouldn't tell me anyway.'

'So you reckon I *am* a liar?'

'Oh for God's sake, we're only going around in circles here. I can't help the way I felt.'

There was tense silence.

'So how did you feel?' he asked. 'Like what exactly did I do to make you think I was after your job?' He paused. 'I worked my arse off for you, Vicky.'

His eyes bored into me, making me feel even more of a heel.

'Well, think about it,' I muttered defensively. 'It didn't make sense for you to come back from London to take a job working under me and Bridie and you O'Neill's son.'

Ed bit his lip. 'I had nothing else,' he said simply. 'As my dad told you, I ditched med school.'

'Yeah, and how come you never told me that!'

He flinched. 'It wasn't your business. And besides, it wouldn't have made a difference. I *told* you all I wanted to do was work. And I bloody well did too. Jesus' – he shook his head – 'if I'd been crap, you'd have been happier – yeah?'

I bowed my head. I could not look into those blue eyes any more. 'Well, you were always making me out to be stupid!'

'How so?' He sounded completely dazed. 'Christ!'

'Doing stuff on the computer, rearranging shelves, being all cosy with Bridie.'

'What?'

'You shoved me out.'

'Shoved you out?' He looked disbelievingly at me. 'Get lost!'

'You did,' I insisted. 'It was always me on my own while you and Bridie talked and laughed. You stole her away just like you were going to steal my job.' My voice had risen and I hadn't meant it to. I was aware of how pathetic I sounded, but damn it, that's the way it was.

'You *really* need to get a life, Vicky.'

He said it as if I was a weirdo. As if he was laughing at me. 'I have a life!' How dare he. He was the one that asked and now he wasn't prepared to face the truth. 'I do have a life.' I searched frantically for something that would impress him. 'I was asked to sing in a hotel.'

He didn't react.

'You're the one that needs to get a life if what your dad says is true.'

My angry words fell into silence.

Ed's face hardened. 'Ta, Vicky.' He turned to go.

I couldn't apologise. I just couldn't. I felt I should but he'd insulted me too.

Bridie came up the stairs, just as he was leaving. 'What is going on up here?' She looked from Ed to me. 'You can hear it in the shop.'

'Bye, Bridie,' Ed said by way of reply. A quick glance at me. 'She's all yours again, Vicky.'

Bridie gawked after him and when the front door slammed she turned to me, horrified. 'Vicky, what have you done? Where's he going?'

I burst into tears.

Chapter Thirty-five

BRIDIE COULD GET no sense out of me. Well, I was hardly going to tell her the full story, was I? I mean, if I told her that I thought Ed had been working so hard and doing so well just so that he could do me out of my job and steal away her friendship with me, I'd sound like one of those sad, obsessive, paranoid people.

As I watched Bridie fussing about, making me coffee and trying to force a huge slice of *that* cake on me, I told myself that we'd manage fine without Ed. I could do windows, I could put up swings. We'd managed before and we would again.

Bridie, of course, was convinced that a huge misunderstanding had taken place. There was no way, according to her, that Ed would have left over his dad wanting to know how he was getting on. He just did not *do* those things. Ed was kind and gentle and funny and charming. Basically, he was heaven on earth. 'He'll be back tomorrow,' she reassured me, 'you wait and see. He loves this job. He told me that only the other day.'

Ed was still AWOL by Friday.

At first, the nasty part of me was glad. I thought it would be like old times, just me and Bridie, working away.

Only it wasn't.

Ed's presence over the last few months had changed things between Bridie and me, or maybe they'd always been that way, I don't know. But I found that Bridie's constant dusting and polishing got on my nerves. At least when Ed was there, I could focus on him rather than feel guilty that I wasn't cleaning alongside her.

And, in the mornings, my eye kept returning to Ed's enormous green mug on the shelf. I wondered how long it would sit there before it became all mouldy. I wondered if I should ring him up and tell him to collect it.

And of course, when a nasty virus threatened to invade our computer system, whom did we have to thank for downloading the anti-virus thingy?

And most irritating of all was that Bridie kept mentioning him. Now that he was gone, I wanted her to forget that he'd been there at all. But she wouldn't. On Friday, she'd spent the morning laughing away to herself because Leeds had beaten Liverpool in some match or other. 'Oh, I wish I could see his face,' she said meaningfully.

I ignored her.

Dominic too wanted to know where he was.

'He's not here any more,' I said to him.

Dominic shrugged, his eyes filling with tears. 'Like Daddy,' he said to his mam.

'Naw,' she said, surprising me, 'he was miles better than your fuckin' daddy.'

But reminders of him were everywhere, not least in the window display, which was still pulling the kids in. It wasn't that I missed *him*, it was more that he was missing, if you know what I mean.

I decided to give him until Saturday before I took action. Though I hadn't a clue what I was going to do.

Of course, when Saturday came around and still Ed didn't show, I lost my nerve. I began to dial O'Neill's number to say that Ed had left, and halfway through I slammed the phone back down. Then, worried and miserable, I had to go back to the flat and watch Sal getting ready for her night out with him. There was no escape.

The guy was haunting me.

I sat on the sofa, pretending to watch a riveting programme about pig prices, while Sal floated in and out of her bedroom in various states of undress. In order to keep him keen, she hadn't talked to him all week, so it was up to me to fill her in or she'd kill me. She was blow-dried, made up and dressed and had just begun painting her nails before I plucked up the nerve.

'I think there's maybe something I should tell you before you go out tonight,' I stammered.

'Yeah?' She wasn't interested. She was holding her nails to the light and trying to gauge if they matched her steel blue trousers or if they needed another coat.

'Well . . .' I licked my lips and took a big, steadying breath. 'Ed has left the toy shop.'

'Oh.' She blinked, confused. 'But he's still coming here, isn't he?'

'I suppose.' That was not exactly the response I wanted. But at least she hadn't blown the top.

'Well then.'

'I'm only telling you so you're prepared for him not staying.' Pause as Sal considered this. 'I mean, we've had a row and he probably won't want to bump into me.' I refocused on Farming Report and waited for the accusations. I tried to look nonchalant but my heart was hammering.

'Him leaving might be for the best,' she eventually pronounced. 'Means you're not his boss any more. Move.' She sat down beside me on the sofa. 'Now, what do you think, do they need another coat?' She shoved her nails under my nose.

I was gobsmacked. Where were the hysterics? 'Eh . . .'

'Oh.' She snatched them away. 'Why am I asking you? Sure you haven't a clue. Where's Mel when I need her?' She studied them again. 'I think they look fine. It's a new non-chip varnish. I'm dying to see how long it'll last.'

That was the sort of stuff Sal found riveting. She even

wrote a beauty page for her paper on stuff like that.

'So, what happened?' she asked, rubbing some hand cream into her nails now that they'd dried to the correct colour. 'Was it over the cake?' Before I had a chance to answer, she went on, 'Honestly, when I told him you'd flipped about the cheesecake, he was so insistent that he get you another one. He didn't even find it funny – imagine?'

'That's because it wasn't funny,' I muttered darkly, cringing yet again.

'She won't appreciate it, I told him, Vicky hates people giving her things. Guess I was right – huh?'

It would have been nice for her to believe that but hey, she was seeing Ed and he was sure to get his slant in on the whole thing and I'd end up looking like a neurotic headcase. 'It wasn't exactly over the cake. He—'

'Aw, well' – Sal snapped her hand cream closed and turned to me – 'something like this was bound to happen. You had it in for him from day one.'

'I did not!'

'You did so.' She stood up and rolled her eyes at me. 'He's trying to take my job, Sal,' she mimicked in my low, husky voice. 'He's not doing what I say.'

'And he wasn't,' I said heatedly. 'He was always trying to undermine me!'

'You think everyone is trying to undermine you,' Sal said back. 'Face it, the guy hadn't a chance. You figured he was trying to steal your job and so you got at him.'

'No, I only asked—'

'It's like the way you are with Mel when we go out. When it's just you and me, we have a blast, but when Mel is there, you think she's taking me over or something.'

'No!'

'You go all out to get drunk, or you make all these smart remarks or you take ages to get ready or—'

'No, I don't!'

'You do. And the time when your German mate came to stay – what was his name?'

I didn't answer.

'Anyway, when he started seeing me, you wouldn't come out with us any more.' She laughed a bit. 'Gee, you flipped bigtime that time.'

'You only went out with him because he had money.'

'You only flipped because you wanted him all to yourself.'

'I'm going out.'

'You want everything all to yourself, Vic.'

'I'm going out!'

'And that's what you always do when you realise you can't have it your way the whole time, Vicky.'

I slammed the door on her.

I had nowhere to go. No money to buy anything. Not, I think, that I could have eaten anything anyway. My stomach was churning, my head was pounding and my throat had a huge lump in it. Sal's remarks had hurt. And what was even worse was that she really believed what she'd said. She hadn't said it in anger or as a joke, but in a sort of amused way. As if I was an amusing oddity or something. As if I was a weirdo. I shoved my hands into the light fleece that I was wearing and began to walk. Ed was due to call for Sal at eight-thirty, which meant that I had thirty minutes to kill before I could go back. It was just as well I had my trainers on; anything else would have crippled me.

I dulled my mind. Tried not to think. Instead, I walked. And walked. And passed flats and roads and roundabouts, schools and shops and the park, which had closed for the evening. I saw couples wrapped around one another, kids playing in their gardens with loads of their little friends, teenagers hanging about in large groups smoking and sniggering, families sitting down to dinner in lighted windows. And I wondered why I'd never been part of a large group. Never. Ever. Not even in school when all the girls had hung about together – there I'd be on the fringes, just watching.

Hovering.

And sort of glad that I was on my own.

I'd always preferred one-to-one relationships. Being part of a gang had never appealed to me. I knew I'd always feel left out. But seeing the kids playing together, I wondered why I'd always shied away from the fun of it. It sure looked like fun. Why had I never—

Because you get scared.

The thought came unbidden and it startled me.

I tried to push it away but it only grew louder. *You don't like crowds because* – I winced as the thought slithered into my consciousness – *because you don't want to have to compete with a group for someone's attention.*

Stop!

I clenched my hands so hard that my nails dug into my palms.

You don't want to compete.

You don't want the rejection.

But so what?

Everyone was different.

And not being part of a team was fine.

Scarily, my disastrous other jobs paraded themselves in front of me. I'd left the flower shop because two new girls had joined. They'd been too cliquey, I'd thought. I left the travel agents because a new boss had brought in new staff and now, well, I'd pushed Ed out.

Maybe not completely intentionally, but I hadn't tried too hard to make him stay after I'd hurt him. OK, so I did think he was after my job, but when I found out he wasn't, what had I done? Accused him of making me look a fool, of trying to steal Bridie. Hurt him by throwing his dad's comments back into his face.

I'd *wanted* him to go.

The chocolate cake *had* earned him some brownie points, but when it came down to it, I'd been glad to see him leave.

But, Jesus, I was the manager.

I was the boss.

I had to have staff. I couldn't go all jealous if the staff happened to get on, could I?

No, some part of me said.

And just because I had good staff didn't mean that they were eyeing up my job – did it?

No.

I saw with a sudden clarity what Ed must have gone through. How it must have hurt to come into the smallest store and be bossed about by the youngest manager. And still, he'd tried to do his best. And what had I done? Never even encouraged him. Never said 'well done' or anything. Because I'd resented him. I'd resented the fact that he was there at all – Daddy's boy with everything to gain. He had it all – looks, charm, a ready-made job, a family, and then he'd topped the lot by making Bridie fall for him. My friend Bridie.

Him leaving was partly my fault.

If I'd really wanted it, I should have been able to persuade him to stay.

I sat down on a wall as the knowledge swept over me.

Sal, with her careless remarks, had opened the door a chink.

And I found suddenly that I couldn't get it closed again.

The lump in my throat dissolved suddenly and I found that I was crying soft, silent tears.

I was a complete fuck-up. Completely weird and alone.

And I didn't know what to do.

Chapter Thirty-six

I WAITED UNTIL Sal went out the next morning before I got up. I'd woken around three a.m. to the sound of voices in the kitchen. There was Ed's unmistakable northern accent as he laughed softly at something Sal had said. It was probably something about me. Anyway, I hadn't been able to sleep until I heard the click of the door as he left the apartment. He mustn't have wanted to face me over breakfast and I cringed in a mixture of shame and relief.

Falling back asleep, I was woken by the sound of the shower. Sal was getting ready for a Sunday afternoon drinking spree with Mel and Lorcan. She'd told me that she hoped it meant what she hoped it meant. Privately, I couldn't see her being offered a job over pints in a pub, but I didn't say that. More importantly, I don't think Mel would have brought Lorcan along if she were discussing business. According to her, Lorcan was pure pleasure.

Like Sal and I *really* believed her.

Anyway, Sal left around twelve and I surfaced. All week, I'd been looking forward to Sunday – well, I had been until I'd rowed with Ed. Marti was due to surprise me. He'd sent me piles of text messages saying how much he was looking forward to seeing me and how well the boys were doing on their first big tour. The audiences had been fantastic, he said, and the only thing that went wrong was when Adam had thrown his cowboy hat up in the air and it had skimmed out over the audience. Some young wan had caught it and had been in tears when they'd made her hand it back. A small piece had appeared in the *Independent* damning the boys but Marti thought it was all publicity. 'How'd you like to lose a hat worth a couple of hundred quid?' he'd texted when I'd told him he should have just left it.

I grabbed a quick breakfast before showering and dressing. Marti had told me to be as flamboyant as I liked. 'It'll be that kind of day,' he said mysteriously. I didn't need to be told twice and I chose my purple jeans, the ones I'd bought for our first date, and a yellow top with Donald Duck on it. I love all the Disney characters. They always look so cheerful, don't you think?

By one, I was presentable, having tamed my hair by plaiting it into two braids.

Marti was on time.

He pressed the buzzer and warbled, '*Something told me it's all happening at the zoo.*' I smiled. '*I don't believe it, I don't believe it's true.*' Then I told him I'd be down in a sec. I glanced in the mirror on the way out. I looked tired, I thought. And there was a frown line between my eyebrows that hadn't been there before. And my eyes were all red so I shoved some powder onto my face, which caked instantly. And Donald Duck looked stupid on me. I was too old for Donald Duck.

I raced back into the bedroom and took out my tie-dyed purple top. Pulling it over my head, making bits of hair stick out all over the place, I left.

Marti was wearing a pair of tight blue jeans and a cream sweatshirt with the words *Boy Five – Five Times Better Than Your Average Boy Bands*. He was sitting behind the wheel of his Boy Five-mobile sporting a pair of cool-looking shades and a navy and cream baseball cap. 'Hey, great to see you.' He leaned over and kissed me as I clambered in.

It was only then that I noticed Leo glowering from the back seat. He had his trusty teddy with him and was holding it tightly. 'Leo,' I said, hoping the shock didn't show in my voice. 'How's things?'

He shrugged and shoved a thumb in his mouth.

'Take that thumb out of your mouth,' Marti said crossly, 'and answer Vicky!'

'Oh, no, it doesn't matter,' I said breezily.

'Then why did you ask it?' Leo said in a bright clear voice.

I ignored him. Marti ignored him. 'Leo's fine,' he said heartily, his hands going white as he clenched the steering wheel. 'And he's looking forward to the surprise too, aren't you?'

Leo shrugged. 'It's the zoo. I heard you talking about it on the phone.'

The zoo?

My surprise was an outing to the zoo?

'The zoo?' I said faintly.

'Sort of.' Marti beamed at me, showing off his gold tooth. 'It's more than that, though.'

'You're shooting the band's video,' Leo chimed in.

Marti gave a loud laugh.

'We're going to the zoo to see the new Boy Five video?' I could not believe this. This was not happening.

'A hard boy to surprise, is Leo,' Marti said through gritted teeth, as he tried valiantly to smile. 'Like his mother, that way.'

'We're going to the zoo to see the new Boy Five video?' I asked again.

'Yep.' Marti beamed at me. 'Isn't that brilliant? I mean, have you ever seen a music video shot?'

'No.' And I really hadn't harboured a secret desire to see one either.

'There you are then.' He looked me up and down. 'And if you want, you can be in it – good-lookers are always needed. We could have you beside the orang-utans – nice contrast with the hair colours.'

'Nah.' I couldn't even muster a grin, that's assuming he was joking. 'I don't think so.' What was happening to my life, I wondered.

'Can I be in it, Daddy?' Leo asked suddenly.

'No!'

'Well, then, I don't want to go.'

Me neither, I wanted to say. I mean, if it had been a video for, say, Juliet Turner or some other brilliant singer-songwriter, I'd probably have been a bit more enthusiastic, but Boy Five?

'What's the new single?' I asked.

'Can't you guess?' Marti took off his glasses and grinned. 'Simon and Garfunkel's Zoo song.'

'Ha. Should have guessed.'

Marti and his crew had hired the zoo especially for the day. When we got there, cameras and lights were being set up outside the lion's enclosure. Boy Five were swaggering around looking very important. They'd been given new hairstyles – floppy blond streaks for two of the lads while Cliff sported an enormous quiff. He looked a bit like a cockatoo. The other two had had their hair completely shorn in order to appeal to the teenagers that liked a bit of rough, Marti later informed me. They were dressed in zookeeper outfits – green overalls that clung in all the right places.

Marti strode on ahead of me, Leo running in his wake. I watched as he clapped the lads on the back and had a few words with the make-up woman. Then he turned to me and beckoned me forward. Introductions were made, the lads nodded briefly at me – all except Cliff who seemed to be a master bearer of grudges.

'Marti,' some fella said then, 'we're ready if you want to go.'

'Uh-huh.' Marti took a seat in a stereotypical director's chair and I sat beside him. From somewhere the music began to boom through the speakers. Boy Five took up their positions in front of the lion's enclosure and proceeded to mime to the song.

'But they're not singing,' I shouted at Marti over the noise.

'Nah, no one ever does on videos,' he said knowledgeably.

The music stopped abruptly. The sound director looked up. 'Too loud.'

The camera guy looked up. 'Too bright.'

Cliff and the lads winced. 'These outfits are too tight, Marti.'

Marti ignored them. 'Back into positions, lads,' he said. A major confab with the cameramen ensued. I sat there, watching the activity going on as the lights were adjusted and the sound was monitored.

Leo trailed around after Marti, who didn't seem to be aware of him.

Eventually they were all ready to go again.

Boy Five took up their positions. They had buckets in their hands and were doing some sort of weird dance routine which involved a lot of jumping over them.

'Action!'

The music blared.

The lads began to mime.

And the lion, which had suddenly arrived on the scene, began to roar. And I mean *roar*. Boy Five jumped about a million miles into the air before legging it. One camera toppled over. Marti yelled out a 'Jaysus' and I had to bite my lip to stop from laughing.

Leo thought it was great.

'Wow, Dad, d'ya hear that! Wow.' He ran up towards the lion to get a closer look. The animal stared at him and then with a disdainful flick of its tail wandered up the hill.

Everything had to be started up again.

And again, just as the lads were about to launch into their dance routine, the lion roared, only it sounded a lot more menacing this time.

'Aw, Jaysus.' Marti glared around at everyone and then glared at the lion. 'Leo, get away from there!' he barked. Leo ignored him. 'Leo!'

Reluctantly, Leo slunk away.

'I only wanted a look,' he muttered under his breath.

'Your dad's afraid you'll get hurt,' I whispered back.

He said nothing.

Marti was striding about the place, wondering what to do.

'Zookeeper,' he pronounced suddenly. 'Maybe the bloody thing is hungry. Get the zookeeper.'

Apparently it was no one's job to get the zookeeper.

'Vicky?' he turned to me. 'Will you go – please?'

'Right.' I stood up. It was better than sitting down and doing nothing. I turned to Leo. 'D'you want to come?'

He glared at me.

'You'll be able to look around the zoo and maybe see some animals?'

He looked uncertain.

'He won't,' Marti hissed, coming over. 'We're on a tight time limit, Vicky. I need you to hurry. This will cost me a fortune.'

I could have strangled the man. Was he completely insensitive to the kid's feelings? Did he even care if Leo liked me? 'I'll bring you around when I come back,' I promised him. 'That's if you'll come.'

He hugged his teddy. 'Will you come too, Daddy?'

Marti gave an impatient sigh. 'Wish I could, Leo, but you can see how busy Daddy is.'

'Then I won't go either,' Leo pouted.

'Fine.' I shrugged. 'I'll just have to go on my own, so.'

'Yeah. After you get the zookeeper,' Marti said, glancing at his watch. 'OK, everyone,' he announced as I walked off, 'take five.'

They took longer than five. I hadn't a clue where a zookeeper could be found. Thirty minutes later, I arrived back with a man smaller than Marti in tow. He hadn't been at all pleased to hear that the lion was roaring. 'I knew this shouldn't be allowed,' he said grumpily as he scampered along beside me. 'I told them that but would they listen?'

I smiled politely and said nothing.

'Now,' he said, as he strode over to where everyone was drinking cups of coffee, 'who's in charge here?'

'I am.' Marti stood up. 'And to be honest, this is not proving to be the most successful of days. The lion, that one there' –

he pointed to where the lion was pacing up and down and glaring at all of them – 'is being very disruptive. I mean, is there any way we can stop it from roaring?'

The zookeeper, whose name was Hugh, smirked. 'I'll open the gates if you want to go in there and try.'

I laughed.

Marti looked offended, though whether it was from me laughing or Hugh's reply, I wasn't sure. 'There's no need for that,' he said placatingly. 'Just shove a few steaks or something in there to keep him busy while we shoot this.'

'That animal is on a strict diet,' Hugh said, somewhat patronisingly, I thought. 'You don't go shoving him a few steaks now and again. What I suggest is that you shoot this somewhere else. You've obviously upset him. I can't have my animals upset.'

'Well, he's upset us,' Marti blustered.

'And I'm sure he's sorry about that,' Hugh smirked. 'But it's not everyone that likes loud music outside their house, is it?'

'So you're saying that that lion has won, are you?' Marti asked.

The lion was lying down now, basking in the unexpected sunlight of the early afternoon. He looked as if he was grinning at us.

'He's smiling,' Leo pronounced delightedly.

'Sure is,' I whispered back.

The child forgot his obvious dislike of me enough to begin to giggle. 'He doesn't like the music – just like my mammy.'

I decided it would be prudent to say nothing.

'So you're not going to do anything?' Marti was still arguing. 'Can't you tranquillise it or something?'

'Move!' Hugh had heard enough. 'Go on now, the lot of yez, move!'

'We've hired the place out,' Marti said back, folding his arms. 'Adam's dad *works* here.'

Adam smiled nervously.

'I don't give a damn if you've *bought* the place out,' Hugh retorted. 'You can't go upsetting the animals – well, not unless you want a huge court case on your hands.'

That did it. Reluctantly everyone began to pack up.

'Well, can you tell us what animals actually like music?' Marti asked, just as Hugh was about to leave.

'That music?' Hugh smirked. 'Animals with severe brain damage, I'd say.'

'So, yourself then?' Marti said, sounding ridiculously polite.

Hugh looked as if he were about to go for him but thought the better of it. 'Excuse me, while I go back to my worthwhile job,' he said instead.

We all watched him saunter off, his small frame looking about a hundred foot high with the swagger he affected.

'Asshole.' Marti raised his eyes heavenwards before turning back to his protégés.

'You ignore that insult, lads. You ignore it. Yez are brilliant. Five thousand pre-teens can't be wrong, sure they can't?'

The five nodded.

They decamped to the monkey enclosure. Once again there began the arduous business of setting up lights and cameras. I really did not want to sit around and watch it all happen. Or not happen as the case may be.

'Marti,' I tugged on his sleeve.

'Yo!' he turned around and bestowed me with a smile. 'What is it?'

'I think I'll just have a wander around. I haven't been to the zoo in years and well . . .' I let my voice trail off. I couldn't say it. I couldn't say that I was dying to look around or that it'd be nice to look around.

'Off you go.' Marti made whooshing motions with his arms. 'You're only in the way here anyway. Enjoy! Enjoy!' He turned back to the make-up woman.

'Now, I want them browner-looking. Brown is sexy.'

'Not if they look as if they've shite smeared all over their faces, it's not,' she grumped.

Marti laughed.

He was still laughing as I turned to go.

I had walked a fair distance away and was heading towards the sea lions when a small voice said nervously, 'Can I come too?'

I was about to smile and say that of course he could come when he added sulkily, 'I mean, I don't want to go with you, not really, but there's no one else.'

'Yeah, well, I don't want to go with you either, but like you said, there's no one else.'

He wasn't sure if I was joking.

But he walked alongside me anyway.

Chapter Thirty-seven

IT WAS QUITE nice having Leo for company, as it happened; at least it took my mind off the fiasco in the shop. It wasn't as if I'd *planned* on thinking about it but it was kind of hard not to. At least with Leo trotting alongside me, I found that I could focus on his hostility, which was heaps better than worrying about O'Neill's impending aggression upon finding out that his problem son had jacked in another job.

'Where d'you want to go first, Leo?' I arranged my face in a big bright contrived smile.

He shrugged and scuffed the ground with his shoe. 'Don't care.'

'How about the sea lions – that's where I was going.'

'Fine.'

'This way, so.' I headed off in what I hoped was the right direction, him trailing behind. Just as we rounded the corner, we came across a sort of mini-playground. I was about to walk past it, when Leo asked shyly, 'Can I have a quick go?'

I was delighted that he'd volunteered an interest in something. 'Yeah. Sure.'

There was a little slide, a swing and a set of monkey bars. I sat down and watched as he made for the slide and scampered up it. Then, in typical boy fashion, he came down head first.

'Don't do that.' I legged it across and caught him just before his head hit the ground. 'You'll hurt yourself. Your dad will kill me if anything happens you.'

'No he won't.' Leo shrugged me off. 'All he cares about is his band.'

'Oh now, don't be silly!' I watched as once again he clambered up the slide. 'That's not true.'

'Is so.' He shoved his teddy down before him this time. 'That's what my nana says to him. She says all you care about is the band, you'll want to cop on. And my mammy used to say the same thing.'

'Oh now—' I couldn't finish. He launched himself down the slide head first again, only faster this time. 'Leo!'

'You can't give out to me.' He jumped up and wiped his hands down the length of his trousers. 'You're not the boss of me.'

'I am when I'm on my own with you.' I met his defiant stare with one of my own. Huh, I thought, this kid thinks he's bad, well, he hasn't met me properly yet. 'Now, you can go back to your daddy and the band or you can see the sea lions being fed – it's up to you, but if you come down the slide head first again, then I'm just going to pick you up and bring you back to your daddy.'

'You're too small.'

I don't like being reminded of that. 'Not as small as you, twerp.'

'That's not nice.'

I shrugged. 'Do you want to see the sea lions?'

He stared at his trainers. Black hair fell forward over his face and I thought how much the kid needed a haircut. And he wore a blue sweatshirt that was way too small for him and jeans that were all frayed and faded. Even his trainers were falling apart. I felt a rush of pity for him. Or compassion. Or something along those lines. Without thinking, I reached out and tousled his hair. 'Betcha can't go on the monkey bars without falling,' I grinned.

Leo's eyes met mine. His bottom lip stuck out in a condescending sneer. 'Can so.'

'Let's see you then.'

I used to be the expert on monkey bars as a kid, maybe

because I'd been so skinny that my arms could support my body easily enough. I figured that Leo would be the same.

He ran across to the bars and launched himself onto the first one.

'Keep your body as steady as possible,' I advised and, though he pretended he wasn't listening, he immediately stopped wriggling his legs. 'Now!'

His hand groped for the second bar.

'Steady yourself.'

His other hand groped for the second bar.

'Steady.'

'I know,' he snapped.

Little by little he eased himself across to the other side and when he finished, there was a grin of triumph in his face. 'See?'

'Good man!' I pretended to be amazed. 'That was brilliant.'

He tried not to smile, but it broke through. 'It's hard,' he said nonchalantly, 'hurts your arms.'

'I'd say so,' I nodded. 'Ice cream is good for fixing up sore arms. D'you want one?'

The wary look was back.

'Only if you want one.'

'Well . . . my arms *are* sore,' he conceded.

One ice cream later, we reached the sea lions. Leo had gone back to monosyllabic mood and all my talk about sea lions went nowhere.

'I thought you said they were going to be fed,' he accused.

I shrugged. For some reason it had never occurred to me that they wouldn't be feeding when I arrived to see them. Any poster I'd ever seen of zoos, it always showed the sea lions being fed. I dunno, maybe I thought it went on all day or something.

'Sorry, Leo, I must have got it wrong.'

'Great!' He rolled his eyes and hugged his teddy closer. 'My mammy wouldn't tell lies like that.'

I said nothing, pretending to be fascinated by the lovely blue pool the sea lions were swimming about in.

'She's going to come back, you know.'

'Guess you miss her, huh?' I hadn't planned to say it, the words just popped out.

He eyed me warily. A slow nod.

I crouched down beside him. 'That's good,' I said. 'And I bet she misses you too.'

He bit his lip. 'I don't know.' His eyes pooled with tears and he turned away.

'No mammy ever forgets her children,' I quoted Lucy. I guessed she should know. 'A very important lady told me that.'

'Who?' He turned back and eyed me suspiciously. 'Pink?'

'Eh – no.'

'The Queen?'

'No – just someone who knows all about mammies and their children. She said that no matter where mammies are, they always remember their kids.'

'Really?' His eyes widened and his mouth parted slightly. It was as if I'd just given him the most wonderful news.

'Uh-huh.'

'Dad says she's not coming back.'

'Yeah, well, I don't know about that.'

'Can you ask your important lady?'

I winced. 'Well, she's not around at the moment. Maybe next time I see her.'

Leo nodded. 'OK, so.' His gaze flicked from my face to somewhere over my shoulder. He gave a squeal that made me jump. 'He's coming! He's coming to feed the sea lions!'

The smile, which lit his face, transformed him into quite a beautiful kid and I wondered how any mother could have walked out on him.

On the way back, Marti moaned on and on about whoever said not to work with children or animals knew what they were talking about. 'The monkeys were worse than the lion,' he said, careering across two lanes of traffic. 'One of them kept screeching every time Cliff had to pretend to feed it. And Adam tripped over his bucket just as we were finishing the shoot and we had to take it again. I swear, he's as clumsy as a three-legged racehorse.'

'I went on the monkey bars, Daddy.'

'Good lad.' Marti flashed him a brief smile. 'And then, right, Logan hurt himself with his costume. Said it was too tight and he could hardly stand upright in it.'

Despite Marti's glowering face, I started to laugh.

'It's not funny,' Marti snapped. 'It's been a disaster.'

'Well, Leo and I had a great day,' I chimed in, 'didn't we, Leo?'

He shrugged. 'It was OK. Vicky said that Mammy misses me.'

The car came to a shrieking halt. Someone blasted us from behind. Marti ignored them. 'I don't encourage him to talk about his mother,' he snapped at me, 'and you shouldn't either.'

'What?'

'His mother left him – she's gone. That's all there is to it.'

'He has to be able to talk about it,' I said, remembering the way I never talked about my own mother. 'The poor kid will go mad otherwise.'

'She loves me,' Leo said. 'And she's thinking of me.'

'Shut up!' Marti ordered.

'And Vicky is going to ask if she's going to come back.' Leo's voice shook slightly, but he kept on going. 'She knows an important lady who knows these things.'

'Vicky doesn't know anyone like that,' Marti said.

'She does!' Leo sounded as if he was going to cry.

'She does not!'

'My counsellor,' I interjected. This was fast becoming a nightmare.

'A shrink?' Marti looked appalled.

'No.' I swallowed. 'It's a woman I see who's, well, she's helping me trace my own mother.'

'What?' Marti looked confused.

'I'm . . .' I closed my eyes. As far as possible, I'd never admitted to being adopted before. It was, I dunno, shameful to me that my own mother had given me away. A stigma. I know it sounds unreasonable, but hey, I blamed myself. I probably wasn't cute enough or something.

'Well?' Marti said, not sounding that supportive.

'I'm adopted.' I mumbled it. I opened my eyes and stared out at the congested Dublin traffic. 'I'm tracing my mother and this counsellor is helping me find her.'

Silence.

Marti was gawping at me.

'What's adopted?' Leo asked.

'It's when your mammy gives you away when you're born,' Marti explained.

'Like, your mammy leaving you?' Leo asked.

'Oh, a million times worse than that,' Marti said.

'Ta, Marti.'

He shrugged, gave my arm a limp pat. 'Sorry, sorry. I didn't mean—'

'Your mammy left you too?' Leo said, poking his face between the two seats.

I nodded, afraid I'd cry. I always cried when I thought of it.

'Poor you.' He reached out and rubbed his small hand up and down my hair. 'Poor you.'

I gave a shaky smile and gently touched Leo's hand.

Marti studied the two of us for a second and his eyes softened. 'Well, she must've been bloody mad,' he pronounced. 'Leaving a fine thing like yourself.'

I gave a bit of a laugh. I wanted to hug the man.

'My mammy was mad too, wasn't she?' Leo said. 'But she still loves me.'

'She does,' I said firmly, daring Marti to defy me.

He shrugged. 'Well, I guess Vicky is the expert,' he conceded. 'Who wouldn't love you, Leo, hey?' He gave his son a broad wink and turned rueful eyes on me. 'Look, Vicky, I'm dead sorry. Talking about Linda makes me angry – I mean she walked out on us – left me with him – I dunno what to do.'

'Leo has to be able to talk about it, Marti.'

'It upsets him.' He inched the car forward and shot a furtive look at Leo, who'd gone back to playing with his teddy. 'It upsets *me*.' Before I could reply, he continued, 'I'm not great with kids. Linda was the one who did all that stuff.'

'Well, learn. It's important.' I bit my lip. 'My folks didn't like talking about my adoption to me. But, like, it doesn't do any good to hide things or ignore things.'

Who was I to talk, I suddenly wondered. Jesus, I was the *expert* in ignoring stuff. But maybe I had a point.

For once in my life.

'You have a point.' Marti gave me his peculiar smile. 'Thanks, Vicky.'

'No,' I said, much to his puzzlement. 'Thank you.'

Chapter Thirty-eight

BRIDIE RANG ME at the flat on Monday to tell me what I'd known would happen all weekend – Ed still hadn't shown. The news, while expected, made my stomach roll. I had tried to ask Sal if Ed had mentioned anything to her about his plans but she was in a big black mood. I took it that Mel still hadn't come up with a job for her.

'I'll be in after lunch to help you out,' I told Bridie. Then, attempting a casual tone, I asked, 'Where does Ed live anyway?'

'Are you going to see him?' Bridie said breathlessly. Before I could answer, she rushed on, 'Oh you should, Vicky. Clear the air and all that.'

'Clear his mug from our office more like,' I muttered.

'Oh now! Oh now!' Uncertain pause. 'You don't mean that. Do you?'

'Just gimme his address, Bridie.'

I heard her tapping some buttons on the computer. 'Here we are now – Apartment five, Abbey Court, Seascape Road, Dun Laoghaire.'

'Ta.'

I put down the phone before she could ask me anything else.

Of course, I hadn't checked to see if he was home. That would have been the sensible thing to do, I realised, as I sat on the dart to Dun Laoghaire. What if he wasn't in? What then? Did I hang about all day in the hope that he'd arrive back? Did I go again tomorrow? Did I ring him up?

There was no point in tormenting myself, I decided, once I got off. The main thing to do was to find the place. There'd be time enough to worry when I got there. I shoved my hands into my jacket pockets and bent my head against the breeze coming in from the sea. Nabbing an old man, I asked him if he knew where Seascape Road was.

'Ohh now,' he said, scratching his chin, 'I *do* know the name. In fact a friend of mine only talked about it yesterday. Hang on now while I think.'

I hung on.

'Seaview Road,' he mumbled.

'Scape,' I said.

'Pardon?'

'Seascape Road.'

'Oh well now, I thought you said Seaview.'

'No.' I fixed a smile in place. 'Anyway—'

'Hang on now while I think if I know of a Seacape Road.'

'Seascape,' I said. 'As in e-scape.'

'Oh.' He looked confused. 'Oh now, hang on . . .'

How is it that when you ask someone for directions they always turn out to be dense? He hadn't a clue. He mumbled something about houses going up everywhere so that a person didn't know if they were coming or going and wandered off.

Eventually I found a woman who lived in the area. 'Second left then take the third right and you'll see it after the traffic lights.'

Still managed to get lost.

It was after midday when I found myself staring up at a nice enough apartment block. All sorts of spring flowers danced in beds outside and the gardener was mowing the grass on a ride-on lawnmower. It all looked so peaceful and nice. Or it would have if I didn't think I was going to be sick everywhere. Not since Mrs Sweeney turned up at our door demanding that I give Lisa's Barbie back to her have I been so scared. I hadn't even planned what I should say. All I knew was that I had to say something to fix things. To put things right. To acknowledge to myself that I wasn't the horrible person Sal said I was. I wasn't selfish.

No way.

My finger shook as I pressed the buzzer for 'O'Kane, O'Neill, Mulligan, Brett'.

'Yeah?'

It was him.

'Ed?'

'Aye – who's this?'

I gulped. I could still run if I wanted. 'Me,' I answered in a sort of terrified squeal.

'Vicky.'

There was a pause that seemed to last for ages.

'You'd better come up.'

He buzzed and I pushed open the door. I didn't even notice what the place was like inside, I was so sick at the thoughts of seeing the guy. He lived in a top-floor apartment and I took the lift up, hoping that it'd get stuck.

Of course, it didn't. It announced pleasantly that we were on the fourth floor and with a swoosh the doors opened.

I patted down my hair, licked my lips and straightened my smock top, which had an annoying habit of riding upwards and revealing my belly button. Then, tossing back my mane of frizz, I tried to stride purposefully forward. I figured that if he heard my footsteps sounding so determined, he wouldn't realise how terrified I was.

He had his door open before I got there. 'Vicky' – he gave a clipped grin – 'what a surprise.'

He made it sound like the worst surprise ever.

I walked into a tiny hall and followed Ed into an average-size sitting room. 'I was just about to go out,' he indicated a guitar standing up against the wall.

'Well, I won't keep you long,' I stammered, still not having a clue what to say.

'What d'you want?'

He was barefoot, I noticed. A pair of navy socks and trainers were sitting on the sofa. His T-shirt was unironed and it had some kind of slogan on it. A pair of faded brown cords completed his 'out-of-work' appearance.

'I, eh, came to see if you'd consider coming back.' I knew the minute the words were out that they were the wrong ones.

'No.' His blue eyes looked kinda like his dad's now.

'Oh.' I bit my lip. 'Well, how about,' I took a huge gulp of air, 'if I, well, if I said that I would *like* you to come back. That as a manager I realise that for the good of the shop you should be working there.'

That sounded good, I thought. Not too grovelling. Not too off-hand.

'And I realise,' Ed said, sitting down on the sofa and beginning to pull on his socks, 'as an employee that for the good of the shop, it's better if I don't come back.'

The smart bastard. I resisted the urge to say that and instead squeaked out, 'But why?'

He began to shove his foot into a trainer and lace it up. 'Let's not do this,' he said, sounding weary. 'We'll only say stuff we regret.'

I winced. 'Look, I'm sorry for what I said about you needing to get a life.'

His only response was a nod.

'Ed, will you stop at your shoes and listen to me!'

He hesitated. Laced up his trainer anyway and, resting his elbows on his knees, faced me.

And of course, the minute I had his attention, I didn't know what I wanted to say. Or what I *should* say. I guessed I should make some sort of an apology. I stared up at the ceiling and observed the progress of a huge spider as he scuttled about making a web. That's what I felt I was trapped in right at that moment.

'I'm all ears,' Ed broke into my thoughts. 'Fire away.'

I wished I could *run* away. Never in my life had I to make an apology to anyone. Maybe that sounds arrogant but I guess I'd just never let myself get into this kind of a situation before. If I wanted to, I could have just walked out. I could have placed all the blame on Ed and I reckoned his dad would go for it, but coward and all as I was, I wasn't that bad. And besides, I didn't want to prove Sal right.

'I'm sorry for what I said to you before you left,' I repeated. 'And, also' – big gulp – 'I'm sorry for not believing you.'

Ed shrugged. 'Ta.'

'So will you come back?'

He looked incredulous. 'Nope.' He sounded as if he might laugh.

'Look, Ed,' I said, 'this wasn't easy for me to come here, you know. I'm doing my best to apologise.'

'Well, apology accepted.' Ed stood up to face me, his trainers now fully laced up. 'But, you know, you've nothing major to apologise for. Basically you were suspicious of me, you checked it out – fine. It's me.' He paused slightly and smiled in such a way that I wanted to touch him. It was so full of regret or something. 'I just can't work where I'm not trusted.' A small shrug before he turned to pick up his guitar.

I stood frozen. I'd honestly thought that he'd come racing back.

'Well.' He signalled the door. 'Let's be off.' He stood waiting for me to move.

'It's not so much that I didn't trust you,' I babbled out. 'I was jealous of you.'

'Huh?'

I could not believe what I'd just admitted to. Jesus, the weirdo label was never going to come off now. Might as well go the whole hog and admit what a pig I was. My face grew all hot and my hands went clammy. He, meanwhile, was gawking at me.

'You're good at the job,' I muttered, minus any admiration. 'I, well, I felt threatened, didn't I? Jesus, if I was your dad, I'd let you run the place.'

'Feck off!' There was a smile in his voice.

I looked cautiously up at him. 'No, I would,' I insisted, gaining courage from his smile. 'To be honest, I wanted you to leave. I can't cope with the competition.'

'Competition?'

Oh God. I was walking right into it now. 'You having such good ideas, you being so friendly with Bridie.' I paused. 'Mainly you being so friendly with Bridie.' I cringed at my honesty. But it was something I had to do, something I had to face up to even if he was going to think I was a sad case.

He was looking at me funny.

'It wasn't personal,' I admitted. 'I reckon no matter who'd started, I'd have resented them.'

'So why'd you come here wanting me back? Surely you're happy now?'

'I was *wrong*,' I gulped out. 'I see that now. It's good you're there. I need you in the shop.'

Now it was his turn to look at the ceiling.

'I just *love* that job, Ed. I didn't want to lose it. I didn't want to lose Bridie. I—' I winced, closed my eyes. 'I guess I find it hard to, I dunno, share. I get possessive about stuff.'

'Like the cheesecake?'

'Forget the cheesecake!' Was that cheesecake going to haunt me?

'So, now, you won't be possessive, is that what you're saying?' Ed asked.

'Yep.'

'Really?' He sounded half amused.

'Yes. Really.'

'So you can turn on and off your emotions, can you?'

He was laughing at me. Suddenly I felt like crying. I had totally humiliated myself and for what? 'I didn't come here to be made fun of.' My voice shook. 'I apologised and did *everything* I was meant to do and now it's up to you.'

'What is?'

'Whether you'll come back.'

'I'm sorry,' Ed said, still smiling a bit. 'I shouldn't have laughed.'

'No you shouldn't.'

'I'll come back on one condition.'

It took a moment to sink in. He was going to come back. 'You will?' A huge whoosh of relief surged through me. Tears sparked my eyes and I had to blink hard. 'Really?'

'Uh-huh.' He winked at me and it made me feel weird. Weird in a nice way. 'I'll come back if we have an afternoon break.'

Jesus!

He was grinning now, his hands shoved into his jeans. 'What d'ya say?'

'Well . . .' I tried to sound disapproving but it didn't quite come off. 'If you think it's a good idea.'

'I do.'

'Fine.' I smiled shakily. 'OK, so.'

'Great. Ta, boss.'

I ignored him calling me boss. 'Sooo – will we see you tomorrow?'

'Aw, no, I'll head in now. Sure Bridie is probably run off her feet.' He grabbed his jacket from a chair and hastily patted his hair down.

I was about to tell him that he couldn't wear that T-shirt in when I stopped myself. I was damn lucky he was going in at all. He could have been a bastard about it and said he'd be back next week. Without thinking, I said, 'Thanks, Ed.'

He paused in the act of zipping up his jacket. Turning around, he studied me, his blue-eyed gaze making me uncomfortable, especially as my belly button was clearly on view. I pulled my top down and straightened my shoulders. To my surprise, he held out his hand. 'No,' he grinned slightly, 'thank *you*. D'you know something – no one has ever apologised to me in my entire life.'

He said it jokingly but there was something in his eyes, something I couldn't quite make out. I took his hand in mine and he grinned. 'Start over?'

'I'd like that.'

We didn't talk much all the way to the dart, each of us busy with our own thoughts. I kept smiling for no apparent reason and perfect strangers kept smiling back. It was a good feeling and I made a few spring resolutions as I walked along, trying to keep up with Ed's long stride. First off, I was never going to get upset about crowds again. Second, I was going to be nice when Mel and Sal were together. And third—

'Hey, tell me about this singing job you have?'

My blood ran cold. 'What?'

'The hotel you said you sing in?' Ed prompted. 'D'you remember you said it when . . . well.' His voice trailed off. He managed a grin. 'During our free exchange of views?'

'Oh, right!' Jesus! 'That!' I hadn't told him I sang in the hotel, I thought. I'd only said that they'd *asked* me to sing. But he'd taken it up the wrong way and now . . .

'Well, go on.'

He looked so interested and encouraging. He'd think I was a real saddo if I admitted that I'd only blurted it out to make it seem like I had a life. Not that I felt I needed a life or anything, but I just thought that being a singer would make me more interesting to Ed. Make him respect me. And it had. I flirted with the idea of lying and telling him that I'd had to give it up due to a madly busy social life, but well, I'd promised him that this would be a new start. And besides, he was bound to mention it to Sal and that'd be even worse.

'I didn't say that I actually *sang* there,' I began, trying not to cringe in humiliation yet again. 'I only said that I'd been *asked* to sing.'

'Oh.' He looked surprised. 'I thought—' Pause. 'So why *don't* you sing there?'

I couldn't admit that it wasn't *actually* the hotel itself that had asked me, that would sound too pathetic for words. So I tossed my hair back, pulled my top down over my belly button again and muttered some rubbish about being too shy to perform in public.

'You should come busking with me sometime,' Ed grinned. 'That'd cure you.'

'You wouldn't want that,' I said. 'Sure I'd outclass you.'

'Ohhhhh!'

We smiled at each other.

It felt good.

And it had only been a *teensy* lie.

Chapter Thirty-nine

I WAS IN good form when I finally got back to the flat. Collecting the post, I found a brown envelope addressed to me. Opening it, I found a blue envelope addressed to the Adoption Board. I recognised the envelope, the handwriting and the postmark. My mother lived in Limerick somewhere. She used blue envelopes and her handwriting was slanted and uneven.

Somehow I knew this letter was going to fill in a piece of me. But I didn't rip it open like I thought I would. In fact, it took me ages to pluck up the courage to read it.

Dear Vicky,

Can I say 'dear'? You called me 'dear' in your letter and it was wonderful. I have read and re-read that letter so many times now that I was almost afraid to write back in case somehow by writing I'd break the spell or say something wrong and make you dislike me. I don't want to frighten you off by appearing needy or emotional but yes, I do want to meet you. I want to meet you very much only I'm not sure if it's too soon at the moment. I don't know how I'll be with you and I so much want to create a good impression.

Can you understand that?

You asked for some background information and I'd really like to tell it to you face to face. Maybe it'd be better that way. But since you asked, you were born three weeks early after twenty-four hours of labour. You were the tiniest baby the nurses said they'd ever seen.

Five pounds exactly. All red and wrinkly with blonde-red hair. Have you still got that colour hair? I used to be red too, you see. I remember looking at you and praying that one day we'd meet again.

I gave you up at three months. They told me they had a lovely couple to take you. A lovely couple. I clung on to those words for years. A lovely couple.

Three months with you was not a long time. I mean, what is a few months of you compared to twenty-eight years of your life? In that time, I experienced more emotion than I have ever felt before or since. I loved you, Vicky. I really did, but I couldn't keep you. I remember holding you and kissing you and talking to you. Trying to explain why I had to do what I had to do. Babbling it all out. And I remember you looked up at me with these blue eyes and I felt you knew. At least that's what I told myself. Then they took you from me. And I tried to be good about it. I didn't want to upset you, you see. I kept wondering if I'd cried more or screamed more would they have brought you back to me? Would we have been in each other's lives? But I didn't cry. Not at all. When you were gone, it was as if I was empty. As if someone had died only worse. There was no body, no visible wounds to mourn, just me the same as I had been for nineteen years. My arms ached to hold you.

They ached.

I think I've been crying inside every day since.

Hearing from you has been the best thing to happen to me. You are alive. You are out there.

I want you to have this. I've had it for the last twenty-eight years and parting with it is painful but everyone should have something of their past and this is yours.

Yours, Barbara

A small picture, faded badly, with the inscription *Baby* and my date of birth. The photo was of a tiny baby peering out from the folds of a white blanket. Red-blonde hair stood up in spikes from my head and, I have to say, I looked truly awful. But then again, I'd just spent twenty-four hours descending down a birth canal.

I stared for ages at the picture, trying to come to terms with the fact that it was me. This was my first baby photo, probably taken an hour after I was born. But I felt nothing, only a curiosity as to who had taken the photo and who had held the baby for the photo. Were the hands, slightly visible, my mother's hands or the hands of some nurse? At the back of my head, I wondered how any mother could walk away from something so defenceless.

But looking at the red face and the horrible hair, maybe it wasn't so hard.

Chapter Forty

BRIDIE DECIDED THAT it would be lovely, in the spirit of reconciliation, if the three of us went out for a drink to celebrate Ed's arrival back in the shop. To be honest, I felt a bit stupid celebrating but I was never one to pass up the offer of a night in the pub. I think Ed felt the same way. 'Just let's go for a drink,' he said to Bridie. 'For no other reason than we all like working together.' He grinned over at me and I flushed.

Whenever I thought of what I'd admitted to him in his flat, I cringed.

Bridie clapped her hands. 'Oooh, yes, yes, that's a *nice* reason.'

I tried to stifle my jealousy as she smiled blindly up at him.

I wondered if he had that effect on all women. Certainly Dominic's mother had been thrilled to see him. 'Aw, Jaysus,' she declared, 'you're like all men, just when we're all used to doing without, back you come.'

Ed laughed.

'Domo has something for you,' the woman said then.

Dominic, smiling shyly, had presented Ed with a hand-drawn card as a welcome-back present and Ed positioned it on the shelf behind the counter. *Welcum back Ed from Dominic and Sylvia.*

The next day, Ed solemnly handed Dominic a voucher for McDonald's. 'I know we were meant to tidy the jigsaw shelves and I'm sorry I left you on your own to do it.'

'Vicky helped,' Dominic said, turning the voucher over and over in his hands.

'It's for McDonald's,' Ed said gently, nudging him. Then,

turning to Sylvia, he said, 'You can order a meal there. I hear they're giving away Action Man meals this week.'

Bridie and I held our breath wondering what she'd do.

She folded her arms and studied Ed. Her big earrings jangled as she cocked her head to one side. 'He *was* dead upset,' she said accusingly. 'So, yeah, I think you do owe him one. And he loves McDonald's.' Without saying another word, she pulled Dominic by the arm and hauled him from the shop.

Huh, I thought, if I'd given them a voucher for McDonald's, she'd have told me to shove it. How the hell had Ed managed it?

So, while they went to McDonald's, Ed, Bridie and I headed to the local.

I hadn't dressed up for the night out – I wore a pair of denim dungarees with a wine-coloured top. My hair hung loose around my face and I'd put on the tiniest bit of lipstick, mainly because my lips were chapped. Ed, on the other hand, *had* made an effort, wearing a dark pair of Levi's and a loose blue check shirt. He'd even abandoned the orange jacket in favour of the nice leather one he wore when he was seeing Sal. Bridie wore a black sequinned top and black trousers – slightly dressy for the pub but really lovely on her. She'd scooped her wispy brown hair into an elegant bun and was radiating happiness as she chose a seat for us right at the back of the bar.

'Isn't this a nice change?' she asked, patting the seat for me to sit down. 'The three of us in here instead of all going our separate ways?'

'It's a change all right,' I said brightly, plonking myself in beside her. 'But I'm warning you, Bridie, don't go getting me too drunk – remember what happened at Christmas!'

She laughed. 'That was no one's fault but your own, miss.'

At Ed's questioning look, Bridie said, 'Vicky and I went to see Joe Dolan and—'

'Joe Dolan?' He smirked at me. 'Really?'

'It was my Christmas present to Bridie,' I informed him

quickly. It was bad enough everyone thinking I liked Boy Five without being classed as a Joe Dolan fan.

'So what happened? Did you go mad and throw your knickers up at him?'

'Oh, Ed!' Bridie went into a fit of giggles and flapped at him with her hand. 'Nothing like that. Vicky just drank a little too much and well . . .' She paused and looked uncomfortably at me.

'Bridie had to escort me home,' I finished.

Ed grinned. 'Aw, sure, I'd get drunk too if I went to see Joe Dolan.'

'Would you?'

'Yeah, it'd make it easier to forget.'

I spluttered out a laugh.

'Oh now, that's *awful*,' Bridie said indignantly. Then she recited her Joe Dolan mantra, the one all the brainwashed fans delivered: 'There's no show like a Joe Show.'

'He's a right show all right,' I giggled.

'Oooh.' Bridie glared at me and at Ed, who'd started to grin. 'You young people have no taste.'

'And you old people can't hear properly, isn't that right, Vicky?'

I laughed. He smiled at me. Then he began to laugh.

And Bridie pretended to look disgusted and we laughed harder.

And it suddenly dawned on me that for the first time, it was Ed and *me* laughing together. *Him* and *me*, the way it had been Bridie and him. And it had been so easy.

And it wasn't because we didn't like Bridie or that we didn't want to include her, it was just fun.

Just fun.

Oooh, Jesus!

How on *earth* could I have accused him of trying to get Bridie onside by having a joke with her? Oooh, how could I have done that? My laughter dried up abruptly as I felt my face go a roaring

puce red. I couldn't look at him. I couldn't look at either c
them. What must he *think* of me?

Jesus.

My sudden descent from laughter to rampant embarrass
ment wrong-footed him. I think he thought he'd done some
thing else wrong. I think Bridie thought so too. He stoo
abruptly up from the table, the laughter fading from his eyes
'Drink, anyone?'

'I'll get this.' I hauled myself up from my seat. I couldn't ge
away from them fast enough. 'I'm the boss.'

'And I asked first,' Ed said firmly. 'Now?' he turned to Bridie

'A glass of red wine, please.'

'Vicky?'

I didn't like the way he'd taken over the situation. I was th
boss. 'No, I'll get this,' I said again.

'You can get the next one.' He sounded a bit narky. 'Now?'
He stared at me as if daring me to argue.

'A pint of Guinness,' I muttered with a bad grace. I was awar
of Bridie looking anxiously at us, so I added in a 'please'.

'Great.' In silence, Bridie and I watched him walk toward
the bar.

I picked up a beer mat and began to peel it apart piece b
piece. It's a habit I have and it annoys the shit out of Sal when
ever we go anywhere. I began to put the little torn pieces int
the ashtray on the table. I couldn't face Bridie. Jesus, I coul
hardly face myself.

'He's a nice boy,' she said suddenly.

I glanced up from my beer mat. 'Who? Ed?'

'Of course Ed,' she said sternly. She held my gaze for a bi
before adding, 'I don't know what the problem is between th
two of you but I hope it'll clear itself up.'

I went even redder and, because I was embarrassed, I snappe
out, 'Isn't he back working?'

'For the moment.'

More silence. I don't know what she wanted me to say

Anyway, I was the boss and it wasn't right to discuss Ed with her. And I couldn't have, anyway.

'You're such a lovely girl, Vicky,' Bridie went on, her voice soft, 'but since Ed's arrived, you've changed.'

I shrugged. Tore the beer mat into tinier pieces.

'I can't be in the middle all the time, Vicky. I like him and I like you and it makes me sad that you both don't get on.'

I made a face.

'I had hoped that tonight would build a bridge.'

'I'm not an architect, Bridie.'

'Now that's just playing with words.' She sounded annoyed. 'You know what I mean.'

It was meant to have been a joke. 'Look,' I said, 'once he sells toys, we'll get on fine.' She didn't seem impressed. 'Haven't we just been laughing together? Haven't we done well this week?'

She sighed and suddenly looked old. She gazed at her tiny birdlike hands and shook her head. 'Oh, Vicky . . .' Her voice trailed off.

She sounded sad and worried and it struck me that she'd probably been worrying about things since the fight, if not longer. And it was my fault that she'd had to do that. My fault because I was a weird wreck of a person. I tentatively touched her shoulder. 'Things will be fine, Bridie.' I gave her a gentle squeeze. 'I promise. Honestly, Ed and I have sorted it. Don't worry – OK?'

'Who's worrying?' Ed startled us as he arrived back. He put his pint of lager down and handed Bridie her wine. 'Well?'

I went red again. I stared at the table.

'Where's Vicky's drink?' Bridie, to my enormous relief, deftly changed the subject.

'I've to get it now. It's not settled yet.'

'Oh, right.'

He stood for a second as if he was waiting for an answer to his previous question.

Both Bridie and I looked blankly at him.

'Drink?' Bridie prompted.

'Oh, yeah. Right.'

We watched him leave.

Bridie and I regarded each other. I smiled awkwardly at he

'I know you think I don't notice things, Vicky, but I do Bridie's voice trembled and she put a hand to her bun and patte it anxiously. 'So far I've kept quiet about it, but please, give hin a break. I think he needs one.'

'He needs a break?'

'Yes. I mean, I think so.' She shrugged. 'I don't know. I jus get the feeling . . .' Her voice trailed off as Ed arrived back wit a lovely creamy Guinness for me.

'There you are, boss.' He placed it on the table, eyeing th decimated beer mat with amusement. 'Sign of nerves, that,' h grinned.

'Yeah, and why wouldn't I be?' I made a humongous effor to grin back. 'I mean, you have never been on the tear wit Bridie, have you?'

Bridie laughed and looked gratefully at me. Ed laughed toc his blue eyes crinkling up and shining a brilliant blue. 'Sound promising,' he said, lifting his pint to his lips.

'Cheers.'

'Cheers.'

'Cheers.'

I bought the next round, Bridie bought the next and soon it wa Ed's turn again. And then mine. And then Bridie's. My heac was spinning nicely, conversation was coming in witty bursts anc already we'd moved from the general to the personal. We wer on the subject of families and relationships. Bridie had just tolc us that she'd never wanted to marry ever since her first love hac died in a car accident. 'I couldn't bear to be hurt like that again, she told us as she ran her finger along the stem of her empt wine glass. 'But sometimes, sometimes, I regret it.'

'Yeah?' Ed, who'd managed thus far to get more informatio

out of her in four hours than I had in the best part of a year, asked, 'Why so?'

'Well, I'm on my own now,' Bridie confessed. 'And it gets lonely.'

We didn't know what to say to that.

'I mean, if I'd taken a chance and fallen in love again maybe I'd be married with children.' Pause. Sniff. 'Oh, I do like children.' She gave us a wobbly smile before standing unsteadily up. 'Now, Guinness again, Vicky? Ed – Carlsberg?'

As we nodded, she wandered off, zigzagging slightly.

'She's had a lot to drink,' Ed observed.

'Too much,' I muttered. 'She'll die when she realises all she's said.'

'Naw, she won't,' Ed shrugged. 'She wants us to know. Anyone that says personal stuff, even if they're drunk, they *want* people to know.'

'Want people to know that you're lonely?' I shook my head. 'Don't think so.'

He shrugged, drank some more.

'I'll tell you something,' I said, jabbing my finger the way I always do when I'm drunk and need to make a point. 'I wouldn't tell *anyone anything* no matter how drunk I was.'

'You wouldn't tell anyone anyway,' Ed replied. 'You're like me.'

Now there was an insult. I sniggered loudly. 'I'm not a *bit* like you!'

He looked me up and down. 'Well, it's true you're not dynamic or sexy or that but—'

'Ha bloody ha!' I raised my eyes to heaven and for some reason my head went down and belted itself off the table. 'Jesus.'

Ed gave a guffaw.

'What?' I knew that even though I couldn't feel the pain, I was going to have a huge bruise in the morning.

'You're nice when you're drunk,' he said.

'*You're* nice when I'm drunk,' I said back.

He laughed again.

I drained my pint and sat back in the seat, waiting for Bridie to return. Ed smiled in a drunken lazy way at me. 'This hasn't turned out to be a bad night,' he remarked.

'Yeah, it's been OK.'

'Well, I wouldn't go that far.'

I sneered at him. He'd been making smart arse comments all night. We both were. It avoided any real serious conversations.

'Here we are!' Bridie was back. She put Ed's drink in front of him. 'I'm just getting yours now, Vicky.'

'Ta.'

She left. 'Poor Bridie,' I said mournfully as I watched her jostle her way back to the bar. 'I never realised she was lonely before. But I suppose, if I'd thought about it, I should have known. I mean she doesn't even have a *family*.'

'So?'

'Well, with a family, at least you can visit them and see them and stuff. Even if you don't want to, at least they're there.'

Ed rolled his eyes and sniggered. 'That doesn't mean *anything*.' He leaned towards me and I could smell a sort of yummy aftershave smell from him. 'I mean, just think, right, if you don't get on with your folks, well, that'd be even lonelier, wouldn't it?' He sat back and folded his arms and regarded me.

He had a point. 'Mmm.' Pause. 'Or if they weren't really your folks, say if you were adopted, that'd be lonely too, I guess.'

He looked surprised. Nodded after a bit. 'Suppose.'

'But it's not something I've ever thought about until tonight,' I said hastily.

'Oh, right. Aye.'

Silence.

'Families are strange, aren't they?' I said then, more to break the silence than anything.

'Aye,' he agreed.

Silence.

'How many in yours? I mean, Bridie and I only ever thought there was one until you arrived in the shop.'

He flinched at my words. 'That's what everyone thinks.' Pause. 'There's just me and Al.' He grinned crookedly at me and traced the condensation on his glass with his finger. 'Like I said before – I'm the one they don't talk about.'

'Oh, I'm sure they—'

'It's not like a big major secret,' he interrupted. 'Half of Ireland knows my brother is the golden boy. The toy boy, that's what his wife calls him.'

'That's pretty lame.'

'Yeah, don't you think so?'

'I do. Yeah.'

He grinned and then looked a bit sad. Or so I thought.

'You're better-looking than him,' I said without thinking. 'Me and Sal saw your brother in a magazine and he's . . .' I stopped. Gulped. 'Well, you're just nicer-looking.'

'Your pity is dead touching.'

'Oh no, it wasn't . . .' Me and my big drunken mouth.

'I've given my dad a lot of grief, that's why,' Ed interrupted me. 'Piles of grief. But anyway, he paid me back.'

'How?' I wasn't sure I wanted to hear this.

'Only gets me a job in one of his bloody toy shops.'

'Hilarious.'

Ed grinned and lifted his pint. 'Cheers.'

He'd been telling the truth, though, I thought as I watched him down his pint. He really didn't get on with his dad. The idea fascinated me. Me, who'd been suffocated with love all my life. I didn't know what it was like to fight. 'What sort of grief?' I asked.

'Just . . .' He stopped. 'The usual.'

As if that explained everything.

'Like leaving all your jobs and courses and stuff?'

'Uh-huh.'

'Why'd you leave med school anyway? Had you only started?'

He stared into his glass. 'Nope. I'd qualified.'

'So you could have been a doctor?' I was impressed. I'd known he was bright – hadn't I?

'Yep.' He smiled suddenly. 'Scary, huh?'

'Stupid, more like,' I said, with a big exaggerated shake of my head. 'I think it must be brilliant to be a doctor.'

'Yeah, well.' Ed gulped. 'Wasn't for me.'

It was making him uncomfortable, this whole conversation. Drunk as I was, I realised it. 'I gave my folks a lot of grief too,' I said then, in an attempt to cheer him up. 'They still love me to suffocation point.'

He smiled.

'I mean, if I set off a nuclear bomb they'd say something like, "Oh well, the world was overpopulated anyhow."'

Ed guffawed.

'And then they'd worry in case I'd broken a nail pressing the button.'

More laughter. I think he was really drunk.

'And then my mother would offer to file my nails all down to the same size so I'd look good.'

He didn't laugh this time. Instead he remarked softly, 'Must be nice.'

I shrugged.

He hadn't a clue.

The night ended with Bridie getting into a taxi with Ed. He'd offered to see her home, though I doubt if he knew where his own place was, let alone hers. I caught a taxi on my own. I closed my eyes as the taxi driver pulled out from the kerb and smiled to myself.

It had been a good night.

Maybe there was hope for me yet. Maybe I could get used to having a third party in the shop.

Maybe I could begin to move out and make friends.

Maybe.

Chapter Forty-one

LEO WAS WEARING a purple Barney sweatshirt. The sleeves were halfway up his arms and Barney was struggling to cover his belly. His jeans were tatty and his hair was blowing across his face because it was so long. He looked like a kid on one of those TV charity ads.

'Hiya, Vicky.' Marti came abreast of me. I'd been waiting outside the apartment for them. 'Were you waiting long?'

'No.' I still couldn't take my gaze from Leo. Jesus, what was he *like*?

'Are you coming out with us today, Vicky?' Leo asked in his bright voice.

I tore my eyes away from his babyish sweatshirt and managed a smile. 'Yeah, if you don't mind.'

'No,' Leo beamed up at me, a big gap where his front tooth should have been.

'Hey,' I grinned. 'Did you lose a tooth?'

'Nope, it just fell out.'

'And did the tooth fairy come?'

'She forgot.' Leo flushed. 'I dunno why. I left it under my pillow and everything and she didn't come.'

Marti took a fit of coughing. 'I, eh, told him that the tooth fairy is very busy and that sometimes she does forget. He's trying it again tonight, aren't you, bud?'

'Uh-huh.'

'Well, she's a very bold tooth fairy to forget,' I said crossly, glowering at Marti. 'She'll probably give you triple money to make up.'

'Yeah?' Leo looked thrilled.

Marti laughed loudly.

'And just to keep you going,' I said, handing Leo two euro, 'get some sweets from the shop up here.'

Leo pocketed the money, grinning.

'You're spoiling him,' Marti hissed as he let Leo's hand go and Leo scampered ahead of us around the corner to the shop.

'Nope,' I said, 'just trying to buy his affection.'

'Well, you've already done that,' Marti half-grumped. 'The kid thinks you're a bleeding oracle ever since you told him Linda misses him.'

'Which she probably does,' I fired back.

He ignored me.

When we got to the top of the road, we found Leo surrounded by a group of rough-looking kids all chanting 'Baby, baby, baby' and laughing.

'Hey,' Marti shouted, scattering them, 'what the hell is going on here – you lot leave my lad alone, d'yez hear?'

'Big baby!' a stick-thin, freckle-faced kid chanted, sticking his tongue out. 'Crybaby!'

Marti made a run at them and they scarpered.

Leo was crying, big silent tears. I tried to hug him but he pushed me away. 'Hey, hey, bud.' Marti knelt down beside him. 'What happened, hey?'

Leo started to blubber.

'Slow down. Slow down. Tell Daddy.'

He buried his head in Marti's shoulder as sobs shook his little body.

I stood by hopelessly, feeling like a spare part. Marti looked different hugging his kid. I liked the picture the two made.

'I can't understand you, Leo,' Marti said eventually. 'Slow down.'

'Was it the sweatshirt, Leo?' I asked tentatively. I thought I'd heard him say the word 'Barney'.

'Baby clothes,' Leo sobbed. 'I'm *not* a baby.'

Marti looked hopelessly at me.

'His sweatshirt, Marti,' I said. 'They were teasing him over it.'

'Were they?' Marti asked Leo, who nodded.

'The little bastards,' Marti declared. He held Leo at arm's length and said fiercely, 'Don't mind them, son, they're just bastards. They're just jealous that they've no sweatshirts like that.'

'Bastards,' Leo formed the new word on his tongue. 'Bastards.'

I didn't know if Marti was handling this quite right, but then again I wasn't a parent.

'A Barney sweatshirt is a bit babyish for a five-year-old, though, isn't it?' I said in an undertone to Marti. 'I mean, does he still *like* Barney?'

'Barney?' Marti frowned. 'Who the hell is that?'

'The dinosaur on Leo's sweatshirt – he's like the equivalent of David Beckham to three-year-olds.'

'Oh right – well, I guess Leo does like him. D'you like Barney, Leo?'

'Barney is a dinosaur, from our imagination, he's six foot tall, farts and all, and he's got constipation,' Leo sang, wiping his tears away and grinning a bit.

'There you are,' Marti said. 'He *loves* him.'

'That's not the Barney song,' I half-giggled and I warbled the real words.

'Hey!' Marti was impressed. 'You can sing!'

'What I'm saying,' I went on, ignoring him, 'is that Leo's sweatshirt is for babies. Sure, look, it's even too small for him. No wonder those kids teased him.'

'So, you're saying it's all right what those kids did?' Marti glowered at me.

'Bastards,' Leo piped up. 'Not kids.'

'I'm just saying that unless Leo gets some new clothes, he'll keep getting picked on.'

'Well, I just won't put that sweatshirt on him any more,' Marti decided. 'We don't want you looking like a baby, do we, Lee?'

'D'you not think that maybe he could do with some *nicer* clothes?'

'Women!' Marti rolled his eyes. 'All yez think about is clothes.'

'Have you *actually* bought him any new clothes since, you know, Linda left?'

'New clothes?'

'Yeah, you know the things you buy in shops – trousers and shirts and socks and—'

'I know.' Marti began to shuffle from foot to foot. 'I know what clothes are – I'm not stupid.'

'Well?'

'I dunno.' His eyes met mine. 'I dunno.' A pause before he said, half defensively, 'Well, *I* haven't.'

'In almost a year, you haven't bought your son any new clothes?'

A guilty look crept over his face. 'Well, no, no I haven't,' he muttered. 'Jesus, Vic,' he shrugged, 'I never *thought* to. Linda did all that stuff, I just ran bands. I never thought—'

'All his stuff is too small for him, Marti.'

He was silent.

'He needs new clothes.'

'It's just – well, I never *minded* him before – Christ, in the beginning I even forgot that he went to school.' He laughed slightly, then bit his lip. 'I'm doing my best but it's so fucking hard.'

'And what about your mother?'

He winced. 'She's turned into Linda – always on my case.' He ran his hand through his own perfectly styled hair. 'Jesus, I cannot believe that I haven't bought him any clothes.'

'Neither can I.'

He stared at his Docs, shamefaced.

'Well—' I gave him a push, feeling a bit sorry for him. 'At least you know now, before the kids in school pick on him. It's not too late.'

* * *

Marti decided that very day to do as I advised. 'Well, I might as well,' he declared. 'You're with me – you'd know what to buy.'

How he figured that out, I do not know. I'd never bought loads of clothes for a kid before but God, it was great fun. And I was touched that he took my advice. Nobody *ever* took my advice. We bought piles of stuff for Leo. Mad bright T-shirts, Action Man shirts and jeans, wrestler shorts, Simpsons pyjamas, you name the programme, Leo got an outfit to go with it. It was kinda sad though and a bit embarrassing when we got him his new trainers. 'Wow, Dad,' he announced in amazement as he bounced up and down in them, 'these shoes don't hurt my feet.'

Marti looked appalled and started shushing him. Then he threw Leo's old trainers, which were two sizes smaller, into the bin and let him wear his new ones for the rest of the shopping expedition.

We discovered a small barber shop on one of the side streets and both of us decided at the same time that Leo could do with a haircut. I think Marti realised just at that moment that taking care of a kid was pretty much the same as taking care of himself. I left them to it, telling Marti that he needed some quality time with his son, and arranged to meet them in an hour.

I traipsed around the half-empty shops, fantasising about all the cool stuff I'd buy if I had loads of money. I wandered into toy shops and gazed at their displays. I watched mothers watching their children playing. I bought an Action Man for Leo to match some of the clothes that Marti had bought him.

Then I grabbed a cuppa in Roche's Stores and bought one of their huge meringues to eat. I sat, drinking my tea and thinking about how much I'd enjoyed the day. At least Leo had Marti, I thought, as meringue and cream smeared my face. It was nice to have someone belonging to you.

There were quite a few people in Roche's and most of them were eating horrible healthy things. I looked around for another meringue-eater, hoping I wasn't the only one. My eye caught a babyish handsome face topped by streaked multicoloured hair. Cliff caught my eye at the same time and he flushed. He was with another man, older. This guy was dressed in very smart casual clothes. His back was half angled towards me so that I couldn't see him properly, but he seemed engrossed in what he was saying to Cliff. Cliff said something to him and then they both looked over at me. I nodded to both of them and the man nodded back and Cliff, to my surprise, plastered a smile on his face and gave me a reluctant wave. I felt quite pleased. Maybe he was beginning to forgive me. I was half-thinking of joining them when they began to talk once more and I got the feeling that I wouldn't be welcome. And besides, neither of them were eating cakes.

An hour later, I met up with Marti outside the barber's. 'Where's Leo?'

'Just there.' Marti pointed to a kid I hardly recognised, jumping up and down off kerbs a few feet away. I'd have liked to say that Leo's new haircut made him so beautiful as to be entirely unrecognisable but I couldn't. Leo's new haircut made him look like one of those kids that roam the streets at night with about a million penknives in their pockets. His head had been shaved on either side and marching down the middle was a jet-black two-inch-high mohican.

'Hey, Vicky!' Leo bounded up to me. 'Don't I look cool?' He bent his head to give me the full effect of his new look. The Barney sweatshirt jarred so completely with it that I had to stifle a laugh.

'He knew exactly what he wanted,' Marti said proudly. 'And I said to the man, just give the kid what he wants.'

Father and son beamed at me.

I gulped. Jesus.

'Are you allowed to have haircuts like that in school?' I asked.

Leo shrugged. 'Suppose.' He pulled Marti's arm. 'Can we go to a film now, can we? Can we?'

Marti laughed. 'Yep.' He glanced at his watch. 'It won't be on for another couple of hours – what say we head for a meal?'

After my meringue, a meal was the last thing I wanted.

'How about McDonald's?' Marti looked questioningly at me. Then whispered, 'I know kids like that at least.'

I grinned. There was hope for his fathering skills yet.

'Lead on.'

We went to McDonald's, saw the film, which Leo loved, and then Marti dropped me home. 'I'll get the sprog to bed and pick you up in a while,' he promised.

Just before I got out of the car, I handed Leo his Action Man. 'For you.'

'Me?' He took it from me reverently. Examined the box. Looked at me with shining eyes. I flinched. I couldn't get used to his gorgeous face under such a vicious-looking thatch of hair.

'Thanks, Vicky. You're the *nicest* of my daddy's friends.'

'I'll second that,' Marti chortled.

'I'm going to tell my mammy all about you,' Leo said, ripping open the box.

I winced. I couldn't help it – every time he mentioned her, I did it.

Marti caught my hand. He pressed it firmly, as if telling me not to worry about it. 'See you later – all right?'

'Sure.'

With a mad beeping of the horn, father and son drove away.

Chapter Forty-two

THE ALARM WENT off at eight-thirty. Bleep, bleep, bleep, it said. I swear, I have the most irritating alarm clock in the world. Its bleep sounds like a nagging mother or something.

'Fuck's sake!' A hairy arm reached over my barely opened eyes and began fumbling about for the clock. 'I thought Monday was your day off.'

Last night came back to me in a blur of hazy colour. Marti had called back for me at nine and we'd gone for a few drinks and on to a band. Someone he was looking at with a view to managing, apparently. They'd been ear-splitting crap and Marti had agreed. 'More talent in Cliff's fingers,' he'd pronounced loudly to all who were around. Then he'd come back for a nightcap and been so grateful to me for all my help with Leo that I found I couldn't resist him when he took me in his arms and started kissing me. The snogging had turned into snogging in my bedroom which had ended up with us in bed. If I'd thought about sleeping with Marti in advance, I'd never have done it, but the drink and the kissing had somehow blurred my reality. Don't get me wrong, I was as nervous as hell. I hadn't slept with a guy in ages, not since Ron the Ride over eighteen months ago. And after that had happened, Ron and I had gone all pear-shaped. 'I'm nervous,' I'd told Marti, as he was sloppily licking my face.

'Don't be,' he'd whispered. 'Just think, in ten minutes it'll all be over.'

I laughed.

But he was right.

Ten minutes later, I lay there, wet and sticky, while Marti grinned into my face.

'Phew,' he winked, snuggling up to me for a final kiss. 'You're fantastic, Vic.'

Then he turned over and conked out.

I lay awake for ages.

Like I always do.

Marti watched me getting dressed. 'Can't you cancel your appointment?' he asked, his blue eyes looking all sad. 'Tell them you've got pressing business to attend to?' He sniggered a bit at his wit.

'No. I can't.' I smiled at him as I reached over him for my jeans. 'It wouldn't be fair.'

'Awww.' He made a face. 'You don't know what you're missing.'

'I do,' I said, as I pulled on my green socks. 'Didn't you give me a demo last night?'

'Aw, yeah. Wasn't it *sensational?*'

I nodded, not sure if he was joking or not. There was silence as I laced up my shoes.

Then he coughed, sort of nervously, and there was something about it that set alarms bells jangling. 'Eh – Vic?'

'What?'

He was staring at the duvet and picking imaginary bits of fluff off it. His face had gone red and he looked as if he was dying with embarrassment or shame or something.

'What?' I asked again, my mouth dry. He was going to dump me, I thought suddenly. Sleeping with him had been stupid. I didn't know if I could bear to be dumped in my own room by a guy sitting in my own bed. I didn't know if I could bear to be dumped, full stop. 'Well?' I asked again, the sick feeling threatening to swamp me. 'What is it?'

'I, eh, wanted to ask your advice. It's all a bit delicate.'

The word wrong-footed me. '*Delicate?*'

Another uneasy look. Then he lifted himself onto his elbow and said cagily, 'Well, last night, after I dropped Leo home, I had a phone call.'

'And?'

'Well, it was Linda.'

'Uh-huh.' I couldn't even lift the brush to do my hair. The very mention of his wife was like a slap in the face. I mean, I know she existed but I didn't want to have to talk about her.

'Well, you see, she always rings for Leo and I always slam the phone down. Well, I did before I disconnected it. But, after what you said before about letting Leo talk to her and yesterday and stuff, I got to thinking. And well – should I let him *talk* to her?' He gulped and looked appealingly up at me. 'Maybe he should talk to her – don't you think?'

'Sorry?' I'd been prepared for rejection and now I hadn't even a clue about what I was being asked. 'What?'

'Leo,' Marti said. 'D'you think it's all right for him to talk to his mother?'

He wanted to know if he should let Leo talk to Linda. I mean, that was *all*. He wasn't splitting, he wasn't dumping me. He was asking my advice. As if my opinion mattered to him. I felt all warm and funny and tender towards him. 'Of *course* he should.' I knelt down beside him, grasped his hand and held it to my face. He caressed my cheek.

'You think?'

'She's his mother – it's important for her to be in his life.'

'You think so?' He looked doubtful.

Jesus, he had to be the least empathic man on the planet. 'I know so,' I said. 'No kid wants to think their mother just walked out on them. It'd hurt too much.'

'Is that the way you feel?'

I froze.

Marti groaned loudly. 'Awwww, that was awful bleedin' tactless of me. I didn't mean it. I mean, I don't mean that I think your mother walked out on you, I just meant—'

'Forget it!' I dropped his hand and stood up.

'Aw, Vic!'

I studied my reflection in my wardrobe mirror. I began furiously tying my hair back – it looked awful, all knotted and frizzy and wild. Then I scrabbled about in the drawer for some lip balm.

'Sorry.' I heard the bed squeaking behind me. He crossed to where I was standing. He wrapped his arms about me, his naked body pressed against mine. 'I'm a fuckin' jerk.' He kissed the back of my ear.

'I have to go.' I wriggled out of his embrace, which felt claustrophobic somehow. 'There's cereal in the top press over the sink.'

'Vic!'

'Bye now.'

I knew he watched me as I left.

Lucy was sitting at her desk when I arrived. Dressed in a petrol blue trouser suit, she looked far more together than she had two weeks ago. I immediately felt intimidated. Shy almost.

'Vicky.' She gave me a big bright smile and indicated a chair. 'Sit down. It's nice to see you again. How's things been? Any more letters?'

I produced the letter. 'And she gave me this.' I handed Lucy my baby photograph and she made the appropriate sounds of admiration. I knew she was only putting it on – no one could possibly think I looked cute or adorable with my big red hair and round face.

'So' – Lucy handed me back the photo – 'how does all that make you feel?'

'Dunno.'

Silence. I think she was waiting for something more. 'I just don't know,' I said again.

Lucy cocked her head to one side. 'Well,' she began carefully, 'how did you *think* it would make you feel before you initiated contact? How did you *expect* it to be?'

I shrugged. I wasn't good at expressing myself. Never had been. 'Just, just different.' I knew that wasn't a great answer, so I added, 'I thought I'd be, I dunno, *complete* or something, as if' – I bit my lip – 'as if I'd suddenly found something to make me me.' Unexpectedly my eyes filled with tears. 'Me,' I repeated again.

Lucy muttered a 'Jesus' and began rifling through her desk. 'I can never find bloody tissues,' she hissed as she yanked out a drawer. Pens and papers tipped onto the floor.

'I don't need a tissue,' I said, wiping my eyes on the back of my sleeve. 'Honest.'

'What the hell—?' She pulled a battered box out from somewhere and pushed it across to me.

I pulled one out, just to be polite, but I wasn't going to cry in front of her.

'Now.' Lucy sat back in her chair and smiled ruefully. 'Now that we're set, what was that you said – that you initiated contact to find your, your roots?'

'Uh-huh.' I began peeling the tissue apart. Two little halves.

'And you thought that this would satisfy you.'

'Everyone needs to know who they are,' I said. 'Where they come from.'

Lucy nodded. 'So how much do you think you need to know?'

'Everything,' I said firmly. 'I want to know it all.'

'And if your birth mother can't supply you with all the facts – what then?'

That was a ridiculous question. 'She had me – she should know.'

Lucy blinked. 'You sound angry.'

I shrugged.

'Does being adopted make you angry, Vicky?'

'No.' I'd answered too fast.

'Really?'

I shrugged again. The tissue was now in pieces on my lap. I had nowhere to put it. I began surreptitiously stuffing it into my pocket.

'Do you think you were abandoned? Unloved? Unwanted?'

Each of those words made me wince. Horrible words. It's what Marti thought. 'I dunno – she says she was sad when she gave me up.'

'And she probably was.'

'But she couldn't have been *that* sad.' I'd voiced it. The thing that haunted me. 'No one does stuff that makes them sad.'

Lucy paused. I could see her wondering what to say. Eventually, she said gently, 'I can't answer for your mother, Vicky. All I know is that I've counselled mothers who've given children up and they've never been the same. Part of them has gone, you see. Just like you feel part of you is missing. At the time, it probably seemed the best option to your mother, but we all do things we regret.'

'It's not like getting pissed on a Saturday night though, is it?'

'No,' Lucy said, sharply. 'It's not.'

The way she said it made me feel ashamed. 'Sorry.'

'Don't be.' She urged me to take another tissue, which I again began to demolish. 'You can't help the way you feel. But it's important to examine this anger before you go meeting your mother or before you say things you regret.'

I said nothing. Examine my anger – what a load of Oprah.

'You want to find your mother but at the same time you're angry at her.'

'Yeah, yeah, I am,' I said back. 'I mean, she didn't come looking for *me*.'

'Maybe she felt she had no right?'

'She didn't!'

Silence.

It went on for ages. When Lucy decided that obviously I wasn't going to contribute anything more, she said, 'So, we've established that you've initiated contact to find out about yourself?'

'Yes.'

'And that you'd like to meet your mother?'

'Yes.'

'And that your mother has thought about you and kept baby photos of you?'

I nodded.

'And that you feel angry towards her?'

I shrugged. 'A bit.'

'Why?'

The anger had never been an issue before. Maybe I'd been too anxious to find her. Maybe that had blotted out the other feelings, but yeah, since I'd got my baby photo, a slow anger had sort of crept into things. But I hadn't known until just that moment why. 'Because I was a baby,' I said. I jabbed the photo, which still lay on Lucy's desk. 'Look. Completely defenceless. And she let me go. Just let me go.'

'To a lovely couple.'

'It could have been *anyone*.'

'But it wasn't.'

'She let me go, she didn't love me enough and she let me go to a couple who were probably so desperate for a child that they'd have loved Satan if they'd been given him.' Now the tears were back. 'I was just someone for them to love. Just something.'

'Isn't that the responsibility of any parent?'

'What?'

'To love unconditionally? To accept what they are given?'

'Then why didn't my *mother*?'

'Maybe she did. Maybe she thought she was doing the best for you.'

'No!'

'Think about it, Vicky.' Her voice was soft, as if my growing hysteria wasn't happening. 'To let someone go is to love them too. To love a stranger as your adopted parents did is a great love.'

'To grow up feeling that everything you have is second-hand – is that great?' I gulped. 'To have *borrowed* parents, a *borrowed* life, a borrowed bloody identity – is that *great*?'

'To have a good life, that's great.'

She didn't understand. No one ever could. Vicky the fucking

weirdo strikes again. I was so angry at myself. So angry at her. 'You've everything off, haven't you?' I stood up and glared at her. 'You're like a bloody priest in confession, all good advice but you don't have a clue. A good life.' I rolled my eyes. 'It's not even *my* life. Not really!' I snatched up the photo from the desk and stuffed it in the envelope. 'I'm going now.'

'Vicky.' Lucy sounded upset. 'Don't. All I'm trying to do is to get you to think about things.'

'And I am.'

'I want any meeting with your mother to be a positive experience for both of you. It's natural to be angry and confused and hurt but is it right to let it colour your life and your future and any possible meeting?'

I paused with my hand on the door. 'It won't.'

She ignored that and went on, 'You've an opportunity now to find out everything you want, you've a chance to meet the woman who brought you into the world, you're so lucky that it was an easy trace – just try to take it easy, try to accept things, try to temper your anger and hurt and use it positively.'

'I'm fine.'

Lucy looked hard at me. So hard that I had to turn away. I heard her patting the arm of her chair. 'Come back for a moment, Vicky – you can go then.'

I didn't like leaving on a row. Slowly I turned around. She smiled at me – a sort of smile that said that she'd seen it all before. She wasn't telling me that she didn't understand or that I was weird. I didn't walk towards her though. I just stood with my arms dangling by my sides, feeling stupid.

'Come here.'

I took a small step in her direction, resenting it.

She continued to stare at me, making me feel like a bold kid. Slowly, I walked back to her. I wasn't going to sit down but she didn't seem inclined to speak unless I did, so I perched on the edge of the chair and tried to look nonchalant.

Still she waited before she spoke.

'Well?' I asked.

She smiled again. 'You're angry – it's OK.'

I said nothing.

'But be aware that you are angry, don't try to hide it. Talk with your adoptive parents – tell them the things you told me.'

Yeah, right, I felt like saying.

'It's surprising how they'll understand.'

It'd be very fucking surprising.

'And write to your birth mother, tell her how confused you are, and even if you don't post it, writing it down will clarify things in your own head – it'll get you accepting the way things are rather than fighting it. You can't afford to ignore these things, Vicky.'

I shrugged.

'And I'm sorry if I upset you.'

She was apologising to *me*. This woman who seemed to know everything was saying sorry to me. I felt I had to acknowledge that. 'It's OK.'

'I'm here to help you, not to send you storming off.'

'It's probably my fault,' I admitted reluctantly. 'I'm a bit sensitive over the whole adoption thing.'

Lucy grinned. 'No!'

I managed a smile.

'Some people are happy being adopted,' Lucy said. 'Others like you, well, they have conflicting emotions over it.'

I bowed my head.

'It's normal enough,' she said then.

I liked being told I was normal.

When I got back to the flat, Marti and Sal had both left. There was a note on the table from Marti. *To the nicest girl in the world – I'm sorry – the jerk.*

I smiled. Marti's writing was large and scrawly and decorative. I ran my fingers over the paper, tracing out the large M of his name. I felt suddenly bad at the way I'd walked out on him that morning. I'd probably over-reacted, just as I had with Lucy. Just as I had been doing all my life at little things that I'd perceived as being directed at me. I was folding the note up and preparing to save it in my 'special things' box when there came a knock on the door.

'These came for you.' Troy spoke from behind a large bunch of flowers. 'You weren't here so I said that I'd give them to you when you came back.'

'For me?'

'Yep.'

'For this flat, you mean,' I said, taking them from him, convinced they were for Sal.

'For this flat,' Troy nodded. 'For you.'

'No!'

'I wouldn't act so surprised.' Troy leaned against the door-frame as I searched for a note on the flowers. 'I mean, if I had money, I'd send you flowers too.'

'Aw, well, it's the thought that counts,' I said, grinning. Then I had the horrible thought that maybe they *were* from him.

'That's what I tell myself,' Troy grinned back. 'And I've thought of bringing you out to the best restaurants in town, taking you to see a film of your choice, driving you in a limo everywhere and necking you senseless at the end of the night.'

The envelope was Sellotaped to the plastic on the front. I was half afraid to open it.

'So, how about it?' Troy said. 'Will those thoughts buy me some Vicky time?'

For yesterday, last night and just in case the note isn't apology enough. Marti. xx

I read it again.

For yesterday, last night and just in case the note isn't apology enough. Marti. xx

'Well?' Troy demanded.

Marti had sent them. *Marti.* I bit my lip and gulped hard. 'Sorry, Troy?'

'Aw, hell, I can see I'll have to think harder thoughts.' He smiled ruefully. 'I dunno, you and Sal, yez play very hard to get.'

'Try lowering your standards,' I joked absently, devouring the note again, the smell of flowers filling my nostrils.

'I have, believe me, I have.'

I made a half-hearted rush at him and he was gone, slamming the door and laughing.

I leaned against the closed door and buried my face in the scented blooms.

I wanted to cry.

I don't know why but I was so deliciously happy and so painfully sad all at the one time.

Chapter Forty-three

'VICKY, LOVE, IT'S MAM.'

Guilt hit me like a freight train. But then guilt followed like a bad smell whenever my parents rang. 'Mam, hi.' I forced a busyness into my voice, as if I was under awful pressure.

'Just rang to see how you are – we haven't heard from you in a few weeks.' I could picture her, settling down at the seat in the hall, all ready for a big chat. 'I said I'd better ring, make sure that you're OK.'

She sounded hoarse, as if she had a cold.

'Have you got a cold?'

'Arragh, nothing that a bit of honey and lemon won't cure. So, how've you been?'

'I'm fine, Mam. It's just, eh, I've been really busy.' More bloody lies. 'You know, with work and everything.' Ed, who was doing a window, shot me an amused glance. Work hadn't been busy, not in weeks, mainly due to the unseasonably good April weather we were having. Ed had decided that all the kids must be outside playing and had no need of 'indoor' toys. As a result, he'd suggested an 'outdoor' window. I'd agreed, only slightly annoyed that I hadn't thought of it myself. We'd decided to erect a mini goalpost in the main window. Ed was slotting it together, his gorgeous backside in full view of any prospective customers.

'Work?' My mother asked.

'Uh-huh.'

'And do you work every weekend?'

'Most of them.'

'Probably because you're the manager,' she stated proudly. 'Well, d'you know something – if you can't come down, sure maybe I'll come up for a day. God knows, I could do with a bit of a break from here. I might get Tommy to run me up some Sunday or Monday. He mainly travels on Monday mornings.'

'You don't need Tommy,' I said. 'Sure the bus will drop you up.'

'Yes, and only get me there in time for lunch,' Mam laughed. 'I want to spend the whole day with my daughter. Isn't Monday your day off?'

'Uh-huh.'

'Well then.' She said it as if it was settled. 'So, any more news?'

'Nope.'

I knew what was coming. 'Have you heard from' – she hesitated – 'from Barbara since?'

What a question to ask me in the middle of work! I turned away from Ed, who was pretending not to listen and making loads of unnecessary noise. 'Just a letter with a photo.'

Mam seemed taken aback at that. 'Of herself?'

I barely got the words out. 'No. Of me.'

'Oh.' I could hear her swallowing hard at the other end of the phone. 'Isn't that nice? I'd like to see that.'

'It's a horrible photo,' I snapped. Why did my mother always think everything was 'nice'?

'Oh now . . .' Her voice trailed off. 'Well, I'd still like to see it,' she said.

'And Dad?' I asked, feeling cruel and horrible and not knowing why. 'Would he?'

'I'm sure anything to do with you would interest him,' Mam said staunchly.

She refused to be upset by me. It had been the same when I was growing up – I'd done everything to hurt them and had never succeeded. Which made the shame and the guilt grow and grow and made me do worse things so they'd punish me and lessen the guilt, but they never did. 'I'll show it to you, so,' I said, 'though it's not worth getting excited about.'

'Vicky—'

'Have to go, Mam, there's someone looking for me.'

Ed, obligingly, called out my name.

'Bye.'

'Bye, love, see you in a couple of weeks.'

I put down the phone and pretended to be busy sorting out money. Eventually, when I couldn't stand the silence any longer, I turned to Ed. He was stringing the nets onto the goalposts. 'Ta.'

He looked up from where he sat, cross-legged, in front of the window. 'I wasn't listening,' he said, 'I just heard you say that you had to go. I do that too.'

'Right.' I didn't need a big story from him.

'D'you want some tea?'

Oh God, he was going to drown me in sympathy. 'I'll get it.'

'Milk, no sugar,' he called out after me.

Chancer!

Marti brought me to dinner that evening. I never normally saw him two days in a row, but he'd rung me to ask if I got the flowers and then told me to shove my glad rags on because he was bringing me to dinner.

'To say sorry and to celebrate Boy Five's new single.'

'Aw, Marti, there's no need. I just over—'

'There's *every* need. And women like going for meals, don't they?' He sounded unsure.

'Yeah, yeah, they do.'

'Well, then, that's settled.'

He hung up.

I couldn't believe that we were heading for a meal. A sort of normal date. And Marti turned up looking normal and he'd even hired a taxi so that we wouldn't be driving about in his Boy Five-mobile. The only thing that was abnormal was that Marti didn't seem to be too comfortable in the restaurant. He kept shifting about in his seat and looking around at everyone.

'What's wrong?' I asked.

'Aw, nothing. I just think it's mad paying to eat. Not my thing.'

'Oh.'

'Like, we could have gone to a music bar for half the price and checked out some new talent. Or down to McCoy's to see that new boy band that Louis Walsh has put together. I hear they're—'

The waiter arrived with our soups.

'Doesn't this look lovely?' I tried to change the subject. Marti was obsessive when he began to talk boy bands.

'Yeah.' Marti barely glanced at his bowl. 'Louis Walsh now, I think—'

I picked up my spoon and began to eat. 'Enjoy.'

There was a moment's silence while I ate and he studied me.

'Rumour has it Louis Walsh's band are bringing out another Garfunkel track.'

'Oh, right.'

'And that the video is really high-budget.'

'Rumour has it that if you don't stop,' I half-joked, 'I'm going and you'll have to sit here on your own.'

'Huh.' He rolled his eyes. 'You remind me of Linda, going on like that.'

'What?' My spoon clattered back into the soup, making it splash onto the linen tablecloth.

'Well,' he half-laughed, 'I just meant that she was always giving out about my musical commitments. I swear, she was as jealous. That's what broke us up in the end.'

'I'm not giving out.'

'Yeah. Yeah, I know.'

There was a tense silence. I cut a roll and began to butter it. I remembered Leo saying that his mother had hated the band.

'Linda, see,' Marti went on, 'she resented my involvement with the music industry – told me I should get a better job – but I didn't. She hated that.'

'Well, maybe she was worried that—'

'Worried my arse.' The venom in his voice surprised me. 'Huh, she wasn't too worried to leave me, was she? I went out to a gig one night, right, and when I came home, she was gone.'

Oh God, I wished he *was* talking about music. People were looking in our direction.

'Marti—'

'And Leo had been dumped over at my mother's for me to pick up—'

I thought his mother lived with him. 'Doesn't your mother—?'

'So, I figured that the best thing I could do, after she left, was to throw myself into promoting Boy Five. You know, to show her that I wasn't just talking shite. She kept telling me I should get a real job but I've shown her, Vic. I've shown her. Boy Five's success is my "up yours" to Linda.'

The waiter was coming over.

'I have to prove to that bitch that I can do it.'

'Sir, if you'll just lower your voice—'

'And another thing' – Marti turned to the waiter – 'she left Leo, that's my son, with me 'cause she thought, right, that I'd go running to her for advice but I haven't. Ha! And she's as mad as hell about that!'

'Well, that's marvellous, sir, but if you don't lower your voice, I'm going to have to ask you to leave.'

'It *is* marvellous,' Marti went on. 'Have you ever tried to bring up a kid on your own?'

'No.' The waiter looked mildly amused.

'It's not easy.' Marti turned to me. 'There's lots of things to remember – isn't there, Vicky?'

I gave a shrug.

'Clothes, tooth fairies, lots of stuff.'

'Can we expect you to lower your voice, sir?'

'What?' He looked around and suddenly seemed to notice people looking. 'Marti Hearty, manager Boy Five,' he announced.

It was met with a blank silence.

'Always say it as much as you can,' he said to me, 'keeps it in people's heads.' He turned to the waiter. 'Sorry.'

The man nodded. 'Just as long as you stay quiet, sir.'

Marti made a face as the guy left. I ignored him and concentrated instead on my shredded bread roll. Crumbs were all over the table.

There was a lot of silence.

'Did I say something?' Marti asked eventually.

Was he serious?

He pouted. 'You're reminding me of Linda again.' He meant it as a joke. When I began crumbling the crumbs between my fingers, he reached across the table and caught my hand. 'Sorry.'

'For what?'

He flushed. 'Aw, Jesus—'

'For what?'

'For, I dunno, being myself.' He lowered his voice and pressed my hand harder. 'Look, I know I'm loud and all but I thought you liked that.'

I shrugged. I didn't like being made to feel like a freak in a perfectly respectable restaurant.

'I'm sorry, Vic.'

'Yeah.'

'I won't talk about music if you don't want me to.'

'Just for tonight or for ever?'

He grinned. 'Awww, don't be like that. I'm mad sorry, right? I really am, and to be honest, with the money I've spent on me band I can't afford to buy you another load of flowers.' Another grin. 'So go easy on me, right?'

I took a quick glance around the restaurant. People seemed to have forgotten about us; they were eating and talking and laughing. Probably at us but maybe not. 'I don't want any more flowers.'

'Good.'

'Just, just let's enjoy the rest of the meal.'

'No problem.'

He bestowed me with his best Marti Hearty smile and made a big deal of slurping up what had to be his freezing soup. 'Lovely.'

It made me smile. 'Make sure you eat it all now.'

And he did.

It was during the main course that I asked him about Leo. 'How's Leo? Has Linda rung since Sunday?'

'Yep.' He stabbed a chip. '*She*,' he said it as if he was spitting, 'rang this evening, before I went out and before *she* had a chance to do all that crying and stuff, I put Leo on.'

'That was good.'

'Well—' Marti made a face. 'The poor kid cried. And when I took the phone off him, she was crying. And then me mother said it was good what I'd done and she cried.' He looked in bewilderment at me. 'It was a fucking nightmare.'

Despite myself I giggled. 'And how's Leo now?'

'Happier,' he said. Stopped. 'Well – he's happier but sadder too. I dunno.' He shook his head. Winced. 'Can't we talk about something else?'

Marti was like me in that way. I felt sorry for him. 'As long as it's not music.'

He groaned.

'How about Boy Five?'

It took him a moment to get the joke and when he did, he flung a chip at me. So I flung one back at him.

And our 'normal' date ended up with us being asked to leave.

But I laughed. Sometimes it was good to be yourself.

Chapter Forty-four

MEL AND LORCAN arrived in their usual flurried state on Thursday evening. 'Hiiiii,' Mel breezed in, blowing air-kisses in my direction and almost knocking me out with whatever scent she'd sprayed on herself.

'Love the perfume,' Sal cooed.

'Lor-can.' Mel looked fondly at her boyfriend.

He smiled in his smug way. 'It's the new brand from Chanel, I was fortunate enough to be able to get a – what would you say – a pre-smell.'

Mel tittered and Sal gave a strained smile.

I flicked on the television.

'I can't wait to see this new boyfriend,' Mel said, sounding like a giddy kid. 'I hope he's as *gorgeous* as you promised.'

'He is,' Sal said back in an equally childish voice.

'Ed?' I said, surprised.

'Well of course Ed.' Sal rolled her eyes. 'Who else would you expect?'

'Ed's going out with you lot?' Somehow I just couldn't see it. I mean, Mel was fine in an acquired-taste sort of way, Lorcan was a complete poseur and Ed, well, Ed was . . . I tried to think . . . Ed was too straight for their company. I just couldn't see him laughing at Lorcan's jokes or sipping coloured cocktails from big blue glasses the way Sal and I did when we went out with them. Ed would think it a load of pretentious crap and he'd be right.

As if in answer, the door buzzed.

'That'll be him now.' Sal ran lightly to the door, her tiny feet encased in an impossibly high pair of black stilettos. Wherever they were going it was posh.

'So' – Lorcan sat in beside me – 'what are you up to this evening, Vicky?'

'Aw, nothing, just catching up on a few of the soaps.'

'I hate television,' Lorcan said, affecting an American accent. 'I hate it as much as peanuts. But I can't stop eating peanuts.'

Mel laughed loudly.

'Orson Welles,' Lorcan said.

'So why eat peanuts?' I asked. 'I mean, if he hated them and all?'

Lorcan blushed.

'Maybe he hated the idea of eating them,' Mel said sharply. 'I mean, they give you spots, don't they? Maybe the man hated the *idea* of eating them.'

'Just like you hate the idea of eating, eh?' I grinned.

Mel was famous for her liquid lunches. And her grapefruit dinners. Her hips should have been classed as dangerous weapons.

She glared at me, glared at her watch. 'I wanted to be out of here for eight,' she muttered.

From the hallway, there came the sounds of Sal laughing with Ed. In they came and I have to say, whatever about Mel and Sal not being his type of people, he could certainly rise to the big occasion. Dressed in a dark grey suit and black shirt and tie, he looked gorgeous. In fact, it was ridiculous, but I felt a pang at the thoughts that Sal had him for herself. He should have been with someone who really cared about him.

He grinned about, his eyes lighting on me. 'Hey.'

'Hiya.'

We were on much better terms now. Almost a month had passed since the argument and I'd done my best to be nice to him, not just for his sake but also for Bridie's. And the nicer I was, the easier it became. In fact, I nearly got on better with him than Bridie did, mainly because of the afternoon break.

'Well, hello there.' Mel stalked towards him, a catlike creature in a black bodysuit. How on earth would she manage to go to the loo, was all I could think. She was almost purring in pleasure. 'Sal has told us all about you.' She made her voice high and teasing.

Ed didn't seem to notice. 'Aye, and I heard about you and Lorcan from her.' He held out his hand. 'Hiya, Lorcan.'

Lorcan gave his a limp shake. 'Pleasure.'

'Well.' Sal was looking about. 'Will we go? We're heading to Blazes,' she informed me. 'Mel's idea.'

'The hardest place in town to get into,' Mel said airily. 'But hey, the editor of *Tell!* has to eat somewhere.'

'Food comes first, then morals,' Lorcan said. 'Brecht.'

Everyone laughed. Well, Mel and Sal laughed. Ed raised his eyebrows questioningly in my direction. I raised him up my cup of tea. 'Good luck,' I mouthed.

He didn't have it. Luck, I mean. Instead there was a huge row between him and Sal when they came back that night. It woke me up and I lay in bed as she screeched at him and he, after taking all the screeching he could bear, told her calmly to 'find some other idiot to screw with'.

To which she yelled that she'd never even got that far with him.

I covered my ears with the pillow for the rest of it.

But I didn't sleep. All I kept thinking about was how could she row with a guy that had made such an effort to look great so he could go out with her.

God, I hoped she hadn't hurt him too much.

Chapter Forty-five

SAL WAS CALMLY eating her breakfast when I got up the next day. She certainly didn't look as if she'd had her heart broken the night before. In fact she looked so great I reckon she'd been up since five getting herself ready. But maybe it was for show. Sal tended to do that. I, on the other hand, liked the world to know when I felt crap.

'It's OK,' Sal said, without even looking at me, as I stood hesitantly in the door of the bedroom, 'I'm not going to blubber over him.'

'You can if you want,' I said. I poured myself a cuppa and slid into the seat beside her. 'I'm not going to tell him.' I looked sympathetically at her. 'Is it over?'

'Is Peter Maxwell a great journo?'

'What?'

'He owns all the big tabloids!' Sal said impatiently. 'Honestly, Vicky, you're so slow sometimes.'

'And what has he to do with you and Ed?'

'You asked was it over, I answered with – oh forget it!' She bit into a piece of horrible-looking bread. 'Yep, it's over.'

I didn't know what to say. I mean, if she'd been upset or cried, then it would have been a cakewalk. But instead she was scary. I hated her like this. 'I'm sorry,' I ventured.

'Well, I'm not.' She bit another hunk out of her bread. 'And you can bet that he'll be sorry for what he's done. He'll be very sorry.'

'Well, I'm sure he is—'

'I don't mean like that. I mean I'll make him sorry. He's only probably gone and ruined my bloody career, d'you know that?'

'Ed?' I was startled. 'How'd he do that?'

'He made a *show* of me, Vicky. I mean, I'd told him how important Mel and Lorcan were for my career and he just wouldn't go along with it.'

'Go along with what?'

'Aw, you know, humouring them – the stuff we do, laughing at Lorcan's jokes, buttering up Mel. He spent the whole time looking completely bewildered by Lorcan and then' – pause – 'd'you know what he said to Mel?' Without waiting for an answer, she ploughed on, 'He only went and told her that he wasn't attracted to her.'

'No!' My tea spluttered all over the table. 'He didn't!'

'It's not funny.'

'I know,' I said, grinning madly and unable to help myself, 'I know.'

Sal glared at me until my smile died.

Silence.

'So what happened?' I asked meekly. Dear God, I prayed, don't let me laugh.

'Well,' Sal began, eyeballing me, daring me to smile, 'Mel was just being Mel, you know. She was flirting with him, rubbing his arm and doing the usual and he says, really loud' – Sal put on a thick northern accent that sounded vaguely like Ed – '"Mel, I don't know what your game is, but I'm not attracted to you. Now that wee lad over there" – and he points at Lorcan – "he's with you, isn't he?"'

I bit my lip. 'And?'

'Well, Mel glares at him and goes all red. Then she says that of *course* she's with Lorcan and that she *loves* Lorcan and that she's only having a bit of fun and Ed says that it takes two to have fun and he's not having it. And Mel says that if he's not having fun then he should go.'

'Christ!'

'A real dry shite,' Sal spat. 'So then, right, he says fine and then he says to me that we are leaving.' Sal looked back at her half-eaten bread and then up at me. 'Well – what am I meant to do?'

'Go with Ed?'

At her dark look, I amended, 'Stay with Mel?'

'Exactly,' she said grimly. 'Only Ed couldn't believe that I was hanging on. He starts saying that Mel was *not* having fun, that she was making a pass at him and what did I need a mate like that for? Imagine, in front of Mel and everything.'

Sal was getting upset now. I took a chance and put my hand on her arm. 'D'you want some more tea?'

She pushed her cup towards me. 'Strong.'

'Sure.'

While I was boiling the kettle, she continued, 'So I took him aside and I tried to explain to him that I couldn't afford to upset Mel. That I needed a job in her magazine and then' – she shook her head – 'he asked me what the hell I wanted to write for a crappy tabloid for. A – crappy – tabloid. The bloody nerve!'

I doused the teabags into the cups and carried the cups to the table. 'Here.' I shoved the carton of milk towards her.

Her hand shook as she poured milk into her cup. 'And I told him that we couldn't all be *noble* toy shop workers, only I made it sound like a rubbish job.' She sounded proud of that then realised that I was one of the rubbish-job people too. 'Oh, sorry, Vic.'

'We noble people don't take offence.'

'Well *he* did.'

'Maybe because he was almost a doctor,' I remarked.

'My arse he was,' Sal scoffed. 'Where?'

'Dunno – somewhere in London.'

Sal rolled her eyes. 'Anyway, this almost-doctor-cum-toy-shop-worker had the nerve to tell me, *me,* that I was a snobby using cow so I told him,' she gulped, 'to fuck off and then we got thrown out.'

'No!'

'Yeah,' she nodded miserably. 'I'll never get in there again.

And then, of course, he tried to apologise and at the same time make out that Mel had been all over him and that he wasn't into cheating on his girlfriends. So I told him to grow up and recognise flirting when he saw it and he said that it would be better if *I* did. Imagine, *me*? Grow up? He said that friends who did that on each other weren't worth it and that you'd never do that on me.'

'Oh.' I felt a small thrill. He'd actually said something nice about me. 'Oh.'

'So I told him that you wouldn't because you couldn't stand the sight of him.'

My tea went all over the place again. 'What?'

She shook her head defiantly. 'Well, you can't, can you?'

'Sal, you shouldn't have said that.' I stared aghast at her. 'You really shouldn't have.'

'But sure he knows it.'

'No he doesn't!' I stood up from the table. 'You should never have said that. That was *awful*. I can't believe—'

'Yeah. Well.' She bit her lip. 'I was upset, wasn't I? I mean, what will Mel think of me?'

It was always fucking Mel. 'What about what I think of you? Huh? You can't go saying that stuff about me to him.'

'I – was – upset!'

'And now, so am I.'

She continued to glare. I continued to glare. Eventually, she stood up and pushed past me. 'Work,' she said, picking up her laptop. 'Bye.'

I was speechless. I watched her walk to the door, take down her coat from its peg and leave.

The silence in the flat overwhelmed me.

My horror at what she'd said to Ed overwhelmed me.

For the first time I realised that I *could* stand him.

That perhaps I actually liked him.

Which made what she'd said all the worse.

* * *

'Have you and Ed been fighting again?' Bridie asked anxiously as I arrived into the office.

Ed was nowhere to be seen. I unwrapped my scarf and hung it on the back of a chair, before answering. 'No.'

Bridie looked unsure. 'Well, he's in a funny humour. He wouldn't even have a cuppa this morning. Said he had stuff to do in stores.'

'Oh.'

'It's not like him not to want a cup of tea. I mean, he didn't even have a biscuit. Now, for Ed to refuse a biscuit, that's odd. So I thought that maybe you'd rowed again.' She waited, presumably for my confession. When I remained schtum, she said with a sort of accusing voice, 'And now you say that you haven't been fighting.'

'No.' I didn't sound entirely convincing.

'Are you sure that maybe you haven't said something to him to annoy him?'

'I've said nothing.'

'Well, he's not himself. Not himself at all.'

'Good,' I grinned. 'Maybe we'll get on even better then.'

'And it's those sort of comments that cause rows, Vicky,' Bridie said, agitated. 'I wish you could listen to yourself. I don't know about you but I find it impossible to work in a bad atmosphere. I don't know if I can take any more of it. I was just thinking on the way in this morning how well we were all doing. How the shop is a happy little place to—'

'Bridie,' I interrupted her flow and she flinched. 'I'll talk to him, right. I'll see what's wrong.'

'You can't just go talking to him,' Bridie said, exasperated. 'He's hardly going to tell you things, is he? I mean, he likes me and he wouldn't tell me and he's hardly likely to—'

I closed the door on her.

Ed was moving boxes all over the place in stores. He was dusty and dishevelled. He barely glanced at me as I entered. I sat down on a box containing a swing and bided my time. Well, it was more a case of me trying to work out what to say. In the end, I squeaked out a 'Hi'.

He flicked me a glance.

'I hear it's all over with Sal.'

'Yep.' He threw an empty box onto a pile of other empty boxes.

'I'm sorry.'

'I'm not.'

More throwing and moving and shifting.

'Look,' I said, my voice a high squeak, 'she's always different around Mel and Lorcan. She, eh, says lots of stuff she doesn't mean.'

Finally he paused. Hands on hips he regarded me. 'Well she can say it to someone else.' He looked me up and down. 'Now if you've come to plead her case, you can forget it.'

'I haven't come to plead anyone's case.' Jesus, what did he think I was? Fourteen?

'So what *are* you doing here?'

I didn't have the nerve. 'Just, you know—'

'No.' He gave me a hostile look.

'Well, Sal told me that she said something to you last night and, well, I just wanted to clear it up.' My palms began to sweat.

'Sal said a lot of stuff to me last night, most of which would take a tribunal to clear up.'

'Oh.'

'So – what was this thing she said?'

He was staring at me again. Making me uncomfortable. 'Oh—' I waved my hand about. Gulped. 'Well, it was just the thing about me, you know, not being able to stand the sight of you.' God, it sounded awful. I wanted to die.

'Oh that.' He turned his back to me and began working again. 'What about it?'

'Well, it's not true. I mean, I don't think that.'

'Right.'

He was still working away. I don't know what he was hoping

to achieve. Our storerooms were always a mess. 'Just so you know,' I went on, babbling to his back, feeling mortified. 'I do like you. I'd even go so far as to consider you a friend.'

He stopped working and turned to me with a speculative look.

'Of sorts,' I added hastily.

He grinned slightly.

'I, eh, just thought I'd say it in case you, you know, were upset about it.'

'Well, I'm not.' He wiped his hands down the length of his jeans and surveyed the mountain of boxes he'd shoved to one side. 'Boys' stuff,' he said, pointing to the left. 'Girls' stuff,' pointing to the right.

'Handy,' I said, my face burning. Why the fuck had I bothered? Did I honestly think he'd be so upset that he'd disappear to the storeroom? Was I that big-headed to think that my opinion of him mattered to him? 'Well, I'll go get my tea.'

'Yeah, I'll follow you up in about ten minutes. Tell Bridie to stick my name in the pot.'

Trust Bridie to be an alarmist. Jesus, if it weren't for her, I'd never have said anything to him. I'd have been extra-nice just to show him I liked him, but I'd never have humiliated myself like that. 'Make your own bloody tea,' I snapped. 'Bridie's old.'

'Spoken like a true friend,' he shouted after me.

Bastard.

Chapter Forty-six

THE REVIEWS FOR Boy Five's new single were lukewarm.

'That's the Irish media for you,' Marti said as he threw one of the rock mags aside in disgust. 'If I'd made it in England, they'd be bloody afraid to write crap like this.' He picked up the magazine again and rifled through it. 'Yeah, here – look at this.' He jabbed a review and read, 'This group should have been left in the zoo and thrown to the lions.'

'Well, they did praise Cliff's voice.' What they'd actually said was that the high notes Cliff had sung were probably only as a result of the tight zookeeper's outfit he wore in the video. 'In a way,' I amended, seeing the dark look on Marti's face.

'Fuckers,' Marti fumed.

'Well,' Sal said from her corner, 'the job of any journalist is to tell the truth.'

'My fucking arse,' Marti said back.

'Shut up, Sal,' I hissed. Between listening to Marti moaning and Sal bitching about Ed at every opportunity, things were at a huge low. Still, it took my mind off the fact that I'd spent the last few days trying to compose a letter to Barbara. So far, I'd managed a 'Dear Barbara'. Everything else I wanted to say wouldn't come out. Or it came out all wrong. All I wanted to know was who I was but it seemed a bit cold just to demand my history from her. It seemed too scary now to meet her. And that photograph that she'd given me still made me angry. It was shoved right to the back of my sock drawer, way down behind my horrible socks, the ones I never wore but couldn't bear to throw out.

Marti topped up his wine and offered me some more.

'How do the lads feel about the reviews?' I asked, as Marti poured a generous measure for me.

'I dunno if they even understand them,' he said in all seriousness. 'I mean, let's face it, the lot of them are a few notes short of a riff.'

'Marti!' I glanced at Sal. There was no such thing as an 'off-the-record' comment as far as she was concerned. 'You didn't hear that, did you, Sal?'

'I doubt my readers would be interested anyhow.' She held up a huge book with a lurid green and blue scarf on the front. 'The art of knitting, that's the feature piece this week.'

Despite her light tone, I knew she was hurting. Mel and Lorcan had been conspicuous by their absence. I knew she'd rung Mel to apologise, but so far there had been radio silence from the other end.

'It'll get better.'

'Yeah,' she said, 'I really think it will. Jesus, it can't get much worse.' She grinned ruefully.

To be honest, she'd been dead nice ever since the row we'd had over Ed. Okay, she hadn't apologised, but she'd done the next best thing. She'd bought us home a take-away and a bottle of wine. I'd forgive anyone anything for a bottle of wine. Especially a twenty-euro bottle of wine. And just to please her, I'd listened as she'd savaged Ed. Then she'd grilled me on him – wanting me to say horrible things about his other relationships, of which I knew nothing. But I did tell her that his dad didn't seem to like him, which had pleased her. 'Sensible man,' she'd spat and forced me to drink a toast to Albert O'Neill's health.

'And what about me?' Marti asked, poking me in the arm. 'Will it get better for me?'

'Oooh' – I made a face and put on a baby voice – 'yes, yes it will.'

'Right, into the bedroom, so,' Marti joked, clapping his hands together and standing up. 'Excuse us, Sal.'

I pulled him down, giggling. 'Will you stop it!'

A lurid wink. 'I haven't even *started* yet.'

'And you won't be,' I laughed. 'Haven't we to go and collect Leo and bring him out?' We always took Leo out on a Friday night.

Marti suddenly looked embarrassed. He shot a look at Sal. Then he sat back down and gazed at his hands. 'Eh, no, actually.'

'What? Is he sick?'

'Nope.' Marti shot another look at Sal, who was pretending to be engrossed in her history of knitting research. 'He's, eh,' Marti lowered his voice, 'he's gone out with his mother.'

'What?'

'What?'

'I thought you weren't listening,' Marti said crossly to Sal.

'A journalist is always listening,' Sal said back. 'So, what's the story? Did she beg to be allowed to see him or what?'

'Sal!' I glared at her. 'It's Marti's business.' She rolled her eyes.

'So?' I asked Marti. 'How did it happen?'

'I was going to tell you,' Marti muttered. 'I mean, it's no big deal.' He made a face. 'Leo talked to her again last night, like *you* said he should and, well, she asked if she could see him and what the hell could I say? I couldn't disappoint the kid, could I? I mean, I don't want him to think he's after being *abandoned*, do I?'

Was he trying to nail this on me? I didn't mind. I felt quite proud of him actually.

'No.' I gave him a light punch. 'You've done the right thing.'

Behind me Sal snorted but we both ignored her.

'Yeah.' Marti sat back in the chair and nodded vigorously. 'I think so. I mean, you'd want to see how happy Leo was when he saw her. So fucking happy.' He smiled a bit, to himself. 'I'd forgotten the kid could smile like that.'

Sal was now making squeaky violin noises. I mouthed her to 'fuck off' but she kept going.

'And Linda, well, she looked fucking terrible,' Marti said.

I was pleased to hear that.

'She'd lost weight and her face was all pale and her hair all scraggy. She's got hair like yours, lovely and bouncy, but it wasn't lovely and bouncy today.'

Brilliant, I thought.

'And her eyes were red, as though she'd been crying.'

Good.

'And when Leo ran to her, I swear I thought he was going to knock her down. And she held him hard, like as if she was going to strangle him. And she was off crying again and telling him how lovely he was and how she was so sorry and that she loved him and missed him and never stopped thinking about him.'

My mother had written that. But she'd never known me.

'Telling you, Vic, I felt guilty for making her suffer. I bloody did.'

I wanted to say that she'd deserved to suffer but somehow I couldn't. Linda had made a mistake – one that had cost her. And she knew it and was sorry for it. 'You've made her happy now,' I said.

He nodded. 'Yeah. I'm not a man to bear grudges. He's her kid, he should see her. She has her rights.'

And I thought, at that minute, that if Marti could forgive his wife, then I should at least be able to write a letter to my mother. It seemed so simple, the idea of writing to her, forgiving her. I leaned over and planted a little kiss on his cheek. 'Hey' – he was surprised – 'what was that for?'

'For you.' I smiled.

'Excuse me while I puke,' Sal said from behind.

Dear Barbara,

Thanks very much for the photo. It was nice of you to send it and I'm glad you kept it with you all this time. And yeah, I still have the red hair and it's a curse. It frizzes out in the rain and curls up at the ends and I've hated it all my life. I've had it straightened, chopped off and nothing works so I've just had to live with it. I mostly wear it in plaits, just to keep it under control.

I'm sorry you were so upset at giving me up. But if it makes you feel better, whoever told you that I was going to a lovely couple was right. They are lovely. They've been lovely all my life.

Believe me, Barbara, you couldn't have done a nicer thing than to give me to these people. There is no point in beating yourself up over what you did or should have done. In the end, you made what you considered the right decision at the time. That's all that counts.

And I thank you for it.

Vicky

By writing it all down, I felt sort of peaceful. I *did* thank her. For the first time I realised that maybe I had been loved. And like Marti with Linda, I didn't want her to feel bad if I could do something about it.

But still, right at the back of it all was the hole.

The part that I needed to fill.

The part that was my story.

Chapter Forty-seven

MY MOTHER HAD to cancel her visit to Dublin. Dad rang me at eight in the morning to let me know. I swear he'd done it on purpose, knowing that it was my day off.

'Your mother has a cold,' he said, in a clipped voice, 'and she can't come to see you.'

'Oh. Right.' I was taken aback. A cold didn't sound too bad. 'Is she all right?'

'I just told you, Victoria, she has a cold. She can't travel. And anyway' – he sucked in his breath – 'it's you that should be coming to visit her, not the other way around. You haven't been down in months.'

It hadn't been that long. 'I already told Mam, I'm very busy in work.' I was glad he couldn't see me because I went bright red.

'There's always Sunday,' Dad said. 'You don't work on Sundays, do you?'

'Depends.'

'On?'

He was so cold. This was my dad and he was like a stranger. 'Dad,' I stuttered, 'don't be like this, please. I'll come down soon.'

'Well, that would be nice,' he said, still in that horrible voice. 'I think your mother deserves it, don't you?'

'Well, *she's* not the reason I'm staying away.' I could have bitten my tongue out.

He didn't reply.

In a miserable attempt to change the subject, I ventured, 'Has she told you that I have a picture of me as a baby?'

'You didn't even come before all this nonsense started,' he said, ignoring me. 'So don't use it as an excuse.'

He was right, of course.

'So I'll tell your mother you'll be down when it suits, will I?'

'Soon,' I said quietly. Guilt. Guilt. Guilt. The feeling that I was horrible hammered into my head.

'I suppose we should be grateful?'

'No.'

'Well, we'll see you when we see you, I suppose.'

I didn't reply.

He seemed to be waiting for me to say something.

'Yeah,' I muttered.

'Bye now, Victoria.'

I waited until the phone bleeped. Slowly I put down the receiver. I don't think, ever in my life, he'd called me Victoria.

Not ever.

Lucy looked quite grave as I took my seat opposite her. There was something in the way she had her hands clasped on the desk in front of her that set the alarm bells jangling. A file, with my name on it, was on the desk. She'd been writing something down, presumably about me.

'What's up?' I asked. I sounded breathless. I tried a smile. 'Looks dead serious.'

Lucy shrugged and patted my file. 'Well, that all depends on the way you look at it, Vicky. It could be good news or it might confuse you.'

'Oh?'

Pause.

'Well?'

She took her time before speaking. It was as if she was figuring out how to tell me. Her words, when they came, were slow and measured. 'Basically, Vicky, I've had a communication from the Adoption Board. Your mother has been in touch with them and apparently she'd like to see you. She feels ready.'

I wasn't sure I'd heard right. 'Sorry?'

'Your birth mother, Barbara, she wants to meet you.'

Time stopped. I stared at Lucy, not knowing what to say. This was what I'd wanted for years. This was why I'd started the search and yet . . . I didn't feel very much of anything. Not joy, or resolution or completion or . . . anything.

Lucy stared back at me. 'Well,' she asked after what felt like ages, 'how do you feel about that?'

'Dunno.' The file in front of her caught my attention. My name, written in blue marker. Victoria McCarthy. Only it wasn't my name, really. 'Why *now*?'

'She wants to meet you,' Lucy repeated softly. 'She says that at the time the letters seemed a good thing but now, what with knowing you're so close, she doesn't want to waste any more time.' Gentle searching of my face. 'I guess it's a normal enough reaction.'

Normal? How could she be normal? Is giving your baby away normal? I nearly laughed but at the same time I was terrified, as if I was standing at the edge of a huge hole. 'So what happens now?'

'Now it's up to you,' Lucy said. 'It's what you want that matters here.'

But I hadn't figured that out yet. 'I know I did want to meet her,' I muttered. 'It's just that, well, talking to you, I realise how big a deal it is.'

She nodded.

'And, like, I wasn't prepared for some of the stuff I felt or thought.' I leaned across the desk. 'I was just thinking the other day, Lucy, what if, right, she wants more than I want to give? What if she tells me my story and I don't want to see her any more? What then?'

'Is that the way you feel?'

'I don't know!' The words tumbled out of me. 'I don't know! But it could happen, yeah?'

'It's common enough.'

Well, that was reassuring. I liked being told things I felt were common enough. 'And then,' I continued, growing in confidence, 'what if my mam and dad get upset or hurt? What do I do then?'

'Have you not talked to them?' Lucy looked stern. 'I told you last time to talk to them, Vicky.'

'Yeah, well . . .' I shrugged.

'There's no "yeah, well" about it,' Lucy said, sounding cross. 'You *have* to tell them. I mean they know you're searching so what's the problem?'

I hated admitting it. I'd only half admitted it to myself. 'I'm scared,' I said in a small voice. I looked up at her; she had her encouraging face on. It would have been mad funny if it had been on the telly, but in the real world, it made me feel a bit like crying. 'My dad,' I sniffed, 'well, he thinks I'm being stupid. He thinks I should be happy.' I took a deep breath. 'I don't know what he'll say if he thinks I'm meeting her.'

'Oh, Vicky, Vicky, Vicky,' Lucy said as she began her usual rummage for tissues. Not that I was going to cry. In the end, she handed me a piece of A4 paper. 'Sorry. Bloody tissues are a curse to find.'

I took the A4 and scrunched it up. Then I pretended to dab my eyes so that she'd think I was using it.

'Vicky,' Lucy said, after I'd finished my dabbing, 'you *have* to talk to your parents. And even if they don't agree, it's still up to you. It has to be what you want. If you choose not to meet Barbara, it has to be because you don't want to, not because of your dad or mam or anyone else.' A swift smile. 'Understand?'

I nodded. How the hell did I talk to them?

I wondered if I could meet Barbara without telling them. They'd never have to know. But I knew if I did that, I'd probably collapse under the guilt.

And if I upset them, I'd collapse under the guilt too.

But at least I'd have been honest.

'You don't have to decide now,' Lucy went on. 'Take your

time. If it's too soon, wait a while. Don't go rushing into things.'

'Yeah.'

'Now.' She lay back in her chair and regarded me. 'what's this about not knowing what exactly it is you want from Barbara?'

Oh God, I hoped she wouldn't pick up on that. The whole thing made me sound like a selfish cow and I wondered how I could paint myself in a flattering light. 'Well,' I began haltingly, 'I've forgiven her, you know, for giving me up.'

'Forgiven her?' Lucy looked puzzled.

'Well, I'm not as *angry* any more,' I clarified.

'OK,' Lucy smiled. 'Good.'

'But, like, how am I meant to forget that she gave me away? And, like, what if she didn't *have* to give me away? I'll probably resent her for that. And then, I was thinking, what if I met her and just didn't like her?'

Lucy looked a little bemused by all the stuff I'd been thinking. To be honest, I was a bit bemused by all the stuff I'd been thinking myself, but it had all come on me once I'd posted my letter last week. I'd had a feeling that things were hotting up and that there was no going back. I always tend to think deep thoughts when my back hits the wall.

'First off,' Lucy said eventually, 'no one expects you to forget that you were adopted. That's part of you, will always be part of you.'

Yeuch.

'And secondly, if you do feel that you don't want to keep in contact with her, it will hurt her, but it's up to you. And like I said, it has happened before.'

'Really?'

'Really.' She smiled. 'And though it's sad on the mother, she's met her child and that's all some of them want. Just to see their kids, to assure themselves that they are OK. It's a wonderful business when it goes well.'

I guess it probably was.

'And here—' Lucy passed a sheet of paper across the desk.

'I got this from the Adoption Board too. It's your mother's phone number.'

Jesus.

'Of course, if you do decide to ring her, you should really have someone with you – especially the first time. If you like, I can be with you or your parents – it's up to you.'

Everything was up to me. Me, whose biggest decision to date had been how many Barbie dolls to order for the Christmas market. Jesus.

'I'll think about it,' I said.

'Good.' Lucy smiled. 'You're getting good at thinking things out, aren't you?'

And I was, I guess. No more jumping in feet first. No more acting on impulse.

'Thanks to you,' I grinned slightly.

'Ring me anytime with a decision,' Lucy said. 'And I'll see you in a fortnight if you want?'

I nodded.

Just as I was leaving, she added, 'Vicky, remember, you can't do this sort of thing without upsetting other people. You'd be surprised at how much upheaval there will be after contact is made. This sometimes is the easy part.'

Christ!

I got back to the flat and drank a can of lager straight down. It was comforting to feel it shocking itself through my body. After that, I lay down on the sofa and let the room spin for a while.

But at the end, I knew I'd still have to think things out sometime.

And I'd have to talk to Mam and Dad sometime.

And I'd have to meet my birth mother sometime.

I closed my eyes and wondered just where everything was leading.

And I'd never wondered about that before either.

Chapter Forty-eight

All that week I walked around in a complete daze. I thought maybe if I didn't think about the decision I had to make, it would all somehow go away. But it didn't. Despite my best efforts to concentrate on work, on Marti, on the fact that much to Marti's glee his separated wife had thrown a wobbler over her son's haircut, nothing penetrated except the fact that by the next time I met Lucy, I had to have made some sort of a decision. *And* I had to talk to my folks. Every time the thought loomed, my heart would sink and I'd get this awful feeling of dread right in the pit of my stomach.

Marti wasn't a lot of help.

'Meet her?' He looked at me as if I was mental. 'Why would you want to meet her?'

'I already told you,' I said. 'To find out who I am. Who I look like. Why I can sing. Why—'

'Phone her. Get a picture of the auld doll. I'm telling you, I wouldn't want to meet any woman that left me. It's bad enough seeing Linda twice a week.'

'That's a bit different. You don't need her to fill in who you are.'

'Thank Christ!'

He was in great form these days, mainly because Leo was now the manageable boy he used to be. And Leo was like a new kid, all chat and jokes whenever the three of us went anywhere.

It was amazing the difference a mother could make.

'I'd like to meet my mammy if I never met her,' Leo chirped

up from the back seat where he was sloppily eating an ice cream.

'You shouldn't be listening into this,' Marti said crossly. 'You haven't a clue.'

'I do too,' Leo said equally crossly. 'Vicky must miss her mammy. I missed my mammy. We went to the zoo yesterday, Vicky.'

'That was nice,' I said absently.

'And Mammy bought me a donut and Daddy said that she was spoiling me.'

'Now, now,' Marti said quickly, a little too quickly, I thought, 'Vicky doesn't want to be hearing about your trip to the zoo.'

'Did you go too?' I asked. 'Did the three of you go? I thought—'

'I was meant to have a session with Boy Five,' Marti whispered, 'but the kid' – he jerked his head at Leo, as if I wouldn't know who he was talking about – 'begged me to come. What could I do?'

He could have said no, I thought. But if I said it aloud, it would sound really mean.

But Marti and Linda and Leo together at the zoo. It made me uneasy. 'And what did Linda think?' I asked. 'You being there.'

'Don't care.' Marti shrugged nonchalantly. 'I only did it for the kid.'

That sort of made things sound better.

'That's what parents do,' Marti said sagely. 'They look out for their kids.'

'Are you the new parenting oracle?'

He laughed his brash laugh. 'Naw. I'm just saying that any kind of a decent parent puts their kid first.' Pause. 'Did *your* mother?'

'Maybe she did.' I shrugged. 'Anyway, your wife didn't and you've managed to put it behind you.' I smiled sweetly. 'I'm just thinking of following your example.'

He looked chuffed at that. 'Oh, right. OK. Yeah. That sounds reasonable. So, you think you'll meet her then?'

'Maybe.'

After you talk to the folks, a part of my mind reminded me.

I felt sick.

Bridie and Ed agreed that I could take a long weekend. Of course, I felt that I had to explain, only I didn't want to tell them the truth, so in the manner of all liars I completely over-explained. 'I haven't been down in months,' I babbled, going red. 'And my dad is freaking out over it and he thinks I don't want to come down, which is completely untrue.'

They stayed silent.

'Completely,' I said cheerfully. 'As if!' I rolled my eyes and snorted a bit.

'Well' – Bridie glanced at Ed, who was giving his irritating slow smile – 'that's nice. To take time off to visit your parents, I think that's nice.'

'Yeah,' Ed agreed, 'I betcha they'll be made up – imagine, who wouldn't? A whole long weekend with Vicky. Three whole days with Vicky. Seventy-two hours of no one but Vicky. They won't believe their luck.'

Bridie giggled.

'Their *bad* luck,' he added casually.

'Ooh, oooh, Ed.' Bridie wanted to laugh and was afraid to. 'Ohh, Vicky, don't mind him.'

I shrugged. 'Seventy-two hours of no Ed,' I said back. 'That's my good luck.'

He laughed. 'Aw, I'm dead hurt. That's not very *friendly* now, is it?'

Ever since I told him I considered him a friend, he'd been dragging the 'f' word into virtually every conversation we had. '"It takes your enemy and your friend, working together, to hurt you to the heart. The one to slander you and the other to get the news to you."' I paused. 'That's from Mark Twain.'

Bridie and Ed were looking agog at me.

I knew that that saying of Lorcan's would come in useful someday. It was the only one I remembered. 'I am both your enemy and your friend, Ed,' I added pleasantly. 'I'm also your boss, so will you ever clean up aisle three.'

'There's nothing sweeter than a girl with a quick tongue.' Ed saluted me. 'That's from Ed O'Neill's disgusting sayings.'

It was the first time I'd laughed that week.

I don't think Bridie understood it though.

Chapter Forty-nine

I CAUGHT THE bus down on Friday night, hoping that the element of surprise would shock my father into accepting what I had to tell him. Well, not that I'd made a firm decision on it, but if he'd been happier about it, yeah, I think I'd have had the courage to meet Barbara.

And it would take courage, I realised. I mean, there was a chance she mightn't like me either.

Every chance.

I mean, I had red frizzy hair, a small skinny body and no boobs. I sure hope she wasn't looking for a supermodel long lost daughter. And that, I realised, was the really scary thing – I'd been rejected once when I was so young that I didn't remember, but now . . . well, I don't know if I could have taken another rejection from her. Of course Lucy had told me that being put up for adoption wasn't a rejection, it was something done out of love or desperation, but hey, Lucy wasn't the one walking about in my head at night.

Anyway, the bus journey was disaster enough to take my mind off things. The fella sitting beside me fell asleep about ten minutes into the trip and his head buried itself in my shoulder. At first I tried to be charitable about it, but in the end, I got tired of not being able to move so I jerked my shoulder really hard to dislodge him and he ended up tumbling out into the aisle and banging his head.

And I got dirty looks all the way down even though I apologised and everything.

It was a massive relief to get off the bus.

On the plus side, I figured that things couldn't be as bad at home.

It was raining as I trudged up the lane to our house. My weekend bag was getting soaked and I cursed myself for not ringing in advance. Dad would surely have driven to meet me. I hefted my bag onto my shoulder and prepared for the half-mile walk home.

I had gone a couple of yards when I heard a car approaching. Its headlights lit up the road before me and I stepped into the grass verge to avoid it. It went by and then came to a screeching halt. A window was rolled down and a dark head poked out. 'Well, hiya, stranger. No one was expecting you tonight.'

Tommy!

Bloody great.

'Hi, Tommy.'

'Get in.' His head disappeared as he reached across and opened the passenger door for me. He grinned at me as I reluctantly climbed in beside him. 'Jesus, you're soaked.'

'Yeah, rain tends to do that.'

He laughed. 'Well, you're lucky I'm heading up your way tonight – Mam has sent me around with one of her crackpot potions for your mother's flu.'

'Flu?'

'Well, whatever she has. A cold or something.' He turned to look at me. 'Jesus, you should have rung me at work, I'd have given you a lift down. I only came down meself this evening.'

'Devoted son,' I muttered.

'Aw, well,' he said easily, not taking offence, 'the mother gets lonely being on her own. I like to keep an eye on her, you know.' He started the car and we didn't talk again until he pulled to a stop in front of the house.

'Ta.'

'No probs. You hang on there while I get an umbrella from the boot.'

'Don't be stupid, sure I'm wet already.' There was no way I was going to let him do me any more favours. I opened the passenger door and was assaulted by sheets of heavy belting rain. I was drenched in seconds.

Tommy was grinning out at me. 'You can get the umbrella for me, so.'

'In your dreams,' I smirked, slamming the door and running as quickly as I could towards the house.

He followed me and waited while I unlocked the door.

'Who's that?' Dad's voice from the kitchen.

'Me and Vicky,' Tommy shouted. 'I've brought medicine from me mother.'

'Did you say Vicky?' Dad appeared at the kitchen door. He was wiping his hands in a towel. From behind, there drifted the smell of coffee and warmth. He saw me and despite the annoyance I'm sure he was feeling towards me, his face broke into a delighted smile. 'Well, well, well. Hello, stranger.'

'Dad.' I felt suddenly shy. And yep, guilty.

'Come on in, the both of you, it's dreadful out there. Did you come down with Tommy?' He was ushering us into the kitchen, which was deliciously warm due to the range being lit.

'Naw, I picked her up on the road,' Tommy answered, placing a brown bottle onto the table.

'Sure you must be soaked, pet.' Dad looked at me in concern. 'We don't want you catching a cold like your mother, now.'

'Where is Mam?'

'Up in bed asleep, thank God. She was up all night with that auld cough. And the pain in her back.' Dad sighed. 'If she's no better tomorrow, I'm getting the doctor for her.' He looked at me. 'Now, take off that coat and I'll hang it up to dry.' He waited patiently as I divested myself of the coat and then he hung it up over the range on a big hook he'd fixed there years ago.

'So, are ye hungry?' He looked at both of us.

'Starving,' I said, sitting down at the table.

'I'll head on.' Tommy indicated the bottle on the table. 'Mam says a spoonful at night – it'll help her sleep.'

'Right, thanks, Tommy.' Dad began to walk out with him. 'Are you sure you won't have anything?'

'Positive.' Tommy looked back. 'See you, Vic. Maybe you'll call over on Sunday to see us?'

'Maybe,' I said, not meaning it. 'I'll be here until Monday.'

Dad looked as if he'd just won the lottery. 'Well, well, that's marvellous. Marvellous indeed.'

I hoped he still thought so in seventy-two hours' time.

He made me waffles and scrambled eggs. 'There now,' he said, dishing an enormous quantity of eggs onto my plate. 'Eat up, there's plenty more.'

'Where did you learn to make these?' I asked. They weren't brown or burnt and they hadn't even stuck to the saucepan.

'Practice,' he nodded, helping himself to some. 'Your mother taught me and I've just got better and better. Sometimes, I put cheese into them or mix salmon through them. Your mother loves the way I cook them.' He beamed at me. 'I've gone very creative in my old age.'

I grinned. He had indeed. There was a time my father wouldn't have even known how to boil an egg.

'We take turns cooking now. Your mother cooks every second day – well, that's providing there's no emergency with the cattle. But we like to have little competitions to see who makes the most imaginative dinners.'

Seeing as all they ever ate was meat, veg and spuds, I'd say the scope for imagination was limited. They both abhorred sauces and dressings and would only eat boiled potatoes. 'Sounds interesting,' I grinned.

He nodded.

'So,' he asked, 'what brings you down? Was it my telephone call the other week? Was I a bit cranky with you?'

'A bit,' I conceded.

'Well, I'm sorry about that,' he nodded. 'I was just worried about your mother. 'Twas me wouldn't let her travel and she was in a huff with me and words were said and I think I took it out on you.'

'It's OK.'

'But it's great to see you. And we do realise how busy you are with everything.'

I was tempted to tell him there and then, to say that I had news for him, but somehow the words got stuck in my throat. I think it was the happiness on his face that I couldn't bear to spoil. And I wondered if I was prepared to spoil it. Prepared to ruin what I had for a pipe dream.

I didn't know.

Lying in bed that night, as usual completely unable to sleep, I heard Mam coughing in the other room. It was a harsh, unforgiving cough that sounded pretty scary. Every time she coughed, my whole body would tense up until the fit was over.

I lay awake, long after they'd both gone to sleep, and worried. What if Mam was really sick? What would I do then? What would I do without her?

I got up at three and went into the kitchen. Pouring myself a glass of milk I realised how difficult the next few days would be.

I loved these people.

I couldn't hurt them.

Not for all the birth mothers in the world.

Chapter Fifty

I AWOKE FROM the weirdest dream to the sound of a car pulling up outside the house. At first I thought I'd imagined it, that it was part of my dream, because it was still night. My room was dark and there were none of the usual farm sounds that you associate with early morning.

Then came the sound of my parents' bedroom door being opened and I heard Dad announcing that 'he'd' arrived. Next thing, Dad was pounding down the stairs and pulling open our heavy front door. There was something in the urgent way he'd spoken that immediately set my heart pounding. Jumping out of bed, I pulled on my old dressing gown – the one Mam always left hanging on a hook in my room. I was just in time to see Dad leading the doctor up the stairs.

'What's wrong?' I gasped, frozen at the sight of them. 'Is it Mam? Is she all right?'

Dad indicated the bedroom and the doctor went inside.

'It's just a precaution,' Dad said, crossing to me. He put his hand on my shoulder. 'It's just that she's been coughing virtually all night and she says that the pain in her back is getting worse—'

'Is she all right?' I demanded.

'That's why the doctor's here,' he sighed. 'I don't know.'

My dad normally pretended to know everything. He sounded defeated, baffled.

I didn't know what to do. Nausea crawled in my belly.

'She just sounds so bad,' he whispered then. 'It's not right.'

Then, with a quick rub of my shoulder, he disappeared inside the room.

I stood, like the spare part I was, awaiting the verdict.

She had pneumonia. According to the doctor, it was mainly confined to her left lung and that was why she had the pain in her back. He told us there was a danger of the other lung becoming affected and that in his opinion she should be brought to hospital immediately.

At the 'h' word both Dad and I jumped.

The doctor didn't seem to notice. 'I'll ring for an ambulance,' he said, taking out his mobile. He turned to Dad. 'Can you pack her clothes?'

'I'll do it,' I said. Dad wouldn't have had a clue what to pack. He'd put in dirty nightgowns and mortify Mam in front of the whole ward. And besides, I wanted to feel useful.

Dad smiled gratefully. He was as white as a sheet and trembling slightly. I don't think he'd have been much good at anything he was so frightened. 'Thanks,' he said. He stroked Mam's hair back from her forehead and I gulped as he kissed her tenderly on the cheek. Mam caught his hand.

'There's nothing too much wrong with you,' he pretended to scoff. 'Honestly, trying to frighten us like this.'

Mam smiled and almost looked like her old self. I was glad I hadn't seen her last night because I wouldn't have been able to sleep. She had become terribly thin, had deep shadows under her eyes and, for the first time ever, she looked old. Or maybe vulnerable is the right word. And the cough. It sounded bad through two feet of wall but hearing her cough now, in the same room, was scary. Every time she coughed my eyes would fill with tears and I'd think of all the nice things she'd ever done for me. And of all the horrible things I'd done on her.

'I'll go and wait for the ambulance,' Dad said. 'They mightn't know exactly where to come.'

'You're only doing that to make sure they take me away.' Mam said thickly.

Dad laughed.

Dad went with her in the ambulance. My mother, who towered over me and always looked so strong and capable, was suddenly tiny as she was wheeled away. Dad seemed to have withered too.

'There's food in the press,' he said before they left. 'You'll manage.'

'Don't worry about me,' I advised. 'I'll be fine.' I tried to keep my voice steady, though I wanted to cry.

'And ring Julia – get Tommy to drive you in later. He'll be around.'

There was no way I wanted a lift from Tommy. I'd find a way to go without asking him. 'I'll be in around dinnertime,' I promised.

Dad gave me a brief hug and was gone.

I watched the ambulance pull out of our driveway, flick on its siren and go screaming up the road.

Then I went inside, sat down at the table and cried.

The phone never stopped ringing all that morning. If I'd paid a plane to fly over the town with a banner headline about my mother being in hospital, the news wouldn't have travelled as fast. Aunt Julia was on around eleven. I actually think she needed reassurance that her potion was not the cause of my mother's sudden admission to hospital. When I told her that Mam had pneumonia, she seemed relieved. Then worried. Then she asked me how I was managing for lunch.

'Dad said there was food in the press.'

'Food in the press,' she scoffed in the bossy way that I hated. 'With a shock like you've had, you'll need something warm inside you.'

'Maybe,' I conceded, just to keep her quiet. The only warm

thing I had a hope of making with any success was a cup of coffee.

'I'm going to send Tommy around to pick you up and you can have dinner with us.'

'No!' Jesus.

'It's no trouble,' Julia went on, 'and then Tommy can drive you in to visit. I'm sure your poor father could do with some company. The man must be out of his mind.'

'I was going to get a bus.' I did not want to be beholden to Julia. The thought of it made my skin crawl.

'You'll not be getting a bus,' Julia answered sharply. 'Not while we've cars sitting in our driveway. Now, Tommy will be up for you in about' – she had a muttered conversation with Tommy. Then she came back on line – 'about thirty minutes – all right?'

'Honestly, there's no need—'

'There's every need,' Julia said. 'Wouldn't your mother do the same for us? Aren't you family?'

She didn't wait for me to answer and I'm not sure I could have. I was family. She'd said it herself. Even if it wasn't strictly true, it sounded nice.

I held the phone long after she'd hung up.

I showered, dressed and, within the thirty minutes, Tommy was at the front door. I nodded to him and, after locking up, went silently to his car.

'I'm sorry about your mother,' he said after I'd put on my seatbelt. 'I'd no idea she was so bad.'

'No one did,' I muttered, not looking at him.

'Mam has a huge dinner ready for you,' he said, grinning wryly. 'I told her you probably wouldn't be hungry, so don't feel you have to please her by eating it.'

Aunt Julia took it as a personal insult if her food wasn't finished.

I bit my lip.

'I mean, she'll probably badger you about it, but don't mind her.' Another grin. 'I know I don't.'

'Ta.'

He started up the car without saying any more but, for the first time ever, I realised how thoughtful he was.

True enough, Julia tried to force every vegetable under the sun onto my plate. 'Ah, you'll have a bit of cabbage, now, won't you,' she said, shovelling what had to be about two cabbages in front of me. 'Cabbage is full of iron, which is good for shock.'

'She's not hungry, Mam,' Tommy said. 'And if you keep forcing her, she'll be sick.'

'There's nothing wrong with my food.' Julia turned scathing eyes on him. 'She'll not be sick.'

'Honestly' – I pushed my plate away – 'I can't eat it, Julia. I mean, it's lovely and all, but I just want to get to the hospital.'

'Ooooh.' Julia was at my side. 'Of course you do. Of course you do. Tommy,' she barked, 'will you get up off your backside and start up the car. Of course she wants to be with her father and mother. You'll eat something later,' she said, more to reassure herself than me, 'you'll be in the mood for it after a day at the hospital. TOMMY!'

Tommy jumped. 'Yeah, Mam, I'm ready. Vicky?' He looked at me. There was a hint of laughter in his eyes which I couldn't respond to. 'Ready?'

'Sure.' I pulled on my coat, which I'd hung over the back of my chair. 'Thanks, Julia. Sorry I wasn't able to do dinner justice.'

'Once your poor mother is all right, that's all that matters.' Julia indicated her groaning table. 'That's only food. There's more important things in life than eating a dinner.'

'Right.' Tommy jangled his keys. 'I'll give you a ring from the hospital, Mam. Let you know what's happening.'

'Take your time.' Julia patted her son's arm. In a whisper, which I don't think I was meant to hear, she added, 'And look after Vicky. You know how highly sensitive she is.'

Highly sensitive? Me? I was about to say that I wasn't when

Tommy whispered back, 'I know, Ma. I'm not going to say anything to upset her.'

I could feel myself begin to bristle. A smart retort formed in my mind. I was about to snap back that I wasn't easily upset when I realised that I'd just become easily upset.

And that being easily upset didn't matter.

All that mattered was my mother.

Chapter Fifty-one

THE NURSE ON duty looked sharply at Tommy and me as we walked into the ICU. 'Mrs Evelyn McCarthy,' I asked. My voice was trembling, as if I was going to cry. Even saying my mother's name was such a precious thing. 'She's my mother.'

'She's only allowed one visitor at a time,' the nurse said, looking sympathetically at me. 'Your dad is with her at the minute. I'll tell him you're here.' She turned to Tommy. 'Are you her son?'

'Nah.' Tommy had his arm about my shoulders. 'Just a nephew. It's fine, I'll stay out here and wait.'

The nurse nodded and padded off down the corridor in her white shoes.

'You OK?' Tommy asked. 'Want a coffee?'

'Yeah and yeah.' I reached into my bag to drag out some change, but he was gone, after first pointing me to a seat. I sat, looking up and down the spotless corridor, feeling more alone than I ever had in my whole life.

Dad arrived about five minutes later. 'On your own?' he asked, sitting beside me.

'Tommy is gone to get coffee,' I muttered. 'How is she, Dad?'

'They're giving her antibiotics and they've got her on oxygen.' He gulped and stared at his huge hands, which dangled uselessly between his legs. 'It looks scary, but apparently she's improving.' He shook his head. 'Jesus, she's had that damned cough for so long, I should have made her go to the doctor.'

'She wouldn't have gone,' I answered. 'You know Mam.'

'At the back of my mind, I knew it wasn't right to have a cough like that, but I said nothing. I was scared, you see.'

'She's in good hands now.' I didn't know what else to say to him. I'd never seen him like this before. It frightened me.

'I was scared in case I'd find out she was sick.' Dad ignored me. 'I didn't want her to be sick so I paid no attention to it. And now look.'

'It's not your fault.'

He buried his head in his hands. 'If anything happens to her, Vicky, I don't know what I'll do. She's my life, you know that.'

'Oh, Dad.' I touched his hand. Rough and strong. 'Don't.'

'The pair of you are my life. I build everything around the two of you. If I lost one of you, I'd be all over the place.' He gave a huge trembly sigh.

'Well, nothing will happen. Nothing.'

He wrapped his big arm around me and it felt safe and secure.

Dad ended up drinking the appalling coffee Tommy eventually managed to purchase because they let me in to see Mam around four. Apparently she'd just woken up, her temperature was down and she'd asked to speak to me. I don't know if it was my imagination, but she did look better. 'You look better,' I said, cautiously approaching the bed. I had a mask over my face and I felt faintly ridiculous. 'You've some colour in your face.'

'I feel a bit better,' Mam croaked. She made no attempt to get up; she just lay against her snow-white pillows and smiled at me. 'My back isn't so sore.'

'Good.'

Isn't it funny that no matter how well you know someone, it's always hard to make conversation in a hospital? It always strikes me as weird that the sick person is expected to do most of the talking. And so it was with Mam and me. All I'd come in to see was that she was looking better and, satisfied with that, I would have sat there in silence with her. But she wouldn't let me. She asked about work, so I told her about Ed and Bridie. She'd always liked the sound of Ed and hadn't been a bit impressed when she'd heard he was seeing Sal. Now that they were broken up, she was happy.

'Maybe there's a chance for you,' she said slyly.

'Nah.' I flushed. I still hadn't told my folks about Marti being married and I certainly couldn't now. 'I'm still with Marti.'

'Oh.' Mam looked disappointed. 'Well, you certainly talk about Ed enough – ever since he started work you've brought him into conversation.'

'That's because you've asked about work,' I said back, feeling embarrassed. I shoved a smile onto my face. 'He's nice, but that's all.'

Mam nodded, giving her smile that said she didn't believe me. 'And Barbara?' she asked. 'Tell me.'

I gulped. The nurse was busy writing stuff down on Mam's chart. 'Nothing much,' I lied.

Mam eyed me.

'Honest.' I gulped out a very forced-sounding laugh.

'I know you better than you think,' Mam whispered. She closed her eyes. 'She wants to see you, doesn't she?'

I didn't say anything. I couldn't. How did she know?

'If it was me, I would never have bothered with the letters.' Mam's voice was getting softer. 'I would want to see you.'

I still said nothing. I didn't want to upset her.

'Well?' Mam asked.

She was expecting an answer.

'She does,' I muttered. 'But now it doesn't seem so important.'

Her eyes opened, slowly. She pinned me with her stare. 'It is important,' she said, stressing each word. 'If it makes you happy, it *is* important. You see her.'

'But—'

'Me and your dad want you to be happy. And don't worry about him, I'll talk to him.' She began to cough suddenly. The nurse shoved me out of the way. She fiddled around with buttons and switches while I gawped uselessly.

'Out,' she said sternly to me.

'No,' Mam spoke up, quite strongly. 'Just a few seconds more.'

The nurse glared at me as if it was all my fault.

'Maybe I'd better—' I indicated the door.

Mam beckoned me forward. 'I'll talk to Sean,' she said. 'He'll do anything for me now.' A quick smile.

It was the smile that did it. Love rushed up through me like a spring from the earth.

'You're my real mother,' I said earnestly. 'I don't *want* any other.'

Mam smiled. 'But think of her,' she said softly, 'missing out on you.'

Then she lay back and closed her eyes.

And it struck me suddenly what I'd spent my years missing out on. I'd missed out on this woman's love because I'd craved the love of a woman who'd given me away. Visions of Bridie holding on to her dead lover in the face of all others came to me. Now she was lonely and wished she'd moved on. I'd spent my time wanting what everyone else had, a real flesh-and-blood mother. And because someone who was meant to love me had given me away, I'd been reluctant to become involved with the love my mam and dad had to offer. Which had made me guilty. And lonely. And unhappy. And what was it all for? I was like Patrick Kavanagh in 'Raglan Road' with his unrequited love. And I had to stop it.

I had to accept love where I found it.

And it was then that I knew I could meet her.

And I could cope with her rejection.

But if my family objected, then she'd have to cope with mine.

Chapter Fifty-two

THE HOUSE WAS a state. Dad and I had spent almost every minute of the past week in the hospital and as a result there was dirt and dust and dirty clothes all over the place. On Saturday, I volunteered to spend the day tidying up. Mam was improving rapidly and was off the oxygen and I felt safe in missing a visit. I was busy trying to burn a shirt with the iron when the guy from the local flower shop appeared at the front door. He was carrying an enormous bouquet of flowers. 'Evelyn McCarthy?' he asked.

'My mother,' I said, as he handed me the flowers. There were lilies and roses and some purple ones that I didn't know the name of. 'Wow.' I caught a whiff of fragrant lily. 'She'll be thrilled with these.'

'And there's some here for a Vicky McCarthy?' The guy produced a smaller bunch. Twelve white roses tied with a white ribbon.

'Oh,' I smiled delightedly. 'That's me.'

'Can't have the mother getting flowers and not the daughter, eh?' he joked as he left.

I was still smiling as I brought the flowers into the kitchen and laid them carefully on the table. There was an envelope Sellotaped to each bunch and I decided to open the envelope on my mother's flowers first. It was pathetic, I know, but I wanted to enjoy the suspense of who'd sent me my flowers for a little while longer. I guessed they were from Marti because I hadn't heard from him all week, except a rushed phone call on Tuesday when he enquired about Mam.

Mam's flowers were from Bridie and Ed. *Get well soon from*

your daughter's slaves was written in Ed's large scrawl. I smiled, slotting the card back into the envelope. Ed in a flower shop? Bridie must have forced him into it.

Then it was the turn of the roses.

To the boss – we thought you could do with some cheering up yourself – Bridie and Ed.

Bridie and Ed.

'Bridie and Ed,' I mumbled, staring at the roses, trying to hide my disappointment from myself. 'Wasn't that nice.'

I stared again at the card as if somehow I could change the words. Then I muttered a 'fuck him' under my breath and then a 'fucking bastard'. Then I repeated both a bit louder, only stringing them together.

It made me feel a bit better.

'Yo, Toys Galore?'

I bristled. 'Is that any way to answer the phone?' I asked before I could stop myself.

'Hey!' Ed sounded delighted. 'It's Vicky. How about you? Things must be all right with you, seeing as you're finding find fault with me again.'

Despite myself I grinned. He had a point. 'Just rang to thank you for the flowers.'

'Ach, you didn't have to. We paid for them out of the money in the till.'

'What?'

'That was a joke,' he clarified. 'No, you're very welcome. How's yer ma?'

'Much better, thanks. We think she'll be out next week.'

'Aw, great.' Then he bellowed, 'Oy, Bridie, Vicky's ma is getting released next week!'

He made her sound like a mental patient. I hoped there weren't too many customers in.

The phone was taken off him. Bridie's breathless voice wafted down the line. 'Vicky, it's Bridie. How are you, pet?'

I smiled. 'Great, thanks, Bridie. Thanks for the flowers.'

'Not at all. Did your mother like them?'

'Haven't been in yet, but I reckon she will. And you shouldn't have got any for me – honestly – the roses must have cost you a fortune.'

She laughed slightly before replying, 'Not at all, sure they hardly cost anything.' She raised her voice. 'Vicky says thanks for the flowers, Ed!'

'Yeah, I know,' Ed yelled from somewhere in the background.

'She liked the roses,' Bridie called out. She came back to me. 'Well, listen, pet, don't rush back, I've got it all under control here. You take your time.'

'Ta, Bridie.' A sort of wistfulness for work washed over me. I missed them. 'I'll probably be back next week.'

'No rush.'

'Take care.'

'You too.'

'Bye.'

Ed yelled out a 'bye'.

I felt lonely when I hung up.

I felt even lonelier when I turned back to face the ironing.

Tommy and John and a few of the cousins arrived around lunchtime. Tommy had some food from his mother. He handed it to me with an apology. 'Couldn't stop her,' he said. 'She's a mad woman when she makes a stew.'

The others with him laughed.

'Ta.' I took the casserole dish from him and baulked at its weight. 'Jesus, how much did she do?'

'Enough for the lot of us.' Tommy indicated the rest of the cousins. 'We've come to help you clean up.'

'What?' I was stunned. I didn't need their help.

'Well, it's a bloody massive house.' John, without being invited, stepped into the hall. 'We figured you'd need a hand.'

The rest nodded and then at my lack of response looked

anxiously at me. I think they were waiting for me to throw a wobbler. Or do something completely weird like tell them that I would be well able to manage, thank you very much. And I desperately did want to do that. But I knew it wouldn't be very grateful. And to be honest, I hated cleaning. 'I guess I do,' I murmured with a bad grace. 'Come in.'

They didn't need to be told twice.

I guess they thought they were family.

'Just don't go into my room,' I warned. 'That's private.'

John was hoovering. Not very well, but he was doing his best. I wouldn't say he'd ever hoovered in his entire life. He was sitting on the sofa, pushing the hose of the hoover over and back, over and back.

'Great job.' I handed him a cup of coffee.

'Thanks.' He flicked off the hoover and wrapped his big hands around the mug.

'You're all very good to come over,' I babbled. I'd never really had a conversation with this guy. Every time we met, I tended to ignore him. But there was no ignoring him when he had planted his backside on our good sofa.

'It's no bother,' he said. He stared into his mug of coffee.

I made to leave.

'And to be honest, Vicky, I owe you.'

I turned back to face him. He was staring cagily at me, studying me. 'Owe me?'

'Yeah.'

Pause. I wondered if he was talking about . . . but nah, no one remembered stuff like I did. I wasn't going to let him *see* that I remembered.

'I've felt bad ever since that time when I told you you were adopted. You've never really talked to me since.'

'You told me I was ready made,' I snapped back.

He winced. 'Ready made,' he conceded. He was grinning a little at the word.

So much for pretending I didn't remember. 'It wasn't nice.'

'No,' he agreed hastily, flicking me a glance. 'I know it wasn't.' He put his coffee carefully on the floor. Then, biting his lip, he said cautiously, 'At the time I didn't *know* just how horrible; I was only a kid and you wouldn't play with us. We all thought you were stuck up. I only said it to get at you, but it was horrible and like, I'm sorry about that.'

I didn't know what to say. The whole thing had happened years ago. His apology made me feel a bit pathetic – I'd been the one that had borne a grudge for sixteen years against a twelve-year-old kid. Maybe I was the one that should be apologising. Only, I was useless at it. So instead, I stammered out, 'I wasn't really stuck up.'

He quirked his eyebrows.

'I wasn't,' I insisted. Again the sceptical look. 'I was scared of yous,' I admitted. 'You were all so tall and dark, and there was me, small and skinny. I didn't feel I fitted in.'

'All you had to do was play with us. We didn't care what you looked like.'

I startled him with a big 'Ha!' Then said smartly, 'Yeah you did. Tommy always pointed at my hair and yelled "Fire!"'

He tried to turn his snigger into a cough. 'Wow, I'd forgotten that!'

Maybe I should have too. Trying to regain some dignity, I said, 'Well, I haven't.'

'Obviously,' he said dryly. Then, in a gentler voice, he went on, 'Vicky, we were kids. All kids do that.'

'Maybe,' I said. 'But it hurt.' At his shamed look, I felt a bit guilty. 'Still.' I shrugged and tried to sound blasé. 'It was all a long time ago.'

I didn't convince him, let alone myself.

We stared at each other a bit more before I again turned to leave.

'We were jealous – right,' John said, sounding almost defensive. 'If you want to know why we did it – we were jealous.'

'Jealous?' I almost laughed.

'You had it all. We had nothing.'

The simplicity of the statement startled me.

'Here comes Miss Perfect with her perfect parents, we used to say.' There was a hint of bitterness in John's voice, despite his grin.

'Here come all my cousins with their *real* parents, I used to say.'

His grin faded. 'I'm sorry for telling you, Vicky.'

I was suddenly ashamed of the elephant in me that wouldn't allow me to forget things. OK, he'd been a nasty little brat, but I guess, in his eyes, I'd been a stuck-up, have-it-all unfriendly weirdo. And people changed. Well, all except me, it seemed. I gulped, made a Herculean effort to be nice. 'You did me a favour actually.'

'Huh?'

'D'you ever see that Steve Martin film where he's adopted by these black people and he can't sing or dance and, like, he's *white*?'

John began to laugh.

'And it's driving him mad that he can't fit in?'

John laughed harder.

'Well,' I grinned ruefully, 'that was me.'

'Must've been hell.' John was still smiling, though he looked sympathetic.

I shrugged. No worse probably than having an alcoholic father. No, I realised suddenly, it wasn't even in the same *league* as having an alcoholic dad.

'Friends?' John asked.

I liked the sound of that. But I didn't want to make out that I was dying for it or anything. 'Hoover this room properly and I'll think about it.'

'Deal.'

We shook on it.

* * *

The cousins left just before Dad came back from the hospital. It had been the nicest day I'd spent at home in a long time. They'd cleaned, polished and dusted so that the house was gleaming. They told me that if I needed anything just to call them. Tommy told me he'd see me the next day with more food. I waved them off, feeling a sort of happy bubble inside me. A sort of semi-belonging to this crowd of people who'd just invaded the house and seen into every corner of it. Not that I didn't want to repay their kindness sometime. Maybe when one of their parents got sick or . . . Jesus, I shook my head. What was I thinking? I didn't want anyone to be sick. Not anyone. I was just closing the door on Tommy when Dad drove up. He'd come back to see to the cows. A few of the neighbours had done the morning milking but Dad liked to do it in the evening himself. I envied Dad his ability to accept favours from people. He maintained that people felt good when they helped you out so it was a favour to let them.

I dunno if I totally believed that.

'How's my girl?' Dad smiled, half shyly, at me.

'How's Mam?' I asked the question I always did when he came home.

'Much better.' He walked by me into the kitchen, almost singing out, 'She'll be home next week.'

'That's brilliant.'

'Yeah. Yeah, it is.' Dad sat at the table and took off his coat. He slung it haphazardly over a chair and beckoned me forward. He suddenly looked serious. 'Vic, come here.'

I didn't want a heavy conversation. All week I'd been dreading this. Mam had obviously talked to him. 'Tea?' I tried to say lightly.

'No, sit down, Vic.' He patted the table. 'There's something I want to say.'

I stood. 'Yeah?'

'It's about all this business with your—' He stopped, waved his hand about and said quickly, 'The other woman. Your, eh, birth mother.'

'We don't have to talk about this now.'

'We do.' The intensity in his voice surprised me. 'Your mother had a word with me.'

'Yeah and she's sick, so it's emotional blackmail.'

'No.' Dad shook his head. Gulped. 'She's right. She told me some home truths and she's right.'

I stared at him. Again, he indicated a chair. I had no choice – I sat down, my hands clenched together in my lap and a sort of mantra running around my head saying, '*Don't fight, please don't fight.*'

Dad's brown eyes met mine. 'I'm not good at all this chat,' he began, flushing. 'But I guess there comes a time when it's time to say things.'

I nodded, not sure why I was nodding.

'There have only been two important things in my life, Vicky,' Dad went on. 'You and your mother.' Pause. 'And I nearly lost your mother because I was afraid to find out if something was wrong with her.'

He stared at me for a few seconds. I couldn't hold his gaze. My eyes dropped to my dirty nails and red hands.

'I'm not a brave man, Vicky,' he said finally. 'I don't like change. I like things to stay the same. I want your mother to be healthy and you to be here. And, well, you looking for this other woman was a lot of worry for me. It was, if I'm honest, rocking my boat a little too much.'

I stole a look at him. He was chewing his lower lip, a sign that he was agitated. When he continued, his voice shook slightly. 'I was afraid we'd lose you, you hardly came home as it was. I was afraid, *am afraid*,' he clarified, 'of you meeting this woman.' He swallowed. 'I mean, she's bound to be younger than us and have more energy than us.'

'So?'

He looked hopelessly at me. 'Can you not see?'

'What?'

'Well, blood's thicker than water at the end of the day. You'll bond with her, want to go with her. You'll—'

'Dad.' I couldn't believe I was hearing this. 'Do you really think I'd drop you and Mam like that?'

'You don't like it here, Vicky, or you'd visit a bit more often.'

Oh God.

Oh shit.

'See,' he said, his face sad, 'you can't even answer me.'

I struggled to find the words to explain. But it was hard when I'd spent years ignoring it myself. 'I do like it here, Dad,' I began. 'But it's hard for me.' He gawped at me, not knowing why it was so hard to live in a comfortable house with good parents. 'See, I know I only landed here from somewhere else and I can't settle anywhere until I find the somewhere else.'

Nothing. He looked blank and hurt and puzzled.

'D'you remember that time, after college, when I went travelling?'

A nod. 'And you were only meant to go for a year and—'

'Well, I did it to see if I could find out where I *should* be.' Pause. 'And there was nowhere I could connect with. Imagine, the whole world and . . .' I gave a shrug. My eyes filled and I whispered, 'Nothing.'

'Aw, Jesus.' Dad shook his head. 'Aw, Jesus, aw, Vic, don't cry.'

'I'm not.' I shook my head. 'It's just hard. I need to know, Dad.'

He bowed his head. Muttered, half to himself, 'I've been so selfish, Vic.'

'That's not what—'

'Yes,' he interrupted. 'All this mess is my fault.'

'No—'

''Twas me that wouldn't let your mother tell you that you were adopted.'

His admission was a hammer blow. I stared dumbly at him.

'She wanted to but I, well, I forbade her to discuss it with you.'

For some reason, I'd thought they'd had an unspoken agreement between them – that by not telling me they could somehow preserve a fantasy that I really was theirs by birth. But his admission sickened me. An order. He'd ordered the other me to be wiped out. My history. He'd wanted me to spend years in Steve Martin limbo. Despite what I'd said to John, finding out after years that I'd been adopted had been horrible. Overnight, my world had crumbled. I realised, to my horror, that I'd lived a lie for twelve years, I'd lived a borrowed life with borrowed parents. My whole story was just a borrowed history. And it was scary, not to know who I was. And that shock could have been prevented.

'I've never thought of you in all this. Well, not properly anyway.'

His words hung in the air. I couldn't think of anything to say to him. In that moment, I wanted to kill him.

He looked desperately at me. 'We were so happy, see, I just didn't want to jeopardise things. But then you found out you were adopted and I've been scared of this moment ever since.'

'Scared?' My dad scared.

'Yes. Because I don't want to lose you, Vic. You're my girl, always will be. But I know I can't stand in your way. Your mother's right – our job was always to see that you were happy and if this . . .' He faltered, coughed and continued, 'So, what I'm saying is, Vic, if you want to meet this woman or whatever, well, I'm not going to stand in your way.'

After that there was a pause. Then he got up from the table and began to put on his jacket.

'I'm scared of change too.' I said it without thinking. 'I'm probably like you like that.'

He smiled briefly but said nothing. He reached for his cap and jammed it onto his head.

'I have my mother's phone number with me,' I blurted out, desperate for him to show that he meant what he'd said. Desperate to show him that there was nothing to be afraid of. 'And before I meet her, I've to ring her.' I swallowed hard. 'Would you be there while I did? Would you like to talk to her?'

I couldn't read his expression. I had the sudden fear that I'd gone too far, expected too much.

'I'm scared of talking to her on my own,' I admitted.

His expression softened. He attempted a smile. 'Well,' he said slowly, 'we can't have that.' He reached across the table and caught my hand. 'We can't have that.'

Chapter Fifty-three

THE PHONE RANG.

And rang.

Slowly, I became aware that it was still dark out. A sliver of light from the landing threw shadows on the floor of my room. It had been a late night. When Dad had got in from milking the cows, we'd talked frankly for the first time in twenty-eight years. He'd apologised again and promised to be right by my side when I rang my mother. I'd told him that I'd never leave him or Mam but that I just couldn't continue to live in a limbo where my past was a huge black hole.

He'd tried to understand, he really had, but despite everything, he didn't get it. He thought that because I was loved that it should be enough.

The phone kept ringing.

I heard the floorboards creak as Dad got out of bed. 'Jesus,' he was muttering as he padded downstairs, 'if this is a wrong number, I'll go fecking mad.'

I grinned and pulled the covers back up around my ears. Poor Dad, just when he was looking forward to a good night's rest, he was being awoken by a bloody telephone.

He would be in awful form in the morning.

Downstairs, he'd picked up the phone. After shouting a bad-tempered 'hello' into it, he'd gone silent.

Completely silent.

Why would he go quiet if it was a wrong number?

And if it was the right number, why would anyone ring us

at – I glanced at the alarm clock – four a.m.?

Uneasily I wondered if anything was wrong.

I waited to hear Dad come back up.

Only he didn't.

He wasn't talking either.

With a sick kind of dread filling me up, I got out of bed and padded towards the top of the stairs. Dad was holding the receiver to his ear and he looked white.

'Dad?'

It took a second before he registered my voice and when he did, he slowly raised his eyes to mine.

'What's wrong?' I could barely get the words out.

'Here.' He held the phone out to me. 'I can't make out what they're telling me.'

I remember every step I took down. It was like I was travelling in slow motion. I wanted to know yet I dreaded it. 'Hello?'

'This is St Anne's Hospital – is that Vicky?'

The hospital? 'What's wrong?' I whispered.

'She was fine today,' Dad said, half to himself. 'Tell them she was fine today.'

'Sorry for ringing so late,' a soft voice spoke from the other end, 'but it's important that you and your father come in. I'm afraid' – she paused and my stomach rolled – 'that your mother has had a stroke. It's very serious.'

'Stroke?' I was falling down, into somewhere. 'I don't understand.'

'She suffered with angina; unfortunately the pneumonia weakened her heart.'

'Angina?'

'Please come as soon as you can.'

I didn't know how we would. Dad was in no state to drive. I couldn't. I cursed the lack of courage that allowed me to back out of learning. 'We'll be in soon,' I said.

The woman told me she was very sorry and hung up.

Neither of us said anything for a moment.

Dad was by the door, staring at his hands. Softly, he asked, 'Is she very bad, Vicky?'

'I don't know, Dad.' I bit my lip. 'But I think so.'

He began rubbing his face, over and over.

'We'll have to get dressed and go in,' I said. 'Go up and put some clothes on. I'll ring for a taxi.'

He stood there, shaking his head.

'Dad.' I gave him a gentle push. 'Please go up.'

He began to shamble towards the stairs. I watched him go. When I was sure that he'd gone into the bedroom, I began to leaf through the phone book, looking for taxi numbers. Then I remembered Tommy. It suddenly seemed important to have someone who cared with us. Someone who could look after us. With a shaking finger, I began to dial.

Tommy answered.

'Tommy,' I said. 'Sorry for ringing so early but it's Mam.' And I couldn't say any more. Just that sentence was enough. I didn't want to say 'ill' or 'stroke' or anything that would make the reality any harder. Anything that would make me cry.

'I'll be there in fifteen,' Tommy said. 'You get yourselves sorted, OK?'

'Yeah.'

The line went dead.

In a complete daze, I walked back upstairs.

Chapter Fifty-four

WE WERE USHERED into the IC unit. Mam was hooked up to machines and tubes and all sorts of things that beeped and blinked. Dad and I tried not to look too shocked.

'It was sudden,' the nurse explained sympathetically. 'We had just put a monitor on her when it happened. No one expected this – she was doing so well.'

'And now?' I asked.

The nurse looked nervously at her chart. 'A doctor will talk to you,' she answered.

I watched her scurry away, feeling a sick dread in my chest.

Dad had barely listened. He was holding my mother's hand and squeezing it hard.

'You'll be fine, Evelyn,' he whispered. 'I know you will. And when you come home, I promise I'll do all the cooking. Everything.'

'I dunno if that will entice her to come home, Dad,' I joked feebly.

He laughed. 'As you can hear, Vicky's with me. We had that little chat. The one you asked me to have with her. Sure, Vicky will tell you herself.' He beckoned me over.

It took every bit of courage I had to catch my mother's hand. It still felt warm and soft and the nails were short and filed, just like they'd been every other time in my life. All the millions of times I'd held that hand. It was as familiar to me as my own. She'd guided me across the road, she'd dragged me kicking and screaming into school, she'd hugged and tickled and loved me.

'Hiya, Mam.' Like Dad I squeezed her hand, hoping for a squeeze in return. There was nothing. Her face looked calm and peaceful on the white pillow. I thought of the last time I'd talked to her, of how she'd been making plans to come home and sort out the flowers for Lisa Sweeney's wedding. And now . . .

'Tell her,' Dad urged. 'Tell her about our talk.'

'We talked,' I said, giving her hand another squeeze. 'And Dad says that you and he will be there when I ring Barbara.'

'I did,' Dad said, his jolly tone sounding forced.

'And we sorted a lot of stuff out tonight,' I went on. 'Lots of things. I even told him why I went travelling that time – it wasn't to get away from you or to hurt you. It was to find out where I came from. That way, I can belong – see.'

Dad was staring at me. 'She always knew that,' he said softly.

'And, Mam,' I went on, trying to sound cheerful, 'you won't believe this, and don't die of shock or anything.' I ignored Dad's intake of breath. Mam loved black humour. 'Well, I'm talking to John now. He came and did the hoovering today at the house.'

'Were you not talking to John?' Dad asked, surprised.

'Dawww,' I said. I squeezed Mam's hand again. 'Imagine not knowing that, Mam. You were right, Dad is hopeless.'

Dad pretended to cuff me.

We both laughed a little self-consciously.

Dad turned back to Mam. He gently lifted up her hand and kissed it. 'I love you, Evelyn,' he whispered. 'And even though you bawled the socks off me today over Vicky, I'm glad you did. We're closer now, aren't we, Vic?' He reached over for my free hand.

'Yep.'

And somehow, I get the feeling that that was all she was waiting to hear, because suddenly the little line that was monitoring her heart began to jump about all over the place and alarms began to ring. Dad and I watched in a stupor as nurses and doctors rushed into the room and began shoving us out. We watched through the doors as they worked frantically to bring her back.

We watched as the activity died down and heads were shaken. We held each other because we both knew that she was gone.

'She had angina,' the nurse tried to explain to me. 'But it was under control.'

I looked blankly at her.

'She'd had tests up in Dublin a few months back and they said that it was quite stable,' the nurse went on. 'But anything can trigger an attack and unfortunately . . .' Her voice trailed off.

I got up, not understanding. Dad was sitting, head bowed, in a chair. Tommy had his arm about his shoulders and was trying to coax him to drink something.

'Angina?' I said. 'What's that?'

Dad had been crying. His eyes were red and swollen. Tears had made tracks across his face. I felt a huge rush of protectiveness for him. I caught his hand and he stood up and hugged me fiercely. 'She didn't want you worrying,' he said brokenly. 'It was under control – she had tests done and everything.'

'But – but I don't understand . . .'

'It's like chest pains,' Dad went on, his voice muffled. 'But they don't do any harm to you. She was getting pains and so she had tests.'

'When?' I couldn't take it in. Why hadn't they told me?

'A few months back – before Christmas and then just after Christmas. She was taking it easy.'

Which was why he'd been cooking and cleaning. And I'd never wondered why, just accepted it. 'But I would have wanted to know,' I said. I couldn't even get up any anger.

'You would only have worried,' Dad said. 'And it wouldn't have done anyone any good.'

'I could have come home more often,' I said, horror at the way I'd neglected her suddenly coming into focus. 'I could have rung her. I could have helped her out.'

'You didn't know,' Dad said. 'And she wanted it that way.'

But I'd been so selfish, so self-centred, so obsessed with how I'd felt.

'She wanted it that way,' Dad repeated, hugging me. 'It made her happy that you didn't know.'

I pulled away from him. I pulled way from Tommy. I turned and walked out of the hospital.

I ignored their calls; I just had to be on my own.

Chapter Fifty-five

ALL THAT DAY and the following are blurry. It was as if I stared out at the world from thick syrup, as if every move took an age. My thoughts were muddled, people spoke to me, shook my hand, and when they'd gone I couldn't even remember what they'd said or what I'd said back.

Dad coped by milking his cows and walking his fields. He tried to speak to me but I couldn't answer. Every time he looked at me, guilt for the way I'd behaved swept through me and I'd be angry at him for not telling me so that at least in the last few months I could have made some effort to come home.

And worst of all, I found it hard to accept that I had no second chance. Life had changed and there was no going back. It all seemed very harsh somehow. There was no court of appeal, no page to re-read and understand, just a huge empty hole where my mother once had been.

Around lunchtime, Tommy tapped on my bedroom door. 'Your dad wants to know if there's anyone you'd like to ring,' he said, holding out the cordless phone. 'He says that maybe not everyone looks at the deaths.'

I hated the way he talked like that. Yesterday my mother had been coming home, now she was a few lines in a newspaper.

At my lack of response, Tommy said, 'I can ring people for you if you like – your workmates and that.'

'If you want.'

I didn't care who came.

'Anyone else?' Tommy asked.

Sal would know, her mother would ring her. Marti would probably need a call. I'd have to do that myself. 'Give it here,' I said, reaching for the phone. 'I'll ring my boyfriend.'

Tommy handed me the phone. 'She's coming to the church tomorrow night at five, Vic, and her funeral is eleven the next morning.'

I flinched at his words.

'It's awful hard to believe, isn't it?'

I gulped. I liked that he'd said that.

'Anyway . . .' Tommy made vague motions with his hands. 'I'll make any other calls you need made.'

I barely remembered him leaving.

Marti's mobile rang and rang. I prayed for him to answer. There was no way I was leaving a message. It just didn't seem right. Eventually, some woman with a warm-sounding voice picked up. 'Hi, Marti's phone?'

'Yeah, hi, is Marti there?'

'Eh, no. Is that a reporter? He's expecting a reporter to ring.'

'No, it's Vicky. Can you get him for me?'

'Are you a singer?'

'Please,' I said, 'will you get Marti for me?'

'He's not agenting any more – just in case you're a client.'

'I'm not . . .' I stopped. Marti not agenting?

In the background, a kid yelled out something. The woman said, 'Leo, I'm on the phone.'

Leo began to whinge, 'Mammmmyyy.'

'Kids,' the woman laughed into the receiver. 'So, Vicky, was it?'

I hung up.

My biggest fear in life has been rejection. Any sort of rejection would send me spinning into a depression. When I'd started applying for jobs, I'd curse the boss that sent me the 'sweet-but-no-thank-you' letter. When I failed to get on with the kids in college, I'd hated them all for what I perceived as their rejection of me.

And until I met Marti, I'd steered clear of falling in love. Sure, I'd go out with guys, but the minute they started to get serious I was out of there faster than a hare at a coursing meet. It wasn't that I intentionally set out to hurt anyone, it was just that falling in love for me was akin to bungee-jumping. I'd get far enough to look over the edge of the cliff but I'd never take that final plunge.

Maybe I'd figured that Marti would be a safe bet – I mean, how much commitment can you get from a guy with a kid and an ex-wife? How much can a guy that's so in love with his career give you? But in the end, it wasn't what he'd been able to give me, but what I'd actually been able to give him. For some reason, I'd fallen for him. There was something about him that had attracted me and kept me dangling. I'd even slept with him, for God's sake. And now, just like I'd always feared, I'd been dumped. But the hurt and the sadness weren't there.

Maybe I was just numb.

Maybe I felt I deserved it.

Chapter Fifty-six

THE CHURCH WAS packed. Mam's coffin, piled with cards and adorned with flowers, stood at the top of the church. As I passed it, I rubbed my hand along its length. I couldn't believe that she was actually in there though I'd seen her myself, lying still and cold in the funeral home the night before. Dad ushered me into a seat at the top of the church, as neighbours and friends looked on.

The night before had been a nightmare – everybody shaking hands with me. Bridie had hugged me and it was the closest I'd come to breaking down. Ed had shook my hand solemnly and then leaned forward and kissed my cheek. 'Hard luck,' he'd muttered before moving on.

Hard luck indeed.

The mass began. Prayers were said. Hymns were sung. I got up and did a reading. I spoke too low, too fast, and I don't think anyone could make head or tail of it, but then again, maybe that was fitting. I certainly couldn't understand why she had been taken from us. From my initial numbness, a slow anger was burning. Anger at the whole world for letting her die.

Dad had persuaded me to sing 'Be Not Afraid' – my mother's favourite hymn at communion time. And I sang it for her, my voice strong. I didn't want her to be afraid all alone. When I'd finished, I'd glared out at everyone.

The priest gave a nice talk, though he told *everyone* that I'd been adopted. I cringed with embarrassment but no one else seemed to notice. Then at the end my father got up and said a few words. His little speech wasn't prepared but he spoke with such love that he could have given a recipe for mince pies and there wouldn't have been a dry eye in the house.

'I'm a lucky man,' he said at the end. 'I've known one of the most wonderful women on God's earth. And I didn't deserve her and I think himself up there finally realised that and decided to take her away.' He paused and I saw him swallow hard. 'But I had thirty-five years with her and even now, when I'm so heart-broken, I don't regret how much I loved her.' Then he took out a handkerchief and dabbed his eyes. When he came down to me, he clasped my hand and smiled.

The graveyard looked nice underneath the spring sunshine. I stared around at all the people that had come and felt a sort of gratitude to them. Bridie and Ed had closed the shop as a mark of respect and were there; Sal and Mel, dressed to kill in short tight miniskirts, were there too. They'd obviously made up their differences and I wondered who'd made the first move. Sal probably. And right beside them, dressed head to toe in tight black leather, was Marti. Even clad in conservative colours, he was attracting a lot of attention. Maybe it was his earrings or his spiky hair. He also looked as if he hadn't attended a funeral in years. He hadn't a clue what was going on and he virtually gawked as they lowered my mother's coffin into the ground. He whispered something to Sal, who rolled her eyes and said something like, 'Well, what did you think the hole was for?'

I resented his presence. How could he come after what he'd done to me? I only hoped he had the sense to make a quick exit.

The priest finished up and announced that a cup of tea would be available back in the house. I had the sudden panicky thought that there was no food laid on until I remembered Aunt Julia and the others working late into the night. It hadn't dawned on me to question what they were doing but obviously they'd been making sambos and cakes and stuff. It was nice of them. Very nice. I felt a lump in my throat at the thoughts of it.

People began to wander away as Dad and I stood side by side accepting condolences.

Bridie and Ed came up. 'Sorry again, luvvie.' Bridie clasped my hand. 'Oooh, I'm so sorry.'

'Dad, this is Bridie and Ed, the people from the shop.'

'Nice to meet you,' Dad said, sounding very formal. 'Vicky has told us a lot about you.'

'Now that *is* worrying,' Ed said wryly and Dad smiled.

'Are yous going back to the house?' I asked.

They looked at each other.

'Please,' I said, and meant it. I suddenly felt that I was closer to these two than anyone else. I barely knew the neighbours and Sal and Mel weren't exactly people you'd turn to in a crisis.

'We will so,' Bridie said. 'We'll see you later.'

'Ta.'

I watched them wander off – Bridie in her brown coat and black headscarf and Ed in his black jeans and jacket.

'What is he doing here?' Sal demanded, arms folded, staring after them too. 'Honestly, as if things weren't bad enough.' She turned to me. 'Vicky, I'm so sorry about your mother. It's terrible.'

'Awful,' Mel agreed, blowing a plume of smoke into the air. 'Sorry about your wife, Mr McCarthy.' She held out her hand with its inch-long fingernails to my bemused father.

'Thank you very much.'

'It's Mel,' Mel said.

'Mel,' Dad uttered, trying not to stare at her fishnet legs.

'We'll see yous back at the house,' Sal said to me. 'It won't be for long though – we've copy deadlines to meet. Sorry to rush. Listen, I rang Marti to tell him, I didn't know if you'd be able to or not. Anyway, he came down with us, so maybe you could get someone to bring him back.'

'Vicky.' Marti arrived over. 'Hey, sorry about your mother.'

He enfolded me in a claustrophobic hug. Sal and Mel slunk away. 'I tried to make it down yesterday but things have been mad.'

'I'll bet they have,' I replied through gritted teeth. How dare he pretend things were normal? I pushed him off and said to Dad, 'This is Marti, a guy I know.'

'Not Marti the—'

'No,' I said hastily. 'Another Marti.'

Marti was looking strangely at me.

'Pleased to meet you, Marti. Thanks for coming,' Dad said.

'No probs, Mr McC.' Marti nodded. His leather squeaked with every movement. 'Hey, Vic, was that Bridie and Ed I saw earlier? I'll catch up with them. Talk later, Vic, right.' He squeezed my hand and was about to kiss my cheek when I turned away.

'Strange sort of fella,' Dad remarked.

'Mmm.' I couldn't say anything.

'And that Mel, she's a bit strange too.'

'D'you think so?'

'She looks like a Dublin girl, that's for sure.'

I smiled. That was my dad all over.

He wrapped his arm about my shoulders. 'We'll be lonely but we'll get through this, Vicky – all right?'

I think he almost believed it.

The house was thronged with people. All I wanted to do was go up to my room and escape them but years of tradition couldn't be ignored. I went from group to group, nodding at their remarks about my mother and only half hearing them. I tried my best to avoid Marti. There was no way I could face him. His loud voice could be heard every now and then floating across the room.

Eventually, I managed to get outside. After the stuffiness and noise of the house, it was a relief to escape into the space and relative silence of the countryside. Beyond the back door, fields of green stretched in every direction. I had a sudden flashback of me as a kid. I'd always run into the centre of a field and turn around and around, until eventually I'd fall with a thump to the ground. Then I'd lie, eyes wide open, and watch the big blue sky spinning like a top and I'd convince myself that I could feel the world turn. Mam used to laugh at me.

So that's what I did. I ran to the nearest field, spun around and around and around, taking my anger and fury out on myself. Eventually, I hit the ground and the world swirled about me. Only it wasn't half the fun I remembered. I thought I was going to be sick. I squeezed my eyes shut to block out the sensation.

'Are you OK?'

Ed's voice startled me. My eyes shot open and Ed's shape was there and was gone. There and gone.

'Oh, Jesus,' I groaned and closed my eyes again.

I was aware of him sitting on the grass beside me. 'Are you drunk?' he asked, his voice a mixture of amusement and concern.

'I'm not about to get drunk at my own mother's funeral,' I snapped. The spinning in my head was slowing down. I took a chance and opened my eyes. Ed was peeling the petals from a daisy and looking into the middle distance. 'Sorry,' I muttered.

'It's OK,' he answered.

'Anyway, what are you doing out here?' I hauled myself into a sitting position beside him.

'Escaping from the dirty looks I'm getting from your friend and my ex-girlfriend.'

'Oh dear.' I allowed myself a smile.

'You?' he asked.

'Just spinning,' I muttered.

'Spinning?'

'Yeah.'

He didn't ask any more and I liked that. 'My mother used to laugh when I'd do it,' I said then, wanting to talk about my mother. Wanting to make her live, I guess. 'So I . . .' My voice trailed off.

'You'll miss her.' It was a statement rather than a question.
I nodded.

'I remember you saying that your folks thought everything you did was great.'

'Yeah.' My eyes filled up. 'Maybe it was because I'm adopted.' I waited for him to say something about me being adopted, but he didn't. So I went on. 'No matter what I did, they thought it was great.' My lip wobbled. 'Especially her.'

He shifted uncomfortably. I don't think he wanted me to cry. He attempted to change the subject. 'My ma does that too.'

'Yeah?'

He grinned slightly. 'When my brother and I turned twenty-one, Dad gave us a pile of money. My brother invested it and made a bloody fortune and so when my turn came, it was a big deal, you know.'

'So what did you do?' My tears were receding. I couldn't cry in front of him. 'Buy over our toy shop?'

He laughed a little. 'Naw. I knew I couldn't compete so I didn't bother. I bought a motorbike and went travelling. Saw the world. Came back with nothing but a pair of jeans and my bike.'

'Jesus!' I gulped out a laugh.

'The old fella went spare.' There was laughter in his voice that made me smile. 'Mam told him that travel broadens the mind. Told him I was like the prodigal son in the Bible.'

'Guess you were.'

'Naw.' Ed shook his head. 'The prodigal son got the fatted calf, I just got earache.'

I smiled.

'Still' – Ed looked wistful – 'it was the best two years of my life. Saw everywhere.'

'Travel is great,' I said, wrapping my arms about my knees. 'I did it too. I feel guilty about it now – I hardly kept in touch with the folks at all.'

'Aw, well . . .' Ed shrugged. Paused. 'You can't change the past, I guess. That's what my mother says, anyway.'

I didn't reply. All the postcards I could have sent. All the phone calls I could have made—

'Where was the best place you visited?' Ed interrupted my thoughts.

I didn't have to think twice. 'Easter Island.'

He looked stunned. 'Me too. Fucking eerie, isn't it – all those statues!'

'And in the middle of nowhere. That's what I liked about it.'

'Yeah.' He nodded vigorously. 'And food? Where was the nicest place you ate?'

I had to think about that one. I hadn't exactly eaten that well. 'Vietnam,' I eventually pronounced.

'Naw.' Ed waved his hand dismissively. 'Nothing like an Irish breakfast.'

'Oh ye of unadventurous taste buds!'

He grinned.

There was a silence.

'So, they were glad when you came home – yeah?'

'Thrilled.' I bit my lip. 'That's when Mam started making the strawberry cheesecakes – she thought it was cosmopolitan.'

He wasn't too sure whether to laugh or not.

'I'm going to miss her so much, Ed.' My voice had gone weepy again. 'I feel so lonely without her – there is nobody who's going to love me like she did.'

'Ach, you'll find someone.'

'No.' I shook my head. 'You don't understand until it happens to you.' My face crumpled up and big fat tears rolled down my cheeks.

'Hey.' Ed wrapped an arm about my shoulder. 'How come I always manage to make women cry?'

I hardly heard him. 'I think it's because I could be a kid with her, see. I could behave badly or anything and she'd still love me. With her gone, I can't do that any more.' A tear plopped onto my hand. 'Now I'm all grown up and it's so lonely. It feels so lonely. She was always there, see, but now, there'll be no one.'

'Your dad?'

'It's not the same.' Snot was coming out my nose and I had no option but to wipe it on my sleeve. 'It's not the same.'

'Naw,' Ed said softly. 'It's not.' He hugged me to him.

It seemed the most natural thing in the world to wrap my arms about him and cry my heart out.

It felt good to cry. To just let go. Of course, it was madly embarrassing that I had to do it in front of, let's face it, an employee. But Ed wasn't just an employee. He was my friend.

When eventually I stopped, I became acutely aware of his arm about me. Of the way he was rubbing my back. Of the way his chin rested on my hair. I could hear him breathing and I could smell the fresh smell of his aftershave and the clean scent of his clothes. It all seemed a bit too intimate for my liking.

Without trying to hurt him, I gently pulled away. I scrubbed my eyes and laughed, mortified. 'You must think I'm a wreck,' I babbled.

'No.' He looked straight into my face. 'Are you feeling better?'

'A bit,' I nodded. 'Thanks.'

'No probs.' He reached out and brushed some hair away from my face. 'You need to tie up your hair again.'

'Yeah.'

'It looks nice though, that way.'

There was a tender look on his face that made me squirm. I had to turn away and there was silence for a bit. In the distance, I could hear the sounds of cars and animals and music – the world going on as if it was just an ordinary day.

'What's angina?' I asked suddenly. I turned to Ed, who was busy decimating another daisy. 'My mother had it and I never knew.'

'Angina.' Ed lay back on his elbows, his long legs stretched in front of him. He frowned, thinking. 'Well, it's not generally considered hugely serious. Chest pains, basically. Your mother would have been on medication.' He paused and glanced uncertainly at me.

'Go on.'

'Well, it can be a warning of a future heart attack.' And he talked of stable angina and unstable angina. And he made it understandable for me – which was good. I needed to understand things.

'You would have made a good doctor,' I said when he'd finished.

He winced.

'Why did you give it up?'

He looked away from me.

I touched his sleeve. 'It's just, you know, you were so good with Domo that time. And now, explaining to me. And you must have really wanted to be a doctor to pay for it yourself.'

He shrugged. He hauled himself back up to sitting. Pulling up a fistful of grass he began filtering it through his fingers. 'I did,' he mumbled. Then he looked right into my face. It was a strange moment. Sort of like the air before lightning. For some weird reason my heart started to pound as Ed reached out towards my face.

'I—'

'So this is where you got to!' Marti hailed us from the back door of the house.

We both jumped.

'Here's Marti,' Ed said, jumping up and dusting himself down. 'He'll cheer you up.'

'No!' I jumped up too. 'I can't see him today. I can't.'

'What? But—'

'Just, just tell him I'm too upset to talk.'

Without waiting for Ed to reply, I turned about and ran off.

Chapter Fifty-seven

I DIDN'T GET back until after five. I walked the farm, something I hadn't done in years. Everything looked so peaceful, so much the same that it hurt me to realise that nothing in the rest of the world was going to change. I wanted to yell out to somebody. I wanted to say, 'Hey, Evelyn McCarthy is dead – don't you realise that?' But even I knew I'd look a complete loon.

The sun was still beaming down as I turned into the back gate. Many of the cars had gone and I was glad. The only ones left were Tommy's and Julia's. As I entered the kitchen, I heard him. Marti was regaling somebody with stories of Boy Five. I didn't notice Dad sitting alone at the table until he said, 'That Marti fella wants to talk to you.'

'Well, he'll have to wait.' I sat down opposite Dad.

'He's been waiting long enough. He even turned down a lift with Bridie and Ed to wait. And if you don't talk to him soon, Tommy won't be able to take him back either.'

'Can't he get the bus?'

Dad stood up. He came across to me and rubbed my shoulder. 'Don't let this make you hard, Vicky. Just remember how wonderful she was. Now' – he looked at me – 'will I bring in your boyfriend and let him talk to you?'

So he knew Marti was my boyfriend.

'I have nothing to say to him.'

'So let *him* talk.' Dad walked towards the door. 'I'll get him. He seems worried about you.'

Worried my arse, I thought. Worried about himself more like. Worried about how poor bereaved Vicky will take rejection. Worried about when to tell her. Well, I'd make it easy for him. I'd dump him.

'Vicky?'

I turned towards Marti as he stood uncertainly by the door. 'What?'

He looked hurt at the way I was behaving. 'I just wanted to talk to you, to say how sorry I was. I didn't get a chance all day and Ed said you were upset so I decided I'd better hang around.'

'There's no need – I've Dad.'

'Yeah, but—'

'And if you want someone to talk to, try Linda.' I hadn't meant to say that – it just sort of spewed out. The anger I felt at Mam dying was a loaded cannon.

'Linda?' he paled. 'What do you mean?'

'She's back, isn't she?'

'No.' Pause as I glared at him. 'Well,' he gulped, 'not exactly.'

'What the fuck does "not exactly" mean?' Before he had a chance to answer, I stood up. 'D'you know what? I don't care. I don't care. My mother has just died and I don't need this kind of shit with you.' He flinched with every syllable. 'Get out!'

He stood his ground.

'Get out, I said!'

'No.' He sat down. 'I have to explain.'

'Why?'

'I wasn't going to tell you – not now.'

'Oooh, that's big of you – so what were you going to do? String me along until I was over all this and then tell me?'

'Aw, Jesus, Vic – I don't think—'

'Get out!'

'She's asked to come back – I haven't said yes yet.' His voice, loud at the best of times, was louder than I'd ever heard it. I'm sure my Dad and Tommy heard him too.

'But you're going to?'

He looked hopelessly at me.

'I mean, you've given up being an agent, you've obviously dumped the lads. Just what Linda wants – eh?'

Marti bowed his head. 'Cliff got a deal on his own – he dumped us.'

That was a bit of a shock; I hadn't expected that.

'And yeah, I've given up the agenting.'

'Because of Linda?'

He glanced at me. 'Leo wants her back. The kid will never forgive me if I don't make a go of it.'

'That's just an excuse.'

'No.' He stared at his hands. 'He's so happy now, Vic, thinking we'll get back together. I can't take it away from him.'

'So you're dumping me, is that it?' The words stuck in my throat.

'Every kid needs a mother, Vic – you're the one that told me that.'

He had me there.

'You'd have liked it – wouldn't you?'

Tears came but I blinked them back. 'I had a mother – a very good one.'

'Yeah.' Marti gulped and looked at me. 'And so had Leo.' He stood up and sighed. 'I was the fuck-up.' It was a few seconds before he spoke again. 'I never told you, Vic, but I remortgaged our house to finance Boy Five. We all would have had to move in with me ma. That's why Linda left.'

I stared at him.

'I owe it to Leo to try to be a good father.'

He was right, of course.

'For once in my life, Vic, I think I'm doing the honourable thing. I think I'm ready to be a dad and I'm awful sorry you have to be hurt.' He paused. Said softly, 'I really liked you, you know.'

I couldn't speak. Now the grief of being dumped was mingling with the grief of being left behind. I'd really liked him too. I dunno why.

'Sorry.'

I nodded, not wanting to cry in front of him. 'Just go.'

He stood uncertainly by the table for a second or two and then turned and slowly began to walk away. I glanced up at his retreating back and felt – I dunno what – regret or sorrow or something, not just for me but for him too. 'Marti,' I said, surprising myself.

He turned back to face me.

'Good luck,' I gulped out.

A small smile. 'Ta, Vicky.' Then he grinned. 'I reckon, with my parenting skills, Leo's gonna need luck more than I will.'

I tried to smile back. There was a silence.

Marti broke it. 'Well, goodbye then,' he said softly.

'Bye, Marti.'

I heard him leave with Tommy about five minutes later.

Dad came in and made me some strong tea. He didn't ask what had happened and I was glad of that.

Chapter Fifty-eight

ONCE THE FUNERAL was over, it was back to reality. In a way, it was a relief. I could, at last, try and get my head together without having to think about funerals and entertaining people. But getting on with things meant that I had to face the fact that she wasn't coming back. And the whole idea of that seemed such a betrayal. I decided to take another week off just to be with Dad. But he said that the sooner he got used to what it was going to be like without her, the better for him and the better for me too.

'And anyway,' he finished, 'you've a shop to run. You're the manager.'

Even through his grief, I could hear the pride in his voice.

'Bridie can do it for me.'

'Not as well, I'll bet.' He patted my hand. 'You go back and get used to things and I'll stay here and get used to things.'

He was braver than I was. 'I'll ring every day.'

He smiled. 'I'd like that.'

Tommy drove me back to Dublin. He hardly spoke on the way up and when he did it was only because I'd spoken first. When we reached the flat, he took my bags out of the boot and asked if I'd be OK dragging them all the way upstairs.

'I'll be fine.' I picked up my suitcase. 'Cuppa?'

'Naw, ta.' He shrugged. 'Maybe we'll do lunch one day?'

'Yeah. That'd be nice.'

'And if you need anything, Vic – just call, all right?'

Jesus, he was such a nice guy. Mam had been mad about him and now I understood why. 'Tommy, thanks,' I said softly. 'You've been great. Aunt Julia has been great. John even.'

He smiled at my inclusion of John. Then in a perfect take of his mother's voice, he croaked, 'Sure, aren't you family?'

I smiled.

'Take care,' he said, giving my arm a brief rub. He climbed back into the car. 'Talk soon.'

As I waved him off, I realised that he was right. I *was* family. Maybe not related by flesh and blood, but in the end, what did that matter? These people loved me. I was beginning to realise just how important that was.

Sal, Mel and Lorcan were in the flat when I got back. Sal and Mel could be heard squealing from the front door. When I actually got inside, I found them poring over some article that Sal had written. Mel was gleefully rubbing her hands. Then, tapping her nose, she said, 'Never let me down yet. I could smell a story in a vacuum.'

'Smells don't exist in vacuums, darling,' Lorcan said laconically. He was lazily flicking through the *Sunday Business Post.*

'No.' Mel folded her arms and glared at him. 'The only thing that seems to exist in a vacuum is our social life.'

'Hiya, folks,' I said, attempting a smile.

There was instant silence.

Sal began shoving her piece into her folder and I have to say, I was insulted. I had more on my mind than her bloody pieces.

'Hey, how's things?' Mel asked, her voice dripping concern.

I made a big deal of putting down my case so that I wouldn't have to answer.

'I am so dreadfully sorry.' Lorcan proffered a manicured hand. 'Losing a parent is a dreadful thing.'

'Yeah. Thanks.'

They all stood looking at me.

'Cuppa,' Sal said, seizing on the word like a lifeboat. 'Would you like one?'

She'd never, ever offered to make me tea before. 'Ta.'

I sat down on the sofa beside Lorcan and inhaled a whiff of his noxious aftershave.

'Isn't it funny how we Irish always make tea to console people?' Lorcan said in his slow drawl. 'And to be honest, all it does is keep you awake at night, tossing and turning.'

'That kind of observation we don't need, thank you,' Mel said stiffly.

'Of course.' Lorcan flashed me an apologetic smile. 'Of course.'

Sal handed me my tea and there was more silence. I soon realised that things must have been booming until I'd entered. Sal and Mel, not being the most empathic of people, hadn't a clue what to do. 'I'll have this in my bedroom.' I stood up. 'I'm tired.'

'Oh.'

'Oh, OK.'

'Bye now.'

Their relief was like a tidal wave washing through the room.

Chapter Fifty-nine

When I got up for work the next day, I found Sal sound asleep on the sofa, her laptop on with a screen saver zooming to and fro across the screen. It was obviously an important story because normally Sal would never sleep in full make-up. She'd probably spend the whole day exfoliating her skin now.

I tiptoed out of the flat, not wanting to wake her and endure some more stilted conversation.

It was hard walking to the bus stop, getting on the bus and walking to work. Hard to get used to the normality of it. Hard to comprehend that I'd be doing this for ever now without the security of my mother at home. A security I'd always taken for granted. I blinked back tears before unlocking the shop and heading into the office.

Ed and Bridie were there.

'Hi yez,' I said awkwardly.

'Vicky.' Bridie enfolded me in a hug. 'Welcome back. Welcome back. We're delighted you're back – aren't we, Ed?'

'Aye,' Ed nodded. 'We've even got you a present to cheer you up.'

'Ed bought it,' Bridie said firmly. 'It was his idea.'

Ed flushed. 'Ach, it's nothing really – but I know you like them, so . . .' He opened the fridge and produced a chocolate cake. 'Here.' He virtually shoved it at me.

'Oh.' I bit my lip as I looked at the cream and the chocolate swirls. I hadn't eaten well in days and I didn't think I'd even manage a slice of it. But it touched me something rotten. 'Thanks. Thanks a lot.'

'It's OK.' He touched me briefly on the arm.

There was a silence.

'Will I cut it for you?' Bridie asked.

'Yeah. Sure.' I knew I sounded completely flat and unappreciative, but I couldn't help it. It was too much effort to put on a show.

I sat down on the sofa as Bridie cut us three large pieces. The largest she put on my plate. 'There now,' she cooed, 'build you up.'

I had to force it into my mouth, piece by piece. I was afraid I'd hurt them if I left it. Bridie made me some tea and began chattering about events in the shop. Finally, after giving me a rundown from stock-taking to the state of her legs, she said, 'And do you know, Ed ended up in Casualty last week?'

'Jesus, Bridie.' Ed rolled his eyes and stood up. 'I think I'll open up.'

Bridie laughed. 'Crashed into the front window because he was giving some kids a demonstration on the skateboard. Walloped his head.'

Despite myself I grinned. 'Where? The front or the back?'

'Back,' Ed muttered. 'Knocked meself out.'

'Oh, right,' I grinned. 'Because you know most bangs to the front of the head are harmless. A med student told me that.'

'Ha, ha.'

We smiled at each other. My heart gave a slow roll and I felt myself blush. I don't know why – it was his eyes or something.

'Well, we could have done with a med student that day.' Bridie crossed to the sink to wash out her cup. 'I thought I'd have to give him the kiss of life.'

Ed put his hand on his heart. 'If you'd have kissed me, Bridie, I'd have died and gone to heaven.'

'Go away out of that,' she giggled. 'Flatterer.'

Ed winked at me and left.

'Gone to heaven,' Bridie said fondly after him. 'He doesn't even go to mass. Prefers the pub, he says.'

'Probably the wine tastes better in the pub,' I remarked.

Bridie giggled, shocked. Then she flapped her hand at me and the whole thing reminded me so much of my mother that tears pooled in my eyes.

'Aw, Vicky, aw, love.' Bridie crossed to me and wrapped her thin arm around me. 'Don't upset yourself.'

'Sorry.' I wiped my eyes hastily. 'Sorry.'

'There is no need to be sorry, love. No need at all. If you want to cry, you go ahead and cry. It'll take time before you're back to yourself. Losing someone you love is the worst thing in life, I think.'

'It is. I didn't appreciate her, Bridie.'

'Arragh,' Bridie half-laughed. 'What child appreciates their parents?'

'And she wasn't even my *real* mother.'

'I know, luvvie.'

Of course she knew. The bloody priest had told her.

'I've spent my whole life wanting my real mother.'

'Oh, luvvie.' Bridie knelt in front of me. Her knees popped but she didn't seem to notice. 'D'you know, even if she was your real mother, you'd have wanted her to be different. You'd have wanted her to be like your best friend's mother or like the one on the television. That's just the way it is.'

'No. No it's not.'

'It is.' Bridie nodded vigorously. 'Sure, I always wanted my mother to be like Veronica Lake.'

'Who?'

'An actress. Very beautiful. My mother, on the other hand, was small and fat and dumpy.' Bridie looked sad. 'I was so embarrassed by her.'

'And did you feel guilty about that when she died?'

'Part of me did. But I had loved her too – just like you loved your mother.'

But when my mother died, I wanted to say, I'd been trying to trace the other woman. I'd been planning to phone her. To get to know her. To meet her.

I despised myself for it.

I flicked off the computer and, after pulling on my jacket, picked up Ed's to bring it down to him. Bridie had left early and there was only Ed and me left. I'd spent most of the day upstairs, inventing things to do because I hadn't felt able to face people. I knew grumpy customers would upset me and as for happy kids with their happy mothers . . .

Ed was on his way up the stairs and we met halfway.

'Ta.' He took his jacket from me. Asked quietly, 'How you doing?'

'Not bad.' I managed a smile. Apart from almost crying in front of Bridie, I wasn't too bad.

'It's great you're back.' Ed began to walk in front of me down the stairs. 'I was going slowly mental on my own with Bridie. Jesus, she kept cleaning stuff all the time.' A bewildered look at me. 'Is that normal?'

I laughed. 'I dunno. You're the doctor.'

He flinched slightly and then tried to smile. 'Not any more,' he said lightly. He turned to unlock the door.

'You never told me why you left,' I said then, suddenly remembering. 'D'you remember, I asked you—'

'Will I put on the alarm?'

I thought perhaps he hadn't heard me. 'Why did you give up medicine?'

A pause, just long enough to be uncomfortable, before he answered, 'Just, you know, decided it wasn't for me.' He walked past me to the alarm and began keying in the code.

'Is that why you left London?'

He froze, one finger on the keypad. I saw him deliberately relax his shoulders before keying the numbers in.

'Well?'

'Well what?' A grin. 'Are we ready to go?'

He didn't wait for me to answer. He pulled open the door. 'After you, boss.'

He wasn't going to tell me and I guess it wasn't any of my business, but there was something weird going on. He'd been brilliant with Dominic, brilliant explaining to me about angina. In fact, his face had lit up just telling me about chest pains and medication. And now, he looked miserable. And I found that I didn't like to see him upset. 'It might help to talk.'

'About?'

'You know what about.'

He stared down at his trainers and bit his lip. 'I'll head off now – OK?'

I watched him leave. I remembered the night in the pub when he'd said that he and I were the same. That we wouldn't tell people things. I'd changed since then, I realised. Sometimes telling people stuff was good. Talking with Lucy had opened me up, made me accept that I was adopted. OK, I still cringed every time someone found out, but I didn't think it was my fault any more. Even if I never met my mother now, meeting and talking with Lucy had made me happier, less paranoid.

I wondered if Ed would ever meet someone he could talk to.

I hoped he would.

I really did.

Part of me was sorry that it wasn't me, though.

Chapter Sixty

FRIDAY EVENING THREE weeks later, Dad and I were watching the last part of *The Late Late Show*. Pat Kenny had just introduced his last guest of the night. A celeb who'd given a child up for adoption when she was just fifteen.

'I think I'll head to bed,' I said.

'This might be interesting.' Dad jabbed the remote at the telly. 'It might help you when you ring your own . . . birth mother.'

'Oh—' I picked up my cardigan and, without looking at him, said, 'I've decided not to bother with all that.'

'What?' He sounded shocked. 'But, but I thought . . .'

'It's better all around,' I went on. 'I mean, she gave me up. You and' – I bit my lip – 'well, you and Mam were my parents – really.'

'Vicky!'

But I was gone.

I got up around one the next day. Dad was downstairs, pottering about the kitchen, probably making himself some lunch. He normally left a sambo for me with instructions as to where he'd be if I needed him.

I pulled my cardigan over my PJs and went downstairs to grab a cuppa and bring it back to bed with me. Every step I took echoed in the hallway below. Jesus, if I'd hated coming home before, it was even worse now. It was as if the house was in mourning for Mam too. All the rooms seemed so empty and big without her to fill them. Dad felt it too, I think, which was why he never seemed to eat in the kitchen any more.

He was in the kitchen when I got down, however. Sitting at the table, with a giant mug in front of him. On a plate beside the mug was a doorstep of a ham and cheese sandwich.

'Thought you'd be up around now,' he said. 'There's tea in the pot, if you want it.'

'Ta.'

As I was pouring the milk into the mug, he said, 'Vicky, about what you said last night—'

'Dad, honestly—'

'Your mother wanted you to do it, you know.' His voice was soft. Whenever he talked about Mam, his voice went like that. 'She told me so herself the day before . . . the day before . . .' He couldn't say it. 'She told me,' he finished.

'Well, I've changed my mind.'

'Can I ask why?'

No, I wanted to say, you cannot. 'Can a person not just change their mind?' I picked up my mug and eyed the sambo he'd made for me. Ham and cheese. 'Thanks for this.' Picking up the plate, I headed towards the door.

'You might want this,' Dad said.

'What?'

'This.' He held out a slim black book. 'Julia found it last week when she was . . . you know . . . going through your mother's things.'

'What is it?' I eyed it suspiciously. I didn't want to get upset. As far as I was concerned, I was doing well at holding myself together. I hadn't made a mistake in work at all that week. Ed and Bridie were being brilliant and I had only thought about Marti forty-two times, which was only seven times a day.

'She wanted to give it to you herself,' Dad said, caressing the little book. 'And I wanted to do it the way she would have done, but with what you said last night and the way you're feeling, I think now might be the right time for you to have it – here.' Again he proffered the book.

I put down my breakfast things and slowly crossed towards him. I didn't think a book would change anything. I was not going to ring my mother, I was not going to meet her. As far as I was concerned, I had a mother and now she was gone.

'She wanted to give it to you when you were meeting the other woman,' Dad said as he watched me slowly open its pages.

To Barbara, with love from Evelyn and Sean.

The sight of her handwriting made the now familiar lump rise in my throat. I realised suddenly that it was a book of me. A photograph album charting my life from aged three months to last year. There were pictures of me smiling, of me riding my first bike, of me in full school uniform, of me making my communion, my visit to the zoo, my confirmation. On and on and on. Loads of happy photos of a much-loved kid. Each photo was marked and dated and, underneath, my mother had written a short description of where we'd been when the picture was taken.

'Oh, Dad,' I whispered, turning page after page.

He stood up and put his arm about my shoulder. 'She wants your mother to know what a wonderful girl you are,' he said. 'To make her feel that she shared her life with you.'

'But—' I took a deep breath to steady my voice. It was no use, it came out all wobbly. 'But I feel like I'm *betraying* her for looking.'

'Not at all, not at all.' Dad's reassuring, loving voice made me begin to sob. 'Sure, you're betraying her by not looking.'

'Nooo.'

'Yes.' Dad caught me by the shoulders and looked hard at me. His own eyes were glistening now. 'A mother wants her children to be happy. This is her way of making you happy. Don't throw it away.'

'But you . . .'

'Were a selfish old man.' He shook me gently. 'I want you to ring this lady. I want to be there when you do. I want her to see what a wonderful job Evelyn did when she brought you up. I want her to remember Evelyn as fondly as we do.'

'Oh, Dad.'

He pulled me to him. 'And I want you to cheer up. Cheer up and start living again. That's what she would have wanted, you know. Go back to Dublin and go out and get drunk—'

'Dad!'

He laughed. 'It's what she would have wanted,' he repeated. 'And Jesus,' he went on, a smile in his voice, 'you never did what she wanted when she was alive, so it's the least you can do now.'

I laughed and cried at the same time.

Chapter Sixty-one

MY FINGER SHOOK as I dialled. Sweat made the receiver slippery. Behind me, Dad was pacing up and down the room, breathing heavily. To be honest, I was more worried about him than I was about myself. He hadn't slept at all the night before – I'd heard him going to and from the kitchen – and I reckon this phone call was to blame.

I'd told Lucy to contact Barbara to say that I'd be ringing on Sunday afternoon, so it wasn't as if the phone wouldn't be answered. My heart really started to pound as the final number was pressed. I listened to the tiny clicking sounds on the line as the phone connected with the phone in Limerick.

'It's ringing,' I said to Dad. My voice was shaking. Part of me felt guilty at the excitement I felt.

Dad froze in the act of walking to the window. He came back and laid a hand on my shoulder. I wished he wouldn't. It was making me claustrophobic. I moved slightly so that I could shake him off without him knowing I was shaking him off. With every ring, my heart hammered more and more furiously until I actually thought I was going to get sick.

'Hello?' A tiny voice from the other end. Then a 'Hello?' Slightly stronger.

'Is that Barbara?' I was surprised that my voice worked.

'Yes.' Pause. 'Is that—' There was a sniff. 'Vicky?' My name was whispered.

'Yeah.'

'Oh my God.' The woman at the other end sounded half

afraid. Then, after a small pause, she went on, 'It is so wonderful to hear your voice. It's so wonderful.'

It was almost like a dream. I couldn't quite take in the fact that I was speaking to someone actually connected to *me*. 'I'm glad to hear you too,' I said. 'It's hard to believe actually.'

'It is, isn't it?' Her voice wobbled. 'I just feel so lucky to have you contact me. I've thought about it for so long.'

'Really?'

'Yes. Since I let you go.' Her voice was husky, like mine. 'And your letters,' she went on. 'Your last letter was beautiful. I cried for days after I'd read it.' She was beginning to cry again. 'Your parents sounded like wonderful people.'

I couldn't speak.

'And' – pause – 'I was sorry to hear about your mother.'

'Yeah.'

'Will you pass that on to your father? Tell him I'm sorry.'

I put my hand over the receiver and said to Dad, 'She says she's sorry about Mam.'

Dad nodded and patted me on the shoulder.

'And will you tell him,' Barbara went on, her voice quivering, 'tell him "thank you" for making me so happy.'

'She says thanks,' I said to Dad. 'Thanks for making her so happy.'

Dad nodded. 'OK.' Then, obviously feeling that that wasn't an adequate response, he said, 'Can I talk to her?'

My heart lurched. 'What?'

'I'd . . . I'd like to talk to her,' Dad said.

What the hell was he going to say? We'd decided last night that he wouldn't *have* to talk.

'Eh,' I said to Barbara, 'my dad is here. He wants a word.' Without waiting for her response, I handed him the phone.

'Eh, Barbara,' Dad said, sounding very businesslike, 'this is Sean McCarthy.'

Barbara said something at the other end.

Dad shifted about uncomfortably. 'Thanks,' he responded.

Then, after swallowing hard, he said, 'I just want to thank you too. No one has ever given us anything quite as precious as our Vicky and, well, I want to thank you for that.' Then he handed the phone to me and left the room.

Barbara was still crying, saying how wonderful it was to have Dad say that. Then I started to cry and agree that it was wonderful. In the end, we agreed to meet at a time to be decided by the social workers.

When I put down the phone I was shattered.

Dad was out in the fields, his boots making huge, squelchy footprints in the muddy soil. He didn't hear me as I came up beside him.

'Thanks for telling her that, Dad. You made her very happy.'

Dad turned to me. 'I just asked myself what your mother would have done,' he answered.

Then he put his arm about my shoulders and together we walked the land until the sun began to bleed across the sky.

Only that Mam was missing, it was almost a perfect moment.

Chapter Sixty-two

'GUESS WHAT? GUESS what?' Dominic burst into the shop. He danced in front of us in a pair of shorts about two sizes too small for him. 'Guess what?'

'You're getting cabbage for dinner,' Ed said, causing Dominic to crease up laughing.

'No, silly,' he giggled. 'Me and my mammy are getting a new house.'

Bridie looked anxiously at me and I looked down at the ground. Sylvia was making her way towards us and she had a thing about Dominic telling her 'private business'.

'Isn't that *great*?' Dominic beamed.

'Hey, Sylvia,' Ed called to her. 'Congratulations on the house.'

'Jesus, Ed,' I whimpered, wanting to kick him. 'Will you shut up!'

'So he's told yez.' Sylvia was actually *smiling*. Her earrings jangled as she turned from one to the other of us. 'And I bleeding told him not to.' She pretended to cuff Dominic, who danced away laughing.

'Mammy says that I can have my breakfast there and that I can stay in it.' Dominic chatted cheerfully. 'She says that we will watch TV in it and the TV will be in a different room to my bed. And that I can have my own bedroom. *And* that we might have a garden. And maybe a dog. And—'

'That is wonderful.' Bridie, having gained courage from Sylvia's smile, clapped her hands. 'I think we'll have to get you a big lollipop to celebrate.'

'Naw.' Sylvia reached into her big black leather bag, the one she always carried with her. 'I, eh, figured yez might prefer this to celebrate.' A bottle of wine was put in front of us.

'A woman after me own heart.' Ed picked up the bottle and grinned.

Sylvia flushed and stared down at her fake-tanned legs and white stilettos. 'Yez have been so good to Domo and me, letting us come in here, giving Domo stuff. I know I've been a cow but—'

'Not at all,' Bridie said. 'We've loved having you!'

Ed looked sidelong at me and raised his eyebrows. I suppressed a grin.

'Well, I've still been a cow,' Sylvia said. 'But yez know, it's hard when other people think you can't provide for your kid. You feel a failure.' She smiled ruefully. 'It makes you hard, you know?'

'You are a lovely girl,' Bridie lied sincerely. 'We were always delighted to see you, weren't we, Vicky?'

'No,' I said, grinning. 'You used to scare the shit out of me!'

Bridie 'tisked'.

'I had to be scary,' Sylvia explained earnestly, looking for the first time the young twenty-something that she was. 'I was scared yez would report me for not being able to mind Domo properly. I didn't want to lose him to some do-gooder.' She shot a look at Domo, who was describing to Ed what exactly he was going to have in his room when he got it. Her face softened. 'Kids are bleeding great, aren't they?'

Ed was promising Domo that when he got his room, he'd give him his very own wrestlers to put in it.

At that moment, I thought Ed was bleeding great.

'Where the hell is he?'

Albert O'Neill's furious voice made me jump. Down at the other end of the counter, Bridie tittered nervously. 'Oh, Mr O'Neill, you gave us a fright, there.'

O'Neill ignored her. Instead, he turned bulging blue eyes on me. 'Where is he?' he demanded. In his hand, he carried a copy of *Tell!* It was rolled up tightly.

There was something about O'Neill holding a copy of Sal's magazine that made my stomach lurch. 'He's bringing up some stock,' I said, as calmly as I could. 'He'll be with you in a minute.'

'I can't *wait* a minute!' He began to stride towards the storeroom, ignoring the stares of curious customers.

Ed chose that moment to appear, his arms piled high with Bey Blade accessories.

'Put those down!' O'Neill shouted.

A few women who'd been browsing made a hasty exit. I could see sales slumping all over the place. 'Please don't shout,' I called over. 'We are open, you know.'

'Then close up!'

It was an order.

As Bridie scuttled towards the door, I watched as Ed calmly put down the boxes he'd been carrying.

'Yeah?' he asked his dad. There was major hostility in his voice and a sulky look on his face that I'd never seen before.

'You've done it again, haven't you?' O'Neill jabbed the magazine. 'Just when I give you one last chance, you decide you're going to throw it right back in my face, aren't you?'

'I dunno what you're talking about.'

O'Neill began to heavy-breathe. He looked as if he wanted to throw a punch. Ed, meanwhile, stood stock-still, his hands by his sides.

O'Neill seemed to square up to him until they were almost nose to nose.

'I think we'd better go,' Bridie whispered. 'Let them sort it out themselves.'

'We'll be in the pub,' I called out.

Neither of them took any notice.

Bridie and I exited the shop without our coats. As we stepped outside, we could hear O'Neill telling Ed that he was a complete and utter waster.

I felt so sorry for him at that moment that I would have gone back to defend him, only Bridie yanked me out the door and slammed it behind us.

We passed a newsagents on the way to the pub. Issues of *Tell!* were splattered all over the window. It was hard for us not to notice the gorgeous picture of Ed that dominated the front cover. It was a recent one – he was wearing his Ireland football jersey and he was laughing into the camera. His teeth gleamed white and his eyes, fringed with dark lashes, were as cute as hell. Underneath was the banner headline – *Is there a doctor in the house?*

'I have to buy that,' I said suddenly. I rummaged about in my purse, found the three euro I needed and barged into the shop. Grabbing a magazine from the rack, I paid for it.

'You must be shocked,' the newsagent said sympathetically. 'Working with him and all.'

Ignoring him, I rejoined Bridie in the street and opened the magazine. More pictures of Ed with an attractive brunette. He looked happy. The headline across the page: *Mental Medic.*

Bridie was peeking over my shoulder. 'Isn't that a nice photo,' she cooed. 'He should be a model.'

He had been a model apparently.

A model prisoner.

As I read the sensational piece, my heart sank. I mean, I was shocked, but at the same time, I felt so terribly sorry for Ed. He was a decent guy despite the magazine's claim that he'd beaten up his hospital boss so badly that the man had needed stitches.

Ed O'Neill, the article read, *was one of the most promising young medics in the renowned Great London Hospital for Children.* There was then a big technical bit about what exactly Ed had been specialising in. *Then, one evening*, the piece went on, *as a dispute arose over how to treat a sick child, Dr O'Neill accused his superior of negligence. The next evening, Dr O'Neill went to his superior's office and witnesses heard a heated exchange of views. There was the sound of a violent fight and Dr O'Neill had to be pulled off his boss. The hospital discharged*

Dr O'Neill and a case was brought against him for assault. He served four months in prison.

Ed O'Neill is the son of toy baron Albert O'Neill and there are reported difficulties in the relationship between father and son . . .

I froze as I read it. I could not believe it.

There had to be some mistake.

'Oooh, there has to be a mistake,' Bridie whispered.

The article was Sal's.

Somehow I knew it would be.

'I'm going home.' I shoved the magazine at Bridie and ran and ran and ran.

Sal was with Mel when I found her. Both of them were drinking tequila slammers in our local.

'Hey!' She patted the seat. 'Come join us.'

'Have a scoop,' Mel said and they both cracked up laughing.

I hated both of them in that instant. But I really, really hated Sal. How could she do that to Ed? OK, he'd made a mistake, but he'd paid for it. Paid for it with four months of his life in an English prison. Paid for it by serving under me in the toy shop.

'You shouldn't have written that piece,' I said, my whole body beginning to shake. 'It was mean and you'll ruin his life.'

Sal looked incredulously at me. 'He ruined it himself.'

'Just because he dumped you—'

'Oh, please!' Mel rolled her eyes and looked at me as if I was a ten-year-old. 'Vicky, I do not use my magazine to settle romantic scores. Please!'

'Well, Sal does!'

Sal eyed me with such disdain that I wanted to curl up and die. People were beginning to look in our direction and I knew they'd think I was the looney one. I told myself to stay calm.

'Vicky,' Sal said, with such smarminess that I could have drowned in it, 'when you told me Ed O'Neill was coming to work in his father's shop as a plain old worker I knew something was up. I mean, what sort of a father does that?'

'So we decided that she should go out with him,' Mel pronounced gleefully. 'Only he was useless, wasn't he, Sal?'

'I mean, I fancied him but, you know, he was just a story at the end of the day. And yeah, he was useless – he refused to talk about his old man. Refused to talk about his old job.'

'Refused to shag *me*!' Mel said indignantly and they both cracked up again.

'So we had to do a little footwork,' Sal went on. 'We talked to every bloody hospital in England and eventually someone said something. And then we located the old girlfriend who gave us photos. And it was easy from there.'

'And Sal is now working for me!'

They clinked glasses.

'Smell a story in a vacuum,' Mel said loudly.

I stood, as if in a vacuum myself, staring at the two of them. A sudden vision of Sal pumping me for info at one stage flashed in front of me. *Oh*, I'd said, *he doesn't get on with his dad.* I felt nauseated. 'You cold bitches,' I said through gritted teeth. 'How could you?'

'Oh, don't get all self-righteous on me,' Sal said scornfully. 'You're not so hot yourself!'

'Sorry?'

'Who's the girl that goes out with guys and dumps them when they get too serious?'

'I *don't*!'

'Oh, yeah.' Sal turned to Mel. 'Ron only got her an engagement ring and she legged it.'

She was twisting the whole thing. 'At least I didn't write about him in a magazine!'

'And who went globe-trotting for five years and didn't even send me a card and then' – Sal turned to Mel again – 'she ended up on my doorstep with her "I'm your buddy" routine. And moved *in*.'

'Not nice,' Mel said as if I wasn't even there.

'And she calls *me* cold!'

I felt as if I'd been slapped and, much as I wanted to run, I couldn't.

'Let's get one thing straight,' Sal said, pinning me with her stare. 'It's my *job* to write stuff about people. OK, I might hurt them, but it's only a job. *You* do it as a personality trait.'

'I do not!'

'You slag off Troy who has the hots for you. I mean, any guy that's worth it, you treat like shit.'

'Fuck off!'

'Now, ladies.' The barman was approaching with an amused grin. 'Put down the handbags!'

'You are a cold bitch, Sal. A cold bitch.'

'No.' Sal raised her glass, mocking me. 'I just know where I'm going. Do you?'

She couldn't have said anything worse. Of course I didn't. I never had. Which was probably why I'd liked being around her. And, in a rare flash of insight, I realised that that's what had attracted me to Marti too. His certainty. His drive. And the realisation of it made all the pining for him disappear. I was suddenly free of him. And free of Sal too.

'I know where I'm going all right,' I said, hating that what I had perceived as friendship should end like this. 'And it's as far away from you vultures as I can get.'

They both cackled loudly as I turned on my heel and left the pub.

I packed everything I had. I cursed and swore as I dumped all my belongings into a small case and five large plastic bags. And I cried. Tears for a friendship that I'd lost. Or maybe it had never been there to begin with – I dunno. I mean, she was right, I had never written to her when I'd been travelling, I hadn't told her about the search for my mother and I hadn't expected her to comfort me when my mam died. What sort of a friendship did we have at the end of the day?

And that made me cry even more.

I rang a taxi after I'd lugged all my stuff into the corridor. There was no way I could carry it back to the shop.

Troy met me on the stairs. He was with some weird-looking girl, both of them dressed in shiny Lycra catsuits. Troy looked like the Spire in O'Connell Street.

'Hey.' He raised a shiny arm in greeting. 'How's the finest thing in the apartment block?'

'Fine.' I smiled weakly. 'How's the space cadet?'

He laughed. 'Not bad. You going away somewhere?'

'Leaving,' I said.

'Aw.' He looked disappointed. 'Gonna miss your smart remarks bigtime. That Sal one is no fun at all.' He held out a hand. 'Good luck and may the force be with you.'

'You too.'

I watched as he and what had to be his girlfriend walked away.

Then I turned and shoved my keys into Sal's letterbox.

I found Bridie back at work. The shop had reopened for business.

'Hi,' she whispered.

'Is O'Neill gone?' I whispered back.

'Both gone,' she said.

'So why whisper?'

Bridie shrugged. 'I don't know. It just seems right. Oh Vicky, what did you think of that awful story?'

'Awful,' I said. I dumped my bag down behind the counter. 'So awful that I've moved out.'

Bridie looked horrified. 'You and Ed?' she said faintly. 'Living together?'

'Oh, Jesus! No!' Despite my shock at the day's events, I began to giggle. 'No! No! No!' I waved my hand about. 'Oh, Bridie!'

She looked confused.

Her confusion made me laugh harder.

'Out of my flat,' I spluttered eventually.

She looked even more confused.

'Sal, the girl who wrote the piece, is my flatmate.'

'Your journalist friend?' Bridie was horrified. 'Oh no!'

'Oh yes.' I sat down. 'Bitch!'

'So where will you go?' Bridie asked anxiously.

I hadn't thought that bit out yet. If the worst came to the worst, I'd bunk down in the shop. 'Dunno. Somewhere.'

'Well,' Bridie said slowly, 'if you like, you can stay with me for a while. I've a spare room.'

'Really?'

'I know we work together but I'll keep out of your way. Now, you've seen my house, it's clean but a bit old, I suppose. I mean, you probably like all this modern furniture and my house isn't like that. Not like that at all.' She raised anxious eyes to me. 'But you'll be comfortable there and, well, I'd like your company, Vicky.'

'And I'd like yours, Bridie.'

She blushed with pleasure. 'Oooh.'

We sealed it with two chocolate muffins.

That evening, after Bridie had cooked us both dinner, we sat inside and watched television. She'd fussed around me all through dinner and then she'd fussed over Ed.

'What'll we say to him if he comes in tomorrow?' she'd asked.

I shrugged. 'Let's see what happens first.'

'But, I mean, do we stand by him?'

'*Of course* we stand by him,' I said. 'You're the one that's always going on about how wonderful he is!'

She took no offence at my sharp tone. Instead she smiled delightedly. 'Oh, I am glad.'

Coronation Street came on. One of the characters was dumping her boyfriend and he was crying and begging her to reconsider. 'Bridie,' I asked suddenly, 'd'you think I'm a cold person?'

Bridie looked confused. 'What?'

'D'you think I'm a cold person?'

'Is it too warm in here? Have I the heating up too high?'

'No.' I bit my lip. 'Forget it. It doesn't matter.'

She peered across the room at me. 'Is something bothering you, pet? You've been very quiet today altogether. I know we've had a bad day and I know you've had a bad time recently but today you've been very quiet and now you feel cold. Are you sick?'

'Sal said that I was a horrible person,' I gulped. 'I just want to know what you think.'

'The cheek of her!' Bridie sounded like my mother. 'And her writing horrible stories in the papers. The cheek of her. You, Vicky, are one of the least horrible people I know.'

Bridie knew hardly anyone.

'If you had a boyfriend and he asked you to get engaged and bought a ring and everything, and you dumped him and he kept ringing you up and crying, wouldn't that be a horrible thing to do?'

Bridie cocked her head to one side. 'Not if you didn't love him. It'd be for the best, I'd say.'

But I had loved Ron. I'd just been terrified of loving him. 'But what if you did love him?'

'Then maybe, yes, it wasn't nice, but everyone has reasons for what they do and most of the reasons are not horrible ones.' She looked keenly at me. 'I'm sure you had your reasons.' She crossed to a sideboard and, opening it, drew out a bottle of whiskey. 'You need a drink.' As she handed me an enormous glass of whiskey, she said softly, 'And you are not horrible, Vicky. For one thing, you make me smile every day and' – she paused and blinked rapidly – 'you make a lonely old woman feel wanted and valued.' She clinked her glass with mine. 'Cheers.'

'Cheers.'

We smiled at each other.

Chapter Sixty-three

NEWS OF ED'S prison escapades was all over the papers the next day. More people crawled out of the woodwork to give their slant on the whole affair. Prisoners who'd done time with him said that he'd been a quiet enough guy that you just didn't mess with. They'd no idea, they said, of who he really was. He played music a lot, they said. More pictures appeared and the journalists seemed to have gone out of their way to find ones of him staring morosely into space. About five or six hacks set up camp outside our shop and refused to budge.

Ed never arrived into work.

I rang his home about midday to be greeted with the answering machine.

'Ed, this is Vicky. Bridie and I just want to say that we don't care what you did in the past. Like, it was a bit of a shock and all' – Bridie frowned at me for saying that, but there was no point in pretending we were OK with it – 'but we still want you to come back.'

At two o'clock, just as I arrived back from lunch, O'Neill rang. 'You and Bridie can hold interviews for a new position,' he said without any small talk. 'Put a note in the paper tomorrow.'

'But Ed—'

'Is gone,' he finished.

'Why?'

'Is that meant to be funny, Vicky?'

'He's the best salesman in this shop,' I said desperately. 'Since he's been here, we've doubled our profits at least.'

'He's a waster. He got a chance and he blew it. I warned him if it happened he was out on his ear. Now' – his voice had a 'don't-mess-with-me' tone to it – 'the last time I looked, I owned the shops. My decision is final.'

The line went dead.

I rang Ed on and off all that day and there was no answer. For some reason, I found that I wanted to talk to him. I couldn't bear the idea that Bridie and I would never see him again. I didn't want him to be just someone who'd passed through my life. With a pang, I realised that I wanted him *in* my life. I wanted to laugh with him, to know what he was up to. I wanted to see his orange jacket and have a laugh with him. I didn't want our friendship to end. The toy shop wouldn't be a happy place without him, which meant that, sooner or later, I'd have to leave.

I think Bridie felt the same.

'Maybe we'll head to his place after work,' I said.

'You go,' Bridie answered. 'I think you might know the right things to say to him.'

I gawped at her. 'If anyone will, you will. Sure he tells you everything.'

She blushed and stared intently at the till. 'Ed is not the sort of man that tells anyone anything,' she said. 'And he's never once told me how cracked he is over you.' She looked up. 'But he is. You go.'

I opened my mouth and couldn't think of a thing to say. Eventually, what came out was, 'That's ridiculous!'

'He never stops talking about you. He buys you cakes. He even bought you those flowers when your mother was ill.'

'What?'

'I only paid for ones for your mother. You told me you got an extra bunch. They weren't from me.'

I suddenly felt scared. 'So?'

'He'll listen to you,' Bridie said gently. 'Call over.'

I wasn't sure I wanted to now.

In the end, the choice was made for me. The phone rang just as we were closing up for the day.

'Hi, Toys Galore.'

I heard someone at the other end swallow hard.

'Ed, is that you?' I turned my back to the gaggle of reporters outside. I'd swear some of them could lip-read.

'Yeah.' He sounded down. 'Listen, I'm sorry about all this hassle. I dunno how you feel about—'

'We want you to come back,' I said. 'I reckon you had your reasons for what you did.'

'Yeah, I did, but they don't sell newspapers.' He laughed slightly. 'Anyway, I just want to apologise. I *was* going to tell you, d'you remember the day of your mother's funeral?'

I gulped. 'Yep.'

'Well, I bottled it.'

'Can we meet?' The words tore out of me. This was not going to be goodbye.

'Aw, I dunno . . .'

'Please?'

He hesitated.

'I'm staying at Bridie's.' I gave him directions. 'We can all meet up there.'

'All?' He sounded taken aback.

'Yeah – you, me and Bridie.'

'I'm not going to be there.' Bridie poked me hard.

I ignored her. I wasn't meeting him on my own.

'I hear Bridie giving out as usual.'

There was a smile in his voice and I pressed the advantage home. 'So?'

He hesitated. 'Naw, I dunno.'

'Please, Ed.'

'Naw. There's no point. Listen, take care – OK?'

'Ed—'

The phone went dead.

For some reason, I knew I'd just failed bigtime.

Chapter Sixty-four

'Is Vicky here?'

Despite my resolve to be strong and firm, my knees suddenly felt very unsteady. Bridie obviously felt the same because there was a slight tremble in her voice as she answered, 'Oooh, Mr O'Neill, it's you.'

'Yes, Bridie,' O'Neill answered ponderously, 'it is indeed me. And I'm quite annoyed at having to call out. I've rung here and none of my calls have been returned. I'm far too busy for this carry on.'

'And we're far too busy to deal with calls,' I said, approaching the counter with what I hoped was an air of serenity tempered with authority. 'There's only the two of us again, you see.'

O'Neill glared at me. 'Not my fault. Three weeks ago I asked you both to place an ad for a new person and that's what I'm here about.'

Bridie and I looked blankly at him. We'd been practising our blank looks in front of her hall mirror.

'Yes?' I prompted.

'Where *is* the new person?' O'Neill asked irritably. 'According to *her*' – he pointed at Bridie, obviously too disgusted to say her name – 'you haven't taken on anyone.'

'It's not from lack of trying, is it, Bridie?'

'Oooh, it's very trying, Mr O'Neill.' Bridie nodded vigorously.

I tried to hold back a laugh.

'So you've interviewed, have you?' O'Neill demanded.

'Isn't this a matter for the office?' I asked, eyeing a woman customer who'd just arrived in.

'Have you interviewed or not?' O'Neill thundered, making Bridie flinch.

'Yes,' I said, 'and none of them came up to the correct standard.'

'Standard?' O'Neill scoffed. 'What standard? They're selling toys, for Christ's sake. It's not brain surgery!'

Bridie was offended. 'It's a *skilled* job,' she said snottily. 'As I'm sure you'll appreciate, Mr O'Neill. I mean, if you didn't have skilled people on the ground, you'd make no money, would you?'

Good on you, Bridie. I beamed at her.

O'Neill flushed. 'I'm not insulting you,' he said. 'But what exactly are the two of you after? Surely you can train the person in? I mean, *Ed*' – he spat his son's name – 'learned very quickly, didn't he?'

'He was a natural,' Bridie said pleasantly. 'Like yourself, Mr O'Neill, a wonderful salesman, could charm money from a miser.'

O'Neill wasn't too sure what to make of that.

'Plus,' I went on, 'he had computer skills, which are a requisite for any job.'

O'Neill rolled his eyes.

'He redesigned the shop floor, he knew the toys inside out, he had a flair for window display, he was good with kids, he—'

'Wore a halo?' O'Neill looked sour.

'No,' I said. 'I never noticed anyway.'

Bridie had to leave at that comment. Her shoulders were shaking.

O'Neill looked furious. 'You find someone, Vicky. You find someone fast. A few months ago you were begging for help and now you won't take it.'

'We had help,' I said firmly. I was not backing down.

'That help is now gone.'

'Excuse me.' The woman, oblivious of the atmosphere between us, had arrived over. 'I was just wondering if I could have a look at the new Action Man toy. There was a lovely lad here the last time and he—'

'Fast!' O'Neill snarled before stomping from the shop.

The woman looked horrified.

'Action Man toy?' I beamed at her. 'Of course you can. Have it on the house.'

'Oooh,' she smiled at me. 'Oooh.'

'Call it being in the right place at the right time.'

It was lonely without Ed; I hadn't heard from him since he'd phoned the shop the day after the story broke. Lying in Bridie's spare room at night, I'd often resolve to ring him. I'd frantically try and think of some problem with the computer that could give me an excuse to talk to him, but in the cold light of day, my courage deserted me. The only thing to do was what we'd decided – that come hell or high water, no one was going to take Ed's job. Only thing was, I reckon our jobs would be the next to go if O'Neill didn't get his way soon.

Chapter Sixty-five

THE MEETING WITH my mother was set for the end of August. During the time in between we rang each other. To be honest, it was hard making conversation over the phone. It was stilted, as if we were both holding our emotions in check. I wondered what it would be like when we met face to face. Would it be different or would we be dancing around each other the way we were now?

Lucy encouraged me to be more open with Barbara. Told me to tell her how I was feeling. Bridie agreed. 'If you want an honest relationship, you should start as you mean to go on.'

'Mmmm.'

'Tell her how you feel about meeting her. Ask her how *she* feels. That's the way for things to survive.'

'Well, I don't see why *I* should be the one,' I muttered.

'Because you never *are* the one,' Bridie suggested in a very sarcastic voice.

'Pardon?'

'Oooh . . .' Bridie, obviously regretting her remark, began to wave her arm about. 'Nothing. Nothing.'

I put down my cocoa. We were drinking it before we went to bed. I'm telling you, old woman habits are contagious. 'It *was* something,' I said. 'Tell me.' I put on a mock-sincere voice. 'I'd like an *honest* relationship with you, Bridie.'

'Oh, *very* clever.'

'Well?'

'We work together, Vicky. I don't think we should get personal with each other.'

'Well, you did it by being sarcastic.'

'And I apologise for that.' She drained her cocoa and stood up. 'Now, I'm going to bed. I'll see you in the morning.'

'Pleeeease?'

She turned in the doorway and studied me. Hard. 'For a smart girl, you're very stupid.'

'I don't—'

'If you had really talked to Ed that day he phoned or phoned him since, he'd still be in the shop with us. He'd never have given up so easily.'

'What?' I gawped at her. 'Are you saying his getting fired is my fault?'

'No, all I'm saying is that he was mad about you, Vicky. And suddenly he's not even around. You should have told him how you felt about him.'

'How I felt about him?'

'Yes.' Bridie nodded, matter-of-factly. 'He'd have fought for the job then. Instead, we're fighting a battle we can't win. He's not coming back and you should face it. You let him go.'

'I didn't! I told him we wanted him back! Anyway, if he liked me, why didn't he say so?'

Bridie shrugged. 'He sent you flowers, bought you cakes. Maybe he felt that's all he could do – maybe he felt he didn't deserve you, him after being in jail and all.'

'My arse.' Bridie looked shocked. 'Anyway,' I went on, 'what am I supposed to tell him – that I love him or something, just to make him come back?'

'Don't you?'

'For God's sake—'

'Then ask yourself – why are you so desperate for him to come back? O'Neill is right – it's only selling toys to the public.'

'He should never have been let go!'

'But he accepts it. Maybe you should too.' She closed the door quietly.

I'd never accept it. I glared into my cocoa. I didn't like unfairness. That's all.

Hey, I thought, wouldn't it be great if Ed sued his dad for unfair dismissal?

I could maybe ring him in the morning with that one.

Barbara rang me the next evening. Bridie was out at bingo with a lady from the house next door. They'd tried to persuade me to go along but there were some things I just did not want to include in my social life. Anyway, this was Bridie's new friend and I didn't want to play gooseberry.

When the phone rang, I was half tempted not to answer it. It'd just be the usual 'hello' and 'how are you keeping' call that had become embarrassing. Then I realised that if I wanted, I could change it. I could ask Barbara how she was, if I wanted. I could take our relationship to a more personal level. Despite what Bridie had said about Ed, she was right. If I wanted it to happen, I had to do it myself.

'Barbara, hello,' I said, forcing myself to sound different.

'Hi.' She sounded surprised. 'How are you? You sound . . . different.'

Normally I'd have answered with a 'fine', but that night, I took a deep breath and said, all in a rush, 'Well, to be honest, I'm a bit nervous about meeting you.'

That threw her. 'Really?' She paused. I heard her catch her breath. 'Why?'

'Well—' I swallowed hard. 'It's just, you know, we seem to have the same conversation every time you ring and I'm afraid that, you know, we won't know what to say to each other.'

There was silence.

'Barbara?'

'I just like talking to you,' she whispered back.

'I know, and I like talking to you, but—'

'And I'm so happy to have found you that I don't want to scare you off by getting too personal.'

'Oh.'

'I let you go once, Vicky, and I'm so afraid it'll happen again.'

'I'm not going anywhere,' I said. 'I contacted you, didn't I?'

'Yes.' Her voice went all wobbly.

So much for being honest and open.

'Barbara, don't get upset—'

'I loved you, Vicky. I loved you when you were born but I was scared to keep you. I was afraid to go against my parents, afraid of what they'd say. I let you go and it was the biggest mistake of my life.'

'Don't—'

'But I learned from it, Vicky. I learned that when you love something you should fight to keep it. That's why I don't want to upset you or have you resent me. I'm so lucky to be getting a chance to know you. I'm so lucky that it's not too late.'

'No,' I said slowly, 'it's not too late.'

'And I very much want to meet you and even if we sit in silence, just to be there with you will be enough for me.' She gulped. 'But if *you're* unsure . . .'

'No.' I was feeling dazed by what she'd said, by the words she'd used. 'I'm looking forward to meeting you too.'

It was the best and most heart-breaking conversation I'd had with her so far.

I was terrified. Unsure. Completely at a loss as to what to do. But I couldn't live for years hoping to meet him again, could I? I couldn't be like Barbara, hanging around waiting because I'd fucked up.

But at the same time, I couldn't just go up and tell Ed that I loved him. I mean, what if what I felt wasn't *really* love, what then? And what if I had left it too late? What if I made a complete fool of myself? What if Bridie was wrong and he didn't fancy me at all? But the flowers and the cakes and the way he looked at me told me that he at least *liked* me.

Concrete physical proof was thin on the ground, though. A Valentine's card would have been handy. But Ed didn't seem like the kind of guy that would secretly send a Valentine card. And maybe waiting until next February would be leaving it a little too late?

And, just as I'd decided to leave, I began to wonder how I'd feel if we went out for a few months and it ended in tears?

And then I remembered my dad's speech at Mam's funeral. How he'd never regretted a single moment of his love for her, how loving her made the grief worse but that he didn't regret it.

It was all about taking a chance.

Oh Jesus!

Chapter Sixty-six

I BRUSHED MY hair, plaited it. Shoved on some make-up – not very successfully – applied a lipstick which clashed with my hair but which was the only one I had. Then I searched out some clothes. I eventually found a long, gypsy-style asymmetrical skirt and teamed it up with my trusty black Docs. A smock top with long, gothic-style sleeves completed the look, which I hoped would make Ed realise what he'd be missing if he rejected me.

Rejection.

The word made me shiver.

It was bad enough what Marti had done but it was nothing like the bungee jump I was about to attempt.

I couldn't let myself think about it. So I shoved a CD into my Discman and left for the dart.

It was after seven by the time I got to Dun Laoghaire.

Upon reaching Ed's apartment, I hesitated. My finger hovered over the buzzer. I made a silent vow – if he wasn't in, it wasn't meant to be.

'Who is this?' A sharp voice. Definitely not Ed.

'Is Ed in?'

'Who is it?'

'Just a mate from his old job.'

'In London?'

'No, Vicky from the toy shop.'

'Oooh' – the voice changed suddenly. 'The Vicky that's going out with the music manager?'

I was a bit taken aback that this disembodied voice knew who I was. 'Not any more.'

'Well, Ed'll be glad to hear that.' A laugh. 'You can catch him in Grafton Street. He's busking there tonight.'

Thursday. Fuck! Why hadn't I thought of that? Aw, well . . . fate had stepped in.

'OK, thanks. Tell him I called – yeah?'

My heart, which had been hammering like mad, suddenly plummeted, making me feel dizzy and sick.

'Well, you can catch him in Grafton Street if you – hey, don't you have a lift?'

'Nope.'

'Hang on a sec, I'll drive you.'

'No. No. It's fine.'

'If Ed thinks he missed you it won't be fine for me – hang on.'

Five minutes later, a tall, dishevelled guy with a broken front tooth and the weirdest accent came down to meet me. He was jangling some keys. 'Vicky, howya.' He shoved out a massive hand. 'Dermo Mulligan.'

'Hi, Dermo.' He shook my hand vigorously. 'There's no need to do this, you know.'

Dermo looked at me as if I'd just said something incredibly stupid. 'Like I said, if Ed finds out you were here and he missed you, he'd fucking massacre me.'

I couldn't imagine Ed massacring anyone.

'You think he's quiet, yeah?' Dermo began to stride towards a battered-looking Focus. 'But he's not. He's mad, is Ed.' Then, as if he'd said something wrong, he amended, 'But in a good way.'

I managed a weak smile.

Dermo opened the door of his car, which squeaked like mad. 'In you get.'

As I climbed inside, he studied me. 'Ed likes you. A lot. You're not coming to wreck his head, are you? I mean, you don't believe all that crap in the papers, do you?'

'I'm sure he had his reasons,' I offered. Jesus, there was no way I was confiding in Dermo how I felt about his friend.

'Bloody right he did. Fecking asshole doctor giving him grief every hour of the day. Anyway' – Dermo started up the engine – 'this is great. Never thought I'd be heading into town with a gorgeous-looking wan this evening.'

I smiled weakly.

'Ed hates his dad,' Dermo informed me as he pulled up on a double yellow line. 'His dad never bothered with him when he was a kid, you know. Well, not that Ed ever says that, but all you have to do is know the family. I mean, if something went wrong, Ed always got the blame – and it was usually Al's fault.'

Dermo offered me a pack of fags and when I refused, he took one and lit up himself.

'I'd ask if ya minded only it's my car – like.' He laughed a bit.

I indicated the door. 'Well, I'd better—'

'One time, right' – Dermo jabbed his fag at me – 'Ed was going out with this girl – mad into her he was – and Al steals her off him.'

'Really?' My stomach lurched. I didn't need to hear of Ed and other women.

'Oh, he's over her now. Well, ever since he met you, he is.' Dermo sniggered. 'But that's Al all over, hates things not being his. Sure he's even getting the dad's business and all. Ed reckoned a long time ago that he might as well be hung for a sheep as a lamb, so he spent his time driving his dad spare, pretending to want to do stuff and then dropping out. Made the auld lad mad.'

'I'll bet it did.'

'Then, for some, like, *bizarre* reason Ed decided to become a doctor.'

He made it sound as if Ed had grown horns.

'And he wouldn't let the auld fella pay. Said he was going to do it himself and he did. Brilliant, he was. Until what happened happened.'

'Yeah.'

A warden was on her way towards the car.

'Now, out you get.' Dermo virtually shoved me towards the door. 'And go see him. I swear, he'll be made up to see you. Not that he'd ever admit that *either*. I mean, me and the lads used to slag him over you and he'd tell us to fuck off but like . . .' He paused as some memory lit up his face. 'Right, just let me tell you one last thing, right.'

He looked hastily around to see where the warden was. She was busy writing up a ticket for the car behind.

'Ed didn't want to work in that toy shop, right. Only did it because his ma begged him to. Ed swore he was going to fuck off after a week or so but that night, the night he started, he came back to the flat and said that he was thinking of staying. Told us there was a nice-looking wan working there.'

'Oh.' I felt a glow of pleasure, then thought that with my luck he'd been talking about Bridie.

'Loved that job, he did. Tried to impress you like mad. First time he's ever done that for someone. Right. Out.'

The warden had drawn level with the car. I jumped out the door as Dermo screeched off, whooping and laughing. The warden gave me a dirty look, which I tried to ignore.

Someone was singing a Bob Dylan song as I neared the end of Grafton Street. The voice, gravelly yet unusually sweet, carried right down towards me. The strum of a guitar could be heard on the early summer breeze. The song was Dylan's 'Don't Think Twice – It's All Right', one of my favourites. There was a crowd gathered around the singer and they broke into polite applause as he finished up.

I had known it would be Ed. I watched from the fringes as he goaded the crowd into paying up.

'Come on now,' he joked, 'you pay for what you get. There's no such thing as free anything in this world. Dig deep.' He looked around. 'Any requests? Anyone want a special song? Special bargain – two euro.'

Without thinking, I yelled out, 'Big Yellow Taxi.'

He turned in my direction.

A slow smile lit up his face. 'That lady there wants "Big Yellow Taxi".' He turned to the crowd. 'And d'you know what, folks, I don't think I'm gonna charge her because she's just too good-looking.'

People laughed while I blushed furiously.

'Instead, I'm looking for another kind of payment.'

An 'Oooh' went up from the crowd.

'I want her to sing with me. She's got a great voice on her, so she has.'

I wanted the ground to swallow me up. I hadn't sung since my mother's funeral.

'No,' I mouthed.

'Come on,' he mouthed back. 'It'll be fun.'

A cheer went up. Jesus, it'd be even more embarrassing to refuse. Slowly I went towards him. He grasped my hand in his and a shock of pure excitement ran through me.

'Here we go.' Ed let my hand go and began to strum.

He began to sing and I followed.

Our voices fitted beautifully together.

At the chorus, he turned to me. I blushed. It was the reason I'd wanted him to sing the song in the first place – *Don't it always seem to go, you don't know what you've got till it's gone* . . .

He smiled at me again. A lovely warm smile.

I knew, in that instant, that this was going to last.

I stayed with him until his session ended, the two of us having a blast, singing and improvising and entertaining. At ten, he slung his guitar over his shoulder and turned to me. I felt suddenly shy.

'Buy you a pint?'

'Sure.'

In silence we walked to O'Neills, a pub off Dame Street. He found a table, ordered our drinks and, pushing mine across to me, he said, 'So, what brought you into town tonight?'

'A battered car with a guy driving who managed to tell me every secret you ever had.'

Ed laughed a little self-consciously. 'Dermo? How'd you meet him? Did you call to the apartment then?'

'Yep.'

'Why?'

Oh good Christ. 'Just, you know, 'cause I missed you.'

'Yeah?' He looked pleased at that. 'It's good to see you too.'

I swallowed hard. If I didn't take a chance now, I never would. 'And the words of that song I asked you to sing – well, it's true, I, eh, didn't realise how much I liked you until you were gone.'

There was a silence.

Ed's smile faded and was replaced by something else. Something I couldn't quite understand. 'What are you saying, Vicky?'

Jesus. 'That I miss you,' I gulped out, my face reddening. 'That, well, that I liked the flowers you bought for me and the cakes and stuff, and that I want you to keep doing that.'

More silence.

'And the stuff in the newspapers?'

I shrugged. 'You already said you had your reasons – I trust you.'

He smiled shyly. 'Good,' he nodded. Then he bit his lip and his blue eyes clouded over. 'It was over a kid who'd presented with sickness and a temperature,' he began.

'Ed – don't—'

He overrode my protest. 'The mother was a bit of a worrier and every week she'd have that kid in the hospital. There was never much wrong with him but this night, I thought something *was* wrong. The kid was kinda listless, not his usual self, so I recommended some tests be done but my boss overruled me. I did argue but it was no good. The kid was sent home.' Pause. He bowed his head. 'He died of meningitis the next day.'

'Oh, Ed.'

'I flipped. Guess I blamed myself really. I mean, if I'd argued a bit more, done more, I dunno.' He shrugged hopelessly. 'So I took it out on my boss. I didn't get on with him anyway, he reminded me of my dad, always getting on my case, nothing ever good enough. Never being trusted – and I dunno, I mixed it all up in my head and went for him.' He looked up at me. 'I regret it every day of my life. I got the sack, which I deserved – I would have left anyway.'

'Oh, Ed.' Tentatively I touched his hand. 'That was awful.'

He nodded. 'So, there you have it. You see what you're taking on?'

'Yep. A guy I'm crazy about.'

We left the pub. Booked into a hotel. Completely seedy but neither of us could wait until we got back to Dun Laoghaire. And there was no chance of any hanky-panky in Bridie's.

I can't even remember what the room looked like. Except as Ed closed the door behind us, I stammered out, 'I never normally sleep with guys on a first date.'

'Just as well we're not on a date then,' he said back, his eyes laughing.

He crossed towards me, so handsome I could hardly believe he was mine. He touched me on the shoulders and ran his hands down the length of my arms, before bending his head to kiss me.

I couldn't stand the distance between us. I moulded my body to his and he pulled me into a tight embrace. His mouth pressed down on mine, harder and harder, making me dizzy with desire.

'Oh, Jesus, Vicky, I've wanted you from the second I saw you.'

'So Dermo said.'

A splutter of a laugh.

He ran his hands to my hair, stopping to undo my plaits. Over my back, up my blouse. Kissing my neck.

I could feel him through his jeans. My heartbeat went off the scale.

Together we fell onto the bed. A tumble of unbuttoned clothes. It was completely frantic. I just wanted him. He just wanted me.

I closed my eyes and took my chance.

Later, he made love to me again. Slower and easier and just as erotic. Just looking at him turned me on something rotten. Just listening to his voice sent my heart pounding. The slow curl of his smile. Everything, basically. And it dawned on me to wonder if I'd been so threatened by him in the beginning because I'd been so attracted to him. It was probably why I'd gone for Marti – the safe, separated option.

We ordered supper to be sent to the room. 'Why'd you go out with Sal?' I hadn't even intended asking him. At his amused look, I muttered, half embarrassed, 'It's just, you know, you said you liked me from the beginning.'

'She asked me out,' he said, unperturbed. 'I didn't like to refuse her. And anyway,' he grinned, 'you had Marti.'

'More fool me,' I scoffed, munching on a chip. 'I guess you seeing Sal had nothing to do with her being gorgeous-looking.'

'Nothing at all,' he said. 'I didn't even get serious with her.' He shoved a chip into his mouth and grinned. 'I think I love you, Vicky.'

'Betcha say that to all the girls,' I joked, feeling thrilled.

To my surprise he didn't laugh. 'Nope.' He sat down beside me. 'I'm not like my dad,' he said. 'I promise I'm not.'

'That's not what I meant!'

'Yeah, well . . .' He took my hand in his. 'I'm not,' he repeated earnestly.

'I believe you.'

'Good, 'cause I fancied you for ages.'

'Even when we had that row?'

He nodded. 'Which was why I left – I was only there 'cause I liked you and you didn't seem to feel the same back so . . .' He shrugged and smiled that orgasmic smile of his. 'And then you apologised and you looked so cute with your belly button showing and your hair all frizzed out and . . .'

'Stop!'

'I love you.'

That was enough to get me back to bed.

Chapter Sixty-seven

'SO, VICKY, THIS is it.' Lucy rose to meet me. She hugged me briefly before surveying me. 'How do you feel?'

'Nervous,' I said, taking a deep breath. 'But, well, happy too, I guess.' I hugged my photo album to me. 'If only Mam was alive, it'd be even better.'

Lucy looked sympathetically at me. 'You've been through a lot this year, you've done really well.'

'Thanks.'

'And you're sure you're up to this?'

I nodded.

'Good girl.' Lucy smiled at me. 'Your mother is waiting in the room for you. She's on her own. Do you want me to go in with you?'

'No,' I said. 'I'll go on my own, if that's OK.'

I left Lucy at the end of the stairs as I walked up to meet Barbara.

Just as I arrived outside the door, I said a silent prayer to my mother. I thanked her for getting me to this moment.

And then I knocked. And I knew that I could cope with whatever lay behind that door. I didn't have any expectations of Barbara and I didn't harbour any anger or bitterness towards her. Parenthood was a damn hard job and all people can do is their best at the time. And no parent or childhood is ever perfect – I understood that from Marti and Sylvia and Ed.

I realised suddenly that all I wanted from Barbara was to

know where I'd come from, just to fill in the gap in my past. Which was my past. Not my future.

And if she wanted to continue to see me afterwards, well that would be fine too.

Whatever I got from meeting her would be enough.

Lucy *was* right – I had come a long way.

Epilogue

THERE IS A silence. A surprised silence where everyone is looking and pretending not to.

Aunt Julia comes forward. 'This must be Ed,' she says, smiling.

Ed nods, shakes her hand and grins. 'Happy Christmas to you.'

'And you too,' she smiles back. Then adds, slyly, 'Doctor.'

Ed grins at me. Holding my gaze with his blue-eyed one. 'Well, I had to do something, Vic always wanted me out of the shop!'

I laugh and he brings his forehead to touch mine.

Then all eyes turn to my father. He coughs slightly and announces, 'Everyone, I'd like you to meet Barbara. Vicky's, eh, other mother.'

Barbara smiles shyly around before reaching for my hand. 'Aren't they all so *huge*,' she whispers.

I splutter out a laugh.

'Welcome to our family,' Aunt Julia says. 'Both of you.'

Our family – my family.

The best bloody night of my life.

Wedded Blitz

For Olive

Acknowledgements

Thanks to all my family, friends and well-wishers who have been thanked before.

Thanks to all my writer friends for understanding how boring and obsessive writers can be!!

Thanks especially to the *Evening Herald* gang – Dave, Sheila and Anna – for their lovely words the last time around.

Thanks also to Ciaran Nevin – fantastic hairdresser – who checked all my hairdressing chapters for me – any mistakes are mine.

Thanks to my agent Ali Gunn and to all at Time Warner – Joanne Coen, Sheena-Margot Lavelle and Rebecca Gray. Thanks to Time Warner too for sponsoring the soccer kit of the Maynooth under-10s. They are top of the league as I write – as long as my book does the same!! Thanks also to Margaret Daly who made the PR for *Something Borrowed* so easy and to Jim Binchy for all his hard work.

Thanks to you, all my loyal readers, for buying my books – hope you like this one.

Prologue

No MATTER HOW many times Jane dusted the mantelpiece, she always had to stop whenever she came to the photo. Matt, with his big wide grin and his tousled black hair, laughed out at her from the frame. It was the sort of photo that made noise. His black hair, the green grass of Phoenix Park and his red Man United jersey all produced a joyous clash of vibrant colours that made her smile. Jim had taken it – one of the few he'd ever taken of Matt. Jim was a good photographer with a great eye for a picture. She was glad he'd taken that one.

It had been a great day, she remembered. Jim had taken his camera out to the park to do some shots of greenery for an ad project he was working on. She and the kids had accompanied him. They'd pulled up in the park, tumbled out of the car and begun walking. Owen had taken his skateboard and was whizzing along in front of them. Matt ran alongside him for a bit, begging for a go, while Di snuggled up to her dad. She was a real Daddy's girl and had yet to discover her love of all things black. Jim had wrapped one arm around his daughter and the other around her. No, he'd put his hand into the back pocket of her jeans, she remembered. And she had put her hand into the back pocket of his. They'd walked along like that, hip to hip, him nuzzling the top of her head and turning her on something rotten.

Then Matt had wrestled the skateboard from a laughing Owen and had stood shakily on it. 'Don't', she'd called out, trying not to laugh, knowing he'd fall.

And he had.

Right onto the grass.

And snap! Jim had left her side and taken the picture. Then he'd snapped her. And he carried that one in his wallet.

Or at least he used to.

'Jane?'

She jumped. Guiltily put the picture back in its place, before turning around. Jim stood, framed in the doorway, his dark hair falling across his face. His eyes flicked to the photo and darted away again. He looked like Matt, she thought suddenly. The notion caused her to wince. 'Yeah?' She made her voice over-bright.

'Look,' Jim swallowed. Moved from one foot to the other. 'I've been thinking.'

'Yeah?' A sort of dread began in the pit of her stomach. Jim was not one for thinking about things, as far as she knew. 'Thinking? About what?'

'Us.'

'Oh.'

'And, well,' Jim swallowed again. 'It's not working, is it?'

She didn't answer. Instead she felt her heart swell up inside her and her stomach gave a weird lurch.

'I think, and well, maybe it's for the best, I think I should move out.'

Move out? She stared at him. 'What?'

He met her gaze for the first time. 'D'you think that would be best?'

Best? Did she think it would be for the best? What kind of a stupid question was that? The memory of that day in the park was only one memory. There were so many more. Like the time they'd bought the house and christened every room. The birth of Di when he'd picked up the wrong baby in the nursery and brought it into her. The time he'd phoned her to tell her that he was coming home early so that they could 'get some decent sex in' before the kids came home from school, only to find he was talking to his mother-in-law, who informed him that she wasn't in the least attracted to him, though thanks for the offer. The time she'd cooked a birthday dinner for him and he'd got food poisoning. The funny times. The erotic times. The bloody wonderful times. And of course the sad times.

'Do I think it would be for the best?' she asked, her tone sarcastic. 'Is that a joke?'

'No.'

'So you actually want me to tell you if you moving out would be for the best?'

'Oh forget it!' He turned around.

'Just like you're trying to forget, is that it?' She was gratified to see his shoulders stiffen. 'There are some things you can't forget, Jim. Leaving is not going to change that!'

He turned around. His dark eyes looked hopelessly at her. 'It's because I can't forget that I'm leaving,' he said, and his voice rose too, though he didn't sound as aggressive as her. He never could. 'We had good times Jane, great times. That's why I'm going – we don't have that any more.'

'But if we tried, we could have.' She hated pleading with him, but this was the only man she'd ever loved.

'We *have* tried,' he said flatly.

'*I've* tried, you mean,' she said. 'You haven't talked to me once. You've never told me what went on in your head that time when—'

'That doesn't matter!' He closed his eyes and bit his lip and when he looked at her again, she knew that no matter what she said, even if she told him that it wasn't for the best, he was still going to leave. But damn it, he wasn't going to take her dignity along with everything else.

'What about the kids?' she tried to hit him where it hurt most. 'What will they think?'

Jim bit his lip again. She used to love seeing him do that.

'I'll tell them – OK? They might be happier anyway.'

She didn't know what to say to that. She never knew what

to say to Jim any more. He wasn't the same person that she used to know. She reckoned that he wasn't the person he used to think he was either.

'And where will you go?'

'Fred said he'd let me stay for a bit.'

Fred. *Jesus.*

She must have rolled her eyes because Jim said, a bit sharply, 'Yeah, well, I won't have much money, will I? I mean, I think we should keep the house for the kids' sake, don't you?'

'I dunno,' her tone was sarcastic. 'Do you think it would be for the best?'

'Jane. Stop.'

She bowed her head. 'Right,' she snapped. 'Let's keep the house.'

'Good.'

'If that's what *you* want.'

Jim winced. It wasn't what he wanted. Of course it wasn't. He wanted things to be the way they used to be. He wanted him and Jane to be happy. He wanted her respect again, but he'd lost that. He glanced briefly at the photo she'd been holding when he'd come into the room. His best shot ever. Bloody photo. Every time he looked at it – which wasn't often – it seemed to mock him. 'It's not what I want Jane,' he said. 'But, I guess it's just the way things are.'

She was about to tell him that the way things were was because they were acting the way they were, but it was too late. He'd turned his back and walked out.

Their marriage was over.

1

Three months later

JANE PARKED HER car and grinned – twenty minutes to get to work had to be some kind of record. Since Jim had left, she was driving to work late in the morning, which meant that the traffic had eased. Patrick, her business partner, had insisted that as she was now a broken marriage statistic it was important for her to be there to see her kids off to school. Jane smiled, thinking that being in work was sometimes preferable to dealing with her daughter's sulks first thing in the morning.

Pulling her bag from the boot, she flicked on the car alarm and began the short walk to the salon. Fifteen years ago, her father had lent her the money to invest in a salon of her own. Jane had thrown her lot in with Patrick, a mate from hairdressing college. Together they'd slowly built up the business. She'd cut and Patrick had coloured. And then, when one stylist wasn't enough, they'd taken on Mir. Much to her mother's horror, however, they'd put Patrick's name over the door. Patrick Costelloe's sounded so much classier than Jane D'arcy's.

Jane hoisted her bag over her shoulder and sighed. It was going to be a quiet morning. They'd closed the salon to do interviews for a new trainee and a quiet morning was not what she was after. Cups of tea and meaningless chat would be the order of the day. But she was good at that. Hadn't she been doing it for the last four years of her marriage?

* * *

His back was killing him. That was Jim's first thought as he woke up. Sleeping on Fred's sofa bed was torture. Not only because the bed was lumpy and small, but because he had to share the room with a manic African Grey parrot that screeched 'Fuck' at least every half-hour. Fred was very proud of the parrot, claiming that it was a real conversation ice-breaker with girls. Jim knew he'd been out of it too long. Girls being fascinated with cursing birds was not something he could envisage.

'Sleep well?' Fred, fully clothed, and stinking of cologne, walked into the sitting room. 'I was going to wake you, but hey, you looked so peaceful there.'

Jim glanced at his watch. Christ! He jumped off the bed and picked up his clothes from the floor. His boss would freak at him being so late. As he shaved and washed he wondered if he'd be stuck with Fred for a long time. The thought chilled him.

It had been crap looking for a flat to rent. Prices everywhere were so high that he'd have had to take out a mortgage on the house just to afford a month's rent. And he definitely didn't want to share with a load of people he didn't know. It had been brilliant when Fred, a mate, had mentioned that he was stuck for someone to share his rent with. At the time, Jim was convinced that it had been heaven sent. He and Fred went back a long way, they got on great and Fred was decent enough, even if there was a major personality clash between him and Jane.

The thought of Jane made him feel a bit sick. He tried not to think of her too much these days. Thinking about her only made the pain worse. When he'd first left he'd thought about her all the time – the Jane of the early years: the warmth of her body beside his in bed, the way she whirled about the house in the morning getting the kids ready for school, the sound of her laugh. He'd loved her laugh. He'd loved *her*. He didn't miss the awkwardness of the last few years but God, he really missed just *seeing* her.

Fred rapped on the bathroom door. 'Listen Jimbo, I'm going!'

'OK.' Jim bit his lip. The whole idea of sharing with Fred didn't seem so brilliant now. For one thing, if he had to sleep on that sofa for much longer he'd be crippled by the time he was forty.

'I'll see you later,' Fred shouted through the door. 'I vote, right, that we have a few beers and make a plan of action – get you circulating in the world again. No point in being free if you're gonna mope like you've been doing – right?' Without waiting for an answer, he called out a 'bye' and a slam of the flat door followed.

Jim looked at himself in the small bathroom mirror. How the hell had it come to this? OK, it was nice not to have that awkwardness every time he tried to talk to his wife, but Jesus, he wondered if he'd ever get over her. She was the only woman he'd ever loved.

'FUUCCKK!' the parrot shrieked from the sitting room.

'Yeah. Fuck.' Jim laid his head against the cool of the glass. 'Fuck,' he said again.

2

MIRANDA, THE OTHER stylist, was on the phone when Jane walked into the coffee room of the salon. Miranda was sitting scrunched up in a chair with her back to the door. She spoke in a low threatening tone into the receiver. Jane smiled. It was kind of reassuring to know that she wasn't the only one with man problems. Mir's love life could have had a regular spot on *Oprah*. If there was a useless waster out there, Miranda would find him. Her latest fella was a musician. He was dead good apparently and his band was called The Condemned. They sang Beatles' numbers and stuff they wrote themselves. How Miranda did it, Jane hadn't a clue. The girl could have had anyone. Miranda was thirty-two, three years younger than Jane, but she looked like a girl in her early twenties. Her jet-black hair was cut short and tight, showing off her perfect oval face and wide brown eyes. Her clothes always had a label whether it was Levi or Calvin Klein, and no matter what she wore it always looked good on her.

Lately, Jane had envied Miranda's free and easy life. There were no kids, no mortgage and if her relationships broke up on a regular basis, at least it didn't impact on anyone else. Mir could still head out the following week and find some other loser, while Jane had spent the last couple of months see-sawing between a sort of grief that her marriage was over and relief that it was finally over. It was only when Jim left that she'd realised how her heart had broken a little bit every day at their inability to laugh and talk together. Every stilted word had been like a piece of glass cutting her open. She wondered if Jim felt that too.

Walking past Mir, Jane hung up her coat and began reviewing the letters from the job applicants. The first one was due in at ten-thirty.

'Bastard,' Miranda said loudly into the receiver. She sniffed a bit. 'No I *won't*!' Slamming down the phone she muttered 'Bastard' again.

'Trouble?' Jane looked up from one particularly badly spelt letter. In normal circumstances the letter would have been thrown in the bin, but these days, for some reason, trainees were very difficult to find. She had to interview anyone who was interested.

'You said it.' Miranda rooted around in her Gucci handbag and pulled out a packet of fags. 'D'you mind?' she asked.

'Just one, right?' Jane replied. 'And keep the window open.' The last thing Jane needed was a stylist grumping and biting the heads off all the applicants.

'That fecker,' Miranda pointed at the phone, 'stood me up last night.' She lit her fag with shaking fingers. Inhaling deeply, she blew a long stream of smoke towards the ceiling. 'He was meant to pick me up at eight and I waited in for him until after ten.'

'That's bad.' Jane braced herself for the details. Miranda shared her problems in the same way that Jesus had shared out loaves and fishes. Most days it was entertaining, and at least today it meant that she could keep her own problems on hold.

'You think *that* was bad!' Miranda exclaimed. She waved her cigarette around and ash fell everywhere. 'When he *eventually* showed up – at around eleven – he was totally locked and reeking of smoke.'

'I hope you told him where to go.'

'Fecker was swaying all over the place, like he was after stepping off the waltzer in Funderland or something. He could barely string a sentence together.' She paused and sighed dramatically.

'Well, I couldn't have him acting like that outside my apartment, sure I couldn't?'

'No. So you told him where to go?'

'Yeah,' Miranda nodded. 'I told him to come in.' She flicked her cigarette in the general direction of the ashtray. More ash fell on the floor. Her face softened a bit. 'Aw Jane, even though he was tanked up he's as cute. He's got this little dimple right here,' she pointed to her left cheek, 'and when he smiles it goes in.'

'That's what dimples do all right,' Jane said, half-amused. 'So what did you do then?' She could guess the rest of this story.

They'd talked.

'Well, we talked for a bit. Straightened things out.'

They'd kissed.

'Had a bit of a snog.'

One thing had led to another.

'A bit of a shag.'

And then he'd pissed off, like they always did.

'Anyway, he fecked off this morning and never even said "goodbye" or "good morning" or anything.'

Jane tried to look as if she hadn't heard the story a million times before. 'So . . . what? He rang you just now to apologise?'

'No, I rang him to see if I could see him this evening,' Miranda bit her lip, 'but he says he's busy.'

'Oh, Jesus, *Miranda.*' Jane couldn't help it. The girl was hopeless.

Miranda shrugged. Gulped. Took another drag on her cigarette. 'Don't gimme the lecture, Jane. Don't tell me what I should have done.'

'I wasn't—'

'It's OK for you. Well,' Mir looked pained, as if she'd just put her size three stiletto in it, 'it *was* OK for you. You've done the great guy bit.'

Jane flinched. 'And look where that got me.' She tried to keep her tone light, to bite down the hurt. She stared hard at one of the applications.

'Yeah, but at least you *did* it,' Mir made a face. 'I don't think I'll ever get a guy to love me the way Jim loved you.'

'*Loved* being the operative word.'

'You have no idea what it's like out there now,' Mir went on, ignoring Jane's bitter comment. 'The whole scene is a fecking cattle mart. Everyone parades about like . . . I dunno . . . like big heifers hoping to get bought up by the highest bidder.'

Jane said nothing. When Miranda began equating dating to anything to do with animals, it was best to keep schtum.

'And when they pick you out they want some action, you know? No one buys a cow and gets milk in the local shop.' Miranda viciously stubbed out her fag.

'Jesus, Miranda, that's awful!'

'Awful world out there,' Miranda said wearily.

There was no hope for her, Jane thought. Every guy she was ever with had done the same thing to her. 'Will you shut up – you're like an auld wan.'

'I feel like an auld wan.'

'Come here and gimme a hand with these CVs.'

'What? All three of them?' Miranda snorted. She stood up and brushed the ash from her clothes. 'I wouldn't mind so much,' she said thoughtfully, 'only he was great in bed. Very considerate.'

'That was nice.'

'I betcha your Jim was like that. I betcha he cared about what you wanted.'

Jane flinched. Mir could be so insensitive at times – not that she meant to be.

'Well?' Miranda looked at her expectantly.

'Mir – I am not going to discuss my sex life with Jim with you.' He'd been great though. *No*, she corrected herself, *they'd* been great. Couldn't keep their hands off each other. And even though the last few years had been bad, and the sex had declined, it had still been explosive when it had happened. 'I'm not!' she said sharply as Mir poked her in the arm. She picked up the second CV. Coffee stains adorned it. Something that looked like jam had stuck to one corner. Her stomach did an involuntary roll.

'I betcha,' Miranda poked her again. 'I betcha Jim didn't do a Koala bear on you.'

'What?'

'You know; eats, shoots and leaves.'

It took a second for the joke to register and when it did, Jane laughed. 'Where do you get them?' she giggled. 'You're disgusting.'

'Not as disgusting as that CV.'

The only person out of the three applicants to show for the interview was the owner of the revolting CV. By the time she turned up, Miranda had worked herself into an even more foul humour.

'You'd think they'd cancel, wouldn't you?' she said as Jane placed a cup of tea in front of her. 'I mean, it's only manners now, isn't it?'

'You're right, but there's not a lot we can do about it.'

'No one has manners any more. I mean, take that fecker last night – did he even thank me for the use of my bed? Did he?' She shook her head. 'Did he fuck! That's everyone these days—'

The doorbell rang and Jane went to answer it. Her head was going to explode if she had to listen to Miranda any longer.

There was a girl of about eighteen outside. She was dressed in what might have passed for an interview suit if it had been ironed: a blue skirt, blue jacket and red blouse. Dark brown tights and heavy shoes did nothing to add to the overall effect. The girl's hair was caught back in an untidy ponytail and she sported oversized glasses through which she peered anxiously at Jane.

'Hiya,' her voice was high and nervous. 'Am I in the right place? I'm looking for the "Patrick Costelloe Hair Saloon"?'

'That's us.' Despite her sinking heart, Jane managed a smile and pointed at the sign above the door. 'Come on in.'

The girl stepped through the doorway and looked around. 'I went to the place up the road, the sort of empty shop where there's loads of work going on, that's where I thought it was.'

'Well, you've found us now.' Jane tried to hide her dismay at the state of the girl behind a frazzled smile. 'Come this way.'

'Yes, yes I did, didn't I?' the girl giggled nervously. 'They said that they were Cutting Edge and that they were opening up next month. They said that you were down here.'

Jane froze. The girl banged into her and her glasses slid off her nose and on to the floor. 'What did you just say?' Jane hoped she'd heard wrongly. Her mouth was dry as she asked, 'Did you say Cutting Edge are moving in up the road?'

'Uh-huh,' the girl located her specs and stood up. Nodding eagerly, she said, 'Cutting Edge is really the business, isn't it? It'll probably get you some customers too.' She looked around the place. 'Isn't it awful quiet?'

'What?' Jane could barely register what the kid was saying now. All she could see was the Cutting Edge hairdressing empire muscling in on her territory. A sort of slow sick feeling spread right through her.

'It's very quiet, isn't it?' the girl repeated. 'I mean, very, very quiet.'

'We're normally busy, it's just that we've closed for the morning to conduct the interviews.'

'Oh.' The girl gave another giggle. 'Ooohh, right. I just thought that . . . well . . . you were . . . well . . .' she paused, unsure. 'Oh, never mind.'

'This way.' Jane's heart had now sunk so far into her boots that she felt as if she was squishing it with every step that she took.

'Interview candidate here,' she announced to Miranda.

Miranda quickly stubbed out her fag and shoved her mirror back into her bag. She folded her hands in front of her on the desk and put on her serious face.

The girl gazed around the office before sliding into a seat. 'Hi,' she beamed. 'Sorry I'm late. I was waiting for the bus and didn't a car come and splash me and I had to go back home and dry myself with a hairdryer and then, after I got off the bus, I lost my way and had to run all the way here.' She stopped and beamed.

'I see,' Miranda muttered.

'So, er . . .' Jane pretended to look through loads of papers, no longer in the mood for talking now. 'You are . . . Rosemary?'

'Rosemary Dalton, that's me.'

'And what experience have you work-wise, Rosemary?'

'Well,' Rosemary licked her lips and frowned. 'I wrote it on my job application.' She smiled and blushed. 'I've got, well . . . none, really. I, er, I just left school and I've always wanted to work in a hair saloon.'

'Have you?'

'Oh yes. I love doing people's hair. I cut all my mates' hair. Your hair,' she gazed in open admiration at Miranda, 'now, that's *fab*. I'd *love* to make people look like you.'

Miranda rolled her eyes and muttered something that Jane couldn't quite catch.

Rosemary didn't seem to notice. She kept going. 'I'd do anything. Like, I know you won't let me loose with a scissors, for like, ooohhh . . .' she bit her lip, '. . . *ages*, but in the meantime, I'll do whatever you want.'

'Well, at the start, Rosemary,' Jane said gently, 'it'll be just sweeping and cleaning and washing the odd head of hair.'

'Yeah yeah, I know,' Rosemary nodded.

'Sometimes the odd head of hair is *very* odd,' Miranda said darkly.

'What?'

'She's joking,' Jane confirmed.

'I'm bloody not,' Miranda hissed.

Jane kicked her. Just because her fella had dumped her there was no need for her to carry on like she was.

'You'll get used to Miranda if you work here,' Jane smiled.

'Ohhhh,' Rosemary gave a few very unconvincing giggles. Then she gave some more. And then some more. Her hands twisted themselves into fists on her lap. 'I know loads about hair. I've got loads of hair books at home. I read all the time about hair, I do.'

'Good,' Jane wondered if maybe she might be suitable. 'Are there any questions you'd like to ask us?'

Rosemary looked at her with huge eyes. 'Any questions I'd like to ask yez? Oooh.'

'It's not a trick question.' Miranda's voice was brittle. 'Any time today now.'

Rosemary giggled again. 'You're funny.' She giggled some more before saying, 'Well, no, that's it really. Is my interview over now?'

Jane couldn't think of anything else to ask. The girl had no experience at all; her average exam results were on her CV, her CV was a mess. But, hey, she read books on hair, she was available, she would do anything and they were desperate.

'Well, thank you for coming Rosemary,' she said as she got up.

'So, when will I know?'

'Soon,' Jane said. 'Maybe tomorrow – we'll call you.'

Beside her, Miranda let out a long slow breath.

'OK,' Rosemary got up too. She smiled brightly at them both as she hitched her glasses up her nose. 'I'll work *really* hard. I promise. Are there many in for the job?'

'Loads,' Miranda answered quickly. 'We'll let you know.'

Rosemary nodded. 'Thank you. Thanks.'

'I'll show you out,' Jane said. She tried to ignore Miranda who was rolling her eyes and pretending to gag. She'd tackle her later. As far as Jane was concerned, beggars couldn't be choosers. They needed a trainee and Rosemary would just have to do. She wondered if, in a few months, they would still be in business.

Patrick was going to flip when she told him about Cutting Edge.

3

JIM FINISHED WORK early that day. His new campaign ideas for Twizters crisps had just gone belly-up and staying in the office and pulling his hair out over it just didn't appeal. He dumped his laptop and his files in the back of his car along with a few packets of the crisps and, flicking on the radio, he drove out of the car park.

Boy, Jim thought, was he glad to have the day over with. All he wanted to do was get back to the flat, order a pizza and have a few cans with Fred. Maybe do a little work. He wasn't going to think beyond that.

The Declan D'arcy radio show was on as he manoeuvred his car on to the M50. Declan was interviewing a guy who'd managed to have sex sixteen times in one night.

'Aw,' Declan said, 'I've never managed that meself now. The auld wife got tired after ten.'

Jim laughed and wondered if Jane was listening.

'So,' Declan went on, 'have you a super-turbo-charged dick or what?'

Jim laughed again. Jesus, Jane was going to go mad. She hated when her dad went on like that on air. She'd be in a foul mood when he got home.

But he wasn't going home.

This was the third time he'd done that this week. Jim indicated and took the opposite lane to his normal one.

The grin disappeared from his face.

* * *

He got a giant-sized pizza and some chips in a little place just up the road from where Fred lived. The food smelt delicious as he carried it to the door of the flat. This was home now, he'd have to learn to love it.

Fred was already inside, sprawled on the sofa, drinking a can of lager and watching the news. 'Aw, Jimbo,' he stood up and looked approvingly at the food. 'Sustenance. Good man.'

'Should still be hot.' Jim put the pizza and chips on the table as Fred handed him a can.

'Cheers.'

'Cheers.'

They ate in silence for a bit, commenting now and again on what was on the news. Jim, though he was hungry, found that he couldn't eat. It was sort of unreal, being here with Fred. Almost as if time had reversed itself and he was still a young lad who'd just left home. He missed the noise of his kids squabbling, the sound of Jane yelling at them to stop, the buzz of the heating system, the way Jane's cold feet always found their way between his legs when she got into bed. All the little things that he'd never really thought about before. The things he knew he shouldn't think about if he was to stay sane.

'So,' Fred asked after a bit, 'what's the story? You left her for good?'

Jim flinched. Fred was a good mate, he'd taken him in without asking any questions but he certainly wasn't going to lay it all out for him now. And, to be honest, even if he'd wanted to, he wasn't sure that he could. 'I guess.'

'Why?'

'Aw, you know, just wanted a younger model.'

'Yeah, figures. What age is she, about thirty-four or something?'

Jim was about to laugh until he realised that Fred was actually dead serious. 'Jesus,' he said instead. 'I was only jokin'.'

'Yeah yeah. I *knew* that.' Fred retorted, blushing. He took a swig of his can. So – did you have an affair? She find you wearing her knickers – what?'

Jim shrugged. 'Na. Nothing like that.' He took a slice of pizza and bit into it. Fred was still staring at him. 'Look, it doesn't matter, right. It's over.' He hated the sound of those words but he guessed he'd have to get used to them. 'Over.'

Fred gulped. He wasn't much good at all this nursemaid crap but his girlfriend, Gillian, had told him to be understanding. 'He's going to be upset, Freddie,' she'd said. 'And maybe he might want to talk about it.'

'Yeah, but what about me? Maybe I *don't* want to talk about it,' he'd said. 'He's better off without Jane. She's an awful bossy bitch.'

'This guy,' Gillian had said emphatically, 'is your *friend*, Freddie. He might need you.'

Sweat broke out on Fred's forehead. He hoped desperately that Jim wouldn't need him. He didn't like being needed. But Gillian had been pressuring him for weeks to talk to Jim and if he didn't report something back to her soon she might dump him. So tonight was to be the night, he'd promised himself, as Gillian, with her huge breasts, was the best lay he'd ever had. So he took a deep breath and asked, 'And how do you feel about it being over?'

Jim almost choked on his drink. Lager came out of his mouth and down his nose. He coughed and his eyes began to water. 'What?'

'Forget it.' Fred shifted uncomfortably in his chair. 'Here, is there anything else on?' He pointed the remote at the telly and began flicking from station to station.

Jim mopped his nose with his sleeve. *How did he feel about it?* He looked at Fred's red face and couldn't help being amused. He'd known this guy for years and they'd never talked about anything. They'd just *done* stuff.

'Have you done a course in the new man experience?' he asked.

Fred's flush deepened. 'I was going to say,' he muttered, still not looking at Jim, 'that if you want a shoulder to cry on, you can piss off out of here.'

Jim laughed.

'And secondly,' Fred, now that he'd managed to save some face, added, 'I'm heading out on Saturday night. You can come if you want. We have to get you circulating again Jimbo – throwing some body shapes.'

'I have piles of work on and I've got to take the kids out that day too.'

'Oh right.' Fred made a face. 'Bummer.'

Fred's momentary lapse into a caring sharing man had been only fleeting, Jim thought. He resisted the urge to tell Fred that he didn't think he'd ever want to go out again. How could he when he'd had it all once? There was no way Fred would ever get his head around that one. For Fred, life was one big party.

Lucky bastard.

4

'I HEARD,' DI SAID nonchalantly, as she sidled up beside Jane, 'that Granddad had sex with Grandma ten times in the one night.'

'Mmm.'

'Imagine,' Diane went on, '*ten* times.'

Jane said nothing, just continued to mash the spuds.

'Is it possible to have sex ten times in a row?' Di asked, plucking out some potato with her finger and eating it.

'I don't know and I don't care.'

'God, there's no need to be so narky – I'm only saying . . .'

'Well don't. Your granddad just makes these things up.'

Diane folded her arms and cocked her head to one side. 'If Dad was here, *he'd* laugh – not like you.'

She'd been hearing this for the last three months. According to Di, Jim laughed at everything. Jane couldn't help her sharp tone as she replied, 'Well he isn't here – is he? He's left us.'

'He hasn't left *us*,' Diane's eyes sparkled with tears. 'He's just left *you*!'

'Thanks.' Jane turned back to the spuds. Di's words hurt her more than anything else she might have said. She gulped hard so that she wouldn't blubber.

'Sorry,' Di said, sounding sulky. 'I guess that wasn't very nice.'

She *was* going to start blubbering. Di issuing an apology was a rare and touching event. 'No it wasn't nice,' she agreed, 'but it was true though.' She attempted a smile. 'He hasn't left you. I'm glad you know that.'

'And he wouldn't have left you if you hadn't been horrible to him,' Di said, sounding hopeful. 'I mean, Ma, you don't have to cry over it, it can be fixed if only—'

'He's not coming back,' Jane said gently. 'It wasn't working. You know—'

'I don't want to talk about it.' Di flounced out of the kitchen.

Jane heard her stomping upstairs before finally slamming her bedroom door. Jesus, she hoped things got easier. Still, they couldn't get much worse.

Dong!

Dong!

Jane dumped the plates on the table and wondered who could be calling at dinnertime. It couldn't be the milkman, he never came on Thursdays, it couldn't be Libby, Di's mate, as Di had come straight from Libby's after school, though Jane, seeing her daughter's rumpled shirt, had wondered, and it certainly wasn't anyone for Owen, because as far as she knew, Owen didn't have any friends – none that called to the house anyway – and it couldn't be . . . She stopped dead halfway to the door. Through the frosted glass, she made out the shape of someone quite tall. Someone quite thin. And if it was who she thought it was, someone quite unwelcome.

'Please God, don't let it be my mother,' she whispered. 'Oh God, don't do this to me, not now.' She opened the door a fraction.

'Oh God—'

'Jane. Dahling!'

It *was* her mother, standing in the porch with two enormous suitcases, four or five plastic bags, and her fur coat draped over her shoulders. Her hair was caught up in a rather elaborate bun and her flawlessly made-up face was spoilt by a sulky pout which pushed her lips out and showed all her fine lines off to perfection.

God was doing his best to really piss her off, Jane thought. The last person she needed to see right at that minute was her mother.

'Mam.' She didn't attempt a smile. 'This is a surprise.'

'Jane – dahling,' her mother said again. She blinked rapidly and tossed her head. 'I've . . .' she gave a big lick of her lips '. . . I've just had the most awful time.' Stepping into the hall, she wrapped her arms around her daughter.

Hairspray stung Jane's nostrils and the stench of perfume made her eyes water. She hoped this display of anguish didn't mean what she thought it meant. Reluctantly she patted her mother on her fur-lined back.

'I've left him,' her mother sighed.

'Again?' Jane wriggled out of her mother's embrace. This was not happening. 'What did you leave him for *this time*?'

'Don't say *this time* as if I'm always doing it,' her mother chastised.

'Mam, you *are* always doing it. Ever since I was a kid you've been doing it. Now, forgive me if I don't take you seriously . . .'

'There's no need to be so cranky, dahling.' Her mother gave a big false smile. 'No need at all.'

'I think there is.' Jane folded her arms and glared at her mother. She was not moving in. There was *no way* she was moving in.

'Did you *hear* your father's show today?' The smile disappeared from her mother's face and the pout returned. 'Did you hear what he said?'

'Nope. You know I don't listen to him.' Jane didn't move. If she went back into the kitchen, her mother would be sure to follow her, bags and all. There'd be no getting rid of her then.

'Well,' her mother closed her eyes. 'He told the whole nation that we,' she shook her head, 'I won't say "made love" because that barbarian wouldn't know the *meaning* of the word, but he told the whole nation that we'd had sex ten times in one night.'

'And?' Jane tried to look as if it wouldn't bother her.

'Oh come on, Jane.' Fluttering hands crept to her mother's throat. 'How would you like it if Jim went into work and bragged about you and him in bed – huh?'

Jane couldn't help it, she flinched at the mention of Jim. Then said ruefully, 'Well, that's not going to be too likely, is it?'

'Ohhh,' her mother flapped her hand about, 'you know, if he'd said it *before* he left. Well, you wouldn't have been too pleased, would you?'

'Mam – I don't see what—'

'That father of yours needs therapy,' her mother went on. 'Huh, he'd need a scaffold to keep it up for ten rounds.'

She really didn't need to hear this. 'Look, Mother—'

'So I'm moving in with you for a while until I decide what to do. Your father knows all about it.'

'You're moving in with me? Like – who decided that?'

'Well,' her mother tossed her hand in the air, 'you'd hardly see me out on the street, would you? You've always been a very good daughter.'

'Mam, my kids have been through enough lately without you dumping your problems on us as well.'

'I'm not dumping my problems on anyone! Just say it – if you don't want me here, just say it.'

Oh for Christ's sake! Jane clenched her fists. 'Where will you sleep?'

'Well, Jim has gone, there's sure to be room, isn't there? Anyway, I don't mind, dahling. Don't worry about me. I'll sleep anywhere. Put me on the floor if you must.'

She'd love to do just that. But she knew she wouldn't. 'OK. But I'm warning you, Mam, you can't go upsetting the kids – right?'

'You are a star, dahling. A star.' Her mother turned and began tugging at her suitcases. 'I'll just leave them here – I'll bring them up later.'

'I'm still not sure this is a good idea, Mam.'

'OK, we'll get Owen to bring them up. He's a big strong boy. Now,' her mother smiled brightly, 'something smells nice. Is that chicken?'

* * *

Diane and Owen accepted the fact that their granny was staying for a bit without so much as a bat of an eyelid.

'So, Gran,' Diane began. 'Have—'

'Less of the "Gran" there now,' Sheila D'arcy said briskly. 'Nana Sheila sounds *so* much *nicer*, doesn't it?'

Jane rolled her eyes.

'So, *Nana*,' Diane stressed the 'nana', 'have you left Granddad *again*?' Even more stress was placed on the 'again'.

Sheila tittered and looked to Jane for guidance.

Jane shot Diane a look which she ignored.

'Well, have you?' Diane demanded.

'Maybe for a little while,' Sheila said. 'Me and your granddad – we're not getting on too well.'

'Oh.' Diane gave her a cheeky grin. 'That's not what he said on the radio today.'

Owen spat out his dinner and started to laugh.

Sheila went bright red.

Suppressing a grin, Jane ordered Di to leave the table.

'I only—'

'Get upstairs and stay there for the night!'

Diane threw her knife and fork on to the table. 'Fine. I *only* asked.'

'Sorry, Mam,' Jane said, unable to stop grinning.

Diane slammed the kitchen door and Sheila winced. 'It's OK.' She mopped her face with her palm. 'That's only the beginning. Things will get worse, mark my words.'

If Diane had anything to do with it, Jane felt like saying, she was probably right.

Her mother went to bed at nine o'clock.

'At my age,' she said, 'I need all the sleep I can get. Twelve hours a night stops one fine line every ten years.'

Where on earth had she heard that load of rubbish? Jane wondered.

'Your father, the barbarian, had a beauty expert on his show last week. She said lots of sleep was a wonderful thing. So I'll say goodnight.'

'You can have my room,' Jane said. 'I've changed the sheets.'

'All right, thank you, dahling. You are a star!'

Jane watched her mother leave. The least Sheila could have asked her was where she'd be sleeping. But that was her mother all over. Once she was OK no one else mattered.

'Oh, and Jane,' her mother poked her head back round the door, 'if your father rings, tell him I've gone out, all right?'

Her dad wouldn't ring. He always let Sheila stew for a week or so before telling her he loved her. He normally did it on his radio show and the audiences loved it. But Jane nodded and agreed.

'Good girl. Tra-la.'

'Where does she get those sayings from?' Owen whispered. 'Tra-la?'

Jane grinned. 'She thinks it sounds posh.'

Owen smiled back at her.

'Don't let your gran see you smiling,' she warned.

'Don't you mean me nana?' he joked.

He really was a great kid, Jane thought.

'So,' he asked, 'are you sleeping with her tonight?'

'Nope.'

'Are you on the sofa?' He looked at her anxiously. 'You can have my room if you want.'

'It's fine. I'll be in . . . ,' a lump formed in her throat before she continued, '. . . your brother's old room.'

'Oh.' He turned away. Stared hard at the telly. 'OK.'

'So I'll be fine,' Jane said.

He didn't answer and she didn't press him. Owen, like them all, found it hard to talk about Matt.

She waited until everyone was asleep before going up herself. There was something about looking in on her kids when they were sleeping that made her happy. Di was in her black bedroom, with her black duvet thrown aside and her long legs sprawled across her bed. An enormous pink teddy, which took up a whole corner of the room, spoiled the Goth effect she was trying to create and Jane smiled. Di looked angelic when she was asleep, no sulky pout, no sneer, just a good-looking fifteen-year-old kid. 'Night Di,' she whispered.

Jane closed the door gently and padded to Owen's room. She knew by his breathing that he was still awake, though she let him think that she thought he was asleep. 'Night Owen.'

Finally, she turned to her own room, well, Matt's room. It was the smallest room for the smallest kid. Painted red for Manchester United, scarves and posters adorned the walls. She'd put a United duvet on the bed. Sometimes it hurt her to come in here, other times it gave her comfort. As she snuggled up under the duvet and found Keano, Matt's old brown teddy named after Roy Keane, she felt close to her child. Burying her face in the soft brown teddy, she imagined that she could still smell the scent of her youngest son. 'Night Matt,' she murmured.

5

THE BUZZ OF the doorbell woke him. Jim rolled over and fell on to the floor. 'Shit,' he muttered as he picked himself up. If he wasn't going to end up crippled from the sofa bed, he was going to end up with concussion. Every morning since last week, he'd rolled over to look at the alarm clock and fallen out on to the floor.

'Shit!' the parrot shrieked.

Jim grimaced. That bird was too clever. Say anything remotely crude and he would pick up on it. It'd be screeching 'shit' the whole day long now. Just as well he wasn't going to be here, he had to pick up his kids at lunchtime.

He tried to focus on what had woken him.

Buzzz!

Yeah, right – the buzzer. He padded barefoot towards the door. It was probably Fred, he hadn't heard him come back last night, and knowing Fred, he had probably lost his key. Jim opened the door without bothering to see who it was.

'Hiya, is Freddie here?'

Jim started at the female voice and then became aware that he was wearing an old T-shirt and boxer shorts. He knew he was blushing as he stammered out an embarrassed, 'Eh, sorry? What?'

A small girl with brown fluffy hair gave him an amused smile. 'Gillian,' she said in what was an unmistakable New York accent. 'Hiya,' she extended her hand towards him, 'pleased ta meet ya.'

Jim shook her hand and gave her a sheepish grin. 'I thought you were Fred,' he mumbled. 'I would've thrown on some extra clothes otherwise.'

Gillian flapped her hand at him and came further into the flat. 'Naw! You look *great.* Men's legs are always nicer than women's. Less fat on them, don't ya know?' She rapped smartly on Fred's bedroom door. 'Hey, you in there! Ged up! Ged up!'

There came a sort of whimpering sound from within.

'He's gonna be in major pain today.' Gillian stalked over to the press and took some Disprin down. 'The guy couldn't even stand up last night. I drove him here and shoved him outa my car. I mean, no way was I gonna carry him up to this place – d'ya know what I mean?'

Jim nodded. Jesus, he must've been totally out of it if he hadn't heard Fred coming in. Maybe the cans of lager before bed had helped.

Gillian poured some water into a glass and dropped in the Disprin. She carried them towards Fred's room. 'Make us a cuppa tea, will you, honey?' she yelled over her shoulder at Jim.

While she was gone, Jim hastily shoved on a pair of jeans. By the time she came back out, he had made a pot of tea.

'Whoever had you, had you well trained,' Gillian smiled, sliding into a seat and watching as Jim poured her a cuppa.

'Sugar?' Jim asked.

'No thanks.' Gillian patted her stomach. 'Dieting – don't ya know.' She picked up her cup and smiled at Jim.

He smiled uneasily back. He knew it was mad, but suddenly, being semi-single again made him really self-conscious about talking to women. He'd always been a bit of a disaster at it before, but with Jane he'd gained more confidence. He used to be a right eejit, taking stuff too seriously and getting tongue-tied, and now it looked as if he was reverting to type. He managed another silly smile at her before turning away.

'So,' Gillian said, 'Freddie tells me you're . . . ,' she lowered her voice and spoke sympathetically, '. . . separated.'

'Uh-huh.' He stared into his tea. He wasn't going to discuss his personal life with a stranger when he still hadn't got used to the idea himself.

'That's tough,' Gillian said. 'And Freddie tells me you've . . . what?' She screwed up her face. '*Piles* of kids?'

'Yeah, well Freddie thinks one kid is too much.'

Gillian cackled and clapped her hands delightedly. 'You're right. You're absolutely right. He hates kids, just hates them,' she giggled. 'I have a niece living over he-a and I take her out with us now and again. Freddie can't talk to her, can't relate to her. He asks her stupid questions.' She nodded and grinned at Jim. 'You're absolutely right.'

Jim grinned. At least the girl was under no illusions about Fred the way that all the millions of others he'd dated had been. 'So, do you want toast?' He stood up from the table. 'I'm just about to make some.'

'Mmm, better not. Fighting the flab, don't ya know?'

Jim shoved some toast under the grill and stood with his back to her. He prayed that Fred would appear soon.

'I hope Freddie is treating you well,' Gillian went on. 'I said to him that if you eva need a night out, to come out with us, there's no problem about it at all. I've loads of girlfriends so it's not as if you'll be, you know, a *spare* or anything.'

'Thanks,' Jim grinned at her complete lack of tact. 'Being a spare would be one of my major nightmares.'

'Yeah. Mine too.' Gillian agreed, missing the irony. She held her nails to the light and said, 'So, anytime – it's no problem.'

'Ta.'

'Now, where is he?' Gillian stood up. 'Freddie,' she said loudly, 'if you don't ged up now, I'm leaving.' She spoke to Jim. 'We're meeting up with some friends and then going hiking.'

'Hiking?'

'Oh yeah, best way to spend a Saturday. Keeps ya fit.'

Gillian must be some girl, Jim thought. Fred on a hike – it didn't bear thinking about.

Just then Fred, dressed in combats, came out of his room. He looked pretty crap, Jim thought. He must have really hit the bottle the night before. 'Hi yez,' he muttered.

'You betta hurry,' Gillian looked at her watch. 'Debbie and Liz and Edmond are leaving in half an hour. I told them we'd bring the food and stuff.'

Fred turned bloodshot eyes on his girlfriend. 'Listen baby, just don't mention food, OK?'

Gillian giggled.

'I hear you're going on a hike,' Jim grinned.

'Yeah,' Fred nodded.

'Freddie loves the outdoor life, don't ya Freddie?'

'Yeah.' Fred shot Jim a look, begging him not to disagree. 'There's nothing like it.'

'Yeah, he always did,' Jim began to butter his toast. 'Sky diving, he loved that more than anything. He was great at it.'

'No way!' Gillian looked impressed.

'Yeah. *And* he was a mean marathon runner, weren't you,' Jim paused and added, '*Freddie*?'

'Aw, no I wouldn't go so far as—'

'Oooh,' Gillian interrupted, wrapping her arms around Fred and snuggling her face into his hair. 'You never told me that – you are just the most modest man eva!'

'Aw, yeah, well—'

'Wait till I tell the others about you. A real marathon runna. Wow!'

Fred disentangled himself from Gillian's embrace. He sneered over at Jim. 'Don't go telling any more of my secrets, OK?'

'Fine by me.' Jim bit into his toast and grinned at his mate. Jesus, the guy must be in love.

When Fred and Gillian eventually left, Jim had a shower. He was picking the kids up at one o'clock and taking them out for lunch. Then they were going to head off somewhere for the afternoon.

He felt weirdly nervous as he drove to the house. Every Saturday and Sunday, before picking them up, he felt the same way – it was almost as if he expected the place to have changed. Of course it hadn't. It looked exactly the same as when he'd left. It was still painted white, the gate going up the driveway still creaked when he pushed it open and the front door was still red. The bell jangled when he pressed it, just like it had for the past fifteen years.

He felt sick as he waited for the door to open. He wondered if Jane would answer. She hadn't answered the door since he'd left, always leaving the kids to do it. The most he'd heard her say was a 'goodbye' to them. He really would like to see her.

From inside the house, he heard an unmistakable voice. 'Diane, Owen, your father's here.'

Oh shit. Jim nervously rubbed his hands through his hair and patted himself down. What the hell was his mother-in-law doing here? That was all he needed – her looking down her haughty nose at him. It was ridiculous, he knew, but Sheila D'arcy always made him feel like a kid with his fly open.

The door opened and Sheila, dressed and made up to perfection as usual, stood looking down at him. 'Hello, James,' she said, a big stiff smile on her face.

'Sheila,' Jim nodded to her and attempted a smile.

'I suppose you've come to collect your poor children from your abandoned wife.'

'You were always dead clever.'

Her big stiff smile stopped and sort of hung on her face like a dirty piece of washing and Jim felt like laughing. But before she could make a retort, Diane pushed past her and flung herself on him.

'Oh, Dad, it's awful here without you!'

Jim was startled at the display of affection. Diane was not normally a hugging type of girl. She had now wrapped her arms around his neck, almost strangling him, and had her head buried in his shoulder.

'That's a fine thing to be saying,' Sheila sniffed. 'And your poor mother working her fingers to the bone to put food on the table.' She looked accusingly at Jim as she added, 'She's working a half-day today.'

'That's because Mir is sick,' Diane retorted, her arm still around Jim's neck.

'She needs the money too!' Sheila snapped.

Diane scowled at her. 'Only 'cause *you're* here,' she muttered.

'What?' Sheila frowned at her. 'What was that?'

'Is Owen ready?' Jim asked quickly, giving Di a dig in the ribs to shut her up.

'I'll go check, Dad,' Diane said. 'Back in a second.' She gave him a huge smile and without looking at her grandmother, sauntered up the stairs.

Sheila glared after her, then turned and glared at Jim. Eventually she said, 'I hope you're proud of yourself, abandoning my daughter.'

'I'd hardly—'

'Goodbye.' She turned and left him standing at the door.

Anne Robinson had nothing on his mother-in-law. Still, he guessed that she was only sticking up for her daughter. He'd often thought that it must be nice to have someone who'd do that.

Unconditional love. He'd never experienced it until he'd met Jane.

The tramp of feet on the stairs made him look up. Owen and Diane stood there.

'Hiya Dad,' Owen muttered.

Jim smiled at his son and daughter. He'd gladly confront ten Sheilas just to see them.

Diane danced out the door, pulling on her black, tattered coat. 'So, where to?' she asked.

'Lunch first?'

'Great.'

Owen said nothing, just followed Diane.

Seeing them together, one so bubbly, the other so quiet, Jim realised how much he was missing them.

6

'THANK THE LORD those two have left for school!' Sheila exclaimed, coming into the kitchen on Monday morning. She wore a nightdress made from yard upon yard of flimsy material that floated behind her as she walked.

She looked like a jellyfish, Jane thought – a big poisonous one with loads of little tentacles floating about all over the place.

'I could murder a cup of tea,' Sheila said wanly, as she massaged her temples. She sat down gingerly on a chair. 'The noise of those two getting up has started a migraine. I mean, *really*,' she gave a humourless laugh, 'does Diane have to shout *all* the time? And the way you scream at them from the bottom of the stairs is quite unnecessary, Jane. I don't know, all this stress and fighting is really getting to me.'

'Stress? What stress? Was it stressful being rude to Jim on Saturday?'

'I wasn't—'

'Diane told me.' Jane pushed a cup of tea in her mother's direction and said firmly, 'It's none of your business, Mam, so keep out.'

Sheila pursed her lips. 'Well, you are my daughter and I have to stand by you.'

'No you don't – I have to apologise to him now!'

'You'll do no apologising on my account.'

'So you'll do it yourself then?'

'I said nothing to him that wasn't true. He abandoned you.'

Sheila picked up her tea and took a sip. 'Mind you, it's not the first time he's abandoned you – is it? He was a disgrace . . .'

'Mam, stop!'

'I'm only saying that I *know* what it's like to be abandoned, dahling. I mean, I'm forty or so years old and all alone. That's no joke.'

'Mam, *you* left Dad. You weren't abandoned.'

Sheila sniffed. 'Well . . . I'm abandoned *now*. Your father hasn't even bothered to pick up the phone.' She emphasised 'your father' as if it was all Jane's fault.

'He'll ring.' He had to, Jane thought. She hadn't time to sort out her mother's life as well as her own. That's if she could even sort her own out.

'I suppose so,' Sheila said, not sounding particularly interested. She focused her gaze on Jane. 'So,' she asked sympathetically, 'how are *you*, dahling? It must be terribly hard for you. I couldn't cope on my own with two children.'

No surprises there then, Jane thought, smiling suddenly.

'What's so funny?'

'Nothing.' Jane picked up her bag. 'Listen, Mam, I've got to go. See you this evening.'

'Oh, I'll be on my own all day again, will I?'

'The kids will be back for lunch.'

'Oh.'

'And if you get too bored, you can do a bit of hoovering.'

Sheila laughed. 'And what would the cleaner say – me hoovering?'

'Mam,' Jane said patiently, not knowing whether to laugh or cry, 'I don't *have* a cleaner. I live in the real world. You should visit it sometime.' She ignored the dismay on Sheila's face as she picked her coat up from the back of the chair. 'I'll be back around six. One of the kids will start dinner.'

She was about to leave when from the kitchen Sheila called, 'But you're only joking about the hoovering, aren't you dahling?'

'Nope,' Jane shouted back, grinning. The Hoover's under the stairs. Plug it in, press a button and Bob's your uncle. Bye now.'

When she arrived into work, Mir was puffing madly on a fag and disregarding the anti-smoking ban as usual. She was also grouching about something. Patrick, who normally made clucking noises and provided her with tissues, was instead mincing up and down the coffee room, shaking his head and alternately opening and fastening the top button of his indigo shirt.

'Hi yez.'

'They've *polished* the windows,' Patrick said frantically as he scurried across to her. Then taking a deep breath, he blurted out, 'They've also put up their shelving and, Jane,' he swallowed, '*you want to see the decor.*'

Momentarily confused, Jane looked to Mir for guidance.

'Cutting Edge,' Mir barked. 'Patrick has been nosing around the competition.'

'And so have you.' He turned back to Jane. 'Go up there now and have a look.'

'Will you let me get a cup of tea first?' Jane flicked on the kettle.

Patrick flicked it off again. 'No, go now, go now. Go on.' He made whooshing motions with his hands. 'You'll be *suicidal* when you see it.'

'And that's supposed to inspire me to go?'

Mir snorted back a laugh then said, 'Fag, Patrick?'

Patrick whirled on Miranda. 'This is not the time for insults – we have to stick together!'

'Naw, I was asking you if you wanted a fag.' Miranda held out the box to him. 'It'll calm you down, stop your frillies getting in a twist. Though with the weekend I've had, I'm the one who needs calming down. It was fuckin' awful.'

Patrick ignored her. 'Jane, I'm telling you, they're going to,' he paused and hissed dramatically, 'put – us – under.'

'No they won't,' Jane flicked the kettle back on. 'Our customers are very loyal.' Even to her own ears she sounded a bit freaked.

'Please, Jane?' Patrick gave her another push. 'Please just go and have a look. For me? I'll have tea made for when you come back. Mir has already seen it. Isn't this going to be a disaster for us, Mir?'

'Not as fuckin' disastrous as my weekend,' Mir said sharply. 'Now, if yez think being put out of business is bad, you should have been there when Drew, that's the musician I was tellin' yez about, left me for a complete bimbo on Saturday.' She made jabbing motions towards them with her cigarette. 'I swear to Christ, I couldn't score if I was a friggin' drug addict.'

Jane did not want to hear about Mir's weekend. It couldn't have been as surreal as hers: sitting watching *Coronation Street* while her mother clipped her toenails and complained about her father, while her daughter went out saying she was meeting a friend and came back with her hair all over the place and love bites on her neck. Nope, maybe heading up the road to view the competition would be preferable.

'A nice strong cup, right?' she ordered. 'And no sugar.'

'I dunno,' Patrick was already getting her cup down. 'Sugar is good for shock and you might just need it.'

The Cutting Edge logo was emblazoned across the window. The C and E intertwined against a neon-blue lightning streak. It was very striking. Not classy like theirs, Jane thought, just striking.

She put her palms up to the window and, pressing her nose against the glass, peered in. Inside, as Patrick had said, stainless-steel sinks gleamed on black marble pedestals. The floor tiles were a mixture of enormous white, black and steel grey triangles. The walls were white as was the ceiling. But what on earth was that yoke hanging from the ceiling? Attempting to get a better look, Jane put her knees on to the window sill and pressed closer to the glass. It looked like the Starship *Enterprise*. It was some sort of light fixture.

'Any more leaning on that window and you'll smash it,' an amused male voice remarked behind her.

'Aw, wouldn't that be a pity,' Jane scoffed, turning slightly. 'It'd ruin the lovely logo.'

'It certainly would.'

Looking back inside, she went on, 'I'm just trying to figure out what that yoke is that's hanging from the ceiling.'

'It's a—'

'It reminds me of something that gave me nightmares when I was a kid.'

'Really?'

'Uh-huh. It's like a giant fungus. Come here and look.'

'No, I've—'

'I mean, honestly, who would put something like that in there?'

'I would.'

The shock of his words and the fact that he obviously had something to do with Cutting Edge, caused Jane to lose her balance. She tumbled off the sill and on to the ground.

The stranger stood looking at her as she clambered to her feet, her ankle throbbing. Huh, she thought, he *could* have offered to help.

'Um, sorry about that.'

'What?' He didn't sound amused any more. 'Falling over or slagging off something I paid a fortune for?'

She couldn't look him in the face she was so mortified. 'Both,' she muttered, making a big deal of brushing down her jeans. 'I was only joking though.' You spineless git, she mentally cursed herself.

'So you didn't have nightmares about giant fungi?'

'Well, no . . . what I mean is . . . well . . .' her voice trailed off. 'Look, I'm sorry, all right?' she said ruefully, finally plucking up the courage to look at him.

He was, as Mir would say, a waste out of bed. Tall and attractive with dark brown hair cut military short. His face was tanned and weather-beaten, which made the pale blue glint of his eyes even more startling. Yet it was his eyes that spoilt his handsomeness. They were, Jane thought, shivering slightly, ice-blue and very cold. They belied the grin on his face. He would have been madly fanciable otherwise.

'No problem.' There was a flash of white teeth. He jangled some keys in his hand, 'You can come in and have a look around if you want. It's always nice to get a female perspective. And I promise, right, that the light won't attack you.'

'Aw, no.' Jane backed away, suddenly wanting to leave. 'I'm late for work now. I'd better go.'

'Hope you're not some kind of fashion-magazine guru, are you?'

Jane gave a weak laugh in response.

'Naw, thought not,' he said and she wasn't sure if it was an insult. 'Anyway, if you do work around here, maybe we'll see you coming in some time for a cut. We're opening up in a week and all cuts will be half-price for the month of February.'

'Half price?' She felt like puking.

'Uh-huh, and we'll be having a big opening, with radio and press and free glasses of wine all day, so do come to that. Tell all your workmates to come too.'

'Oh,' Jane gave a brittle smile, 'I'll be telling them *all* about it.'

'Pete Jordan by the way,' he thrust out his hand.

Pete Jordan? *The* Pete Jordan? Jane gulped. He of the Cutting Edge empire. Shit! Shit! Shit! 'Jane McCarthy,' she muttered with bad grace. This guy was out to bury her and he didn't even know it. Well, she certainly wasn't telling him who she was – it was the only advantage she had over him, so far.

'Nice to meet you, Jane, see you around some time then?'

'Aw, I shouldn't think so.' She couldn't resist it. 'I go to the place down the road. They're very good. Very talented.' She stressed the 'talented'.

'What place?'

'Patrick Costelloe's.'

'Oh, *that* place.' He spoke with disdain. 'Sure all they do is OAPs.'

OAPs? *OAPs?* The nerve!

'Actually,' her voice had an indignant edge, which she couldn't curb, 'they do all sorts of people.'

'Do they? That's—'

'They've a loyal clientele,' Jane carried on, unable to help herself. 'Everyone loves the cosy atmosphere there.'

'Aw, sure, well if ever you want a change, you know where we are.'

'I won't be changing.'

'Eh, right.' Pete sounded as annoyed as she felt. 'Well, it's up to you. Anyway, we'll be around a long time. This'll be our flagship store.'

Which meant that her place would probably be the *Titanic*; the thought came unbidden and she quashed it. No way. No bloody way! She'd worked too hard to let him come and mess it up for her now.

Pete started unlocking the door. 'Sure you won't come in?'

'Yeah. Thanks. Bye.'

Without even waiting for him to reply she left.

'Good luck,' he called after her.

Good luck? She'd need a miracle.

A miracle was what they all needed when Rosemary started work. Jane had done her best to explain to Patrick that Rosemary was the only applicant to turn up for the interview and that she wasn't exactly what they had been looking for. Patrick had been OK about it, but Jane got the feeling that he hadn't completely grasped the situation. He was so caught up with Cutting Edge moving in on their doorstep that when Rosemary arrived with her crazy ponytail and disastrous clothes, he mistook her for a customer.

'Sorry honey, can't fit you in today, we're fully booked. You'd need a good two hours, minimum.'

'No,' Jane heard Rosemary giggle uneasily, 'I'm Rosemary. Rosemary Dalton – your new person.'

'My new—?'

'She's the trainee,' Jane tried to sound unfazed. She wished she could stop Patrick from gazing in such horrified amazement at Rosemary's hair and clothes.

'The new trainee,' Patrick muttered. 'Oh, right.'

'Rosemary, this is Patrick,' Jane tried to cover up the awkwardness, 'he's my partner.'

'Hiya,' Rosemary grinned brightly, 'pleased to meet ya.'

'Yeah. Sure.' Patrick was having difficulty getting his composure back.

'Listen,' Rosemary went on, 'Thanks a *million* for giving me this job. No one believed me when I said I'd got a *real* job. My dad laughed and everything.' She stopped. 'But now I'm the one laughing, isn't that right?' She didn't wait for a reply. She took off her coat and looked around. 'Is there somewhere I can put this?'

'Don't tempt me,' Miranda whispered, coming up behind Jane.

'In the office.' Patrick still couldn't tear his eyes away from Rosemary's hair, though he was attempting to smile at her. 'Jane,' he said faintly, 'show her, will you?'

'Sure.' Jane was glad to get away from him. She knew he'd have something to say to her later.

She smiled at Rosemary. 'This way.'

The girl followed her so closely that Jane could feel her breath on the back of her neck when she talked. And she talked non-stop.

'Thanks. Wow.' On entering the office she gave a squeal of recognition. 'This is where I had my interview, isn't it?'

'Yes.' Jane hung her coat on the coat stand.

'And it's really an office, is it?'

'Office-cum-coffee-break-room.'

'Right, I see.' Rosemary nodded sagely. 'An office-cum-coffee-break-room,' she murmured as if committing it to memory. She gave another bright smile. 'So – what will I be doing? I can't wait to start. I've been looking forward to it all weekend.'

'Well, you'll be sweeping the floor,' Jane said, leading her back out into the salon. 'It's important to do it at least after every haircut.'

'No problem. I can do that. I like sweeping floors.'

'And we need fresh towels for every customer. And eventually we'll let you shampoo hair.'

'Wash hair. Wow!'

'The towels are in here,' Jane showed her a large press at the end of the room. 'Every evening we take them down the road to the launderette and then we collect them again in the morning. You can do that from now on.'

'Yes, yes. Brilliant.'

'And you can work out front too.'

Rosemary's face dropped. 'Oh . . . oh, right.'

'Is something wrong?'

'Well, I . . . you know . . .' Rosemary winced. 'I want to be a hairdresser – not a billboard. I mean, if I have to, I will, but it's not, not me, really. I get cold easily too.'

'Out front,' Jane repeated, trying not to grin, 'on the reception desk. Taking appointments?'

'Ohhhh. Right.' Rosemary blushed. 'Oh OK.' She nodded. 'Fine.' More nodding and blushing. 'I mean, that's brilliant. Glamorous even.'

Her enthusiasm was kind of endearing. Jane smiled at her. 'We'll try not to work you too hard.'

'Oh right. OK. Yes. That's fine.'

Jane handed her the brush. 'Off you go then.' She pointed to where Mir was just dusting a customer down. 'Sweep up over there.'

Rosemary giggled. 'Oh, this is going to be brilliant, I just know it.' She held the brush to her and sighed happily.

'It'll be the best job in the world. Everyone seems so friendly. And so *glamorous.*' She stared at Miranda. 'With my first pay packet I'm going to buy a pair of the jeans that Miranda's wearing.'

Four of Rosemary's pay packets would hardly pay for a pair of Miranda's jeans, Jane thought.

Patrick beckoned Jane over a little while later.

'There you go,' he said to June Rodgers as he helped her on with her coat. 'Enjoy your bridge party.'

'Thank you,' June croaked, smiling at him. 'You do a lovely colour, Patrick.'

He smiled as she left, and then turned to Jane. 'Jane,' he said quietly, 'I don't know what it's going to take, or how much it'll cost us, but for Heaven's sake, do that child's hair.' He looked sorrowfully in the direction of his new trainee. 'She'll put us out of business quicker than you can say "Cutting Edge" walking about with a head like that on her.'

'I think we've more important things to discuss,' Jane said, ignoring him. 'Like what are we going to *do* about Cutting Edge?'

Patrick looked stricken. 'I don't know yet. We'll have to talk about it.'

'When?'

'Ooooh.'

'How about Sunday? My place?'

He nodded. 'Right. We'll draw up a plan of action.'

A plan of inaction more like, Jane thought in amusement. Patrick was useless when he was panicking.

'Around two or so all right? Jim'll have the kids and my mother's heading into town.'

'She still with you?'

'Yep.'

'Poor you.'

'Aw, she'll be heading home soon anyway – Dad'll start begging her to come back any time now.'

'So Sunday's fine then?'

'Yep.'

'And Rosemary's hair?'

'I'll have a word.'

'That's my girl.'

They grinned at each other and then turned their attention back to Rosemary. She looked over at them and started sweeping vigorously. Miranda's customer tripped over the brush.

'Ooohhh, sorry!'

Patrick sighed resignedly and went over to apologise. 'Soon, sweet cakes,' he begged as he left.

Patrick left work at four. The minute he went, Rosemary scurried over to Jane. 'Can I ask you something?' she whispered.

'Yeah.' Jane wondered how to broach her own question.

'Is he *gay*?' Rosemary whispered.

'Who? Patrick?'

'Uh-huh.'

'Yep. Eh Rosemary?'

'Wow!' Rosemary shook her head. 'Wow! Imagine. A real gay person. Wow!'

'It's not such a big deal, you know.' Really, Jane thought, Rosemary was exhausting. She was like a two-year-old kid the way she went on. Every experience appeared to amaze her completely. There seemed to be no bored cynical teenage side to her at all. 'Rosemary, I was wondering—'

'It's not a big deal to you 'cause you're *old*,' Rosemary was almost hyperventilating with excitement. 'You've seen loads of mad stuff. But like, I haven't. I didn't think gay people were really like that. I mean,' she said, as she leaned on her brush, 'he's good-looking, right? That's a dead giveaway. *And* the way he dresses. It's cool and yet it's too nice for a *real* guy.' She shook her head. 'Wow.'

Jesus, Jane thought. She couldn't remember the last time she'd been that amazed by anything. 'Look, Rosemary, about your hair—'

'Yeah, it's nice, isn't it?' She began to fiddle with the elastic band that tied it up, making Jane wince as it got caught time and time again. 'I got it done at Cutting Edge a few months back. I saved my dole for two months to get it done, but it was worth it. It's held its shape well, hasn't it?'

Once free of the band, her hair, which had appeared dishevelled, fell across her shoulders in glorious curls. In parts it was frizzy but it was still possible to see how it must have looked when she'd had it done.

'Wow,' Jane said.

Rosemary went to tie it up again.

'No, leave it.' Jane took the band from her. 'It looks well and maybe I can trim it for you and do a conditioning treatment on it.' She touched the ends of Rosemary's hair. 'It'll stop the frizz.'

Rosemary looked doubtful. 'Aw, I dunno. You might mess it up.'

'What?' Jane almost laughed.

'Well, I sort of trim it myself, you see,' Rosemary went on. 'Like, I don't want an old person's style.' She gazed around at the four waiting customers. 'I'm not after a blue rinse.'

'I know how to do hair,' Jane gawped at her. So much for thinking that the kid would jump at the offer.

'Yeah. Yeah. I know you do.' Rosemary smiled a big bright false smile.

Jane watched her hair as it caught the light. Bright, vibrant, slightly frizzy hair. Her fingers itched to style it. Still, if Rosemary wouldn't let her, she couldn't force her. Well, not for the moment anyhow. 'Just don't go telling the customers that you got it done at Cutting Edge,' she said. 'It's not good for business.'

Rosemary giggled and rolled her eyes. 'I'm not *stupid*, you know.'

'Wear it like that in future, it's nice.' Again she wanted to touch it. She'd always loved good hair.

'OK.' Rosemary blushed with pleasure. 'I will then. Yez are all so nice here.' Off she waltzed with the brush.

7

'WHAT THE HELL are you doing?'

What the hell was he *trying* to do more like, Jim thought in irritation. It was impossible to bring any work back to the flat, what with the noise of the parrot – who was currently screeching 'Fuck me sideways' courtesy of *Father Ted* – and the constant bombardment of talk from Fred.

'Well?' Fred asked as he buttoned up a lurid green shirt. 'What the hell are all those pieces of paper?'

'Statistics,' Jim muttered.

'Boor-ing!' Fred gave a giant yawn and plonked himself down beside Jim. 'Statistics on what?'

'On boring things,' Jim snapped.

'Ouch.' Fred made a face. 'Honest Jim, you are such a dry arse. Where's the craic in you gone? Jaysus, all you ever do is work. You never used to be like that.'

'I have two kids, half a mortgage and rent on a flat to pay.' Jim didn't look at Fred as he spoke. He studied the data for Twizters crisps and tried to stop himself from groaning. Philip, his biggest client, was going to flip unless he came up with a new angle pronto.

'I vote,' Fred was nudging him on the arm, 'that we head out on the town and get locked. I'll ring Gillian and cancel. It'll be just you and me – right?'

'Naw.' Jim shook his head and indicated his papers, 'I have to analyse this stuff.'

'Tonight? You have to do it tonight?'

Jim shrugged. He didn't, but working kept his mind off other things.

'Well?' Fred asked.

Maybe going out with Fred would be a blast. It always had been in the past, but they'd been a decade and a half younger then. Still, a few gargles wouldn't hurt and maybe getting drunk would be more fun than sitting in the flat. It might open up his mind too.

'Just for the one, right?' He folded away his papers. Grabbing a few packets of crisps, he said, 'I might bring these with me – leave them on a few tables – see what the reaction is.'

'Aw, sure, fuck it, bring the laptop too.' Fred rolled his eyes in exasperation.

Jim ignored him. 'Where to?'

'That's the Jimbo I know,' Fred grinned. He pulled his mobile from his pocket. 'Hang on till I give Gillian a ring. She'll be cool about it.'

'Na, it's OK,' Jim shrugged. 'Tell her to come too. The more the merrier.' Plus, if he wanted to leave, at least Fred would have Gillian for company.

'Great.' Fred gave him the benefit of his shiny smile. 'Let's head, shall we?'

The pub was hopping when they arrived. Fred was a master at pushing people out of his way and Jim trailed in his wake. He felt a bit out of it in his good suit trousers and shirt. At least he'd taken his tie off and worn a denim jacket instead of his suit jacket. If he hadn't, he'd have been completely overdressed. They probably wouldn't have served him because he looked too old or something mad stupid like that. Jesus, it was ages since he'd been out. Fred was king of everything. He ploughed towards Gillian's table hailing people along the way, slapping others on the back and roaring with loud laughter over the most inane comments.

'Hey,' Fred elbowed Jim, 'get a load of Gillian's mate Debbie – is she like Catgirl, or what?'

Jim looked. Jesus, what was that girl like?

'Catgirl', who was beside Gillian, was poured into and pouring out of a low-cut, skintight leather catsuit. Black hair cascaded over her shoulders.

'Hi,' she said. She gave Gillian a nudge, 'Hey, Gill, it's Freddie.'

'Aw, hiya baby,' Gillian blew him a kiss across the table. Her voice rose, 'And hiya Jim. Good for you. You finally came out!'

'He's not bleedin' gay,' Fred squeezed his way in beside Gillian. 'You want to watch what you say.'

People laughed.

Gillian patted the seat on the other side of her and wriggled towards Fred. 'Hey, Jim, sit down here.'

The last thing he wanted to do was to sit beside the catsuited girl, but he hadn't much choice. He sat down gingerly between them. 'Hi,' he muttered to her.

'Hello. It's Jim, is it?'

She had a deep, husky voice – very sexy. Jim gulped and nodded. 'Uh-huh.'

'Hey everybody, quiet.' Gillian clapped her hands and waited for people to look at her. 'This is Jim – Freddie's friend. He's staying at Freddie's for a while.'

'Hiya,' someone said.

More people introduced themselves and Jim promptly forgot their names. He just grinned self-consciously and wished that he'd told Fred to cancel with Gillian. He thought it was just going to be the three of them. His head was spinning. He hated crowds.

'News flash ov-a,' Gillian announced. She leaned towards Jim. 'So, whatcha having?'

'Na, it's OK, I'll get it.' Jim stood up and dug his hand into his pocket.

'No!' Gillian pulled him down. 'Freddie is going to the bar – it's ya first night out wid us, he'll buy.'

'The bitch has me broke,' Fred grumbled good-naturedly. 'Carlsberg, is it Jim?'

'Yeah. Thanks.'

Jim watched Fred leave and wondered if he'd get away with having just the one pint before heading back. It was stupid, but he felt guilty about being out.

'So, Jim,' Catgirl spoke, startling him, 'I'm Debbie. It's nice to meet you.' She extended a perfectly manicured hand.

Jim took her hand in his and stammered, 'Nice to meet you too.'

'So, how come you're with Freddie?' Debbie asked, releasing him and studying him with dark eyes.

'Well, I, eh—'

'Things that desperate?'

His bumbling reply shuddered to a halt. He looked up to see her smiling at him. He grinned back and nodded, 'Pretty much, yeah.'

Debbie laughed. She didn't look quite so vampish when she did that. 'Poor you. What happened? Did you take a vow of masochism or something?'

Jim grinned again, then saw that she was looking expectantly at him. 'Well,' he shrugged, 'it was more the "or something".'

'Yeah?'

Jesus, she really wanted an answer. He guessed that he'd better say it. Saying it made it awful real though. He began threading the beer mat in and out of his fingers.

'I, eh, I'm separated.'

'Oh. Right.'

Fortunately she didn't seem to know what to say to that. He wondered when Fred was coming back with the drinks.

'I think your reply has just stalled our conversation, huh?' Debbie said. 'I thought you were gonna say that you'd been evicted from your flat or that you'd lost your job or something.'

'No such luck.' He hadn't meant it to come out sounding so

bitter. Attempting to get things back on a less personal level, he muttered, 'I hate me bloody job.'

'You do?' She angled her body towards him. She had long, slim legs that seemed to go on forever. Jim wished he'd sat beside someone else. 'What is it you do?'

'Market crisps.'

'Sorry?'

'You're not the only one.'

She laughed. Her laugh was like her voice, deep and husky. 'No, I meant, what exactly is involved in marketing crisps?'

'Believe me,' Jim shook his head, 'you don't want to know.' He reached into his pocket and pulled out a few bags. 'I've got to market these. They want them to be called Twizters. Here, try a pack.'

'Is he fucking working again?' Fred's booming voice cut in on the conversation. He dumped a pint in front of Jim. 'Here, drink that up and forget about those bloody twistery things.'

Debbie had opened her packet and was busy examining the crisps. They were tight spirals. She took a nibble of one. 'Tastes fine.'

Jim nodded. 'Yeah, but would you have bought a packet of crisps called Twizters? Or would you have stuck to your Tayto or Hunky Dorys?' He looked eagerly at her.

Debbie shrugged. 'Stuck to what I know I guess.'

'That's what I figured,' Jim said glumly as he observed the others messing about with the bags he'd brought. One of the guys, whose name he couldn't remember, was making funny shapes out of them. He'd joined a few together and had the crisp chain dangling from his nose. Everyone was laughing. Jim grinned. Philip Logan would not be at all impressed to see his sophisticated snack being abused in such a way.

'So,' Debbie said, breaking into his thoughts, 'besides giving out freebies to a load of drunken adults, what else do you have to do to make these the next big thing?'

'You sure you want to know?' Jim looked at her doubtfully.

It was one thing not knowing what to say to women, but it was even worse boring them stupid.

Fred elbowed him in the ribs. 'Whoa Batman,' he whispered. 'You're away there.'

There was no way that Debbie could have failed to hear. Jim took a gulp of his drink so that he wouldn't have to look at her for a second. 'Don't mind him,' he eventually muttered.

'He's an asshole,' Debbie said loudly.

Fred didn't hear, he was busy regaling the table with his mad days at school. Gillian was clinging on to his arm and giggling frantically.

'I don't know what she sees in him,' Debbie said, quieter this time.

'Aw, he's all right.' Jim felt he had to stick up for Fred. 'He's been a good mate to me.' And he had. He'd rescued him more than once. 'I've known him years, he's good fun.'

Debbie shrugged, obviously not convinced. 'So, tell me about marketing these things,' she said. 'What do you do? Design cool new foil-wrapped packets for extra freshness and give them extra-strength onion flavour, or what?'

'Now you're attempting to trivialise my job,' Jim said in mock annoyance. 'I'll have you know, marketing the latest Cheese and Onion is damn hard work.'

'Cheese you off, does it?'

Jim laughed.

Debbie was good company. Jim talked to her for most of the night. She was easy to talk to, not at all as scary as he'd imagined. By the time he left, he was quite drunk. He'd had more than he'd had in ages and his head was spinning nicely.

'Thanks for the chat,' he smiled.

'Thanks for telling me all about crisps,' Debbie said back. 'I'll definitely buy your ones in future. What are the company called again?'

'Incredible Crisps.'

'Inedible Crisps?'

Jim grinned. 'Bye.'

'Nice to meet you. See you again maybe.'

'Maybe.' Jim nodded.

Debbie walked off. Jim couldn't help noticing the looks that she got as she walked through the pub.

Such a body.

She'd make some fella a very happy man.

He pulled on his jacket and left the pub.

It was later that night when the idea struck. He was just dozing off when it came to him – one of the best bloody ideas of his career.

8

HER MOTHER HAD finally gone out. Jane heaved a sigh of relief as she heard the door slam. Sheila had been hard work this past week, monopolising the bathroom and leaving her false eyelashes in the sink. Jane had been forced to draw up a bathroom rota, much to her mother's chagrin.

Flicking on the television, Jane decided that she needed a break. The sounds of her two kids squabbling upstairs, she decided, was not going to interfere with her enjoyment of the Sunday film. They'd be heading out with Jim soon, so she figured she could put up with the noise of their arguments until then.

The title *Calamity Jane* appeared on screen. *Wonderful*. Doris Day had just begun to sing about her secret love being a secret no more when the doorbell rang.

She glanced out the window and saw Jim's Volvo at the gate. It sort of shocked her, seeing the car like that. Normally it was parked in the driveway with her car blocking it in. Jim used to tease her that the sight of her car would frighten any would-be thieves away. She smiled sadly as the memory washed over her.

The bell rang again.

'Di! Owen! Your Dad's here!'

'Just getting my jacket, Mam. Owen has hidden it,' Di yelled.

'Have not!'

They continued to fight and once again, Jim rang the bell. Jane willed one of the kids to come downstairs.

Nothing.

'Owen!'

'Down in a sec.'

It'd be pure childish not to answer the door, she thought, as she uncurled her feet from under her. After all, it was *only* Jim.

The sight of his tall silhouette through the glass made her realise quite suddenly how very weird things were. When she'd married Jim it was for ever. There was nothing about him that she hadn't loved. And even though she'd been expecting Di at the time, it had only made the two of them happier. She remembered him proposing to her in a McDonald's car park and when she'd said yes, he'd shoved an onion ring on her finger. It had been one of those rare moments when happiness is recognised and enjoyed and she wouldn't have traded it for anything. Even then, she hadn't really realised how lucky she was. But then again, neither had he.

Heart thumping, she plastered a smile on her face and opened the door. 'Hi.' It was the first time she'd seen him in months. On weekends she normally made sure she was out of the way when he called. Damn, he looked good, she thought before she could stop herself, his dark hair clean and shining, his liquid brown eyes, even the way he half-smiled.

'Hiya,' he nodded back.

'The kids aren't ready yet,' she gabbled, opening the door wider and catching a whiff of his familiar aftershave. 'Step in for a sec.'

'Ta.'

Another attempt at a smile as he brushed by her. She wanted to touch him all of a sudden, just to feel the warmth of his hand interlocking with hers. It took everything she had to stop herself. Instead, she let him walk to the bottom of the stairs and stand facing her. His eyes were fixed firmly on her face. She wondered if he was trying to show that he wasn't uncomfortable with the situation. Then he shoved his hands into the pockets of his jeans and his jacket fell open, revealing his shirt.

A new shirt.

A new *bright orange* shirt.

Huh, she thought, as her semi-sad feelings were washed away by a tide of indignation and hurt, there *she* was looking after his kids and there *he* was out gallivanting and buying new clothes. And bloody bright orange clothes at that. *And* he hated shopping – she'd always had to do it for him – but now, they were barely three and a half months apart and he'd reinvented himself. She'd never have bought that shirt for him.

'How's things?' Jim asked. His eyes drank her in. He hadn't seen her in months and it was like seeing her for the first time. He didn't want to stare at her but he couldn't help himself.

'Things are great,' she answered and he thought that he detected an edge to her voice. 'Just great,' she repeated.

'Why – has Sheila gone home now?' He meant it as a joke. He wanted to see her smile.

Instead she glared at him and said, 'No. She's staying for a while. I enjoy the company.'

He flinched. It was a barb and aimed straight at him. His heart sank. He knew when he'd moved out that it was for the best. He'd hoped that at least they could stay, well, maybe not friends, but he didn't want her to hate him. He didn't think he could bear that. So he ignored her dig and forced his voice to sound glad. 'That's good then.' The light from the hall window was catching the auburn glints in her hair, forming a sort of halo around her face. He wished that he could touch her, just one more time.

'Yeah. Great.'

More silence. Where the hell were the kids?

'Down in a sec,' Diane yelled, breaking the tension that seemed to have arisen between them. 'I have to get my Docs.'

Jane shrugged apologetically at him.

He shrugged back. Wondered what to say.

She broke the silence. 'I hear my mother was a bit abrupt with you last week.'

He forced a grin. 'No more than usual.'

It was the grin that did it – it made her realise that he wasn't hers any more. It hurt. She had to swallow the huge lump in her throat and force her voice to be normal. 'Sorry anyhow.'

'You don't have to apologise,' his voice and his smile were like the Jim she'd known before the edgy silences. 'You never did before.'

She couldn't answer him. Instead, she turned away and yelled up the stairs for the kids to come down. When she turned back, she was glad to see that his gaze was now directed at the floor. She didn't like the way he had been staring at her.

'Dad!' Diane appeared at the top of the stairs.

The smile she gave Jim was so bright that Jane felt irritated.

Diane flung herself down the stairs as if she was welcoming the Messiah into the house. 'Hi!' She gave him a big cuddle. Then pulling back, Diane nodded approvingly. 'Hey, nice threads, Dad.'

'Sorry?'

'Your shirt, Jim,' Jane said nonchalantly, delighted to know what her daughter was talking about before he did. 'She likes your, er,' she tried to sound slightly amused, but it didn't quite come off, '*tangerine* shirt.'

'Yeah, it's cool.' Diane gazed at him adoringly.

Jane rolled her eyes behind Diane's back, as if to say, 'Huh, kids, what would they know?' Jim looked, Jane was gratified to see, very alarmed at the eye-rolling. He obviously wasn't *that* confident in his choice of clothes just yet. 'Well,' she said, knowing she was being awful, but unable to help herself, 'I'll leave you to your children, Mr Tangerine Man.'

She closed the kitchen door and tried to block out the happy-sounding voices of her kids as they left with their father.

'Hey, I have a life.' That's what Jim's shirt said, Jane realised. He had a life: he'd been shopping, he'd been out hunting for things to make himself look good. And what had she done? Worked. And worked. And worried.

Damn him anyway.

Damn him and his new shirt.

She opened the fridge to get the bottle of wine she knew was in there. She felt like getting drunk.

The wine was gone. Typical. Her mother had probably drunk it in bed or something. She'd kill her if she'd taken the red too. But, nope, it was in the press. Uncorking it, she poured herself a glass and took a huge slug.

The fecker had even looked good. Maybe he'd wanted to leave. Maybe he was relieved it was over. She squeezed her eyes shut to block out that thought.

But then again, *she'd* been relieved when he'd moved out.

Not relieved enough to go out and buy new clothes though. She hadn't been *that* relieved.

There was a fuzziness in her head and a huge lump in her throat, and the lump hurt when she tried to swallow it. She was damned if she was going to cry over such a waster.

But he *wasn't* a waster, the fair-minded part of her tried to say. Not always.

Not always.

Something plopped into her wine glass. And then something else.

Tears, she realised. Tears.

Closing her eyes, squeezing them tight shut, she tried to make herself stop. There was no point – just like there had been no point when—

Dong! Dong!

Jane froze.

'Jane!' Patrick's voice came through the letterbox. 'It's meeee!'

She stayed very still, willing him to leave. Maybe she could pretend that she had forgotten their business meeting? She put down her wine glass and hastily wiped her face. Jesus, her eyes must have been leaking like mad. There was no way she could answer the door when she looked like this.

'Jane!' There was more tapping on the door. 'Open up!'

Outside Patrick began to mutter to himself. 'Television on, that's a sign she's in. Mmmm.' He began to walk around the house. 'Windows open, definitely in. There is no way Jane would leave windows open and go out. A security freak, that's what she is.' He tapped on the door again. 'Jane! Jane! Hello!'

He was not going to go away. In fact, knowing Patrick, he'd call the police if she didn't answer. The kettle was stainless steel and hastily she studied her reflection in it. Her eyes looked red. Sort of tired. Maybe she could get away with saying she had a headache or hay fever or something.

She kept her head down as she answered the door. 'Hiya. Come in.'

Patrick, dressed to kill in a big orange mohair jumper and red jeans, bent down anxiously to look at her. 'Ohhh, have you been crying? Your eyes are all red and swollen-looking.'

'Hay fever,' she mumbled, reddening.

'Really? At this time of year?'

Jane shrugged.

'Isn't it unusual to get it at this time of year? I hope that's what it is and that it's not the flu or anything. The last thing we need is you sick.' He turned from her. 'Hey, great wallpaper. Did you get that in Habitat?'

'Yep.'

He smiled. 'I can tell, you see. An eye for good quality, that's me.' He held up a briefcase 'Plan of action,' he grinned.

Jane held up her wine glass. 'Plan of action.'

Patrick giggled. 'Is there some for me?'

'Loads.'

He ruffled her hair and walked past her into the kitchen.

After Jane had topped up her own drink and poured a generous glass for Patrick, he opened his briefcase. 'I've just jotted down a few ideas that might work. You've probably done the same.'

'Well, jotted down, no,' Jane admitted, 'but I've been thinking about the best way to market ourselves.'

'And here they are.' Patrick ignored her as he drew a tatty little notebook from the depths of his case.

Jane would have smiled only it was hard to get the image of Jim in his orange shirt out of her head, especially as Patrick was wearing orange too.

Patrick coughed and she smiled.

Jim had looked great.

Patrick smoothed out his notebook and after a small silence began, 'We're going to have to up the profile of the salon somehow – are you with me?'

Jane hoped that the rest of his stuff wasn't so blindingly obvious. She nodded, only half-listening. *And the gentle way he'd said that she didn't have to apologise. She loved his voice when he sounded like that . . .*

'Firstly,' Patrick said smugly, 'I'm going to spy on Cutting Edge – see what sort of shampoos and colours they use and then do something with that information.'

As if on cue the tune to *Mission: Impossible* began on the telly. Jane smirked.

Patrick didn't seem to notice. 'The next stage involves your father, Jane.'

'Sorry. What?'

'The next stage involves your father, Jane. Are you listening at all?'

'Yeah. Yeah. Sorry.' She took a gulp of wine. 'Fire away.'

'Are you all right? You don't seem your usual sunny self. Is there something wrong?'

She shook her head. The concern in his voice was making her weepy and she was not about to cry in front of Patrick, especially as the future of the salon was at stake. This was probably the most important meeting of her life so far.

'Right.' Patrick sounded doubtful. 'If you're sure.'

'I'm fine – go ahead.' *Patrick had an orange jumper on.*

'I was wondering if he'd give us a plug or two on his show.'

Jane had thought of that idea and immediately discarded it.

She managed a grin. 'Patrick, if we'd topless lap dancers prancing about as we cut hair, he'd mention us, but otherwise . . .'

'Mmm,' Patrick bit his lip, 'yes, I suppose it *is* that kind of show.'

'And if he did mention us,' Jane continued, 'we'd get every pervert in town coming through the door.'

'Business is business.'

He meant it too, Jane knew. 'I'll see what I can do.' She bit her lip. 'It might be difficult though, seeing as Mam is still here.'

'I thought you said that she was going back soon?'

'Yeah, well, I don't know about that.' Her dad had phoned the night before just for a chat and to ask how she was coping without Jim. At first Jane had been convinced that it was a cover for asking about Sheila, but her dad hadn't mentioned her once. The signs for an early reconciliation were not looking good.

'Ohhhhh, you poor duck.' Patrick squeezed her hand. 'I did think you looked a bit down today, and I thought that maybe you'd been told you only had a week to live or something, but I never envisioned anything this bad!'

Jane smiled weakly. Tears pricked her eyes again.

Patrick noticed. 'Heeey, it's not *that* bad, is it?'

It was no use. His big orange jumper was making her cry. His kind, sympathetic face was making her cry. The way he was squeezing her hand was making her cry.

'Hey.' His big scratchy orange arm wrapped itself around her. 'Hey, what's wrong honey pie?'

Tears were plopping into her wine, her nose was running, her shoulders were shaking and her sleeve was getting wet. Damn it! Attempting to swallow the hurt only made things worse.

'Cry, pet,' he whispered. 'Get it out.' He pulled his hanky out of his pocket and pressed it into her hand. 'This isn't hay fever at all, is it?'

'No.'

'Well, then, what is it? Is it . . .' he hesitated, 'Jim?'

She nodded. 'He's wearing new orange shirts that I didn't buy for him.'

Patrick had been great. Their business meeting had gone by the board as he'd listened to her sniff and snuffle her way through the miserable story of the last four years of her marriage. Of course, he'd known some of it, but not everything, and anyway, half of what she'd said hadn't made any sense but it didn't seem to matter. She just couldn't pretend that it was fine to be separated any more. OK, so it was a relief not to have the silences or to be walking on eggshells all the time, but she felt like a failure.

'No,' Patrick handed her a cup of coffee. 'You're not a failure. You and Jim, well,' he sat beside her, 'you've had it tough, you know. At least you both tried.'

'Not hard enough though.'

'And what is hard enough?' He pushed her hair behind her ear. 'Suits you better,' he murmured. 'You were together for a long time. You had good times. You've done well, honey pie, to be where you are today.'

Jane shook her head.

'You've got your own business, two kids, me and Mir. Some people would have given up, but not you, you kept going.'

'I had no choice.'

'You did, you know.' Patrick hugged her. 'You could have given up, but you didn't. You are a fighter, Jane. Always will be – that's what I like about you. *Love* about you,' he clarified.

Jane said nothing. She was a fighter all right. She bloody well seemed to fight with everyone these days, her daughter and mother included.

'And,' Patrick went on, 'have you considered the possibility, Jane, that maybe Jim *needed* the orange shirt?'

'He needed an orange shirt like I need smallpox.'

Patrick laughed loudly and for the first time that day, she smiled too.

* * *

At five, he left. They hadn't managed to discuss any of Patrick's other plans for the salon, but he'd told her there were more important things to worry about.

'We'll discuss them another time,' he tapped his folder and smiled. 'Meantime, I'll work on them and then when you're emotionally stronger you can see them come to fruition. There's loads we can do. And you,' he pointed a stern finger at her, 'don't go getting drunk. That's the worst thing to do. Have a lie in tomorrow – I'll go in for nine. Give yourself a nice bath with some smelly candles and you'll feel a lot better.'

'Maybe I will,' Jane watched him leave, feeling sort of lonely when Patrick drove up the road and out of sight. But it had been nice to confide in him. It had been a long time since she'd talked so frankly to someone and it left her feeling lighter, more able to cope.

9

'THANKS FOR THE shirt.' Jim peeled the orange shirt off and threw it on top of the stack of other stuff that he had to take to the laundry.

'No probs,' Fred grinned. 'Jaysus, I can't believe you forgot to get your washing done.' He grinned at the mountain of clothes in the black sack. 'What sort of a moron does that?'

'The sort that keeps forgetting to go to a laundry,' Jim said sheepishly.

'So wifey looked after you well, then?'

Jim shrugged. He didn't like discussing Jane with Fred. The two had never liked each other, mainly because Fred had advised Jim not to marry Jane under any circumstances. 'She'll turn out just like her mother,' he'd warned.

On that count, Fred had been dead wrong.

'Tell ya what,' Fred went on, cutting into his thoughts, 'I'd rather do me own laundry than be stuck with a woman for ever. Couldn't stand that.'

'And that's what you tell Gillian, is it?' Jim grinned.

Fred shrugged and searched around for his jacket. 'Gillian knows the score. She's cool.'

'And you'd never consider her as potential wife material?'

'Listen, Jimbo, I'd never consider any woman as potential wife material. The shine doesn't last, you know what I'm saying?' Fred pulled on his leather jacket. 'Things go great for a while and then it's . . . bang!'

'Lots of bang,' Jim grinned again.

'Dirty fucker!'

They laughed.

'Anyway,' Fred said, 'Gillian knows how I feel. And while you're here, she can't move in, can she?' He smiled at his brilliance.

'I can move out.'

'Don't even think about it! D'you want to ruin me life?' He grinned, poked his finger into the bird cage where he was given an affectionate nip and then, giving himself the final once over in the mirror, he left the flat.

So that's why Fred had asked him to stay, Jim realised – to stop Gillian from trying to get him to commit. He felt oddly let down. He wondered, not for the first time, how a guy could go through life without caring for anyone. Still, maybe Fred was one of the lucky ones. He'd never be in this mess if he'd listened to Fred all those years ago.

But then again, he wouldn't have had eleven happy years with his kids. He wouldn't have woken up with Jane beside him every morning. He wouldn't have seen her all tousle-haired and sleepy-eyed as she stretched like a cat under the covers. He wouldn't have kissed her until she cried out.

He wouldn't have had a life, he realised.

But he wouldn't be in such a mess now, either.

Jane got the call just as she was about to step into her camomile-scented bath. For a second she thought of ignoring it, but the fact that her mother hadn't yet arrived back from her shopping spree decided her. Sheila loved shopping, but there was nowhere still open at nine on a Sunday night. Maybe, Jane thought hopefully, as she picked up the receiver, she's gone back to Dad and she's ringing to tell me.

It *was* her mother.

'Jane, dahling,' she whimpered. 'Come and get me, please. I'm in Pearse Street Garda station. Oh, come quickly, dahling. Please.' Without further explanation, Sheila hung up.

Jane, sick with worry, abandoned her bath, told the kids to be good and raced across town to her mother.

Apparently, from what Jane could gather from the guard on duty, Sheila had been arrested for using a stolen credit card.

'Honestly,' her mother said, pale-faced, as she tottered out of the station behind Jane, 'they didn't even know who I was.' She glared at the policeman on the desk. 'I told them I was Declan's wife and they just kept sniggering at me.'

'Come on.' Jane took her mother by the arm and began to lead her to the car which was double-parked outside. 'You'll be fine.'

'I'll never get over this,' Sheila gulped. 'The *humiliation*.' She clutched her daughter's hand. 'Not being believed is the worst ordeal that anyone could suffer.'

Jane grinned. In her mother's life, it probably *was* the worst ordeal she'd ever suffered.

'I mean,' Sheila continued, 'I must have said about a hundred times who I was, but they just kept saying, "Of course you are, dear."'

'Maybe they didn't recognise you because the photo the press use of you is about twenty years out of date.' She unlocked the car.

'That's the best photo that's ever been taken of me.' Sheila sank into the passenger seat and pulled down the mirror. 'I got it professionally done. It was the time they did the big spread on our house in that celebrity magazine. D'you remember?'

Did she remember? She'd been fourteen and the slagging she'd got at school for having a picture of her bed in a national magazine had been awful. And the picture of her parents lolling across their bed with her dad in his boxers and her mother in her baby doll haunted her to this day.

Jane knew that she should have been annoyed with her mother. After all, the lovely bath she'd prepared for herself was growing cold at home, her bubble bath was wasted, her precious store of scented oil gone, and all because her mother had been arrested. But God, it had almost been worth it to see her sitting in all her finery in a holding cell.

Sheila began to examine herself in the mirror. 'Well, at least my make-up stood up to the stress of the day,' she murmured. 'Thank God I looked well through my ordeal.'

'That's the important thing,' Jane said drily.

'But my hair now,' Sheila began pulling fistfuls of hair out of position, 'that's very untidy. That hairspray didn't do a good job at all. I'll never buy that again. This,' another bit of hair was yanked out of place, 'shouldn't happen with a really good quality spray.'

'So tell me, what *did* happen?' Jane was still unclear on the details.

The subject change caught Sheila off balance. 'I already told you,' she snapped. 'Your father reported a stolen credit card. Stupid man didn't realise that I'd taken it.' She brushed a tendril of hair from her face. 'Of course, if he'd bothered to ring me, he'd have known. So there I was, in the middle of BT's, buying some fabulous clothes – oh, dahling, you'd just die for them. There was this exquisite cerise top with the most gorgeous beading on the sleeves. And some of the shoes were really lovely.' She looked pointedly at Jane's trainers. 'Much nicer than those things you wear, dahling.'

'So, what? You went to pay and . . . ?'

'I went to pay, and this gangly girl on the till – I don't know how she got the job, really, you should have seen her, dahling – working in a supermarket would be too good for her. She had an awful voice and her make-up was moving all on its own. Awful.' Sheila shuddered.

'And?' Jane prompted.

Sheila looked blank for a second and then gave a brittle laugh. 'Oh, yes. Well, this horrible girl tells me to go to the manager's office. And when I get there, I'm told that I'm under arrest – I mean, can you imagine it, dahling?'

'Must've been a shock,' Jane murmured, trying to sound sympathetic.

'A shock!' Sheila rolled her eyes. 'I didn't believe it. I laughed. I asked them if they knew who I was. I said, "I'm Sheila D'arcy", and they said that *of course* I was. Then I was taken away. And then, hours later, I was told I could go.'

'Did they ring Dad?'

Sheila shrugged. 'I don't know. I don't even want to think about it.'

'Well I do,' Jane said. 'I mean, did Dad know they'd arrested you? What's happened to the credit card?'

'Gone.' Sheila sighed. 'It was his card as it happens. Mine is in the red. I can't pay it now.'

Wonderful! Jane clenched the steering wheel tightly. 'Well, Mother,' she said, through gritted teeth, 'maybe you should ring Dad tomorrow and find out what you're going to do about money now.'

'Ring him?' Sheila laughed. 'You have got to be joking. He'll have to ring me – to apologise. He'll be on that phone quick smart tomorrow, I can tell you.'

'How can you say that?' Jane demanded. 'He hasn't rung you at all, he had you arrested for using his card and he's left you with no money – *you* have to ring him!'

'I don't *have* to do anything,' Sheila said. 'The man is a barbarian, I'm always telling you that. And please don't rub in the fact that I was arrested, I thought you were better than that, dahling.'

Jesus, the woman was impossible!

Jim liked the silence of night-time. He found it easier to work when everyone else was asleep. It hadn't always been like that, but for the past few years, he'd done his best work at night. It was far better, he figured, to work productively, than to lie in the darkness trying not to think. It had been a good day, first he'd had the kids and they'd been great and then after he'd dropped them home – without seeing Jane – he'd gone back to the flat. Gillian was there with her six-year-old niece in tow and she'd let Jim study her as she played with the Twizters crisps. Fred hadn't been impressed. He'd spent the whole time yawning and complaining loudly about how bored he was. But Gillian, much to Jim's amusement, had ignored him. She knew how to handle Fred all right.

'Don't ya mind him,' she kept saying to Jim. 'Selfish, that's whad he is. Ignore him.' Then, blowing a kiss in her boyfriend's direction, she said, 'Why don't ya make yourself useful honey and put the kettle on?'

So Fred had made them all coffee and been sent out to buy biscuits. When Gillian left, Fred had gone to bed, but Jim was still up at four in the morning, contemplating perhaps the biggest idea of his career so far. The preliminary artwork was completed; the idea was beginning to take shape. He reluctantly decided that maybe he should get some sleep, he was running on empty by this stage, so he lay on the sofa, fully clothed, with the duvet thrown over him. It was no use – ideas were pounding his brain. He finally conked out around five, but by seven-thirty he was washed, shaved and ready for the off.

Philip Logan was expecting a great campaign and if Jim had anything to do with it, a great campaign he would get.

10

'AW, HERE SHE is,' Diane called as her grandmother came down to breakfast. 'Owen, have you got your valuables locked up?'

Owen half-smiled but said nothing.

Sheila looked wearily at Diane as she sat down. 'Honestly, dahling, have you so little in your life that you have to make the same silly comments every morning?' She poured herself some tea. 'I feel sorry for you.'

'Huh,' Diane muttered, 'if you felt that sorry for me you'd go home.'

'Diane,' Jane caught her daughter's eye across the table. 'Stop it!' she mouthed.

Di gave her a cocky look in return, which made Jane smile. Jesus, she was as cheeky as hell, but you had to admire her spirit.

'Haven't you your school books to organise?'

'Yep,' Diane agreed. 'Better make sure they're all still there. After all,' she threw mock-dark looks in her nana's direction. 'We've a thief in our midst.'

Owen started to laugh, which made Jane laugh. Owen was normally so quiet that it was good to see him laugh at something. Spotting her mother's anguished look, she spluttered out a 'Sorry, Mam,' and turned from her mother's martyred face to Owen. 'Come on Owen, will you get a move on? You'll be late.'

Owen stood up. 'I'll go now. Me bag is ready.' He found his coat amidst the tangle of clothes hanging on the end of the stairs and, with a brief nod at his mother and nana, he left.

'You've very strange children, dahling,' Sheila observed. 'One attacking me constantly and another who hardly talks at all.' She took a slice of toast from the plate in the middle of the table and examined it. Putting it back, she took some fresh bread out and looked around for the toaster.

'What's wrong with the toast that's already there?' Jane asked, her smile disappearing. 'You're wasting food.'

'I like a nice crisp toast,' Sheila explained. 'That slice is too thick. Bad for the digestion,' she said. 'Very bad.' She busied herself trying to figure out how the toaster worked, then she sat staring into it, as if willing it to hurry up. Jane tidied the kitchen, picking up cups and saucers and stacking them in the dish-washer. She then wiped the table down. She wondered how to broach the subject of her father with her mother. It was best to wait until her mother was sitting comfortably.

It took about five minutes. Sheila got her toast, buttered it, poured herself some fresh tea and began to nibble the crust very daintily.

Even the way her mother ate was beginning to get on her nerves.

'Mam,' Jane slid onto the seat beside her, trying to ignore the little crunchy sounds she was making. 'Dad still hasn't rung, has he?'

Sheila stiffened. She swallowed hard and drank some tea. 'Too busy trying to impress the nation with filthy comments,' she said airily.

'But he must know you're still here?'

'Well of course he knows.' Sheila rolled her eyes. 'The news-papers saw to that, didn't they?'

Jane took a deep breath and said the words she swore she'd never say again: 'Maybe I should go and see Dad, try and sort this thing out?'

'Maybe you should just mind your own business,' Sheila said smartly. 'If I were you, I'd sort your rude daughter out. Honestly, I've never met such a cheeky child. You were never like that.'

'I'm surprised you noticed,' Jane said. 'It's not as if you were around much.'

'Well *of course* I noticed.' Sheila was offended. 'You were such a good girl. Really good.'

Jane rolled her eyes. 'Anyway, we're not talking about me,' she got the subject back on track. 'We're talking about you and Dad.'

'No, dahling,' Sheila gave a bright, brittle smile, 'you are the one talking about Declan. I most certainly am not.' Without finishing her toast, she left the room.

'Well, the nerve!' Patrick, who had just collected the post from the door, was waving a bright red and white envelope about. 'Honestly, I can't get over it.'

'The nerve of what?' Jane was studying her appointments for the morning and to her dismay Eileen Simms had booked a cut. Eileen's hair was the pits to style as she couldn't keep her head still for more than two seconds and she constantly talked about her dogs.

'The nerve of this!' With a dramatic flourish Patrick laid a flashy card down in front of her. 'An invite from Cutting Edge to their big opening today. I mean *really*.'

'From Cutting Edge?' Rosemary sounded excited. She abandoned her towel folding to peruse the invite. 'Can you not go, Pat – is that it? I'll go if you want – I think the place up there is deadly.'

'No one from here is setting foot in that place,' Patrick said sternly. 'Not unless they want to lose their jobs, that is.'

Rosemary giggled. 'Sure that'd be unfair dismissal, wouldn't it?'

'Yes,' Patrick nodded, 'indeed it would, but that's never stopped me before.'

Rosemary gaped at him as he stalked past her. 'Grumpy knickers,' she muttered, copying Mir's expression. She adjusted her glasses and, with a sulky pout, returned to her towel folding.

Jane idly studied the invite. It was a no-expense-spared gold embossed card. Addressed to the staff of Patrick Costelloe's, it invited them to share a celebratory drink at the opening of Cutting Edge's flagship store. Pete Jordan had signed it himself, his signature scrawled across the page like a man in a hurry. Such a wanker, Jane thought. Did he honestly, *honestly* think that they'd amble up the road to wish him success in his business when he was in direct competition with them? Even more, did he think they'd have *time* to amble up the road? Crumpling the card up, Jane fired it at the bin.

'That's where you and your stupid salon belong,' she smirked.

The card missed the bin and rolled on to the floor.

Cutting Edge's opening started at noon. It was loud and noisy and seemed to be achieving the desired effect of being hugely noticeable. Jane, on her way up the road to grab a paper from the local shop, hurried past it, not wanting to be seen to be interested. The local radio had a broadcast unit set up outside and was asking queuing customers why they liked Cutting Edge.

To Jane's horror, Eileen Simms was being interviewed. The traitor. 'Ohhh,' she was simpering, 'Cutting Edge is the business and with everything half-price for today—'

The DJ interrupted her. 'That's half-price folks!' he boomed. He thrust the mic back at Eileen. 'Yo!'

'Well, with everything half-price for today,' she went on, giggling, 'it's good value.'

'Did you hear that?' the DJ announced. 'Good value!'

A cheer went up from the crowd waiting outside.

Jane felt sick. Cutting Edge were welcome to Eileen Simms. She'd like to see them cut her hair when she couldn't sit still.

'Some wine, madam?'

Jane hardly heard. Her eye had been caught by Cutting Edge's window. Where it had once been blank, now it was covered with classy framed prints of fabulous-looking hairstyles. Every style that they'd ever entered in competition was there.

Jane remembered some of them from her own visits to the IHF competitions. Most of the styles had won too, she thought faintly.

'Wine, madam?' the offer was repeated.

She shook her head.

They'd won the IHF championships four years running. Pete Jordan himself had won last year with a fantastic fantasy style.

'Canapé, madam?'

'No!' Jane abandoned any thoughts of getting her paper and headed back down to Patrick. Something drastic would have to be done. And fast.

'Ohhhh, I dunno.' Patrick bit his nails. 'My own ideas were going down other avenues. You know flyers and . . .' he paused. 'Well, flyers, basically.'

'Yeah, well, we can try everything,' Jane said, pacing furiously up and down. 'But for now, if we can't beat them, we have to join them. I vote that we enter the IHF championships this year ourselves.'

'With what?' Patrick squealed. 'We've no model.'

'Rosemary,' Jane said. 'Have you seen her hair?'

'Yes,' Patrick gave a semi-hysterical nod. 'It's frizzy and out of shape and she won't let you touch it.'

'It's fab hair,' Jane replied smartly. 'Secondly, are you forgetting that I won Trainee of the Year when I entered years ago?'

Patrick stopped his agitated nail-biting. 'I could never forget that, honey cakes,' he said affectionately. After she'd won, Jane had been beset with offers from big salons all wanting to offer her work, but instead she'd gone it alone. Well, alone with him. He'd been in her debt ever since. But it had been at least sixteen years ago.

'It was a long time ago though,' he reminded her gently.

'Yes, I'm probably a little rusty, but I'll do a few courses beforehand. They've a great one with Julian Waters this year – I can book myself on to that.' She looked pleadingly at him. 'I need you in on this Patrick. I need you to advise me about colour. I can't do it on my own.'

'What if we make a balls of the hairstyle?'

'Then we say it's a bun.' She cracked a grin. 'Come on – they'll,' she nodded in the direction of Cutting Edge, 'they'll wipe the floor with us, otherwise. And Patrick, they can't do that. That man is so arrogant. If you'd met him, you'd know what I mean. I'll bet he bullies other hairdressing salons into liquidation, but not us. Come on!'

Patrick hopped from foot to foot. 'You've your mind made up, haven't you?'

'Almost.'

'Oooohhh,' he winced and waved his hand about. 'Fine. OK, fine.'

'Great!' She hugged him. Tried to do a little dance around the room with him, but he pushed her off, laughing.

'You've to persuade frizzy-head first.'

'Don't call her that – she's our model.'

There was a second's silence, before Patrick asked, 'And it won't be too much for you – what with home and everything?'

Jane shrugged. 'I won't have a home if I don't do something soon.'

'That's not what I mean.' Patrick said gently.

'I *know* what you mean.' Jane bit her lip. Patrick had not mentioned their chat yesterday, knowing that if she wanted to talk she would. 'To be honest, it'll be a diversion. Something to keep me going.'

'Well, if you're sure . . .'

'I'm sure.'

He smiled and nodded. 'And while you organise that, I'll organise something more short-term.'

'Like?'

'Flyers. They're a surprise.' He tapped his nose. 'I think you'll be pleased though. Now, go,' he whooshed her away. 'Talk to frizzy-head – see what she says. She's washing hair at the moment.'

* * *

Rosemary was thrilled. 'A model?' she gaped. 'Me?'

'A hair model,' Jane clarified. 'You'll be modelling your hair. Of course, we'll provide you with the clothes and shoes and accessories that you'll need to go with your final style.' Rosemary didn't look so certain now. 'All free,' Jane added.

'Ooooh.'

'Would you like that?'

'And would *you* cut my hair?'

Jane braced herself. For some reason, Rosemary had got it into her head that she was a crap stylist. It was a bit annoying actually. 'Well, initially I wouldn't.' She pretended not to see the relief on Rosemary's face. 'I'd condition it and trim off the split ends – just basically get it into peak condition for the competition. Then, as the time gets nearer, I'd try out a few ideas, play around with a few styles.'

'Like?'

'I don't know yet. I'd have to see what inspires me. For instance . . .' Jane tried to think of what Rosemary might like, '. . . I could do a colour and some highlights, stuff like that.'

'In a cool way, though?'

'Well, yeah.' Jane felt insulted. 'Rosemary, I am a qualified hairdresser, I have won competitions before!'

She must have sounded annoyed because Rosemary flushed, then attempted to explain. 'You see,' she sat down on a chair and frowned. 'I like my hair a lot.'

'You've good hair.'

'Yeah, and I don't have good much else.' Her forehead wrinkled as she tried to explain. 'I mean, I'm a bit spotty and my glasses are awful, but they're the only ones I can afford, and my clothes make me look fat, but my hair see,' she ran her fingers through her hair and her face softened, 'well, that always looks good no matter what.'

There was something so vulnerable about her that Jane's eyes filled up. She thought of Di stalking about in the latest Goth fashion and wondered if the girl ever thought about how lucky she was. Most likely not.

'Well, when I'm finished with you,' Jane put her arm around Rosemary, 'you'll look like a princess.'

'Getting a head transplant is she?' Mir asked sourly, as she led a customer to the basin.

Rosemary giggled nervously.

'No,' Jane said, eyeballing Mir firmly. 'Rosemary is our model for the IHFs this year.'

Mir gawped. 'No way!'

'I am actually.' Rosemary sat up straighter. 'No joke.'

'Well, can you wash Mrs Boylan now please?' Mir snapped.

Mrs Boylan sat down. 'Hello Rosemary,' she said brightly. 'How's the boyfriend?'

'Great, Mrs Boylan and how's your boyfriend?'

Jane left her to it. Rosemary was great with the auld ones.

11

'JIM? JIM? JIM, are you with us?'

Jim jerked awake at the abrupt voice. He looked around and the whole table was staring at him.

'Yeah? What? Sorry.'

Dave, his boss, was looking annoyed. 'I was just explaining how much work we've put into designing a concept to market Incredible Crisps' new Twizters crisps, Jim. It'd be nice if you could contribute something.'

'Oh yeah. Right.' Jesus, what on earth was he thinking, nearly falling asleep on what could turn out to be the most important meeting of his life? Well, either that or the meeting that would end up with him losing his job. With the strain of it all, he hadn't bloody slept the last few nights.

'And Jim has been researching the campaign for us, haven't you, Jim?' Dave spoke loudly, his face fixed in the chummy smile he seemed to think the clients went for. 'Jim?' Dave was staring at him again.

'Yeah. Sorry.' Jim gave a bright false smile. 'Just getting my thoughts together, you know?'

Dave continued to glare at him. Thoughts were meant to be gathered prior to meeting clients. Incredible Crisps were big. Westbury Marketing's biggest client, in fact. Jim had come up with a brilliant angle on their first foray into the crisp market and as a result they wanted him to head all their campaigns.

'Well, Philip,' Jim nodded to Philip Logan, the brain behind the crisp empire, 'I commissioned a report for you.' He took a sheaf of papers from his folder and handed them around the table. 'Basically, it's not good news. If you cut out all the jargon, the bottom line is that Twizters is about the crummiest name for a packet of crisps you can get. All sorts of connotations there, you know – only twizters eat Twizters crisps, that sort of thing.'

Philip nodded, looking slightly pissed off. 'Oh, shit. Yeah. I see where you're going.' He folded his arms. 'So, what? What happens now?'

'I decided to brainstorm a couple of the lads in the marketing department and we've come up with a few names you might like. We've a few rough ideas for the packets too.' On autopilot, Jim began showing Philip the concept behind what the designers had come up with: blue packets calling them Spirals, green packets calling them Incredible Edibles.

'And mine.' Jim took out a bright-yellow design. 'Now hear me out, right? When the report came in a few weeks ago, it was really depressing, I kept thinking that there had to be some way out of it. And well, I only have the tiniest proof on this, but it kinda dawned on me that kids would go for the crisps in a big way.'

'Kids?' Philip didn't look impressed. 'They're an *adult* party snack.'

Philip Logan's men nodded and mumbled.

Dave gave Jim a dig. 'Jim, this had better be good,' he hissed.

Jim ignored him. He knew when he was right. OK, so it was suicide to suggest a campaign with very little research to back it up, but he'd got that tingly feeling up his spine when the idea had struck. Tingly feelings meant that he was on to a good thing, and Gillian's niece had kind of confirmed it for him.

Everyone was gawking at him. He took out a sample packet of the Twizters. 'Gimme a sec to demonstrate.' He opened the bag and began to join the spirals together. 'Crazy, isn't it? Cool too. Crisps that make chains, necklaces, bracelets. Kids, girls in particular, will go mad for them. See,' he held up a necklace and grinned. 'Great piece of jewellery, isn't it? And when I get bored,' Jim popped a couple of the Twizters into his mouth and with supreme effort, his stomach turning somersaults, he chewed them, 'I can eat it.'

Some of the guys around the table laughed.

Philip looked confused. 'But they were meant to be a sophisticated snack,' he protested.

'They'll sell better this way,' Jim explained. 'And as for the name, they could be called "Incredible", he made a big production of holding out his design, "Chains Bond".'

There was more laughter.

Jim grinned. When clients laughed, you were just about to nab them.

'And the name, being similar to James Bond, will appeal to the boys, so you'll get both groups buying the crisps,' Dave explained unnecessarily. He kicked Jim under the table again.

'Mmmm.' Philip jabbed a finger at Jim. 'Once again, you have totally disregarded what I wanted.'

'I didn't.' Jim held up the other two designs. 'If you want boring, it's right here.'

Dave sucked in his breath. He could never get used to Jim showing such disrespect for clients, but Jim called it honesty. He was a funny guy, Dave thought, he was so quiet that sometimes he was easy to overlook. He was hopeless at general chit-chat, but give him an abstract concept and ask him to come up with an angle and the man was a genius. Philip was going to buy. Dave could smell it.

'And you think these Twizters would sell if we went after the kids' market?' Philip asked.

'Like hot cakes.'

'I'm not interested in the hot cake market,' Philip snapped.

'They'll outsell hot cakes,' Jim amended. 'If you go this way, you'll be on a winner.'

Philip stood up. 'I'll think about it. I'll need more research done, though.'

'Gimme two weeks.'

'Done.'

Philip shook hands with Jim and Dave, then Dave saw him and his entourage down to the front door. Jim was suddenly on his own in the big office. He looked out of the huge glass windows at Dublin. The city looked so orderly from where he was standing, he thought. He packed all his papers back into his folder. Standing up, he poured himself a black coffee from the pot on the table and stood for ages just staring down on to the street.

When he got back to his office, Jim buzzed his secretary. 'Maud, will you come in here for a sec?'

'I will, angel face.'

Jim grinned. Maud had started calling him that about two months after she'd begun working for him. She was in her sixties and needed someone to baby. 'And you'll do,' she'd clucked. 'You'll do.'

She walked in now, grey hair in a bun, ample bosom and a wide smile. 'Yes?'

'Maud, will you take that box of Twizters and give a few packets out to anyone here who has kids under ten? Tell them they've to give the crisps to the kids and then fill this form out. Will you do that?' Jim handed her a sheet of paper.

'I will.' Maud took the form from him. She cocked her head to one side. 'You're very black-looking under your eyes. Are you sleeping all right?'

'I'm sleeping fine. Now how about—'

'You're pale too.' She lowered her voice. 'Now look, I know it's not my business, but leaving your own place takes its toll. It makes it hard to sleep at first. You should get yourself a tonic or something.'

'A gin and tonic, maybe.'

Maud clucked disapprovingly. 'I don't know how you can make light of the situation. It's no joke. You work too hard, you know. Always have. You need to relax now and again.'

'Yeah. I know, Maud. Now look, can you please just give out the crisps?'

'I already said I would.' Maud was not pleased. She threw him a withering look before exiting.

Jim rubbed his hand over his face. Jesus, he was wrecked. He laid his head on his desk and closed his eyes.

'Tired?' Dave startled him as he closed the office door. 'Not a good idea when meeting our biggest client, Jim.'

Jim could feel his face flushing. He glared sullenly at his boss. 'So, what is it you want?'

Dave walked slowly towards his desk. Placing his hands on it, he leaned towards Jim and said slowly, 'Never, ever, pull a stunt like that again. You only tell clients what you know, not what you think. Is that clear?'

'It's a good idea. He'll buy it.' Jim kept his voice even.

'But it might just have easily been a crap idea,' Dave said. 'And we can't afford that.' He was silent for a second before saying, 'You get away with a lot of shit here, Jim, but don't cross the line like that again.'

'Sorry.' Jim gave a half-shrug. 'You're right.'

'And another thing, don't tell Philip Logan his ideas are boring ever again.'

Jesus, Dave was really milking this. Jim decided to ignore him. He indicated his computer. 'Dave, I've two weeks to get a survey together, so can I start now?'

'Yeah, start now,' Dave ordered. 'If you're sure you don't want Maud to bring you in a cup of cocoa.' Laughing to himself, he left.

'Asshole,' Jim muttered. 'Bloody asshole.'

12

ROSEMARY ACCOSTED HER before she'd even taken her coat off. 'Jane. Hi. I'm all set for today.' She stood in front of her, beaming.

'Are you?' Jane smiled. 'That's good.'

'I thought I'd bring you this in,' Rosemary said triumphantly as she produced a tatty book from her bag.

'Did you?' She wondered idly if Rosemary was on drugs.

'Here!' The book was shoved at her. 'It's my favourite hairdressing book – it'll give you ideas.'

'Ideas?'

'On my *hair*,' Rosemary said, as if it was the most obvious thing in the world. 'For tonight. For my conditioning treatment. See, this page,' she frantically tore through the book, 'somewhere here it gives you ideas on dealing with long hair like mine.' Finding the page, she thrust it under Jane's nose. 'Dealing with long hair,' she read out. 'See.'

'Is there nothing called "Dealing with disgusting hair?"' Miranda asked laconically.

Rosemary stopped, looking puzzled. 'But your hair *isn't* disgusting, Mir, it's *lovely*.'

'I wasn't—'

'Now, now,' Patrick cut in, 'I think it's time for you to man the ship, Rosemary, isn't it?'

'Woman the shop,' Rosemary giggled.

'Ha. Ha.' Patrick managed a passable laugh before saying

briskly, 'So off you trot, we've a customer due in any second now, give me a shout when she arrives.'

'OK. No problem.' Rosemary handed the book to Jane. 'Now, you study that and we'll have a chat about my hair later, OK?' She gave herself a sort of hug. 'Ohhhh, I just can't wait.' She danced out of the door, letting it slam behind her.

'Thank God for that,' Miranda gave a sigh of relief. 'Bloody headache tablets should use her to boost sales.'

Patrick laughed.

'She's a good kid.' Jane found herself sticking up for Rosemary. 'Yez should give her a break.'

'Yeah – break her arm,' Mir chortled.

Again Patrick laughed. 'Well,' he defended himself as Jane glared at him, 'I know it wasn't nice, but it *was* funny.'

That evening, after the salon closed, Jane gave Rosemary her first conditioning treatment. She pretended that she'd read the book Rosemary had given her, just to make the girl less apprehensive.

'Now,' she began as she tested the water and motioned for Rosemary to put her head back, 'I'll do this after work at least three times a week from now on. The idea is to make your hair shine and stop it from getting frizzy.'

'And you won't cut it?'

Jane didn't bother to answer. She'd jump that fence when she came to it.

Rosemary, sensing that she'd somehow offended Jane, babbled, 'I mean, I wouldn't mind you cutting it if I knew how it'd turn out.' She paused, 'I mean, all I ever see you three do is bouncy hair for old women and, well, I don't—'

'Bouncy hair for old women!' Patrick said aghast, as he wrapped his scarf around him. 'We don't do that!'

Rosemary's eyes widened as she realised what she'd said. 'Well, maybe not,' she amended hastily. 'Not quite, like. But, well, this place is not exactly Cutting Edge, is it?'

'No. No, it's not and . . . and thank God!' Patrick spluttered as he flounced away.

'Ohhh, he's mad at me now, isn't he?' Rosemary said mournfully. 'I didn't mean to annoy him.'

'He'll get over it,' Jane muttered, wondering how on earth she was ever going to get the kid to trust her. 'But Rosemary, we are all as good as Cutting Edge in here, you know.'

Rosemary remained schtum.

She began rinsing Rosemary's hair, running her fingers through it, massaging the scalp.

'Ohhh,' Rosemary closed her eyes. 'That's lovely.' Then she asked, 'How come all you get in here are the wrinklies?'

'We do get some young people coming in,' Jane said, trying to recall when she'd last seen one inside the salon. She remembered the guy from Cutting Edge saying that he thought they were an OAP joint. And they weren't. At least that wasn't the intention. 'Would you not normally come to a place like this to get a haircut?' she asked.

Rosemary shrugged. 'Well . . .' she hesitated. 'Maybe.'

'Cutting Edge or here?' Jane asked, more firmly.

'Ohhhh.' Rosemary giggled. 'Ohhhhh.'

'Well?'

'Cutting Edge is dead cool though, isn't it?' Seeing Jane's face, she said unconvincingly, 'But here is good too.'

She meant 'Cutting Edge is better'. Jane decided to say nothing more. It'd only stress her out and you couldn't be stressed doing hair. She concentrated instead on rubbing in the conditioner, running it through the hair from root to tip. Working with hair relaxed her. She loved it. As she massaged Rosemary's head once more, she wondered why Mir never got either her or Patrick to style her hair. Maybe Mir also thought that they just weren't up to scratch. It sent a chill right through her.

Rosemary was delighted with her shiny hair. 'Wow.' She turned her head from side to side in front of the mirror. 'Wow.'

Jane smiled, feeling vindicated.

'And it's free?' Rosemary asked.

'Yep.'

'That's brill.' Rosemary beamed at her reflection.

'It still needs some work.' Jane picked up a ragged-looking section. 'I'll trim it soon, but for now we'll just condition it. And here,' she rummaged around in her bag and took out some fancy scrunchies that she'd bought for Rosemary that lunchtime. 'No more elastic bands, right? From now on, if you want to tie your hair up, use these.'

'For me?' Rosemary hesitated.

'Yep. All of them.'

Slowly Rosemary took the proffered bands. BT's best. She stared at them wonderingly. 'These are *lovely*. Aw, thanks Jane.'

'Naw,' Jane waved her away. 'Thank *you*.'

13

'DI,' JANE YELLED, 'I've your lunch made.'

'All this shouting,' Sheila moaned. 'Is it really necessary?' She took a shaky sup of tea.

'WILL I PUT IT IN YOUR BAG?' Jane yelled even more loudly, amused at the way her mother shuddered violently. Without waiting for Di to answer, she opened her daughter's schoolbag and was just about to put the lunch box and an apple in, when a bright-pink envelope caught her eye.

Di came galloping down the stairs just as she pulled the envelope from the bag.

'Hey, you've no right to go poking in my bag!' Di hurtled into the kitchen, grabbed the envelope from her mother and furiously zipped up her schoolbag. 'I don't like being spied on!'

'I wasn't spying.' Jane looked at her mother for support. Sheila turned away. Jane turned back to Di who was scowling, her hands on her hips. As calmly as she could, she explained, 'I was just putting your lunch in your bag for you.'

'Yeah, well, you've no right to go taking out my *private* things.'

'Oh for God's sake!' Jane rolled her eyes. 'It's only a valentine's card. I thought it was a note from school. It's not as if I read it or anything.'

'Oh thanks,' Di drawled. 'Thanks for not reading my *private* things.'

'Don't talk to me like that!' Jane snapped. 'Don't you dare. I'll ground you tonight if you keep it up.'

Di stuffed the envelope back into her bag and began stomping around the kitchen.

Jane ignored her. She set Owen's place at the table and vowed that if he wasn't down in two minutes she was going to brain him. He was the world's worst kid for getting up. But at least with Owen that was about as bad as he got. She'd have gone mental if she had two of them like Di.

'So you've a boyfriend, have you, dahling?' Sheila asked, sounding interested. 'What's he like?'

Jane paused in what she was doing. How her mother had the nerve to ask that question she didn't know. She wouldn't have dared. Di had the uncanny knack of making a person feel about two feet high. She began to hum, making it appear that she wasn't listening.

'He's dead nice,' Di said nonchalantly. 'A good kisser, knows how to Frenchie really well.'

'Ugh!' Sheila sounded as if she was going to be sick.

'For God's sake,' Jane hissed. 'Your nana only asked you a question. One more cheeky remark and that's it.'

Di picked up her schoolbag. 'I was only *answering* Nana,' she said innocently, her big brown eyes open wide. 'Sorry if I *offended* you Nana.'

'You disgusted me, dahling, that's what you did.'

Di nodded, unconcerned. 'Aw, well, at least one person in the house will have a valentine's card.' She swanned out of the door.

'Oh,' Sheila sniffed. 'Now *that* hurt. That was deliberately aimed at me, dahling. She knows Declan wouldn't even think of it.'

Jane didn't bother to disagree with her. She didn't tell her mother that it was her sixteenth wedding anniversary that day. She didn't tell her mother that Jim, in the good days, had made a huge fuss of her on Valentine's Day. It was their day. Always had been. She tried to ignore the empty feeling Di's words had given her and went to haul Owen from his bed.

* * *

Valentine's Day – his sixteenth wedding anniversary, Jim thought despondently as he crawled out of bed.

'Good morning,' Fred boomed, as he emerged, clean-shaven, from the bathroom. He gawked at Jim. 'Jaysus, you look like shit!'

'Thanks.' Jim flicked on the kettle. 'And you just smell like shit.'

Fred chortled good-naturedly. 'I'll have you know, this after-shave is dead expensive. The last mot I had bought it for me.'

'Trying to put the rest of humanity off you, was she?'

'Aw, you can be very fuckin' funny in the morning, can't ya?' Fred rooted around in the press and, taking a packet of corn-flakes out, began to eat them from the box. With his free hand, he flicked on the radio.

'. . . the question is – how many valentines will you get?' the DJ asked. 'It's lurve all the way today folks!'

'Fucking asshole,' Fred fiddled with the dial. 'Love me arse.'

'So, you going anywhere tonight?' Jim asked.

'What?' Fred found a station that he liked and sat down.

'Are you taking Gillian out somewhere tonight?'

Fred guffawed. 'Are you joking? I hate all that crap. It's a bloody money-spinner, that's all.'

Jim shrugged. 'Yeah, I'd say Gillian will really understand all those moral sentiments, Fred,' he deadpanned.

'And what does that mean?'

'Have you even got her a card?' It was a stupid question. He knew bloody well that Fred hadn't. Fred hadn't even given it a thought.

Jim felt that he had to say something because Gillian had told him that she had a huge surprise lined up for Fred. She'd tapped her nose, giggled and said, 'I want you to be there, Jimmy, I want everyone to see his wee-action.'

'A card?' Fred rolled his eyes. 'No way. Anyhow, she'll be cool about it. Gillian is a cool girl.'

'She'll freeze you out, she'll be that cool,' Jim said.

'Oh yeah,' Fred sneered, 'and what makes you the expert on women, all of a sudden?'

Jim flinched. 'I'm not an expert,' he muttered. He paused, then continued, 'It's just, women like that shit. A bunch of flowers, a card, it doesn't cost much.'

'It's not the cost, it's the principle.'

'Well, once a year is a weird time for you to have principles. They've never mattered before.'

'Fuck off.' Fred slammed down the flakes and glared at him.

Jim returned the glare. 'She's got something for you – it's a surprise.' He felt like a heel for ruining Gillian's thunder, but what else could he do?

Fred flushed. Gulped. 'Well then . . .' His voice trailed off. 'I guess I'd better . . .' He looked at Jim. 'Thanks.'

Jim turned his back and pretended that he was busy making a cuppa. Jesus, he hated Fred sometimes. The guy didn't deserve any girl, let alone one who was mad about him.

'Sooo,' Patrick waltzed into the salon with a grin the size of America on his face. 'Anyone get any valentine's cards?'

Mir narrowed her eyes. 'Yeah. I got one,' she snapped. 'From fucking Harry.'

Harry was Mir's fall guy, the one she used when there was no one else available. He gave her lifts to and from work, got drunk with her when she was mourning the break-up of a relationship and was generally a nice guy. He was also crazy about Mir and a complete doormat. This year, he'd obviously decided to declare his feelings and take the plunge, thus committing the ultimate insult in Miranda's book – a card from a friend.

'As if I wouldn't know it was him!' she sneered.

'Well, I think it was nice of him,' Patrick said sweetly, still smiling. 'Wasn't it nice of him, Jane?'

'Uh-huh,' Jane nodded. Attempting a grin, she added casually, 'Look at me, no cards at all.'

'You've had them for the last, I dunno, fifteen years, haven't you?' Miranda spat. 'It's about time I got my turn in the sun.'

'You will.' Patrick reached out to pat her on the arm.

Miranda pulled away. 'I don't need your sympathy, Patrick. And I don't need sympathy cards. If I wanted a sympathy card, I'd, I dunno, kill my mother or something.'

Patrick tut-tutted. 'Rosemary?' he asked.

'One,' she giggled. 'From Jaz.' She blushed. 'Me fella.'

Patrick and Jane made 'ooohh' sounds which had Rosemary giggling frantically while Mir looked on sourly.

'And moi,' Patrick beamed. 'Did I get a card?'

'A wild guess – I'd say you did,' Jane smirked.

'How did you know?' Patrick feigned surprise. Then, reaching into his bag, he drew out a box of chocolates. 'Well, to be honest and if I'm not going to depress Mir over there too much, I got a card *and* a box of chocolates this morning.' He offered the box to Mir. 'Want one?'

'That's right, make me feel miserable.' Miranda dug her hand into the box and pulled out a handful.

'Who from?' Jane asked.

Patrick grinned and tapped the side of his nose. 'Oh, I'm not sure, but I've got my hopes up.'

'Not the only thing that's going to be up, is it?' Miranda gave a dirty laugh and Patrick and Jane joined in.

Jesus, Declan D'arcy was a great laugh. Jim grinned as he pulled into a space in front of the Incredible Crisps' offices. His special Valentine's Day show was based on love – though what Declan knew about love could probably be written on the back of a postage stamp – and he'd got people to phone in and tell him their experiences of love. Jim wondered if there were really that many weirdos out there. Some people were so completely mental. The show should have had an 'X' rating. But it had been compulsive listening, as horribly irresistible as looking at a car crash.

It hadn't been too bad a day at all, Jim thought. OK, so it was crap that it was Valentine's Day and anyone with a partner was grinning from ear to ear – but it had been liveable. He'd coped the only way he knew how, by working his butt off. He was going to fill Philip Logan in on the latest details and he knew that Philip would be impressed with what he'd done. The Chains Bond crisps idea was a good one. Most people at work had filled out the form for him and it seemed that their kids had loved them. He was feeling the way he'd felt when he'd started marketing Incredible Crisps at the beginning. A bubbly excitement was beginning to build. He knew that with careful marketing, his idea could be big. Bloody big.

Di's card had pride of place on the mantelpiece. She'd moved the picture of Matt to one side so that her card took centre stage. Jane took Matt's picture and straightened it. She wanted everyone who came into the room to see that happy picture. Jane reached out and let her finger trace the face of her youngest son. He'd been such a happy kid. It had been the only consolation left when he'd gone.

She gulped, drawing her finger away, and stared determinedly at Di's card. It was small and completely unromantic. She hoped her daughter wasn't about to make a fool out of herself. *Darling*, the card said, *seven days spent with you makes one week*. Inside, the fella had scrawled, *To Di, loads of kisses on V day*. He'd signed it *Guy*.

Guy was a nice name, Jane thought. Sort of film star-ish.

She wondered where Di was now. She'd said she was heading to Libby's house but on Valentine's night it was highly unlikely that she was going to stick with Libby all night. God, it was a worry. She guessed she'd just have to trust her daughter, but trust and Di didn't seem to go together in the same sentence. She tried to reposition the card on the mantelpiece so that Di wouldn't know it had been disturbed.

'Here Ma.' Owen made her jump as he shoved a video under

her nose. 'It was the only decent film they'd left. I dunno what it's about though. Something about a hairdressers, I thought you might like it.'

Why couldn't Di just be the teeniest bit like Owen? She smiled at her son and took the video from him. 'Ta. *Steel Magnolias*,' she read, 'I've heard of that.'

'Great.'

'You going to watch it with me?'

Owen shrugged. 'Seeing as Da's not here, I guess I'd better.' He gave her a tentative grin.

'You're great.' She hugged him and he pushed her off, embarrassed.

God, she loved that kid.

Jim wished he could fall asleep, but the sound of his flatmate moaning and urging Gillian to 'Do it to me' made it impossible.

'Asshole,' he whispered.

'Asshole!' the parrot screeched.

Jim put a pillow over his head and tried humming.

It was no use.

He tried to think of something else besides what was going on in the bedroom.

That didn't work either.

How come Fred could get a woman to love him as much as Gillian obviously did? Fred with his dying bunches of flowers and his cheap tacky card. Still, it had been a good laugh when Gillian had presented Fred with a voucher for a parachute jump.

'I did try to get the sky-diving thing,' she said, 'but, nah, it was impossible.'

Fred should have got an Oscar for his mock-delight.

'He hates it, doesn't he?' Debbie had whispered.

'He's shitting himself,' he'd whispered back.

They hadn't been able to stop laughing all night.

Fred was now hoping to screw Gillian's brains out to put her in good form so that he could exchange the parachute jump for something else.

Steel Magnolias was too emotional. Owen left to get a coffee halfway through it and didn't come back. Jane wasn't surprised. She heard him playing his PlayStation in his room. She stuck out most of it, but eventually couldn't take it any more. Flicking the telly off, she went to bed.

She lay awake for a while until Di came home. She heard her daughter whispering to someone outside. It had to be *him* as the voice was too deep to be a girl's. She resisted the urge to peek out the window. Di would probably never talk to her again if she saw her. After a while she heard the sound of a key in the lock and Di whispering 'goodnight'.

Jane closed her eyes, willing herself to fall asleep now that her kids were safely home. Well, now that two of her kids were safely home.

'Night Matt,' she whispered to the silent room.

14

'HELLO, MAY I speak to Mrs Jane McCarthy, please?' Jane didn't recognise the voice. Long ago, she had grown wary of voices she couldn't identify. Sometimes journalists phoned up looking for quotes about her father. And with every tabloid in the land writing snippets of gossip about her parents each week, there was no way she was adding fuel to the speculation. A bookie had even started taking bets on when they'd get back together again. Apparently the odds on Declan having a new woman by the end of the year were two-to-one.

'Who's speaking?' She made her voice gruff to put any would-be hack off.

'Eh, it's Deirdre Mulvey – your son's tutor?'

'Sorry?'

'Owen's tutor. You *are* Jane McCarthy?'

'Yes. Yes I am.' God, what must the woman think of her? 'Sorry about that. I thought you were someone else.' The woman at the other end made no reply, so Jane continued meekly, 'What can I do for you?'

'It's about Owen – I was wondering if we'd see him in school this week?'

'Sorry?'

'He's been out sick rather a lot this term – this year in fact,' the woman amended. 'Frankly, Mrs McCarthy, it's a bit worrying, seeing as it's exam year next year.'

Owen? Out sick? She must have the wrong Owen.

'I'm sorry, Miss Mulvey,' Jane said pleasantly. 'Owen hasn't been sick at all. Are you sure you've the right Owen?'

'Yes.'

'Owen McCarthy. He's in second year?'

'That's right.'

There was a pause while she tried to digest what it meant. 'Are you saying that Owen—'

Miss Mulvey's voice, when it came, was sympathetic. 'He hasn't been showing up for school,' she said gently. 'He's missed about six weeks at least this year.'

Six weeks!

She wondered if she was dreaming. Owen went out every morning. He took his lunch, his bag, everything. He wasn't the sort of kid to bunk off.

'Owen's not the sort—'

'Well, he hasn't been in school.'

'He's a good kid,' Jane stammered. 'I-I can't believe he would deliberately miss school – there must be some mistake.'

'There's no mistake, Mrs McCarthy. Maybe you could have a word with him about it?'

She sounded quite firm. Jane gulped, her head reeling. 'I'll try,' she muttered, 'but I can't believe—'

'Now, I know that you and your husband have separated recently,' Miss Mulvey went on delicately, 'and that certainly would be a factor. Children react in different ways to these things. But Owen—'

'Owen is a good kid,' she repeated.

'Owen is very quiet, he never says much in class, maybe he needs to talk to someone?'

She didn't need advice on how to mind her kids. She tried to recall a picture of Miss Mulvey and she remembered a twenty-something with cropped dark hair and trendy clothes. The woman was only a kid herself! 'I'll talk to him,' she said. 'He'll be in school tomorrow.'

'Well, if he needs to talk, we've a social worker in the school.'

Owen didn't need a social worker. 'OK. Fine.'

'Thank you Mrs McCarthy. I'll be in touch.'

'Bye. Thanks.' She put the phone down and stared at it for ages. There had to be some sort of a mistake. There just had to be.

She was so preoccupied with what to say to Owen that after dinner she almost let Diane out of the house in a black handkerchief. A black handkerchief masquerading as a skirt.

It was the happy tone in her daughter's voice that caught Jane's attention. The skirt or lack thereof was the next thing to get her attention. Short and tiny and way too tight, it had been teamed with a pair of thigh-length boots. If she'd been touting for business she'd have made a fortune. 'Off,' was all she could manage.

Diane turned to protest and Jane nearly died. Her skirt had been bad enough but her *top*. Well, that's all it was. It certainly hadn't a middle or an end.

'You are not going anywhere in that,' Jane spluttered. 'Go upstairs and change.'

'What?' Diane gawped and put her hands on her hips. 'What do you mean?'

'I mean that you look ridiculous. You are not leaving this house half-dressed.'

'I look fine,' Diane said, her voice quivering. 'Libby said it was gorgeous.'

'Libby?' Jane rolled her eyes. 'Well, I don't think it's Libby who you're meeting, Miss, and believe me, you are not going to meet any fella looking like that.'

'Well a fella gave me the money for it,' Di said indignantly. 'Dad gave me and Owen money last week and told us to buy what we liked – didn't he Owen?'

Owen nodded.

'So I got this and he didn't see any problem with it.'

'Your dad is not one for acknowledging problems.' The words

were out before she could stop them. She hated the way Di flinched. 'Look,' she said, in a gentler tone, 'just change.'

'Yes, dear,' Sheila spoke up. 'Put on something a bit more flattering. That top does nothing for your chest.'

'Does it not?' Diane narrowed her eyes and wiggled her minute chest about. 'Just 'cause your generation was sexually repressed. I'll have you know, Gran, I'm very proud of my 36C bust.'

'It's Nana,' Sheila corrected. 'And dahling, if you're a 36C then my eyesight is worse than I thought. I really can't see very much there at all.'

Jane snorted a laugh and then pretended to cough.

Diane's eyes widened at the put-down. She opened her mouth to say something but no words came out.

Her mother was improving, Jane thought, amused. A few weeks ago she'd never have been able to come out with something like that. 'Upstairs, Diane,' she said.

'You wouldn't know what fashion was if it hit you over the head,' Diane said sulkily.

'Up.'

Bestowing a final glower, Diane stomped out, her skirt riding higher and higher up her backside with every step she took.

'I'll tell you,' Sheila cackled after her granddaughter, 'that new boyfriend of yours is going to be blind before long, the get-up of you will make the eyes pop out of his head.'

'I wish I could pop the tongue out of your mouth,' Di yelled back.

Sheila laughed good-humouredly.

Jane stood up to clear the table. Her mother had obviously decided to play Di at her own game, trading insult for insult.

'Ahh,' Sheila said fondly, dabbing her mouth with some kitchen paper. 'Di reminds me so much of Declan.'

Jane laughed.

Owen began helping Jane clear the table. He scraped the left-over food from the dinner plates into the bin and stacked the plates neatly for her.

'Thanks,' she smiled at him.

He shrugged and kept his head down.

He did that a lot, she suddenly realised, shrugging and not looking her in the eye. He'd always been quiet, but he used to laugh and talk with her. She tried to remember when he'd become so withdrawn, but couldn't. It had happened gradually. Maybe it was his hormones. Or maybe it was just guilt over bunking school that made him unable to meet her gaze?

But he'd been like that for years, another voice told her.

She studied him as he went about clearing up. He looked pale, she thought. But he was so dark that his skin had always seemed pale, especially in winter. She wondered if it was normal for a fourteen-year-old lad to help around the kitchen without being asked, to never go out, to have no friends that she could see. A sort of dread crawled into her stomach.

'How was school, Owen?' she asked suddenly.

He dropped the plate he'd been holding and it clattered on to the table.

'Mind my dress!' Sheila barked.

'Look, Mother, if you're not going to help, get out!'

Her mother made some comments that Jane only half heard, before self-righteously exiting.

Owen stood, head bent, still staring at the table.

'Well?' Jane asked again. She knew it was true, sure as anything. The way he'd dropped the plate told her everything. 'Owen?'

He shrugged, then picked up the plate. 'OK,' he muttered. He still didn't meet her gaze.

'OK?' Worry made her grab the plate from him and crash it down on to the draining board. 'How would you know it was OK? Well?'

His silence seemed to go on forever.

'Well?' she demanded again.

'Who told you?' he asked.

'Who the hell do you think? Your tutor told me! Can you

imagine how I felt being told that my son is not turning up for school? Can you imagine?'

'No.'

The way he answered her and his anxious, flickering glance stopped her dead. There was something there . . . she couldn't get a handle on it. He wasn't brash or cocky about it. He wasn't upset. He was just . . . nothing. 'So why, Owen?' she asked uncertainly, her annoyance evaporating. 'What's wrong?'

More shrugging. This time his head sank even lower, he tapped the toe of his trainer off the tiles on the floor.

'Is something wrong? Are you being bullied? What?' God, don't let anything be wrong, she prayed. She thought of what Miss Mulvey had said. 'Is it because of your dad leaving? Is that it?'

'Sort of. Kind of.' His voice caught. 'I just . . . I dunno, Ma. I can't face it – school and stuff.'

'What? You can't face school because your dad has gone?'

'Well . . .' He shrugged. Seemed to struggle with the words. 'I just feel it's stupid, Ma. A waste.'

'A waste?' Jesus, she was like a parrot. But she just couldn't get her head around it. 'A waste?'

'Uh-huh.' Owen gulped. He rubbed his face. 'Since . . . since Matt—'

She flinched. 'Matt?' she asked.

'I'm going out now!' Diane screeched from the hallway. 'And don't try to stop me this time.'

Jane hardly heard her. Instead she waved her away and studied Owen some more. She couldn't make herself get annoyed with him, though she knew she should. There just didn't seem to be a point to it. For the first time in four years he'd actually mentioned his brother and surely that was progress. She didn't want to make too big a deal of it though. Instead she refocused on his truancy. 'Nothing is a waste,' she said gently. 'Tell me, how much school have you missed?' She closed the kitchen door so that her mother wouldn't walk in on them. 'A lot?'

'A few weeks.'

'Owen!'

'Sorry Ma.'

He sounded genuinely sorry. She didn't know quite what to do. Maybe lads did this sort of thing all the time. She knew Jim had. Maybe it was nothing. 'And what did you do?' she asked. 'Where did you go?'

'Nowhere much. Just around the place. Playgrounds. Parks.' He looked at her. 'Sometimes I even climbed the tree in the field at the top of the road and just sat there watching people come and go.'

'The tree at the top of the road?' Jane rubbed her hands over her face. This just got worse and worse. 'That's thirty foot high – at least.'

'It's easy to climb.' His eyes grew sullen. 'It's not a big deal.'

'It's too dangerous!' She surprised both of them by yelling into his face. 'You never, ever climb that tree again, do you hear me? Never, ever!' She poked him hard in the chest. 'You do, Owen McCarthy, and I will, I will . . .' her voice broke. She bit her lip and fought to regain control.

'Ma—'

'Just, just don't climb it. OK?'

A second or two elapsed before he answered. 'OK.'

'Promise me?'

'Yeah.' He touched her arm briefly.

'OK.' She caught his hand in hers. Said fervently, 'And you'll go into school tomorrow, won't you?'

His shoulders slumped. 'Yeah.'

'And it's not a waste. Nothing is ever a waste. It'll only be a waste if you let it. Don't you know that?'

'Yeah.' He didn't sound convinced.

'I'll be checking up on you, you know. I just can't believe . . .' She didn't finish. What else could she say? 'It's not a waste,' she said again.

He didn't answer.

'And if you want to talk to me, Owen, you can. You know that, don't you?'

'Aw, Ma . . .' Owen rolled his eyes, mortified.

'About Matt, about anything – OK?'

He stared at the floor.

Jane tossed his hair. 'Now, start showing up at school and we won't mention it to Dad – all right?'

'All right.'

Jim would have done nothing anyway. He was too soft with the kids.

'Go on now, go and get your books for tomorrow.'

'OK.'

She watched him leave. Even though she believed he would go into school, she was sure she'd handled the situation all wrong. She felt she'd missed something, but she wasn't sure exactly what.

It came to her, just as he was climbing the stairs – it had almost been too easy.

15

PHILIP LOGAN WAS smiling. His team were smiling. Dave was even managing a grin of sorts.

Jim tried not to look too relieved as he pressed the remote control for the DVD. 'This is the ad campaign we've come up with,' he explained. 'We've a series of ads that'll run over the next few months. Slightly off-the-wall humour that kids go for.'

'I smell expensive,' Philip half-grumbled.

'Good sense of smell there, Phil,' Jim grinned.

Dave gave a cough and glared at him. Jim ignored the glare and continued, 'It's a great concept. Worth every penny.'

The screen lit up and Jim pulled down the blackouts on the windows. 'Make him like it,' he prayed silently. He'd spent ages with the ad people throwing about ideas until they'd all found something they could work with. It had taken him two solid weeks of sleepless nights and crazy days to get the thing exactly the way he'd envisioned it.

'Bitch!' Mir hissed as she put the telephone down. 'Another cancellation,' she called down the salon. 'Julie Edwards can't come today.'

'Why?' Jane asked.

'Dunno, she was dead evasive,' Mir reached under the desk and took out her nail file. 'What's the bet she's heading up the road – huh?'

Jane gritted her teeth and looked around the empty salon. Her business was coming apart at the seams and she was powerless to stop it. For the past couple of weeks, the amount of customers had dwindled to almost half. God, if she'd Pete Jordan in front of her she'd give him a piece of her mind, so she would. She could only hope that the novelty of Cutting Edge would wear off. And soon.

'Where is Patrick?' she asked, suddenly aware that he'd been missing all morning.

'Doing something important somewhere,' Mir answered and then cursed quietly as a nail broke. 'It's just not my fuckin' week,' she hissed.

It hadn't been the salon's week either.

'That's it folks, one hundred per cent of all kids prefer Chains Bond crisps to any other.'

The voice over: 'Chains Bond, the crisps with a twist.'

There was a spatter of applause and laughter. Jim grinned.

The follow up ads were equally bizarre.

When the DVD had finished, there was silence. Jim flicked it off and looked expectantly at Philip.

Philip shook his head and grinned. 'Fucking brilliant.'

'It is, isn't it?'

'You're not going to be able to make enough Chains Bond to meet demand,' Dave said. 'We'll see to that.'

There was more loud laughter.

Philip shook Dave's hand. 'You, gentlemen, have got yourselves a deal. I want all that stuff out mid-May.' He turned to Jim. 'And you – well done.'

Jim smiled. 'It's what you pay me for.'

'Yeah, I guess so.' Philip gave a final grin and a nod before being ushered out of the door by Dave.

'Now, Jane, have you missed me?' Patrick swaggered into the coffee room around four holding a box. He glanced around. 'Not much going on here, eh?'

Jane put down the phone on Owen's school. At least he'd

shown up. That was two weeks on the trot now. She felt she'd been stupid to worry so much. All lads bunked off.

'Sorry, Patrick, what?'

'I said,' Patrick dumped his box on the coffee table, 'not much going on here.'

'We'd only three customers in this afternoon,' Jane replied glumly. 'I let Mir go early, she's got some kind of hot date tonight. And Rosemary is down at the launderette. I'm doing her hair later. She's heading to the cinema so I told her I'd do a conditioning treatment. I might try and trim it as well if she'll let me.'

'Aw, well, maybe I have something here that might just boost things up a bit.' Patrick located a knife and sliced open the tape at the top of the box. Taking out a sheaf of papers, he handed Jane one of them. 'My flyers.'

'Oh good.' Jane had heard about nothing else all week. 'Let's have a read.'

Patrick smiled proudly. 'It's dynamite,' he grinned.

Patrick Costelloe's was written in red across the top. *Hair to have affairs with* was the cringe-making slogan.

'Hair to have affairs with?' Jane said faintly.

'Three days it took me to think up that one,' Patrick said smugly. 'Now, keep reading. It's a touch of genius if I say so myself.'

The leaflet went on to say that Patrick Costelloe's used far superior hair products compared to their chain-store rivals. At the end was printed, *You pay half the price – you'll get double the hairstyle.*

'Well?' Patrick asked.

Jane bit her lip. 'I dunno if we should use this Patrick.'

'And why not?' He sounded seriously offended.

'Well, for starters,' Jane began, 'we'll be sued. I mean, it is Cutting Edge you're talking about, isn't it?'

Patrick took the leaflet from her and made a big deal of examining it. 'Is it?' he smirked. 'Where does it say that?'

'Well, it doesn't but—'

'But nothing!' Patrick rubbed his hands together gleefully. 'I've consulted with a friend of mine, he's a brilliant solicitor and there isn't a thing they can do.' He jabbed the leaflet. 'Everything there is fact. No names are mentioned. It's all above board.'

Jane wasn't exactly sure that this was the right way to go about things, but as she hadn't an alternative to offer she didn't think it was right to criticise too much.

'I mean,' Patrick continued, 'if you'd still been with Jim, maybe we could have come up with a better idea, but I really, really think this is a winner. People are bound to take notice. Everyone likes good hair, don't they?'

'I suppose so.' Jane jabbed the leaflet, still trying to figure out what bothered her so much about it. 'It'll make us enemies,' she said eventually.

'And Pete Jordan is our friend?' Patrick opened his eyes wide in mock surprise. 'Oh, pardon me. Stealing all our business is a *friendly* thing to do? Robbing our customers is doing us a *favour*?'

'You know what I mean.'

'Stabbing us in the back is *nice*?'

'OK, you've got a point.'

'So,' Patrick waved a leaflet about. 'Are you in or are you in? We're going to be distributing them in the next couple of weeks.'

'Well, I guess I'm in.'

'Atta girl!' Patrick winked at her.

16

FRED WAS BRICKING it. 'It's all your fault,' he snapped at Jim.

'No it's not.' Jim unlocked his car door and Fred climbed in beside him. 'If you'd told Gillian from the start that you hate all this outdoor stuff, she wouldn't have bought you a parachute jump.'

'She bought me a parachute jump because you told her I liked abseiling or some crap like that.'

'Sky diving,' Jim corrected, grinning. He was driving Fred to the aerodrome as Fred didn't think his nerves would stand it. Gillian and her mates were going to meet them there to cheer him on.

'For fuck's sake.' Fred buried his head in his hands. 'What am I going to do?'

'Tell her the truth – that you're terrified.'

'The truth?' Fred guffawed. 'Jaysus, that's mad. I can't do that.'

'Well then, it's the high jump for you.'

'You're fucking enjoying this, aren't you?' Fred spat.

'Me? Naw!' Jim laughed.

'Well, I'm glad something can make you laugh. You've been so bloody miserable these last few months that I was beginning to get depressed meself.'

'As long as you don't get compressed, eh?'

'Fuck off!'

They arrived at the aerodrome at eleven. Fred was due to jump at eleven-thirty.

'Oh fuck,' he kept saying over and over.

'Look, Fred, you've trained for the past couple of weeks, it can't be that bad.'

'Oh yeah, say the parachute fails or I get it caught in the engine of the plane or something?'

'You could sue them.'

'Ha. Ha.'

'Here's the fan club,' Jim said, spotting Gillian across the tarmac.

Gillian saw them at the same time and began a sort of skipping run towards the car.

'Hiya boys.' She poked her head through the open window. 'All set, Freddie?'

'Oh yeah.' Fred gave a confident grin. 'Just have to, you know, get kitted up and have a chat with the instructor.'

'Well, you wanna hurry honey, aren't you gonna jump at eleven-thirty?'

'That's right.' Fred gave Jim a shaky grin as he climbed out of the car. 'Not likely to forget that, am I?'

'Naw. Come on. I'll go with you.' Gillian linked her arm through his and beamed up at him.

He smiled back down at her.

'Hi yez.' Debbie knocked on Jim's window. 'Hey, is this it? The "See Freddie Meet His Maker" fan club.'

'Just the four of us?' Jim queried. 'I thought—'

'Way too busy,' Gillian said. She pulled on Fred's arm. 'Come on, hon. Get your kit on.'

'That makes a change, I'll bet,' Debbie remarked.

Both of them laughed. Jim managed a grin. Jesus, it'd be just him and Debbie watching Fred jump. Well, Gillian too, only she didn't count. It felt suspiciously like a set-up.

Debbie went around to the passenger's side of the car and climbed in. 'Just the two of us, huh?' she remarked drily.

'Looks like it.' Jim gave her a brief smile and turned away. He'd met Debbie a few times since that night in the pub and

Fred was always slagging about how much she fancied him. It made him uneasy.

'Gillian's all excited about this,' Debbie went on. 'She hasn't talked about anything else for ages.'

'Fred hasn't talked about anything else either,' Jim grinned. 'For an entirely different reason of course.' He was aware of Debbie crossing her slender legs. She was wearing an ankle-length skirt, split at the side, and as she crossed one leg over the other, the split opened and revealed long tanned limbs. Jim stared out of his window with a forced intensity. He didn't want to look. He wasn't interested. And even if he was, he wouldn't know what to do about it.

'Nice car,' Debbie remarked. She pushed a switch and a little door overhead opened, revealing a pair of sunglasses. 'Hey, cool.'

Despite his jangling nerves, he laughed. 'Jane,' he winced a bit at saying his wife's name, 'used to call me "Gadget Man". The more gadgets in a car, the better I'd like it. Here, look at this.' He pushed another button and a little tray popped out between them. 'For McDonald's takeaways or whatever.'

Debbie gave a delighted laugh. 'And this one?'

'Heats up the seats in winter.'

'No way. Like an electric blanket for your arse?'

Jim grinned. 'Uh-huh.'

They caught one another's eyes and he gulped. He kept the smile fixed on his face, but a scary, uncomfortable feeling seemed to be creeping across him.

'Hey, hey, you guys.' Gillian broke the moment by hammering on the window. 'Come on, he's almost ready to jump. They'll let us watch it from that building over there.' She indicated a grey, small building with a tower. 'Hurry.'

Jim and Debbie climbed out of the car and followed behind her. She kept up an endless stream of chat the whole way across. 'Freddie's plane is going up any second now. He'll be number two to jump.'

'Number two,' Debbie whispered. 'How appropriate for a shithead.'

Jim pretended not to hear. Fred wasn't *that* bad.

They gathered with a small group of people who must have been there for other parachute jumpers.

Further down the strip a little plane was revving up. 'There it goes,' Gillian announced in a high-pitched, excited squeal.

The plane lifted off and began to gain altitude.

Jim winced at the small size of it. Jesus, Fred was some man to go up in that. He didn't know if he'd have the nerve. It looked a bit shaky too. Soon it was just a dot above them.

'*I think someone has just jumped!*' Gillian shattered the silence with her shriek. Everyone craned towards the window. Sure enough, a tiny dot could be seen floating downwards. And then another.

'*There's my Freddie!*'

Fred's parachute could be seen opening and, after an initial hurtling upwards, he began to float towards the ground. Jim realised he'd been holding his breath and clenching his fists.

'Isn't he wonderful?' Gillian breathed, turning adoring eyes on both Jim and Debbie. 'Such a man, such a nerve.'

'Such a nerd?' Debbie asked. But she was laughing as Gillian hit her.

The drive home had been celebratory. Fred was puffed up. 'Parachute jumping is like drinking a pint,' he declared. 'Second nature to me.'

'You are a wonderful human being,' Gillian breathed. 'Wonderful. Grabbing life by the throat like that. Me, I'd never have the guts to jump out of a plane.'

'Aw, well, that's probably because you're the nervous type.' Fred ruffled her hair fondly and ignored the guffaw of laughter from Jim. 'So, let's go grab a drink.' He talked loudly, just in case Jim was planning on laughing too much. 'Are yez on, folks?'

They were standing outside Fred's flat. Jim jangled his car keys and shook his head. 'I've to pick up the kids in an hour, so I'll pass.'

Fred gave Gillian a squeeze. 'And you?'

'I'm for a drink,' she said. 'Debs?'

Debbie smirked. 'And play gooseberry? Naw, I'll head home.'

'You won't be a gooseberry,' Gillian cuffed her. 'And anyways, how'll you get home? I'm driving.'

'Walk? Catch a bus? Taxi?' Debbie answered.

'I'll drive you.' Jim felt he had to offer. He could hardly leave her to go home on her own when he had a car.

'A better offer you won't get,' Fred gave Jim a meaningful wink.

Both of them ignored him.

'Well?' Jim indicated his car.

'But your kids?'

'I'll have plenty of time.'

Debbie shrugged. 'OK, if you're sure.'

'Oh,' Fred chortled, 'he's sure, aren't you, Jimbo?'

Gillian giggled.

'Asshole,' Debbie muttered.

This time Jim didn't disagree.

As he drove Debbie back to the flat she shared with Gillian he couldn't think of a thing to say. He was completely useless at making conversation with beautiful women. Well, with any woman that wasn't Jane, actually. Being away from her was getting harder instead of easier.

When he pulled up outside she invited him in for a coffee. 'Kill some time before you see your kids?'

'Naw, thanks. It's cool, I'll, eh, just, you know . . .' his voice trailed off and he began studying his hands.

'Suit yourself.' Debbie pulled the door handle and made to leave.

'Thanks for the company today,' he found himself saying before he could stop it. 'The other two would have driven me mental otherwise.'

A smile lit up her face. 'And thank you for yours,' she said back.

Silence.

'Well,' she muttered. 'See you again.'

'Sure.'

'Maybe next Saturday? We're all heading out that night. It should be a blast.'

He let himself give a non-committal sort of a nod. She climbed out of the car and walked up the driveway to her apartment.

A sigh of relief escaped him. It was as if he could breathe again.

'I think you could do with a night out.'

Jane looked up from her hairdressing magazine. So far Patrick's flyers had failed to produce any more customers. If anything, numbers had continued to dwindle. The only thing she could do to stop herself from worrying too much, was to read the latest hairdressing mags. At least that way she'd be prepared for the young trendies when they eventually came.

'You need a night out,' Mir said again, as she leant against the reception desk. She took one look at what Jane was reading and grabbed it from her. 'That's boring!' she declared. 'Come on, Jane. How about a night out? My treat?'

There was no way she was going out with Miranda. Their conceptions of a night out were wildly different. 'Aw, I—'

'You can come back and stay at my flat, so you won't have to drive home and Sheila's in your house, so she can keep an eye on the kids.'

'My mother only has eyes for herself.' Jane snatched the magazine back and folded it up. 'Naw, thanks anyway Miranda.'

'Oh, go on. Don't be such a dry shite. D'you remember you,

me and Patrick used to always go out every Saturday? We haven't done it in ages – not since . . .' Mir trailed off.

'Not since Matt died,' Jane finished for her, her voice quiet.

'Yeah,' Mir said. 'So come on – we'll ask Patrick too.'

If Patrick went, she could be tempted. 'Well . . .'

'Oh, go on.' Miranda, sensing victory, gave her a poke. 'It'll just be the three of us, the way it used to be. Please – come out with us?'

'Are you going out?' Rosemary bustled up, all business. 'Like as in a staff outing? Can I come?'

'You have as much chance of coming as I have of liking you,' Miranda scoffed.

'Jesus, Mir—'

'Oh thanks,' Rosemary beamed. 'That means "yes" – right? That means I can go? Ooooh brilliant. I'm dying to go out with you, Mir. I'll bet you go to the coolest places. D'you go to that place – the Kitchen place? I've never been there. I bet you go there. Oooh great.' She looked at Jane. 'And will you do my hair for it? Jaz loves the way you do it.' She did a dance of some sort before waltzing back down the salon with some conditioner.

'What a complete loser,' Miranda said, sounding bewildered.

Jane giggled.

'You *have* to come now Jane. I mean, if you don't I'll end up killing her.' Her voice rose. 'Patrick isn't man enough to stop me.'

'Are you having a go at my sexuality again?' Patrick chided. 'Honestly, if I wasn't the boss, I'd sue you.'

'I'm trying to persuade Jane to go out with us one Saturday,' Miranda explained.

'Like we used to?' Patrick's face lit up.

'Only instead of convincing her, I've bloody well got Rosemary coming.'

'Aw well,' Patrick rolled his eyes. 'Enjoy yourself, sweet cakes.'

'What?' Miranda paled. 'No way am I going out with her on my own. No bloody way. Yez have to come.'

'I'll go if Jane goes.' Patrick looked at her questioningly.

Jane smiled. Talk about being railroaded into something. But still, the idea of a night out with Patrick and Mir appealed to her. 'OK,' she nodded. 'That'd be great.'

'Good girl,' Patrick grinned. He turned to Miranda. 'The three hairdressers ride again.'

'Ride being the operative word, I hope,' Miranda giggled.

Patrick gave her a clout. 'You bad bitch.'

'I'm a very bad bitch,' Miranda nodded. 'Thank you for noticing.'

17

IT WAS AS if she'd just told them she was going to bare all for *Playboy*.

'You're going out?' Diane glared at her. 'When?'

'Saturday night.'

'With who?'

'Patrick and Miranda,' Jane answered patiently.

'Oh.' Di seemed happy enough with that. Then she said, '*Where* are you going?'

'Diane,' Jane leaned towards her daughter. 'Do I ask you to fill in a questionnaire every time you sneak off to see your boyfriend?' At Diane's sullen look, she nodded. 'Well, then, mind your own business. I'm going out. Your nana will be here to see that nobody gets up to anything.'

'Who?' At the mention of her name, Sheila stopped studying her reflection in the teapot. 'What did you just say, dahling?'

'I said that you're going to be keeping an eye on Owen and Di for me on Saturday.'

'Me?' Sheila was horrified. 'Me? Keep an eye on those two?'

'Yes, Mother. Your grandchildren.'

'I don't need *her* to keep an eye on me,' Diane said scornfully. 'I'm fifteen.'

'That's right, dahling, you are.' Sheila gave her a beatific smile. 'Far too old to have Nana minding you.' She turned to Owen. 'And you're a big boy, too.'

'That's what all the girls say, isn't it, Owen?' Diane smirked.

Owen smirked back but didn't reply.

Sheila tut-tutted at their crudeness and turned to Jane. 'Now, dahling, you've heard them. They don't need me.'

Jane gave a tight smile. 'You'll be here on Saturday so you can keep an eye on the place. I'm going out and that is that.'

'I might need to go out myself—'

'Well, if Dad rings, I'll cancel my plans, OK?'

Sheila pursed her lips. 'There's no need for that sarcasm,' she quivered. 'No need at all.'

But there was, Jane realised. Her dad hadn't been in contact once since Sheila had left him and, despite Sheila saying that she'd handle it, she didn't seem to have done anything. There was nothing else for it, Jane realised, but to do what she'd spent her life doing. She had to go and sort it out herself. It might also be an opportunity to ask her dad to put in a word for the salon on his show. Desperate times called for desperate measures.

As Patrick said, business was business and the way things were going they needed all the perverts and loonies they could get.

18

'And Jaz, he jumped on the lad that was jumping on the other lad.'

'Did he?' Jane, combing conditioner through Nash's hair, tried her best to sound interested.

Nash was a friend of Rosemary's who'd decided to pay her a visit and at the same time get her hair washed and blow-dried and be waited on hand and foot by her mate. She thought it was a great laugh to have Rosemary scurrying to and fro making her cups of tea. Rosemary was throwing poisonous looks in her direction.

Nash nodded. 'He did. Flattened him with a magic right hook, nearly took his head off.'

Jane wondered if it would be possible to take Nash's head off. The girl never stopped talking and Jaz, Rosemary's fella, featured prominently in every story. He was like some kind of malevolent Superman, always around when fights broke out.

'The cops arrived soon after and we all had to scatter. Hey, hey Rose,' Nash bellowed across the salon, 'were you around when Jaz got carted away by the cops?'

'No,' Rosemary answered sourly. 'I had work to do at home.'

'Last Sunday night?' Nash scoffed. 'Hate that.'

It was just as well there were no other customers in the salon that afternoon, Jane thought. Nash wasn't exactly good for business. OK, she was young and she was a customer, but she'd spent the last visit describing in lurid detail how Jaz had lost his index finger. Eileen Simms, who had come back after her initial defection, had made a big deal of fanning herself and declaring that she felt sick.

'Now, Nash, lie back and relax.' Jane put the comb down and tucked a towel in around Nash's shoulders. 'I'll wash the conditioner out in about five minutes, all right?'

'Yeah, yeah, no problem. Hey Rose, get us a cuppa would you?'

Rosemary bristled. 'I'm a trainee, I've other stuff to do, haven't I, Jane?'

'It's all right Rosemary, I'll make it,' Jane said.

Immediately Rosemary scuttled over to the office. 'No, no, it's OK, I'll do it. I mean, I don't mind making tea I just don't like,' she paused, 'people – taking – advantage.' She scowled over at her friend. In a lower voice, she hissed to Jane, 'She's already got me to make her two cups. I just don't think it's fair that she comes in here, getting hairdos and ordering me about.'

'Well, it's not as if you're exactly busy, are you?' Nash cackled over. She had ears like a bat. 'Jane says that your hair reflects your inner health – isn't that right, Jane?'

'Yes.' Jane smiled ruefully at Rosemary who was giving her friend the fingers.

'In which case,' Nash went on, grinning broadly, 'Rose must be about to drop dead!'

'You bitch!' Rosemary tore across the salon and belted her friend.

Nash screamed with laughter.

'Girls!' Jane bellowed. 'Stop—'

She was halted mid-sentence as the door slammed closed. It would be bloody typical for a potential customer to see her trainee trying to strangle a regular. She was relieved to see Rosemary hastily drop a fistful of Nash's hair and instead pretend that she was doing something with the towels. The kid was learning.

'Hello,' a male voice said, sounding slightly annoyed. 'Can I speak to the manager?'

His voice was familiar though she couldn't place it. Turning around, she came face to face with Pete Jordan. Shit. Double shit. She assumed a vacant expression and wondered if she could get away with pretending that she was a customer.

'Hey.' Pete's irritated expression vanished and he crossed to meet her. 'We meet again. Jane something or other, isn't it?'

'Pardon?' She hoped her puzzled expression would put him off, make him think he'd made a mistake.

'Jane,' he said instead, more confidently. 'The woman that hates my light fittings.'

'Ooh, I'd say your fittings are heavy enough,' Nash called over.

Pete looked mildly disgusted as Jane started to laugh.

Rosemary belted her friend, hissing, 'That's rude. You don't talk rude to customers.'

'So,' Pete said, smiling patronisingly at Jane. 'I see you haven't defected from your local.'

'Er, no, ha.' God, how was she going to get out of this?

'So, where is he – the manager?' Pete asked. 'I need to see him.' He paused. 'Urgently, in fact.'

'But sure, Jane owns the place,' Rosemary said as if Pete Jordan was a complete idiot. 'She's the manager!' She gazed proudly at a mortified Jane, 'Aren't you?'

'Rosemary, will you wash Nash's hair, please?' Jane strove to sound normal, even though curling up and dying would have suited her better. 'Lukewarm water, OK?'

'Yeah, Rose, wash me hair,' Nash said, throwing her head back into the basin. 'Nice and gentle. Jane says that you can destroy it if—ooooh!'

Rosemary had turned on the water full force and squirted it into her mate's mouth. Her voice dripping with false concern, she said sweetly, 'Sorry 'bout that, Nash. You OK?'

'Bitch.'

Jane gave a nervous laugh. 'Mad,' she tittered.

'Just like you, eh?' Pete lifted an eyebrow. Not sounding quite as friendly as he had initially, he continued, 'Imagine forgetting that you owned this place when I talked to you last.'

'Imagine,' Jane said briskly, hating the fact that he'd caught her out.

'You taking tablets for it?'

She was not going to have him sneering at her. 'So, what is it you wanted?' She kept her voice neutral. For some reason, she felt embarrassed to be seen looking the way she was. Hair neglected, face make-up free, she was wearing old jeans and a sweatshirt with the words *Boston Chick* scrawled diagonally across it. He, on the other hand, looked quite the successful businessman. His clothes casual, yet madly expensive. No fear of getting hair dye on them, she thought. He was probably one of those owners that did no work yet took all the glory.

'What I want to talk about is this.' He pulled a folded-up piece of paper from his pocket. 'Your salon's back-stabbing advertising campaign.' He thrust the paper towards her. 'One of my stylists was handed it yesterday.'

Oh wonderful.

She folded her arms, realised it was a defensive gesture and immediately unfolded them. 'What's the problem?'

He raised his eyebrows. 'Do I have to spell it out?'

'That'd be an unusual way of doing it, all right,' Jane said.

Behind her, Rosemary started to giggle.

'The problem is, *Jane*,' Pete stressed her name, 'that in this leaflet you are basically having a go at us. At Cutting Edge. At our credibility.'

She took the leaflet from him. 'We are?' She was proud of her surprised expression. For some reason the fact that he was annoyed gave her a bit of a buzz. 'And where does it say that?' She arched her eyebrows and made a big deal of perusing the flyer. Looking up at him she shook her head. Copying Patrick, she said in a baffled tone, 'I can't see your name on it anywhere.'

Pete's eyes narrowed. 'Well, if it was we could sue you, couldn't we?'

Jane shrugged.

'Yeah. Yeah, yez could,' Rosemary piped up. 'Patrick told me we have to skid a very narrow line.'

'Rosemary, please keep out of this,' Jane said icily.

'I'm just putting him in the limelight.'

'Well don't!' Jane turned back to Pete. 'So, if all you have to go on is your own suspicious mind, I suggest you leave now.'

'I'm not going anywhere.'

'Well there's no reason why you should stay.' Jane indicated the salon. 'There are no more of our customers that you can actually steal.'

'Competition, dear girl,' Pete snapped, 'if you can't stand the heat, then get out of the kitchen.'

'I prefer to turn the heat off myself,' Jane said calmly, relishing his annoyance. 'Saves a lot of energy.'

The front door slammed and Mir struggled in with some leaflets of her own. 'Only came back to do Bridie Doyle's hair. I've her booked in for two. The leaflets are going a bomb. Jane wait until . . .' Her voice trailed off and her eyes lit up. 'Hiya,' she said, grinning at Pete. 'Hey – great hair.'

'Got it done in the overpriced place up the road.' Peter eyeballed Jane.

'Aw, well, we all have our crosses to bear.' Mir chortled.

'He owns Cutting Edge,' Rosemary, busy towel-drying Nash's hair, said. 'He's Eddie Jordan.'

Mir's mouth dropped so far open that she could have swallowed him whole. 'You own Cutting Edge?' she gasped. She made an unsuccessful attempt to hide the leaflets behind her back. A pile of them tumbled from her hands on to the floor where they lay face up.

Jane winced.

'Uh-huh.' Pete looked pointedly at the leaflets.

'You own it?'

'Uh-huh.'

'And Jane and Pat have let you live?' Mir said, recovering her composure. 'Well, things are looking up.'

Jane stifled a laugh.

Pete looked from one to the other. 'I'm leaving.'

'Just you or your actual hairdressers?' Jane asked, making Mir giggle.

'I won't dignify that with a response.' He glared at the two of them and then turned to Nash. 'And obviously your prices in this place are as low as your standards – your trainee just messed up towel-drying that lady's hair. It'll take the shine from it. It's no wonder you've lost all your business.' He gave a mock-pleasant smile and added, 'I can swat you like flies from a cow.' So saying, he strode from the salon and let the door slam after him.

'Asshole,' Jane, Mir and Rosemary said together.

19

IT WAS STRANGE to be going out, Jane thought. She hadn't really gone clubbing in years. And any time she'd gone for a drink in recent years, it was usually with Jim. They'd sit in a pub, trying to make conversation and failing miserably. She wondered why they'd bothered. Tonight was going to be different. Miranda and Patrick were a great double act and even though Rosemary was coming along, it should still be a good laugh.

She pulled a brush through her hair before heading downstairs. The kids had just come in from being with Jim and she wanted to chat to them before leaving. They were in the sitting room watching telly while her mother sat in state on the sofa with her nails soaking in some putrid-smelling liquid.

'Hi yez,' Jane smiled, 'Good day?' She tried to make it sound as if she hoped they'd had a good time.

'Brilliant,' Diane answered. 'Dad's great fun to be with.'

'People are always fun when you don't see them that much,' Sheila said smartly.

Jane was oddly touched by the comment. Her mother flashed her a sympathetic smile and Jane smiled back.

'True,' Diane surprised them by agreeing. 'Maybe you should remember that, Gran.'

'It's Nana,' Sheila corrected, stiffly. 'And I—'

'Oh God,' Diane talked loudly over Sheila's reprimand, '*What* are you *like*, Mam?'

'What?' Jane looked down at herself. 'What's wrong?'

'You. In bootlegs. Jesus.' Diane gave a snigger.

Her daughter's laughter fazed her. OK, so she'd expected Diane to be like this, Di didn't want her to go out, after all, but maybe she did look stupid. Maybe her new clothes *were* a bit on the young side for her. Maybe she should go and—

'I think you look great,' Owen said quietly. 'Really, you know, nice and all.'

Relief flooded through her. But Owen had been bunking school and it was probably his way of making it up to her. He'd say anything, she reckoned.

'You do,' Sheila agreed. 'You look lovely, dahling. Don't mind that sourpuss over there.'

Di glowered at her nana.

'Thank you,' Jane said, pleased. 'Now, Mam, I'm staying at Mir's tonight, I've left her number in the kitchen in case of any problems.' She picked up her bag from the chair and grabbed her fleece.

'And Di, if you're heading out, be in by midnight.'

'Oh,' Di smiled sweetly, 'I don't think I'll be going anywhere tonight.'

'Really? Why? Is it—'

The doorbell rang.

She had been going to ask Di if it was all off with the mysterious Guy, but she appeared to be in good humour so that didn't seem a possibility. Maybe they were cooling things, which would be nice. After all, Di did have her exams later in the year, it wouldn't do her any harm to study a bit more.

The doorbell rang again.

'You might as well answer that, Mam, seeing as you're on your way out,' Di remarked.

'I will. Bye now.'

They mumbled their goodbyes.

Pulling on her fleece, she opened the front door.

Outside, standing on the step, was an unshaven, ear-ringed, nose-ringed youth. He wore a long black coat and baggy black jeans. His eyes, which could have been nice, were outlined in thick black eyeliner. Long dreadlocks hung down to his shoulders like pieces of frayed rope.

'Sorry,' Jane tried to inject some sympathy into her voice, 'I've no money.'

The guy looked surprised and then drawled out a sympathetic, 'That's shitty.'

'Yes, it is, so would you mind—'

'Gooey!' Diane pushed past and to Jane's horror enfolded the youth in a bear hug – the kind of hug she'd recently started using on Jim. Turning to her, she announced proudly, 'Mam, this is Gooey.' Dragging him into the hall, she dismayed Jane further by saying, 'He's my boyfriend.'

Whoever she had imagined as her daughter's boyfriend, it certainly hadn't been *this*. The lad looked like an abused animal or something.

Gooey shoved his hand towards her. 'Hiya, Mrs D'arcy.'

'McCarthy,' Jane corrected faintly. He was some boyfriend if he didn't even know Di's second name. 'And you are – again?'

'Gooey.'

She watched, in a kind of frozen stupor, as Di beamed from her to him and back again. Where was Guy, the film star she'd imagined for her beautiful daughter?

'Interesting nickname,' she said pathetically.

'It's his real name,' Diane said. She gave Gooey a shove. 'Go on, tell my mam how you got it.'

Gooey looked mortified. He coughed and shuffled and mumbled away to himself.

'His mother was looking through a magazine when she was expecting him,' Di said, cutting Gooey off mid-sentence, 'and she saw a gorgeous fella in a magazine and she said that if she had a boy she'd name him after this fella.'

'A fella called Gooey?' Jane found that hard to swallow.

'She wasn't good at reading,' Gooey spoke. 'Me name – it's spelt G-U-Y.'

'Oh, right.' Jane didn't know if she should sympathise, laugh or cry.

'Gooey is heaps nicer than Guy,' Di smiled at him. 'Heaps better.' She turned to Jane and raised her eyebrows. 'So, you're going out, aren't you Mam? See you.'

She bloody well wished she wasn't going out now. What would those two get up to in her absence? Satanic rituals sprang to mind.

Di pulled Gooey by the arm, giggling into his face. 'Now, Goo,' she said, 'see, meeting my family wasn't so bad. You can meet my brother later and just ignore my nana. So, will we head upstairs? We can talk privately there.'

'There'll be no private talk in any bedrooms in this house,' Jane managed to splutter out. Then, knowing that Di would hate her for saying that, she conceded, 'If you want, there's always the kitchen.'

'Oh, brilliant!' Di said, her face contorting to convey how square her mother was.

Jane ignored her. She watched them head into the kitchen before going back into the sitting room. 'Mam,' she whispered, hoping Di wouldn't hear, 'Diane has,' she lowered her voice, 'a boyfriend outside. I wouldn't trust him with me let alone with her. You're not to let them go upstairs. I've told them they can use the kitchen. It's up to you to try and get rid of him, soon.'

Sheila looked stricken. 'Dahling, how do I do that? You know she won't listen to me. Maybe you'd better stay—'

'Are you joking?' Jane suddenly understood. 'That's the only reason I'm getting an eyeful of him.' She bit her lip. 'Now, Mam, please, will you keep an eye on her?'

'I was never much good at that sort of thing,' Sheila said mournfully. 'But I'll do my best.'

'It's okay Nana, I'll help you.' Owen grinned. 'I'll keep an eye on them, drive Di mad.'

'Oh, now, I don't want any fighting. Your mother never fought when she was a child.'

'I was an *only* child Mam.'

'So?'

Jane stared at her in exasperation. She was so tempted to ring and cancel, but she knew she couldn't. Di would have her trapped in the house for ever if she did that. 'Now just keep an eye on them, Mother. It's no big deal. Keep going into the kitchen to make tea or something. Do anything – I don't care.'

Sheila moaned slightly.

Poking her head into the kitchen, Jane noted that Diane had poured Gooey a cuppa and that he was eating the nicest biscuits. It all seemed innocent enough. 'Bye.' She managed a smile at Gooey who looked even more unattractive under the light. 'Nice to meet you, Gooey.'

'Enjoy yourself,' Diane said sweetly. 'Don't think of us *too* much.'

'Oh, I'll enjoy myself all right,' Jane smiled back. 'Thank you, Di.'

Her daughter's sour look almost made her laugh.

Jim showered and shaved. He hadn't wanted to go out with Fred and his mates, but the alternative – staying in with a laptop and a heap of figures – had decided him. Running his fingers through his short hair, he let it dry naturally. Now, he wondered, what did he wear? He'd never been much of a clothes man, Jane had bought most of his stuff for him. He tried to remember what she'd liked. There was a black shirt that she'd bought him once, so he put it on. He'd a black pair of jeans that would match it. Dressed, he sat down and flicked on the telly. Fred wouldn't be ready for ages. He was worse than a woman the length of time he took. Everything was tried on and discarded until he was looking the best he could. Which, Jim grudgingly admitted, was always pretty good.

'Bless me father, for I have sinned,' Fred chortled when he did eventually emerge.

'What?'

'You.' Fred gestured to Jim's clothes, 'You're like a priest.'

'What?'

'You don't want to be giving out the wrong signals to Debs now. A priest is definitely *not* what that lady wants.'

Jim scowled. He'd had enough of Fred's comments about Debbie. 'Fred, get lost. I don't give a toss what Debbie or anyone else thinks, right?'

'Oh yeah, right,' Fred drawled, in such a way that Jim knew he didn't believe him.

'Leave it, Fred.'

'It was just a joke.'

'Jokes are funny.' Jim tossed the remote control on to the sofa. 'You're not.'

There was an edgy silence until Fred muttered, 'I'm fucking sorry, all right? Jaysus, you're as narky as an auld wan. It's worse than having a woman in the place.'

Jim gave a reluctant grin.

'Comes from the lack of a sex life, Jimbo.'

20

MIRANDA WAS WAITING for her outside the salon. The minute Jane saw what Miranda was wearing, her new clothes seemed frumpy and old. Miranda was dressed for clubbing in a tiny white mini-skirt, impossible heels and a backless white top. Over her shoulders she wore a diminutive red-denim jacket. Her make-up was subtle except for the crimson lipstick which gave her a Marilyn Monroe pout.

'Hiya.' She gave Jane the once over. 'You look great.'

'Not as great as you though,' Jane said enviously.

Miranda shrugged modestly. 'Well,' she said, 'I just wish Patrick would hurry up or I'll freeze the arse off myself. At least you'll be warm.' She shivered slightly.

Wouldn't she just? Jane thought glumly. She wondered what had possessed her to bring her navy fleece. The lack of any other coat, maybe? She'd no fancy little bits of jackets to wear on a night out. Everything was sensible and warm. She wanted to kick herself.

'Hi yez,' Rosemary called, tottering up the road towards them. 'Is Pat not here yet?'

'Naw, just the cow pat,' Miranda mumbled.

Jane elbowed her to shut her up. Honestly, Miranda could be awful cruel sometimes.

'What on earth is she wearing?' Miranda whispered. 'Jesus tonight, what *is* that?'

'It's a skirt,' Jane whispered back. 'Will you stop?'

'Would you let your Di out in it?' Miranda asked.

Jane didn't answer.

Rosemary came towards them. Her legs were lathered in fake tan. The bits that she'd missed stood out as white streaks. She wore a huge pair of platform heels that made her legs look slightly deformed. Her skirt was a short wrap-around that didn't quite wrap. She sported a top which proclaimed to the world that her other job was as a porn star. Her hair, which Jane had washed for her that evening, stood up in massive peaks on the top of her head. She wore no glasses and, as a result, was squinting madly. And her neck, wrists and fingers dripped in bright, fake gold. However bad Di could be, Rosemary was worse.

Rosemary stopped a few feet from them and gazed at Miranda in awe. 'Wow! Great minds think alike – huh?' She indicated their short skirts.

'Wha—!' Miranda spluttered before beginning to cough as Jane gave her another dig in the ribs.

'I'm not mad into white myself,' Rosemary confided, standing close to Miranda, as if they were best friends, 'but on you it looks great. And your top!' Reverently, she fingered it.

To Jane's relief, Patrick chose that moment to arrive.

'Hi!' He waved at them from his Celica. 'Climb aboard you beauties.'

Rosemary giggled frantically. 'Aw, stop. Go away.' Then she asked, 'Can I sit in the front?'

'You can indeed, madam.' Patrick opened the door for her. 'In you come.'

Rosemary looked at Jane and Miranda. 'Yez don't mind, do yez? I mean, if one of you wants to sit in the front . . . ?'

'Go ahead,' Jane grinned.

'Mir?'

'Yeah. Yeah.' Miranda gave a bored sigh.

Looking as if she'd just won the lottery, Rosemary scuttled into the passenger seat. 'Oooh,' she squealed, 'this is like being important.' She gazed around in wonder. 'This is a *lovely* car, Pat. Ohhh, I hope someone sees me sitting in it.'

Miranda yawned widely as Jane grinned.

'Where will you be driving?' Rosemary asked. 'Will you be going by St Anne's Park?'

Patrick shrugged. 'If you want.' He gave the dash an affectionate pat. 'I'll drive this little goer anywhere.' He started the car and pulled out.

'Oh *please*, let's go there,' Rosemary begged, looking at them all with shining eyes. 'My friends live around there, I'd just love them to see me.' She giggled a bit, 'I told them I was going out with my boss from work and that he drove a cool car and none of them believed me. Of course,' she added seriously, 'I never told them you were, you know,' she flapped her hand about a bit, 'sort of gay.' She shrugged. 'That would have spoilt the story a bit.'

'And why spoil a good story with the truth, eh, Rosemary?' Miranda said drily.

'Yep. True enough,' Rosemary agreed. 'So,' she turned to Patrick, 'can we go around there?'

'Only if you promise to snuggle up to me if they're around. No point in letting the whole world in on my shameful life, huh?' Patrick grinned and winked at Jane and Miranda.

'It's not shameful,' Rosemary said. 'Just, like, really really *weird*.'

Miranda exploded in a laugh and Rosemary gave her a puzzled look, before giving a fake laugh herself.

'St Anne's Park detour, here we come,' Patrick said.

'Oooh.' Rosemary almost wet herself with excitement. 'The last time I was in a car this big was for my mother's funeral. Ooooh.'

Jane settled back into her seat, smiling. She was glad she'd come. Still, a call home wouldn't hurt. She took her mobile out and began to dial.

Gillian drove Fred and Jim to the pub. There was no way Fred was driving. 'I'm having a few jars, doll,' he said, patting his belly. 'A man like me needs his drink.'

''Course you do.' Gillian patted his belly too. 'I'll drive.' She fished her keys from her bag. 'I don't wanna drink anyhow. There's this psychotherapist back home who says that drink is bad—'

'That's all there is in your country,' Fred said knowledgeably, 'loonies with qualifications telling the rest of the world how to live. I'd have none of that meself now.'

'I dunno that loonies—'

'Would you, Jimbo? Would you let some looney tell you how to face your fear and all that crap?'

Gillian looked offended. 'It's not crap.'

Jim shrugged. 'Facing me fear, I don't mind. But someone telling me it's bad to drink, now that's a looney.'

Both Gillian and Fred laughed.

After half an hour looking for Rosemary's mates Patrick decided that the night out had better start. Rosemary reluctantly agreed, while peering desperately out the window.

'It's like the Wild West around here,' Miranda whispered to Jane as they drove back up Rosemary's street, which was a sad affair of boarded-up houses and burnt-out cars. 'No wonder no one's around; probably all out joyriding.'

Jane shot Miranda a warning look. It wasn't a bit funny. No wonder poor Rosemary never looked well, the poor kid probably did her best with what she had. Her affection for Rosemary grew. She was glad the kid was working for them. Maybe it'd give her a chance.

'So, where to?' Patrick asked. 'Pub first and then a club?'

'Fine by me.' Miranda crossed one perfect leg over the other. 'Let's go to The Orange Tree and then hit,' she frowned, 'The Kitchen maybe?'

'The Kitchen?' Rosemary said the words reverently. 'As in *The Kitchen*?'

'Naw, as in The Dining Room,' Miranda deadpanned.

'As in The Kitchen,' Jane smiled.

'Wow.' Rosemary was seriously impressed. 'That's brill. The last time I tried to get in there, they wouldn't let me.'

'Well, they'll let you in tonight.' Patrick gave her a fond smile. 'You're with us.'

Rosemary's eyes widened. A slow smile broke over her face. 'Yeah,' she said, as if hardly daring to believe it. 'Yeah, I am, amn't I?'

'Hey, competition alert,' Patrick called.

A Cutting Edge salon came into view.

They rolled down the windows and, to the amazement of passers-by, gave the building two fingers while Patrick shouted out 'crap styles' at the top of his voice.

Debbie wasn't there when they arrived at the pub and Jim, to his surprise, felt slightly let down. It wasn't as if he was interested or anything, but she was good company. Talking to her was better than hearing about Fred and his parachute exploits for the millionth time.

'Some of the other guys were shitting themselves,' Fred said to an agog table. 'But I wasn't. Naw, if I died, I died, but yez know, there's no point in dying if you haven't lived – is there now?'

Jim had had enough. He excused himself and went to the bar to get in a last round. The barmen were rushing about like mad things.

'Yo?' one of them said.

'Two Guinness, one Carlsberg, Heineken, Southern and white.'

'And a vodka and lemon,' a voice from behind said. 'Get you later.'

Jim turned around to find Debbie smiling at him. He grinned back before confirming the order with the barman. 'You're late,' he commented.

'Yeah.' Debbie shrugged off her jacket, revealing a tight top with plenty of cleavage. 'Work was a bitch today so I went home and took it easy. There was no way I was coming straight in and heading straight back out. I'd a nice Chinese,' she grinned slightly, 'dinner, that is. Then a big bubbly bath and, 'cause I'd the flat to myself, I spent ages just mooching about in my dressing gown before I got ready. It was brill.'

Jim tried to push the image of her in a bath out of his head. Jesus, what was he like? 'Well, it's good to see you,' he said awkwardly. Then, smiling, added, 'I'd no one to talk to in the Snigger-at-Fred part of the night. It was awful hard trying to smile and look impressed along with everyone else.'

Debbie laughed her husky laugh. 'Spineless git.' She gave him a puck on the arm and suddenly looked embarrassed. There was a small silence before she said brightly, 'Here's your drinks. I'll give you a hand to carry them over.'

The barman began placing the pints along the bar top. Debbie picked up two pints and the Southern Comfort and told him that she'd see him at the table. Jim pointed out where they were sitting and watched her shapely form disappear into the crowd.

Two pints of Guinness and the vodka were banged down in front of him and absently he handed over some notes. His head was a mess. Here he was barely separated, yet thinking of someone else. Rebound city here I come, he thought morosely.

To hell with it, he thought, as he got his change back from the barman, Jane didn't want him any more, so what did it matter what he did?

21

AFTER THE PUB they headed to a club. They had no problem getting into The Kitchen. Patrick put his arm around Rosemary, making it look as if they were a couple and they were waved in. Garage music pumped out of speakers and the place was beginning to fill up.

'You've a nerve trying that.' Miranda rolled her eyes at Patrick. 'The dogs in the street know you drive on the wrong side of the road.'

'Well, he didn't on the way here,' Rosemary said, confused. She looked even more confused as the other three started laughing. 'What's the joke?'

'Nothing,' Patrick said as he headed to the bar.

Coming back laden with drinks, he said, 'Mir, you're going to freak. Guess who I just spotted on the other side of the room?'

Miranda froze with her pint of Guinness halfway to her mouth. 'Who?' There were about a million people who would cause her to freak if she met them when out. All of them male.

'Harry.'

'Aw, Jesus! Aw no!'

'What's wrong with him?' Jane asked. 'It's not as if he ever, you know . . .'

'He never what?' Miranda snapped.

Jane tried to think of a tactful way to say that Miranda hadn't ever been dumped by him. 'Well,' she eventually muttered, 'you've never been in a relationship with him, have you? He's your friend.'

'And who the fuck wants a male friend hanging around them when they're on the prowl?'

'Well, Patrick is our friend,' Rosemary piped up. 'We don't mind him being here.'

'Patrick is one of us,' Miranda snapped. 'He's looking for a man too. Here,' she stood up and pushed Rosemary off her seat, 'let me sit there, with my back to the room. You take my place.'

Rosemary was only too delighted to be of help. 'Oooh,' she said as she was about to sit down in Miranda's seat, 'there's a fine thing on his way over. He's definitely coming this way. Ooooh, I wonder who he wants.'

The 'fine thing' slapped Miranda on the back, making her drink splash on to her brilliant white skirt.

'Oy! Watch it.'

'Sorry,' the guy grinned. He turned to Patrick. 'I *thought* it was you at the bar. How's it going, folks? Hey, Jane, long time no see!'

'Hiya, Harry.' Jane smiled at the tall, dark, good-looking guy that had plonked himself right next to a scowling Miranda.

'You'll pay for this to be cleaned,' Miranda grouched, furiously trying to wipe the stain out of her skirt.

'Sure. No probs. Take it off and I'll take it away with me now.'

Rosemary giggled in near hysteria.

'And who's this?' Harry asked, turning great brown eyes in Rosemary's direction.

'Rosemary,' she said, her eyes big with awe. 'Hiya.'

'You've ruined my skirt!' Miranda gave him a puck. 'Don't mind Rosemary.'

'I told you I'd get it cleaned,' Harry said mildly. He held out his hand. 'Hiya, Rosemary. How's it going?'

'Great. Brill. Thanks for asking. Hiya.'

'D'you work with this shower then?'

'Yeah. Just started a few months ago.'

'Well don't let this one boss you about.' He jerked his head towards Miranda. 'She can be a right bitch. Tries it on with me sometimes too.'

Rosemary tittered violently.

'Are you here with friends?' Jane asked swiftly. Miranda was going to brain Rosemary if she didn't stop hyperventilating.

'Yeah, a few of the lads from work. One of them is getting hitched on Monday, so we're getting him plastered at the moment.'

'Well, don't let us keep you,' Miranda snapped. 'You go and enjoy yourself.'

'And it was great seeing you too, Mir. Listen, making any sweet music lately with musician man?' He winked at the others as he said it.

'Making a symphony actually,' Miranda said, flicking him a disdainful glance. 'Now, go on and toddle off to your friends. We don't want to keep you, they need someone with your dazzling wit to entertain them.'

'Save a dance for me, huh?' Harry caressed her shoulder briefly before she shrugged him off.

Jane gave him a sympathetic smile but he didn't return it. Instead, he nodded briefly and sloped off.

'You're horrible to him,' Jane chastised. 'He was only being friendly.'

'If I want him to be friendly, I'll call him. That's our arrangement.'

'Bloody stupid if you ask me,' Patrick said mildly. 'I wouldn't throw him out of bed for eating crisps.'

'Well, with your performance record, that's all he would be doing, isn't it?'

'Mia-ow.' Patrick made scratching motions with his hands.

Miranda picked up her little bag, 'I'm going out for a smoke. I hope the record will be changed by the time I get back.' A guy passing the table threw her an admiring glance. 'Hiya,' she smiled at him, her face one high-voltage beam.

The guy grinned back and a conversation ensued.

'That's him for the sack tonight,' Patrick observed wryly.

Jane winced. Now where would she sleep?

He was at the stage where he was aware he was drunk. He knew what he was doing, but he didn't care that much. He was conscious of laughing a lot and making other people laugh. He was also aware of Debbie hanging on to his arm and snuggling into him and he liked it. Damn it, he was a free man. He had nothing to feel guilty about.

When the others said that they were heading off to a club however, the guilt set in. 'I'll, eh, give it a miss,' he mumbled.

'Aw, come on.' Fred looked devastated. 'Don't be a fucking . . .' he frowned, searching for a word to describe guys that didn't go to nightclubs, '. . . a fucking *tissue*,' he finished.

Gillian squealed with laughter. 'You!' she belted him. 'Whatta word. Don't be a tissue! Gweat!'

'Well,' Fred asked Jim, 'coming?'

'Nope.' Jim stared into his pint glass. 'I'll, eh, just hang on here and finish my pint.' He wished Debbie would let his arm go.

'I'll hang on too,' she said, startling him.

'Oh,' Fred winked lewdly, 'hey, hey, hey.'

'Yeah, make hay while the sun shines, isn't dat wight, Debs?' Gillian hooted.

Fred guffawed at his girlfriend's wit. 'See yez,' he said, injecting a wealth of meaning into his words.

'You don't have to—' Jim turned to Debbie, but she was watching the others leave.

'Fred is as bad as Gillian,' she said when they'd all disappeared.

'Naw, Fred's definitely worse,' Jim grinned. Debbie didn't grin back. 'You didn't have to stay,' he said quietly, 'there was no need.'

The long, appraising look that Debbie gave him made him squirm. He busied himself draining his pint glass.

'I stayed because I wanted to ask you something,' Debbie said coolly.

He was aware of the heady scent of her perfume and his heart began to speed up.

'Don't you want to know what it is?' she asked.

'Sure.'

Debbie coloured slightly. She glanced at her perfect nails, rubbed her hands together and looked back up at him. 'I like you, Jim, I really do.' As he made to interrupt, she held up her hand and talked over him. 'I've gone out with you a few times in the past couple of months and we always end up chatting together—'

'You're good company.'

She went on as if he hadn't spoken. 'Tonight, I hang on to your arm, I brush off your leg and you enjoy it. Then you say you're not going to the nightclub. The other week we had a blast at the parachute jump and you drive me home but wouldn't even come up for a coffee. Every time we go out it's the same, you're blowing hot and cold on me. I guess,' she swallowed, 'I just want to know where I stand.'

Jim stared at her. Jesus, she was honest. *And* she liked him. 'Debs,' he began, 'I'm thirty-five, I've two teenage kids and I'm barely separated. It's all wrong for you.'

'Let me decide that.' She turned from him and said quietly. 'I hope you don't think I come on like this to every guy—'

'You're not coming on to me. I understand what you're saying.'

'And?' She paused. 'Where do I stand? Am I wasting my time? 'Cause I really like you Jim.'

Jim could not believe it. She really liked him. This beautiful woman with the gorgeous body and great personality was into him. 'I like you too,' he said quietly. His heart twisted as Jane's face flashed into his head. 'But, like, I'm all over the place at the moment. And, well, I don't want to hurt you.'

'What makes you think you will?'

'I dunno. I just want to be fair to you . . .'

'Forget about me,' Debbie said, 'what do *you* want?'

He wanted his wife and kids back, that's what he wanted. But that was never going to happen. 'I guess if I hadn't so much baggage and well . . .' The drink was making it hard to say what he wanted to say. He wasn't much good at saying things anyway, preferring to do things instead. So he cut to the end. 'I'd want you,' he said simply. 'Any guy would.'

'We can work on the baggage.' Debbie's eyes were shining. 'Can we not just go for it? The way you feel, the way I feel. Isn't it worth a try?' She moved nearer him on the seat.

The proximity of the woman was making it difficult to think. He was alone. She was available, desirable and he liked her a lot. Everything seemed so simple. 'You sure you want to?'

'I've never been more sure of anything in my life.'

Jesus.

'OK,' he said slowly. 'Why not?'

Jane ended up at Patrick's flat. Miranda had left with the guy she'd picked up and there was no way Jane was heading back with them. Patrick had eventually persuaded her against getting a taxi home in favour of staying the night at his place.

He drove Rosemary back to her house first. She insisted on being let off at the top of her road.

'It's best if you don't come to the door,' she said.

Patrick didn't argue. Rosemary's estate was frightening enough during daylight, at night it looked even more terrifying.

Once Rosemary had left, a silence descended on the car. Jane spent the time staring out at the darkened streets, amazed that so many people should still be wandering about at this late hour.

Eventually Patrick spoke. 'She does it all the time,' he muttered.

'What?'

'Mir. Every time I go out with her, she leaves with some horror.'

'Jealous, are you?' Jane teased.

Patrick shrugged, slowed the car down. 'Naw. It's just that she never seems to learn. He'll be gone by Monday and we'll have tears everywhere. Did you see the way he was groping her when she was telling us that she was leaving with him?'

Jane nodded. She'd wondered how on earth Miranda could put up with it. 'And she's so good-looking too – she could have anyone.'

'She *does* have anyone,' Patrick said, causing Jane to smile briefly. 'She's a bloody idiot.'

'You've changed your tune.' She gave him a puck. 'Normally you're all over her, getting the juicy gossip.'

'I know, I haven't the heart to slate her,' Patrick sighed. 'The tears are real.' He stopped talking until he had negotiated his way on to the motorway.

'I dunno why she does it,' he muttered. 'It's like she thinks that's all she's good for. When I try to have a serious talk with her, she loses the head. I don't bother any more.'

'Harry's mad about her.'

'Harry's mad full stop.'

They laughed quietly and said nothing more until they were safely ensconced in Patrick's apartment. It was a shrine to minimalism, Jane marvelled at his good taste. 'Well, if the salon fails, you could always become an interior designer.'

'You think so?' Patrick looked chuffed as he handed her a glass of wine. 'Barney says it's cold. No personal things around.'

He dropped the name Barney into the conversation so casually that Jane wondered if she should know who he was. A brief search of names and she couldn't put a face to him. 'Barney?' she asked, looking at Patrick over the rim of the John Rocha wine glass.

Patrick smiled. 'The valentine's card and chocolate box man.'

'Get lost!'

'He made himself known to me a few weeks ago.' Patrick sounded as if he'd been waiting all night to divulge the details.

He leaned towards her, his eyes bright and a big stupid smile on his face. 'And I did have an idea that it was him – well, hoped actually. Only I couldn't be sure. He's a guy I met last year and we'd kept in touch.'

'*And*?' Jane asked. It was nice to see Patrick so happy, he'd been let down badly in the past. It gave her a sort of pang though, to see the way his eyes lit up just talking about Barney. She used to be like that. Ages ago.

'Well, we're taking it slowly – you know – best thing really. But he's lovely.'

There was a small silence before Jane said softly, 'Good. I'm glad. It's important to be happy.'

Another silence descended, punctuated only by the clock ticking.

'And you?' Patrick asked cautiously, 'are you happy, Jane?'

'We're not talking about me.' She forced a bright smile on to her face.

'We are now.'

He expected an answer, but she didn't have one. Was she happy? She never much thought about it. Sometimes it was better not to analyse stuff too much. There was a time she'd been sad, devastated, angry, guilty, but was she happy? Not as much as before, she had to admit. But then again, she could never hope to be as happy as before. 'Happy enough,' she said without conviction. 'I mean, things have changed for me. I've just got to make the best of it. I reckon if Mam wasn't living with me, things might quieten down. Her and Di knock sparks off each other.'

'So she's still with you?'

'Yeah, and there's no sign of her leaving,' Jane muttered. She refilled her wine glass. Talking about home could only be done when well plastered. 'I'm going to have to go and see Dad in the next little while. Mam told me not to, but I'm beginning to think she was only saying it for show.'

'Mmmm.' Patrick studied his best mate. He'd known her for

ages. She'd been the quietest, most unassuming woman he'd ever met. Yet she'd known what she wanted and had gone for it. Why she'd chosen him to go into business with, he could never figure out, but she did and they'd had a blast together. It was Jane's organisational skills that had kept their heads above water in the early days. 'And how's Jim?' he asked, wondering if she'd snap his head off. 'Do you see much of him?'

'Only when he picks the kids up.'

She was *definitely* sounding snappy. He took a risk and said, 'And that's it? Yez don't talk any more?'

She shrugged, saying nothing, about to tell Patrick to leave it. But he looked so concerned that she couldn't. Instead she said softly, 'I dunno Patrick. It was after Matt . . . things changed . . . he blamed me.'

'He'd never do that,' Patrick said with quiet conviction.

Jane shrugged again. A sort of sadness washed over her. She clamped it back. 'Sure,' she muttered.

'That man loves you, Jane.'

'Loved me,' she corrected.

'D'you remember when he first met you and he couldn't screw up the courage to ask you out?'

She didn't want to remember.

'Three months solid he came into the salon looking for a wash and blow dry – d'you remember?'

'Patrick—'

'Mir thought he fancied me,' Patrick chuckled. 'Of course *I* knew he was straight, but I kept serving him anyway, hoping for a road to Damascus type conversion.'

'He was a bit scared of you, all right,' Jane grinned.

'But he kept coming back,' Patrick said. 'And then one day you served him because I was busy with someone else, and he asked for a wash and blow job by mistake! Poor Eileen Simms nearly died.'

Jane smiled. 'So did Jim,' she said softly. 'He was mortified. He started stammering and apologising and everything.' She had fallen in love with him then, she remembered. His shyness, his awkwardness. Later, she'd loved his laugh and the passion he had for his work. All the stuff that had annoyed her more recently.

'He'd never blame you.' Patrick touched her arm.

She didn't bother to answer.

'And anyway, there's nothing to blame you for.'

She wished he'd stop. 'Any more wine?'

'Yeah. Sure.' Patrick took her glass and padded across to the drinks cabinet. He uncorked another bottle of red and poured her some. 'Here. The best stuff in the flat for my wonderful partner.'

Jane smiled and took it from him.

They clinked glasses and sat in silence for a while.

Jane wondered why Patrick was staring at her. She gulped down half the glass and liked the way her head swam.

Patrick reached out and tipped some more wine into his own glass before saying, 'Sometimes . . . I dunno, Jane . . . life is shit hard.'

'Tell me about it.'

'And there is nothing you can do about it.'

'Huh.' Jane closed her eyes. She didn't want to think like that. She let Patrick's words wash over her.

'I remember when I was about twelve, suddenly realising that I was different to all the guys I knew. At fifteen, I had a massive crush on the captain of the rugby team. I fantasised incessantly about him, tried to stop, but couldn't. I went out with piles of girls to make the thoughts stop.'

Jane heard Patrick laugh a bit, but it wasn't a humorous type of laugh. It was sad. She opened her eyes. Patrick was swirling his wine around as he talked.

'It was no good, I couldn't shake it. I became the biggest stud in school instead. And underneath, I knew I was a complete weirdo.'

'You're not weird, don't mind Rosemary,' Jane smiled sleepily.

'Naw, that's not what I'm saying,' Patrick said intently. 'I mean, I sort of knew what I was inside, only I denied it to myself. Couldn't face it. Couldn't even look at myself in the mirror. I spent my life running from my life, you know?'

'Did you?' Jane, her thoughts fuzzy, wondered why on earth Patrick was telling her this.

'Eventually I cracked up. Got counselling. And I remember the day I told the counsellor that I thought I was gay, he just looked at me. I think he knew it anyway, but I had to say it. I guess by saying it I accepted it.'

'Well, I'm glad you're you.' Jane gave another sleepy smile.

'I am too, now,' Patrick said. He laid his glass down on the glass coffee table and said, 'I learnt, Jane, that accepting stuff is the best freedom there is. You know, it stops you fighting things you can't change.'

'And we wouldn't change you, not for the whole world.' Jane squeezed his arm. 'You're the best mate there is.' Her head was spinning. 'I'm glad you told me that, Patrick.'

'You are?' He smiled at her.

'Yeah, I love bedtime stories with a happy ending,' she grinned and then wondered why he looked sort of disappointed.

He lifted himself off the sofa. 'I'll get you a few blankets.'

'Ta.' She sprawled out, too lazy to undress.

Patrick gave a small smile. '*And* maybe a bucket.'

Jane giggled. It was ages since she'd been drunk and it felt great. 'I won't be sick, I'm not that bad.'

'You're not bad at all.' He tousled her hair.

Debbie didn't come up to the flat and Jim didn't ask her. Instead he accompanied her back to her flat and kissed her outside her gate.

'I feel like a teenager,' she giggled.

'Do you?' Jim asked, smiling. 'Well, I hope I'll do instead.'

'You'll do nicely, so you will.'

She wrapped her arms around his neck and he could feel the

softness of her breasts pushing against him. It turned him on so much. They kissed again, his tongue probing her mouth. He felt he was going to explode if he did it any more. Breaking apart, he cupped her face in his hands, 'Call you tomorrow – OK?'

If she was disappointed, she didn't let on. 'Great.'

He waited until she was safely inside and then turned and began the long walk back to Fred's flat. Part of him was singing, but the other part was dead confused.

'Night!' She'd opened her flat window and was yelling at him.

He grinned and lifted a hand in salute. 'Night yourself.'

The dead confused part wondered what the hell he was doing. The singing part told him that he was moving on.

22

JANE TOOK A deep breath as she pulled up in front of a big square house set well back from the road. This was it. The claiming back of her life. Of her house. She tried to block out the fact that she was only doing what she'd done from infancy, sorting out her parents' lives yet again. It had been four months now, the longest split ever, and she was becoming slightly concerned that her mother would be a permanent fixture in her bed. And, after avoiding Matt's room for so long, sleeping in it every night now was hard. Sometimes hugging his teddies comforted her, other times she cried herself to sleep. She didn't know if she could stand it much longer. But it was better than letting her mother sleep in it. Sheila wouldn't hug Keano, wouldn't say goodnight to Matt.

Jane climbed the five large stone steps that led to the front door of the house. The door was a huge oak affair, complete with stained-glass windows on either side. The sound of the bell echoed inside the hall and she soon heard footsteps. The door was answered by a small, narrow, dude-ish looking man. His voice, when he spoke, was all cigars and whiskey.

'Yo, Jane.' He pulled the door open wider. 'How's things? Long time no see!'

'Dad.' Jane gave a nod and, pushing past him, entered the hall. 'Is there somewhere we can talk – in private?'

Declan D'arcy shut the door. 'Hey Dad! How ya doin'? Gee, it's great to see you. How's things?'

'Can we talk?' Jane asked again. She was not going to be sidetracked by her father's trendy jargon and funny jibes.

'Straight to the point – that's my Janey,' Declan grinned. 'Ever consider a career in radio?'

'Dad, I didn't come here to be entertained. I want to talk.'

'Nothing I like better than talkin'!' There was a pause as he awaited her laughter. When none was forthcoming, he continued, 'It's gonna be difficult. I've a few lads here from the station. We're having a big confab on the direction the show is gonna take in the next few months. I dunno. You're lucky you caught me here, normally I'm down the station.'

'So, can you talk or not?'

'In about an hour,' Declan said. 'You can make yourself a cuppa if you want.' He followed her into the kitchen. 'You're wasting your time if it's about Sheila,' he warned.

Jane froze for a second, before choosing to ignore the comment. How many times had she heard that in the past? 'Go back to your important meeting, Dad,' she said airily.

When she turned back, he'd gone.

Typical.

The meeting finished up exactly an hour later. It ended with much laughter and backslapping. Her dad insisted on dragging a pile of men into the kitchen to say 'hello'.

'This, fellas, is my daughter, Jane,' he bellowed. He did a big flourishy thing with his hand. 'She owns a hairdressing place on Yellow Halls Road.'

'Cutting Edge?' someone asked, impressed.

'No,' Jane answered a little too brightly. 'The other one. Patrick Costelloe's.'

'Don't know that one,' the guy replied, sounding puzzled. 'My wife now, she went to Cutting Edge the other day. Dead expensive it was. I dunno how they can justify those kinds of prices.'

'Send her to us next time,' Jane said. 'We're reasonable and the products we use are of a higher quality.'

The guy shook his head. 'Naw, she thinks if she pays a lot,

she'll look good. Jaysus, all I keep telling her is that plastic bags are cheaper.' He slapped his thigh at his wittiness and some of the others laughed along.

'My wife Sheila takes out a mortgage whenever she goes anywhere,' Declan guffawed. 'I'm telling yez, if we spent as much on property as she does on her hair, we'd own New York City by now!'

'Hair-raising or what?' some other guy said.

Her dad's show was going to go down the tubes if this was the sort of stuff they thought was funny, Jane thought.

'I cut me own hair,' a completely bald guy said.

There was more laughter.

'My wife sued me when she found out I had a hairpiece. She thought it was one of those sexually transmitted diseases!'

Hand-clapping and knee-slapping this time.

'Hey, maybe we should do a section on hair and hair tales on the show,' Declan said.

They all agreed that this was a fabulous idea. It got scribbled down in the bald guy's notebook and, after saying goodbye to Jane, they all trudged off. Declan saw them to the door, laughing every inch of the way. When he got back into the kitchen, he still had a grin on his face. 'Mad bastards or what?' he said.

'Definitely mad and most definitely bastards,' Jane couldn't resist answering.

'Aw, now, Janey,' Declan placated.

She hated it when he called her that.

He flicked on the kettle. 'Tea?'

'I've had about five cups in the last hour,' she said. 'So, no thanks.'

'Five?' Declan gave her a look of mock horror. 'I only said "a cuppa". Jesus, women, yez all take advantage of my good nature.'

She smiled despite herself. 'Yeah, right.'

There was a silence while Declan made himself tea and a sandwich. For the first time Jane took in what he was wearing.

He was dressed like a guy in his twenties as usual. Jeans with turn-ups, Doc Martens, a sweatshirt saying: *DJs do it on air*. His hair was closely cropped and he sported a gold stud in one ear. The stuff of teenage mortification.

'So, what's this chat you want to have?' Declan sat across from her. The grin was gone from his face and he looked uneasy. Not for the first time, Jane became aware of a weird role-reversal taking place.

'It's about Mam.'

'I fucking knew it.'

'She can't stay with me for much longer.'

Declan took a bite from his sandwich. He munched it for a while, before saying matter-of-factly, 'So, throw her out.'

'Dad!'

'Well, why not? If I know her, she's monopolising the bathroom, the shower and the hairspray. She's eating her rabbit food all the time and refusing to do any cleaning – yeah?'

Jane squirmed. 'It's not that bad—'

Declan gave a snort of laughter. 'Neither was Boyzone.'

'I want you to ask her back.'

There was more laughter. 'You have *got* to be joking!'

'Dad—'

'No way. And Janey,' he reached across and tugged her hair affectionately. 'You know I'd do anything for you – but I sure as hell won't do that.'

Jane was confused. Normally, to get her dad to make it up with her mam, all it took was a bit of grovelling on her part. OK, so she hadn't done that much grovelling. 'Please, Dad, tell her you miss her. Beg her to come home. It'd make her so happy.' She paused. 'And me too.'

'Has she sent you?'

'No, she doesn't even know I'm here.'

'Well, at least she has some pride.' He stood up and shoved his plate and cup into the dishwasher. 'But there is no way I'd have her back. Getting rid of her has been the best thing I ever did.'

'You didn't get rid of her.' Jane felt some sympathy for her mam. 'She left you.'

To her surprise, her dad chuckled. 'So that's what she told you – is it? She left me. Well, I guess she *would* say that.'

'What do you mean?' Jane tried to keep her voice angry, but she couldn't help feeling uneasy at his laughter.

'I just got fed up with her,' Declan said, as if he was talking about some piece of furniture. 'She was always moaning on about something – when she wasn't *leaving* me that is. So that day, when she rang up the radio station and gave me major earache for telling everyone about our sex life, I just told her to go. "Piss off," I said. And when I got home, she'd pissed off. Best thing ever.'

This was new territory for her. Her dad had never done that before. Delicate handling was called for. 'You were wrong to tell everyone about your sex life,' she said, forcing her voice to be gentle. 'That sort of stuff is private.'

'I said that we'd had sex ten times in one night,' Declan explained, his mouth curving up in yet another smile. 'Jaysus, sex ten times in one century would be more like it. I'm a showman, Jane, an entertainer. I tell great big fat ones.'

'Yeah, well, no one else knew it was a lie. It was horrible.'

'It made your mother out to be every guy's dream date – will you get a grip, babe!'

'Not every woman wants to be perceived like that, Dad.'

'Oh, yeah. Sure.'

He really didn't get it. He never had. He'd done the same to her when she was a kid. Her love life had been the nation's favourite topic and the break-up of a relationship was greeted with cards from every corner of the country with people telling her how sorry they were. He'd never understood the meaning of the word 'private'. 'So,' Jane said eventually, 'you're not going to ask her back?'

'No, I am not.'

A major grovel was called for. 'Dad, please—'

'Jane,' Declan interrupted, 'it's about time you let your mother stand on her own two feet. She doesn't need a babysitter. You're a grown woman now, you've your own life. Butt out of ours.'

Butt out!

Butt out!

She was only the one who'd kept their lives together for the past thirty-odd years. And now she was being told to 'butt out'. It hurt. She picked up her bag and coat. 'Don't worry, Dad, you've made your point. You don't need me. Fine.'

'Aw, now I didn't mean—'

'Get your listeners to advise you instead. After all, they've plenty of opinions.'

'Aw, Jane—'

But she was hurrying towards the door and refusing to listen to him. Why had she bothered?

'Jane, please,' her dad was saying.

'I'm going, Dad. And,' she whirled around to face him, 'don't even think of apologising on your pathetic show, because I never listen to it anyhow.'

'So *you're* the one person who doesn't,' he joked feebly.

'I'm out of your life.' She slammed the door in his face and revved up her car so hard that she was surprised the engine didn't explode.

Well, that was it. If he wanted her to butt out, she would.

And JESUS, she was going to *kill* her mother when she got home.

'How come you didn't tell me that Dad had thrown you out?'

'Pardon, dahling?' Sheila took the cucumber from her eyes and sat up gingerly. 'What's that you said?'

'I said,' Jane flung her coat across a chair and advanced on her mother, 'why didn't you tell me that Dad had told you to leave?'

Sheila paled. 'Have you been to see him?' she demanded.

'Have you been to see him after I expressly told you not to? Have you?'

'Yes, yes I have, Mother.' Jane stood over her mother and glared at her. Sheila seemed to wilt before her eyes. 'And it's just as well too, or you would have gone on making a huge fool out of me for God knows how long!'

'I'd never make a fool out of you, dahling, you know that.' Sheila pursed her lips. 'I mean, I didn't technically lie to you – I was going to leave him anyway. I told him I was leaving and he said fine.'

'He said, "piss off"!'

'Oh, now really dahling, there's no need for that type of language.'

'Isn't there? *Isn't there?*'

'Well, no. Not that I can see,' Sheila said primly. She swallowed hard and continued, 'I *told* you not to go and see him. I knew he'd only upset you.'

'You lying to me upset me, Mother,' Jane gulped. 'How dare you not tell me the truth? I went around to sort it all out and I made a right eejit out of myself.'

'Well, whose fault is that?' Sheila asked sharply. 'I told you not to go and you went. It's about time you realised, dahling, that you cannot control our marriage.'

'I'm not trying to control—'

'Yes you are dahling,' Sheila said, sounding quite cross. 'You always thought you could sort us out, but we would have sorted ourselves out anyway. You know your father, he only does what he wants, when he wants.'

Jane gawped at her mother. She had never spoken to her like this before.

'And really, dahling, what happens in everyone's marriage is private, isn't it? I mean, you've told me to mind my own business over you and Jim plenty of times.'

'That's different!'

'How?' Sheila demanded. 'How is it any different?'

'Well . . .' Jane bit her lip. 'Well, I dunno. It *seems* different.'

'Well it's not. It's the same. And I could be interfering and say to you that maybe you and Jim should talk to each other more, but I don't, because it's not my business. If you *asked* me my opinion, I would give it, but you haven't, so I won't. Because it's – not – my – business.'

Jane stared, stunned, at her.

'So, to finish,' Sheila said, 'I am sorry that I didn't tell you Declan had asked me to leave.' She made a big deal of examining her nails. 'I suppose,' she said, with difficulty, 'I suppose, I just wanted to save face, in front of my daughter and grandchildren.'

There was a silence.

Jane studied the top of her mother's bent head. Saving face was so important to this woman and she had ruined it for her. And of course, she was right. She shouldn't have gone around to her dad when she'd been told not to. 'I'm sorry, Mam,' she said, half-choking on the words. 'You're right.'

Sheila gave her a watery smile.

'And I won't interfere any more.' Jane sat down beside her. 'What's your business is your business. And Di and Owen won't find out.' She took the risk of touching her mother on the shoulder. 'We'll let them go on thinking that Granddad Deco is suffering big-time.'

'Thank you, dahling.' Sheila patted Jane on the arm. 'I think I'd like that.'

They smiled hesitantly at each other.

'And,' Jane bit her lip, 'what you said about Jim and me . . .'

'Not my business.'

'I know. But, it's just that we tried to talk and, well, we, we physically couldn't do it. He'd end up walking out all the time or I'd cry. That's all there was to it.'

Sheila said nothing, just squeezed Jane's hand.

'So it was the best thing for both of us, for him to leave. The silence wasn't good for the kids.'

'No, it couldn't have been,' Sheila said. 'And if there's anything I can do to help, dahling, you only have to ask. I mean, the time you went out and I minded the two kids wasn't bad at all. I managed perfectly well, so if you need me to do it again – I'm here.'

'Thanks.'

Sheila squeezed her hand again. 'Anything at all.'

She felt happy as she waited for Jim. The talk with her mother had done her good. Maybe now that they'd come to an understanding, it'd be nice to have her around. At least it'd be another adult to talk to in the evenings when the kids had gone to bed. And Sheila had offered to watch the kids, which meant that she could get out for a drink after work with Patrick some time.

The future was looking decidedly upbeat.

At half past eight Jim pulled up in front of the house and let the two kids out.

'Tell your father I want to see him,' she said to Owen as he came up the driveway.

'If it's about Gooey, don't bother,' Di said, 'I've already told him.'

'It's none of your business what it's about, miss,' Jane said. She gave Owen a gentle push. 'Owen, go now, before he drives off.'

'Will I tell him to come in, like?'

'Yes.'

'Are you going to take him back?' Di startled her with the question. She was looking at her mother with eyes that barely concealed her hope and delight.

Jane touched Di on the shoulder. God, the poor kid, thinking like that. 'No baby, I'm not. I just—'

'Yeah. Yeah. Right.' Diane stomped upstairs, taking her frustration and embarrassment out on every step.

Owen was coming up the drive with Jim. Jim was wearing the black shirt she'd bought him ages ago and a pair of black Levi's. A bit priestly, but he got away with it.

'You wanted to see me?' he asked, grinning in the way she remembered from back when he'd first asked her out.

'Uh-huh. Just for a chat,' she clarified. She turned to Owen. 'We'll be in the sitting room, you can get yourself something to eat in the kitchen.'

Owen sloped off.

Jane ushered Jim into the sitting room. 'Tea?' she asked.

'Naw. Thanks.' Jim shoved his hands into his jeans pockets. 'I'm heading out later, so I need to get back.'

'Heading out?' She hated the lonely sound of her voice.

Jim gulped. Scuffed his shoes on the carpet. Brought his dark eyes up to hers. 'Yeah, just like you last week. Di said you didn't come home.'

'No. I stayed with a friend.' She deliberately didn't mention Patrick and was glad to see the slight wince he gave.

There was a silence.

'So, what do you want to talk about?'

'Our daughter.'

'If it's about her boyfriend, she told me.'

'Did she now?' Jane quirked her eyebrows. 'And what exactly did she tell you?'

'That she's seeing a guy called . . . I dunno . . . something weird, and that she's very happy.'

'A guy called Gooey,' Jane said slowly. 'An eighteen-year-old guy called Gooey who looks like a cross between a down-and-out and a dog with mange.'

'Right.' Jim nodded.

'Right?' Jane couldn't believe this. 'Is that all you can say?'

'OK, so he's not good-looking – big deal.'

'Di also told me that he's unemployed and left school at fifteen. Jim, he's a bad influence. And God, the last thing she needs is a bad influence. She's difficult enough as it is.'

'Well, if he's wrong for her, I'm sure she'll find out herself. She's an intelligent girl.'

'More intelligent than her father, that much I can see.'

'Well, what do you want me to do?'

'Tell her not to see him.'

'Oh for Christ's sake, I can't do that! I don't even know the lad.'

'I know him.'

'So you tell her, if it bugs you so much!'

Jane bit her lip and turned away. 'She won't listen to me,' she muttered.

''Course she will,' Jim said, softer now. 'She's always talking about you when I take her out. She keeps tabs on all the stuff you do.'

She didn't need his sympathy. This, this fecker who was heading out for the night. 'It's not the same.'

Jim flinched. 'Well, there's nothing I can do, Jane. I'll have to wait until I meet him.'

'Well, if it takes as long as it took me to meet him you'll have some wait!'

Jim shrugged helplessly. 'What do you want me to do? I can't force her to let me meet him, can I? Be reasonable.'

God, she hated being told to be reasonable, especially by Jim, Mr Rational himself. Oh, he could put everything into neat little boxes and only open the ones he wanted to. No matter what happened, he went out to work, he came home, he went to work. His bloody life could fall apart and he could still go out. She glared at him, feeling tears of frustration well up inside her.

'Hey.' Jim had reached out to her and she pulled away as his hand brushed her shoulder.

'Get out! Just . . . just get out and come back when there *is* something you can do!'

Startled, he gazed at her. 'Jane—'

'Out!' More in control now, she walked to the sitting room door and held it open for him. 'Bye now.'

He looked steadily at her for a few seconds before walking past her. At the door he turned. 'I'll talk to her about it,' he muttered.

'I won't hold my breath.' She couldn't help herself. 'You were never much good at talking.'

He bowed his head and shrugged. 'Sometimes words are just too fucking hard.'

He caught her off balance. 'No words at all are even worse,' she said back softly. 'Sometimes—'

'I'll talk to Di, OK?' Jim interrupted her. 'That's all I can do.'

'Ohhh,' Jane nodded furiously. 'I agree with that.'

Jim looked hopelessly at her before walking out through the front door and off down the driveway.

He drove until he reached a little lay-by. Pulling in, he cut the engine of the car. He stared out of the window for a long time.

It was the first time Jane had been angry with him in years. He didn't know if it was a good sign or not. Maybe he should have stayed and rowed with her. Maybe he should have just stood on his front step and shouted at her and let her shout back at him. Maybe it was just what they needed.

He laid his head on the steering wheel and wondered what would happen if he went back and told her that she was being unfair, that talking to Di was not the only thing he could do, that he could do so much more if he had the chance.

But he'd had the chance, he thought.

Four years ago he'd had a chance to stand by her and he'd messed it up.

He started his car and knew that he'd never go back and say those words to her. Never.

23

IT COULDN'T BE right, Jane thought, staring hard at her bank statement. Surely there had to be a mistake. She ran down the list of standing orders and checked it off against her bills – yep, everything had been paid, nothing had been done on the double. Her half of the mortgage had gone through and her wages had been lodged.

Her *pathetic* wages.

She and Patrick were now earning less than Mir. Business was falling off rapidly, despite days upon days of handing out Patrick's leaflets. He'd printed thousands of them and so far they'd had about three extra customers. But lost about fifty to the salon up the road. If things continued like this, there'd soon be no business left and then what would she do?

A small flutter of fear began in her belly. She couldn't ask Jim for more money, he was giving more than his share as it was. Despite the fact that he was no longer living with them, he still paid half the mortgage. And the money he gave for the kids was more than enough. Well, it had been until she'd started to earn peanuts.

And of course there was her mother. Cast adrift without a penny from her father, she was now an extra drain on the household. Especially as she kept forgetting to turn off the immersion and spent all day huddled beside the fan heater, saying that she was cold. The electricity bill had gone through the roof since she'd arrived.

There was nothing for it, Jane decided, if her mother had

pledged to do anything to help, well then, she'd just have to prove herself.

She found Sheila and Di sitting together on the sofa. For once they weren't sniping at each other. In fact, they looked quite cosy.

'Now, dahling,' Sheila was saying, 'you only file in one direction. That way you'll have lovely strong nails.'

'Like this?'

'It's not a sander you know,' Sheila laughed, taking the nail file away from her granddaughter. 'It's a delicate piece of board and you must treat it as such.'

Jane smiled, before noticing that Sheila had again raided the kitchen press as a bowl of hot olive oil was on the floor. Expensive olive oil. Obviously they'd both been soaking their nails.

'Mam,' she said, trying to keep the irritation from her voice, 'I need a word.'

'Just a minute, dahling, I'm doing your daughter's nails. Honestly, what are you teaching the child about grooming? – she hasn't a clue.'

'Will you French polish them too?' Di asked.

'I'll put a coat of strengthener on them,' Sheila said. 'They're too short for French polishing just yet.' Seeing Di's disappointed look, she added, 'I'll see if I've some falsies in my room later.'

'Great. Thanks.'

Jane waited as Sheila filed Di's nails for her and applied some varnish. Di was in her element and Jane smiled to see the happy expression on her face. Sheila, too, was happy. There was nothing she liked better than talking about hands or toes or hair.

Finally, Di held up her fingers and grinned. 'Libby will be raging when she sees these. She's not able to file her nails properly at all. They're all chipped and broken.'

'Bring her over some evening,' Sheila said. 'I'll do them for her if she wants. Honestly, the world is in a terrible state when girls can't look after their appearances properly.'

Di danced out of the room. 'Hey, Mam, aren't they nice?' She fluttered them under Jane's nose.

'Gorgeous,' Jane grinned. 'You'll have every fella after you with nails like that.'

'Don't want every fella, just one.'

Jane tried to keep the smile plastered on her face as Di left.

'Well, dahling,' Sheila began tidying up her nail-care products, 'what is it you wanted?'

'You're not going to like it, Mother.'

'Well, it can't shock me as much as Di not being able to file her nails properly.'

Jane smiled at her mother's naïveté. 'OK, well, that's reassuring because I'm stuck for cash and I've no way of supporting two kids, a mortgage and you.'

'Oh.' Sheila froze in the act of putting her emery board away. 'Well, I have no money to lend you, dahling, and I can't go asking Declan for money.'

'I know.' Jane nodded. 'So that leaves just one option.'

'You want me to go!' Sheila's hands fluttered to her throat. 'Oh, dahling, where will I go?'

'No, Mother, I don't want you to go,' Jane said softly. 'But you will have to start paying your way.'

'But I've no money!'

'Yes, which is why you'll have to get a job.'

'A job?' Sheila mouthed, barely whispering. Then she gave a brittle laugh. 'Oh, dahling, I couldn't possibly get a job.'

'Why not?'

'Well,' Sheila licked her lips. 'I'm Sheila D'arcy, aren't I? Wife of the most popular entertainer in the country.'

'Who is not supporting you,' Jane put in gently.

Sheila looked aghast. 'But,' she stuttered, 'but what will I *do*?'

'I don't know,' Jane said. 'Anything. Mam, I wouldn't be asking if I wasn't strapped. The salon is doing badly at the minute and I can't afford . . .'

'Ask Jim for more money.'

'To support you? You want my ex-husband to pay for you?'

'Ohhh,' she curled her lip disdainfully. 'I never thought of it like that. Yes, I wouldn't take money from a wife-deserter. But, dahling, I can't get a job. There has to be another way.'

'Well, unless you're any good at robbing banks.'

'That is just not funny.' Sheila stood up shakily from the sofa. 'Oh my, I've a headache coming on. I'm going for a lie down.'

'You said you'd do anything to help me, Mother,' Jane said as Sheila began to climb the stairs. 'I believed you.'

Sheila turned stricken eyes on her daughter. 'Dahling, I meant it. I truly did. But this . . .' She swallowed hard. 'Oooh, my head.'

24

JANE AND ROSEMARY spent the morning handing out the last of the flyers to uninterested passers-by. The whole thing was made worse because it was lashing with rain. And, after going to the effort of handing leaflets to people, it was disheartening to see them crumple them up and shove them in their pockets without even glancing at them.

'I think this is worse than being a billboard,' Rosemary remarked as the rain streaked down her face, making tracks through her heavily applied false tan. 'At least if you're a billboard, you've wood protecting your clothes. My skirt is soaking now. And look at me legs!'

Her legs were purple with cold. Purple and brown.

Jane wondered if she looked as bedraggled as her trainee. If she did, she'd be in no fit state to cut anyone's hair that afternoon. 'Come on,' she said, taking the leaflets from Rosemary. 'Let's head back. I think we're wasting our time with these anyway. We handed out loads last week and no one has come in because of them.'

'No, they haven't.' Rosemary clumped alongside her, pulling her jacket over her hair. 'Just the granny brigade and they come in every week anyway.'

'Rosemary, don't call our customers that.'

'I don't. Nash does.' She giggled a bit. 'Nash says you'll probably blue rinse me for this IHF competition, but I said that you won't.'

Jane resisted the urge to brain the kid. Confidence-boosting she was not.

'You won't, sure you won't?'

'Rosemary, please stop saying stuff like that. If you don't want to do it, just say so – right?'

'Aw Jane—' Rosemary looked contrite. 'Sorry. It was a joke.'

Jane couldn't bring herself to smile. 'I won't blue rinse you, but you'll just have to trust me and let me get on with it. Otherwise there is no point in agreeing to be my model.'

'OK.' She looked at the ground.

'OK,' Jane said.

Silence descended as the rain got heavier.

'What is this IHF thing anyway?' Rosemary broke the silence. 'All me mates want to know – they don't believe that I'm going to be a model. Is it an important thing?'

'Yeah.' Jane nodded. 'It's sort of like the Oscars of Irish hairdressing.'

'The Oscars?' Rosemary let out a little squeal of delight.

'Basically, what happens is that the hairdresser styles the hair, then the model gets her make-up and clothes done, and later there's a reception where the models parade their hairstyles in front of the judges.'

'Oooh.' Rosemary hugged herself. 'And can anyone go?'

'Anyone with a ticket. Everyone dresses up and has a bit of craic. It's good fun.'

'And have you ever won before?'

'Once. Years ago.' Jane smiled at the memory. 'I won Trainee of the Year.'

'Trainee?' Rosemary looked impressed. 'Ooooh, that was good. Maybe I'll enter one year.'

'Maybe you will.' Jane smiled at her.

'My dad wouldn't laugh then,' Rosemary said cheerfully. 'He thinks I'm mental, see. He thinks I want too much. He says that aiming high is only for people with bad shots. He says we should always aim level with what we're given. That's crap, isn't it, Jane?'

'Oh, I don't want—'

'I mean, you didn't aim as high as you could have, did you? I mean, what with you winning that competition, you could have done much better. But you didn't.'

'Sorry?'

'You're happy styling oldies' hair in a small place.' She paused. 'Though,' she amended, 'you can do young hair too.'

Jane nodded approvingly. 'Yep, I can.'

'So that means, me, well, I can aim as high as I want. There's no law says I have to stay where I am, is there?'

'No.' Jane wished she'd stop. It was really great to think that an eighteen-year-old kid with nothing behind her thought she was a failure.

'I like your salon,' Rosemary said. 'But—'

'I have kids,' Jane said suddenly. 'Kids curb your ambitions, you know?'

'Mir said your fella had a big job. It didn't curb his.'

And it hadn't, Jane thought bitterly.

'No man is going to stop me,' Rosemary smiled brightly. 'Especially not me da.' She paused again. 'Or Jaz for that matter.'

She'd been like that once, Jane thought. All she'd wanted was to be a hairdresser. A top stylist with a chain of stores named after her. But it hadn't happened.

She wondered what exactly *had* happened.

It was turning into a wonderful day. First getting soaked in the rain, then two of her customers cancelled and to top all that, because she'd left the house in such a hurry that morning, she had forgotten her lunch. It was probably sitting in its foil wrapper on the counter top at home. She'd made her favourite too, egg, cucumber and tomato. Now Sheila would probably eat it, after taking out the egg, of course. And scraping off all the butter. And the mayo. So far, Sheila hadn't succeeded in getting any interviews and was lolling around at home, plucking her eyebrows and saying how useless she felt.

Jane searched her purse to see if she had any change to get a sandwich at the local shop. She had three euros. It was so long since she'd bought a sandwich that she didn't know how much one would cost. 'How much for a sambo at Lisa's?' she asked.

'Too bloody much,' Miranda muttered. 'They're meaner than a gang of Rottweilers.'

'Pack,' Patrick corrected absently. 'Dogs are pack animals.'

'Why don't you pack it in?' Miranda suggested as she towel-dried some poor victim's hair.

Rosemary giggled, then stopped suddenly and scurried away to the other end of the salon.

She was copping on, Jane thought, getting to know when to steer clear of Miranda. 'Three euro be enough?' she asked.

No one answered her. 'Anyone else want anything?'

'Yeah, the guy from Saturday night cut to ribbons and salt poured into his open wounds,' Miranda snapped.

'I feel like that about my husband sometimes,' Miranda's customer ventured.

'Well, at least he stayed around long enough to marry you,' Miranda said. 'At least he didn't treat you like a cow on the first date.'

'What?'

'Hit the hay and milk you for all he could. And then shit all over you.'

'He does that now . . .'

Jane left before she heard any more. It was a typical Monday with Miranda. She passed Cutting Edge on her way to the shop. The place was hopping, which was a bit depressing. They'd only had three customers in so far that day. And they'd only come because Cutting Edge was booked solid.

Lisa's was packed too. They made up fresh sandwiches and there seemed to be crowds waiting to be served. It seemed every business on the street was doing well, except them. Jane joined the end of the queue and again cursed herself for leaving her lunch behind. It wasn't like her, she was normally so organised. And now her mother would find it and . . . She concentrated hard on the menu on the wall, wondering what she'd have.

'Yeah?' a woman asked. 'Whaddya want?'

'I'll have—'

'Hurry up now, we've not got all day!'

'A white sandwich with—'

'No white bread.'

'A brown sand—'

'No brown.'

'A white roll? Have you got that?'

'Are you being smart? I've no time for smart-arses. Now, what do you want?'

'A white roll with ham, cheese, spicy chicken, crisps and tomato.'

The woman began flinging food everywhere as she made up the roll.

Suddenly, a bright orange sign on the wall behind the woman caught Jane's attention. *Staff wanted. Apply within.*

'Is that job gone by any chance?' she asked.

The woman paused in her shovelling of food. 'Is dat job gone, she asks?' She flung back her head and let out a bellow of a laugh. 'D'you think there'd be a queue a mile long waiting to be served if the job was filled?'

God, she was horrible, Jane thought. So rude. It was no wonder people weren't queuing up to work for her. But maybe . . . naw, she couldn't. But maybe . . .

'Two euro seventy.' The woman peeled off her glove and held out her hand for the money.

'I might have someone who'd be interested,' Jane said as she paid. 'Can she come for an interview tomorrow morning?'

'An interview.' Again the woman laughed. 'And where would I get time to give an interview? Look,' she said as she handed Jane her roll, 'if this person can speak English, make rolls up and take money, she can have the job.'

'Really?'

'You think I've time for joking?'

Jane shook her head. 'No. No, of course not. Well, I'll, eh, let this person know.' God, it had been so easy. Now her mother was set. 'Keep the job open, won't you?'

'Luv, it's been open for the past month.'

A man behind Jane banged on the counter. 'Oy! Anyone serving here?'

'I'll have her here tomorrow,' Jane promised, but the woman wasn't listening. Angry words were being bandied about between her and her customer.

Jane grinned. Patrick's words came to mind. Business was business and a job was a job. If her mother could work here, she'd work anywhere.

'Serving sandwiches?' Sheila could barely get the words out. 'Dahling, I can't serve sandwiches.'

'It's easy. People tell you what they want and you shove it between two slices of bread.'

'No. I don't mean it like that. *I mean,*' Sheila took a deep breath, 'I'm Sheila D'arcy. I just don't "do" serving sandwiches. I mean, what will my public say?'

'Dad's public,' Jane corrected briskly. 'And Mam, I don't care. You will do this job until you can find another that suits your needs better.'

'I'm quite capable of finding my own job, thank you,' Sheila said crossly. 'I was hoping at worst to be a sales assistant in somewhere like BT's, not—'

'They don't take credit card scammers, Nana,' Di, who had just entered the room, piped up in a mock-helpful voice.

'Right, for that, I'm not plucking your eyebrows,' Sheila said smartly.

'Awww,' Di looked devastated. 'Please, Nana.'

'No.'

'Mam, I mean it.' Jane decided to finish the conversation

before Di and her mother went for each other. As her mother went to protest further, she added, 'And I am not having this conversation again. I'll drive you to work tomorrow and after the shop closes you can call in on me at the salon and we'll go home together.'

Sheila moaned despairingly. 'You're a hard woman, Jane,' she sniffed. 'You never used to be like this.'

'Like what? Anxious about money? Well, sorry, Mam, but my business has never been in trouble before – all right?'

'Oh, dahling, you're so dramatic!'

'Tomorrow,' Jane nodded. 'You'll start work tomorrow.'

As she left, she heard Di promising to show her nana how to butter bread with hard butter if only her nana would do her eyebrows.

'I'll do one eyebrow,' Sheila replied.

'Cool!'

25

JIM FLICKED OFF his mobile phone and frowned.

'So, who was that?' Fred asked as he leaned over Jim's dinner. 'The gorgeous Debbie?'

'Nope. Just Di.'

'Oh.' Fred looked disappointed. 'So, what is the story with Debbie? Have you two, you know . . . ?'

'Have we two, what?' Jim asked flatly as he bit into a slice of pizza. Jesus, he'd really have to start eating properly. Most days it was pizzas or chips or, if he felt like cooking, waffles and sausages. It was all getting a bit monotonous. A bit like Fred actually.

'You and cat-woman – have yez shagged each other yet?'

'Her name is Debbie and it's none of your business.'

'So you haven't.' Fred pulled back with a look of bitter disappointment on his face. 'I dunno what the hold-up is.' He paused. 'Or,' he said slyly, 'maybe *that* is the problem? *A hold-up.*' He chortled loudly.

'Is Gillian around?' Jim asked. ''Cause like, she's the only one who ever laughs at your jokes – don't go wasting them on me.'

'You are so narky since you left yer woman,' Fred muttered. 'I dunno, she's managed to turn you into a right ballet shoe.'

'I'd rather be a ballet shoe than someone who walks around with their foot permanently in their mouth.'

Fred laughed. 'Good one, Jimbo.' He nicked a piece of pizza from Jim's plate and, munching on it, asked, 'D'you fancy heading out somewhere mad later?'

'Nope.'

'Aw, come on, I sold three cars today.'

'Nope.'

'Seeing Debs are you?'

'Nope.'

'Then why not?'

''Cause I've a busy schedule. The Chains Bond crisps are being launched tomorrow and there are a couple of other promotions that I've to handle as well.'

Fred yawned in pretend boredom.

'Is Gillian not around?'

'Naw, she's a bit narky this week, so I said I'd stay well clear. I asked her if it was her time of the month, you know, trying to be understanding, and Jaysus, she belted me.' He touched his face gingerly. 'So, like, I'm letting her sweat. I'll give her a bell in a day or so.'

'Aw, Fred, you know how to treat a woman, that's for sure.'

'There's only one woman in my life,' Fred said, as he went towards the parrot cage. 'And it's Parrot here.' He shoved his nose in and the parrot rubbed her beak on it. 'Who's a lovely girl?' he crooned. 'Say, "Gillian is a narky bitch" for me.'

'Bitch,' Parrot squawked.

Fred laughed. 'And say, "Jimbo is a wanker."'

'Takes one to know one,' Jim grinned.

He was rewarded with a piece of parrot food right smack in the middle of his pizza.

'Seriously though,' Fred sat down beside Jim on the sofa. 'Is it hot and heavy with Debbie?'

Jim glared at him in exasperation. 'Fred, you're sitting on my projections.'

'Ouch! Painful!' Fred smirked and, removing a pile of paperwork from under him, he handed it to Jim. 'I just want to tell you, right, and it's not my business, right, but that Debbie is big into you. Gillian says she's mad about you.'

Jim continued to gaze at his laptop. He was sure Fred was just fishing for information.

'Now,' Fred moved nearer to him. 'You don't want to be getting too involved with her, you know. Women let you down, Jimbo. Look at Jane and what happened there.'

'Jane didn't let me down.' Jim started to type.

'She got pregnant and trapped you.'

'Fred—'

'And your mother let you down.'

'My mother let me down?' Jim stopped typing and gazed incredulously at his mate.

'Well, she died, didn't she? How permanent is that?'

Jim couldn't speak. He simply couldn't say a thing. The guy was unbelievable. After staring at Fred for a while, he turned back to his computer.

'And your grandmother – what a ball-buster!'

'Fred – leave it!'

'Women let you down. It's their nature. They want you and when they have you, they don't want you any more. That's why,' Fred jabbed him, 'you can't fall for any tricks she might pull on you.'

'Fred—'

'It's time to enjoy life now. You and me and the lost years – eh?' Fred gave him a friendly thump on the arm.

Jim managed to smile. 'I will enjoy life when I get about a million people to buy a million bags of crisps.'

'All work and no play makes Jim a dull boy.'

'And all play and no work makes Jim an unemployed boy.'

He was glad to see Fred sigh deeply, as if something pained him very much. Shaking his head, Fred got up from the sofa and left the room.

26

SHEILA WAS BARELY recognisable as the groomed, sophisticated woman that had left with Jane earlier that morning. She staggered into the salon at six, breathing heavily. Clenching the back of a chair, she lowered herself into it with the air of one who has seen too much. 'Oh my God,' she half-heartedly fanned her face. 'I just want to die, right now, this second.'

'Good day?' Jane asked, ignoring the hysterics.

Patrick laughed and tried to turn it into a cough. 'Would you like a cuppa, Sheila?' he asked solicitously.

'Patrick, dahling, I would kill for a cuppa. Strong, no sugar, skimmed milk.' Sheila closed her eyes. 'Oh, I just want to die, this second,' she said again.

'So, you won't be looking for a lift home then?' Jane began putting her combs and brushes into the steriliser. 'Has Rosemary gone with the towels?' she asked Miranda.

'Gone with the bloody fairies, if you ask me,' Miranda snapped.

Jane didn't reply. Miranda still hadn't been coaxed out of her bad mood. It'd take another worthless fella to do that.

'I had such a dreadful day, dahling,' Sheila moaned loudly. 'That woman, Lisa, is as hard as nails. And talking about nails, she bawled me out when one of mine fell into the coleslaw.'

'Your nail went into the coleslaw?' Jane said in disbelief. It'd be typical of her mother to get fired on her first day. Well, not typical, as she'd never *actually* had a job before, but still . . .

'And she wouldn't even let me look for it. Thank you,

dahling.' Sheila blew a small, weary kiss as Patrick laid a cup of tea before her. 'It would only have taken a minute or so, I mean, how many bright red things can one find in a tub of 'slaw? But no, she dumped it all into a big bin and told me to file my nails and dress more appropriately.' Sheila looked down at herself.

'"This is Louise Kennedy," I said to her. And she said she didn't care if it was the Pope.' Sheila lowered her voice, 'She used the "F" word, no less. She didn't care if it was Pope eff John Paul, I shouldn't wear it in her shop in future. Vulgar. That's all she is – no breeding.'

The door of the hairdresser's burst open and a red-faced Rosemary ran in. 'Hi yez. I dropped the towels off and I'm just . . .' She stopped mid-sentence, then blushed and smiled delightedly. 'Oh, oh, oh, are you Mrs D'arcy? Declan D'arcy's wife?'

Sheila preened herself. 'I am indeed.'

'A famous person.' Rosemary's jaw almost hit the ground as she turned and looked at the other three. 'A famous person right here in our salon.'

'She's my mother,' Jane said, rolling her eyes. 'She was working up the road today.'

'Declan D'arcy is your father?' Rosemary looked at Jane with new respect. 'Wow, Jaz loves Declan.'

'Unlike myself,' Sheila said, causing Patrick and Mir to laugh.

'You look fab,' Rosemary said, awestruck. She touched Sheila's cardigan reverently, 'Your cardigan is the biz. I saw something like that in Dunnes. Is that where you got it?'

Miranda laughed and so did Jane. Sheila narrowed her eyes. 'Was that a joke?'

'No.' Rosemary gulped. 'Twenty-five ninety-nine, Dunnes, last Saturday.'

'Well, it most certainly is *not* Dunnes,' Sheila hissed. She pursed her lips and looked with deep disdain at Rosemary. 'So, Jane,' she said imperiously, 'are we leaving now?'

'Eh, yeah.' Jane fetched her coat and came out in time to hear Sheila whispering to Patrick that if he didn't hire people with a bit more class the place would go down the tubes.

'Are you volunteering your services?' Patrick asked smartly. 'A more mature trainee is just what we need. A floor-sweeper, cleaner-upper, head washer—'

'No, no Patrick, I don't think so,' Sheila said, not amused. 'And that's in *very* poor taste if you don't mind me saying. It's no fun to be working at my time of life.'

'It's no fun to be working at any time of life,' Jane said.

A rap on the door stopped the conversation.

'That'll be Harry,' Miranda said, 'let him in Rosemary.'

Patrick raised a quizzical eyebrow at Jane, who shrugged.

'He's only picking me up,' Miranda shouted over at them.

'Ohhh,' Patrick grinned. 'Picking you up, very nice.'

'I've to go to my mother's tonight.' Miranda stalked by him. 'It saves me getting two buses. So yez can put yer dirty thoughts away.'

'Did I hear dirty thoughts being mentioned?' Harry poked his head through the door. 'Are you having dirty thoughts about me, Mir? Are you?' He jabbed her in the arm as she stalked by him. 'Bye fucks, eh folks!' A quick wave and he was gone.

'Isn't he funny?' Rosemary smiled. 'Dead nice too. Dead good-looking.'

'Dead stupid,' Patrick muttered.

Jane tugged Sheila's arm. 'Let's head, Mother. That's if you're not going to drop dead on me.'

Sheila threw an anguished, look-how-badly-I'm-treated grimace at Patrick before sighing, 'Coming, dahling.'

Di and Owen were plonked in front of the TV when she got in. There was a smell of burning coming from somewhere. Both the kids seemed oblivious to it. 'What's burning?'

'Oh shit.' Owen pushed past her and ran into the kitchen. Jane was in time to see him grab the grill pan and run over to the sink with it. He turned on the tap and the meat for dinner turned from a burning inferno to charred blackness.

'Sorry, Ma,' he muttered.

Sorry? Now, on top of having to listen to her mother moaning about her day, there was no dinner. Jane dropped her bag on to the table and glared at him. 'Sorry!' she mimicked. 'Sorry! The one thing I ask you and your sister to do and you mess it up. Is it too much to ask that you at least keep an eye on the dinner for me?'

Owen gulped, his eyes downcast. 'It was just, well, Dad's—'

Dad! 'Oh God, well, if it was Dad who asked you to do it, you'd do it, wouldn't you? Huh?'

'Naw, it's just—'

'But me, I don't count, do I?' She stalked over to the meat and glared at it. She opened the kitchen window to let the smoke out. Turning back to her son, she said in a big mock-sarcastic voice, 'I mean, I only wash, iron, clean and clothe yez, don't I?'

'Aw Ma—'

'Well, d'yez know something? You can make your own dinner. I'm not doing it.'

'Dahling, don't you think, you're maybe overreacting . . . ?' Sheila said hesitantly from the doorway. 'It's only a little meat.'

'A little meat that I paid for,' Jane whirled on her mother. 'Me! Me! D'you hear that?' She poked her face into Di's, who'd come out of the sitting room and was standing, pale-faced, at the door. 'I paid for that meat you've just incinerated. My business is struggling and the last thing I need to see is burnt bloody meat!'

'Dad's ad is on tonight and we wanted to see it,' Di said quietly.

'And I wanted dinner when I came home. But, oh no, that didn't matter to you, did it? Well, yez can make your own.'

'Oh dahling, now . . .'

'Don't "darling", me, Mother!' She stomped up the stairs. God, it felt good.

She couldn't stop shaking as she sat down on Matt's bed. Huh, they wanted to see Jim's ad. He was obviously more important than her. It was typical, Jim took them out at the weekend, showed them a good time and they thought he was wonderful. Easy now he didn't have them all week. And now there was no dinner for her and she'd been out working for the lot of them. Well, to hell with it. She stood up from the bed and brushed herself down. She was going out herself, to a nice restaurant to have a nice meal. The other three could go and starve for all she cared.

'Mam?'

She jumped, startled. 'What?'

It was Owen. 'We're sorry, OK?'

'It was a mistake, Ma,' Diane said, as she pushed her way into the room, 'it was Dad's ad, see—' She stopped. She bit her lip, then shrugged. 'Well, sorry anyway,' she muttered.

It was as if she was a balloon that someone had just deflated. There she was, all ready to head out and now . . . well, there was no way she could *now*. In fact, she didn't know what to do. It was hard to do anything. It touched her more than she cared to admit that Diane had apologised. Owen was a pet, he'd do it no problem, but Di – she swallowed, blinked rapidly and looked at her two kids; one brazen-looking, despite the apology, the other gaping at the room he probably hadn't entered in four years. 'OK,' she said, hoping she didn't sound too humbled. 'Thanks.'

'I'll find something else and put it on,' Owen mumbled. 'Maybe some sausages?'

'Thanks pet,' Jane smiled at him. 'And I'll send out for chips.'

All three stood there exchanging awkward smiles.

'Go, go on,' she said gently to Owen, breaking the silence. 'Get those sausages on.'

'Yeah. OK.' He hesitated for a second, stared around the room and then backing out, he pounded down the stairs.

She was alone with Di. 'Go on down and see your father's ad.' She gave her a hesitant smile.

Her daughter didn't seem to hear her. Instead, she reached out and touched a red and white scarf that was hanging from the shelf. 'He was mad into United, wasn't he?'

'Sorry?'

'Matt,' Di whispered. 'He loved United.'

'Yeah.' Jane gulped at the mention of her baby. 'Yeah, he did.'

'I got him this for his birthday.' Di smiled suddenly as she ran her fingers down the length of the scarf. 'He was thrilled with it. D'you remember?'

How could she not remember? Every little thing that had made that child happy was etched into her mind in technicolor. 'Yeah.'

'He was such a funny little guy.'

Jane said nothing. She couldn't. She just watched Di stroke the scarf until the physical pain of it was too much for her. 'Just, just, let's just go and get some dinner,' she said. Her voice, sounding so normal and assertive, made her feel good again. 'Come on.' She put her arm around Di's shoulder.

Di put her arm around her too. 'We really are sorry Mam. Nana told us how hard you work and how worried you are and we really are sorry.'

Jane felt a lump in her throat. 'I'm not that worried,' she soothed. 'And don't you worry either – we'll get through this – OK?'

'The ad for the crisps is on,' Sheila shouted wearily. 'It looks stupid.'

'Ohmigod!' Without waiting for her, Di legged it out of the room.

'Well, I'm not watching a wife deserter's ad,' Sheila's voice came from downstairs. It rose quite substantially as she added, 'My daughter might shout at me, but I'm still loyal to her. Go on Owen, you watch it, I'll do the sausages.'

Jane smiled. Absently she readjusted the scarf so that it was centre shelf. A sudden, bright picture of Matt dancing around the kitchen in the scarf flashed before her. He was five and laughing. Jim was picking him up and holding him upside down, while she begged Jim to stop. Jim saying fine and grabbing her instead. Tickling her hard. Matt almost getting sick with laughing so much. Jane squeezed her eyes tight shut. The pain seemed to lodge in the hollow space right inside her. Sometimes, like now, it was as if she could feel Matt beside her, sense him standing, looking at her with his big eyes. But of course, he never was and her arms ached so badly to cuddle him and hug him that it was easier not to acknowledge it. She took deep breaths, opened her eyes and, with an effort of will, smoothed the duvet down. Then she exited the room, closing the door behind her.

She met Sheila in the kitchen. 'Just minding the sausages, dahling, making sure they don't burn.'

Jane smiled. 'Sorry for snapping at you.'

'Oh snap away. I feel I'll get used to it in my new job.' She turned a sausage over, wincing as some fat landed on her blouse.

'Thanks, Mam.'

'No problem, sausages I can do.'

'No, I mean for having a word with the kids, for making them apologise.'

'I didn't make them do anything. They know when they've done wrong. Despite being so weird, they are nice children, dahling.' She paused. 'You've done well.'

And sometimes, like now, despite everything, she felt that she actually had.

27

'EMERGENCY STAFF MEETING,' Patrick announced the first Monday in May. 'Very important.'

All three of them looked up. Mir was plucking her eyebrows in the salon mirror, Jane was reading the paper and Rosemary was reading aloud her horoscope.

'Someone is going to enter my life,' she proclaimed breathlessly. 'Someone will be a force of change for the better.'

'Yes,' Patrick said, tapping her on the shoulder, 'me.'

Rosemary looked devastated. Then unsure. And finally she erupted in semi-hysterical giggles. 'Ohhh, that's a joke, right? You don't really mean that, sure you don't?'

'Staff meeting?' Patrick gently took her magazine away from her. 'Emergency staff meeting?'

'Oh, right. Yes. Of course. Of course.' She jumped up from her chair and knocked her knee against the counter. 'Ooooh.' Hobbling behind Patrick, she babbled, 'Gee, thanks for including me on this. Emergency staff meeting. Wow.'

She followed Patrick into the staff room. She stood by the door while Patrick took the swivel chair and Jane and Mir shared the sofa.

Patrick waited until there was silence before he began. 'Well,' he licked his lips. 'As you can see from the lack of clients, the flyers didn't really help things a whole lot.'

'They made things worse,' Jane pointed out. 'No offence Patrick, but please don't say you've spent money on anything else.'

'No, I haven't.' Patrick sounded offended. 'In fact,' he went on, 'what I'm about to say will actually *make* us money.'

'Do I have to sit in on this?' Mir asked. 'Like, it's your business and—'

'Yes, you do,' Patrick snapped. 'I need everyone's opinion on this.'

Jane resisted the urge to tell him that it was her business too. But there was no point in getting his back up. Time enough for that when he came up with another hair-brained scheme. 'So, what's this idea?' She strove to make her voice sound interested.

'Well,' Patrick smiled smugly. 'I was trying to figure out, over the weekend, what it is that makes people go to Cutting Edge instead of coming here.' He nodded encouragingly at them.

'So, what does?'

Silence descended.

Jane hoped this wasn't going to go on too long. Thinking about stuff like that was enough to start a major depression.

Patrick clucked. 'OK,' he said, turning to Rosemary, 'let's start with their number one fan over there.'

'Where?' Rosemary asked.

'You,' Patrick said patiently. 'Why would you go to Cutting Edge?'

Rosemary blushed and squirmed. 'Well, I'd come here,' she said. 'Like *now* I would. Now that I know you all.'

'Why would you go to Cutting Edge?' Patrick was striving to sound patient. 'Come on,' he cajoled, 'tell the others what you said to me the day we handed out the flyers.'

'Ooooh, I couldn't.' Rosemary looked as if she wanted to blend into the wall. 'You got all annoyed and offended and wouldn't talk to me.'

'She'd go to Cutting Edge,' Patrick stated, 'because they're better than us.'

'Aw, thanks,' Mir glared at her.

'But *why* are they better than us?' Patrick was now standing over an embarrassed Rosemary. 'Tell them, Rose.' Turning to Mir and Jane, he added, 'You won't believe this.'

'Then why bother telling them,' Rosemary asked sullenly.

'Why?' Patrick asked again.

He really was composed, Jane thought. Normally Patrick would be hopping about in semi-hysteria if things were going wrong.

'Well?' he asked Rosemary again.

''Cause they charge more.' Rosemary looked defiantly at all three. 'They charge more so they should be better.'

There was a silence.

Patrick looked triumphantly at Jane and Mir. 'And therein lies our next plan of campaign.'

'You're going to up the prices?' Mir asked incredulously. 'You can't do that, we just slashed them last month.'

'Don't you see,' Patrick looked at them as if it was obvious. 'By not valuing ourselves, no one else did either. Like Rosemary, people do think that paying more means a better service. For instance,' he nodded at Mir, 'why don't you ever let Jane cut your hair?'

Mir squirmed.

'You also go about in designer clothes when you can buy the same stuff in Dunnes.'

'Designer gear is better,' Mir spat. 'Everyone knows that.'

'And so is,' Patrick clapped his hands, 'designer hair!' He looked at Jane and Mir. 'Well?'

It was true, Jane realised. Even that mate of her father's had said that his wife went to Cutting Edge because it was expensive. Maybe it would be worth a try, it couldn't make things much worse. Fair play to Patrick for thinking that one up. 'I agree,' she nodded slowly. 'Sure, when you think of it, my mother is a prime example of that sort of thinking.'

'Isn't she just,' Patrick smiled delightedly.

'OK,' Jane grinned. 'Let's hike up the prices. Only, well—'

It was as if Patrick knew what she was going to say. 'Don't worry, the granny brigade will still get a special OAP rate.'

'Don't call them that,' Jane glared at him and indicated Rosemary. 'For God's sake!'

'So basically we're all now working in a high-class place as opposed to the low-class place of last week,' Mir said laconically.

'And it's all thanks to me!' Rosemary looked as if she couldn't believe it. 'I'm helping to save the salon. Imagine!'

'Yep. You did your bit,' Patrick smiled at her. 'Now scoot. You too Mir. There's a gran – a senior citizen due in for ten. Gimme a shout when she arrives, OK?' He turned to Jane and giggled. 'Come on partner, let's decide how much to charge.' He pulled a piece of paper from his pocket and waved it about. 'I took the liberty of writing down a list of Cutting Edge's prices.'

They spent much of the morning talking. Well, there wasn't a whole lot else to do. Three customers in three hours. They agreed to charge two euros more than Cutting Edge for all their cuts. 'After all,' Jane said, 'the stuff we use is better quality.'

Patrick rang the printers and asked if they could get a list of charges run up. He e-mailed the information over and when that was done, he turned back to Jane.

'I've a few more ideas to run past you.'

'Well, if they make as much sense as the last one, I'm all ears.'

'OK, first one, and don't get offended, is that you, me and Mir should do a few advanced styling courses. If we're to compete we need to know what's going on. I think we've grown lazy because we've never had competition before.'

'Fair enough,' Jane nodded. 'Makes sense.' She smiled brightly at Patrick. 'God, you've been a busy little beaver, haven't you? Thinking up all these wonderful ideas.'

'Well,' Patrick blushed, 'to be honest, that was the only idea of mine he did agree with.'

'He?'

'Barney,' Patrick said. 'I ran my ideas past him at the weekend.'

'Oh.'

'You're going on the first course,' Patrick went on, 'seeing as you'll be in the IHFs. As soon as we see the right one, I'll book you on to it. That Julian Waters one you were on about should be good.'

Jane bit her lip. 'I was on about it before we started losing money. I dunno if we can afford to go to him now.'

'We can't afford not to,' Patrick said sternly.

Jane liked that he'd said that. Making a mock-glum face, she said, 'OK, I'll *force* myself.'

Patrick grinned. 'Now, for the next idea, I had a think about what it is that Cutting Edge is doing and how we can do it better.'

'We are not having a light fitting like theirs.'

Patrick laughed and flapped her away. 'No. Nothing like that. Cutting Edge salons are big, quite anonymous really, aren't they?'

'Uh-huh.'

'And we are small and intimate. So let's go for that. Let's make that our selling point if you will. We'll chat to the customers, find out about them and keep the information on the computer. That way, when they come in again, it's like we remember them.'

'But we remember them anyway.'

'But when we get more business we won't.'

Jane made a face. 'I dunno, it sounds a bit mercenary.'

'OK, forget that for the moment.' Patrick was impatient to get on. 'Still on the intimate theme, let's give them some cakes and nice biscuits with their cup of coffee. Cutting Edge,' he rolled his eyes, 'only offer coffee. We can do better than them on that.'

'Patrick, it's a hairdressers, not a restaurant. And what happens if hair gets into the cakes?'

'Mmm.'

'Maybe some kind of packaged biscuits instead?' Jane suggested.

'Yeah. Yeah. Sounds good. Now, Barney said to give the ideas a month's trial. That way we can see what's working and what's not.' He bounced up off the sofa. 'Oh, I can't wait. Declaring war on Cutting Edge has to be about the most exciting thing to happen to us in decades.'

He was seriously mental, Jane thought, grinning.

28

On the first day of June, Jane took a day off work, bought a bunch of carnations at the florist's and drove to the graveyard. It was a beautiful day, the sky was baby blue and the sun seemed to bounce off the streets. All around her, people flaunted acres of flesh, tanned or otherwise, as they strutted about in shorts and T-shirts, or thigh-high skirts and belly tops that exposed flabby stomachs. Jane wore a pair of wide black hipsters and a white cotton shirt. A white scarf held her hair back in a ponytail.

She didn't want to dress too summery – visiting a graveyard didn't merit the bright greens and yellows that fashion seemed to favour this year. She wasn't a big believer in graves, but twice a year, on Matt's anniversary and birthday, she came to say hello and tidy it up a bit. She liked to come on her own, without the kids, so that she could talk to Matt without upsetting them. She'd bring Di and Owen some other evening, though she knew that Owen in particular hated coming.

As she neared the plot, she saw that someone was already there. Down on bended knees, this person was throwing weeds into a black sack.

Jim.

Damn! Why had she come so early? She should have known he'd be here, and there was no way she wanted to talk to him. But now that she was here, it couldn't be avoided.

Hearing her footsteps, Jim turned around. 'Hiya.'

He looked tired, she thought. 'Hi.' She gave him a brief smile and, crouching down with her back to him, she set about arranging the flowers in the little jar that always stood in front of the headstone. Firstly, she took out the dead carnations from her last visit.

'Throw them in here.' Jim offered her his plastic bag.

'Ta.' Without looking at him, she tossed them into the bag. Then she concentrated on her flowers. She didn't hurry herself, hoping that he'd take the hint and go. He didn't, instead resuming his cleaning of the grave.

'Surprising how many weeds gather,' he muttered.

'Yeah.' She made a big deal of arranging the flowers. She took the yellow carnation from the middle of the bunch and put it at the front.

'There's a freshly dug grave backing this,' Jim said conversationally. 'It must have been a child – see all the teddies?'

Jane looked and immediately wished she hadn't. It was a child all right. A smaller child than their Matt. Seeing all the flowers and toys resting on top of the clay brought a lump to her throat. 'Poor parents,' she muttered.

'Yep.'

They didn't speak as they worked on. Jane had nothing else to do so she sat hunched over her flowers, not willing to do anything else that might involve interaction with Jim. From behind her, Jim pulled and smoothed and cut. She wished he'd go so that she could just be on her own. He'd never been so attentive when they were together, preferring to walk around the graveyard rather than listen to her talking to Matt. Not that Matt was there or anything, but—

'Is Di all set?'

His voice broke into her thoughts. 'Sorry?'

'Her exams. The Junior Cert is starting Wednesday, isn't it?'

'Yep.'

'Betcha she's swotting away today, isn't she?' Jim asked.

Jane shrugged. 'That's Di, everything at the last minute. Having a school dropout for a boyfriend can't help matters, mind you.' The barb just popped out of her mouth and it wasn't the right place for it. 'Sorry,' she muttered.

'I've spoken to her, if you must know.' Jim put down the scissors he had been chopping the grass with. 'And I don't know what else I can do.'

'You can meet him,' Jane said. 'You wouldn't be so bloody complacent then.'

He shook his head helplessly. 'Let's just stop this. Just for today – OK?'

The way he said it hurt her, though she didn't know why. Quickly turning away again, she tried to look as if she'd suddenly become interested in something. A plane flew overhead just in time. As she gazed at it, she could sense Jim looking at her and the fine hairs on her arms seemed to be standing to attention. Why couldn't he just go?

'When you're finished there,' his voice was hesitant, 'd'you want to go for a coffee?'

No, she did not bloody want to go for a coffee! Why the hell did he think she'd want a coffee?

'It's just, you know, well, it's . . .' Jim didn't finish his sentence. Instead, he gazed into the middle distance and muttered, 'Mattie would've been ten today and like, well, we're his parents and no one understands like us, do they?'

He'd never understood, that was for sure. But he wouldn't even understand *that* if she said it to him. She was about to refuse, but the sight of him putting the weeds into a plastic bag that he must have brought with him touched her. 'No,' she said. 'They don't.'

'So – a quick coffee?'

'Just a quick one,' she agreed.

'Fine,' Jim nodded. 'I've got to head back to work this afternoon anyhow. How about you?'

'I took the day off,' Jane said, then wished she hadn't said it in quite such an I'm-better-than-you-for-doing-that manner as hurt flashed across Jim's face. Instead of apologising she stood up and dusted herself down. Jesus, why the hell had she agreed to go for a coffee with him? Chit-chat with her estranged hubby hadn't exactly been on her agenda.

Jim stood back from the grave and observed his handiwork. 'Looks great – huh?'

She didn't even bother to answer that. Instead, she walked ahead of him, away from the grave and once outside had a mad urge to jump into her car and drive off. Instead, she waited while he dumped his gear into the boot of his car and wiped his hands clean down his jeans. Thank God she wasn't doing his washing any more.

'There's a coffee shop over there that I sometimes go to,' Jim said, pointing at a small dingy place across the road. 'They do nice stuff. How about that?'

'Fine.'

She followed him across the road, not wanting to walk beside him in case they looked too cosy. It was childish, but necessary.

Once inside, he told her to grab a table. 'Coffee and a danish?'

'I don't eat them any more.' Why was she saying these things? She only ate about two a day. 'Just a coffee.'

'Fine.' He joined the queue and she sat down. It was a typical Jim place, she thought absently. She used to find it cute and endearing, the fact that Jim always sought out the crummiest places to eat and drink. It was almost as if he felt sorry for the people running them or something. Still, when he arrived back at the table she was sorry that she had been so pig-headed about the pastry. His looked lovely.

The coffee wasn't bad either.

'Want some?' He moved his cake towards her.

'No. I told you, I don't eat them any more.'

'Why not?'

'I saw a programme on telly where a guy said that they can cause cancer.' Actually, it had been barbecued sausages, but she wasn't telling him that.

Jim looked at the cake doubtfully before taking a huge bite. 'Good way to go.'

Jane didn't answer. No way was a good way to go.

'How are you?' Jim asked. 'You know, with it being his birthday and all?'

Too late for all this, Jimbo, she wanted to say. 'I'm fine,' she answered instead. Her voice was a little too bright. 'You?'

He shrugged and sipped some coffee.

'I saw your ad the other night.' Jane felt desperate to change the subject. 'It's good. Funny. The kids love it.'

'Thanks.' Jim grinned and the flash of his white teeth made her heart flip over. 'The crisps have taken off in a big way. We weren't expecting it to be so successful. It's like a craze.'

'And it was your campaign?'

'Uh-huh.'

'Great.'

'Your dad gave them a great plug on his show last week.'

'My dad always liked you.'

'Yeah.' Jim fell silent again.

'I—'

'Listen, Jane—'

They stopped.

'You first,' he said.

'I was going to say that I have to go now.'

'Oh . . . right.'

'You?'

'What?'

'What were you going to say?'

Jim peeled a piece of pastry from his cake and flaked it between his fingers. 'Doesn't matter,' he said flatly. 'See you.'

'Yeah.' Jane stood up. 'And, er, thanks for the coffee.'

'No probs. Wish Di luck for me.'

'Sorry?'

'In the exams?'

'Oh, right. Sure. But maybe you should ring her yourself.'

Jim nodded. 'OK.'

It was painful, this conversation making. Every time she talked to him, she was reminded of the gulf between them. She brushed a stray hair from her face. 'Bye now.' She didn't wait to see if he'd reply or not, she just made a bolt for the door.

Di and Owen were waiting for her when she arrived home.

'Are you not studying, Di?' Jane asked as she flicked the kettle on. 'It's maths tomorrow, isn't it?'

'English,' Di said. From behind her back she produced a bunch of flowers. 'I was just going to put these in water. They're for you.'

'Me?' Jane said, surprised. 'Why?'

'They're from me and Owen,' Di said, handing them to her. Then gulping slightly, she said awkwardly, 'Because it's a hard day for you, today.'

'Oh guys.' Jane thought she was going to cry. 'Come here.'

They crossed to her and she wrapped her arms around them. 'Owen wanted to get you a box of chocolates but Nana said that it would ruin your skin and your figure.'

Jane half-laughed, half-sobbed.

'So we got them instead,' Owen said.

Jane closed her eyes. 'You could have got me anything and I'd have loved it,' she whispered. She hugged her kids hard. 'Thank you so much.'

29

JIM WAS AT work by five-thirty. He badly needed to get some sleep and a quiet office seemed the ideal place. There wasn't a hope back at the flat between Fred and Gillian and the bloody bird.

Fred had told him to spend the night with Debbie. 'Or maybe you'd get even less sleep then, huh, boyo?'

'Ha. Funny.'

Only it hadn't been that funny. It had been quite tempting actually. But staying the night with Debbie was taking their relationship into deeper waters and he didn't know if he wanted that just yet. She was a great girl, loads of fun, dead gorgeous and when they were together he could forget about Jane for a while. But a while wasn't enough. He needed to be sure he was doing the right thing.

He unlocked the front door of the building, punched in the access code and strode towards his office. Posters of Chains Bond were everywhere. The crisps had been the firm's greatest success story to date. Philip was due in that day for an update, hence the posters. It made it look as if the whole firm was behind his snacks. Though Jim felt pretty sure that Philip wasn't stupid enough to believe it.

He sat down at his desk and flicked on his computer. At least if someone did come by, it'd look like he was working. He laid his head down and closed his eyes.

Jane wrote a card for Di and left it on the table. *Good Luck in your exams* she wrote. She signed it *Mammy* and *Owen*. It looked sort of lonely with just the two names there, so she added Jim's in too.

Beside Owen's.

He felt as if he'd just drifted off to sleep when the ringing of a phone woke him.

'Sleeping beauty, there's a call on line one for you.' Maud was waving at him through the glass door.

Jim grinned sheepishly at her and, yawning widely, picked up his phone. 'Jim McCarthy here.'

'Jim, it's Dave. My office, now.'

The phone was put down at the other end. Jim rubbed his face and yawned again. Glancing at his watch, he saw that it had just gone nine. Jesus, he'd slept for hours. He wondered what Dave wanted. He couldn't figure out if he'd sounded pissed off or excited. Still, he'd know soon enough.

'You want to get a tonic.' Maud poked her head in the door. 'You look wretched. An iron one would do the trick. Will I get it for you at lunchtime?'

'Nope,' Jim said firmly, 'just tell Dave I'm on my way if he rings again. I have to have a shave and tidy meself up.'

'Aw, you're gorgeous anyway,' Maud said, as if talking to a five-year-old. 'Wrecked-looking, but lovely.'

'Just tell Dave – yeah?' Jim tried not to grin too much as he walked out past her.

'That woman,' her mother always referred to Lisa as 'that woman', 'asked my advice yesterday on what to wear.'

'Did she?' Jane was only half-listening. The traffic was totally gridlocked and she was wondering if she should cut down Merrion Square or just keep going.

'Of course, I told her that nothing I'd seen on her to date would do her any justice. I mean, she's a big woman, Jane, and big women do not wear small prints.'

'That's right.'

'So she asked me what she should wear to make her look good and I was tempted to say that even I wasn't able to solve that problem for her, but instead I told her that if she let me have the afternoon off, I'd have a look around the shops and come back with a list of recommendations. Now, wasn't that a brainwave?'

'That's right.'

'It must be important – I thought at first it might be a man, but what sort of a man would inflict someone like her on himself? So I really don't know. What do you think Jane?'

'That's right.'

The punch her mother gave her made the car swerve into the wrong lane and from behind someone beeped long and hard. 'Mother, do you mind? I'm trying to drive!'

'You weren't listening to me.'

'I was. You were talking about the woman you work with.'

'Yes, and?'

'Mother, I'm trying to concentrate on the road here!'

Sheila glared at her and Jane glared back. The traffic began to move again and Jane turned away.

'Well, I've a half-day today, dahling, when you'll be working, so I suppose I can't complain.' With that, Sheila took out her nail case and began to clip her nails on to the floor of the car.

To Jim's surprise, Philip was in Dave's office. 'I thought we had a meeting scheduled for two?'

'We did, but I've taken the liberty of rescheduling it,' Philip boomed. He crossed to Jim and pulled him towards a seat. 'Sit down while I tell you my news.'

Jim looked at Dave, who gave a grimace of a smile.

'These bloody crisps have exploded,' Philip said loudly, 'and it's all thanks to you, wonder boy.' With that he clapped Jim on the back.

Jim shrugged. 'Aw, well now, everybody did—'

'Rubbish,' Philip said expansively, 'if you hadn't come up with the chain angle we'd all be trying to market them as sophisticated snacks. Oh no, you are the man of the moment.'

'Yeah?'

'Absolutely!' Philip turned to Dave. 'Isn't this fella a bloody genius, Dave? Isn't he?'

Dave had difficulty answering with a smile on his face. 'He does what he's paid to do,' he eventually choked out.

'He bloody does,' Philip agreed. 'So that's why,' he paused dramatically, 'that's why I want him to come on the show with me.'

'Show?' Jim glanced at them both, trying not to sound alarmed. 'What show?'

'The business type thing,' Philip gestured with his hand, as if that'd make it clear. 'You know, the yoke on Tuesday nights!'

'*The Angle is All*,' Dave put in. 'Prime-time TV.'

'I've been asked to go on,' Philip nodded proudly, 'seeing as Chains Bond are now the biggest-selling snack in the country! And,' he crossed to Jim and put his huge hand on Jim's shoulder, 'they want my marketing people there too. Brilliant publicity for this firm.'

'So let Dave go,' Jim said, trying not to panic. 'He's the boss.'

'I don't bloody want Dave,' Philip said. 'Sure I don't, Dave?'

'No. You've made that *very* clear, Mr Logan.' Dave began to tap his pen on his desk as he said to Jim, 'He wants you, wonder boy.'

'Well he can want all he likes,' Jim stood up. 'There is no way I'm going on television.' Turning to Philip, he said, 'It's not in my brief to do TV appearances.'

Philip looked taken aback. Jim heard Dave's sharp intake of breath.

'Well it is now,' Philip said sternly. 'You've marketed my crisps brilliantly from the outset and now you are going to take the credit for it.'

'I get paid for it. If you want, pay me more, Philip, but I am not going on telly.'

'Now hang on Jim—' Dave was up out of his seat.

'How much more?' Philip asked. 'Say it and I'll do it, but only if you go on telly.'

'He'll do it anyway,' Dave said, trying to sound calm. 'It's not our business to go ripping off our clients.'

'It's not our business to go on telly either,' Jim stated. Jesus, there was no way he was doing it. No way. He'd make a bloody eejit out of himself. The thought of everyone gawking at him as he sweated under TV lights in a shirt and tie was nightmare territory.

'Mr Logan,' Dave said smoothly, 'could you excuse us for a minute please?'

Philip, looking disgruntled, stomped out of the room. He was a man used to having his own way.

'What?' Jim said once the door had closed. 'You gonna tell me off?'

Dave came around his desk and glared at the younger man. They were nose to nose. 'If Philip Logan wants you to shovel his shite up, it's your job to do it,' he said evenly. 'If he wants you to turn cartwheels, you bloody take lessons. Have you got that, Jim?'

'No, actually, I haven't,' Jim said calmly. 'I market his crisps. That is all I do. I do not make TV appearances. If I wanted to do that I would have done a communications course instead of a marketing course. Now, Dave, while you're shovelling shite up and turning cartwheels, maybe you can shove that up your tight arse as well. OK?'

Dave went white, then red and finally purple. 'I will ignore that,' he said, his whole body trembling. 'But only because Philip Logan seems to have taken a shine to you.' Pushing his face nearer Jim's he went on, deliberately slowly, 'It is in your contract that you will do whatever the firm deems *necessary* and *reasonable* in order to promote a customer's products. This, Jim, is *necessary* and *reasonable*. You will get yourself a new suit and new shoes, and you *will* be available next Tuesday week for recording, or else you'll be in breach of contract – understand?'

The implication was only too clear. Breach of contract meant he'd be out on the street with no bloody job and he couldn't afford that. He was beaten. Swallowing hard, he pushed past Dave and out of the office. From behind, he heard Dave say, 'He's doing it, Philip.'

Oh, good Christ.

Four customers were in the salon at the same time. Patrick was orgasmic with delight. 'Two trendy twenties,' he said excitedly to Jane as he escorted her into the office. 'And two bouncy hair beauties.'

'Patrick, don't—'

'Rosemary came up with that name. It's better than the Granny brigade. Really that girl is quite bright when she's not being so irritating.' He held the door to the office open for her and when she was sitting comfortably, he handed her a leaflet. 'I was wondering what you'd think about this?'

'A course in advanced styling,' Jane read. 'Yeah, great. Is this the one I'll be going on?'

Patrick beamed. 'Yep. Two weeks from now in Killarney, for a whole weekend.'

'Killarney?'

'Uh-huh. It's with Julian Waters too.'

'But Killarney? I can't. I've the kids, and here and—'

'You've Sheila. She'll keep an eye on them.'

'For a whole weekend? She'd run a mile!'

'So much the better.'

Jane chuckled slightly. 'Look, Patrick, I'd love to go, but I can't, I really can't.'

'Two nights in The Abbey Hotel?'

'Don't!'

'A massage and hairdo thrown in?' Patrick looked at her beseechingly. 'Please?'

'No.' Jane stood up. 'No, I can't. Sorry.'

'Well,' Patrick tittered nervously, 'you'll have to find a way. I've booked it already.'

For a second, she was dumbfounded. He'd booked it without consulting her – that was going a bit too far. Drawing herself up to her five foot two she glared at him. 'Patrick, you seem to forget that I own half of this place too. You can't go booking courses and spending money without telling me.'

'But we agreed that you were going on a course!'

'Yeah, but not for a weekend! Jesus!'

'Oh for God's sake, Jane! Don't be so negative! Where's the fighter in you? If you want to win this competition you need to learn from the master. You are going. And anyway,' he paused, 'you need a bit of a break, you know.'

Jane opened her mouth to protest, but all that came out was an indignantly spluttered, 'Break?'

'You've had a hard time lately,' Patrick muttered. 'I just thought, well, Killarney and all . . .' his voice trailed off.

'When I feel I need a break, I can pay for it myself,' Jane said with dignity. 'I don't need charity.'

'You do need a break though, honey chicks,' Patrick said gently. 'You look tired.' He paused. '*And*, you'd be doing yourself a favour – learning from a master so that you stand a shot in the competition come October.'

'I thought you said I'd win?' Jane retorted. 'I thought you had great confidence in me.'

'Oh I do. I do,' he placated. 'But a weekend away can't do any harm. And to be honest, until business picks up a bit more, we can afford to be a stylist down. And Jane, how can you turn down Julian Waters?'

'Seeing as he's gay, I don't think it'd be a problem.'

'Oh, very witty.'

Jane smirked at him.

'Come on, Jane. In your heart you know this has to be done. You need this course just to get a few hints. He's one of the judges this year, you know.'

He had a point, Jane reluctantly admitted. If she stood any chance at all . . .

'Do you want to win this thing or not?' Patrick dangled the tickets in front of her. 'Do you want to save our business?'

'Don't be so melodramatic.'

'I don't care if you don't want to sleep in the hotel – get yourself a cardboard box on the side of the road if you want – but do the bloody course.'

He was right. These days it seemed that Patrick was always right. 'OK then.'

'Now don't pretend you're not delighted. You'd cut your arm off to do a course with this guy normally.'

'If I cut my arm off, I wouldn't be able to do it at all, would I?'

He grinned. 'Smart bitch.'

'That's me.' Jane grinned back.

'Oh yeah,' he gave another nervous laugh, 'I booked Rosemary in as well. She can be your model for the weekend. You don't have to hang around with her or anything.'

He left before she could react.

'I am *so* excited.' Rosemary sat herself down on the chair as Jane got out her brushes. 'A *real* hotel. And being with other real models. It's like a dream or something.'

'It's a nice hotel too,' Jane found herself smiling. 'The food is lovely and they have a swimming pool and a jacuzzi.'

'*No!*'

'Uh-huh.' Jane began to brush Rosemary's hair. It had grown terribly bushy in the last while. It badly needed a cut. There was an enormous knot that wouldn't come out.

'And will there be servants and everything?'

'Waiters at dinner time to serve you your meals.'

'Get away!'

'And anything you like for breakfast – you can even have it in bed.'

Rosemary curled up her lip. 'Sure me dad has that all the time at home. That's not a big deal. Ouch!'

'Sorry. Sorry.' Jane braced herself to deliver the bad news. 'Rosemary, this hair has to be cut.'

'I know.' Rosemary seemed unperturbed. 'I've saved up and I'm booking myself into Cutting Edge next week.'

'You are not!' Jane almost laughed. 'You can't do that. You're our model.'

'But—'

'I'll do it for you now – remember our bargain – you have to trust me.' Without even waiting for Rosemary to say anything, Jane just chopped a piece of her hair off. It was slightly unprofessional, but there was no alternative. 'Now, relax.' She tried to ignore the big horrified eyes of the kid in front of her. 'Your Jaz will love it,' she said. 'Promise.'

Rosemary smiled nervously.

It was the most satisfying hairstyle she'd done in ages. All the little frizzy bits that had bugged her for months lay in a pile on the floor.

Rosemary was not looking too happy though. 'You're cutting loads off, aren't you?' she asked faintly.

'Just the dead ends,' Jane replied cheerfully.

When she'd finished, Rosemary had lost a third of her hair.

'Now,' Jane said, plugging in the dryer. 'Wait until you see what I've done – it's the same, but shorter.'

Rosemary couldn't speak. Her eyes were focused firmly on all the hair sitting in her lap.

Jane began to blow dry. Rosemary's hair was a pleasure to work with – its natural curl lent itself very well to scrunch drying. When she'd finished, the highlights in Rosemary's hair gleamed with good health. She'd cut it well, Jane thought proudly. OK, it was an easy style that wouldn't win any prizes, but Rosemary looked about a million times better.

'Jaz likes my hair long,' Rosemary whispered.

'It is long,' Jane said. 'See.' She held a mirror to the back of Rosemary's head.

'Oh, it sort of goes in a triangle at the back!'

'Yeah, I layered it like that so that it wouldn't frizz out so much. It stops your hair from getting too full.'

'Oh.' Rosemary looked as if she couldn't quite make up her mind about it. 'It looks, well, young-looking.'

'You are young.' Jane tweaked Rosemary's nose affectionately. 'Now, go on and ask Jaz what he thinks of it.'

'I will.' Rosemary paused. 'And, eh, thanks Jane. Thanks for doing my hair. I quite like it.'

30

JIM PICKED THE kids up on Saturday as usual. He was mortified, he'd left his wallet behind in the flat and his car was low on petrol. Unless he asked Jane for a loan there was no way there'd be any trip that afternoon. He cursed himself as he rang the doorbell.

'It's Dad.' He heard Di's cheerful voice coming from her bedroom. 'I'll get it.' Her feet pounded down the stairs and a second later the door was flung open. 'Hi. Stand in Da, won't be a second.'

Jim moved into the hall. 'Is your mother in?' he asked.

Di looked hopeful, then suspicious. 'Yeah. D'you want her?'

'Just for a sec.'

'Are you going to fight?'

Jim winced. Jesus, what did the kid think of him? 'No. Not unless she wants to.' He gave her a grin.

Di looked sceptical but called Jane. She stood sentinel beside him as Jane emerged from the kitchen. Jim's first thought was that Jane looked fantastic. She'd had her hair done differently and it really suited her. His next thought was why the bloody hell had she got it done? It had looked fine before, long and shiny. So he decided to say nothing about it. 'Eh, this is a bit awkward,' he began, 'but I've left me wallet in the flat and I've no money for petrol, so I was wondering—'

'If I could lend you some?' Jane finished for him.

'Bang on. Just until tonight.'

'Oh, a likely story,' Sheila called out her tuppence worth. 'Neither a borrower nor a lender be.'

No, Jim thought, just a bloody sponger be.

'So, how much?' Jane interrupted his malevolent thoughts. 'All I have is a tenner.'

'That'll do.'

She disappeared in search of her purse and Di ran up the stairs to hurry Owen along. Jim waited in the hall, praying that Sheila would be content to call out insults rather than appear in person.

Jane came back a second later. 'Here.' She held out the money towards him.

As he reached out to take it, their eyes locked. The words popped out before he had a chance to stop them, 'Your hair is beautiful. You look . . . beautiful.'

Jane flushed.

'Oh, it's amazing what ten euros will buy these days,' Sheila shouted.

'Don't mind her,' Jane whispered. 'She's just tired. She's to go into work today and she's taking it out on everyone.'

'Work?'

'Yep. Making sandwiches.'

He couldn't help the laughter that bubbled up. 'Feck off.'

Jane smiled at him and it felt good.

They stopped at a petrol station and he half-filled his tank. Then, driving Northside, he said, 'I've just to get my cash from the flat and we'll head off somewhere. Anywhere you want to go?'

Owen shrugged as Di's brow furrowed in thought. 'What about the beach at Malahide? We always used to go there as kids.'

'It'll be freezing,' Jim said.

'I don't care.' Di tossed her head. 'We always had such a laugh there. You used to chase Mam with fistfuls of sand, d'you remember?'

Jim wished that his daughter wouldn't do this. She was about as subtle as a neutron bomb. Every time she came up with a suggestion for somewhere to go, happy families always played a part. 'The beach will be too cold,' he said firmly. 'How about a movie?'

Di nodded. 'Suppose.'

'Owen?'

Owen shrugged. 'Don't care.'

Jim wondered if Owen cared about anything. Not for the first time he felt uneasy as he studied the sombre set of his son's face. He wondered if he should mention it to Jane. He decided to wait and see how the day went.

Di wanted to see his flat. So far, he'd avoided having to show them the place, but now it couldn't be helped. 'It's a bit small,' he explained as he ushered them into the flat itself. 'I'll be getting a place of my own soon, but for now I'm stuck here.' As he drew near the door, he heard voices. He hoped to Christ that Fred and Gillian were decent. That would be all he needed to nail his coffin with Sheila.

'Does Fred live here too?' Di asked.

'Well, it's Fred's place, he lets me kip on his sofa bed, but like I said, I'll get somewhere myself soon.' Jim pushed open the door, striding ahead of his children in order to shove Fred and Gillian out of the way if he had to.

To his horror, Debbie was there. She was perched on the edge of the kitchen table, drinking coffee.

'Eh, hi guys.' Jim strove for a normal tone. 'Forgot me wallet.'

'Men – huh?' Debbie, dressed in a denim miniskirt and tight top, crossed to the coffee table and tossed it at him. 'Still, when you're so gorgeous we can—' She stopped abruptly as Di and Owen filed in behind him.

'My kids,' Jim gulped, shoving his wallet into his back pocket. 'Di, Owen, this is Gillian, Fred's girlfriend, and this girl here is, eh, Debbie. She's eh—'

'I'm Gillian's friend,' Debbie said smoothly. 'Hi.'

Jim gave her a grateful smile.

Diane was staring in open admiration at Debbie. 'I like your skirt,' she said. 'D'you get it in TopShop?'

'Yeah, could have,' Debbie smiled. 'You look like your Dad you know. Both of you.' With that she winked at Jim.

Jim turned to the kids. 'So, will we head?' he asked hastily, wanting to get out of there before anything incriminating was said.

'Oy, Jimbo, have you got the sprogs?' Fred walked out of the bathroom, freshly washed and shaved. He smelt like a flower shop. 'How're yez?' He tossed Di's hair with his hand. 'How's things? Long time no see.'

Di hastily flattened her hair back into place and scowled at him.

The lack of response didn't bother Fred. 'So,' he asked, 'what do yez think of yer old man being on telly?'

Jim glared open-mouthed at him. The one bloody thing he'd told Fred not to say and the bloody eejit had just blurted it out.

'Telly?' Diane, Owen, Debbie and Gillian said in unison.

'When?'

'How?'

'Why didn't you say?'

'Sorry.' Fred did look sorry. 'I kept telling myself not to say anything and then it just came out.' He looked around at them all. 'Let's just try and forget it.'

'Forget it!' Gillian squealed, belting Fred. 'How can we when we've a celeb in our midst? Oh, Jim, tell us all!'

'Are you on telly, Dad?' Di asked. 'When?'

'Tuesday week at eight,' Jim said resignedly. 'I've to talk about the crisps.'

'Aw, that'll be a real cruncher.' Debbie pinched him affectionately.

Everyone laughed. Jim moved slightly away from her, he didn't want his kids getting any idea about what was going on between them. Not that there was an awful lot. 'Anyway, we'd better go,' he said. 'A film to catch.'

'You must tell us later about you being on telly,' Gillian warned.

'Sure. Bye.' He was aware that Debbie was looking slightly hurt as they left. He felt like a heel.

Jane was in the garden when he dropped the kids off. As he handed her her money, he said, 'Is Owen OK, Jane? He seems a bit, I dunno, down.'

'Down?' Jane said sharply. 'What d'you mean?'

Jim shrugged. 'He's just really quiet or something.'

'That's Owen – he is quiet.' Jane stood up from where she had been weeding the flowerbed. 'He's like you, as you'll no doubt discover in a fortnight's time.' She pushed her hair from her face and shielded her eyes to look up at him. 'I'm going away for the weekend and I need you to keep an eye on them.'

'What? Here?'

'Yes. You can take the sofa or the, the other bed.' She shrugged. 'Matt's old bed.'

'Oh.'

'You *can* do it, can't you? I don't want to stand in the way of your social life.'

He couldn't figure out if she was being sarcastic or not. 'You know the kids come first with me,' he said. 'I'll get the days off work. So, where are you going?' He knew it was none of his business, but he couldn't help it.

'Just to Kerry.'

She was being evasive. 'With?'

'Someone I know.'

'Right.' He paused. 'Anyone I know?' He didn't think he imagined the smirk on her face as she shrugged.

'Nope. Bye now. See you next week.'

'Yeah. Sure.'

Ha! That showed him, Jane thought, as she went inside. She grinned. Maybe it was horrible of her, but if he could buy orange shirts and go out, well then, so could she. Difference was, he probably was really going places and she really wasn't, she thought ruefully. Still, he'd never know.

The kids were in the kitchen, eating as usual. 'So,' she smiled brightly at them, 'did you have a good time?'

Di declared that she'd had a brilliant time. 'We got to see a really sad film and it was great,' she said. 'And we had something to eat. And, oh yeah, we saw his flat.'

'Oh?' Jane tried not to sound too interested. She knew that he was living with Fred, he'd told her that much, but as to what the place was like, she didn't know. It was probably a pigsty knowing Fred. And Jim.

'It was gorgeous,' Di said. 'Wasn't it Owen?'

'Didn't really notice.'

'And we met Fred's girlfriend and her friend – didn't we Owen?'

'Uh-huh.'

'Gillian and Debbie,' Di said. 'And Debbie was so glamorous. She had this fab skirt on.'

'She fancied Dad,' Owen put in.

'What?' Jane and Di said together.

'She did,' Owen said matter-of-factly, 'she pinched him on the arm and he moved away. *And* she winked at him.'

Di rolled her eyes. 'She'd never be interested in Dad,' she scoffed. 'She's nice. Dad's too old for her. Debbie looked about the same age as Fred.'

'Fred's older than Jim,' Jane said, trying not to sound alarmed.

'Is he?' Di said mildly. 'Well, he looks younger and no way would an old person wear a skirt as short as Debbie's.'

'I think she liked him though,' Owen said.

The nerve of the girl, Jane thought. And pinching him. Huh, she hoped that Jim wasn't going to fall for it. After all, he did have two kids to consider.

'Dad must go out with them,' Di mused. 'They said they'd see him later.'

'Isn't it well for him going gallivanting,' Jane muttered. 'Easy now he doesn't have two kids to mind. And give me that!' She grabbed a packet of biscuits from Di. 'They have to last all week you know.'

'They'll be stale by then,' Di pouted.

Jane ignored her and put the biscuits back in the press. She longed to ask more about this girl, but knew she'd sound too anxious if she did. And besides, there was probably nothing in it. After all, Di, the big romantic, hadn't noticed anything. Owen was the one who'd made the comment and he hadn't even noticed what the flat was like, for God's sake. Not that it mattered if someone fancied Jim. It didn't matter at all, really. She just didn't want him to forget about his kids.

'Don't you have study to do?' she asked Di.

'In a bit.' Di poured herself some juice. 'I've to go and wash my hair now.'

'D'you want me to style it for you?' Jane asked suddenly. It'd give her a bit of practice before this course. 'I can do something really nice with it if you like?'

'Mam!' Di rolled her eyes. 'Nice? God, no. Who needs "nice" hair?'

'You never told us you were going to be on telly,' Debbie said, as he walked her up to the door of her flat. 'How come?'

Jim grinned. 'If I'm going to make a right eejit out of meself it's not something I want witnessed by all my friends.'

'You won't.' Debbie put her hands lightly on his shoulders and moved towards him. 'You'll be brill. You look the part anyhow – sexy and interesting. I'd watch the telly just to look at you.'

Jim laughed. 'Better turn the sound down then.'

They kissed briefly before Jim said quietly, 'Look, Debs, I owe you an apology. About today, when my kids were there—'

She put her finger to his lips. 'No you don't. I know you have to take it slow with them. I'm happy to be Gillian's mate.'

Jim nodded. 'Thanks.'

'Coming in for a coffee?' She turned to unlock the door. 'It's just us. Gillian is going back with Fred. Well?'

He wondered if she just meant a coffee. 'Aw, I dunno. I'm pretty wrecked. And I've some work to catch up on.'

'A coffee won't take long. Well,' she amended, 'not if you don't want it to.' He followed her inside.

Jane sneaked a peek through the crack of the kitchen door. Di and Gooey were sitting on opposite sides of the table. Di had done her hair so that it stuck out all over the place. It looked completely awful. Gooey was much the same. Reluctantly, Jane had to admit that in this respect anyhow, they were well matched.

'Hi Ma,' Di called loudly, making her jump.

Jane flushed, then stood up and tried with some dignity to walk into her own kitchen. 'Hello,' she said, making an attempt to smile at Gooey. 'How are you?'

Gooey mumbled something incoherent.

'Great,' Jane beamed. She indicated the kettle. 'Mind if I make some tea?'

'Well, it *is* your tea and your house,' Di said nonchalantly. There was silence as Jane filled the kettle. Silence as she waited for it to boil. Then, just as she was carrying her cup out the door, Di said, 'Oh yeah, I forgot earlier, Dad's going to be on the telly.'

She almost dropped her cup. 'What?'

'I said,' Di repeated, 'that Dad is going to be on the telly.'

'Really?' Jane walked back to the table and sat down, ignoring the glare Di gave her. She could stay now until Gooey went. 'When?' she asked. She smiled brightly at the two of them.

Gooey stared hard at the table and bits of his biscuit seemed to explode all over the place as he bit into it.

'Next week on some business show or other.'

'When did he tell you this?'

'Today.' Di had on her bored voice. The voice that was really saying, go away, Mam.

It made Jane more determined to stay.

'He didn't mention it to me.'

Di sighed but didn't reply.

It was amazing how her daughter could make her feel like the class nerd, Jane thought. She took a sip of her tea and wondered what to say next. 'Why is he on the telly?'

''Cause he's going to dance naked in St Peter's square.'

Gooey gave a strangled laugh and bits of biscuit landed on the table.

'Why is your father going to be on the telly?' Jane asked again, keeping her voice even and ignoring Gooey as he surreptitiously tried to rescue his mashed biscuits.

Di rolled her eyes and gave a martyred sigh. ''Cause of his crisps.'

'Thank you, Di.'

'You are most welcome, Mother.'

Jane gritted her teeth at Di's fiercely polite tone. That kid was heading for big trouble if she kept—

'Gotta go.' Gooey stood up. In his haste he banged against the table and knocked over his cup. His tea went everywhere. 'Aw, shit!' He attempted to stem the flow with his hands. Di grabbed a cloth from the sink and began a mopping up operation. Gooey muttered an apology and announced again that he had to go.

'Aw, Goo, hang on. It's only ten.'

'Naw, better go. Bye.' His eyes barely met Jane's as he muttered, 'Bye Mrs D'arcy.'

He still didn't know her surname, Jane thought.

'*Now* see what you've done,' Di whispered furiously, flinging down her cloth and flouncing out of the room after her boyfriend.

Lovely. If she hadn't talked to him, Di would accuse her of being a snob and because she did, it was somehow her fault that the guy had spilt his tea all over the place and then legged it out the door. Typical!

31

IT WAS THE click of a kettle that woke him. Opening his eyes, Jim noticed that he was in a strange room. Well, not strange, 'cause he'd been there before, but what the hell *was* he doing in Deb's flat? On Deb's sofa? Still, his head felt less stuffy than it had in weeks. He must've had a good night's kip.

'Morning, sleepyhead.'

Deb's teasing voice, coming from behind, forced him upright. Peering over the rim of the sofa he saw Debs coming towards him, holding a cuppa.

'You were great company last night, I must say,' she grinned. She perched herself on the arm of the sofa and handed him his tea.

'Ta.' Looking down at himself, Jim noted that he was still fully clothed except that someone – Debbie probably – had taken off his trainers. 'Jesus, did I fall—?'

'Yep. You conked out while I was making you a coffee last night. I didn't have the heart to wake you. You looked so . . .' Debbie screwed up her face and rubbed her nose against his, '. . . so *cute*.'

'Jesus, sorry about that.'

'Naw, I don't mind.' Debbie laughed, 'It'll give Fred and Gillian something to talk about over breakfast.'

Jim grimaced, thinking of the slagging he was going to get. And it'd be no use protesting that nothing had happened, Fred thought everyone operated the same way he did.

'Toast?' Debbie asked as the toaster popped.

'Yeah. Great.' Jim stood up and stretched. He felt great. Amazing what a good night's sleep could do. He couldn't remember the last time he'd had eight hours. Following Debs out, he sat down at the table and watched her potter her way about the kitchen. The white dressing gown she wore accentuated her dark hair. The dressing gown ended at her knees and Jim found himself wondering just what she was wearing underneath.

'Butter's on the table.' A plate of toast was shoved towards him.

Jim started, then gulped. 'Ta.'

He sensed her watching him as he buttered his toast. Glancing at her, he saw that she was looking thoughtfully at him, her chin cupped in the palm of her hand. 'What?'

'You talk in your sleep, d'you know that?' She sounded amused.

'So I've been told,' he muttered. Jane used to belt him whenever he woke her. And he always seemed to be saying . . .

'Who's Matt?' Debbie asked. 'You kept calling out that name. Jesus, I didn't know whether to wake you or not.'

The toast was like sandpaper in his mouth. He took a gulp of tea to help it down.

'Well?' Debbie asked, still grinning. 'Who is it? Some secret woman? Mathilda?'

Jim gulped. 'My son,' he said, wishing she'd stop grinning so much. 'He's, he's dead now.'

The grin left Debbie's face. 'Oh,' she said. 'Right.'

Jim suddenly wanted to get out of there. He'd no appetite for the toast now.

'How long ago?' Debbie asked, her voice gentle.

'Sorry?'

'How long ago did he die? Your son?'

'Four years.' Jim rubbed his hands through his hair and stood up. 'I better go now. It's, eh, late and I've to go into work before I pick up the kids.'

'But you haven't finished your breakfast,' Debbie exclaimed. 'There's no rush. It's only gone ten.'

'Yeah, well,' he attempted a smile as he searched for his trainers. 'You know Fred. If I don't get into the shower, he'll hog it all morning.'

'Under the sofa,' Debbie said, still staring at him. 'Look, Jim, did I say something wrong?'

'Nope.' He located his trainers and shoved his feet into them. He was all fingers as he tied his laces. 'I just have to wash and stuff. Get new gear. I'll call you.'

'OK. Sure.' She sounded slightly shell-shocked.

'I really will. See you tonight – OK?'

She just nodded.

Once outside in the sharp morning air, he cringed at his behaviour. Jesus, the girl probably thought he was mad. And maybe he was. Talking about Matt was never going to be on the agenda. It was too late for talking now, it was fine to remember him inside – Jesus, he couldn't seem to stop remembering – but the time for talking had come and gone.

32

FRED'S FLAT WAS full to bursting and Jim wondered despondently if there was anyone in Dublin that Fred didn't know.

'Good turnout, eh, Jimbo?' Fred boomed on his way to the kitchen to dump a pile of cans. 'And all in your honour.'

Since his gaffe with the kids – when he'd announced that Jim was to be on telly – Fred had decided that there was no point in crying over spilt milk. It wasn't every week that one of his best mates was on the telly and fuck it, he was going to throw a party. Unfortunately, it had been a surprise party and Jim hadn't been able to protest.

It was now seven-fifty, everyone was getting tanked up and Jim was due to be on in five minutes. *The Angle is All* was a highly successful business show where businessmen discussed their marketing ploys in an accessible way. For some reason, the show attracted audiences in the hundreds of thousands.

Jim wished that there was somewhere he could just die.

'Not your scene?' Debbie came across and linked her arm through his.

Jim grimaced slightly. 'The party's great, it's the entertainment I'm not going to enjoy. Jesus, Fred is a right bastard for doing this to me.'

'We can go off somewhere if you want?' Debbie suggested, taking his hand in hers and squeezing it.

'Aw, I dunno.'

'They won't notice you're gone,' Debbie whispered. 'Come on.'

It was tempting. He'd made such a bloody fool of himself at the recording. His sentences kept getting all twisted up and once he'd even forgotten the question he was asked.

'It'll be OK,' the producer had said, 'we'll edit all that out. Take your time.'

After that he guessed he hadn't been so bad, but still . . .

The signature tune came on and Fred stood up on the sofa and loudly told everyone to 'Shut the fuck up.'

Parrot started screeching and he yelled at her to stop.

Everyone began shushing each other.

'Let's head,' Jim grabbed Debbie's hand and she giggled as he pulled her out of the flat.

It was like watching an accident, Jane thought grimly as the signature tune of *The Angle is All* blared out of the telly. She didn't want to see Jim, yet she was drawn to watch it. Curiosity was a killer.

'Oh God, oh God,' Di began to mutter. 'Oh, he's on.'

Owen lolled back in the sofa, watching through slitted eyes.

Sheila haughtily exited the room. 'I'm surprised at you,' she said in an undertone to Jane. 'Encouraging this sort of thing. He left you, you know. I'd like to see him watching you if you were on the television.'

'Shut up, Nana,' Di hissed. 'We're trying to listen here.'

'Ohhh, don't let me stop you,' Sheila sniffed.

'Shush!' Di glared at her.

Sheila slammed the door.

The presenter introduced Jim and Philip.

'Ohhh, look at him,' Di shrieked excitedly. 'Look!' She began an ooh-aah session over Jim's clothes.

Where the hell had he got his new suit? Jane wondered. It had cost a bit. Dark grey with a dark grey shirt and tie. He'd had his hair butchered too, shaved close to his head. He looked like a holocaust victim. His hairdresser should be shot.

'Now,' the presenter said, 'Jim McCarthy is largely responsible for Incredible Crisps' incredible success. Jim,' he swivelled to Jim, 'how so? Take us through it all step by step. Where did you succeed? What did you do that was so right?'

Jim's expression was one of a rabbit caught in headlights, Jane thought. She was just beginning to feel sorry for him when he began his answer. His voice and smile and sincere eyes coupled with his obvious enthusiasm for the marketing business made her heart twist up something rotten. The joyous look in his eyes as he described the search for the Chains Bond kid reminded her of when he'd talked about all the things they were going to do together. He hadn't looked like that in such a long time. It was like rediscovering all the things she'd fallen in love with as she watched him – the way he sat forward in his chair as he became animated about the ad campaign, the way he used his hands, the way he raked his meagre bit of hair, the half-embarrassed laugh he gave at the end of his answer. God, it hurt. She half-hated him for his enthusiasm. The show seemed endless with answer coming thick upon answer.

She was so busy feeling something akin to grief that she only registered that the programme was over when Di jumped to her feet.

'I'm going to ring him.'

'You can ring him tomorrow, it's too late now.' For some reason, she didn't want to have to talk to him. Or listen to the kids talking to him.

'It's only half nine,' Di said, sounding surprised. 'He'll be up.'

There was no arguing with that. 'Well, you can ring his flat, I'm not paying for mobile calls.' She glanced at Owen. 'D'you want to ring him?'

Owen shrugged. 'Well,' he answered, 'he was good, wasn't he?' He sounded as if he was looking for her permission to like his own dad.

Jane nodded and tried to inject some enthusiasm into her voice. 'He was,' she agreed, even managing a smile. 'And you should tell him so. If I know your dad, he'll be worried about what you think.'

Diane was busy pressing buttons when Owen and Jane joined her. 'It's ringing,' she told them excitedly. Then, 'Hi, may I speak to Jim please? Jim McCarthy . . . he's what? Out? D'you know where?'

Jane watched the smile on her daughter's face suddenly disappear.

'Sorry. No, Jim *McCarthy*. No. No, he couldn't be. Are you sure?'

Di put the receiver down slowly and stood looking at it.

'Is he not there?' Owen asked.

Diane shook her head. Jane noticed that her eyes were glistening. 'Di, she began, 'what's—'

'He's gone out,' Diane said, looking at the two of them. 'Out with his girlfriend.'

'What?'

'The girl that answered the phone said that Dad had gone out with his *girlfriend* and they didn't know where he was and I said it was Jim McCarthy that I was looking for and she said that he had done a runner with, with, with Debbie. And she sounded a bit drunk and there seemed to be a party going on, so I didn't know if I believed her or not, but then in the background someone said that Jim had gone out with Debbie.' Her words were tumbling from her mouth and tears had begun to spill from her eyes. 'But, but maybe they made a mistake, I don't know.'

'Come here.' Jane pulled Di into an embrace, desperately hoping that her own shock didn't show.

When she looked around for Owen, he had gone.

Debbie wanted him. She was scrunched up beside him in the front seat of his car, her hand was fumbling with the zip on his jeans and her mouth was making mincemeat of his resolve.

His hands found their way under her blouse and up the front of her bra. As he rubbed her nipples, she moaned with pleasure.

His interview would be over by now.

Debbie slid her hand inside his boxers and began to rub him up and down.

'Aw, stop,' he whispered, not wanting her to.

'Why?' she asked, her brown eyes teasing. 'I've got you exactly where I want you.'

He pulled her on top of him and fumbled with the seat. Jesus, he hadn't had sex in a car in years. Not since Owen was conceived. Jim closed his eyes and gave himself up to the pleasure of being with Debs. There was no point in thinking of Owen and the rest. It was time to move on.

It was so long since a woman had loved him like Debs was doing.

Jane sat downstairs with a glass of wine and tried to block out the sound of Di sobbing upstairs. There was nothing she could do, nothing she could say to Di to make it all right. Because it *wasn't* all right. It didn't seem right. She'd tried ringing Jim but his phone was switched off. The bloody tomcat, she thought, gutted. Off with his latest fling. Debbie had probably bought that orange shirt for him too.

It was strange how hurt she was. OK, so they hadn't been happy, but to be replaced so easily by someone he probably hardly knew! It just showed what she meant to him. No wonder their marriage had fallen apart. She closed her eyes and took a sip of wine. She honestly thought he'd have more sense. He had two kids, a wife, and half a mortgage to pay. He had responsibilities. And this girl – well, she was bound to fall for him, wasn't she? Jim was shy, but when you got to know him, like she had, he was funny and quirky and romantic and mad. And Jim must like this girl.

And that hurt. More than she'd thought it would.

Well, she'd ring him tomorrow at work and ask him all about Debbie. She'd tell him how much he'd upset his kids. That should put a stop to his gallop.

In that moment she hated him. She really, really hated him.

33

JIM WATCHED APPREHENSIVELY as Jane slid into the seat opposite him. What should have been a brilliant day had suddenly turned sour. There he was, hero of the hour at work, everyone delighted with the interview he'd done and telling him jokingly that they were going to make him PR man for the firm.

The only person with any negative comments had been Dave. He'd sniggered and asked what had happened to his hair. 'Fall out with fright, did it?'

But he hadn't cared about that.

What he did care about was the scummy way his wife was looking at him across the table. Thoughts of the wonderful night with Debs faded as he studied Jane's face. Jesus, she was angry.

'Hi.' He gave her a smile. 'Want a coffee?'

'This is not a social meeting, Jim,' she said. She put her hands on the table and leant her head forward. 'Who the hell is Debbie?'

He was glad that he wasn't eating as he'd have choked. 'Debbie?' He attempted nonchalance and shrugged. 'Just, eh, a mate.'

'A mate?' Jane glared at him. 'In the physical sense of the word?'

'Aw, Jesus, Jane—'

'Well, that's what Di was told when she rang to congratulate you on the television thing last night.'

His stomach lurched. 'What?'

'Some girl in your flat told Di that you'd disappeared off with your girlfriend.'

Jim felt his world begin to flake. 'Di rang the flat?'

Jane nodded. 'So – is it true? 'Cause if it is, you've some explaining to do to the kids.'

He contemplated lying, but he could never bloody lie to Jane. She saw through everything. Slowly he nodded.

'You didn't waste much time, did you?' she asked. God, she wanted to kick herself as her voice broke.

He had to stop her. Reaching out he caught her hand, 'It's not like that, Jane. It just—'

'Save it for the kids.' She got up and left him.

She didn't want to go back to work but she couldn't face going home either. Maybe if she concentrated hard on her job, thoughts of Jim with some faceless female wouldn't bother her. And it did bother her. If she was honest, she'd say that she was jealous that he'd found someone so quickly. Not even her dad had done that. Jim, shy boy Jim, had actually scored. It was hard to believe really. Hard to take in.

Someone banged into her and glared at her. Jane hardly noticed.

'Hiya Jane,' Rosemary said brightly, when she arrived at work. 'I saw your mother in the shop at lunchtime. She was fighting with one of—'

'I'll be in the back.' She couldn't face anyone.

'—the customers. She was telling him that if he skipped the queue, she was going to skip over him and she wouldn't serve him and then . . .' Rosemary's voice trailed off as Jane pushed past her.

'You took a short break,' Patrick said from the doorway. He smiled, 'You're a glutton for punishment.'

'Patrick, can you just leave it – please?'

'What?'

'Just, just leave me for a second.'

'You all right?' Patrick ignored her, as he always did.

She couldn't bring herself to tell him. It would be too humiliating.

'You making a cuppa?'

'I, I dunno. Maybe . . .'

'I'll get it.'

She watched Patrick, through a sort of emotional fog, as he fussed with the teapot, humming tunelessly all the while. He poured some tea, got her two biscuits and, after neatly folding away the packet, crossed the room and handed her her mug.

She nodded her thanks. There was a small silence while she sipped some tea. She wished he'd leave.

He moved in beside her. 'Now, chicken,' he began, 'you tell me to mind my own business if you want—'

'Mind your own business.'

He gave a laugh that made her want to cry. 'What has Jim done?'

'What?' How did he know?

There was a hint of a smile on Patrick's face. Nudging her gently, he went on, 'You've been acting strangely all morning, chicken. Normally you're so in control it scares me. The only time the "in-control" mask ever slips, it's to do with Jim.' He tweaked her cheek gently. 'So, come on – spill.'

Was she really that obvious? Jane cringed.

'Well?'

He was going to sit there until she told him something. She didn't want to tell him, but if she lied, he'd know. It was hard to meet his eye as she muttered. 'He's, well, it looks like, as if, well . . .' It was hard to say it. She took a deep breath. 'He's seeing someone.'

'Seeing someone?' Patrick sounded confused. 'As in . . . ?'

'As in, you know, *seeing* someone.'

'No!' Patrick looked shocked. 'Well, he didn't waste much time, did he?'

'Nope.'

'And it's upset you?'

'Yeah. Yeah it has.' Jane bit her lip. 'I was married to the guy for almost sixteen years, Patrick. I just didn't think—'

'That it was as over as this?'

She shrugged, not trusting herself to speak. Last night, when he'd been on the telly, she'd seen him the way he used to be, but now . . .

'Do you want him back?'

'I don't know. I didn't think so. I don't *know*.'

'If you want him back, maybe you should talk.'

'Talk?' she laughed slightly. 'I've tried to talk. No. I guess I'm just, well . . . anyway,' she shook her head, 'I don't think I do want him. Not after everything.'

'Oh, right, I see.' Patrick looked confused. 'So, you don't want Jim any more – right?'

'Yeah.'

'Oh.' Silence. Then, 'Sooo, what is the problem?'

Men, even gay ones, could be so stupid sometimes, Jane thought. 'I'm not the problem!' She forgot she had a mug of tea in her hand and it slopped out all over the place. 'Oh *great*.'

'Here. Here, let me.' Patrick fetched a towel from the sink and handed it to her. He watched as she furiously wiped her clothes down. 'You're not the problem?' he probed gently.

Jane looked up. Auburn hair fell across her face and she brushed it away. 'No. I mean, it was a shock for me, yes. It was. But really, see, it's the kids. They're devastated. And it's me who has to pick up the pieces.'

'Why?'

'Oh, Patrick, don't go completely stupid on me.'

'I'm not.' Patrick took her cup and refilled it. Handing it to her, he said, 'It's not your problem. They're Jim's kids, it's his new relationship – it's up to him to talk to them.'

'Well, I'm the one who has to live with them.'

'Oh, I know, I know,' Patrick placated, patting her on the arm.

'Do you? Have you a wife and kids stashed away somewhere?'

'Now, don't *you* be stupid,' he admonished gently. 'But, look, you can't go about explaining Jim's actions to them. If he wants to go tom-catting and find sexy new women, it's his choice. You stay well clear.'

'I never said she was sexy.'

'No, no I know you didn't. She's probably *not.* In fact, she's probably a desperate hag whose biological clock is ticking away like some neutron bomb—'

'Patrick, you don't have to make me feel better.'

'But I have, yeah?'

His gentle smile was so concerned that tears pricked the back of her eyes. Blinking hard, she managed a watery smile, 'Yeah, I guess.'

He patted her head affectionately. 'So,' he said, 'let him explain – OK?'

Of course he was right. Jane wondered why she hadn't thought of it. 'What made you such a rock of good sense?' she asked, half-begrudgingly.

'Life, darling.'

They smiled at each other.

34

As Jim threw some gear into an overnight bag, he was aware that Debbie was watching him. She'd spent the night with him in the flat as Fred and Gillian had gone to Gillian and Debbie's place.

She sat cross-legged on the sofa, with a sleeping bag pulled over her. Dark hair spilled on to her shoulders and a rueful smile curled her mouth. 'I'll miss you,' she said, poking his leg with her foot.

Jim shrugged, 'You'll manage,' he muttered.

The last couple of days had been awful. Neither of his kids would talk to him. He'd called over the same night that Jane had confronted him in the café and it had been hell. Jane, to give her credit, had tried to make the kids see him, but they wouldn't.

Jane hadn't sneered as he thought she would. Instead, she'd been apologetic. 'I did try my best,' she said. 'But, well . . .' She'd shrugged and looked helplessly after her two offspring.

'It's fine,' he said, knowing that Jane knew it bloody well wasn't.

'Maybe Friday,' Jane said, 'you know, when you mind them, things will be different.'

He'd forgotten about it until that moment. And he was sick at the thought of it. Two kids and a mother-in-law from hell.

And even though he was tempted to call a halt to the whole thing with Debbie, he didn't think it was fair. It wasn't her fault and anyhow, she made him laugh and he hadn't laughed in what felt like years. She was dead nice and he felt good when he was around her. He turned to her now and smiled, 'I'll try and give you a ring when the kids are out,' he said. 'No point in rocking the boat.'

'Poor Jim,' she said softly. 'It's all my fault, isn't it?'

'Nah,' Jim shook his head. 'It's just a shock for them.' He shoved some aftershave into the front of his bag and zipped it up. 'Anyway, I'd better go. Jane said she's heading off early this morning.'

Debbie nodded. 'Take care,' she stood up and pinched his arm, 'Incredible Edible.' She planted a soft kiss to the side of his neck.

Jesus, where was he? Jane paced the hall from the front door to the kitchen and back again. She'd *told* him she was leaving early and that she wanted to be on the road by nine at least. Jim was always late for everything. The only time he'd ever been early was their wedding day and a fat lot of good that had done either of them. She wondered whether she should just go, but the fact that she was dressed in new clothes, with fab new auburn and red highlights running through her hair stopped her. It might be petty, but she wanted to show him just how gorgeous she could look. Plus, she hadn't told him where she was going; for all he knew, she could have a new relationship herself. She'd told the kids that she was going on a break for the weekend, so they couldn't spill the beans either. Not that they would. They still weren't talking to Jim though she sensed a thaw in Owen. He seemed unsure of what to do. She'd told him that Jim was still his dad and that it was OK to see him. 'I won't mind if you do,' she'd told him.

'But what about Dad's new girlfriend?' he'd asked. 'What about her?'

She had deliberately misunderstood the question and tried to make a joke of it. 'Well, I'm sure if you want him to bring her along, he will.'

Owen hadn't smiled back, just nodded.

Di was another matter. Jesus, the girl could do hysteria as an Olympic sport. Even the mention of Jim's name freaked her out. Jane couldn't understand it. 'But why won't you see him?' she'd asked, trying the same argument out on her that she'd used on Owen. 'He's still your dad and having a girlfriend doesn't change that.'

'Well,' Di had said, 'he's still your husband and the fact that he's moved out doesn't change that.'

Jane gulped. 'That's different.'

'Yeah?' Di had widened her dark eyes. 'Sure.'

That had finished the argument for Jane. There was no way she was going in any deeper. Anyway, Di would cool off. She always did.

The ringing of the bell broke into her thoughts. Jim's tall silhouette was framed in the glass doorway. Opening the door, she snapped, 'Well, you took your time. Out late last night, were you?'

Jim flinched. 'You wanted to be on the road by nine. It's nine now. Off you go.'

God, she hated herself for the barb. There she was, trying to pretend all was cool to the kids, but the minute he showed up in she went with the delicacy of a scud missile. 'I'm going now,' she replied, trying to keep her voice neutral. She'd already dragged her case to the car, so all she had to do was to don her newly acquired jacket, a little one like Mir had, and leave.

He had the nerve to close the door the minute she left the house.

Jane could be a right bitch, Jim thought. Jesus, asking him if he'd been up late. He'd killed himself to be on time – it wasn't his fault there'd been an accident on the motorway. Still, no point in explaining that to Jane. She knew everything. He found himself taking out his frustration on the cups and sugar and milk as he made himself a cup of strong tea.

He wondered if the kids were awake. Maybe he should do some toast as a kind of peace offering. He always used to do toast for them in the mornings. Well, the mornings when he was at home. He'd bring Jane a cuppa up too, to wake her up. He used to love looking at her first thing, all tousle-haired and sleepy-eyed. He sometimes thought he loved her more in the mornings than at any other time of day.

He smiled suddenly at the memory.

'I don't want any of your vomit toast,' Di said from the door. 'I'd rather die.'

His daughter was still in her nightclothes and her face was red and furious.

'I could help there,' he deadpanned, ''cause the way you're blanking me out makes me want to kill you.'

'You'd be up for murder then,' Di sneered, 'and you wouldn't be able to screw around.'

Jesus. He was sure no daughter should talk to her father like that. 'Don't talk to me like that!' He made his voice stern. 'I don't behave like that.'

'OK, I won't bother talking to you at all then,' Di said. 'So, have a happy weekend here – right, Dad?'

Rosemary was waiting, with an anxious look on her face. 'Hiya Jane, ooohh, isn't this great? I've never stayed in a hotel before. Jaz is dead jealous.'

'Is he?'

'Yeah. I had to promise him that I'd bring him some fancy soap and shampoo back. He said if I could get a shower cap and some polish that would be great too. He said they leave it in the rooms for you for free.'

'They do.'

'Wow!'

By three Jim was ready to surrender to depression. Di had gone out to meet Gooey and told him that she'd be back later. She refused to say when later was. She told him that she didn't want a vomit dinner. Owen too, had left the house. He hadn't even said that he was leaving, he'd just sneaked out.

If things had been normal, it wouldn't have bothered him. But with everything in their young lives being turned upside-down, he didn't know what to do for the best. He flirted with the idea of ringing Jane to ask her if he should let Di out, or if she had any idea on where Owen could be, but chickened out. Jane would kill him. He wondered what the hell he'd say to Sheila if she asked where his kids were. She'd be sure to make a disparaging remark. Well, damn her, he thought viciously, she hadn't exactly clamoured to look after them, so he'd just tell her to mind her own business.

The hotel was gorgeous. Their room was spacious, with twin beds, a wardrobe, a dresser and a little table bearing a bowl of fruit. Munching on an apple, Jane inspected the bathroom. A shower, bath, toilet and washbasin in brilliant white. Black and white tiles gleamed on the floor and the walls were also decorated in black and white. This was going to be brill.

She was suddenly overcome with a sense of freedom. She could be anyone. She was away from home and God, it felt great.

'Gorgeous room,' Rosemary said, staring around, awestruck.

Jane grinned and plonked herself down on the bed. Picking up the phone, she ordered dinner for the two of them.

'I never believed in heaven until now,' Rosemary declared.

Jane laughed.

35

THE COURSE STARTED at nine sharp the next morning. As Jane showered, she found to her surprise that she was quite looking forward to it. It'd been years since she'd done one. There was a time when she'd known every trick in the book, every gel, every mousse, every type of roller. Her wish of opening a chain of salons had never materialised though. Jim kept trying to make her take the plunge, he'd even told her he'd do the marketing for her if she wanted, but having the kids made her wary about taking risks.

She pulled on a pair of white jeans and a bright pink T-shirt. Her hair shone thanks to Patrick's ministrations. He'd insisted, that as she was to be representing the salon, the least she could do was have decent hair.

Jane knew he'd only done it to cheer her up.

As she rubbed some bungee gum into the layers, she wondered how Jim was getting on. He hadn't phoned anyhow, so it must be a good sign. Maybe the kids were taking to him again.

Despite her bruised ego at his fickleness, she did hope they were.

'You are grounded,' Jim said. He kept his voice calm the way he'd promised himself and he looked Di straight in the eye.

'What?' There was a barely concealed sneer in her voice. The way her lip curled up as if she smelt something rotten hurt him.

'You heard.' He came around the table to face her full on.

'You weren't in until after two last night. You never phoned to say where you were or anything.'

'That would've been hard, seeing as I wasn't talking to you,' Di said, cool as a cucumber. 'What d'you want me to do, ring and then do some heavy breathing down the phone?'

'I expect you to ring at least. And anyhow, I'm sure your mother doesn't let you out that late. She never did when I lived here.'

'Well, you don't live here any more, do you? And things have changed.'

'Well, I'm living here this weekend and my rules stand. You are grounded for today.' Jim glared at her. He'd never before understood how Jane could get so annoyed at Di, but he did now. 'You can have the run of the house, but that's it. How dare you come home so late? What were you doing?'

'Want me to draw you a picture?'

'I want you to give me an answer.'

Di folded her arms and cocked her head to one side. 'Can't. I'm not talking to you.'

'Well, you'd better start. Otherwise you're grounded tomorrow too.'

'I did nothing much.' Di's eyes narrowed into slits. 'Just messing about with Gooey and a few mates.'

'Until two in the morning?'

'Yeah. It's no big deal. It's not like I stayed out all night, is it?'

'You're fifteen years old for God's sake.' Jim rubbed his hands across his face. 'Jesus, Di, talk to me, will you?'

Just for a split second, he thought he saw the old Di underneath the hard exterior. But it was brief. This new version of his daughter gave him another scum-of-the-earth look and shook her head. 'Ground me if you want, Dad, I don't care.'

She walked out.

Jim bit his lip. One down, one to go.

* * *

The course was run in the hotel's salon, so Jane didn't have to hurry. She left Rosemary eating a full Irish breakfast in the restaurant and walked into the foyer where a receptionist directed her to a small room where coffee and biscuits were being served. She was asked her name and received a name badge.

'Grab a coffee, Jane,' the woman said, 'we'll be starting in about fifteen.'

As Jane made her way across to the coffee table, she was dismayed to see a tall figure chatting and laughing with a group of scantily clad hairdressers. What on earth was Pete Jordan doing here? she wondered. It wasn't as if he needed a course, he kept winning the bloody championship year after year anyway. You'd think, she fumed, that he'd let other people have a chance now and again.

She managed to get to the table without being spotted, but to her horror, as she took a coffee, Pete Jordan began to cross the room towards her.

'Hey,' he greeted her, patronising to the last, 'how's it going?'

Dressed in dark jeans and a bright blue T-shirt, he looked every inch the successful, happy businessman. And why wouldn't he be, after stealing all their clients? She shook her head, it was important to at least *appear* civilised.

'Are you on those tablets again?' Pete asked, eyebrows raised. 'Forgotten who I am?'

'How could I forget that?' Jane took a sip from her coffee cup and regarded him over its rim. 'Your business set up in direct competition to mine. It's a hard thing to forget.'

He nodded. 'And now your business happens to be the most expensive one in town.'

So he'd noticed. Jane allowed herself a smirk. He'd probably sent a little spy haring down the road to see how much they were now charging. 'Only because it deserves to be,' she said sweetly. 'After all, we use very high quality products.'

'And do OAPs appreciate that?' He actually sounded as if he wanted to know.

'Everybody appreciates that,' she said, gritting her teeth. 'As I'm sure you'll find out when all your business diverts to us.'

He threw his head back and laughed. 'Right,' he said, sounding amused.

Jane took a sip of her coffee. 'Now, if you'll excuse me, I've to drink my coffee and I'd like to do it without feeling sick.'

He didn't like that and she probably shouldn't have said it.

'Claustrophobic,' she said unconvincingly. 'I hate crowds.'

'Just as well you don't have to worry about that ever happening at work,' he said.

Bastard. 'Bye now.' She tried to say it pleasantly. 'See you on the course.'

'Yes. It'll be good. Joules is great.'

Joules! Pretending that he was well in. Was there no end to the man's arrogance? She didn't bother to reply, just smiled again and walked off, hoping to find a quiet corner where she could fume in private.

'You're grounded.'

'What?'

At least Owen didn't shout. He just looked a bit surprised and not too devastated.

'You heard.' Once again, Jim walked around the table and faced his other child. 'I said, you're grounded.'

Owen blinked. Once. Twice. 'OK.'

It took a second to register. There was to be no battle. 'Don't you want to know why?'

'I'm sure you've a good reason,' Owen said calmly. He picked up a slice of toast from the table. 'Eating this?'

Jim shook his head. 'No. And I'm surprised you can eat either. What the hell were you at coming home drunk last night?'

He saw his son gulp. Then shrug. 'I wasn't.'

'You were.' Jim took the toast out of Owen's hand. 'D'you think I'm stupid?'

'No, course not, Da.' Owen shrugged and admitted quietly, 'I was only a bit drunk. It won't happen again, OK?'

'Oh.' Taken aback, Jim was at a loss for words. 'OK, fine. But you're still grounded.'

'Uh-huh.'

'Where did you get the booze, anyway?'

Owen flinched. 'A few of the lads brought some cans.'

'And that girl?'

'What?'

'The girl that carried you home, did she bring drink?'

'Dunno. Could have.' Owen was shuffling from foot to foot. 'Can I go now? Is there anything else?'

'Yeah, as a matter of fact,' he said. Then as Owen showed no trace of emotion, he said in a stronger voice, 'Just 'cause your mother's away, don't think you can do what you like. I'm still your father.'

Owen gave a funny sort of a grin and nodded. 'Right.'

Jim watched Owen pick up the toast and leave the kitchen. He felt somehow as if he'd lost the battle with him. Maybe he should have asked him more about where he'd been. Owen going out was unusual enough in itself, Owen hanging around with a girl was even weirder. Still, maybe it was a sign that he was growing up. Most young lads drank at some stage and to be honest, he'd rather Owen out doing a few mad things than cooped up in his room the way he'd been the last few years. That had been unnatural.

The course was brilliant. Julian Waters talked about what styles suited what faces. With his model he demonstrated how to change a hairstyle simply by cutting into the guideline. Then there was a short break for coffee and after that, the models began to arrive.

There was no sign of Rosemary.

Jane waited and waited, her heart soaring and sinking every time a new model walked into the room. Eventually, trying to quell her rising panic, she walked out into the foyer to look for her. She stopped dead at the sight of Julian and Pete talking and laughing with one another. So Pete did know him. Typical. That's probably why he won every year, she thought, he probably knew all the judges. He'd enough money to bribe them anyway. He seemed to be in the middle of introducing Julian to a beautiful ethnic woman with glorious black hair. It looked very much as if this woman was going to be Pete's model. If so, she needed to find Rosemary quickly. There was no way she was being upstaged by him.

She crossed to reception. 'Excuse me,' she asked the receptionist, trying to keep her voice from spiralling upwards in panic, 'did a small auburn-haired girl pass by here by any chance?'

The receptionist looked blank and then said, 'Well, a girl had to go to the doctors with a burnt hand about half an hour ago. She left a message for a,' the woman consulted a card, 'Jane McCarthy.'

'That's me.' Frantically, Jane took the card. On it, Rosemary had scrawled: *Jane, have burnt my hand. Was eating breakfast and the coffee spilt all over me. Doc bringing me to his surgery to dress it. Will be back as soon as I can. Really, really sorry, but the bitch on reception,* Jane looked at the bitch, *wouldn't let me in to you.*

Jane closed her eyes and scrunched up the note. She hoped poor Rosemary was all right.

'Bad news?' the woman asked sympathetically.

Jane didn't bother to reply. Instead she stood looking resentfully at Julian and Pete and the beautiful woman. Eventually Pete and his model left Julian and returned to the room. Julian, after consulting some notes, made to follow them.

'Excuse me.' Jane rushed across to him as he looked at her impatiently. 'I'm Jane.' She tried a smile, which wasn't returned. Flustered, she babbled, 'And, eh, well, my model has had an accident, so, eh, I've no model.'

'No model?' Julian looked at her in disbelief. 'You come to *my* course with *no* model? I specifically said that everyone had to bring a model.'

'Well, she had to leave early, see, and well, I was wondering if you had a spare—'

'A spare model?' Julian quirked his eyebrows. 'Where? In the boot of my car?'

What a bastard. No wonder he and Pete got on. 'No. But I'm sure one would fit in your mouth,' Jane muttered.

'What?'

She flushed. What had possessed her? Still, he didn't seem to have heard or if he did, he obviously didn't seem to think he'd heard correctly. 'So the answer is "no" then, is it?' she asked sullenly, reminding herself of Di.

'The answer is "no".' Julian looked impassively at her. 'I do not bring extra models with me in case someone's gets lost. Now,' he said briskly, 'you may sit in and watch or alternatively, you can look for someone else, it's up to you. We start in five minutes.' He walked off.

Jane gave him two fingers. Well, she thought, no matter how good he was, she was never, ever going to spend her hard-earned cash on him ever again.

'Hello, hello,' the receptionist was waving at her.

What now, she wondered?

'I couldn't help overhearing,' the woman said, 'and, well, if you're really stuck, will I do?'

Jane winced. Marge Simpson was only in the halfpenny place. Still, beggars couldn't be choosers. 'That's very nice of you,' she smiled, 'but aren't you working?'

'I get off in five minutes,' the woman said. 'I'm June by the way. Now, I'll just wait for my replacement and I'm all yours. I'm glad I can help. That young lady wanted to go in to you and I wouldn't let her and now, well, I think it's all my fault.'

Jane smiled. 'Not at all.'

It was ten minutes before the second receptionist arrived and then June announced that she had to use the toilet.

Fifteen minutes late, they entered the room. Everyone looked up at them and she fancied that Pete Jordan was smirking at her. Ignoring Julian's grimaces, she quickly set up.

'Now,' June said, settling herself at the basin, 'I don't want anything really adventurous. I know what you hairdressers are like. Something nice and fluffy, I think.'

All through breakfast Jane had fantasised about the wonderful things she'd do with her scissors, but now, it just looked like being a straight curlers-and-hairnet job.

'Really, it's me who should be deciding,' she whispered. 'I won't make a mess, I promise.'

'No, I know you won't,' June said. 'Because I won't let you.'

Jane gritted her teeth and glanced across at Pete. He was deftly combing through his model's wet tresses. There was no way she'd even come close to him today.

'Now,' June said briskly, 'I don't want much off as I said, I like it fluffy – lots of body.'

Jane nodded, pretending to consider. Jesus, she thought, any more body and there'd be two of her. 'How about I layer it tight in at the back,' she suggested, 'and I even out the top? I think it'd look great on you.'

June shook her head. 'Nooo, I don't think so dear. That's the kind of thing my daughter has. I'm not into all that. I just want it fluffy.'

Jane wondered what on earth you did with someone who had definite ideas on what they wanted when what they wanted was completely wrong. She knew what she normally did. She gave it to them while trying to talk them out of it.

Diplomacy was called for.

She winced, thinking of Jim, Di and Owen. Diplomacy was not her strong suit.

An hour later and June's hair was a disaster. Jane had done her best to talk her out of her suicide style, but no way would that woman be deterred. She was delighted with the finished result, while Jane cringed. All she wanted to do was run out of the room before Julian caught sight of it. Pete had done a really radical style on his model's hair and while Jane wasn't mad on it, it was a damn sight better than what she'd done. More challenging too.

All around her fantastic styles were being invented and what had she done? Bloody 'fluffy'. Jane cursed her dowdy model who was singing her praises.

Julian came around and commented individually on everyone's work. It was amazing the hints he gave that could pull a style into a better shape. When he arrived at her, Jane blurted out, 'It's what she wanted.'

Julian nodded, frowning. Everyone was looking to see what he'd say.

Instead, he turned to June. 'And how about you, madam? Are you happy?' he asked.

'It's wonderful.' June patted and preened herself in front of the mirror. 'The nicest it's ever been.'

Julian patted Jane on the back. 'One happy customer who'll return again.'

'Yeah, but her friends won't when they see her hair,' she muttered in an undertone.

He gave a guffaw of laughter which transformed him from surly hairdresser into human being. 'Don't be so hard on yourself. The style is technically perfect. It's the best that could be done.' Giving her another grin he went on to the next student.

She hadn't looked at it like that, she thought. OK, it was a mess, but out of the mess, it was the best that could be done. She ought to be happy with that.

'Hey,' Pete came towards her, 'I see you've stuck to type.' He thumbed towards June.

'Absolutely,' Jane nodded, 'one happy customer, one technically perfect hairstyle.'

'That's not what I meant.'

'Is it not?' she said innocently. 'Why – what *did* you mean?'

He shook his head and stomped off. He even looked a bit rattled.

Later that night, when he was sure that the kids were asleep, he rang Debbie. She picked up and from the background noise, he deduced that she was in a pub. There seemed to be loads of loud laughter. Debbie said that she couldn't hear him properly, so he had to wait until she went somewhere quiet.

'Hi you,' she said. 'How're things going? Are they talking to you yet?'

'No.'

'Aw, poor Jim. Well, you've missed all the news while you've been away doing your domestic duties.'

'Yeah?' He found he was smiling as he listened to her bubbly voice.

'Liz and Edmond got a place of their own and they're having a housewarming right now, which is where I am. And, big news flash, Fred and Gillian have had a huge row and Gillian is at home bawling her eyes out, while Fred is here getting plastered and half-heartedly feeling up anything on legs.'

'Fred and Gill?' Jesus, he couldn't believe it. Still, it *was* Fred they were talking about – he'd probably just got bored.

'So, be prepared for a very sick flatmate tomorrow,' Debbie laughed.

'Great,' Jim muttered. 'Just what I need after this weekend.'

Debbie giggled.

That night, after Rosemary had fallen asleep, Jane picked up the phone to call Jim. She'd had such a wonderful weekend that she felt sort of guilty about him. He was bound to have had a terrible time. Besides, she wanted to check up on the kids. She couldn't help worrying whenever she left them.

His phone was engaged.

36

IT WAS WITH a heavy heart that Jane pulled into the driveway of her house. She felt even more depressed as Jim gave her the run-down on the weekend.

'I grounded both of them yesterday,' he said, as he helped her pull her bags out of the boot. 'Di was out until two the night before and Owen came home drunk. Of course, he tried to dodge upstairs on me but—'

'Drunk?' Jane laughed slightly. 'Don't be ridiculous, Owen wouldn't get drunk.'

'Well, he did on Friday. I thought grounding him would be a good idea.'

'How drunk was he?' she asked, wondering suddenly if it had any connection with Owen bunking off school.

'Well, I don't think he was really bad, but you know, he can't come home in that state.'

'Yeah. Right. Good.' She'd have to talk to Owen later – find out what had happened. 'Did he say why he was drinking?'

'Nah,' Jim shrugged. 'I reckon it's just a phase. All lads do it at some stage.'

He was probably right, but it was still worrying. 'I'll have a word.'

'Yeah. Good.' Jim nodded at her. He helped carry her case into the kitchen, then asked if she wanted it upstairs.

'I'll do it later. I'll just get a cuppa now. It's been a long drive.'

'Yeah, sure.' Jim moved out of her way. 'There are bars in the press you can have. I bought them for the kids only they

. . . well, apparently not talking to me means rejecting my grub as well.'

God, things must have been bad if Owen refused to eat chocolate, Jane thought as she fished them out of the press. They were his favourite too. 'So,' she asked Jim, 'where are the kids now?'

He shrugged. 'Dunno. They just went out. Wouldn't tell me. Another part of the not-talking-to-Dad clause, I guess.'

God, the man was hopeless. Couldn't he have just demanded that they tell him? Jane bit her lip so that she wouldn't say something stupid. That was Jim all over, come the heavy one minute and be completely walked on the next. 'And my mother?' she asked instead.

'Gone back to Hades in her burning chariot.'

The comment was so quick that Jane giggled. 'Stop!'

Jim grinned back at her. 'Sorry.' He shook his head. 'But Jesus, she's made my life a complete misery this weekend. Every time I walked into a room, she walked out. Then the kids started to copy her.' He paused. 'Anyhow, she's gone to work.'

'Oh, right.' Maybe this afternoon wouldn't be so bad, Jane thought. She'd have the house to herself. She could do a big clean-up and maybe read a book or something. Feeling more generous, she asked, 'D'you want a cuppa before you head off?'

He looked surprised, but pleased. 'Yeah, sure. If you want.'

She filled the kettle halfway and flicked it on. She was aware of him looking at her, but she couldn't turn around and meet his gaze, instead she got cups from the press and pretended she couldn't find the tea bags. The silence seemed to grow and grow.

Just as the kettle clicked off and she was pouring them both some tea, Jim asked, 'Did you have a good weekend?'

'Brilliant.' She sat down opposite him and pushed his mug across. 'I learnt loads.' She stopped. Decided not to be so childish. 'It was a hairdressing course.'

'Oh, right.' Jim didn't seem to know what to say to that. He sipped his tea and peeled open a bar of chocolate. 'It's a long time since you went on one of those – isn't it?'

'Years.'

'So, like, what did you do?'

It was weird at first, talking to him about the course. They hadn't really talked about small things in ages, but as she described Julian and saw him grin at her description of June, she grew more confident. 'She wanted "fluffy",' Jane said. 'I mean, can you *imagine* it? I might as well have just glued a cat to her head.'

Jim laughed and the sound of it was bittersweet.

'Julian thought it—'

The ringing of Jim's mobile cut her off. He looked at her apologetically.

'You better get it.'

'Yeah, right.' He seemed embarrassed as he fumbled it out of his pocket. He got even more embarrassed as he talked into it.

Jane knew it had to be Debbie and she cursed herself for being so nice to Jim. She was glad that he'd had a bad weekend, he deserved it. The bloody – she racked her brains to think of Mir's joke – the bloody koala bear that he was.

She noisily began to clear away the mugs.

Jim wished he'd turned his mobile off. Jesus, he'd completely forgotten that Debbie had said she'd ring him. He was meant to be back at the flat by now. He tried to talk to her as if she was just a mate, but he knew Jane wasn't fooled.

'Listen, talk later,' he eventually said. 'I'm not at the flat yet.' He flicked the phone off and turned to Jane.

'Well, you'd better go,' she said brittlely. 'You've got your orders.'

The moment was spoilt. She had her efficient face on, the one that completely closed him out. 'Yeah, right. I'll just get my bag from the sitting room.'

As he left the kitchen, he wished he didn't have to go.

* * *

'I believe you were drinking on Friday,' Jane said.

Owen was watching TV, the remote in his hand, his feet up on the sofa. 'Yeah,' he muttered, without looking at her. 'I told Dad I was sorry about that.'

'He told me.' Jane pushed his feet off the sofa and sat beside him. He squirmed away, still looking at the telly. 'D'you want to tell me why you found it necessary to come home drunk?'

He grinned slightly. 'It wasn't like that. One of the lads had a few cans, that's all.'

'One of the lads – what lads?'

'From school. He bought them and we all just shared them. I only had a couple.'

'Owen, you're only thirteen – it's illegal!'

'Yeah, sorry.'

Jane took the remote from him and flicked the TV off.

'Hey!'

'Perhaps you'll look at me now?'

Owen stared at her with solemn brown eyes. 'I told Dad it won't happen again. What more can I do?'

'You can tell me.'

'It won't happen again.'

'And it's got nothing to do with bunking off school?'

'Ma!' He refocused on the telly. 'Gimme a break. I go in now, don't I?'

And he did. Perhaps it was just as Jim suggested, a lad thing. She decided to let it go. 'All right,' she tousled his hair. 'I forgive you.'

Owen shook his head and flicked the telly back on.

37

FRED BARELY GLANCED at him when he arrived back. Instead, nursing a can of lager, he kept his gaze on the telly.

'How goes it?' Jim dumped his sleeping bag on to a chair and grinned at his mate. 'I believe you had a wild night last night?'

Fred shrugged. He slugged some more lager. 'Goodfilmzis,' he muttered.

'What?'

'I *said*,' Fred repeated very deliberately, ''Sagoodfilm.'

'Oh, yeah, right.' For the first time, Jim noticed the stench of beer, then he noticed that the normally immaculate Fred hadn't shaved and was dressed in a shirt that looked as if it had been puked on. 'Are you OK?' he asked cautiously. 'You look a bit rough.'

'Feel great!' Fred waved his can about and drink sloshed everywhere.

Jim tried not to wince as most of it went on to the sofa. Jesus, it'd smell like mad tonight. 'Good. How's Gill?'

'Don't talk to me about her.' Fred wiped his mouth and stood up. He jabbed his can towards Jim and swayed dangerously. 'I told her, I told her to go. I said I didn't want her. Women are all the same. Think they can pin you down. But not me. "Not me," I said to her. "I mean," I said, "look at Jimbo. Jimbo's wasted," zats what I said.'

'Thanks.'

'No, no, no, no,' Fred waved his arm expansively and yet more drink fizzed to the floor. ''Snot an insult. Right. Right?'

'Yeah, whatever you say.' Jim studied Fred who was now

stumbling towards the fridge in search of more cans. 'So, what happened with Gillian?'

'It's over. That's all. Now where are the bloody cans?'

It was the first time Fred had ever taken a break-up so hard, Jim thought. Normally, after ruining some poor woman's dreams, Fred would be out enjoying himself for weeks afterwards. Still, it was not the time to say anything as the guy was going to pass out on the floor if he didn't shift him somewhere. He was just trying to coax him to sit back down again when the buzzer went.

'It's me!'

Jim buzzed to let Debbie up. Then he hauled Fred to his feet, saying, 'Come on – get your head down. Don't let Debs see you like this. She'll tell Gillian.'

'Couldn't give a shit,' Fred spat. 'Gillian fucking who? That's whad I want to know. Gillian who?'

'Yeah right.' Jim rolled his eyes and dragged Fred into his room. 'Just get some kip.'

'The fucking room is spinning.'

Jim closed the door on him. He'd be fine. From the look of him, he'd been up all night, so he was bound to conk out.

'Hi you,' Debbie, dressed in the catsuit he'd first seen her in, looked fantastic. 'Are you not going to let me in?'

'Well,' he shrugged apologetically, 'Fred is smashed. I should stay with him. Maybe you'd better—'

'Gillian is crying her eyes out at my place, but she doesn't *want* me to stay. So, come on, Jim, let me in – I've nowhere else to go. And besides, I haven't seen you in days.'

Reluctantly he let her past. Jesus, the way her bum looked in that tight black leather. And her hair . . .

'So,' Debbie crossed her legs and surveyed him, 'did you miss me?'

'I missed having someone to talk to,' he said ruefully.

'You look awful,' she said, sympathetically. 'Was it a bad weekend?'

'Bad doesn't even come close.'

'Aw, poor Jim,' Debbie said in mock-sympathy. She made a face and said, as if talking to a five-year-old, 'Come over here. I'll make sure no one else does anything bad to you.'

'Aw, pity about that.' Jim sat down beside her. Grinning, he added, 'And here was me thinking I'd just love someone to do bad stuff to me.'

'Yeah?' Debbie snuggled into him.

'Yeah. But seeing as there's no one around—'

'Come here, you.' Debbie pulled his face to hers and kissed him hard on the lips.

Jesus, she was gorgeous.

Just as she began unbuttoning his shirt, Fred stumbled out of his room and into the bathroom, where he was violently sick.

'Ugh, Jesus,' Debbie winced and pulled away.

'You all right, Fred?' Jim called.

'Fuck off!'

'Charming.' Debbie rolled her eyes. 'I dunno what's happened between the two of them, but whatever it is, Gill's better off.'

'He's cut-up over it.' Jim felt he had to defend Fred. 'Honest, I've never seen him like this. Normally he just gets on with life. He never gets in this kind of state.'

Fred re-emerged from the bathroom, wiping his mouth with his sleeve. Taking a look at Jim and Debbie he said, 'Can yez not go and fuck yourselves somewhere else?' He gave his bedroom door a hard slam.

'Fecker,' Debbie said. 'Come on, Jim, let's go.'

'Naw,' Jim shook his head. 'You go if you want. I'd better stay, just in case he does anything mental.'

'He won't,' Debbie said impatiently. 'Come on!'

'He's me mate, Deb, I can't.'

'Fine.' She didn't sound as if it was fine. 'Stay.'

'I'll call—'

But she was gone.

God, he was upsetting them all these days.

38

MONDAY MORNING. MIRANDA was stomping about the place as usual. Nothing ever changed, Jane thought as she pulled the appointments book from under the desk to check her clients for the day. It was funny, she'd been away for a weekend and somehow she was convinced that something had to have happened while she was gone. No such luck.

Still, at least something had changed, even if it was only slight. Ten customers were booked in, four of whom she didn't recognise. Business was on the up.

'Hey.' Patrick startled her, as he tweaked her hair. 'The wanderer returns.' Leaning over the appointments book so that she couldn't read it, he asked, 'Tell me, what did you think?'

'Oh, it was great,' Jane smiled. 'He was brilliant.'

'Yes, I know.' Patrick beamed delightedly. 'So, go on, tell me all about the weekend. What did you do?'

So Jane told him about Rosemary burning herself and the model that she had as a stand-in. 'And, yer man was there,' she added, 'Pete Jordan. He's not the smiley guy he once was. I think we've got him rattled.'

'Take a lot to rattle a guy like that,' Patrick said. 'Barney met him on a course once. Said everyone was eating out of his hand.'

'I wish one of them had *eaten* his hand,' Jane muttered.

Patrick giggled.

'Oy, Pat,' Mir held up the phone, 'For you. Some guy, says his name is Barney?'

Patrick scurried over to take the call and Mir stared grumpily at him before mooching over to Jane.

'That's the fourth time that fella has rung in the past week,' she grumped. 'And every time he rings he sounds different. He's as gay as Christmas now.'

'Probably because he is,' Jane grinned. 'He's Patrick's partner, I think. He's the guy who sent him the valentine's card.'

'Oh,' Mir's eyes narrowed. 'He never told me.'

'Told you what, Mir?' Rosemary looked at both of them. Her hand was wrapped in a big bandage.

'Well, someone obviously never told you to mind your own business.'

Rosemary's face dropped. 'Oh. I just thought, well, never mind . . .'

'Never mind what?' Patrick asked brightly.

'Oooh, don't ask,' Rosemary gulped. 'I think it's private.'

'Who is Barney?' Mir sounded annoyed. Patrick's grin only seemed to annoy her further. 'Well, go on tight knickers, tell me.' She poked him with her elbow. 'Who the hell is Barney?'

'Aw, he's that flippin' purple alley-gator that all the kids love,' Rosemary said, delighted to be of help and redeem herself for her nosiness. 'Yez know, he sings that sick song about everybody loving each other.'

'That's not the Barney we mean,' Patrick laughed indulgently. He'd grown quite fond of Rosemary in the past while. 'No,' he paused, then said half-shyly, 'Barney is my partner.'

'You've gone inta partnership, have ya?' Rosemary gawped.

'His *sexual* partner,' Miranda sniffed. 'God, Rosemary, you're awful thick.'

'Yer boyfriend like?' Rosemary's jaw nearly hit the ground as she stared wide-eyed at Patrick. 'Like, as in a *relationship*?'

'Yes,' Patrick nodded. 'He's the man who sent me the valentine's card and now, well . . .' he beamed happily, 'we're very close.'

'Awwww,' Rosemary smiled. 'That's lovely, so it is.'

'Well, I don't think it's fair,' Miranda snapped, not looking a bit pleased at Patrick's happiness. 'Jesus, straight guys far outnumber gay guys in this poxy city. So how come you can get someone and I can't? How come?' She glared at Patrick as if it was all his fault.

'Give it a rest, Mir,' Patrick said, sounding irritated.

Rosemary tittered. 'It's not that hard to find someone. You'll *easily* do it. I mean, even I have a fella.'

Jesus, Jane thought, *why did Rosemary have to say that*? Miranda did not like people to be happy on a Monday morning.

'I met him last—'

'I'm not on the lookout for blind, brain-damaged specimens,' Miranda almost spat into Rosemary's face. 'So save it.'

There was an uneasy silence.

'He is not brain-damaged,' Rosemary said, her eyes filling up. 'He's—'

'Whatever he's like, I wouldn't want him.' Miranda turned to leave.

'No, Mir,' Patrick said quietly, 'you prefer the louts that use and abuse, don't you?'

Miranda froze.

Jane wished she could be somewhere else. A fight between Miranda and Patrick would be awful. 'Look guys, let's just—'

'What?' Miranda asked, '*What* did you say?'

'You heard.' Patrick's voice sounded harder than Jane had ever heard it before. His eyes seemed to bore into Miranda, who flinched.

'I don't go out with guys that . . . whatever the hell you said,' Miranda said defensively. 'The guys I go out with are fine.'

'Oh right,' Patrick said in pretend nonchalance. 'So *that's* why you were crying this morning, is it? That's why you waltz off with every deadbeat you find in every club we go to, is it? That's why *every* Monday, after these guys dump you, me and Jane have to try and coax you into semi-good form so that our customers won't get their heads bitten off – is it?'

'Piss off!'

'Well?' Patrick demanded. 'Is it?'

'Don't you dare! Don't you dare. That's – not – fair.'

'It's true though.'

Jane didn't know what to do. Jesus, they'd been mates for so long it'd be terrible if this fight ruined things between them.

'I, I, was wrong about you,' Miranda said to him. Her voice wobbled dangerously. Gulping hard, she said, 'You *are* a real man. A complete bastard.'

'And when in doubt, curse like a trooper, eh, Mir?'

Miranda jerked at his words. Blinking rapidly, her voice trembling, she said, 'I think I'm going home.' She looked Patrick up and down. 'I'll be *sick* if I stay here.'

'If you put as much effort into styling as you do into chasing hopeless losers, you'd have a bloody chain of salons of your own by this stage.'

'Aw, Patrick!' Jane interjected.

'Are you saying that I'm no good? That I'm lazy?' Mir shoved her face almost into Patrick's. 'Well?'

'Mir!' Jane said. 'Please. It was just said in the heat of the moment.' Desperately, she turned to Patrick. 'Wasn't it, Patrick?'

The silence seemed to last for ever. Eventually Patrick said gently, 'It was said as a friend, Mir. Look at what happened at the weekend—'

'I don't need your friendship!' Miranda grabbed her coat from the chair where she'd tossed it. 'And, seeing as I don't put any effort into my work, I don't need your poxy job, either.'

'Miranda!' But Miranda was storming to the door. Jane pushed Patrick. 'Jesus, Patrick, go after her!'

Patrick let the door swing shut behind Miranda. 'No,' he said, 'leave her. She's better off on her own.'

'I'm sorry,' Rosemary piped up. 'It was my fault. I shouldn't have said—'

'It was nothing to do with you,' Patrick patted her arm. He

glanced at Jane. 'Listen, Rosemary, hold the fort while I have a chat with Jane, will you?'

Rosemary, looking very pale and subdued, agreed.

Inside the coffee room, Jane tried to get him to go after Miranda. 'Jesus, she's left her—'

Patrick held up his hand. 'Jane, don't.' He shook his head. 'Don't give me grief. She had it coming.'

'No,' Jane shook her head. 'Not like that. What you said was awful.'

'Do you know what she did last weekend?'

'No, but Pat—'

'Well, I'll bloody tell you.' He paused for a second, as if willing himself to calm down. He closed his eyes and began slowly, 'We went out to a club. This band were playing and that musician fella, the one that dumped her ages ago, was playing. Well, Mir goes up and makes a complete fool out of herself. Laughing with him, flirting with him, she even kissed him. And when I tried to have a word in her ear, she turned around and told me to mind my own business and to get lost. So I did. I went home.'

'Yeah, well—'

'And then she rings me up on Sunday, crying her eyes out 'cause musician man had left with someone else and she had a go at me, *me*, for leaving her on her own.' He tossed his head. 'I mean, honestly!'

'She always does that.'

'Yeah, well, I've had enough. I'm tired of being good enough until something better comes along.'

He was very hurt over it, Jane realised. Hurt and furious. Patrick didn't get annoyed often, but when he did, he was immovable.

'She's, she's unhappy,' Jane said, understanding for the first time that Miranda probably was. 'She's just looking for love. OK, she gets it wrong but—'

'But why the hell is it our fault?' Patrick snapped. 'With her, it's always someone else's mistake. Yours, mine, Harry's. Never Miranda's. Never. And yet she goes about attacking kids like

Rosemary who – Jesus Christ – have absolutely nothing in their lives besides a fella and a two-bit training job.'

He walked to the door and just before he opened it, Jane said, 'Patrick, she's packed in her job. I mean, do you want your friendship to end because of it?'

'What friendship?' His desolate tone shocked her. 'It's all take, take, take with her. Harry will tell you the same. That man puts up with some crap. She's treated him far worse than she's ever treated me.'

'Yeah but—'

'No buts.' Patrick opened the door. 'Anyhow, she'll be back. I know she will. I mean,' he made a face, 'how else will she afford all her designer gear?' He gave a twisted sort of a smile and left.

Jim took out his organiser and keyed in 'Debbie'. Her home and work numbers flashed up on the small screen. He was about to reach for the phone to dial her work number when the phone rang.

'Philip Logan for you, honey pie,' Maud said cheerily. 'Your number one fan.'

Jim sighed. Philip would keep him for hours. Reluctantly he flicked his organiser off and prepared himself for the onslaught of orders from Philip.

'Philip,' he said in a tone that implied he was under pressure and couldn't talk for long. 'What can I do for you?'

'Ask not what you can do for me, but what I can do for you,' Philip chortled.

There was a brief silence. Jim took a deep breath, told himself to have patience and in a remarkably even voice, he asked, 'So, what can you do for me, Philip?'

'Atta boy!' Philip boomed so loudly that Jim had to take the phone away from his ear. 'You want to know, meet me in, mmmm, let's see . . .' He hummed and hawed and seemed to press a lot of buttons before he said, 'Meet me at Jury's at one.'

'I've got a lunch appointment at one,' Jim said firmly. Jesus, there was no way he was meeting Philip. Philip's idea of lunch was wine and food in that order. Dave would have jumped at it, but he didn't fancy sitting in a restaurant while Philip ordered the staff to jump through hoops for him.

'Cancel it,' Philip ordered.

'I can't,' Jim replied. 'My clients are important to me, as you know.'

'Fuck off with the bullshit and cancel,' Philip laughed. 'It'll be worth your while, I guarantee it.'

Jim sighed. Dave would go through him for a shortcut if he found out that he'd refused a potentially lucrative lunch with Philip Logan. 'Right. I'll rearrange my whole schedule to accommodate you,' Jim said with a bad grace. 'It won't be easy though.'

'Nothing worthwhile ever is, Jimbo. Did no one ever tell you that?' Philip gave another boom of a laugh and hung up.

The day had been a complete disaster, Jane thought as she pulled into her driveway. There had been an upturn in business, but because they were a stylist down, there were queues. It hadn't looked good, but it had felt great.

As Jane let herself in, Sheila drifted out of the dining room. Her mother was wearing a dressing gown, her head was swathed in a towel, her nails had been painted and the stink of them was all over the place.

'Hello, dahling,' Sheila smiled. 'Good day?'

'Terrible.' Jane brushed past her mother and had a look in the kitchen. Owen was standing over the cooker stirring a stew. He smiled at her and she smiled back. 'Where's Di?' she asked.

'In the shower,' Sheila answered. 'Honestly, that girl will have herself washed away – *if* we're lucky.'

Jane smiled despite herself and Sheila looked pleased. She sat down gingerly on a kitchen chair, being careful to keep her French-polished nails away from the furniture.

French polish and her mother usually meant only one thing. Her mother was going out somewhere.

'Are you going out, Mother?' Jane couldn't keep the surprise from her voice. Perhaps she was meeting her dad, Jane thought. They hadn't heard from him in weeks. Maybe tomorrow she'd tune into her dad's show and see what he was up to. There was no way she was ringing him, not after what he'd said.

'A woman doesn't have to be going anywhere to try and look her best,' Sheila said defensively.

'No, but she doesn't normally use expensive nail vanish unless she is,' Jane shot back. Her mother, much to her horror, had been forced to use cheap make-up in the last while as all her expensive stuff had run out. Bits and pieces of her former life's make-up had been hoarded away 'just in case'.

'Well, if you must know,' Sheila looked slightly embarrassed, 'I'm going to Lisa's.'

'Your boss's house?' Jane gawped. 'Why? Is she suddenly your best friend or something?' The last she heard, Lisa was as common as muck, with a mouth like a sewer and skin like barbed wire.

'A friend? *No.*' Sheila looked revolted at the thought. 'A woman interested in making the most of the little she's got? Yes.' She blew on her nails to hurry them up, before continuing, 'It was her idea. She was so delighted with the outfits I chose that she wants to learn more about looking well. Apparently, she's separated and she wants to show hubby what he's missing. Now, I'm not a miracle worker, but I did say that I could give her a few hints on how to look after her nails and things. So she thought it'd be wonderful if I did a sort of,' Sheila screwed up her face as she tried to think of the right word, 'a sort of class in grooming, I suppose you could say. So I said fine.' Sheila smiled, 'And best of all, if I do this, she lets me off work for the next two days.'

'What? She's going to pay you two days' wages to file a few nails?'

'Apparently,' Sheila nodded. 'I mean, she's invited her friends to hear me talk and everything – wonderful, isn't it?'

Jane nodded. And what was more, her mother actually looked happy. Something like that would suit her down to the ground.

'And I'll tell you something else wonderful,' Sheila said, 'if this goes well, Lisa thinks there might be a business in it. People listening to me talking. Imagine!'

Jane winced. She didn't think it bore imagining. 'Eh, great.'

'She might *look* awful,' Sheila had her charitable voice on, the one she used for talking about travellers and refugees and ugly people, 'but she's very sharp. Always thinking of new businesses. She's more money than Jack Benny hoarded away. So, there we are.' She got up and went to the fridge. Taking out some natural yogurt and a grapefruit she proceeded to eat.

'Owen, is dinner ready?' Jane asked.

Owen peered into the pot. 'It's hot, I reckon so. Will I get the plates?'

'How can you eat that stuff?' Sheila shuddered. 'Nice fresh food, that's what keeps your skin intact.'

'Yeah, but your tongue keeps wondering what the hell it was invented for.' Di strolled into the kitchen. Staring down at Sheila's 'dinner' she made a face. 'Taste? Hello? Where are you?' she mocked.

'Well, dahling, I'd rather have bland food than a bland body.' Taking her food with her, Sheila exited.

Jane suppressed a smile. Sheila had really copped on to how to infuriate Di. 'What does she mean, "a bland body"?' Di whispered furiously. 'I'm thin. Amn't I thin, Mam?'

'Anorexic looking,' Jane soothed.

Pacified, Di sat down.

After dinner, Jane dialled Miranda. There was no answer, so she left a message on the machine asking Miranda to ring her.

Jim left the lunch with Philip at eight. He was locked and he knew he couldn't drive. He'd have to leave his car overnight and get a taxi home. Philip had offered to call him one of his cars, but Jim had refused. He needed to think. His head was spinning with Philip's proposal. It'd mean a complete change. Philip had told him he needed to know within the next couple of months. 'It's all a bit up in the air at the moment,' he'd said. 'But it'll definitely be happening, by the end of the year at least. I want you on board.'

It'd mean giving up everything he'd really wanted. But, Jim thought as he hailed a taxi, everything he'd ever wanted had given him up, so maybe . . .

39

IT WAS LUNCHTIME the following day before Jim realised that he still hadn't called Debbie. Between Philip's offer and Fred going on another bender, ringing Debbie had completely slipped his mind.

As Jim listened to Debbie's phone ringing, he half-hoped she wouldn't answer. He knew if she did, she'd probably be feeling a bit pissed at him.

'Hello?'

'Hiya, Debs, it's me. Jim.'

'Yes?'

She *was* angry. Jim gulped. 'Listen, sorry about the other night, Fred is in bits. He even got drunk again last night and he didn't go to work this morning.'

'Am I supposed to feel sorry for you both or something?'

'Aw, Debs, don't be like that. Listen, can I call around tonight? I promise I'll make it up to you.' Debbie said nothing. Jim took her silence as a good sign. 'Please?'

'Well,' she still sounded a bit annoyed, though not as much as before, 'don't come to the flat. Gillian is swearing vengeance on all things Fred at the moment – you included. I'll meet you after work, say around seven, outside Cleary's?'

Outside Cleary's. Jim felt his heart twist. He and Jane always used to meet there. Under the clock at Cleary's was the big meeting place. It was funny how stupid things like that could affect him. 'Sure,' he said. 'See you then.'

She hung up on him without even saying goodbye.

* * *

Miranda didn't show for work but Patrick wasn't too worried. 'Give her a week,' he said. 'She'll be back.'

'But what if she's not?' Jane asked. 'I think you should ring her and ask her if she's really left. Talk to her, tell her you didn't mean what you said.'

'But I did mean it.' Patrick wasn't going to budge. 'I meant every word. She *is* lazy, she *is* a tart.' With that, he asked Rosemary to get one of the customers a cuppa while he mixed a colour.

Jane took it that the subject was closed.

Sheila was relishing her lie-in. Getting up for work in the mornings was so tiring. It was now after three and she felt rested and refreshed. Maybe she would get up – after all, the sun was splitting the rocks outside and if she lashed on some suntan lotion, she might even get a bit of a colour. She tried not to think of the foreign holiday she would be on if she'd still been with Declan. Still, losing a foreign holiday and a tan was a small price to pay for not having to put up with Declan's fumblings in the bedroom. Sheila shuddered as she remembered. Don't even *go* there, she thought.

Instead, she let her mind wander to the previous night. It had been a screaming success and Lisa, who owned a lovely house – even if the interior designer had ballsed it up – had seemed pretty sure that more bookings would follow. It was the easiest thing to do, Sheila thought, hair and nails were so *interesting*. Talking about them to a room full of women was sheer heaven. And getting paid for doing it was the icing on the cake.

She stretched and savoured the silence in the house. The kids had gone out. Di had made her a cup of tea before leaving, in exchange for a lend of some pink nail polish. Sheila smiled. Di was a scream; moody as hell, but so quick-witted and smart. It was fun sparring with her. Owen, on the other hand, was the weirdest boy going. But then again, he had more of his father's genes than was good for him.

She turned on to her stomach and flicked on the bedside radio. It was nice to know what was happening in the world before getting out of bed. Although sometimes the news wasn't very interesting; all that political stuff could be mind-numbing. She didn't know why they bothered reporting it. Who would be interested in all that malarkey? Give her a good bit of gossip or scandal any time.

The news was as boring as ever. Sheila had virtually given up on it when the newscaster said, 'And finally, DJ Declan D'arcy's show has been voted the number one radio show in the country for the eighth year running. Declan says he's going to celebrate in style.' Then Declan's voice came on, 'No point in growing old unless you're going to do it disgracefully – huh?' There was the sound of loud laughter in the background before it cut to the studio again. The newsreader gave a giggle. 'Well, that's our Declan,' she tittered.

She went on to give the weather forecast but Sheila hardly heard it.

'That's my *pig* of a husband more like,' she muttered. 'I'll show him.'

She wasn't quite sure what she'd show him, but it'd be good.

40

JANE HAD DECIDED to go into town. There were a few things that she needed to buy. First on her list had been new trainers for Owen, but she'd crossed them out. He'd bought himself a pair last week out of some money he'd saved. They'd been in a sale, he said, and he just had to have them. Jane grinned. It was nice to see Owen getting enthusiastic about things for a change. He sort of coasted through life with no particular interest in anything much. Still, he'd started calling for some girl recently and Di had been slagging him about being in love with Charlotte the swot. It had caused a bit of friction at breakfast, with Owen sullenly denying that the girl was anything but a hanger-on.

Di had tapped her nose and giggled and waltzed out the door, leaving the usual trail of exasperation in her wake.

Jane kind of hoped Owen did have a girlfriend. Even though she had disputed Jim's comment the time he'd ventured his opinion on Owen being a bit down, it still bothered her. Maybe Owen was upset over the split? Maybe they'd handled things all wrong? Hadn't he bunked school? At least if he was socialising a bit more, it might mean that he was adjusting to things. She couldn't bear for her kids to be unhappy. They were the most precious things in her life and she didn't like to think that she and Jim had upset them.

She parked her car along the quay, shoved a pile of change into the parking meter and, hoisting her haversack on to her back, began the short walk into the city. She had just reached the beginning of O'Connell Street when a tap on her shoulder startled her. She whirled around and found herself face to face with a small man with peroxide-blond hair and a stud in his ear. He was wearing jeans and Doc Martens.

'Dad,' she said, the tension leaving her. She gave him a sullen look. 'Hi.'

Her dad grinned. 'Thought it was you. Nearly didn't recognise you, it's been that long.'

Jane nodded. 'Well, you didn't exactly put a time limit on the "butt out" section of our last conversation.'

Declan laughed loudly, causing passers-by to stare at them. 'Amn't I always saying that you should be on the radio?' He slapped his denim-clad thigh. 'Honestly, you're so quick with the one-liners when you have to be.'

Jane folded her arms. 'Surprised you noticed, seeing as the only person you like listening to is yourself.'

Again he laughed, a big, hearty laugh, which boomed out across the street. He always laughed at stuff that made him uncomfortable. 'So,' he asked finally, 'how're things with you?'

'Pretty good.' Damned if she was telling him anything.

'Hiya, Declan,' a pretty blonde girl called out as she walked by. 'Love the show!'

'Thanks.' Declan blew her a kiss and she giggled and nudged her mate. He turned back to her. 'Fame is pretty good too, Jane,' he chortled.

Jane remained impassive.

'Have you time for a coffee?' There was a certain awkwardness about the invitation. An almost embarrassed shyness which wasn't like him.

'OK,' she shrugged reluctantly, 'why not?'

'Why not indeed!' Declan slapped her on the back – nearly crippling her – his reserve of a second ago forgotten. 'I know just the place.'

'It'll have to be quick,' Jane lied. 'I'm meeting someone later.'

'No problemo,' Declan began to lead her through the crowds. 'I know a cool place, does great coffees, juices, whatever. And no worries about a table, they've a special one for me. Jaysus, it's been so long since I've seen ya, we'll have loads to talk about.'

That'd be something all right, Jane thought sardonically. In her whole life she'd never had a proper conversation with her dad, unless you counted all the ones where she'd begged him to make it up with her mother.

Declan was as good as his word. Walking into the restaurant, he managed to attract everyone's attention by calling the head waiter's name at the top of his voice. In a cringe-inducing Italian accent, he yelled, 'Pablo, see Declan. Uno tablo par fuck-er.' Loads of gesturing followed and Jane, ready to die with shame, was ushered by her dad to a table in the very centre of the restaurant.

'Si?' the head waiter asked, pen poised.

'I'll, eh, have a coffee with the frothy bits and the spicy stuff,' Declan said with authority. 'Jane?'

'Just an ordinary coffee,' she mumbled. 'Thanks.'

The coffees arrived quickly, along with two small cream cakes. 'To congratulate you,' the waiter said.

Declan gave a self-deprecating bellow. 'Aw, thanks. Thanks.'

Some of the customers clapped politely and Declan stood up and took a bow. 'This is my daughter,' he said loudly, gesturing to Jane, 'in whom I am well pleased.'

Laughter was followed by more clapping. Jane had to smile like a performing seal. She wanted to die.

When the fuss had abated, Declan pushed one of the cakes towards her. 'Eat up there now, feed your face. Getting something for free always makes it taste better.'

'Why did he congratulate you?' Jane asked. The cake was nice though she'd have preferred a Danish.

'The best show on radio,' Declan said. 'I won it again.'

'Great.'

'Great indeed,' her dad said, totally missing the fact that she was being sarcastic. 'No one else can come close. My listenership figures are in orbit at this stage.' He beamed at her but there was a certain something missing from his eyes. It was the sort of smile she used sometimes when she didn't really feel like smiling.

'So, how's everyone?' he asked.

Jane shrugged. 'Fine.'

'Di?'

'She's just finished her Junior Cert and has managed somehow to latch on to an appalling boyfriend.'

'Yeah. How so?'

He actually sounded interested. But she didn't feel like elaborating. With her dad, he was liable to announce it over the airwaves. 'Dunno. But he's awful.'

'Aw, you're doing a Sheila on it. She never liked Jim. D'you remember?'

'I am doing nothing of the sort!' Honestly!

Realising that he'd put his foot in it, her dad changed tack, 'And how's my grandson?'

'Fine.'

'Good. Good.' Declan spooned sugar into his cappuccino. 'He still doing the skateboarding?'

That had been years ago. It just showed how much interest her dad had in her family.

'He stopped doing that,' she said icily. 'It was too dangerous.'

Declan chortled. 'And what lad stops doing something when it's too dangerous?'

'I *made* him stop.'

Silence.

'Oh, yeah. Right. Of course.' Her dad flushed. 'Very sensible too.'

And it had been. Even if Owen had been the best skateboarder around. Jane swallowed the last of her coffee and wondered how best to leave. This conversation-making was hopeless.

'And how are you?' Declan asked, 'since you and Jim . . .' his voice trailed off. Apologetically, he muttered, 'I met him a while ago – gave his crisps a plug on the show. He looked tired, I thought.'

All his socialising, Jane thought morosely.

'So,' he asked again, 'how are you?'

'Single.' She gave him a bright smile. Indicating her coffee cup, she said, 'I have to—'

'And Sheila?' He blurted the question out, his face flushing. 'Has she moved out yet? Set up in digs?'

The idea of her mother in digs brought a smile to her face. 'No, she's still with me. Why don't you ring and talk to her yourself?'

He ignored that. 'And I suppose she's helping out around the house, is she?' He looked cockily at her. 'Cleaning and dusting and hoovering to earn her keep.'

Jane felt sorry for her mother. 'Actually, Dad, she has a job.'

Coffee spluttered all over the table as Declan began to cough. 'A job? Sheila? My arse she has!'

'She makes sandwiches and rolls in a shop up the road from the salon.'

Declan gave a huge belt of a laugh. Coffee went everywhere. Jane was practically drowned.

'Sheila, a sandwich-maker? Jaysus!' He wiped his nose with his sleeve as coffee started to run down it, then, unable to stem the flow, he pulled his napkin out of his wine glass and began a mopping-up operation. 'That's a joke – right?'

'No,' Jane said weakly as she fished her own napkin out of her glass to wipe her face. She probably shouldn't have said anything. Her mother would kill her. But she was only sticking up for her when all was said and done. 'It's true,' she confirmed, remaining stony-faced. 'It's a good job. She works on her own in the shop on Sundays. And she's even started giving *nail* demonstrations.'

'And – makes – fucking – sandwiches!' Declan was coiled up laughing. His body shook trying to keep it in. 'The woman who has trouble buttering bread is making sandwiches for the good people of Dublin.'

Jane had to leave. To minimise the damage it was important to make a dignified exit. 'Thanks for the coffee,' she said briskly, refusing to be drawn into his laughter. 'Bye now.'

She didn't think her father even noticed. Well, there was a surprise.

41

IT HAD BEEN a good night, Jim thought, as he awoke in Debbie's bed. It hadn't started out too promising though, with Debbie being really narky at first. But when he'd told her of his seven-hour liquid lunch with Philip and his subsequent humongous hangover, she'd begun to thaw. A dinner and a few drinks later and he was feeling dead guilty as she radiated warmth and adoration for him once again. The night ended with her suggestion that they go back to her place.

'But what about Gillian?'

'She'll have gone to bed,' Debbie said.

So he'd followed her into her apartment and up to her bedroom. She'd flicked on the bedside lamp, which gave a dim yellow glow to the room. Taking his hand, she'd led him to the bed.

Sleeping after sex was a damn sight better than sleeping after downing a few cans, Jim thought.

It was five-thirty. Dawn light was just seeping into the bedroom and Jim knew he wouldn't sleep any more that night. He decided to get up, grab a coffee, and head back to his place to pick up some gear for work. He'd leave Debs a note or something.

He dressed silently, half-buttoning his shirt and shoving his socks into his trouser pockets. Carrying his shoes, he tiptoed towards the door. Debbie didn't stir. She looked great with all her black hair fanned out on the pillow. Jim opened the door and closing it silently behind him, made his way to the kitchen.

He jumped, startled, at the sight of Gillian nursing her own coffee.

'Hiya,' she mumbled.

Her eyes were red and her hair, normally so bushy and bouncy, was flat and uncared for. Snot was running from her nose and Jim, after staring horrified at her for a while, handed her a piece of kitchen tissue. 'Thanks,' she muttered, as she rubbed her face vigorously.

'Another coffee?' he asked. At least she was being civil to him.

'Yeah.'

They sat in silence as the kettle boiled: Gillian sniffing and blowing her nose, and Jim wishing he'd just done a runner when he'd woken up. Pouring the water into the coffee, he carried two mugs to the table. Shoving one of them across to her, he asked, trying not to sound too hopeful, 'D'you want me to go?'

'I thought he loved me, Jim,' Gillian said. A big fat tear rolled down her face and plopped into her mug. 'I really, really did.'

He was useless at this weepy stuff. Useless. Gulping hard, he wondered what to say. The truth maybe? 'I think he did,' he said. 'Does,' he amended.

Gillian looked up at him. 'Naw. He wouldn't have treated me so bad if he did.' More tears. More sniffing. More snot. More kitchen paper.

Jim wrapped his hands around his mug, gripping it as if it were some sort of lifeboat. 'He's been in a bad way since you broke up,' he consoled.

It was the wrong thing to say. She got hysterical. Hyperventilating and glaring at him, she said through her tears, 'And I'm not? Is that what ya saying?' Her bottom lip curled downwards and she sniffed loudly. Pointing to herself, she snuffled, '*I* am the injured party· hee-a.'

'Naw,' Jim hastened to explain, 'I meant that I've never seen him so cut up about anything before. Like, he normally doesn't care if it's over, but he does this time. He's in bits.'

Gillian blinked her swollen eyes. 'Then why won't he ring me? What's stopping him?'

Jim shrugged. 'Dunno.'

'He's a shit, that's what.' A fresh batch of tears loomed.

'Why don't *you* ring *him*?' Jim asked.

Gillian looked at him as if he were mental. 'He's the one who told me to get lost! Are you joking? I do have some pride, ya know!'

Jim winced. Why couldn't he just keep his mouth shut? 'Look Gillian,' he said, trying to sound concerned yet not concerned, 'I dunno the ins and outs of the situation, so I can't comment. I don't want to say the wrong thing, OK? All I know is that Fred is more upset than I've ever seen him before – OK?'

'Do you wanna know the ins and outs?' Gillian virtually shrieked. 'Do you?'

Oh sweet Jesus. 'Naw,' he shook his head.

'What the hell is going on?' Debbie, white-faced, tore into the kitchen. Seeing Jim and Gillian there, she demanded, 'Well?'

There were more tears from Gillian. Jim stood by helplessly as Debbie put her arms around her friend and sat her back down on her chair. Jesus, give me Fred's binges any time, he thought.

Eventually Debbie calmed Gillian down. Getting her a fresh coffee, she made her sip it. 'Now, what's all this crying about, Gill?' she prompted. 'Come on. You'll have to tell me sooner or later. You can't keep things to yourself like this.'

'I'll, eh, just go . . .' Jim began to back out of the kitchen.

'No!' Gillian's sharp tone stopped his getaway cold. 'No, I want you both to hee-a what a swine Freddie is. He hasn't the nerve to tell you, so I'm gonna.' She sniffed, pulled herself upright in her chair and announced loudly, 'I'm pregnant!' Then she burst into more sobs.

Debbie looked at Jim. He looked at her.

'Aw, poor baby.' Debbie cradled Gillian's head in her arms.

'Don't mention babies,' Gillian wailed.

Jim was rooted to the spot. Gillian pregnant, he should have guessed. What else would send Fred into such a tailspin?

'How far gone?' Debbie asked, gently pushing Gillian's hair back from her face.

'Five months.' Gillian had begun to hiccup. 'And Freddie don't wanna know and I can't get rid of it, I can't.'

'Has he asked you to?' Debbie glared up at Jim as if it was all his fault.

'He just says he don't wanna know.' Gillian buried her head in Debbie's shoulder. 'And he says that . . . that . . .' She began to sniff again.

'It's OK,' Debbie soothed.

When Gillian got herself back under control, she continued, 'He says that I didn't really know him. That I nevea did. He says he hates sports and hiking and stuff and that we'd nothing in common and that it wouldn't work out and . . .' Her voice grew jumbled as she explained everything that Fred had said.

Jim was suddenly reminded of Matt, the way, if he fell, he'd cry and blubber and no one would have a clue what he was on about.

'What the hell are you smiling at?' Debbie snapped.

He hadn't been smiling, he didn't think. 'Nothing,' he mumbled. Images of his little boy disappeared and he was left with the heartbreak that was going on in front of him. 'Look, I'll go. I'll call you later, OK?'

Debbie barely nodded. She continued stroking Gillian's hair and telling her to 'let it all out'.

Jim, feeling as if somehow it was all his fault, let himself out of the flat. Jesus, he thought, Fred was a right bastard.

When he got back to the flat, Fred was sprawled out on the sofa, snoring loudly. He stank of beer and sweat and vomit. Jim's stomach did an involuntary roll as he surveyed his friend. There was a tiny part of him that actually felt sorry for Fred. It was no fun when your worst nightmares suddenly became reality.

Jim flicked on the switch for hot water and soon he was washed and shaved and ready to head off. Fred seemed to stir slightly at the sound of the electric razor so Jim moved closer to him and began to shave into his face.

'Uuuggh!' Fred moaned as he turned his head away. He put his hands over his ears and curled up in a foetal position on the sofa.

'How's Daddy today?' Jim asked, before he could stop himself. 'Enjoying drowning your responsibilities in drink?'

It was as if he'd put a bomb under him. Fred sat bolt upright, decided that it wasn't a good idea and sank back down again. White-faced he looked at Jim. 'She told you,' he said, sounding completely terrified. Then he groaned, 'Out of me way.' He stood up, pushed Jim away and staggered towards the bathroom.

Jim flicked off his shaver and waited for Fred to re-emerge.

'Sorry 'bout that,' Fred muttered sheepishly.

Jim said nothing, just continued to stare at him.

'Well how the hell do I know it's mine?' he snapped defensively.

'You said that to her, did you?'

'Damn right, I did.' Fred attempted to regain some dignity. He stood upright and walked in a straight line to the sofa. 'Women will all try and sucker you.'

'You know damn well it's yours,' Jim snapped. 'Unless it's a bloody immaculate conception. Yez were always together.'

Fred looked mutinously at him. 'It's none of your business – so keep out.'

'She's in bits you know. It's not good for her to be like that, not if she's pregnant.'

'Well, that's her fault, isn't it?' Fred stood up and faced him. 'Now, Jimbo, if you want to stay here, just keep that,' he jabbed at his nose, 'out!'

'You can't keep drinking and just hope it'll go away, you know,' Jim said.

Fred said nothing for a second. Then, a sneer curling his lips, he said calmly, 'So what? I should copy you, is that what you're saying?'

'What?' Jim was puzzled. 'Copy me?'

'Yeah.' Fred nodded. 'Work all the hours in the fucking day and hope things will go away that way.'

For a second, Jim was stunned. 'I bloody well don't,' he snapped. 'My job is a busy bloody job. I have to work, otherwise I go under.'

'Yeah, you'd go under all right, having to face things, wouldn't you, Jimbo?'

'Aw, Jesus.' Jim turned away from him, his heart hammering. 'You're still drunk. I'm going to work!' Hands fumbling, he zipped up his laptop.

'The solution to everything!' Fred called as he left. 'Work.'

'Naw, the solution to this is that I'm leaving.' Jim turned back to him. 'As soon as I get a decent place, I'm gone.'

'That's what you said to Jane too, was it?' Fred sneered.

Jim's answer was a slam of the door.

42

NERVOUSLY, JANE PRESSED the buzzer. A crackled voice answered. 'Who is it?'

'Me. Jane.'

There was a silence, then a very grumpy, 'What do you want?'

'Well, seeing as you've returned none of my calls, I thought it'd be nice to talk.' Jesus, she wondered, was she doing the right thing? Miranda was prickly enough, without her making things worse, but it had been two weeks now and she still hadn't come back to work. For some reason that she couldn't understand, she felt she needed Miranda to come back. Patrick was talking about advertising her job and Jane just couldn't let it happen without doing something.

The buzzer went to allow access to the building and as Jane climbed the stairs, admiring the wallpaper and carpets in the foyer, she thought that though Miranda might be stupid where guys were concerned, she was dead clever with money. The apartment block was beautiful.

Miranda was waiting for her at the door to her apartment. 'Come in,' she said, not sounding a bit pleased to see her, 'you'll have to excuse the state of me, I haven't had a chance to shower yet.'

She wore a long silk gown, patterned with large flowers. Her dark hair shone and even the fact that she looked as if she'd only just climbed out of bed couldn't obscure how good-looking she was.

'Tea?'

'Yeah, if you're making some.'

Without a word, Miranda padded out to the kitchen and reappeared a few minutes later with two mugs of tea. 'No sugar, loads of milk, right?'

'Ta.'

Sitting down in a chair opposite her, Miranda curled her feet under her and cupped her mug in both hands. She regarded Jane with cat-like eyes. She was a bit like a cat, Jane thought. Unapproachable and unreachable.

'Why didn't you return my calls?' Jane asked, trying not to sound hurt about it.

Miranda shrugged. 'And say what?' She arched her sculptured eyebrows. 'You only rang to ask me to go back, and until he apologises, I'm not setting foot in that place.' She took a sip of tea, all the while regarding Jane. '*Is* he going to apologise?'

Jane attempted a smile. 'Aw, Mir, just come back – he won't mention it. It'll be forgotten about.'

'Forgotten about?' The cool woman evaporated, to be replaced by the Mir Jane did know. Eyes blazing, she spat, 'Patrick called me a slapper—'

'He didn't!'

'Like hell he didn't – it's what he meant. He said I was stupid about fellas. Well,' she tossed her head defiantly, 'he can't go about saying stuff like that to his staff. I could sue him!'

'Don't be ridiculous. It was a fight. Said in the heat of the moment. I mean, look at what you said to Rosemary. That wasn't very nice either.'

'Rosemary is a twit. Full of big ideas and stupid dreams.'

'There's nothing wrong with having dreams.'

'There is if you're as thick as Rosemary.'

Jane left it. Arguing about Rosemary was not going to solve the situation. 'Look, forget about her, let's talk about you.' She attempted a smile. 'Will you come back?'

'He said I was lazy,' Miranda said next. She scowled at Jane, 'Am I lazy?'

'No.' Jane shook her head. 'No more than the rest of us anyway.'

'What?' Mir glared at her. 'So I *am* lazy?'

'He just meant that you'd grown complacent about cutting people's hair. We all have. It's important to keep up to date, branch out, attract younger customers. If there is one thing Cutting Edge has done for us, it's that.' She paused. 'You are not lazy, Mir.' Mir's softening expression made her say, 'If he'd been rowing with me, he would have said the same thing.'

It was the wrong thing to say. Mir's eyes darkened. 'Only thing is,' she said bitterly, 'you and Patrick never row, do you? He tells you all his little secrets and you tell him yours and I'm left out in the cold the whole time.'

'What?'

'I'm like a spare in that place. You and him are as thick as thieves.'

'He's my partner, Mir. We have to be.'

'He goes out with me at least once a week and does he tell me about his new fella? No.' She folded her arms and glared at Jane. 'But I bet he told you the first chance he got.'

'He told me the night we last went out together. You were too busy with a fella to bother.'

'Well, he had a chance to tell me after that.'

'When?' Jane found herself annoyed all of a sudden. This was petty. This was not what she'd come to talk about. 'You're too busy talking about your own disasters to listen to him.'

'Ooooh.' Mir stood up. 'So now you think I'm a slapper as well!'

'Oh, for God's sake—'

'If all you've come for is to have a go, then, then, then go!' Mir pointed to the door, her hand shaking.

Jane stood up. This was not meant to happen. She'd never rowed with Mir before, but then again, Mir had never shouted at her like this before. 'I didn't come to have a go.' Jane tried to keep her voice steady. This was awful. It was like her whole life was crumbling down around her. First Jim, then her parents and now Mir. 'I just want you to come back to work. Please. We need you. Business is even picking up.'

'Well, bully for you and Patrick. But I don't let my employers call me a slapper and get away with it.'

'Mir, we're your friends.'

'Some friends.'

'Well, we care more about you than the ones you pick up on a Saturday night.'

Her words hit home. She was sorry she'd said them the minute they were out. Miranda looked as shocked by her as she had been by Patrick.

'Get out.'

'Mir, I'm sorry. I didn't—'

'OUT!'

'I'm sorry.'

'You can still get out.'

Jane stood her ground. There was no way her friendship was going to end like this. 'You can't keep letting people treat you like that,' she said.

Miranda began physically shoving her towards the door.

'That's all Patrick meant. You have to cop on Mir. You could have anyone, don't go for the dregs. You deserve—'

'Out!'

'—better!'

'What in the name of Jaysus is going on?'

The male voice froze both women in their tracks. Miranda glared at whoever was behind Jane. 'Fuck off and let me deal with this.'

'Hi, Jane, nice to see you.'

Jane turned around and saw Harry looking at them both in amusement. 'Did I miss something?'

She was flustered. What the hell had possessed her? Other tenants were looking at them from the safety of their doors. 'I, eh, was just going,' she mumbled.

'So I see,' Harry nodded. 'Mir was helping you. She's awful helpful is Mir.'

'Fuck off back to your cave, Harry!' Miranda made to slam the door.

Harry stuck his foot in the gap and got a right wallop for his troubles. He looked unperturbed by it. 'Jane, maybe you can enlighten me as to why she's lost her job? She won't tell me. I'm awful worried about her. I keep calling in to see how she's doing. Bringing her,' he fished out a naggon of vodka from his pocket, 'little treats to loosen her mouth, but she still won't tell me.'

'Loosen my legs more like,' Miranda said darkly.

Hurt flashed across Harry's face. 'You know that's not true,' he said quietly.

'Isn't it?' Miranda arched an eyebrow at him.

Harry flushed and shoved the vodka back into his pocket. 'See you around, Mir.'

His voice was cold and Jane saw that even Mir looked stunned by it. But she recovered. 'In your dreams,' she spat after him. When Harry carried on walking, Mir turned blazing eyes on Jane, 'Now, see what you've done! You made me say horrible things to him.'

'I didn't make you say anything,' Jane said, startled. 'You—'

'You put me in a bad mood. Now,' Mir said, 'go and sort someone else's life out. Your parents, how about them?'

The hurt started in her heart and spread into every part of her. How could Miranda drag her folks into this? What had her parents ever done to her?

'Thanks Mir.' Jane swallowed hard and forced herself to keep looking at her. Taking a breath, she said, 'Patrick was right. You bloody well blame everyone else, but your life is in this mess because of *you*! No one else. You were horrible to Rosemary, horrible to—'

The door was slammed in her face.

Patrick *was* right, she thought. With Mir, it was all take, take, take.

Trying to retain some dignity, she walked down the corridor. She didn't see Harry, who'd obviously been waiting for her.

'Jane,' he asked, 'what the hell is going on?'

In a pub in Rathmines, she told him the whole story. She was fair to everyone, she thought. When she'd finished, she looked at Harry. 'She won't talk to me or Patrick – maybe you can get her to come back to work?'

Harry shook his head. 'Naw, I'm finished with all that. The girl is more trouble than she's worth.' He took a gulp of his pint and smiled ruefully, 'Never too old to learn – huh?'

'Aw Harry—'

He held up his hand. 'That stuff she said to me today? Well, she can't think too much of me, can she?' His finger, long and slender, traced patterns on the cool of the glass as he continued, 'I've loved that girl since I first met her. But, I dunno, she's just not happy, is she? Not with anything she has.'

Jane nodded. 'She doesn't realise how bloody lucky she is,' she said, her bitter voice surprising them both. At Harry's sharp look, she said, 'You know, she's good-looking, she's got a nice apartment, a good job and, if she wants it,' she paused, 'a nice guy.'

Harry smiled. 'Thanks.'

She smiled back. 'Hang in there, Harry. Maybe one day she'll realise just what she's missing.'

His smile disappeared. 'I dunno if I can. Maybe it's time to move on. Maybe the best thing to do sometimes is to walk away.'

Jane thought of Jim. She thought of how he'd left. Slowly she nodded. 'But to move on,' she said, 'it's nice to know where you're going first, isn't it?'

'Suppose.'

Jane touched his hand. 'Hang in there, OK?'

43

ANOTHER SATURDAY MORNING. Jim climbed into his car, not sure how much more rejection he could take. It had been five weeks now and his kids still refused to see him. He did get the feeling, however, that Owen wasn't angry at him any more, but that only made it more confusing. Why the hell wouldn't the kid go out with him then?

Debbie had said to give them time, it'd work out she said. Then she announced that Gillian had asked her to be godmother to her baby. 'It'll be me and Gillian,' she'd told him, at the top of her voice one evening, in the hope that Fred would hear, 'two mothers is better than a whole *heap* of fathers.'

Jim had cringed, wondering if it was true. He felt like just about the worst dad in the world. And the laugh of it was that he'd been determined to be the best dad in order to make up for his own miserable excuse for a father. Maybe Gillian's baby *would* be better off without Fred to mess its life up.

Fred, of course, was refusing to talk about Gillian or the baby, denying the fact that the whole thing had anything to do with him. He'd come off the booze and was now working as if his life depended on it. 'I'm doing a Jim on it,' he kept sneering every time he left the flat.

Relations between the two had become so bad that Jim had announced that he was leaving. Fred had barely blinked at the news.

That was the effect his leaving seemed to have on most people, Jim thought ruefully.

* * *

Jane was mortified. Well, part of her was mortified, the part of her that remembered the way Jim loved his kids. The other part of her, the nasty part, couldn't help feeling that it was his own fault. If he wanted to have a new woman, he had to pay the price.

'Sorry Jim,' she said. 'I'll kill Di when she gets back, I didn't even know she'd left and . . . well, Owen isn't feeling well.' She bit her lip. 'Or so he says.'

He nodded, blew air out through his lips. 'OK.' Then he said, 'Anyway, I guess I might as well tell you my bit of news now. I was going to let you know this evening but, well . . .' He looked questioningly at her. 'Can I come in?'

Caught off balance, she stammered out, 'Yeah, sure. Sure.' As she led the way to the kitchen, she wondered what the hell he was going to spring on her. Maybe he was dead serious over this Debbie? Jesus, her ego couldn't take that. She actually felt physically sick at the thought of it. Suddenly she wanted to shove her fingers in her ears and chant like she had when she was a kid to block out horrible stuff. Without even offering him a cup of tea, she stood in front of him with her arms folded. 'Well?' she demanded, 'what's the big news?'

'Two things.' Jim looked slightly intimidated by her aggressive stance. 'First is,' he fumbled about in his shirt pocket – a shirt she'd bought for him about five years ago, she noted. Pulling out a piece of paper, he handed it to her. 'It's my new address. I've, eh, moved out of Fred's place.'

His new address was in Rathgar. So he was moving in with this Debbie, was he? She was shocked at the sinking feeling in her stomach.

'I, eh, got a good bonus from work over the crisp thing,' Jim said as he pulled a wad of notes from his pocket. 'So I put a deposit on me own flat and here's some cash for you – well, for the kids really.'

His *own* flat. So he wasn't sharing it with Debbie or anyone. That was good, at least. Good for the kids, she thought.

'Here.' Jim held the money towards her.

Honestly, that was another bloody idiot thing he always did. No matter how much she'd badgered him, Jim had never bothered with a chequebook. He carried cash about everywhere. 'I don't need money,' she muttered, touched by his generosity. 'What we agreed on is enough.'

'It's not for you.' His voice grew intense and she saw his Adam's apple bob as he swallowed hard. 'It's for the kids. Save it for them or something.' He threw her a quick smile. 'Sure, I've probably saved as much by not taking them out on weekends.' Again, he shoved it towards her.

'The kids'll come round,' she said gently. She took the money from him and thrust it in a drawer. 'Thanks.'

'No probs.' He smiled briefly again before beginning a study of his hands. 'And, eh, another thing, eh,' his eyes met hers, 'I've been offered another job.'

'Yeah?'

He nodded. 'Uh-huh. It's marketing crisps full-time.'

Jane tried not to smile. Jim's job, though important and well paid, had always seemed funny to her. 'But isn't that what you do anyway?' she asked.

'Yeah, it is,' Jim agreed, 'but Incredible Crisps are going to do their own in-house marketing in future and they want me to head the team.'

'Oh, right.' Jane nodded. 'Well, that's great. Congratulations.'

'It'll be well paid, so that'll be good, but, well, I dunno. I dunno if I want to do it for ever.'

'Do you not?' What did he want, career advice?

'Like, if I turn the offer down, I'll get a chance to market other stuff 'cause I won't be doing the crisps any more.'

'Right.' She wondered why the hell he was telling her this.

'Plus, if I take the job,' Jim paused, 'it'll mean loads of travelling. Maybe even a move to England.'

The words hit her. 'A move?'

'Yep. It's a big job.' He looked into her face. 'Well?'

It was as if he was seeking permission from her. Well, damn

him, if he wanted to go, he could go. There was nothing stopping him. 'Well what?' she croaked out, her throat dry.

He looked taken aback. 'Well, d'you think the kids will mind? D'you think it'll work, me there, you lot here?'

'I don't know, do I?' She suddenly hated him. How could he even contemplate it, this move? How could he just up and leave them all? 'It's your choice. Why don't you ask the kids?'

'I will, but . . .' She was suddenly aware that there was only inches between them. 'What do you think? Do you want me to go?'

His brown eyes were so intense as they gazed at her, the smell of him was so familiar, she could even feel the heat from his body. Her heart flipped about in a weird way within her breast.

'What?' she stammered.

'Do you want me to go?' he asked softly.

She was aware that one word could change everything. One word and he'd probably kiss her. It was like being suspended in time, the way things seemed to slow down. 'Do *you* want to go?'

He moved closer to her. She could feel the back of his hand as it brushed hers. He didn't answer, just kept staring at her. She was vaguely aware that his hand was holding her wrist and that his thumb was caressing her palm. She wished he'd kiss her, just to feel his lips on hers.

'Well?' he asked, and there was a tremor in his voice.

She could almost taste his breath.

'Do you think I should go?'

His lips brushed hers as he asked the question. She delighted in the feel of them, the sensation of their closeness, the barest touch of them, the slight pressing of lip upon lip. His hand caressed the small of her back, his other hand creeping up to hold her head, entwine his long fingers through her hair. God, she loved that. He gave her a long, steady gaze before he kissed her, just long enough to turn her on. She arched her back and felt his body bearing down on hers as his kiss grew more passionate. She caressed the back of his neck, slipped her other hand into the back pocket of his jeans and savoured the sensation of him being so close.

He was pressing harder against her. His breath was ragged and she could feel his erection through the denim. For one glorious second she wanted him. Wanted him to love her the way he used to. Wanted to love him the way she used to.

'Oh, God, Jane,' he whispered. 'Aw, Jesus, Jane.'

His voice broke the spell. 'Get away from me!' She turned her face away and pushed him off. She was aware that somehow the top button of her shirt had become undone and her bra had been unclasped. 'Just,' she held up her hands, as if to ward him off, 'just get out, OK?'

He stood uncertainly by, looking at her and then turning his gaze to his hands.

She wondered if he managed to sound so excited when kissing Debbie. She wondered if he ran his hands through *her* hair.

'You do what's best for you.' She moved away from him, towards the sink, trying to fasten her shirt. 'It's your choice. Have a word with the kids if you like.' Pulling a bag of spuds from the press, she said, 'Now, sorry to rush you, but I've to work this afternoon, so I'm a bit busy.'

What the hell had happened there? Jim wondered. One minute he was normal and the next . . . well he didn't know. His heart was pounding like mad and there was an unmistakable bulge in his jeans. Jesus, he'd really wanted her. Did really want her. In fact, just looking at her standing by the window turned him on all over again. He opened his mouth to say something, he wasn't sure what, when she said, 'Go on, go.'

'Oh, yeah . . . OK.' He bit his lip. 'I'll talk to them next week.'

'Fine.'

'And, eh, you have my number at the new flat and . . .' his fingers tapped the leg of his jeans, 'and well . . . bye,' he finished up. Jesus, he was pathetic.

'Bye.' She gave him a weird smile. 'See you next week.'

'Bye.' He didn't move. Couldn't move. 'I would have liked to kiss you some more,' he blurted out.

Her eyes hardened. 'Jim, you've got someone else now. You're not the two-timing sort, are you?'

He seemed to stand there for an age, just looking at her. Finally he bent his head. 'No.'

Once he'd left, she put down the potato peeler and sat down at the kitchen table. She touched her lips and closed her eyes. Part of her wished she'd kept kissing him.

44

JIM STUDIED HIS two kids. Jane was working that morning and had given him the house so that he could tell the kids that he was taking the new job.

Neither of them would meet his eye. Owen was staring at the table as if he'd never seen it before and Di was alternately smiling nervously at him or else glaring in a very confrontational manner.

'Will this take long?' she asked in a pissed-off voice. 'I'm meeting Gooey in an hour.'

He didn't bother to say that he'd hoped they could go out later, he knew that would be the thing most likely to make her leave the room. 'I just want you both to know that I'm taking a new job from the beginning of December.'

No reaction.

'It'll be based in the UK so I'll probably be living over there from then on.'

Owen jerked his head up to look at him. He didn't say anything though.

Di gave a laugh. 'Oh, that's just great,' she said, in a voice that implied it was anything but.

'I'm glad you feel that way,' Jim said mildly. 'I just want—'

'Not only have you left us, not only have you found a bitch to shag—'

'Di, don't you dare—'

'—but now you're going to shirk your responsibilities as well. But I guess we shouldn't be surprised, should we Owen?'

Owen jumped as his sister barked out his name. 'Leave it, Di,' he said softly.

'No, no I won't.' Di stood up from the table. She blinked. Once. Twice. 'I hate you, Dad,' she said. 'I really hate you. How can you go and leave us?'

Her voice shook and Jim made a move towards her, but she backed away from him.

'But I haven't left you,' he said desperately. 'I'll be home every weekend if I can. You'll still see me just as often.'

'I don't want to see you. Can't you understand that?' She walked towards him then looked up at him. I – don't – want – to – see – you.'

'Look, I won't take the job if you don't want me to.'

'I don't care what you do.' Di turned on her heel and left.

'Di!' Jim made to go after her, but stopped when Owen said, 'Leave her, Dad. She's just upset.'

Jim paused, unsure.

'She thought,' Owen again stared at the table, 'well, she thought that you were going to get back with Ma, didn't she?'

'What?' Jim ran his hands through his hair. Jesus, this was a mess. Jane had asked him if he wanted her to be there, but he'd told her he'd handle it. Some job he was doing. 'Did Di tell you that?'

Owen shook his head. 'Naw, but like, it's what she always thinks. That's the way she is.'

Jim didn't know what to say. Owen was surprising like that. He was always dead wide where people were concerned. When he was a kid he'd stare at people for ages, as if he was figuring them out. It took a while before he'd ever speak to someone. 'Maybe you're right,' Jim conceded. 'And you,' he asked, as he slid into the seat opposite Owen, 'how do you feel about me taking this job?'

'It's your life.'

'Yeah, I know Owen, but you're my son.'

There was a long pause.

Owen, when he lifted his head up, had a funny look in his eyes. 'And so was Matt,' he barely whispered.

Jim felt as if he'd been hit.

'Take the job, Da, it's your life.'

With that, his son also left the kitchen.

Patrick arrived at the salon, rubbing his hands with glee. 'I talked to Barney yesterday,' he told Jane, 'and he's come up with more great ideas.'

'Yeah?' Barney was proving to be quite a powerhouse of ideas. 'What?'

Patrick glanced around the salon, which was fuller than it had been in months. 'It can wait,' he winked. 'Tell you after work. We can get a few jars and have a very interesting business discussion.'

Normally Jane would have jumped at the chance, but the last thing she wanted to be doing that night was talking business. Especially as Jim had phoned to say that it hadn't gone too well with the kids. When she'd phoned home, Di had answered, referred to Jim as a prick, told her she was glad to see the back of him and asked her did she want to speak to Owen. Owen had said that it was Jim's life.

'But how do you feel about it?' she'd pressed, wishing she could see the two of them.

'I dunno, Ma.'

And that's all he'd said on the matter.

There was so much more she felt she should say but couldn't. She knew he didn't want to hear it and it all sounded so trite anyway. I mean, she thought, as she put down the phone, were there words to apologise for messing up your kids' lives?

'So,' Debbie purred into the phone, 'how'd it go?'

'Rotten.' He didn't feel like talking to her. He didn't feel like doing anything much, except working and getting plastered, in that order.

'They'll come round,' Debbie was sympathetic, 'want company?'

'Naw,' he shook his head. 'I've a pile of work to get through. And I've to sort out the flat and stuff. Better if you stay away.'

'Sure you don't want to talk about it?'

'Positive.'

'Oh.' She sounded a bit hurt by his monosyllabic answer. 'Oh, OK then.'

'Bye now.' He ended the call and turned off his phone.

He just wanted to be on his own.

Patrick had ordered a cab for Sheila and waved her on her way. Looking distinctly put out, Sheila had muttered something about dinner and food.

'The kids will get their own,' Jane said, 'you just concentrate on mixing your yogurt into your stewed prunes.'

'Oh, OK, dahling.' Sheila air-kissed her and tottered off to her waiting cab. As she climbed in, she told the driver sternly to take her straight to her destination. 'No funny routes to up the price,' she said imperiously. 'And I don't want any opinions on politics or religion or racism discussed, please. I've done a hard day's work and I'm exhausted.'

'Can I put on deh radio?'

'As long as it's not Declan D'arcy, you may do as you please.'

'Hilarious, your mother,' Patrick commented once she was on her way. 'Highly irritating, but hilarious.'

'Highly *glamorous*,' Rosemary butted in. 'Even though she's old and all, she's an inspiration.'

'Really?' Jane glanced incredulously at Rosemary. She'd never much thought of her mother as an inspiration to anyone. 'How so?'

'Well,' Rosemary blushed, 'she's on her own and she hasn't let it get to her, has she?' She didn't wait for a reply. 'She's working in a crap job and she still does it. *And* despite all that, she always looks great, well, for an old person, I mean,' she clarified.

'Mmmm,' Jane smiled. 'I guess so. But you try living with her!'

'*And* she speaks really well, and she just looks classy. I mean, I could dress like her and stuff, but I'd never—'

'Excuse me,' Patrick tugged her sleeve. 'Jane, we've things to discuss now. Rose, you finish sweeping up the floor and you can go, all right? Don't bother to let us know, just leave.'

'Right.' Rosemary didn't like being interrupted by Patrick. She began to sweep up with bad grace.

Once in the office, Patrick outlined Barney's plans. He could barely contain the grin on his face. 'Well, you know the way Cutting Edge has all those posters in their window, showing all the winning hairstyles they've done?'

'Uh-huh – they've done the most damage to our business,' Jane said.

'Well, not any more,' Patrick almost sang. Then, as if imparting some magical secret to her, he whispered, 'He says to make out that we've won stuff too.' He sat back in his chair and observed her reaction.

'Make out we've won stuff too?' Jane couldn't believe she was hearing correctly. 'What do you mean "make out we've won stuff too"?'

'Just, you know, make out we've won things.'

'What things?'

'Hairdressing things, you fool.'

She really didn't get it. 'So, like, I go about telling everyone I've won competitions?'

'No!' Patrick chortled. 'Not exactly.'

She was smiling, but only because he seemed so hyper. 'So what the hell are you talking about?'

'This is what is so brilliant about it.' Patrick giggled slightly. 'Barney says that we can hang posters of our own models in the window and title the hairstyles. For instance, you do Rosemary's hair in a certain way and just call it "Winning Style". No one will know the difference.'

It took a second for Jane to absorb the news. 'Naw, I can't do that.' She paused. 'Can I?'

'You can!' Patrick was triumphant. 'You can call it "Championship" or "Prize-Winning" or pretty much whatever you want.'

'Jesus.' Jane was laughing. 'Are you serious?'

'As serious as cancer, darling lady.'

'And our prices – did he say anything about Cutting Edge upping their prices?'

'He said that Cutting Edge are now way overpriced. They'll have to come down at some stage.'

'Hopefully when they've lost all their business.'

'That's what he said too,' Patrick chortled.

'I like this guy,' Jane grinned. 'Can't wait to meet him.'

Patrick turned to the appointments book. 'Sooooo,' he tapped the pen against his teeth, considering, 'will I pen Rosemary in for a colour and cut next week? Can you do anything with her yet – will she allow you?'

'I won't cut,' Jane said, 'it won't have grown back in time for the IHFs. Get Nash in, Rosemary's friend, she's got good hair, I'll do some rolls and plaits and things and we'll shoot some photos. Call a few of the other models too, ones we've used before, I'll give them all a free haircut.'

'Marvellous.' Patrick rubbed his hands gleefully. 'And we'll say that you won the IHFs if anyone asks – OK?'

Jane nodded.

'Even if it was a lifetime ago,' Patrick chortled. He picked his coat up from the chair. 'So, will we celebrate with a drink or two?'

'Lead on.'

45

THANK GOD SHE was driving, Jane thought grimly, otherwise she'd be up for – what was it called when you killed your mother? – matricide or something. Her mother had spent a good part of yesterday and all of this morning wittering on and on about her dad's radio show. Of course, it didn't matter to her mother that *she* was worried too. Worried about the kids – Owen had flunked his second year exams in spectacular style. She'd have to ask Jim to have a word with him and, thinking of Jim, she was worried about his new job and the effect it was going to have on all of them. She was worried *sick* about the bloody hairdressing competition because she couldn't make up her mind what way to style Rosemary's hair. But did any of that matter to her mother? Nope. With Sheila, her dramas had to take centre stage.

Her mother jabbed her in the arm.

'Mam, how many times do I have to tell you not to do that?' Jane glared at her.

Sheila sniffed disapprovingly. 'Well, maybe if you showed some respect and answered me once in a while, I wouldn't have to.' She paused, obviously waiting for something. When nothing happened, she demanded, 'Well?'

'Well, what?' Jane snapped.

'Oh, you're in a lovely mood today, dahling.' Sighing resignedly, Sheila fished some hairspray from her bag and sprayed it all over the place.

Jane started to cough as the stuff went up her nose. 'Mother! Will you open a window!'

'And have my hair ruined? You *are* joking, dahling.'

'Uggghhh!' In exasperation, Jane tried to keep the car straight as she rolled down her own window.

Sheila looked at her as if she was acting peculiarly. 'Now, I'm not being nasty, dahling, but if you bit Jim's head off like that, it's no wonder the alley cat walked out. Not that he should have. That man had nothing before he met you. Nothing.'

'Mam,' Jane said. 'Not your business?'

Sheila smirked slightly, before patting her hair and tucking stray strands back into place. 'Point taken. Now, all I asked you was whether you'd been in contact with your father or not, that's all. I don't expect to be attacked for a simple question.'

Count to ten. One. Two. Three. 'I wasn't attacking you and the answer is "no", I haven't.'

'No need to snap, dahling.'

Jane bit her tongue and remained silent. Maybe, if she let it go, that would be an end to the conversation.

And indeed, the subject was dropped for a few minutes. Her mother shifted about uneasily in the car seat and made a few doleful remarks about the way the passenger mirror always made her look awful. She then rubbed cream into her hands and plucked her eyebrows. Eventually, when she'd finished preening herself, she muttered, 'Well, someone – I don't know who – has been telling tales. Why else is Declan running the best made-to-order sandwich competition in Dublin – tell me that now?'

Jane almost swerved into the wrong lane. Someone behind blasted her out of it. 'What?' she asked faintly.

'You heard.' Sheila gave a martyred sigh. 'I am to be humiliated yet again. Your father is running a best sandwich competition. He knows where I work. He has to.'

'It could just be a coincidence,' Jane said, a sort of sick feeling invading her.

'Not at all,' Sheila said dismissively. 'He's running it because he knows I make sandwiches – that's why.'

Oh God.

'He's trying to humiliate me. He's doing a tour of Dublin sandwich bars and the best one is going to win some piece of stupid equipment. I mean, what will Lisa say when she finds out who I am?'

'I don't know.'

Her mother continued on and on until she got out of the car.

Jane wondered if she should ring her dad and ask him what the hell he was playing at? But maybe he'd tell her to butt out again. Yep, she thought, she'd been given her orders and there was no way she was going to interfere.

But a showdown on national radio between the two of them . . . It didn't bear thinking about.

She spent the morning working on one of the models that Patrick had got hold of. OK, it meant that they couldn't take as many appointments, but it would be worth it for the posters they'd shortly be hanging in their windows. She spent ages with the model, studying her face, working out what sort of a style would suit her best. Then she'd washed, conditioned and discussed with Patrick the best colours to use. He'd suggested a mixture of highlights and lowlights and she'd run with that. And then she'd begun to cut. At first she was slightly nervous, but then her creative instincts took over and she forgot that she was copying a style from a magazine and began to add in her own touches. As she cut and shaped, Jane blotted out everything else. That's what she loved about styling, all her worries disappeared. There was nothing more satisfying than creating a new look for someone. She and Jim had often thought how similar their jobs were – he marketed products while she marketed people. She was only vaguely aware of Rosemary watching agog from her corner of the salon.

Eventually, she finished up and, standing back from the model, she studied her. It was looking good. A sort of excitement began to build at the thought of blow-drying and seeing the finished result. God, she hadn't felt like this in ages.

'Not long now,' she told the girl who was looking doubtfully at herself in the mirror. 'Thanks a million for being so patient.'

The girl smiled.

'Photographer is due in half an hour,' Patrick said.

Jane nodded. She'd be well finished in half an hour. Out with her brushes and off she went, drying the roots, smoothing the hair down, getting it as shiny as it would go.

'Wow!' Rosemary said when she'd finished. 'Wow!'

'It looks great.' The model was overwhelmed. 'Jesus, it really suits me.'

Patrick came over. 'Looking good.' He put his arm about her. 'You haven't lost it, honey chicks, you haven't lost it.'

The haircut was a mid-length style with broken up layers. The ends were textured to give a soft but edgy feel and Patrick's colours made the whole thing look quite stunning.

'I think we'll call that one "Champions Hair".' Patrick kissed her on the cheek. 'Done by a champion.'

Jane smiled. Patrick was right. She really hadn't lost it. In fact, as she looked at it, she conceded that it was bloody brilliant. 'I reckon Cutting Edge will be 'edge cutting by the time we finish with them,' she joked.

'Stick to the hairdressing,' Patrick patted her on the head. 'Don't go it as a comedian.'

46

JIM TOOK A deep breath and tapped on Owen's bedroom door. It was the last thing he needed, a row with a son that he was barely on speaking terms with. If anything, the talk Jane wanted him to have with Owen would finish the relationship completely. On the other hand, if he didn't talk to him, Jane would be mega pissed off.

'I'm not asking you to row with him,' she'd said, 'just urge him to do better next year. I've already had a go at him over the results so I want you to give him some positive encouragement. We have to present a united front on this, Jim.'

Of course, she was right.

Just before he entered Owen's room, Jim glanced again at the results. How had the kid done it? One pass in English and an across the board fail in everything else. He didn't know whether to be angry or upset. 'Owen,' he called, 'can I come in?'

'Uh-huh.' Owen muted the television and sat up straight on his bed. His face was pale and wary-looking. 'Is this about me exam results?' he asked.

'Yep.' Jim sat down on the chair beside his bed. 'They're pretty appalling.'

'I know.' He paused. 'Sorry.'

'I want your promise that next year you'll do better. Or at least try to.'

'Yeah.'

This was going well, Jim thought. 'And if you've any problems that you'll talk to us and we'll try and sort them out. Get you extra tuition, whatever – OK?'

'Uh-huh.'

Jim wondered what else he should say. The whole thing had been very easy. And the fact that Owen was actually talking to him for the first time in weeks made him want to stay there and try to bridge the gap between them. 'It's not that we want you to be a genius, Owen,' he said, 'but you can do better, I know you can.'

Owen gave him a quick glance and shrugged.

'So,' Jim continued, 'what went wrong? Did you just go blank?'

'Nah,' Owen sighed, shot him a weary look. 'It was all the bunking off. I already told Mam this.'

'What?' Jim asked. 'What bunking off?'

Owen's face went even paler than normal. 'Nothing,' he stammered. 'Sorry.'

'What bunking off?' Jim asked, his voice rising. 'What are you on about? Did you bunk school?'

Owen looked at his hands and didn't answer.

'Answer me!'

'It was nothing. I don't—'

'Jesus Christ, Owen, why the hell did you bunk school?'

Owen seemed to flinch at his words. Jim attempted to touch him but he shrugged him off.

'D'you not like it? Do you not?' Owen still didn't respond and Jim looked at him despairingly. 'Well?'

'Is there something wrong?' Jane poked her head in the door. She looked ready to avert a fight. 'I thought I heard—'

'Did you know he bunked school?' Jim asked, turning to her. 'He's after telling me that—'

'I know,' Jane said, a bit too calmly, he thought.

'But sure, that's why he failed his exams,' Jim went on. He felt relieved that at least now he had a reason for the crap results. At least Owen wasn't completely stupid. 'How long has this been going on?'

Owen looked at him. 'I went in for the last couple of months.' He glanced quickly at his mother and then his gaze returned to his hands.

It was the gaze that did it. The silence that followed. The way Jane blushed furiously and averted her eyes from his. Jim looked in bewilderment from one to the other. Finally, he said, as he pointed at Owen, 'Am I getting this right – he's been bunking off and you never told me?'

'I think we should discuss this downstairs,' Jane said firmly.

'I'm his dad,' Jim stood up. He held the exam results towards her. His fist was clenched and the paper had crumpled. 'D'you not think I've a right to know that kind of stuff?'

'I sorted it,' Jane said. 'There was no need for you to know.'

'There was *every* need.' Jesus, he couldn't even shout at her and he wanted to, he really did, but the hurt seemed to have won out over the anger. 'I'm his dad,' he repeated despondently.

At least she had the decency to look ashamed. 'Yeah, maybe you're—'

'Maybe?' This was his wife, this was his son. His bloody family for Christ's sake. '*Maybe*?' he repeated. He felt as if he'd been hit with a sledgehammer.

'I'm sorry—' Jane began.

'Save it.' Jim threw the results at her as he walked out of the room. 'Draw me up a list of stuff I can be included in, OK? Gimme a call when it's done.'

From behind, he heard her go 'Aw, Jim' and he heard Owen stammer out an apology for landing her in it. After she'd told him not to worry, he heard her come out of the room after him.

He took the stairs two at a time and she'd only just managed to wrench the front door open as he drove off.

He knew Debbie was getting a bit pissed off with him, but he couldn't help it. She'd be in the middle of telling him something about work or a funny story and he'd come out with, 'I didn't think she'd exclude me like that. I never knew she could be so fucking horrible.'

This time, Debbie folded her arms and glared at him. 'Well, if you didn't think she could be so fucking horrible – why did you leave her?' she snapped.

'Sorry,' he apologised. 'I'm sorry – what's that, what were you saying?'

Debbie regarded him through narrowed eyes. He knew enough to know that that meant she was quite mad. 'Forget what *I* was saying,' she said. 'I'd much rather know why you left your wife.'

Jim turned from her and walked towards the window. Jesus, where had that come from? Tell her why he'd left Jane?

Debbie came to stand beside him. She too stood gazing out on to the back yard. Her voice softer now, she said, 'It's something we've never discussed, Jim. In fact, you've discussed nothing with me about yourself. OK, I know what you do for a living, I know you like junk food and gadgets,' she gave a small laugh, 'I know *The Simpsons* is your favourite TV programme, but do I know anything else?' There was a pause. 'Nope.'

'There's not a lot else to know,' Jim said as casually as he could. 'It's not important.' His eyes stayed glued on a wheelie bin with a big smiley face stuck on to it. It was so naff, yet it touched him.

'It's not important that you spent almost sixteen years with a woman that Fred said you were so cracked over you practically kissed her knickers every night?'

'What?' Jim turned to face Debbie. 'You talked about me to Fred? Jesus,' he laughed crazily, 'I thought *he* was an asshole!'

Debbie flushed. 'Well, I got Gillian to ask him about you when I first met you. That's what she said that he said.'

'Oh yeah, and what else did he say?'

'Nothing.'

'What else?' Jim poked her with his finger. 'Go on.'

'Nothing!'

He began jabbing her with both fingers. That normally got Jane into fits of giggles. Instead, Debbie pushed him off and told him to grow up. 'So, you gonna tell me what happened between you and wonder wife or what?'

'Nothing happened,' he muttered, feeling a strange sense of loneliness. His hands dangled uselessly by his sides and he shoved them into the pockets of his jeans. 'We just, I dunno, drifted apart.'

'You drifted apart?' Debbie sounded as if she was either madly disappointed or completely disbelieving. 'Your marriage ended because you drifted apart?'

'Yep.' Thank God all that explaining was over. Jim wondered if she wanted to head out for a drink. He could do with a few to try and forget the hurt of earlier. 'Do you—'

'Did she drift or you drift?'

'Both. Eh, do you—'

'Where? Into someone else's arms or what?'

'Naw, nothing like that. We just . . .' Jim gulped. How did he explain? He'd never had to explain stuff before. 'It just ended.'

'But you loved her?' Debbie asked. 'At the end, did you love her?'

The way she asked the question was so intense that Jim knew it was important how he answered. It made him feel a bit trapped. 'Yeah,' he said simply. 'I did.'

Debbie gulped.

'But, and I swear to this,' he gave her a small grin and crossed his heart, 'I never spent me time kissing her knickers.'

Debbie smiled. She reached out and pulled him towards her. 'I'm crazy about you,' she whispered, entwining her arms around his neck. 'It makes me feel weird to think that there's another woman out there who had you first. I feel I have to compete, you know?'

He hadn't a bloody clue, but he nodded anyway.

'Come here, you.' She kissed him slowly on the mouth. Pulling away from him, she smiled suddenly. 'One day, Jim McCarthy, I'm going to figure you out. I swear I am.'

He gave a weak laugh. What was she on about?

The ringing of his phone shattered the moment. Jim was glad of the interruption, as he still couldn't get the fact of Jane not telling him about Owen out of his head. Even when Debbie was covering his neck with kisses, it wouldn't shift. Debbie was bound to notice his lack of interest if she carried on. 'Hang on a sec, Debs.' He moved away from her, ignoring her pout, and began his usual search for his mobile. He eventually found it under his jacket and flicked it on. 'Hi. Jim McCarthy.'

'Jim, it's Jane.'

Jim glanced at Debbie, mouthed, 'It's Jane', then watched Debbie flounce over to the table, fold her arms and glare across at him. 'What?' he said shortly.

'I'm sorry about earlier,' Jane muttered. 'I know I probably should have told you about Owen, but it all happened so quickly, it was all over so quickly that there didn't seem to be much need.'

'So, like, I'm not needed, is that it?' He didn't know whether he was being nasty to impress Debbie or to hurt Jane.

'No. That is not it.' Jane sounded hurt and he was glad. 'I'll tell you things in future.'

'OK.'

'But eh,' Jane hesitated slightly and Jim knew she was about to hammer him. She could always do it. Whenever she apologised and caught him off guard, she'd then land in with the big guns. It was something he'd slagged her over before, but now he knew it wasn't going to be funny.

'Well,' she began innocently, 'when I told you about Gooey and attempted to involve you, you said that there was nothing you could do.'

'And there wasn't.'

'Oh, yeah, like hell!' Jane scoffed. 'You just couldn't have been bothered. I mean, how am I supposed to know what you will be bothered to sort out and what you won't? Di is out every night with that waste of space. But can I do anything? No. Have I tried? Yes! Have you? No. Will you? Not bloody likely!'

Jim said nothing. Debbie shot him sympathetic looks across the room which he ignored. He kind of wished that Debbie wasn't there.

'Anyway,' Jane went on, not seeming to have noticed his lack of reply, 'I'll write down and inform you of all the comings and goings from now on. It'll be great to have some support at last.'

The last bit hurt. She would never forget, or let him forget, for that matter. 'I thought you rang to apologise,' he said steadily.

'Yes.' She sounded flustered.

'Well, you've done that. Thanks.' He flicked the phone off and immediately wished he hadn't. He stood staring at it for a couple of seconds and was startled when Debbie gave him a cheer.

'Way to go!' She giggled. 'Jesus, I'd hate to have a row with you. All that ranting and raving for nothing.'

Jim pocketed his mobile. He'd never rowed with Jane over the phone before. In fact, he'd never cut her off full rant in his whole life.

He'd never had to. He could always make her laugh instead.

As Debbie put her arms around him and buried her face in his neck, the sense of loneliness he'd felt earlier washed over him again.

47

WITH LONG, CONFIDENT strokes, Jane brushed Rosemary's hair until it fell like shiny springs down her back. All the conditioning treatments had made it gleam like something from a shampoo ad. With the right style, it could look fantastic. Jane still hadn't decided exactly what she was going to do, the shape of Rosemary's face would support quite a few styles well. Tonight she was just going to trim it to get rid of split ends and then cut it in a basic shape that could be manipulated without too much trouble.

She had just finished a section of Rosemary's hair when someone knocked on the front door.

'We're closed,' she shouted. 'Come back in the morning.'

'I want to talk now. We need to sort things out.' Pete Jordan was peering into the salon. 'This is getting ridiculous.'

Jane almost dropped her scissors in shock. For a second, she didn't quite know what to do. Then, after telling Rosemary not to move, she ran to fetch Patrick from the office. 'It's Pete Jordan and he wants to talk,' she whispered. 'What'll we do?'

'We let him talk,' Patrick said matter-of-factly. 'You open the door, we'll chat in here.'

'But I've Rosemary.'

'OK, we'll chat outside.' Patrick stood up. 'Now, just remember, concentrate on Rosemary's hair, don't go making mistakes at this stage. And for God's sake, honey pie, don't lose the head!'

Jane glanced quickly at him. *Don't lose the head.* He'd come a long way in a few months – Patrick used to lose his head on a regular basis.

She smiled and watched as he opened the door.

'Hello.' Pete Jordan nodded curtly at them before taking the seat that Patrick proffered. 'I thought it would be the best time to call, seeing as we've both shut up shop.'

'I've just this style to finish.' Jane brought Rosemary down to where Peter sat. 'I'll listen in.'

Pete hardly heard her. He was gazing in open admiration at Rosemary. 'Hey, great hair,' he said, impressed.

'Ooooh,' Rosemary giggled uncontrollably. 'Thank you very much. That's very nice of you. It's only really because Jane has been putting stuff into it every week.'

'Your model?' Pete asked.

'My model.' Jane tried not to sound too smug. Rosemary would be a match for his any day.

'And the girl in the posters?' Pete indicated the window.

'What about her?'

'Is she someone you used to use before?'

'Patrick.' Jane turned to him with a smile. 'Can you answer that?'

'I know,' Pete said, without giving Patrick time to answer, 'that this salon has never won a single thing. That shit,' he indicated the posters, 'is false advertising.'

'Oh,' Patrick managed to sound as if he'd never heard the word 'shit' before. 'Do we have to trade obscenities? Can we not just talk about things in a civilised manner?'

Pete made a sound very much as if he was choking.

'What exactly seems to be your problem, Pete?'

'Your signs. They're completely bogus. And I've also checked and no one from here has ever won an IHF award.'

Little feck, checking up on them, Jane thought. 'I've won it actually,' she said.

'Oh yeah, right,' Pete made a face. 'There is no record of a Jane McCarthy *ever* winning,' he folded his arms.

'That's because I registered under Jane D'arcy,' Jane said. 'I won Trainee of the Year.'

Pete looked taken aback. 'Sure, but that must have been years ago,' he spluttered.

'It was,' Jane nodded. 'But I don't like being called a liar, Mr Jordan, and if all you can do is sling insults, why don't you just leave? Right now.'

'I'm only here to try and sort things out,' Pete said.

'You're only here sorting things out because your pockets are feeling the pinch,' Jane retaliated.

Pete glared at her.

'Competition, Mr Jordan,' she continued, 'ever heard of it? If you can't stand the heat, then get out of the kitchen.'

Pete Jordan glared at her for a second. Flicking a glance at Rosemary, he nodded. 'See you in October at the IHFs. I'll turn your heat right off Miz McCarthy.'

'Hot or cold, it doesn't bother me.'

'Well,' Pete licked his lips. 'I can see calling down here was a waste of time. Maybe you and I will make more progress on our own, Patrick?'

God help him if he agreed, Jane thought. She'd brain him so she would.

'Ooooh,' Patrick hugged himself. Putting on a camp voice, he said, 'I'd love to make progress with you Pete. Come on, come on in here.'

All three burst out laughing as Pete rushed out the door.

'You know, I rang her this afternoon,' Patrick said as he came back from the bar with two pints. He sat down opposite Jane and looked expectantly at her.

They had decided to go for a drink to celebrate annoying Pete Jordan.

Jane took a sip of Carlsberg before putting the glass down. 'Who?' she asked. 'Who did you ring?'

'My old drinking buddy,' Patrick answered mildly. Before Jane could say anything, he held up his hand. 'It was a disaster.' He spread his arms wide and made a tragic face. 'I just told her that her job was open if she felt like coming back. I mean, it was nothing we hadn't said before.'

'And?'

'Oh, she said some dreadful things.' Patrick tut-tutted, making another face. 'I think she wanted me to grovel, but honestly Jane, what more could I do?'

With that question, his drama-queen mask slipped and Jane saw that he really did want to know. She reached out and patted him on the hand. 'Nothing,' she said. 'You've done your best. She knows she can come back.'

'She said some really quite horrible things,' Patrick said, sounding hurt.

'That's Mir though – isn't it?'

Patrick nodded morosely. 'Her own worst enemy.'

They drank in silence for a bit before Patrick asked hesitantly, 'And, dare I ask, how's your life going?'

'Awful.' Jane bit her lip. 'Jim is pissed at me, Di is in love, Owen failed his exams and my mother and father are about to launch World War Three live on radio.'

'What?' An amused smile danced across Patrick's face. 'Your mother and father what?'

So Jane told him, in clipped sentences, all about the sandwich competition.

Patrick cracked up. 'No way!' He tried to stop laughing and couldn't. 'Aw, God, no way! And he's going—'

'Next Tuesday,' Jane said through gritted teeth. 'And I don't know why you're laughing.'

'Because it's *funny*.' Patrick winked cheekily at her. 'And you should laugh too. Sure, your parents love it. Everybody knows that!'

'Well I don't. It's embarrassing.'

'Jane, honey.' Patrick reached across the table and took her hand. 'You have got to stop taking responsibility for everyone else. Stand back and look at the full picture. It's *hilarious*!'

His laughter was kind of infectious. 'And I thought you lot were supposed to be sensitive,' she tried to say grouchily. 'Can't you see I'm dying here?'

'Well, all the more reason to laugh.'

48

IT WAS ALMOST one o'clock. Jane glanced uneasily at her watch. Where on earth were the kids? Owen had told her he was heading to a friend's house and she hadn't been able to help the look of surprise on her face. She'd told him to be in by eleven thirty. Di had gone clubbing to celebrate her Junior Cert results. They hadn't been great, but compared to Owen's, they looked fantastic.

She knew she had to stop worrying about them, but the truth was, since Matt had died, she couldn't help it. Anytime they went out she dreaded getting an unexpected phone call or someone ringing the bell in the middle of the night. She knew she had to keep things normal for their sakes and not go all over-protective, but it was hard. She flicked on the telly to see if there was something she could watch to take her mind off things.

Nothing, as usual.

She went and got a coffee and carried it back into the front room. Sitting there, she'd be able to glance out the window from time to time. She was going to kill Owen when he came back.

It was two o'clock and she was wound up like a spring with worry, when she heard giggling. There was the sound of a key in the lock and to her relief, her two kids walked in the door. Owen came in first, then Di, with her hands on his shoulders.

'Where were you?' she demanded, trying to sound cross but just wanting to cuddle them. She glared at Owen first, 'Didn't I ask you to be in for twelve-thirty?'

'Uh-huh, but then I met Di and we walked around for a bit.'

Jane stared incredulously at him. 'You walked around for a bit with your *sister*?'

'Yeah.'

Behind him, Di giggled. Well, at least, Jane thought, there was a smile on her face for a change. 'And was the club good?' she asked, making a supreme effort to be nice.

Di looked blankly at her.

Owen poked his sister hard. 'Did you have a good night, Di?' he asked her. 'Ma wants to know.'

'Fanilliant,' Di slurred. 'Over early but.'

There was no mistaking her thick voice or the fumes that seemed to wash across the hall. Jane took a few steps towards her. 'Have you been drinking?' she asked, her nice voice gone.

'Me? No.' Owen said. 'Now, Di says she's knackered—'

'I was talking to your sister,' Jane snapped, pushing him out of the way. She stood in front of Di who'd begun to giggle helplessly at her mother's expression. 'You have.' Jane was shocked. It wasn't that she thought Di wouldn't try a drink, but to end up in that sort of a state was a bit much. Christ, she must have had loads. She poked her face into Di's, knowing that it was no use confronting her in this state, but unable to help herself. 'Where the hell did you get the drink?'

'Chill out,' Di said between giggles, 'it's, it's Junior Cert, they all do it.'

'Yeah, they do, Ma,' Owen said helpfully.

'Am I asking your opinion? Am I?'

'No, but I'm just saying—'

'Well don't. Just keep quiet.'

'Aaahhh,' Di nodded sagely. 'The thing everyone is best at in this house, keeping veery, very quiet.' She bent forwards and made shushing noises.

Owen poked her again.

Jane closed her eyes and rubbed her hands over her face.

Di shoved Owen off and stood upright, swaying unsteadily.

'Where did you get served drink?' Jane asked.

Di bit her lip and gave an exaggerated shrug.

'You are not setting foot outside this house until you tell me.'

'So?' Di answered cockily.

'Di, stop it,' Owen said. 'Just stop it.'

'Awww, my brudder, the best boy.' Di put her arm around his shoulders and squeezed him. He smiled reluctantly at her. 'I love you, Ownie boy, do you know that? He walked and walked and walked me so that I could come home in a reasonable state. He's a lovely brudder. Just like Mattie was.' She gave him another squeeze. 'I love you Ownie.'

'Great.' Owen rolled his eyes at Jane and grinned.

It wasn't funny. Jane didn't smile back.

'You will not be able to see that boyfriend of yours unless you tell me,' Jane said again. 'Think about that now, Miss!'

'Poor Gooey, I got sick on his docs, didn't I Ownie?'

'So you said.'

God, she must have made a right show of herself. 'Where did you get the drink?'

Di righted herself. She shook her head defiantly and had to grab on to Owen to stay upright. 'I come from a dys . . . dys . . .' she stopped, started again, 'a fucked-up family, it's no wonder I drink.' The last part was said almost triumphantly.

Jane didn't know what happened then. All she knew was that she heard a crack and only then did she realise that she'd walloped Di right across the face.

Owen gasped.

A huge red slash instantly appeared on Di's cheek. Di put her hand to it and tears pooled in her eyes.

'Oh God, Di—' Jane stared at her hand, which was stinging, and then she stared at Di. 'Oh, I'm sorry,' she gulped, 'I'm sorry.' She held out her arms, 'Come here.'

Di backed away.

'Owen drinks,' Di said, her face screwed up to stop tears leaking all over her cheeks, 'and you don't say anything to him. Why do you give out to me all the time?'

'Thanks, Di,' Owen said, sounding annoyed. 'Thanks a bunch.'

'And he bunks school and I don't, but you don't give out to him, and then he fails his exams and you *still* don't give out.'

'None of that is dangerous,' Jane said, trying to make herself understood, but not knowing what she should be saying. 'Anything could have happened to you in that state. For God's sake, Di!'

'All you ever do these days is give out,' Di said, half-sobbing. Pushing past Owen, she stumbled awkwardly up the stairs.

Jane gazed after her.

There was a silence. Jane turned to Owen, who was also looking after his sister. 'Go to bed,' she said.

'Everyone drinks, Ma,' he said. 'It's just 'cause it's Junior Cert year, you know?'

'Yeah Owen – thanks for minding her.' She tousled his hair, wanting to hug him but knowing he'd only get embarrassed.

He smiled slightly before going upstairs.

49

JANE AWOKE BEFORE the alarm went off. The house was silent, sun sneaking in under the curtains. She lay still for a few blissful seconds in a cocoon of warmth under Matt's duvet before suddenly remembering the row of the night before.

Her heart sank and she groaned. After Matt had died, she hadn't slept for days. She'd been afraid to. Afraid to sleep and forget and then suddenly wake up and remember. It'd be like losing him all over again when she woke. Recalling that made her feel that she could cope with whatever the morning brought. OK, Di had been drunk, but she was home. She was safe. She was healthy and alive. They'd sort something out. She dragged herself from the bed and pulled on her dressing gown. Shoving her feet into tatty blue slippers she shuffled out of the room.

'Owen, school. Up. Now.' She gave his door a good hard thump. From behind it, she heard groaning noises, so at least he was awake.

She was about to tap on Di's door when she wondered if it would be better to go down and get her daughter a cuppa. She'd be feeling rotten this morning and maybe if she brought her up tea and a couple of Disprin, the gesture would help break the ice. Anything to help, Jane thought as she turned from Di's door and made for the stairs. The sound of a radio drifted up from the kitchen and Jane realised in shock that her mother was already up. In the whole history of their relationship, Jane could never remember Sheila being up before her. In fact, getting her mother up for work was harder than getting the kids out to school.

Her mother was eating a slice of thin, dry toast when Jane joined her. 'Hi, dahling,' she said, wiping her mouth daintily with some kitchen paper, 'I have the kettle on for you.'

'Ta.' Jane took a cup from the press and dropped a tea bag into it. Taking a couple of slices of bread, she shoved them into the toaster.

'What was all the fuss about last night?' Sheila asked. 'I heard shouting at around two which woke me.' She spoke in a faintly accusatory tone, which Jane ignored.

'Di came in drunk last night.' The kettle boiled and she made tea. 'We had a row.'

'Oh yes, teenagers do that, don't they?' Sheila gave a martyred sigh, as if she was used to handling drunken teens. 'Junior Cert results come out and they all get smashed.'

'And how would you know?' Jane asked. There were two Disprin in the press and she snapped them out of their foil.

'Your father's show, dahling. Every year, after the Junior Cert, he does a special on teen drinking. All those stupid parents ringing in baring their souls,' Sheila gave an affected laugh, 'they're wasting their time telling Declan about it. That man is only interested in hearing about one thing.' Jabbing her finger towards Jane, she spelt out, 'S-E-X. But you know what they say: what you can't have you always covet.'

Jane didn't bother to answer. Running down Declan had become routine by this stage. Her mother was definitely much stronger than she had been, especially now that Lisa was on side. When Sheila had revealed her 'true' identity to Lisa, a big bonding session had apparently taken place. Lisa had been dumped too and bore a chip the size of Everest about it. She'd told Sheila, who'd told Jane, that all her grooming was an effort to get hubby to notice her so that she could tell him to shag off. Lisa was the first friend Jane could remember Sheila ever having.

'A psychologist on your father's show said that teen drinking could sometimes mask deeper feelings,' Sheila called out as Jane ascended the stairs. 'If that's any help, dahling.'

If she'd wanted to feel any worse, it would have helped all right, Jane thought.

'Di,' she called, tapping on the door, 'may I come in?'

There was no answer.

'Di!'

There were some groggy mumblings from within.

Owen appeared at his bedroom door. His uniform looked as if he'd dragged himself through a wringer, but Jane didn't bother to comment on it. 'There's toast downstairs,' she said. 'Go and get it.'

Owen gave her a shaky grin and, barefooted, he ran downstairs.

Owen's grin gave her confidence. At least he wasn't blaming her. And to be honest, it wasn't acceptable for a fifteen-year-old to be drunk. Feeling better, Jane pushed open Di's door.

Di, bedclothes pulled up to her chin, glared balefully at her. 'I never said you could come in,' she muttered.

Jane swallowed. Oh, how she longed to snap at her, but it wasn't the way. And what if Di told Jim that Jane had hit her? It'd make Jim hate her even more than he already seemed to and Jane didn't know if she could bear that. For the first time she was actually glad that the kid wasn't talking to him.

'I brought you up some tea,' she said softly, laying the cup beside Di's bed, 'and a couple of tablets for your head. They work well.'

Di looked suspiciously at her.

'It'll be hard to go to school with a hangover,' Jane said by way of explanation. 'And it's time you were up.'

Di winced. 'I don't feel well.'

'Most people don't when they drink too much,' Jane answered. Then, her heart hammering, she added, 'And I'm sorry I hit you last night. I shouldn't have.'

Di shrugged.

'But it hurt, you know, what you said about this family.'

Di looked up at her. 'Yeah. Sorry.' She gave her a big sullen look.

Jane decided that was the best she'd get out of her. 'Just don't do it again, eh? I was worried.'

She made her way to the door and was just opening it when Di said, 'Thanks for the tea, Mam. And the tablets.'

Jane smiled. 'No problem.'

Di smiled a little back. 'And sorry for making you worry.'

Jane's eyes filled with unexpected tears and she could only nod.

'Well, wish me luck,' Sheila said as she smoothed down the light green and pink skirt she was wearing. Picking up a baby-pink cardigan from the chair, she put it on. 'Your dad is coming to our shop today around four.'

Jane's toast felt dry in her mouth and her heart lurched. *How could she have forgotten?* 'Mam, do you have to?' she asked. 'I mean, do you want all the world to know your business?'

Sheila laughed tolerantly. 'Lisa says if she could tell the world what a faithless abuser she had for a husband, she would. She says I'm lucky to have such a platform. Anyway,' she tossed her head, 'he's the one doing the sandwich contest. He's out to humiliate me, well, the boot will be on the other foot.'

'Yeah, but Mam—' Jane didn't get to finish her sentence; Sheila left the table and went upstairs to get her bag.

Jim was on his way to Galway when the Declan D'arcy show came on. He almost crashed the car when he heard that his father-in-law was standing outside the sandwich shop his mother-in-law worked in. At least, Jim was pretty sure it was Sheila's shop.

'And now, folks,' Declan said, in his gravelly voice, 'we're outside Lisa's for today's sandwich challenge.' People cheered in the background. 'Now, let's give a description of the place for those of you listening in and not able to see it – which is all of yez, I guess.' He laughed at his wit and continued, 'Northside Dublin. Very salubrious lookin' indeed with its cool wood finishings, in keeping with the general up-your-arse poshness of the place. And speaking of posh, the Patrick Costelloe hairdressing salon is just down the road from here and it's brilliant. My daughter works there – she's the best hairdresser in the country.'

Jim grinned as he changed lanes. Patrick would be well pleased with that plug. From the radio came the sound of someone squealing. 'I work there too,' the squealer squealed, 'I'm Rosemary. I know Jane. We all work there. Yeahhhhh.'

Jim cringed. That bit wasn't so hot. He could picture the kid getting yanked by her hair all the way back down the street by Patrick.

'Yeah, rock on Rosemary,' Declan said, sounding mildly amused. 'I'm sure you do. Anyway, plugs aside, let's enter this emporium of sandwich-making and meet the staff.'

Oh shit, Jim thought.

There came the sound of footsteps and then Declan began describing what the place looked like inside – how they had adorned the walls with flags and how posters with funny sayings were scattered about. 'What about this one?' Declan read aloud, '"Give a man a fish and he'll eat for a day, teach him to fish and he'll destroy the world's oceans."' He chortled a bit and said, 'So, everyone, I'm now standing beside Lisa, who owns this place. Bit of an environmentalist are ya, Lisa?'

'Naw,' a woman replied, in a thick Dublin accent, 'just anti-man. The rest of the poster should read, "teach a woman to fish and she'll do it properly".'

'Yeah, but only after she's put on her make-up, eh?' Declan bantered.

His comment was met with deafening silence from Lisa.

'Well, now,' Declan sounded a bit flustered, 'I'm told ya make great sambos, Lisa? Is this true?'

'Only after I put on my make-up, Declan,' Lisa answered smoothly.

There was a huge guffaw of laughter from the people gathered. Declan graciously laughed as well.

'And is it just you working here?' Declan asked. 'I was, eh, told by my researcher that there's two of yez?'

Jim, about to take off at a green light, held his breath. Jesus. This was great.

'Go Sheila!' someone yelled.

The customers broke into a 'Go Sheila' chant.

'I have my very valued assistant,' Lisa said. 'As you can see, she's popular with the punters and is a brilliant worker.'

'She is?' Declan sounded doubtful.

'She is?' Jim also asked.

'Come on out here, Sheila.'

There was a lot of clapping as Sheila appeared.

'It's your wife, Declan,' Lisa said. 'The one you dumped like a dose of the runs a few months back? Huh, I bet you knew she worked here. Out to humiliate her, you were!'

There were a lot of gasps and giggles from the shop floor. Declan made amazed spluttering sounds, but just from knowing him, Jim knew he was spoofing. Declan had known Sheila would be there.

'Hello, Declan.' Sheila sounded very composed.

'It's my wife everyone,' Declan announced.

People clapped. 'So, hey, how are you?' Declan asked, sounding as if they were best buddies. 'Long time no see. You're looking well. You've obviously been busy in the make-up department. Ha, ha.'

'Indeed,' Sheila replied drily. 'Well, when you've been kicked out of your home and not given any financial support, you do what you can to survive.'

In the background, people gasped.

Declan attempted to laugh it off. 'Aw, now, that's not true. You were well provided for. Anyway, we're here to taste the sandwich—'

'When your only daughter takes you in *despite* being left by her own cad of a husband, you try to make the best of things.'

'Bitch!' Jim shouted at the radio.

'Aw now—' Declan attempted to say.

'And if you want a sambo, it won't be free,' Lisa interrupted. Her voice turning to a holler, she shouted, 'You'll pay like everyone else. We do have a living to earn, you know, and no fecker of a man is getting it free from us any more!'

'Well said!' Sheila cheered.

Declan laughed along as if it was just a big joke, but there was an edge of panic to his voice as he asked, 'How much for a cheese salad with ham?'

'To you – three-fifty,' Lisa answered.

'Gimme one then.' Declan no longer sounded jovial or civil, just extremely pissed off. 'And just for the record, folks, this interview was not meant to go like this.'

'Lettuce?' Lisa barked.

'Yeah.' Declan said. Into the microphone, he announced, 'Service is not great. No smiles here at all.'

'Cucumber?'

'Yes.' Back to microphone he commented, 'She's only giving me two slices.'

'Oh, Declan, don't be so petty,' Sheila muttered. 'Judge the sandwich on its merits.'

'I have to judge the service too,' Declan said self-righteously. 'And just because you're my wife, I can't show favouritism.' Then, sounding frustrated, he added, 'And anyway, I don't care about the bloody sandwich, I only came here to see you.'

'To humiliate me, more like!' Sheila sniffed.

'*No*,' Declan stressed. 'To see you. I set this whole thing up.'

There were gasps from the spectators and someone groaned in the background.

'I mean,' Declan clarified, 'there *is* a real sandwich bar competition, but I wanted to see my wife because I missed her and . . .' his voice stopped its upward swing and instead he muttered, 'I want her back.'

'Yeah, right.' Jim muttered. It was a typical D'arcy ratings booster.

'Yeah, right,' Sheila laughed.

'And don't do that don't-mess-with-my-knickers laugh,' Declan hissed. 'I bloody mean it. I'm sorry. I want you back.'

'Tomato?' Lisa barked.

'Eh, yeah.' Sounding distracted, Declan said, presumably to Sheila, 'Well?'

There was a long, long silence. Then Sheila said, 'Three-fifty for the sandwich, Declan, and to be honest, I wouldn't go back to you if you were a magnet and I a pin. Well, unless it was to stick myself into you very, very hard.'

'Sounds promising,' Declan joked.

There was more silence.

'I even got you this ring,' Declan said shakily, his voice unsure. There were more gasps from the audience as he produced something from his pocket.

'Why, thanks,' Sheila said. From what Jim could gather she took the ring and then said, 'Three-fifty please.'

It was a quiet and sober Declan that parted with his money. The shop seemed to have fallen silent.

In an effort to divert what was a highly embarrassing situation for the host, a drum roll was started up. 'And the verdict on the sandwich?' the speaker boomed.

'Not hungry,' Declan muttered.

They cut to a commercial break.

Jim let out a whoosh of air and wondered what the hell would happen now.

What happened was that Declan walked out of the shop and down the road to the hairdressers. Shoving open the doors, he strode past a chastened Rosemary, five agog customers and a wide-eyed Patrick. 'Tell her she has to come back to me,' he shouted at Jane who was busy cutting a client's hair.

Jane felt her stomach heave, especially as people had gathered outside the shop to have a gawk in the windows. Rosemary had filled her and Patrick in on all the details and Jane just wished she was dead. Years and years of humiliation welled up inside her.

'You tell her to come back to me,' Declan said again. 'I bought her a ring and she bloody took it off me and she still won't come back. Jesus!' He strode closer to Jane. 'You were the one who told me that she wanted me back!'

'That was months ago, Dad,' Jane hissed, trying to keep her voice down, but knowing it was futile. The whole story would be all over the place tomorrow. 'Things change. I mean, you didn't want her back then . . .'

'Well, I do now.'

'So tell her!'

'I bloody well did and she threw it back in my face.' He looked like a kid who hadn't been invited to a birthday party.

'Well, I can't do anything,' Jane said. 'It's not my business – you told me to butt out, remember?'

'Why do women never forget these things?' Declan shouted. 'You lot are descended from bloody elephants.'

From outside came the flash of cameras.

Jane gritted her teeth and turned to her customer. 'Just tilt your head a little please?' The customer obliged and muttered a 'Hiya' to Declan who ignored her.

'Well?' her dad demanded.

'I'm at work, Dad, I don't conduct my affairs in the glare of the public. OK?'

'Well, it wasn't meant to happen like that! She was meant to give me a sandwich and I was going to give her the ring. But she got all snotty on me.'

Jane said nothing, instead she stared pointedly at her customer's head and hoped that by ignoring her dad, he'd get the hint and go away.

'Hey, Deco.' A customer, arm outstretched, came towards him. 'Love the show.'

Declan glared at her, then he glared at Jane. He glared at everything around him and finally stomped out.

No one said much when he left.

Eventually after about ten minutes, the customer muttered, 'Someone told me he's dead nice to his fans. Some story that was.'

And that was when Jane realised that her dad probably did want her mother back. Her dad never snubbed fans. Even when things were bad, his fans always came first.

Only now, it looked like Sheila had.

She attempted to explain it to her mother when she got home. Sheila was having none of it. Drunk on victory, she kept admiring the ring he'd given her. 'My arse,' she kept saying, whenever Jane tried to get her to see things properly.

She'd recently started saying 'my arse' to everything she didn't agree with. It was a new expression, one she'd presumably learnt from her employer.

Jane was about to tell her mother that she couldn't stand much more of it when the phone rang.

'What?' she snapped into the receiver.

'It's just me.'

Hearing Jim's voice made her heart lurch. What was he going to have a go about now? 'Yeah?' she said warily.

'I was just wondering,' he paused, 'if you're OK? You know, with the stuff on the radio today? I know how much you hate all that.'

She couldn't speak for a second. It touched her that he'd rung. 'Thanks for calling,' she said, hoping her voice wouldn't tremble. 'It was nice of you.'

'No probs.' He sounded quite cheerful, not like the guy that had glowered at her last Saturday. 'Just remember what I always used to say – d'you remember?'

'Yeah.' She remembered how he'd wrap his big arms around her, kiss her head and tell her that although they were her parents what they did was nothing to do with her. She was still Jane and she had her own life and they had theirs.

'Just thought I'd remind you.'

'Thanks,' she said softly. 'Patrick said the same.'

'He's right.'

Jane didn't want to let him go. Even if he didn't say another thing, she just wanted to know that he was on the other end of the line. 'I had a row with Di,' she confessed suddenly. 'She came home drunk after her Junior Cert results came out.'

'Oh . . . right.'

She knew he was wondering why she was telling him this, and what it had to do with anything. And it had nothing to do with anything, yet everything to do with it. 'I hit Di across the face,' she confessed.

'Jesus!' Jim sounded shocked. Then he said, 'And now, how're things?'

'Well, not too bad, but she's well hungover.'

He gave a splutter of a laugh.

His laughter warmed her.

He paused. 'Thanks for telling me.'

'You're her dad, you should know.'

'Right.' He sounded as if he was smiling and that made her smile. 'Listen, Jane, gotta go. I'm in Galway and I've to go to a business dinner in an hour. See you Saturday?'

'Sure. Bye.'

When he hung up, she felt lonelier than she'd felt since he'd left. But to feel anything other than angry with him was weird. In a nice way.

50

'PHILIP LOGAN HAS offered me a job,' Jim told Dave as they sat across from each other in Dave's office. 'I've accepted it provisionally, but I'll work until Christmas here and then I'll leave after that.'

Dave didn't congratulate him, instead he regarded him through narrowed eyes. 'So that's it. You're just going to up and leave us in order to market crisps?' There was a bit of mockery in his voice and Jim flinched. Normally he didn't care what the hell Dave said, but this time he felt the blow.

'You were always quick on the uptake, weren't ya, Dave?' Jim said, rising from his seat. 'There's no flies on you.'

Dave gave a bit of a chortle as Jim stomped out.

In the corridor, Jim laid his head back against the wall and closed his eyes. In his heart he knew that Dave was just jealous, but the slur hurt. Marketing crisps was not how he'd seen his life, he'd wanted to do so much more. There was the anti-drinking campaign that Dave was working on, he'd have loved to get that project, but Incredible Crisps was his baby and he supposed he should feel honoured that he was in charge of them.

But, Jesus, even the Chains Bond thing was boring him now.

He guessed it was because he'd no one to share it with. Not really.

It was all over the papers. 'End of the Road for Sexy Sheila and Deco D'arcy' was the banner headline in one of the tabloids. There were pictures of them on their wedding day, the infamous picture of them both in their sexy night attire, posing on their bed, and pictures of Jane as a baby.

'Awww, you were so *cute*,' Rosemary remarked.

Pictures of Patrick Costelloe's adorned the front page too. It was described as 'the place where a rejected, dejected D'arcy sought refuge from his humiliating show'.

Patrick was trying not to show his delight with the salon getting front-page publicity. He was all tea and sympathy, but every so often his face kept breaking into a huge grin.

And the customers had been pouring in all morning. Just like they'd been queuing up at Lisa's to get a sambo made by Sheila.

Jane felt like an animal in a circus.

Jim picked up the paper. He was bored out of his tree. Debs couldn't come over that night as Gillian had been advised by her doctor to rest. 'If I leave her, she'll start cleaning the flat,' Debbie giggled, 'so I'll see you another night – right?'

He was going to offer to go over, but he knew that the sight of him and his connection with Fred would only upset Gillian, and if Gillian got upset, Debbie would kill him.

Turning over the front page of his paper, Jim saw yet another spread on the D'arcy marriage. Declan was still declaring that he hadn't left Sheila destitute and she was keeping a noble silence on the matter. 'I've said all I can,' was her response.

My arse, she has, Jim thought in amusement.

A sudden longing for home seemed to wrench his heart. In a flash of clarity, he realised that this single man status wasn't him. Dating Debbie wasn't him. Living in this flat wasn't him. But the deafening silence at home wasn't him either.

Trouble was, Jim thought, he didn't know what *was* him any more.

Di wanted to take sixty euros out of her savings. She stood petulantly before Jane, ready to do battle if she had to.

'Why do you need it?' Jane asked.

'It's Gooey's birthday in a couple of weeks and I want to get him something nice.'

'OK.'

There was a moment of stunned silence.

'You mean I can take the money out?'

'Yeah, you can.' Jane turned from her. 'It's nice that you want to buy him a birthday present.'

'Can I take seventy instead?'

'Di, why do you always want more than—'

'OK, OK, I only asked.' Shoving her savings book into her pocket, she slouched from the kitchen.

Jim had just begun to type up a schedule for one of his projects when the buzzer went. It had the sound of a trapped bluebottle magnified by a million. Every time he heard it, it made him jump.

'Yep?'

'Hey, how's it going, my friend?' Fred's booming baritone almost took the intercom off the wall.

Jim winced, wondering what he wanted. They hadn't really been in contact since Jim had left, but enquiries had yielded information to the effect that Fred was still working furiously and had stopped the heavy boozing.

He buzzed Fred up and stood waiting for him at the door.

'Nice pad,' Fred said as he walked towards him. 'You must've been pretty well paid by your crispy friend.'

A girl from the flat opposite came out on to the landing. She gave Jim a shy smile as she locked her apartment door.

'No views like that at my place,' Fred said wistfully as he watched the girl's retreating back. 'You are one lucky man, Jimbo.'

'Shag off,' the girl hissed, turning back.

'You offering?' Fred called after her.

Jim smiled despite himself. He'd missed Fred's awful sexist remarks and his un-PC views of life. 'I suppose you want a can?' Jim asked as he led the way inside.

'On the ball, there, Jimbo,' Fred nodded, shutting the door behind them. He looked around and made more admiring remarks. Taking an opened can of Bud from Jim he drank thirstily. When he'd finished, both men stood staring at each other.

Fred broke the silence. 'Can we shove all the shit, you know, about Gill, behind us?' he asked. As Jim was about to interrupt, he held up a hand and continued, 'Look, I know you think I treated her badly, but fuck it, that's me, you know. I didn't judge you when you upped and married what's-her-face.'

'Jane,' Jim suggested.

'Yeah, her,' Fred said dismissively. 'I mean, right, you took one road and I'm just taking the other one.' He paused, then said quietly, 'But, like, it's got nothing to do with you and me, has it?'

Put like that, Jim still didn't agree. 'I think what you've done is crap,' he said.

'Yeah. Right.' Fred shuffled from foot to foot. He gulped, before saying haltingly, 'But, Jimbo, we've been mates a long time. I don't want to lose that.'

Neither did he, Jim thought. Fred had always been there, through everything, his dad leaving, his ma dying, everything. Through Matt.

He hadn't been a lot of help, but he'd been there.

'Yeah,' Jim agreed, wondering if he was doing the right thing, 'Me neither.'

Fred looked as if he'd been pricked with a pin. He grinned in relief. 'Knew that,' he said cockily.

Jim grinned back.

They clicked cans.

'Anyway, any news?' Fred asked.

Jim shrugged. 'Nothing much.'

'I had a bleedin' scare last week,' Fred made himself comfortable on Jim's sofa. 'All Parrot's feathers fell out. Had to take her to the vet. Cost me a fortune. She's fine now though.'

'Good.' Jim found it a bit bizarre to be talking about Fred's parrot when the subject of Gillian lay between them.

'She's as right as a good screw,' Fred nodded. 'The bleedin' vet said she was the cleverest bird he'd ever met.' He said it with the pride of a doting parent. 'I told him I'd taught her meself. Dead impressed he was.'

Jim smiled. Bloody vet wouldn't be impressed if he'd to listen to her every night, he thought. They talked about other things, Fred mostly leading the conversation. He wondered how Jane was putting up with her mental parents and Jim gave him a censored version of events.

Eventually, as midnight drew in, Fred got up to leave. 'Better head.' He pulled on his jacket and just as he turned to leave, he asked casually, 'How is Gillian, anyway? I haven't seen her in ages.'

Jim wondered if he really expected Gillian to call him with progress reports. He thought not, it was just Fred asking the question he'd bloody well come to ask four hours ago. 'She seems grand,' he answered, equally casually. 'Debs said her blood pressure is up and she's to take it easy, but other than that, she's fine.'

'So she's having the baby – yeah?'

'Well, unless they've invented some other way of doing things.'

Fred didn't smile. 'Righto, thanks for the drink. Maybe we'll head out somewhere one weekend?'

'Sure.' Jim agreed. 'Gimme a ring.'

Fred left and Jim polished off the last remaining can. He fell asleep on the sofa.

51

JANE AWOKE FEELING nervous. It was fifteen minutes before the alarm was due to go off and she lay staring at the ceiling, trying to quell the queasiness. This was it. Make or break time. It was funny how the competition had crept up on them all so quickly. All week she'd been having awful dreams about her colours going wrong, or cutting Rosemary's hair in a weird style, or Rosemary transforming into a different model with a funny-shaped face. Every time she woke, her heart was hammering like a drum, but the sense of relief was wonderful. She wondered if it would backfire completely on the salon if things did go wrong. Having been featured on the front pages of most of the nationals, the salon didn't need the publicity any more. They had plenty of customers and Patrick had reluctantly advertised Mir's job last week.

Still, Jane thought, entering this competition had given her focus for the first time in what felt like years. No longer was she just existing from day to day, no longer was she just putting in the hours at the salon, she was actually improving her skills and come what may, it was good for her, despite all the pressure and the nightmares. She was out to prove herself – to show that she was good and not some hick, OAP hairdresser.

And Patrick was fired up too. He seemed to love the back-biting that was going on between themselves and Cutting Edge. There was a great buzz around their salon that had never been there before.

Her alarm began to bleep and she hauled herself up in the bed. Time to get the kids up and out.

Di wanted to ask her something. It was so obvious. She was passing the butter, bread, and teapot without so much as a grumble. She had even given her a sunny smile and asked her if she was nervous.

'So Di,' Jane was determined not to be taken for a fool, 'what is it you want?'

Her daughter paused in the middle of lifting her teacup to her lips. She flushed, put down the cup and shrugged. 'Oh, that's typical,' she snorted. 'I try and be nice and I get accused of wanting something!'

'Which is?' Jane asked patiently.

There was a pause. 'Just, well, there's a party on tonight. Gooey's party. And I was wondering if I could go?' The last part of the request was muttered hurriedly.

'So you didn't want anything,' Jane said pleasantly and resumed eating her breakfast.

Di said nothing. Did nothing. Then, when the silence got too much for her, she snapped, 'Well, can I? Can I go?'

'Will there be drink there?'

She gave a mutinous shrug.

'More importantly, will you be drinking?' Jane asked.

'No, I won't. I promise, all right?'

It was said with very bad grace but Jane believed her. Di was many things, but she was not a liar. 'Be back by one,' Jane said.

'One?' Di rolled her eyes.

'Yes.'

'Fine.' Di muttered a 'dorky' under her breath and stomped off to get her coat for school.

'I can't *wait* for tonight.' Rosemary swung her legs back and forth in her chair. She'd been on a sunbed for the past few weeks and she glowed like a shiny brown penny. Her hair cascaded down her back and Jane, blow drying it, felt a little tremor of excitement at the thought of working on it that evening. It hit her like a small shock, the fluttering anxiety she felt. She found, quite unexpectedly, that she was looking forward to it.

Sheila was still in bed when the phone rang. Lisa had given her the day off after another successful 'ladies night' the evening before. She was going to get up, nibble on a grapefruit, make up a face pack and do her hair. After that, well, the day was hers to do with as she wanted. Only thing was, she didn't want anything much. There were only so many episodes of *Oprah* or *Ricki* one could take. And afternoon television was so bland. It wouldn't have been too bad to go to work really, mix with the outside world, share a bit of scandal. But, it was her day off and enjoy it she must.

The phone stopped ringing but started up again a few seconds later.

Honestly, Sheila thought, as she put her feet into her crocodile slippers, she just hated talking to people first thing out of bed, but maybe it was Lisa asking her to come in. She wouldn't want to let the woman down, not after she'd been so supportive of the 'Declan debacle' as they'd affectionately nicknamed it.

She lifted the receiver and put on her posh voice, 'Hello?'

'Aw, it's yourself!' Declan's unmistakable accent boomed down the line.

'Jane is not here.' Sheila was deliberately frosty. 'Bye now.'

'No, no,' Declan sounded flustered. 'No, it's you I want to talk to.'

'Oh, are you taping this for your show?'

'No!' he sounded annoyed. 'What do you take me for? I was just wondering if I could drop over tonight.'

'Drop over? Why?'

'To see you.'

'No,' Sheila said, relishing her power. 'I will not meet you tonight. I'm not a pushover – I'm not easily swayed.'

'So you still haven't had the operation then?'

'I beg your pardon?'

'You know, the one to remove the pole from up your arse.'

'Oh Declan, that's you all over. Can't get your own way and you immediately make crude jokes. Your adolescent humour may woo the public, but it does nothing for me.'

'Sorry.' He paused. 'Anyway, I'm going to come over.'

'I don't care what you do Declan. You can come or not, I don't care.'

'Fine.'

'Fine.'

He put down the phone.

Damn it, she thought. She should have done that first.

Jane couldn't concentrate at all. Patrick sent her home with strict instructions to relax. 'I'll pick you up at four and we'll drive over there. You get a bath or whatever and calm down.'

So she'd gone home, only her mother was ensconced in the bathroom and about an hour later, smelling like the entire contents of The Body Shop, she emerged, oblivious as usual to other people's needs.

'Oh, dahling,' her mother smiled pleasantly at her, 'will you style my hair? You see your—'

Jane made herself take deep breaths before she said crossly, 'I'm doing a competition tonight Mother. I'll see enough hair there, so I don't need to be looking at yours. And right now, I need a shower.'

'But your father said he might call around,' her mother said. 'I think he's going to ask me back.'

Jane rolled her eyes. 'He already has Mother. It's been all over the papers these last two weeks, now if you'll just get out of my way . . .' Saying this, she elbowed her mother aside and stalked into the shower.

Of course, her mother hadn't even cleaned it and the floor was sopping. So that took another ten minutes. By the time she emerged, she had just two hours to kill.

* * *

Jim wasn't in the mood for going out but Fred had rung him and he felt he had to. Of course, Debbie had flipped. 'Oh,' she said, 'that's lovely. He left my friend in the lurch and there *you* are going out with him.'

What was it with women? Jim wondered. Couldn't she see that his going out with Fred had nothing whatsoever to do with him and her? Or him and Gillian for that matter? So he'd listened to Debbie rant on with no idea of what to say to her.

Eventually, when she'd run out of steam, he said, 'I'll give you a bell tomorrow, OK?'

'It'll have to be, I suppose,' she'd said.

He didn't know why she was so huffy. She'd told him that she wouldn't be able to go out anyway as she was having a girls' night in with Gill. They were going to get videos and paint toenails and stuff, so he'd thought that it'd be fine. He'd squeeze Fred in and they'd all be happy.

Some hope.

52

IT WAS THREE-THIRTY. Jane couldn't stop pacing up and down the kitchen. If she'd had a packet of fags, she would gladly have smoked the lot.

Oh God! she thought.

'Will you sit down?' her mother said irritably. 'You're making me nervous.'

Through her own fug of nerves, Jane managed to register that her mother looked totally ridiculous sitting at the kitchen table in a six-hundred-euro, off-the-shoulder, sequinned black dress. Sheila had also tried to do an overly elaborate hairstyle which now sat like a squashed blonde cat on the top of her head.

'Here,' Jane reached for her bag and pulled out her comb, 'let me fix that for you.' She felt that if she was doing something with her hands, it might get rid of the nerves. She worked rapidly, the deft way her fingers parted, sectioned and styled giving her reassurance in her ability.

She'd already rung the salon to check on Rosemary's clothes and to double-check that Rosemary had actually made it to the beautician's without any mishaps.

Jane had just inserted the final pin into her mother's hair when the doorbell rang. Four on the button. Shoving her comb back into her bag, she took a deep breath. 'Wish me luck,' she said.

'You don't need luck, dahling,' Sheila kissed the air around her, 'you're a D'arcy – talented and wonderful.'

They smiled at each other, Jane basking in her mother's approval.

'Bye.'

'Bye, dahling.'

From upstairs came the shout, 'Good luck, Ma.' The two kids, who were on a half-day Friday, were smiling at her from the landing.

'Give it loads, Ma,' Owen smiled.

Di managed a fairly friendly, 'Do well,' before sauntering back into her room.

Her heart filled with trepidation, Jane opened the door to Patrick. 'Your carriage awaits.' He did a big bow for her and, taking her hand, led her outside.

The minute her mother left, Di scooped up Gooey's present from under her bed, shoved it into a plastic bag and went downstairs. 'I'm going out, Nana,' she said, 'I'll be back later.'

Her nana looked ridiculous in that black dress, she thought.

'What time, dahling?' her nana asked. 'I'll need to know in case your mother rings.'

So her mother hadn't told her nana what time she had to be in at. 'Four,' she said nonchalantly, chancing her arm.

'I'll take that as one-thirty, dahling and no later.' Sheila gave her a clipped smile.

One-thirty wasn't so bad, she conceded reluctantly. Without answering she left the house.

Fred called around at nine and together they headed for a local pub. For the first time in his life, Jim found it hard to talk to Fred. If the conversation became any more stilted, it'd keel over and die.

It was going to be a bloody long night.

At nine-thirty the doorbell rang and, peering through the curtains, Owen saw his Granddad Deco shuffling nervously from foot to foot. There was no way he was staying in the house listening to the two of them squabbling. He legged it down the stairs, wrenched open the front door, yelled to his nana Sheila that she had a visitor and was gone.

Declan looked quite well, Sheila thought, as she walked towards him. Dressed in a shirt, tie, and a well-cut pair of Louis Copeland trousers, he almost looked like an adult.

'Oh,' she gave a sniff, 'so you decided to call, did you?'

Declan shrugged, quirked an eyebrow and said, 'Well, you look like you were expecting me.'

'Ha, ha, ha.' Even to her own ears, the laugh sounded false, so she stopped. 'I always wear this old thing about the house,' she said. 'It saves my good clothes getting destroyed.'

'The good stuff you wear for work – like?'

'I do beauty sessions,' Sheila answered scornfully. 'They're my *real* work, you know, since I—'

'Was flung out and left prostitute, yeah, I know.'

'*Destitute*, Declan,' Sheila corrected.

'It was a joke, oh fair one,' he grinned.

There was no way she was smiling back. After all he'd put her through, was still putting her through. Who on earth did he think he was? Did he *honestly* think he could snap his fingers and things would go back to normal? Did he really think that she was going to stand being slagged off regularly on the radio? And who was he to slag anyone anyway?

'So, what's the occasion, Declan?' Sheila folded her arms. He attempted to move inside the door and she asked again, 'What's the occasion?'

'Well, if you'd let me in, I might tell you. I don't want the world knowing what I'm gonna say.'

'Well,' she said in mock surprise, '*there's* a first.'

She was startled to see the shamed look on his face. So startled that she moved sideways to let him sidle by her. He carried on past her and into the kitchen.

'Is Janey not here tonight?'

'She's at a hairdressing competition with work.'

'Oh right.'

'And you're not having tea or anything else,' Sheila said imperiously. 'This is Jane's house, I can't go throwing about good food and drink. She's been left by Jim you know.'

Declan nodded. 'D'you know, Sheila, being poor suits you almost as well as being rich. You could get drama from a bleedin' roll of Sellotape.'

'Well, at least I got something out of nothing. I wish I could have got some money from my husband when I needed it.'

Another ashamed look. Really, Sheila thought, Declan wasn't arguing with his usual flair at all this evening. 'Well, what can I do for you?' she asked again.

Declan sat down. 'Come back,' he said.

It was the simple way he said it that touched her. But it was also extremely strange. 'Oh, come on, you can do better than that,' she scoffed. 'Come back?' She arched her eyebrows and thanked God that she'd plucked them earlier that day. 'You really expect me to drop everything and go back to you?' Her dress clung in all the right places as she walked towards where he sat. 'Declan, we hadn't made love in over four months and you told everyone you, you . . .' Sheila shuddered. 'Well, that we did it ten times or something like that. I can't remember.'

'Call it wishful thinking.'

'I call it lying. I call it making a laughing stock out of me. I call it the words of an impotent man.'

She knew she'd hurt him, but it was about time it was voiced. He couldn't perform and as a result he kept talking about it and making out he was some sort of sex god. The whole thing was killing them – this dancing around the subject, pretending it wasn't there. 'Declan,' she said, 'you've got to see someone.'

He looked at his hands for ages. Then he turned them over and looked at the backs. 'And what will the papers say to that?' he asked quietly.

Sheila knelt down. There was a tearing sound as the fabric

of her dress caught on the heel of her shoe. Still, if she got back with Declan, she could always get another one. 'We'll find out if it happens, dahling.'

He looked at her. 'We'll?'

'Yes. *If* you'll see someone.'

He sat there for a while then slowly nodded. 'I've missed you,' he whispered.

Sheila nodded. She'd known he would. She'd known when he kicked her out that he was going to regret it, so she'd bided her time.

'I thought, you know, it was cool at first,' Declan swallowed. 'Kicking you out saved me from, well, you know – I couldn't bear for you to . . .' he stopped, '. . . witness my failure all the time.'

'I know, dahling.' God, she'd have to stand up soon, her knees were killing her.

'But then, when I won that bloody award thing, it wasn't the same, not being able to share it with you or even Janey. And, Jaysus, I didn't know what to do. I didn't know how to get you back. I felt if I did a big public thing, you'd come back.'

Sheila nodded. Really, men felt they had to explain everything. *Of course* she knew.

'Why didn't you come back that time?' Declan asked. He reached out and touched her face.

Sheila spent a few seconds just enjoying his fingers as they trailed their way down her cheek before answering. 'I knew it would be no good, that you weren't ready, dahling.' She put her hand up to stop him from going any further. 'I stayed away because it was good for you. For us.'

'Oh Jaysus.' Declan wrapped his arms around her, totally ruining her hairstyle. His finger pierced itself on one of her hairgrips and cursing, he pulled away.

Sheila smiled at him as he sucked on his bruised finger. Thank God she could now go back home. How Jane and Jim had ever slept in that bed was beyond her. She looked at Declan and he looked at her at the same time.

He was so much nicer when he wasn't being a famous DJ. Their eyes locked and bending towards her, he kissed her. She'd missed that – the warmth of someone loving her.

'Tell you what,' Declan said, 'if things in this house aren't too tight, I'd kill for a cuppa.'

Sheila smiled at him. He smiled back. They were going to be OK again.

53

IT HAD BEEN a long night, Jim thought. He resisted the temptation to look at his watch and when he did, he almost groaned to see that it was barely ten o'clock.

'Another?' Fred stood up and put his hand into his pocket. 'My shout?'

'Yeah, go on.' Jim hoped that if he got drunk it would help the conversation flow better. It kinda made him sad that he and Fred should be scrounging around for something to talk about, but he was too aware of what a bastard Fred was for it to spur him on to try harder. Fred either didn't notice or was hell bent on ignoring the atmosphere. He filled in the gaps in the conversation with mad stories that made them both laugh. And while they were laughing, the world seemed to right itself for a few seconds.

It was while Fred was up at the bar getting the drinks that Jim's mobile rang. Who the hell would be ringing him so late? he wondered. He hated late calls, they always spelt bad news. He'd just answered the phone when Fred arrived back with two creamy pints of Guinness.

'Tell ya what, Jimbo, you're lucky with your local. They do a good pint.'

Jim barely heard him. It was Debbie on the other end, sounding as if she was about to have a breakdown. In the background, Gillian was telling her to calm down.

Gillian telling Debs to calm down – something must definitely be wrong.

Debbie blabbered something that Jim couldn't make out.

'Who is it?' Fred asked, taking a gulp of his drink.

'Debs, I can't make out what you're saying.' Jim tried to sound patient.

'He-a.' There was a bit of a tussle and Gillian came on the line. 'Jim, we decided to ring you 'cause you probably are dee expert.'

'On?'

'Childbirth.'

'Sorry?'

'What are dee symptoms? I've been in already this week with a false alarm and no way am I going in again.'

'She's going to have it on the floor,' Debbie, missing her usual sexy huskiness, shrieked down the line. 'She's been holding off these last couple of hours. And I just couldn't deliver a baby. Oh, God.'

Jim had to hold the phone away from his ear. Christ, he wouldn't want Debs on his team in a crisis. 'Have you a pain?' Jim asked, feeling like a total fraud. What the hell did he know about childbirth? His last kid was born ten years ago.

'Pains in my stomach,' Gillian said. And as if to demonstrate this fact, she let out a yowl and all he could hear was Debbie telling her to 'bloody breathe'.

'That sounds bad,' Jim said. 'Maybe—'

'Sounds bad,' Debbie shouted. '*Sounds* bad – you should *see* her. Oh God, I'm going to throw up.'

'She's a bit upset,' Gillian confided. 'I dunno. I didn't think she'd be like this.'

'I think you should go in.' Jim was not going to be responsible for her having the baby in the apartment. 'Even if it's a false alarm—'

'It's not a false alarm,' Debbie shrieked. 'Haven't I been telling her that for the last few hours?'

'Call a taxi,' Jim said. 'You're in no fit state to drive.'

'Have you ever tried to call a taxi on a Saturday night?' Debbie was hyperventilating. 'It'll be hours. Oh God!'

'An ambulance?'

'Yeah. Yeah, OK. And Jim—'

'Just get off the phone and call an ambulance,' Jim ordered. 'I'll meet you in there, OK?'

The line went dead.

Jim clicked his phone off and looked at Fred who'd turned as white as the line of foam on his upper lip.

'Was that Gillian?' he asked nervously.

'Yeah.' Jim pocketed his mobile. 'She's going in to have the baby.'

'Oh, yeah, right.' Fred turned from him and, lifting his pint up, drank thirstily.

The action infuriated Jim. 'Oh. Yeah. Right,' he said, copying Fred's laid-back voice. 'Is that all you can say?'

Fred looked up. 'Yeah. What else is there?'

'That girl,' Jim jabbed his finger towards his mate, 'has gone in to have your baby and all you can say is "oh, yeah, right"?'

'Yeah.' Fred glared at him. 'I didn't ask her to have it, did I? I don't want a bloody kid. It's her lookout.'

Jim had had enough. He stood up abruptly, almost upending the table. People from other tables glanced at him uneasily. 'You make me fucking sick – d'you know that? All you care about is you. *Hey,*' he yelled, '*this fucker's girlfriend is having his baby and he's dumped her.*'

'Shut up!' Fred jumped up too and poked his face into Jim's.

'Lads, lads,' the barman attempted to intervene.

'He has a parrot that he calls Parrot and he gives her more affection than he does to anyone else!'

'She bloody well deserves it. She doesn't hightail it out when things go wrong, does she?'

'She's in a fucking cage, how can she?'

'Lads – out.' The barman caught them both by the arm and attempted to push them towards the door.

Both guys shrugged him off.

Jim jabbed a finger into Fred's chest. 'You're a loser Fred. A fucking loser.'

'Oh yeah?' Fred's curled lip gave him an ugly look. 'And you're not? You don't even have a bloody home any more. You fight with your wife, your kids wouldn't talk to you for fucking ages, you work all the time and you shut everyone out. Don't call *me* a loser.'

Jim grabbed Fred by the shirt and Fred pushed against him. The barman gave up and went back behind the bar. Picking up a phone, he started dialling. 'Lads, I'm calling the cops.'

'But at least I had that,' Jim snarled, shaking Fred like a rat. 'At least I had all that, and d'you know what? I'd chop me right arm off to have it back. And you, you fucking wanker, you could have it all. A girl that loves you, a kid. Jesus,' he threw Fred from him and stalked from the pub, 'you make me sick.'

He didn't wait to see if Fred was all right. His head hammering, his heart racing, he stumbled out into the inky black night.

The mansion house was packed. The hairstyling had been done and the ramp and the lights had been set up for the various competitions. Entrants for the fantasy hair competition were receiving the most attention, with photographers fighting to take their picture. One girl was trying to balance what looked like a birdcage on her head. Inside, hanging from a loop of hair, was a perfect stuffed budgie.

Everyone was dressed in up-to-the-minute fashion, backless tops, tight trousers, short skirts. Jane, as usual, felt completely unhairdresserish in her black trousers and tight T-shirt.

Drinks were being served at the bar and loud music was pumping from the speakers.

It was ten minutes before the start of their competition and she was behind stage giving advice to Rosemary on how to walk. 'Modelling is just as important as the hairstyle,' she advised. 'Just walk on, don't acknowledge the applause and be untouchable, unreachable, OK?'

'Yeah. Yeah.'

'A bit like the hairdresser herself, eh?'

Pete Jordan must have sneaked up behind her. Jane flushed. The man had been studiously avoiding their party all afternoon and now, when he could get a dig in, here he was, sniggering away.

'I'll give that comment the attention it deserves,' Jane muttered. 'None.'

'Not a bad job,' Pete nodded to Rosemary. 'Still, I'm told the judges this year favour the brunettes.' With that, he waltzed off.

'Bastard,' Jane hissed.

Sheila had located some sausages and an egg in the fridge and had decided to show Declan that she could now attempt a fry-up with the best of them. He was sitting down, looking at her in admiration.

'You look nice beside a cooker,' he told her seriously. 'It sort of suits you.'

'It's quite easy really.' Sheila brushed a tendril of hair from her face. 'Jane is marvellous at it. She can even get the eggs from the pan without breaking them.'

'Aw, she's a great girl, all right,' Declan mused. 'Turned out very well.'

'She did,' Sheila pricked a sausage and the grease spat back at her, burning her wrist. 'Oh, honestly,' she exclaimed, as more grease splattered on to her dress, 'this will be ruined.'

'So what?' Declan stood up and wrapped his arms around her waist. 'Can't you buy twelve of them now if you want?'

The words gave Sheila a nice warm glow inside.

They were both startled as the front door slammed open, crashed closed and pounding footsteps legged it up the stairs.

'Jaysus.' Declan looked at Sheila in concern.

'Di,' Sheila said wearily. Then, deciding to show Declan what else she'd learnt, she said, 'I'll go and have a word with her. See if she's all right. Honestly Declan, she's a very difficult child. You would not believe the hostility that emanates from her.'

She handed the frying pan to him and gingerly approached the bottom of the stairs. 'Di, dahling,' she called, 'is everything all right?'

There was no answer, though she fancied that she could hear the child sobbing. She walked up the rest of the stairs and commented, 'You're back very early.'

'Ten out of ten for observation,' Di replied in a hostile but shaky voice.

From downstairs she heard Declan give a guffaw of laughter.

'Are you all right?' She took the risk of tapping on her door. 'Are you crying?'

'No. Go away!'

'Di, dahling.' Sheila tapped the door again, praying that Di would stay inside. She'd have no idea what to do if the child appeared. But Jane would expect it. Jane would like to know what was wrong. 'Are you sure? Your mother will—'

'I'm fine!' Di shouted, her voice spiralling upwards and not sounding fine at all. 'Leave me alone!'

'OK.' Sheila couldn't help the relief she felt. But she'd done her duty. She was a concerned grandmother. 'If you're sure.'

Di didn't bother to reply.

Thank God, was all Sheila could think.

The hospital was packed when Jim arrived. He asked at reception and was told that Gillian was up in a labour ward. Following directions, he found himself outside the glass doors. A passing nurse located Debbie for him and she arrived out of the labour ward, pale but smiling.

'Oh Jim.' She crossed towards him and caught his hand in hers. 'Thanks for coming.' Squeezing his hand, she added glumly, 'Sorry about earlier, I think I got a bit nervous. Hot water and towels seemed to be on the agenda.'

Jim laughed. 'A *bit* nervous?' he teased.

Debbie punched him lightly. 'Will you hang around? D'you mind? They say it'll be born tonight sometime.'

'No probs. How's Gill?'

'She's great.' Debbie made a face. 'Better than I'd be anyway. I mean, the *pain* she must be in. She's high with the gas, but she won't have the, you know, injection thing?'

'Epidural?'

'See,' Debbie said, 'I *knew* you were an expert. Two kids qualifies you to know these things.'

'Three,' Jim corrected automatically.

Debbie blushed, 'Sorry. I didn't—'

'No, it's OK,' Jim said hastily, wishing he'd kept his mouth shut. Giving her a gentle push, he added, 'Maybe you'd better get back in there. You might miss all the action.'

'Yeah.' Debbie squeezed his hand. 'Thanks for coming.' She paused just before she pushed open the doors. 'Was Fred with you when I rang?'

Jim nodded. 'I told him, but he, eh, he didn't want to know.'

Debbie bowed her head. 'She keeps asking for him. I dunno if it's the gas or what, but it's like she thinks he's coming.'

'Well, he's not.'

'Bastard.'

Jim nodded slowly, 'Yeah.' He watched the doors swing shut behind her and saw her go into the first room on the right. Walking back down the corridor, he found a small waiting room with a telly in it and sat down. It was going to be a long night.

54

THE BELL RANG for the start of the competition and one by one the models and their stylists walked on to the ramp. The stylists stayed at the top of the ramp while their models walked down it, turning their heads left and right to show off their hair. The judges, one of whom was Julian Waters, were placed at tables on either side. As various salons appeared, huge cheers went up. Pete Jordan's model looked stunning in a tight, black velvet dress, with a plunging neckline and a thigh-high side split. Her hair, glossy and curly, fell to her shoulders and was a mixture of coffee, gold and caramel lowlights. It was simple, yet very effective, though not exactly a competition hairstyle, Jane thought.

'Cutting Edge of Yellow Halls Road,' was called out as they took to the ramp. Flash bulbs popped and Pete stood proudly by, acknowledging the applause and attention. He was the hot favourite to win and Jane couldn't help envying him his smooth composure. She was a wreck.

'And now, representing Patrick Costelloe's, Jane McCarthy and her model, Rosemary Dalton.' In the crowd, Patrick was giving her the thumbs up and beside him, a tall, peroxide-blond man, who must be Barney, was nodding in approval.

Rosemary looked like the princess Jane had promised. Her style was funkier than Pete Jordan's. More modern. And best of all, Rosemary loved her hair. The colour scheme that Jane had chosen for her was red and orange. Rosemary wore a retro orange and red sunburst top and red, figure-hugging jeans.

She had a lovely figure, they'd discovered, and tight things suited her. The hairstyle Jane had decided to go for was the look Di was so fond of – a bed-head. She'd done a mixture of highlights and lowlights and Rosemary's hair was now a glorious blend of reds and oranges and yellows. Then, free-hand, Jane had texturised the hair and the result was pretty good.

Rosemary, after initially looking terrified, walked down the ramp with confidence. As the applause grew, so did her poise. Some guy in the crowd wolf-whistled her as she passed and Jane saw her face light up with pleasure. Once her walk was over, she took Jane's arm and together they left.

Backstage, she flung her arms around Jane and hugged her hard. 'I look so lovely,' she half-sobbed. 'And it's all thanks to you. I feel like a film star or something.'

Jane hugged her back. 'You look like a film star, Rosemary.'

'You and Pat,' Rosemary wiped her eyes, causing her mascara to run. 'You have made my year. I am the luckiest girl ever. I really am.'

She was the loveliest girl ever, Jane thought fondly, giving her another hug.

Back in the hall, Jane looked for Patrick and Barney. Patrick spotted her immediately and greeted her with a smile.

'Well?' Jane asked anxiously.

'It looked good, hard to tell though. Cutting Edge will be difficult to beat. And that other guy, what was his name?' He looked to Barney for support.

'Vernes or something, wasn't it?'

'Uh-huh,' Patrick nodded. 'Fantastic use of colour. Very original. They did the floodlights, did you manage to see it?'

Jane nodded, her high hopes disappearing. Maybe she'd flop completely.

'And where is our star?' Patrick shouted, spotting Rosemary hiding behind Jane. 'Where is she?'

Rosemary giggled.

'This, Barney,' he pulled Rosemary forward, 'is Rosemary. Isn't she lovely?'

'Beautiful.' Barney gravely took Rosemary's hand and kissed it.

'Aw, stop!' Rosemary flapped them away.

'And this is Jane.' Patrick introduced her to Barney.

Jane smiled. 'Patrick has told me so much about you.'

Barney smiled and clasped her hand firmly. 'Likewise, only he never said you were so talented.'

'Flattery will get you places I'm sure you've no desire to go,' Jane giggled.

Barney laughed.

'Hey, great job,' a guy with a huge scar on his face crossed to Jane. Nash trailed in his wake. 'Jaz,' he said, nodding to Jane.

'Aw, hi Jaz,' Jane nodded to him. He was worse-looking than Gooey, if that were possible. Thin and scrawny with hair like a badly peeled spud. 'So, d'you like what I did to your girlfriend then?'

'Aw, she's lovely any time.' Jaz winked at Rosemary who seemed to melt just looking at him.

Jane smiled. It was a nice thing for such a rough-looking lad to have said. 'She is, isn't she?' she agreed.

'How about we go and get a drink, eh?' Barney asked.

'Does that include me too?' Jaz asked, rubbing his hands together and looking hopefully at Barney.

'Sure.' Barney flashed Jane and Patrick a grin before disappearing with his new-found friends.

'And I thought Di's fella was bad,' Jane said in bewilderment. 'Jesus!'

Patrick laughed.

'Hey, hey, Jimbo.' Someone was shaking him. He felt stiff and sticky. Opening his eyes, he saw a lurid black and white print and his mind went into a tailspin.

'Jimbo!' Once again he heard the voice. The print disappeared and a face gawked at him. 'Hey, it's me.'

It was Fred. Jim sat up and rubbed his eyes. The last he remembered he'd fought with Fred or maybe he'd only dreamt it. But no, he was in a hospital, 'cause he felt hot and the smell of disinfectant in the air would kill most living things. 'Fred?' Jim said, swallowing hard as his mouth was dry. 'Is that you?'

'Yeah.' Fred hunkered down beside him. 'Is this where she is?'

'So you decided to come, did ya?' Jim was unable to help the smile that crept into his voice.

Fred gazed at his hands, the normally cocky look gone from his face. 'I tried not to but, well . . . I thought about the stuff you said and, well . . .' he paused, then coughed. 'Anyway, I'm here now and I can't get anyone to tell me where the fuck she is.'

'She was asking for you earlier.' Jim stood up. Jesus, his legs were stiff. He looked at his watch. It was only eleven-thirty, but it seemed much later than that. 'Debs is with her now.'

'Is she OK?'

'She's in the labour ward,' Jim said. 'The baby's due tonight.' He watched the terrified look that crept over Fred's face and decided not to say any more. Instead, he left the television room and walked Fred up the corridor. Pointing through the glass doors, he said, 'It's the first room on the right, that's where she is.'

Fred stared at the doors as if they were the gateway to hell. He looked at Jim in desperation. 'Will she want to see me?'

'Only one way to find out.' Jim opened the door slightly. 'Nothing ventured, nothing gained.'

'Yeah. Yeah, right.'

Taking huge whooshes of air, Fred readied himself. He squared his shoulders and had one foot inside the door when from down the corridor, someone called, 'Hey, hey you two, what are you doing?'

Jim turned and saw a woman in a green coat striding towards them. 'This is Fred,' he indicated Fred. 'He's going in to see Gillian Rodgers. She's in that room there.'

'Well, if she's in that room there,' the doctor said sharply, 'she's in labour and from what I can remember, she already has someone with her. Only one person allowed, I'm afraid.'

'Well, that's it.' Fred sounded relieved. 'Did me best.'

Jim glared at him. 'He's the baby's father,' he said to the doctor, 'and the girl with Gillian will let him in.'

'And will Gillian?'

'I dunno—'

'Yep.' Jim gave Fred a dig in the ribs. 'No probs. Just ask.'

At that moment, Debbie came hurtling out of the room, shouting at the top of her voice, 'Doctor, Doctor? God, is there a doctor?'

Pushing them aside, the doctor hurried towards Debbie.

'I think the baby's coming,' Debbie said, sounding as if she was going to cry. 'She says she wants to push. Isn't that a sign?'

The doctor nodded, closed the door firmly on Fred and Jim and bustled into the room. Debbie was about to go after her when she looked up and spotted Fred. Her eyes narrowed and tossing her head, she walked off.

'She can't do that,' Fred spluttered. 'I'm here now. She can't just go and ignore me like that.'

Jim resisted the temptation to tell Fred that he'd ignored Gillian for months, but he didn't. The fact that Fred had come to the hospital at all was a miracle, it couldn't go wrong now. 'Go in,' he said, decisively, 'go on.'

'It's my baby in there,' Fred said, as if he was psyching himself up.

'Yep, and you've more right than Debs to see it born.'

'Right. Yeah.'

'So, what are you waiting for?'

'Dunno.' After more deep breathing Fred pushed the door

aside and strode through it. Jim followed. If Fred hesitated again, he'd never go in, and Jim was damned if he was going to let that happen.

Fred stopped outside the door to the room and he almost turned and fled when he heard all the commotion from inside.

'Go on,' Jim urged, looking around desperately in case they'd be thrown out. 'This is it, Fred. Hurry up, would ya!'

'Right!' He shoved open the door and strode into the room. 'Gill,' he said loudly, 'I'm . . .' Whatever else he was going to say died on his lips as he took in the scene inside. *'Jaysus!'*

'What are you two doing?' The doctor turned furiously to them. 'Someone get them out. This girl is about to give birth.'

'Hey, I've something to say—' Fred protested, his hands in the air as a nurse made to shove them out.

'Is that, is that my Freddie?'

'Get them out!' the doctor shouted.

'Yeah – it's me.' Fred shoved the small nurse aside and stood, arms dangling, gazing at Gillian.

'I'm here, Gill – I came.'

Jim pushed him nearer the bed. If Gillian got another pain, Fred would do a runner. This had to be settled quickly, especially as the nurse was gawking indignantly at Fred and seemed about to summon help.

'Oh, Freddie.' Gillian sounded as if she was close to tears. 'Come he-a.'

'Jesus!' the doctor and Debbie said in unison.

'Out!' The nurse tried to ferry Jim towards the door.

'I missed you.' Fred stood beside Gillian but stopped short of taking her hand. Instead he wiped damp hair from her brow and said tenderly, 'I've been a fucking jerk.'

'Naw. You just got scared, it happens.'

'Jesus!' Debbie said on her own this time.

'Jim told me I was a lucky fucker to have you, said he'd cut his arm off to have his family back, he said—'

Gillian grasped his hand. 'I knew you'd come. Didn't I say he'd come, Debbie?'

Debbie nodded.

'Do you want this person at the birth?' the doctor demanded impatiently.

Gillian nodded and then let out a yell. 'Owwww.'

'Oh fuck – what's happening? Fred glanced around in terror. 'Jesus, someone help her.'

'Just hold her hand,' Debbie said to him as she kissed Gillian on the cheek. 'Come on, Jim, let's go,' she said as she pushed past him.

As Jim made to follow Debs, he saw Fred reaching for the gas mask and shoving it over his face. 'No, it's for her,' the doctor shouted.

It was going to be a rough night for Fred, Jim thought, grinning.

There was silence in the hall as the president of the hairdressing federation began to speak. Jane had just finished thanking Barney for all his help with the salon. He'd been dismissive of it, told her not to mention it. Then he'd shuffled away to get a few more drinks in.

The president was now talking about what they looked for in the winning styles. Jane felt Patrick reaching for her hand and squeezing it. Jane grinned at him and squeezed his hand back. It had been a brilliant night, the best she'd had in ages. Of course it would have been better if Mir had been there, but it couldn't be helped.

'And now to our decision,' the president continued. 'As you know, we mark under various categories . . .' Jane tuned out. It was the same speech as all the other years. The next thing he'd say was that the standard had been very high.

'Of course, this year's standard was exceptionally high . . .'

It was a difficult choice.

'. . . and the choice was very difficult.'

But in the end . . .

'. . . it came down to what I personally liked the best and in third place is . . .

The name of the winner was lost to her as her mobile rang.

Jane's heart went cold as she saw that it was her home phone number.

Debbie was in a funny mood, Jim thought. It wasn't that she was angry exactly, it was more that she was answering all his questions in monosyllables. Her arms were folded, her legs were crossed and she was sitting angled away from him, in the chair beside the telly.

'What's up?' he asked uncertainly. He couldn't figure her out. Surely she should be glad that he'd managed to get Fred to come, last minute and all as it was.

Debbie fixed him with a gaze that made him catch his breath. Her huge eyes were pooled with tears and she said quietly, 'Well, if you can't figure that out, then there's no hope for us, is there?'

Why did women always do that? Why did they always give a cryptic answer to a perfectly simple question?

'Is it because you wanted to see Gill's baby being born?' he asked. He moved nearer to her, but she flinched. 'I mean, I think it was great that Fred came—'

'So do I.' Her tone was clipped.

So it wasn't that. Jim sighed. He tried again. 'Look, Debs, either tell me what's wrong or else I'll probably say something else to annoy you.'

'You couldn't do any worse than you already have.' Deb's voice shook and she sniffed.

What had he said? Mentally, Jim ran over everything that had happened that night and he still—

'You'd "chop your right arm off to have your family back", would you?' Debbie asked, her voice shaking. 'That's what you told Fred, wasn't it?' She jabbed her chest. 'What does that make me feel like? Huh?'

Oh Jesus. Jim winced at the look of hurt on her face. He reached out to touch her, but again she moved away. 'I only said it to make Fred realise what he'd be giving up,' he explained. 'It's nothing to do with you. And I value me arm, I really do.'

'Sure.' A tear rolled down her face.

'Debs—'

'You've never told me anything about yourself, Jim, never confided in me why you and your wife split—'

'I did so,' Jim raked his hand through his hair. 'I told you we drifted—'

'Wonderful,' Debbie sneered. 'You never talk about your son that died—'

'That's . . . that's . . .' Jim shook his head. 'That shouldn't affect us.'

'You are *going out* with me.' Debbie stood up. More tears had spilled out and were running down over her nose and plopping on to the floor. She came towards him and held her hands in front of her as she said fiercely, 'I tell you everything. I get nothing back.'

'You do. I tell you stuff.'

'Nothing – that – matters.' Debbie brushed her face with her hand, smearing her lipstick all over the place. She shook her head. 'You and Fred are the same. Neither of you gave me or Gill anything concrete. You even took a job without thinking about me.'

'Aw, now—'

'Is that why it ended with your wife?' she asked suddenly. 'Did you shut her out too?'

'Does it matter?'

'Yeah, if you still love her. I mean, you don't love me, do you?'

'I—'

'You love your wife, Jim. You should go back to her.'

'It's over,' he said desperately. 'Jesus, Debs—'

'Either you leave this hospital, or I will,' Debbie said, ignoring him. 'And I think that since I've been with her all evening, I deserve to be here.'

'There's no need for this,' Jim said, knowing he was only saying it for the sake of it. He'd hurt her and he knew there was no going back. And what he'd said to Fred *was* true. He *would* chop his arm off to have his family back and maybe while he felt like that, he shouldn't be seeing Debs. He'd thought he was moving on, but maybe in order to move on he had to have somewhere he wanted to go. 'Debs—'

'Stop.'

They stared at one another. Jim was the first to drop his gaze.

'So, will you go, Jim? Please?'

'How'll you get home?'

She gave him a weary look. 'Just go.'

He nodded and picked up his jacket from the chair. When he looked at her again, she was facing the other way, pretending to look out the window. 'I'm sorry,' he said quietly. He didn't know if she heard.

He had just unlocked the car door when his mobile rang.

It was Jane and she was crying.

55

JIM DROVE LIKE a maniac to the hospital. This could not be happening again, he thought. Please, God, not again. It became a sort of prayer in his brain as he drove through the Dublin streets on the way to the Mater. He hadn't been able to get much out of Jane until his mother-in-law came on and told him that there'd been an accident and to get to the Mater as quickly as he could.

When he got there, he parked his car assways and ran up the steps. Jane met him in the hallway. Sheila had her arm around her. Jim stared at the tableau the two made and, his voice contracting with fear, asked, 'What's happened?' Jane covered her face, so he looked to Sheila. 'Jesus, tell me!'

'It's Owen,' Sheila said, as Jane let out a moan, 'he's been knocked down.'

The words hit him like blows. No way, not again.

Jim covered his face and sat down on a hospital chair. Jane and Sheila sat beside him. Almost out of instinct, he put his arm around Jane's shoulder.

He knew she was remembering that awful night too.

Matt danced by her out of the house, saying that he was getting his bike out of the garage. She meant to tell him to put his helmet on, but for some reason decided not to. Maybe it was because Matt lost everything and if she asked him to put on his helmet, they'd be looking for it for hours, and by the time they found it, he'd have decided not to bother going out. And she wanted him out. He had been watching telly all day; it was about time he got a bit of exercise. Five minutes later, she heard a scream. And she knew it was Matt. But she hadn't moved, just stood in the kitchen with her eyes closed, until one of the neighbours had come running up her driveway. And she'd been so afraid to go outside, because she'd known . . .

He'd died that night.

Jim had made it to the hospital just as Matt died. He'd been away on business and the minute he walked into the little room and held his son's hand and said, 'Hi, Matt, it's me, Dad,' Matt had just gone.

Like a light being put out.

The nurse said that often happened. 'It's like they hang on until everyone important has come,' she'd said.

Jim had spent months wondering what would have happened if he'd never arrived.

'Excuse me.' A doctor tapped Jim on the shoulder. 'Are you the McCarthy boy's parents?'

At his question, Jane wrenched herself free from his embrace and stared wildly at the doctor. 'Yes, yes, we are. What's happened? Is he OK?' Grasping his arm, she said, 'Please, don't say any fancy words, just tell us.' Her voice broke, 'We lost another boy, you see and—'

'Jane, dahling,' Sheila smiled uneasily at the doctor and put her arm around her once more. Softly, she said, 'Come on now, just listen to the doctor.'

'Yeah.' Jane nodded and blinked rapidly. 'Yeah,' she said again.

The doctor smiled sympathetically at her and indicated the chairs. 'Would you like to sit down again?'

'No.' Jane shook her head frantically. 'We just want to know – don't we, Jim?'

Jim nodded. He had to swallow hard. He looked at the doctor, a young guy with a chart. He probably didn't even have kids himself . . .

'Your son has been in a serious accident,' the doctor began.

Jane moaned and covered her face. Sheila pulled her close. Jim felt himself drifting.

'We've done all we can to make him comfortable.' The doctor looked at the three of them. 'He had some internal injuries and we've done a scan and, well, at the moment he's stable. Other than that, it's hard to say, at the moment.'

'He's alive.' Jane mouthed the words cautiously. 'He's alive and might get better?'

'It's early days,' the doctor said. 'But, yes, he's alive.'

'Can I see him?' Jane asked.

The doctor nodded. 'Don't get upset by the machines,' he said, as he led the way to ICU. 'They're the things keeping him alive. It might be frightening at first.'

The ICU was scary and the sight of Owen, looking so small and pale, did shock her. Jane went towards the bed and touched her son's face. He didn't react. Beside him, machines bleeped and whirred.

'Owen, it's Mam,' she said softly. *Mam.* She wanted to cry at the sound of the word. She caressed his cheek and kissed his face. She rubbed her finger up and down his hand. His skin was so soft, so vulnerable. Never had he seemed more precious than he did in those moments.

He could die.

It was too enormous to take in. Too much to think about.

She felt her mother rubbing her back, trying to calm her. She turned to the doctor, 'How did it happen?'

'There was a girl with him,' the doctor said, 'she's being treated for shock. I can take you to see her when she's ready, but maybe it's too much—'

'No,' Jane shook her head. 'I need to know.'

Jim didn't want to touch Owen. He didn't want to acknowledge the fact that the horribly bruised body in the bed was his son. It was like his whole existence had frozen over. He was in a little pocket of air and all about him was ice. It'd been like that after Matt had died too. It'd been like that a lot in his life.

The doctor led them towards a cubicle where a young girl lay on a bed. Her name was Charlotte, the doctor had said, and she was a friend of Owen's.

Jane's first thought was that the child was stick-thin and earnest-looking. Black bushy hair fell to her shoulders and pale blue eyes, swollen with tears, gazed fearfully at them as they entered. On either side of her were her parents.

They smiled awkwardly at each other and then Charlotte's mother said softly, 'I'm sorry about your boy. How is he?'

Jane opened her mouth to answer, but nothing came out.

Jim stared hard at the wall.

'Not good,' Sheila said softly. She put her arm around Jane and forced her to sit down.

'Is it all right if we talk to Charlotte?' Jane asked, gulping. 'It's just, well, I just need to know what happened.'

'Charlie?' her mother asked.

Charlotte nodded.

'Will we stay with you?' her dad asked, ruffling her hair.

'No. No, it's OK,' Charlotte spoke. She had a light, nervous voice. 'I'll be fine.'

Her mother opted to stay anyway, while her dad went to get them all some tea.

Jane licked her lips nervously. It had all happened so fast. She wondered if she was in some sort of horrible nightmare. She was upset, but it hadn't got right in yet. Not right in, under her bones. 'Hiya,' she managed. 'I'm glad you're all right.'

'Thanks.' Charlotte bit her lip.

'So, can you tell me what happened?' Jane asked.

Charlotte sniffed and a tear plopped from her eye on to her bedcovers. She took the tissue her mother offered. 'He was running,' she said, in a barely audible voice. 'And he didn't see the car.'

'Running from what?' she asked. 'Was someone chasing him?'

Charlotte nodded.

'From who?'

Charlotte looked at her mother.

'Go on, Charlie,' her mother coaxed. She looked at Jane. 'It might upset you both, the way it happened.'

Jane didn't feel she could be any more upset. 'Just tell me the truth, Charlotte, *please*.' She touched the girl gently on the hand. 'I need to know.'

Just as Charlotte was about to begin, Jim stood up and walked out.

'Jim—' Jane said, but stopped. Refocusing on Charlotte, she said gently, 'Please go on.'

Charlotte nodded. 'OK,' she said softly. 'Owen, well, he was running away from the guy in the off-licence.'

'The off-licence?'

'Yeah. He'd gone in to nick some whiskey.'

Nick? 'Steal?' Jane whispered.

'Yeah.'

Owen stealing? No. No, it couldn't be true. She stared blankly at the girl, unable to say anything.

'He only does it now and again,' Charlotte went on. 'For a buzz, he says. He normally takes crisps and once he took a pair of trainers, but he's not bad. He only does it for the buzz and tonight he wanted a buzz.'

'Buzz?'

Charlotte nodded. 'Yeah. To get a buzz he does mad stuff like climb really high trees and nick things.'

It seemed to Jane that she was about to fold in on herself. 'And he stole the whiskey?' she whispered.

Charlotte nodded. 'Yeah, but you see, the guy in there had chased Owen before, over some crisps, and, I guess he must have spotted him tonight, because when Owen took the whiskey, the guy chased him and then . . .' Charlotte gulped, 'and then . . .' she couldn't say it. Her voice wouldn't let her.

'It's OK.' Jane reached out and patted her hand. 'It's OK.'

Charlotte began to cry. Her mother pulled her into an embrace and she cried harder. 'He was my friend,' she sobbed. 'My friend.'

'He *is* your friend,' Jane said firmly. 'Is.'

Sheila left the room. There was no need for her to be there. There *was* a need for Jim, however, and there was no way he was going to leave her daughter to do all the worrying alone.

It was hard, traipsing the slippery corridors in high heels and a tight velvet dress which was ripped at the seams. Her hair was coming undone too, and wisps of it hung like cheap thread down the sides of her face. But that paled in comparison to the rage she felt building inside her. From the moment she'd set eyes on Jim McCarthy, Sheila had disliked him. She'd been right then and she was going to be right again. Well, to hell with it, things had gone far enough.

She spotted Jim, his forehead pressed against the cool wall tiles. He was standing beside the coffee machine though Sheila didn't think he'd even got himself a drink. 'So this is where you've got to, is it?' she asked archly. 'You've abandoned my daughter yet again to press your head against the wall.'

'Sheila, don't start.'

'I haven't. Yet.' Sheila gave him a poke. 'What do you think you're playing at? My Jane is up there, devastated, and what do you do? Walk off as if it's no concern of yours.'

'I said, don't bloody start!'

'Well, you did it to her before and there's no way you are doing it again. Pull yourself together and be a man for a change.'

Jim turned around. The bleak look in his eyes made her half-sorry she'd been so harsh.

'You let her down over Matt—'

'Don't talk about Matt, *please*.'

Sheila paused. 'Sorry,' she said softly. 'I know it hurts.'

Jim squeezed his eyes tight shut and turned away.

'But Jim, Jane needs you now. You have to be there for her.'

Jim said nothing for ages. He rubbed his hands over his face and Sheila felt like shaking him. However bad Declan was, he certainly knew how to cope in a crisis. He'd driven her and Di to the hospital and then he'd taken Di home because she was so upset.

'Jim?' she said again.

'I dunno what to do,' he said dazedly. 'I dunno what she wants of me.'

Sheila was tempted to tell him to do the opposite of what he'd done the last time, but she held it back. 'Just be there. Don't leave her on her own.'

'But she wants to know things and I don't.'

'Jim,' Sheila said, 'you don't have to listen, you don't have to talk. All you have to do is *be there*.' She waited for a reaction. 'Now, I'm going back to the house to see if Di is feeling strong enough to come in now. For your own good, Jim, go to Jane.'

'And she'd want that?'

She'd known he was stupid from the minute she'd met him. A crisp man, how are you? '*Yes*, she'd want that.'

Jane thought it was her mother returning and she didn't even look as the person walked into the room. It was only after Charlotte was taken home by her parents that she turned around and saw Jim sitting beside her.

So he'd come back.

She wondered how long it would last.

56

JANE DIDN'T THINK she'd ever been so aware of time as on that night. It had the slow, sluggish quality of a nightmare. Everything she did seemed steeped in a million moves, a million little details and throughout it all, there was a sickness in her heart and a granite-faced stranger by her side. Jim hadn't said much at all. He'd asked her if she wanted coffee and she'd wanted to tell him that no, she wanted her son to be bloody all right, but instead she'd nodded and he'd got up and taken ages to come back. The coffee had now grown cold and she spent her time staring into it.

Jim walked to the window, walked back. Walked to the window, walked back. If he didn't stop soon, she was going to scream. All that fucking endless movement and the loneliness of him being there. It would have been better if he'd done what he'd done before – just bloody fucked off for a week.

He began to walk to the window again and Jane gritted her teeth, it was not the time for an argument. As he walked back towards her, she surprised both of them by flinging her cup of cold coffee at him. It hit his shirt and dripped down the front of his jeans.

God, it had felt good.

Jim stared at the stain as it spread over the crotch of his jeans. 'What did you do that for?' He sounded more bewildered than annoyed.

'I did it because you are fucking pissing me off.' The words forced themselves from her. She could hardly talk, she was clenching her teeth so tight. 'All you can fucking do is walk and bloody walk and meanwhile our son, our son—'

'And what the hell am I meant to do?' Again he sounded bewildered, though at the mention of Owen, she noticed him flinch.

'Forget it.' Jane turned away and picked up the coffee cup from the floor.

'No. No, I mean it,' Jim said savagely. 'What *would* you like me to do? Make him better? I can't do that! In fact, I can't seem to do anything right, can I?'

'Oh, bring out the violins!'

It was as if she'd slapped him. He seemed to snap out of whatever mood he'd been in. Making a grab for his jacket, he haphazardly started shoving his arms into the sleeves.

'Jaysus, I'm going. I can't take this any more.'

'Yeah, go on. Leave me like you did when Matt died.'

'Don't say that – I didn't leave you.' He poked his face nearer hers, 'I *didn't* leave you.'

'You just couldn't bear to be with me, could you?'

'That's not—'

'You went away for a week after the funeral. What do you call that – huh?'

'But I came back,' he said. 'I came back.'

'No you didn't,' Jane said bitterly, the hurt of that time filling her up. 'You never came back.'

Jim opened his mouth to say something then, defeated, he turned away from her and left.

He walked and walked and walked. Clear of the hospital, he kept going. Somehow, he thought that if he walked far enough, he could leave his thoughts behind. But it didn't work. His whole rotten life paraded itself in his head. The dazzling, shining, eleven years of bliss with Jane outdone by the early stuff and the later stuff.

Eventually, Jim stopped. He didn't know where he was exactly, but he knew it wasn't where he should be. The only problem was, he didn't know where he should be. With Matt, he hadn't been able to handle anything, not the way Jane cried, or the way the kids had been, or the way he'd felt himself.

But what he'd done then hadn't worked.

He thought that no matter what he did, things couldn't get much worse.

'Now, here you are.' Sheila placed a cup of tea in front of Di.

'How is he?' Declan asked. 'Did you see him?'

Sheila glanced at Di, then, knowing that the child wasn't stupid, said, 'He's . . . he's comfortable.'

Di sniffed.

'And Jane?' Declan asked. 'How's she bearing up? Is Jim with her?'

Sheila nodded. 'For the moment,' she muttered disapprovingly. 'However long that lasts.'

Di glanced at Sheila. She didn't want to hear her giving out about her dad like that. But maybe if her dad hadn't done what he did, things might have been different. After Matt's funeral he'd left for a week and no one had known where he was. When he came back things had changed, no one talked to anyone any more and no one mentioned Matt. She wondered if Owen died would they just forget about him too? Would she have to remember him all on her own again? She'd be the only kid left and she'd be on her own. There'd be no Owen to tease and—

'Hey, hey,' a warm arm was wrapped around her. The smell of smoke enveloped her. 'Don't cry.' Her granddad shook her affectionately. 'Your Owen, he'll be fine, he's a fighter, so he is. He bleedin' takes after his granddad, so he does.'

Di wiped her face. She didn't want to cry in front of them. A lace handkerchief was pushed towards her. Her nana's. Di thought of all the times Sheila had blown her nose in it and it took every ounce of courage she had to dab it on her eyes.

'Owen's far *better* than your granddad, dahling,' Sheila said smartly. 'Don't let him scare you – it's bad enough that he has his arm around you.'

Di managed a smile. The two of them were getting on famously, bitching and backbiting. 'I don't mind his arm – it's fine,' she said.

'And your brother will be fine too.' Her granddad cuddled her. 'Jesus, it's nice to have a young wan to cuddle,' he said. 'Your mother would never let me near her. Like a porcupine, she was – all spikes and bristles. Born with a pole up her arse, just like her mother.'

'I'll shove a pole up your arse if you don't stop it,' Sheila bantered back. She poured more tea into Di's cup. 'Now, I've put sugar in it, don't worry – it won't ruin your skin or anything – but it's good for shock. I know you want to look well for that creature you're seeing.' She turned to Declan. 'He's an unusual boy. His name is Gooey. Jane isn't keen on him at all.'

'Neither am I, any more.' Di wiped her eyes again. She was not going to cry over Gooey, not when Owen was so sick in hospital. 'It's . . .' she blinked rapidly. 'It's off.'

'Oh.' Sheila didn't know what to say to that. 'Oh dear.'

'And I'm not upset over it.' Di tossed her head. Her voice was a bit wobbly as she added, 'Not a bit.'

'That's the spirit, dahling.' Sheila smiled proudly at her. 'No man matters enough to cry over. Like the worms they are, they all come crawling back in the end.'

'Yeah. Look at me,' Declan said, without a trace of embarrassment. 'Didn't I come crawling back? And your mother can vouch for how many times I've done it in the past. He'll come back or else he's a fool.'

'You stay strong, my girl,' Sheila went on, 'keep yourself looking well and don't show him you care. That's the secret for a contented life.'

'Really?' Di asked.

Sheila nodded. 'Now, if your mother would only take some

of that advice, Jim would have come back long ago. But that's Jane all over – never tries to impress anyone. Slobs about—'

The shrill ringing of the phone shattered whatever else she had to say.

'He's still stable, the doctor's just finished letting me know,' Jane said. 'It means that he hasn't got any worse, which apparently is a good sign.'

The reaction to the news was celebratory. They couldn't have been more excited if they'd won the lotto. Jane hadn't meant to get their hopes up like that and when a tearful Di came on the phone, she felt that she had to bring things back down to earth.

'There's a long way to go,' she said.

'Can I come in?' Di asked, ignoring her. 'I promise I won't get upset. I'd like to see him.'

There was no way Di could come, Jane thought, not with Jim missing. Jesus, she hated Jim for this. 'Tomorrow Di,' she said. 'It's not as if you can see him now anyway.' Then before Di could say any more, she said, 'I'll have to go. I'll ring later on.'

Putting down the receiver, she walked back up to ICU and stared in at Owen, still as frozen snow. If anything happened to him, it'd be her fault. He'd been too quiet, she should have known, but because it suited her, she'd ignored all the signs. What kid bunked school unless there was something up? And Jim had told her he was drunk. He'd even asked her if Owen was a bit down. As for the things that Charlotte said he'd done . . .

She was a hopeless mother. If only she could turn the clock back . . . if she could borrow back some time. If she could just have another chance. Just one more chance. She wouldn't mess it up this time. When Matt had been in this position, she'd wondered how it could have happened to her. How could her lovely life be ruined so much? Why had it happened to her and Jim?

Worst of all was the irreversible nature of it. The suddenness. The shock. It was like being told by a very stern parent, 'that's that, now get on with it'. And getting on with things after her precious child had disappeared out of her life had been so hard. Too hard to explain with words, with tears, though she had cried, but she could have cried twenty-four hours every day for the rest of her life and it still wouldn't have filled the empty space inside her.

Now, looking at Owen, she knew that even with Matt gone, she *had* been lucky. So bloody lucky. She had two kids that she loved. If only she'd seen it like that . . . Please, she grovelled with any God that existed, I won't mess up this time. Just another chance . . .

She was vaguely aware of someone standing beside her.

The someone said, 'I was looking all over the place for you. How is he?'

Even when he'd first asked her out in the sunshine days of her youth, it didn't compare with her relief at having him with her at that moment.

'I'm glad you came back,' she said simply.

He managed a half-smile and together they turned to look at their son.

57

SHEILA FOUND THEM together in the waiting room the next morning. Jane, her head on Jim's shoulder, was fast asleep. Jim was trying to drink a coffee without waking her.

Unable to help the sarcasm, Sheila asked, 'So you stayed, did you?'

Jim just flicked her a look that said he wasn't going to get involved in her pettiness.

Sheila tried not to flinch. He was right of course, it wasn't the time for any of that. She tried again, 'Any news?'

'He's stable,' Jim answered. 'The doc said that he had a good night and it's a case of wait and see. We can go in to him in a while.' He looked at Jane and the tenderness in his face caught Sheila by surprise. 'She's only just fallen asleep,' he said. 'She was pacing the floor all night. The minute she sat down, she conked out.'

'Poor dahling.' Sheila patted Jane on the wrist and she sat bolt upright.

'What's wrong? Any news?'

'Jesus!' Jim glared at Sheila. 'What did I just say? She'd only just fallen—'

'I'm sorry. I didn't know I wasn't allowed to *touch* my own daughter.' She turned to Jane, ignoring another 'Jesus' from her son-in-law. 'I patted your wrist, dahling, and you woke up.'

Jane rubbed her eyes and yawned. 'I didn't want to sleep anyhow.' She shot Jim an accusatory look. 'I told you that!'

'What harm is a bit of sleep?'

'I told you I didn't want to.'

'Men, they never do what they're told.' Sheila smiled up at Jim who'd stood up and was now scowling at them. 'Any chance of a coffee Jim? I want to talk to Jane.' Dismissing him, she added a 'thanks'.

'Jane?' Jim asked sourly, 'do you want a coffee?'

'Yeah. A strong one.'

Jim dumped his coffee cup down and left the room.

Sheila embraced Jane awkwardly. She wasn't into hugging or holding, mainly because it tended to crease linen suits, but in these circumstances she knew that Jane needed all the hugs she could get. 'How are you, dahling?'

'OK.'

Sheila glanced at Jim's retreating back. 'Is he,' she said the 'he' as if Jim were something that had just evolved from the swamp, 'minding you all right?'

Jane nodded. There was no point in giving her mother more ammunition. 'A bit shaky at first, but he's doing his best. He finds it hard, Mam.'

'And you don't?' Sheila scoffed.

'Yes, but that's just Jim, it's the way he is.'

'Abnormal,' Sheila confirmed. 'What man runs away from his own son's funeral?'

Not this again. Jane sighed wearily, the last thing she needed, today of all days, was her mother bitching about Jim. 'He was devastated, Mam. You saw the way he was. I don't think he was thinking straight.'

Sheila felt like saying that in her opinion, Jim had never thought straight, except of course when he'd married Jane. But she didn't. Instead she changed the subject. 'Your father wants me to move back,' she said. 'I told him I'd think about it.'

In ordinary circumstances, Jane would have been ecstatic, but now it didn't seem to matter that much. 'Good,' she nodded. She wondered when the doctor was going to come. He'd said last night that he'd be around first thing. Well 'first thing' had been and gone. She glanced quickly down the corridor.

'And I'm keeping my job,' Sheila went on, studying her nails and tut-tutting at one that had chipped. 'I quite like work actually.'

There was a doctor coming towards them.

Sheila fell silent, but the doctor walked on, obviously on his way to someone else.

'Jesus,' Jane muttered.

Sheila patted her hand.

After a second or two, she said, 'By the way, just to warn you, Di is coming in later. She insisted.'

'OK.'

'And she's a bit delicate. Neanderthal man is off the scene.'

'Oh?' Well at least that was some good news.

'She's very upset, though she's being very brave about it. Won't tell anyone what's happened, but I'd say she's the one that got dumped.'

Poor Di. Jane wished she was there so she could comfort her. It was no fun being dumped.

Her two beautiful kids, one in hospital, the other at home crying her heart out, and where had she been? Out enjoying herself.

She felt terrible.

She didn't deserve a second chance.

But God . . . didn't that mean she needed it even more?

They were let in to see Owen that afternoon. 'Two people only,' the doctor said.

Jim looked at Di, who'd just arrived. 'You go in,' he said. 'I was in last night.'

Jane said nothing. Jim was drinking coffee constantly and had become edgy. The hospital was slowly driving him mad. The strain of waiting for news was killing him. He was coping, but only just. And the only just was for her sake. She didn't want to push him any further.

'Come on, Di,' she said. 'It's not as scary as it looks.'

To her surprise, Di took her hand and together they walked into the room. Owen looked exactly the same as he had done the previous night, he was still pale, though Jane didn't know if it was wishful thinking or not, but his face didn't look quite as white.

'Can I touch him?' Di asked.

'Yeah, take his hand,' Jane whispered. 'The doctor said we can talk to him. Just say "hi" or something.'

'Hi, Ownie.' Di pressed her brother's hand and told herself not to start crying. 'It's me – Di.' She felt a bit weird talking to him like this, but she'd seen a programme where a girl had talked to her brother and her brother had woken up.

'I just want to tell you that what I said that night, the night I was drunk, well, it was true.' She hoped he knew it was when she'd told him she loved him. 'And also, Ownie, please don't leave me on my own – sure you won't?' The last part came out in a sob.

The next thing she knew, her mother's arms were around her shoulders. It felt nice. 'My poor baby,' her mother rubbed her back. 'Don't say that.'

'Oh, Mam,' Di sniffed and knew snot was going to run out of her nose and go everywhere. 'Oh, Mam.'

Holding each other tight, they walked out of ICU and past Jim, Sheila and Declan.

'What's the matter?' Jim caught up with them as they reached the empty coffee room. He looked at Jane over the top of Di's head. 'Did she get upset?'

What an idiotic question; Jane glared in exasperation at her husband. Jesus, if he'd been man enough to go into the room and see his son, this would never have happened.

'Sit down Di,' she said gently, prying the sobbing teenager away from her. 'I'll get you a coffee.'

'I'll get it,' Jim offered, digging in his pockets for some change.

'You stay with Di.' He went across to the machine and began shoving coins into it.

Jane continued to rub Di's back as Jim crossed towards them with the coffees. He placed Di's on the table beside her. Looking uncomfortable, he muttered, 'Di, there's a drink there for you if you want it.'

'No. No, I'm fine.'

'You're not fine,' he said gently. 'You're upset. But it looks worse than it is. Maybe you shouldn't have gone in to see him.'

'And who *told* her to go in?' Jane asked, before she could help herself. At least that was one thing he couldn't blame her for.

'Yeah, I know,' Jim said ruefully, seemingly unaware of her anger. He ruffled Di's hair. 'But I thought she was able to cope with it.'

'Like you are, you mean?' Jesus, she couldn't help it. There was a slow rage building up inside and if she didn't let it out, she was going to explode. The stunned look on Jim's face only infuriated her further. 'You'd rather subject Di to it than go in yourself. You really are hopeless, do you know that?'

Jim slapped his styrofoam cup down and hot coffee slopped out over his hand, burning his fingers. 'And you are such an expert in reminding me, aren't you? You and your stuck arse mother.'

'A stuck arse? Wow! A new word!'

'STOP IT!' Di stood up, tears running down all over her face and plopping from her chin on to the floor. 'Just stop! You both make me sick! Sick!'

'Di—' Jane attempted to touch her, but she pulled away.

'You are always angry at Dad, Mam. And you,' she shot a look at Jim, 'are just useless. Owen is sick and all you can do is fight. Huh, if he dies, you'll probably forget about him the way you did with Matt.'

'What?' Jim paled.

'You won't talk about Matt. *You*,' she turned venomous eyes on Jim, who visibly flinched, 'you didn't even *cry* when he died.

And now it's Owen's turn and I'm not going to forget about him. You can fight all you like, but I'll remember him.'

'Aw, Jesus, Di—' Jim looked helplessly at Jane.

'And I'm sorry that you had to get married because of me, I know you both probably hate me for ruining your lives.'

'Di!' Jane stared at her, appalled.

'Gooey was right, you know,' Di sniffed. 'He said I only went out with him to annoy you, and it's true, I did. You only notice things that annoy you, Mam.'

Which was why she'd never noticed anything wrong with Owen.

Jane closed her eyes. What Di said was true.

'You two are so wrapped up in being miserable that you don't care about me or Owen.'

'That's not true,' Jane gulped. 'We care so much. We do. Honestly.'

Di said nothing. She just gulped and scrubbed her eyes with her hand.

'I always worry about you,' Jane whispered. 'Always. When you're out late, I worry. When we fight, I worry. Wasn't I worried when you came home drunk? And I'm worried now.'

'Gooey used to tell me he loved me,' Di cut across her, 'and it was nice.'

'But *we* love you too,' Jane said desperately, making a move towards her. 'Don't we Jim?'

He blinked hard, then gulped. 'Yeah. Of course.'

Di backed away from both of them.

'You and Owen and Matt were the best things to happen to us,' Jane said. She stood in front of Di, not knowing whether to touch her. 'Me and your dad,' she said softly, 'we loved you all so much. If we didn't, we wouldn't be so upset now.'

'And it's because we're upset, we're fighting,' Jim said. 'Isn't that right?' He looked to Jane for support.

'Yep.'

Di's body sagged as she looked from one to the other. 'So why don't we ever talk about Matt?' she asked.

Jim gazed at his shoes and bit his lip.

Jane wanted to shake him. Why couldn't he just say how he felt? As usual he was leaving it up to her. Oh, she'd wanted to talk about Matt – wanted to talk about him to anyone who'd listen. But the person who'd mattered most to her, the person who she'd wanted to talk to the most about him hadn't been able to handle the memories. So she'd choked it all back.

'When he died,' Jane began, 'it broke our hearts. And when things break, it's hard to mend them again, Di. Things like this leave you changed, because the bits get rearranged in a different way.' Jim slowly brought his eyes to meet hers and she turned to Di. 'But if it upsets you so much – I'll try. Honestly I will.'

'We'll both try,' Jim promised softly.

It hurt her heart to hear him say that.

His words seemed to do the trick. Di gave a watery smile.

Maybe a better relationship with her daughter was what she'd have to settle for out of this whole mess, Jane thought. She held out her arms. 'Come here.'

Di fell into them and Jane thought of how good it was to hold her daughter so close. She gave Jim a half-hearted, apologetic smile and he returned it despondently.

58

PATRICK ARRIVED ON the third day. He handed her a huge 'get well' card and a basket of fruit. Seeing him was so comforting. He enfolded her in a tight hug. 'You poor, poor thing,' he kept muttering as he rubbed her back. 'You poor, poor thing.'

She hadn't been able to cry. It was as if all her emotions were frozen. It was better that way, because she couldn't have kept going otherwise.

Jim, after some polite conversation, wandered off and left them on their own. He wasn't into talking to visitors. Even when some of his mates from work had arrived, he'd been unable to say very much. Jane took Patrick down to the canteen and bought him a coffee. It seemed that she'd done nothing but drink the bloody stuff for the past few days. Patrick looked great, full of the joys of life. He was like some kind of exotic bird in the general gloom of the hospital canteen.

'So,' he leant across the table, giving her the full benefit of his acrid aftershave, 'how are you coping?'

Jane shrugged. 'We're coping. Just doing what has to be done, you know?'

There was silence.

She didn't want to talk about it, didn't want to voice her fears. Instead, she sought for another subject. 'Hey, how'd we do in the IHFs?'

Patrick waved his arm around. 'Oh, you don't want to talk about that now,' he said dismissively.

'I guess that means we didn't win?'

'Second.'

Second was good. Well, it would have been good if they hadn't so desperately wanted to beat Cutting Edge. 'Second?' She tried to look pleased.

Patrick had a grin the size of America on his face. With a sort of squeal, he said, 'And Cutting Edge got *third*!'

'*No!*' She laughed for the first time in days. 'No!'

'Pete Jordan was disgusted. He was disgusted!' Patrick chanted loudly, making people look at him. 'He came over to us at the end and said that we'd only come second because Rosemary had good hair to begin with. He tried to make it sound like a compliment, but d'you know what Rosemary said?'

'What?' She found it hard not to smile at his enthusiasm.

'She said, right.' Patrick straightened up in his chair and squinted his eyes in the way Rosemary did, causing Jane to giggle. 'She said, "I suppose your model had good hair to begin with too, Mr Jordan. It's kind of hard to tell now!"'

'No!'

'Uh-huh. Then he stomped off, after saying that we were the most ignorant crowd he's ever come across.'

'Great.'

Patrick grinned, pleased to have made her smile. 'So,' he continued, 'we got loads of photos of Rosemary for the window and, eh, well, Barney said that it might be nice to do a few bill-boards.' Before Jane could protest, he held up his hand, 'It won't be expensive and besides, we're doing so well now. You wouldn't believe it Jane, the posters and the fact that your dad was in has them flocking to the place. We need to keep the ball rolling. Cutting Edge has been the best thing to ever happen to us.' He beamed delightedly at her. 'There's always a silver lining.'

She wished she could believe that.

'Oh, by the way,' Patrick reached into a plastic bag and pulled out a pile of envelopes. 'A lot of our regulars have dropped in cards for you.' He pushed them across the table to her.

Jane stared at the pile and touched them. 'Tell them thanks very much,' she said softly.

'I already did.' Patrick reached out and clasped her hand.

Jane laid her free hand on top of his and never wanted him to let go.

Jim arrived back at five. He'd showered and shaved and still didn't look any better for it. 'Sorry I was so long,' he said, 'but there was stuff I had to take care of.'

Bloody work.

Jane made no comment.

'You can head home if you like. I'll be here. I'll ring you if anything happens.'

There was no way she was going home. And his assumption that she would angered her. 'You only want me to go because your fancy piece is probably coming in,' she said, glaring at him. 'I know the way your mind works, Jim.'

He looked hurt and she knew she'd been way off the mark.

'I want you to go home because you need a break, Jane.' He raked his hands through his hair. 'You've been here three days now, you need a decent wash and a sleep. Your mother wants you to go with her. She's waiting in reception for you.'

Jane bowed her head. 'Sorry.'

'Don't be.' He poked her with his finger, then stopped suddenly. 'And it's off with Debbie, if you must know, so she won't be calling in.'

'Oh.'

There was a pause.

'Sorry.'

'Don't be.' His eyes met hers. 'Don't be,' he said again, softly. He held her gaze for a few seconds and then indicated his mobile. 'I'll ring you, OK?'

'OK.'

Jane didn't know who initiated it first, but suddenly she was in his arms and he was holding her fiercely.

There was no need to say anything.

59

THERE WERE NOISES coming from somewhere, weird noises that seemed vaguely familiar and yet hard to place. They sounded like . . . it flitted away again before he could catch it. There was a lot of darkness around him, and pain. A kind of deep pain, like an army marching on his brain. He felt the pain seep down into him, like water on sand. Through the pain he felt his neck and shoulders and hands. His stomach and hips and legs. It was as if he was sliding slowly into his body, visiting it after a long time, and he couldn't quite fit any more.

Light seemed to be filtering into his head, filling the darkness and frightening it away. The sounds seemed to be getting louder.

There was a pressure on his hand.

A voice.

He tried to catch what the voice was saying – he could make out words, but there were too many. It was hard to make sense of them. He just let the words pour over him like light rain. Refreshing him. The voice was lilting and soft. His hand was pressed again.

Slowly, he moved his head towards the sweetness of the voice and a buzzing sound, coupled with shouts, disorientated him.

It might be safer to stay where he was.

'He moved his head!' Jane said to the doctor. 'I was telling him about work and he moved his head.' She watched anxiously as the doctor peered at read-outs and stuff that she couldn't understand.

'Are you sure?' he asked. He flipped open his chart, wrote notes, then replaced the chart at the end of the bed.

'Of course I'm sure.' Jane didn't know whether to celebrate or kick herself. 'He moved it very slightly, but it was a movement.'

'Well, he does seem to have settled down a lot.' The doctor kept his voice cautious. 'Just keep talking to him, if he did it once, he'll do it again.' He touched Jane. 'It's a good sign, the earlier he responds, the more chance he's got of making a full recovery.'

As he left the room, Jane felt her heart sink. Somehow, she'd expected more. She'd hoped that this was it, that Owen would be fine. But they never told you anything.

Once more, she took Owen's hand and began talking.

Jim, coming back from the canteen, met the doctor in the corridor.

'Your wife thinks Owen might have moved his head,' the doctor told him.

'Yeah?' He was too numb to take it in. If he didn't get out of here, he'd crack up.

The doctor put a hand on his shoulder. Very gently, he pulled him aside. 'If I were you,' he advised, 'I'd get into that room while I still have the chance. If that boy wakes up and you're not there, well . . .' He shrugged. 'Women find it hard, things like that. Take it from me, I've seen it happen a lot.'

Jim looked after the doctor. How the hell did he know what their relationship was like? But maybe he was right, maybe he should go in and just sit there.

The thought terrified him.

Jane looked up as Jim came in. He sort of edged around the door and walked towards the bed as if there were needles on the floor.

'His head moved,' she said.

Jim nodded. He took a seat on the opposite side of the bed.

'Talk to him,' Jane said. 'He might want to hear your voice.'

Jim shook his head. What could he say?

'*Please* Jim,' she said. 'Just a "hi" or something? He might be waiting to hear your voice.'

Yeah, like the way Matt had been. But they knew Matt was dying that time. There had been no hope, but Owen was alive. He'd moved his head. Jane was looking at him and Jim knew that if he was to salvage anything out of this, he had better talk to his son.

Slowly he took Owen's thin hand. It was lukewarm and felt soft. His heart lunging about in his chest, he whispered, 'Owen, it's me. It's Dad.'

The figure in the bed didn't move.

He remembered holding his mother's hand when she'd died and talking to her just like this. But he'd been a kid then and hadn't really known what death was. He felt sick.

'Owen, I dunno what to say. Just get better.'

Jane started to talk to him then, while Jim continued to hold Owen's hand and listen to his wife talking on and on and on. She told Owen about all the happy things they'd done together. The time they'd gone to the beach and the five of them had gone swimming and lost their way back to their towels. How they had searched for hours for their gear and they'd been freezing. How Matt had stolen someone's towel to wrap around himself and they'd come after him. Jim found himself smiling at the memory, smiling at Jane as she recounted the tale.

He could make out what the voice was saying now. The words had meaning and shape and form. Putting them together built up pictures in his head. Funny pictures that made him smile and want to see the voice. It was as if he was pulling at himself from the centre, from some dark place deep inside. Rising up towards the surface of himself, touching the water and breaking through the surface.

Lights and noise.

A face, bending over him.

Another.

Both bewildered. One with tears dripping, tears that touched his own face.

A word, formed in his head, bubbled into being. 'Mam.'

Chaos.

60

FRED CAME OVER that night with a bottle of champagne. Jim let him in and took two glasses down from the press. Running them under the tap, he tried to locate a tea towel. The only one he could find was a rather mouldy one that had been in the press from before Owen had gone into hospital.

'Aw Jaysus,' Fred looked in disgust at the towel. 'Here, give the glasses here.' He took them and rubbed them on his shirt sleeve. 'I dunno, Jimbo, this place needs a woman's touch.'

'I've hardly been in it for the last five weeks,' Jim said. 'Can't bleedin' do everything.'

'And sure it's not as if you'll be here much longer.' Fred poured two generous glasses of champagne.

'Another week and then it's London,' Jim agreed.

'Ummm.' Fred handed Jim his glass. Raising his own in the air, he said, 'To your job and to Clinton and Owen.' Clinton was his baby son's name.

'Job, Clinton and Owen,' Jim said.

'So how is Owen?' Fred asked. 'He came home from hospital today – yeah?'

Jim nodded. 'He's great. He'll recover completely, the doc says. It's a big relief.'

Fred nodded sagely. 'I never really understood how awful it must've been on yez to lose Matt,' he said. 'I guess, being a father meself now, I'd have a better idea.'

Jim didn't answer. He drank some more champagne.

'It makes you see stuff differently, doesn't it, Jimbo?'

'Yeah.' Jim drained his glass and held it out for some more.

'Thanks for making me see how stupid I was being,' Fred said.

'No probs. Any time,' Jim grinned.

Fred didn't smile back. 'And I know this is gonna be completely out of character for me, but, well, Gill has told me to say what's on me mind to you.'

'If it's about Debs—'

'Naw, naw, not about her. She thinks she had a lucky escape. Says you love your wife too much.' Fred paused, as if waiting for a reaction.

'And?'

'Well, do you?'

'She won't have me back,' Jim said into his glass. 'I let her down.'

'What? When?'

He'd never voiced it aloud before, never wanted to admit it. 'The time that Matt died.' He had to force the words out. 'D'you remember, you and me left the funeral and went on a bender for a week?'

'*You* went on a bender,' Fred said. 'I made you go home in the end.'

'Yeah. You told me to get my act together and go home.'

'And you did.'

'Naw,' Jim shook his head. 'I just went home. I don't think I've ever got my act together.'

Fred said nothing.

'Jane needed me and I wasn't there. It was the worst thing ever to happen to us, and I wasn't there.'

'But did you not explain to her? You know, tell her why you did it?'

Jim shrugged. '*I* hardly knew why I'd done it. I'd never have explained it to her.'

Fred put down his glass and said sagely, 'Jim, women like explanations. They need to understand things. I mean, Gill wanted to know why I was so afraid of commitment and I found it hard to explain, but eventually we figured it was because of me ma leaving me when I was a kid.'

'Awww, poor baby,' Jim grinned.

'Fuck off, right?' Fred flushed. 'I'm just saying that women like that shit. You have to tell her something, even if it's just to say you made a mistake. And you did make a mistake, didn't you?'

Who the hell was Fred to be advising him? 'Just forget it.'

'I would if you didn't look so bloody miserable.' Fred poured him another glass of champagne. 'Did you never, ever, ever talk about it?'

Christ, Jim thought, Gillian was having a weird effect on Fred. 'D'you know something, I preferred you before you had that baby.'

Fred laughed and drank some more booze. 'All I'm saying is that it's good to talk,' he said.

'It's too late now.'

'It's never too late. Look at me, I thought Gill would tell me to take a flying fuck out of the hospital and did she? Nope.' He punched Jim on the arm. 'You gotta go for what you want in this life, Jimbo. It's too bloody short. I know that from experience.'

All Jim knew was that it was a night for getting smashed.

Jane pulled a bottle of wine out of the press and, uncorking it, set it on the counter to breathe. It was the first night she'd had to herself in a long time. Owen was safely in bed, fast asleep. He was going to be tired for a long time yet, the doctor had told them. But he was alive and healthy and she didn't care how much hard work lay ahead. Di was out with Libby, and her mother – who had insisted on staying around while Owen was in hospital – had retired to bed. She'd been a revelation, Jane thought, the way she'd looked after Di. OK, so she'd wrecked all their clothes in the hot wash, and anything that had been lucky enough to survive had scorch marks from the iron, but she'd tried.

Di hadn't seen it quite that way and there'd been a bit of a scene, but Jane had promised her new stuff.

Her mother was going home the following day and Jane actually thought that she would miss her.

As she pulled a glass out of the press, the doorbell rang. She wondered who it was, if maybe it was Jim. He'd offered to stay the night to help with Owen, but she'd told him to go. It hurt having him around.

From the frosted glass in the hall door, Jane made out the silhouette of a woman. Maybe it was one of the neighbours, they'd been so good to her these last few weeks. It'd be nice to share the wine with someone.

She unlocked the door and was startled to see Mir standing on the doorstep. Her surprise must have shown in her face because Mir began to back away. 'If this is a bad time,' she began, 'I'm sorry, I can—'

'No, no, it's not. Come in.' Hastily, she opened the door wider. 'Please.'

'Sure?' Miranda looked questioningly at her. She was terrified, Jane could see it in the way she kept fidgeting with her hands. Mir had never been like that in all the years she'd known her.

'Of course I am,' Jane said in a softer voice. 'It's great to see you.'

Mir stepped into the hallway. Holding a bag out to Jane, she said shyly, 'For Owen. I heard he came home.'

'Thanks.' Jane smiled at her. 'Today.'

They stood looking at each other.

Breaking the silence, Mir said, 'I rang you at the salon the day after the competition to see how you'd done, a sort of peace offering, and Patrick told me about Owen. I didn't want to come any earlier.' She paused. 'I thought you'd have enough on your plate.' She stared at a point over Jane's shoulder.

'I'd have loved to have seen you earlier,' Jane said quietly.

Mir brought her eyes to meet Jane's. To her surprise, Mir's eyes were glistening. 'I've been such a bitch, Jane. I know I have. I'm sorry.'

'No.' Jane shook her head.

'Yeah.' Mir brought her hands to her face and hastily scrubbed some tears away. 'Well, that's all I came for.' Her voice broke and she made fumbling motions for the door.

Jane reached out and touched her. 'Don't go. Not yet. Look, I've a bottle of wine open. Stay and have some.'

'You don't want me.' Mir's hand slipped on the door lock.

'True. But I reckon you're the best I'll get tonight.'

As Mir spun around to see if she was serious, Jane gave a hesitant smile. 'Come on,' she began to walk to the kitchen.

Her eyes strayed to a photo of Matt that Di had put on the hall table. Life was too short for fights. Way too short.

Fred showed Jim snapshots of his son before he left.

The pictures seemed to mock him, Jim thought. Fred's happy smiling family. Gillian, looking radiant, holding by turns the 'cleverest', the 'strongest', the 'most gorgeous' son in the world.

'Who ever thought that a kid could be so interesting, huh, Jimbo?' Fred kept saying. 'We're getting a video camera next week. Nothing like live action, I say.'

Jim smiled, remembering how many pictures they'd taken of Di when she was born. They hadn't taken as many of Owen. And as for Matt – they were lucky to have a baby picture of him. If only they'd known . . .

'Anyway, have ta go,' Fred broke into his thoughts. Tucking his pictures into his jacket, he zipped it up. 'I'll call around soon, we'll head out for a few jars before you go – huh?'

'Sure.'

Jim watched as Fred, with half a bottle of champagne and three cans inside him, made unsteady progress down the hall. Jesus, he envied him starting out on a whole new life. Looking at his suitcases, which he'd bought for his move to London, he guessed that he'd be starting out on a new life too.

'I hit rock bottom when Harry told me he didn't want to be my friend,' Mir said, downing her glass of wine in one gulp.

Jane refilled it. 'He didn't mean it, though,' she said, her mind going back to the last time she'd seen Harry, staring dejectedly into his pint.

'He did.' Mir gave a bitter laugh. 'Serves me right too. I treated him like dirt. I always have. Serves me right.'

'What happened?'

There was a slight pause before Mir said, 'The day after you called, I went around to his place – just for a few beers, as I'd nothing else to do – and he told me that he was going out and he didn't want to see me. So I called the next day and the next day and it was the same thing every time. Eventually I snapped. I mean, you were gone, Pat was gone and I was losing him too, Jane. I did a complete psycho on it. I started yelling at Harry, through his letter box, telling him that he was a prick for not seeing me.'

'You didn't!' Jane could just imagine it. A small grin curled her mouth.

Mir smiled uncomfortably and said sheepishly, 'Yeah, well, it has always worked before. He'd usually be on bended knees the minute I'd raise my voice. This time though, he opened the door and he gave me a look that would have stopped two rabbits shagging.'

Jane grinned, despite Mir's doleful tone.

'He said, right, that he wasn't as much of a prick as I was a cold selfish bitch.'

'That was awful!'

'No, it was true.' Mir shook her head and managed a watery grin. 'He told me that I was always blaming someone else for the way I acted. He said that maybe if I grew up, I'd realise that. He said that I, well, that I was a slapper.'

Jane handed her a piece of kitchen paper.

'Thanks.' Mir dabbed her face. Looking at Jane, she whispered, 'He was right. I mean, I picked up every shithead in Dublin 'cause I think, well, I think I felt superior to them or maybe, I dunno, maybe I felt I didn't deserve much better.'

'But you do.'

'I know,' Mir gulped, 'and I didn't realise it until it was too late.'

'That's when most of us realise things,' Jane said softly. 'You don't have to tell me all this, you know.'

'I do, I owe it to you. I said some awful things to you, and then when Pat rang I really went to town on him. Called him all sorts.'

'Nothing he hasn't heard before.'

'Yeah. Well . . .' Mir took a gulp of wine and when her voice was slightly stronger, went on, 'When I finally realised that I'd lost Harry, I understood how bloody lucky I'd been all along. It was that simple. I had a job, friends, a nice place. But I just wasn't happy with that. I dunno why. I've always wanted more. I wanted the husband, the kids, anything I hadn't got. Guess that's why I picked up the dregs, they were the excuse for my life not being the way it should have been.'

'What?'

'Well, I guess if I never made the effort, I could still have my dreams, you know?'

Jane nodded slowly. 'You didn't want to fail.'

'Yep. But I failed anyhow. I think that's why Rosemary got up my nose so much, she was so enthusiastic and ambitious and bloody *happy*. I used to think, Jesus, how can anyone be happy looking like her?'

Jane grinned, despite herself.

'But she's happy because she's trying,' Mir said. Then added wryly, 'Very trying.'

Jane laughed.

'I'm only joking,' Mir said.

'You haven't failed, you know.' Jane poured her some more wine. 'You're here, aren't you? You've still got me. And I know Pat will have you back like a shot at the salon. He's only got a temp until the end of the week. All you've got to do is ask.'

'I've never been much good at asking for things.'

'And then you trot around to Harry and apologise. Get down on your knees and yell through his letter box.'

'Oh, I couldn't.'

'You have to go for what you want, Mir. At least you can always say you tried.'

And it was true, Jane realised. It was better to try to fix things than ignore them.

Jim switched off his mobile and grinned. The billboard posters were being delivered on Tuesday. When Jane saw the photos she was sure to guess. Maybe, just maybe she might give him a second chance. There'd be no need for any talk then.

It was the first time in months he felt he'd done something right.

In bed that night, Jane felt calmer than she had in months. Mir coming around had made her see that maybe if you faced things head on they could be sorted out. It gave her the courage to face something else she'd been putting off these last few weeks.

61

SHE CHOSE A time when there was little chance of them being disturbed. Di was at school and her mother was packing her thousands of belongings in readiness for going home.

Owen was watching the telly, sitting on the sofa with a duvet thrown over him. He'd lost weight in hospital and his once handsome face looked pinched and old. His black eyes seemed to have sunk deep into their sockets and there was a scar on his forehead where his head had hit the road. Jane's heart twisted as she looked in at him.

She laid a glass of orange juice on the table beside him.

'Ta.' He gave her a smile.

Her hands clammy, Jane sat at the end of the sofa and took Owen's feet on to her lap. She began, absently, to rub his toes. 'Owen,' she said casually, though her heart was pounding, 'can I ask you something?'

His gaze flitted from the telly and rested on her. His eyes were wary. 'What?'

'Why did you steal from the off-licence?'

Owen jerked. 'Dunno.' His gaze returned to the telly, but he wasn't really watching it. He pulled his feet from her grasp and picked up his orange juice. 'Dunno,' he repeated.

'Did it give you a . . .' Jane sought for the word Charlotte had used, 'buzz?'

Owen didn't answer. His profile gave nothing away.

'Please, Owen, tell me. I need to understand – don't you see?' When he still made no reply, she got up and stood in front of him. 'Just tell me why you did it – please?'

Nothing.

And then, from way back, she remembered something he'd said about why he'd bunked off school. Hunkering down, so that he could see only her face and not the TV screen, she asked softly, 'Is it to do with Matt?'

His brother's name sparked something. Owen screwed his eyes up and shook his head. 'Ma, please—'

'Owen, you've got to tell me. I'm going out of my mind here. It's not like you to steal stuff.'

Owen bit his lip. He stared her in the face. 'Yeah, yeah it is, Ma. I've been doing it for ages. I've stolen drink from you, sweets and crisps and drink and fags from shops.'

'No!'

'Yeah.'

'Why?'

He looked dejectedly at her. 'The buzz. The high. Makes me feel . . .' he took a breath, '. . . alive.'

Jane didn't understand. 'Alive?' she repeated.

Owen nodded and stared over her shoulder to the wall beyond. 'Ever since Matt,' he began haltingly, 'ever since he died I've been scared. So scared.'

'Scared?' Jane could only stare dumbly at him.

'Yeah. Like he got up that day and ate his breakfast and then by lunchtime he was dead. How did he not know, Ma? How did he not know that he was going to die?'

'Aw, Owen—'

'It's such a *big* thing Ma.'

'I know.'

They gazed at each other. Owen broke the silence. 'And after that, Ma, well, nothing seemed to make sense any more. I mean, I could die any time. And, well, I dunno, I just couldn't take anything seriously. And not taking stuff seriously meant that nothing mattered. And then I just needed to feel as if stuff *did* matter, you know?'

She didn't.

'I stole just to *feel* something. I climbed trees just to be dizzy. I drank to laugh.' He bit his lip. 'I bunked off 'cause what did school matter in the end anyway?'

Jane touched his hand. 'You should have told me,' she gulped.

'You were too sad. You wouldn't have understood. I didn't really, not then. And afterwards, it was too hard.'

'You mean with me and your dad?'

'Uh-huh.'

'We let you down, didn't we?'

'Naw.'

'And now,' Jane touched his damp hair. 'How are you now? Still scared?'

Owen didn't answer for a bit. Then he said softly, 'Since the accident I know I want to live.'

'Good.' Jane sat down on the sofa beside him. She rubbed his arm and said fervently, 'Know this, Owen, no one knows when they're to die. I wish I could make it easy for you, but I can't. No one can.' She gulped. 'Mattie just died, his little life was over, there was no sense to it, but it happened. We have to accept it. You, on the other hand, are very much alive.' She cupped his face with her hands. 'So *brilliantly* alive. Just live, please. Just do that for me and I promise, I'll listen to you and be there for you and never let you down again. It's my fault for not talking about it with you at the time. I should have, I know that now. Di gave me grief over it at the hospital.'

'No one better than her to do that.' Owen gave a shaky grin.

'You'd better believe it,' Jane smiled back.

'I'm sorry, Ma,' Owen said.

'No,' Jane cuddled him to her, 'no, I'm the one who's sorry.'

Sheila looked up as Jane came into the kitchen. Her daughter looked exhausted. 'There's tea in the pot, dahling,' she said.

'Ta.' Jane poured herself a cup and sat opposite Sheila at the table.

Really, Sheila thought, Jane had to sort herself out. If she kept going the way she was, she'd be nothing but a shadow. Her hair was a mess, you'd never think she was a hairdresser, and all that stuff she'd just said to Owen – she wondered if . . .

'What?' Jane asked. 'Why do you keep looking at me?'

'Did you mean what you said to Owen in there?' Sheila hadn't planned to ask that, it just popped out.

Jane's eyes narrowed. 'What?'

'When you told Owen that he had to accept that Matt was dead?'

'Were you listening? You had—'

'I was bringing you a cup of tea, dahling, and I heard all the emotion, so I decided not to intrude, but nevertheless, I did hear you tell Owen that he had to accept things.'

'You had no right—'

'Maybe not, but still, I heard you tell Owen that,' Sheila's eyes glistened slightly, 'well, that Mattie's life was over and that though it didn't make sense he had to accept it.'

'You must have glued your ear to the door,' Jane muttered.

Sheila said nothing.

'Well, it's true,' Jane snapped. 'Makes things easier.'

Sheila reached across and patted Jane's hand. She said quietly, 'So why don't you also accept it, dahling, and make things easier on yourself?'

'What?'

'You heard.'

'Mam, I don't need . . .' Jane didn't finish. She pushed her cup away from her and stood up.

Sheila blocked her way. It was about time someone said something. 'Don't run away now, dahling,' she said.

'It's harder to accept things when you're responsible for them happening,' Jane said, trying to push past. 'It's my fault he died, how can I accept that – huh?'

'Making him wear his helmet wouldn't have saved that child.'

'Looking for it would have.'

'Maybe. Maybe not.' Sheila caught Jane by the arm. There was no way Jane was leaving the kitchen until she faced facts. 'But you said it yourself to Owen. Matt just died. There was no sense to it.' Tightening her grip on Jane, she continued, 'You can't keep blaming yourself any more than you can blame Owen or Jim. It's *ruining* you, dahling.'

'Let – me – go.' Jane tried to wrench herself free.

'You can't take responsibility for everything, Jane. You can't sort everything out with a phone call or by wishing it never happened, you know. You have to accept that some things happen that are no one's fault.'

Jane twisted her face away. '*Stop.*'

'You are *not* to blame.'

'I am.' Jane pushed against her, trying to free herself.

Despite her angry face, there were tears in her eyes and Sheila was determined to make her shed them. She'd only seen Jane cry once for Matt and then that waster of a husband had gone and left and Jane hadn't cried or talked about Matt since. Instead she'd turned all her unhappiness in on herself. 'Jane, dahling,' she said, 'look at me and I'll let you go.' At first she thought that Jane wouldn't, then slowly, her daughter brought her eyes up to her face. 'You are *now* looking at a hopeless mother,' Sheila said. 'You, dahling, are a shining light by comparison.'

Jane gulped out a laugh but shook her head. 'No.'

'Yes!' Sheila said emphatically. 'I know I neglected you terribly when you were growing up, Jane. The truth was, I just didn't know what to do with you. I mean, if you were a dress or something, there'd have been no problem. And then, off you went and had Di, and I couldn't believe the way you were with her. You shamed me. I knew how bad I'd been, but that was me. And now, now I'm trying to be a good mother, so for God's sake don't ruin it for me!' She shook Jane gently. 'You are *not* to blame. And, dahling, you have to let people back in again.

Di and Owen need you – you know that. You've been great with them, but they need more than you just keeping it together. They need someone who's living fully in the world. And your father and I have always needed you. I think even Jim needs you, though,' she sniffed, 'that's not surprising.'

'He doesn't need me. He shut me out. I killed his son.'

Sheila shook her gently again. 'Well, if he thinks that, then he's the fool I always said he was,' she said with passion. 'You are a *great* mother and you learnt it all on your own. You are not to blame.'

'I am. I should have looked after him – I was his mother.'

'You still are, wherever he is, you still are.' She pulled Jane to her. It was lovely to feel her so close. 'It's time now to go on and make the best of what's left. Accepting things makes you free, you know, it stops you fighting stuff you just can't change.'

Patrick had said that to her once. Jane closed her eyes to squeeze away the tears. 'I try, but I can't . . .'

'You have to. Look at me and your father. I'm making the best of the fact that he can't perform and he's making the best of the fact that I'm going to spend all his money when I get back. But we accept . . .' Sheila stopped. Against her, Jane was sobbing, her shoulders heaving.

Sheila, only vaguely aware that tear stains would not come out of the suit she was wearing, pulled Jane tighter. 'Let it out,' she soothed. 'Just *cry* for God's sake.'

62

IT WAS HER first day back at work since the accident and Jane was looking forward to it, despite the fact that she'd probably spend all day worrying about Owen. She'd made him promise to ring her if he needed anything and he'd rolled his eyes and said that all he needed was for her to stop nagging him. He'd changed since they'd had their talk, Jane had to admit. Even though he still looked ill, there was a brightness to his eyes that had been missing for a long time. And he'd begun fighting with Di, which was another good sign.

Jane too felt different. Lighter somehow. The only black cloud on the horizon was that Gooey had begun sniffing around again. However, Di was now relying heavily on her nana for advice, so it was highly unlikely they'd get back together.

Jane parked her car and made her way to the salon. Despite the fact that she hadn't been to work for almost six weeks, nothing about the road had changed. Lisa's was open and a sign in the window announced that Sexy Sheila's rolls were on sale. A picture of her mother, taken at least thirty years ago, was plastered to the window. Jane grinned and carried on down, past Cutting Edge, where she noted that their prices had reverted to normal. Ha. Ha. Finally she arrived outside her own place.

She stood still, savouring the fact that this was her salon. Her little business. The prices were still the same, the posters of their 'Winning' hair were still up in the windows. A new, funky one of Rosemary had been added. 'IHF prize-winner' was scrawled in bright green along the side of it. It looked cool and modern.

Inside the salon, Jane could see Mir escorting one of the customers to a seat. She was chatting and laughing and it was a Monday. Patrick was studying something at the reception desk and Rosemary was washing some poor victim's hair. Taking a deep breath, Jane pushed open the doors of the salon and walked in.

All activity stopped. There was a moment's silence before Patrick ran to embrace her.

'Welcome back! Welcome back!' He beamed delightedly into her face and, grasping her hand, tugged her up the salon. 'Hey, everybody, Jane is back,' he called.

Eileen Simms was the first over. Grasping Jane's arms in a vice-like grip, she said passionately, 'I'm so glad about your son, *so* glad.'

'Ta.'

Rosemary's client managed a wave before beginning to cough violently. Rosemary, in her excitement, had squirted what had to be at least half a pint of water over the woman's face and into her mouth. Rosemary, oblivious to her client's distress, rushed towards Jane, stood in front of her and then, unsure of what to do, stood beaming stupidly up at her. 'It's great to have you back, Jane,' she eventually gasped out.

'You're drowning Mrs Lyons,' Patrick said in disbelief as water squirted everywhere.

'Ohhhh.' Her hands splayed out in panic, Rosemary rushed off.

'Fucking idiot,' Mir muttered darkly as she came abreast of Jane. They smiled at each other. 'Hiya boss,' Mir smiled. 'It's great you're back.'

'It's great to be back,' Jane grinned.

Patrick was doing big pointy things with his fingers. Dancing from foot to foot, he was pointing at Mir.

'What?' Jane asked.

Mir rolled her eyes and held out her hand. On it, a ring inset with a row of diamonds gleamed.

Jane grasped her hand. 'Is this what I think it is?' she asked delightedly. 'Is it?'

'Nope.' Mir rolled her eyes again. 'It's a friendship ring. Harry bought it for me.'

'My arse it's a friendship ring,' Patrick chuckled. 'The man just wants everyone to think you're engaged to him, that's all. And it'll double as an engagement ring when the time comes.'

'It is *not* an engagement ring.' Mir sounded fed-up. Patrick had obviously been saying the same thing to her for days. 'What part of "not" don't you understand, Pat?'

'Ohhh, touchy.' Patrick rubbed his hands gleefully and headed back up to the reception desk.

Jane turned to Mir. 'So, what? Harry is back on the scene, is he?'

'And it's all thanks to you.' Mir blushed. It was the first time Jane could ever remember her doing that. 'Come over here and I'll tell you.'

In-between cutting her customer's hair, Mir told Jane that she'd gone to Harry's and yelled through his letter box that the cold, selfish bitch wanted to try to apologise.

'He was a bit off at first, but I just said that all I could do was apologise, isn't that right, Jane?'

'Yep.'

'I mean, I couldn't change the past, but I could make the future a lot more enjoyable for both of us. It was the "enjoyable" part that got him in the end. I think he liked the idea of that.' Mir gave a dirty laugh.

Jane smiled. 'Well done.'

'Hey,' Patrick sauntered over, 'what do you think of this as a billboard poster?'

He held up a picture of a grinning Rosemary with an enormous yellow lollipop in her hand. Her head was tilted to one side and her hair was the funky mix of colours that Jane had done. The picture was laid against a brilliant green background. *Hair To Dye For* was the caption.

'Well?' Patrick asked.

'Cool, yeah,' Mir nodded.

'It's me!' Rosemary squealed. 'I'm going to be up on a billboard.'

It was like the one outside, Jane thought. Very quirky, very modern. Very Jim. The thought came unbidden, but as soon as it hit her, she knew. 'Jim did that, didn't he?' she asked slowly. 'That's one of his, I'd know his design ideas anywhere.'

Patrick flushed. 'No, Barney arranged—'

'Patrick!' Her voice was sharp. He hated when she sounded like that. 'Tell me the truth.'

'He didn't want you to know.' Patrick looked guilty.

'What? What? That you'd used him to do up a billboard?'

No answer.

'Well?'

No answer.

'Has he been helping you and Barney from the start?' Jane asked incredulously. 'Did you ask him to?'

'No!' Patrick said hastily. 'Well, he rang me, see. Apparently one of the kids told him the place was in a bit of trouble and, well, he gave me a few ideas.' He smiled ruefully. 'He almost flipped when I told him we'd slashed our prices. He's a bit of a tyrant, your Jim. He told me I was a complete idiot and to hike the prices up pronto.'

'That was Jim's idea?'

'Uh-huh.'

'And the coffee and biscuits? And the posters in the window?'

'All Jim's.' Patrick gave a nervous laugh.

'So Barney was never a part of it?'

'Well,' Patrick bit his lip. 'He agreed to pretend that he was, you know, in case you ever met him.'

'No wonder he always sounded different on the phone,' Mir said. 'One day he'd sound dead sexy and the next, well,' she giggled, 'well, he'd sound like Jim.'

She laughed as Jane belted her one.

'I'm sorry, honey chicks,' Patrick said contritely. 'I didn't like keeping things from you, but, well, you'd never have agreed and Jim, well, he's good at marketing, isn't he?'

'You should have told me,' Jane said flatly.

'He made me swear not to.' Patrick rolled up the poster. 'And anyway, it's dead nice of him, isn't it?'

'He's just dead.' Jane made her way to the door.

'Where are you going?' Patrick asked alarmed.

'To see my husband.'

'But, but, we've customers booked in for you.'

'Get *Barney* to help.'

She dialled Jim and told him she wanted to meet him. He told her he was in the flat packing away a few things and she said she'd meet him there.

Jim's apartment block was very nice, she thought as she pulled into the visitor car park around the back. The gardens were well taken care of and the whole place had an air of newness about it. Now, what apartment number was he again? 3b or something? Oh well, she thought, as she pressed 3b, even if it wasn't his they'd be sure to know where he was.

'Hi,' a woman's voice answered. 'Is that Jane?'

A woman? A bloody woman!

'Yes.'

'Come on up.' She was buzzed in.

She stood in the foyer, uncertain about what she should do. Was that Debbie? Was it back on between them? Huh, she wouldn't be a bit surprised if it was. Jim was easily swayed like that. Well, she decided, she might as well get a dekko at the woman who'd managed to replace her. She wished she'd worn something a bit more exciting though. Her jeans were just boring blue ones and her T-shirt was the only clean one she'd been able to find that morning and it didn't really do her justice. But, feck it! She ran her hands through her hair, squared her shoulders and gave the brass bell of 3b the most aggressive ring she could.

A 'Fuck's sake' was heard.

Someone opened the door and it wasn't Jim. It wasn't Debbie either. It took a second for her to realise that it was Fred. She hadn't seen him in ages.

'Jane,' he managed some sort of a grimace, 'come in. We're just going.'

Jane, feeling awkward, entered the bare room. Well, it was bare except for a sofa and two chairs. 'Hiya Fred,' she mumbled.

'This is Gill.' Fred indicated a bushy-haired, slightly plump girl with a friendly smile.

Not Debbie, Gill. Whoever that was.

'Gee, hiya.' The girl held out her hand. 'So you're Jane. You look different to what I expected.'

'Naw, honey.' Fred gave her a nudge. 'I wasn't serious when I said she had a black hat and a broomstick.'

Gillian looked mortified as Fred laughed. 'Underdeveloped sense of humour,' Gillian said. 'Comes from his mother leaving him when he was a kid.'

More like his mother dropping him from a height when he was a kid, Jane thought mutinously. Still, she managed to smile politely. Where the hell was Jim? she wondered.

As if reading her mind, Gillian said, 'He's just nipped out to buy biscuits seeing as you were calling. I was just feeding junior here while he was gone.' She indicated the sofa where a small baby lay curled up in a white baby blanket. Jane hadn't noticed the baby at all because there was a pile of boxes blocking her view. 'A baby?' she said. 'Yours?'

'Mine and Freddie's,' Gillian said proudly.

'Well, congratulations.' Fred a father, the very idea sent shivers up her spine.

'You wanna see him?' Gillian didn't wait for an answer. Dying to show her child off, she placed him gently into Jane's arms.

He was beautiful, Jane thought. All clean and innocent, with that gorgeous baby smell. She put her nose against his scalp and inhaled the sweet scent. 'He's lovely,' she said softly. 'Really lovely.'

'He is, isn't he?' Fred peered in at the baby too. 'The blanket sort of ruins him, though. Gill bought lovely clothes for him and he looks nicer when you can see his clothes.'

Gillian giggled.

Jane smiled.

The door opened and Jim walked in. He stopped dead at the sight of her holding the baby.

'Jim,' she said, not able to make her voice sound as hard as she wanted because the baby had now opened the most navy blue eyes she had ever seen, and was staring at her.

'Jane. Hiya,' he muttered.

'Let us get out of your way.' Fred gently took the baby from Jane and after gathering their bits and pieces they left.

Jane and Jim stood looking at each other.

'So Fred's a daddy,' she said at last.

He nodded. 'Scary, isn't it?'

They smiled at each other. Briefly.

'So, what's the occasion?' Jim walked past her and into the kitchen. 'Come to say goodbye?'

'No, actually.' Her anger flared again. 'Just came to tell you that I don't appreciate you butting into my business.'

'What?' He began to fill up the kettle.

'You helped Patrick market the salon.'

He actually had the nerve to smile at her. 'Yeah.'

'Well, you had no right!'

His grin faltered. 'Sorry?'

'So you should be! It's my salon. Not yours. If I'd wanted your help I'd have asked for it. I don't appreciate being kept in the dark by my own partner. Being made a fool of by my own husband.'

'I wasn't making a fool of you.' He genuinely looked bewildered. 'I was only trying to help. To show—'

'The thing is, I don't want your help. I don't want anything from you.'

'Fine.'

'Good.'

The kettle flicked off.

'Do you even want tea?'

The question caught her off guard. She smiled. Then stopped. 'No. I'd better go.'

She wasn't prepared for the look of devastation on his face. 'OK.'

There was a pause.

She indicated his boxes. They looked so final. So lonely. 'Good luck with the new job.'

'Ta.'

She was leaving. Walking out without even having a cup of tea. And he'd bloody well gone and bought her favourite biscuits and everything. Her hand was on the door. Now she was pulling the door open. *And* she was mad at him.

That wasn't meant to happen.

He stood by helplessly as the door began to swing shut behind her.

'No!' His voice seemed to work all by itself. His legs, of their own accord, sprinted across to the door and he yanked it back open. 'Jane! Jesus, don't go.'

She turned to face him, puzzled.

Silence descended.

Damn it. Why couldn't he ever say what he wanted?

'Yeah?' she asked.

'I only did it because I couldn't think of any other way to tell you that I loved you,' he said.

'What?' She thought he was mental.

'The posters and marketing and stuff,' he said. 'At first I, well, I did it 'cause Di was upset. But, well, I wanted to do it. There was no other way I could make you see that I still cared. You shut me out, see, and, well . . .' He stopped.

Fucking words.

'No,' she said simply. 'You left me.'

He ran his hands over his face and gulped. 'Yeah. Yeah, I know.' Why did everything always have to come back to that? 'I made a mistake. A big mistake.'

To his surprise, her eyes filled with tears.

'Aw, Jane, Jesus, don't.'

'I didn't mean to let him go out without his helmet,' she said, blinking really hard. 'It was an accident.'

'Jesus, yeah. Yeah. I know *that*.' He didn't know if he should hold her or leave her. 'I know that.'

'So why did you blame me? Why did you leave me, Jim?'

'I didn't blame you.' Not this again. She never believed him.

Women like to talk. To know things. Fred's voice cut in on his thoughts.

But he couldn't explain to Jane. He'd never explained to anyone. It hurt too much.

'Then why?'

He looked up at the ceiling then down at his trainers. His heart began to pound, sweat broke out on his forehead. 'I couldn't cope,' he said eventually. 'When Matt died, I just couldn't cope.'

Jane stared at him. He couldn't cope. He'd never admitted that before. Instead, he'd shut off, or change the subject, or walk out of the room. Or leave.

'Talk to me, Jim,' she said. 'Please.'

There was no other way. If he had to have a shot at getting her back he had to talk. He couldn't just do stuff and hope she'd understand. How had he ever thought that would work anyway? For the first time in his life, it looked like Fred was right.

He opened the door wider and stood aside to let Jane walk back inside. Taking a deep breath, he followed her.

Jane sat on the sofa while Jim took a chair.

There was an expectant silence.

He bowed his head, clasped his hands between his knees and haltingly said, 'I just couldn't cope when Matt died, Jane. You were crying and the kids were crying and I didn't know what I should be doing.'

She didn't say anything.

Jim looked quickly at her. Said, 'I couldn't cry. I felt bad. So I left with Fred.'

'But I wouldn't have cared if you hadn't cried, as long as you were with me,' Jane said softly. 'I thought you couldn't bear to be near me.'

'Naw.' He shook his head. 'Don't put that on me. It's not true. All I ever wanted was to be with you.' He gave her a half-smile.

She smiled a bit in return.

He closed his eyes. He'd never really told Jane much about his family and she, knowing how valuable his privacy was, had never really pushed him. He'd liked that about her. But now, well, that had to change. 'See,' he stopped, then started again. 'See . . . I never knew my dad. And when me ma died, my gran, she wouldn't let me cry. She told me that big boys didn't cry.' He gave a bitter laugh. 'I was only seven, you know.'

'Jim.'

He shook off the pity in her voice. 'And I went to live with her then. You were lucky you never knew her, Jane. Fred called her The Ball-breaker and she was. I couldn't cry, get mad, get upset, nothing.' He looked at her. 'I don't think I've ever cried in my whole life, Jane.'

She looked upset.

'The point is, right, that no one ever talked to me about any of it. And then when Matt died, I wanted to cry, but I didn't know how. I wanted to talk to you and I didn't know how. It was like,' his eyes closed, 'well, like I was trapped in myself . . . words just, you know, wouldn't come.'

'Oh Jim, I'm so sorry.' She crossed towards him and knelt down beside him. 'I thought it was me, see, and I—'

'No.' He reached for her hand and she clasped his. 'Never. I've always loved you, you know, but I let you down. I know I did. And, God, I'm so fucking sorry.' He wiped her hair from her face and let his palm caress her cheek. 'I know it sounds crap, but it's all I can say. I can't change the past.'

Neither of them could, she realised. 'Nope,' she said. 'But we can try to change the future, can't we?'

It was like coming home, feeling her arms around him again. Feeling her hair against his face. He'd lost so much in his life that to find her again was better than finding her for the first time – a cute brunette with hair dye under her fingernails. His lips sought hers and he felt her tears on his face.

He was crying, Jane realised. She could taste the salt of his tears on her lips. He was holding her fiercely and telling her how much he loved her, and he was crying.

At long last.

63

THEY TALKED NON-STOP all the way to the graveyard. She made him laugh when she told him about the card Cutting Edge had sent congratulating them on their second placing in the IHFs.

'He'd written on it that he was looking forward to beating us next year and Patrick sent him a card back saying that as the standard of entry was so low, he didn't know whether he'd bother entering next year.'

'Well, at least Patrick is a bit smarter with his comments than he is as a marketing agent. Jesus, he was bloody hopeless, you know.'

'Not like you, eh?'

Jim grinned modestly.

Since turning down the job with Incredible Crisps, he'd been headhunted by every firm in town. He was finally doing the kind of stuff he'd always wanted to do. 'Great thing I'm working on now,' he said, beginning to tell her all about it.

Jane smiled at the enthusiasm with which he talked. He was like a kid that had seen something wonderful for the first time.

He paused mid-sentence and looked at her with sparkling eyes, 'I'm boring you, amn't I?'

'Naw,' she smiled back. 'I'm just thinking of how much I love you.'

His eyes grew sombre. 'We'll always be like this, won't we, Jane? Let's never mess up again.'

She put her arm around his waist and he slung his arm over her shoulder. They kissed softly.

The grave was neat and tidy. Together they began replacing old flowers with fresh ones, talking quietly as they did so and touching off each other as much as they could. It was like the thrill of new love all over again.

'Sorry, excuse me,' a tearful voice said.

Together they looked up and a woman who couldn't have been more than twenty-five was gazing down at them. 'Sorry for disturbing you,' she said, 'but I come here every week and I couldn't help seeing that your boy was only six when he died.'

'That's right,' Jane said quietly. 'Why?'

'Well,' the woman pointed to the grave that backed on to Matt's. 'My baby died a few months ago. She was almost three and, well . . .' Her eyes filled up, 'I was just wondering how you cope. I'm not, you see. Not at all.'

Jane jumped up, flowers falling from her lap. She took the woman's hand and pressed it. 'You are,' she said. She moved nearer the woman and said more firmly, 'Believe it or not, you are. It takes time—'

'But you two seem so happy,' the woman whispered, looking from one to the other. 'Me and my partner aren't like that.'

Jane put her arm around the woman's shoulders. 'Come on,' she said, 'Jim can cope here. I'll buy you a coffee and a danish in this coffee shop outside and then . . .' She looked at Jim, who smiled up at her. Turning back to the woman she said softly, 'And then, I'll tell you a story . . .'